Robert Kemp Philp

# The Lady's Every-Day Book

A Practical Guide in the Elegant Arts and Daily Difficulties of Domestic Life

Robert Kemp Philp

**The Lady's Every-Day Book**
*A Practical Guide in the Elegant Arts and Daily Difficulties of Domestic Life*

ISBN/EAN: 9783337121211

Printed in Europe, USA, Canada, Australia, Japan

Cover: Foto ©Andreas Hilbeck / pixelio.de

More available books at **www.hansebooks.com**

IN THE

# ELEGANT ARTS AND DAILY DIFFICULTIES

OF

# DOMESTIC LIFE.

BY THE

AUTHOR OF " ENQUIRE WITHIN," " BEST OF EVERYTHING," ETC.

No condition is hopeless when a lady possesses decision, firmness, and economy.
" She looketh well to the ways of her household."—*Proverbs.*

NEW EDITION.

LONDON;
BEMROSE AND SONS, 10. PATERNOSTER BUILDINGS ;
AND IRONGATE, DERBY.
1880.

# PREFACE.

An "Every-Day Book" may be properly defined as a repertory of knowledge on a variety of those subjects upon which we are continually wanting information. The definition we have now given has practically animated us throughout the compilation of this volume, with this difference only, that the subjects contained herein are restricted to those of feminine interest. This is the "Lady's Every-Day Book;" and we have spared no labour of research to make it a complete and useful book of reference upon *two thousand* topics, more or less connected with the utilities of a Lady's every-day life.

The extent of the subjects embraced in our Volume numerically prohibit us from referring to them in detail. Everything interesting to Ladies that may be classified under Domestic Economy, Elegant Arts, Etiquette, In-door and Out-door Games and Exercises, Pet Animals, Legal Matters, Gardening and Botany, Laundry and Nursery, Accomplishments, Management of Children and Servants, Dress and Fashion, Home Decorations, Income and Expenditure, Health Resorts, Phenomena of the Months, Histories of Domestic Articles——We must pause from further particularising, and say, in brief, that we have occupied our four hundred closely-printed pages with such subjects as cannot fail to be of interest and importance to every-one desirous of obtaining social distinction as an accomplished and well-informed woman.

The enormous success of our " ENQUIRE WITHIN " is at once a public admission of its practical value.  One million copies of that work have found their way into circulation in Great Britain and in the United States.  Some fifteen years ago the compilation thereof was a labour of love with the Editor, who received the assistance of a large number of acquaintances skilled in the various arts and duties that tend to render home happy, and to lessen the cares and pains of life.

But, in such lapse of time, even in simple matters of the household, new discoveries are made, novel arts introduced, fresh amusements suggested, etiquette assumes new affectations, and even legislative wisdom steps in to modify the laws affecting husband and wife, landlord and tenant, and parent and child. Old Books, like old clothes, require repairing and renovating— but, better than repairs and renovations is a new garment, if it be made of sound and tasteful material.  These pages of the " LADY's EVERY-DAY BOOK " are designed to supply the gleanings of fifteen years of later experience in matters of domestic utility.  The hand that compiled " ENQUIRE WITHIN " writes this ; and some old, and many new friends, have aided the work.  The heart that conceived the usefulness of a domestic " friend in need " still beats with sincere regard for those simple altars of home life where olive branches wave around patriarchal trees, and a sweet voice whispers—" A strong title to Heaven is the love of Home."

# LADY'S EVERY-DAY BOOK



## ELEGANT ARTS AND DOMESTIC ECONOMY.

---

**Hints for Hot Weather.**—The numerous fatalities and sickness that attend hot weather, renders it important to guard ourselves against it as much as possible. The sun that ripens the corn for our daily bread, and allures us abroad by its brilliant beams, is, nevertheless, fraught with our destruction if we expose ourselves too much to his powerful rays.

From 6 to 11 a.m. are the established hours of work in India, and those who can would find it conduce to their comfort and health to adopt the same hours for their labours during the prevalence of almost Indian weather that July and August are so constantly attended by. Above all, the children should be carefully looked after in hot weather; they should, as a rule, be allowed to sleep throughout the day, and take their exercise only in the morning and evening. This caution may be more particularly recommended while on the accustomed sea-side visit. True, there may sometimes spring from over the sea a cool refreshing breeze to those sporting on the sands, yet we admonish all that they would be safer within doors while the sun's power is scorching up everything that comes in its fiery way.

Heat, too, stimulates thirst, and it is important to remember that all alcoholic drinks and high feeding are great aids in hot weather in producing sickness and even sunstroke. Light wines, plentifully diluted, and ærated waters, are the only safe and suitable beverages for summer temperature; sulphuric acid, lemonade, lime-juice, and similar preparations, are at once refreshing, and excellent antidotes for diarrhœa, loss of appetite, and other disturbances of the system caused by hot weather.

Never open windows while the sun shines on them, and the blinds should be wetted, or, better still, a wet blanket be hung behind them. In this way any room may be kept comparatively cool, especially those exposed to the rays of the sun.

A flat vessel filled with water, on which are floated branches of trees covered with green leaves, is a very efficacious and pleasant means of imparting coolness to an apartment, and is much employed in Germany.

The suspension of Indian matting, previously damped, at the open window, tends much to diminish the heat. This matting may be imitated by any kind of plaited grass.

But the most important thing to observe and watch is the temperature of the body—we mean that we should be very careful not to increase the heat of the blood by animal food, either fresh or seasoned, or by stimulating drinks. Nothing could be more dangerous, and many deaths arise from the too prevalent practice of indulging in animal food and alcoholic drinks, during the hot seasons. It is opposed to the great physiological rule, which is to keep the body cool.

Moderately acid drinks are both very grateful and wholesome, and are, moreover, cheap.

We learnt from Franklin a century ago that the solar heat is absorbed with greater or less facility according to the colour of the object exposed to its rays. Every one remembers how he put pieces of cloth, similar in texture and size, but different in colour, upon fresh-fallen snow in the sunlight, and how he found the snow melted under the pieces of cloth quickest when the cloth was black, less quickly under the blue, green, purple, red, yellow, in the order enumerated, and very slowly indeed under the white.

Each day's experience shows us that we do not need to be made of snow in order to melt rapidly under a black dress. What we require for comfort for summer wear is of course a light or white material, in order that the heat rays may be reflected as much and absorbed as little as possible.

The material should be porous— should imprison, that is, large quantities of air in its texture, and serve, therefore, as a very bad conductor of heat, while at the same time facilitating evaporation of the moisture from the surface of the body.

These qualities are possessed in the highest degree by white flannel, and there is no reason that we can find, remarks the *Lancet*, why this material should not be generally adopted.

**Propriety of Speech.**—1. You must be quite as anxious to *talk* with propriety as you are to think, work, sing, paint, or write according to the most correct rules.

2. Always select words calculated to convey an exact impression of your meaning.

3. Let your articulation be easy, clear, correct in accent, and suited in tone and emphasis to your discourse.

4. Avoid a muttering, stuttering, guttural, or lisping pronunciation.

5. Let your speech be neither too loud nor too low, but adjusted to the ear of your companion. Endeavour to prevent the necessity of the person you are speaking to crying "what do you say?"

6. Avoid a loquacious propensity; you should never occupy more than your share of conversation, or more than is agreeable to others.

7. Beware of such vulgar interpolations as "You know," "You see," "I'll tell you what."

8. Learn when to use and when to omit the aspirate *h*. This is an indispensable mark of a lady's education.

9. Pay a strict regard to the rules of grammar even in private conversation. If you do not understand those rules learn them, whatever be your age or station.

10. Though you should always converse pleasantly, do not mix loud bursts of laughter with it.

12. Above all, let your conversation be intellectual, graceful, chaste, discreet, edifying and profitable.

**Furs and Moths.**—Ladies are very properly anxious about keeping their furs free from moths during the summer months. A writer who may be relied on, says darkness is all that is needed. This little grey moth, or "miller," which deposits the eggs, moves only in the light. Enclose the article loosely in a paper box, put this in a pillow-case, or wrap it round with a cloth, and hang up in a dark closet. Camphor, spices, or perfumes, are of no use. Continual darkness is sufficient. And do not take out the furs in June or July to give them an "airing," for even then cometh the enemy, and it may be that in ten minutes after exposure to the light and sun has deposited a hundred eggs in the article. If you consider an airing indispensable, give the furs a good switching and put them quickly back.

[We do not see why the old preventives for keeping furs from moths, such as camphor, &c., could not be persisted in combined with the darkness recommended by the writer we have quoted from, and thus make twice sure of preserving our furs from the ravages of the moths.]

**Best Treatment of Cough.**—For a simple cough, we consider the following treatment by Dr. Searle as the very best :—

" A simple cough, attended with little or no fever, is often relieved by the application of a mustard-plaster to the chest. The mustard should be fresh mixed with hot water as for the table, but a little more fluid, and spread upon a napkin about the size of a cheese-plate, and then applied to the chest and windpipe, and kept on for ten or fifteen minutes, or as long as it can be conveniently borne. If necessary it may be repeated every evening ; immersing the feet and legs at the same time in hot water, and taking also a teaspoonful of a mixture consisting of syrup of poppies, antimonial wine, and paregoric elixir, in the proportions of half an ounce of the first, with a quarter of an ounce of each of the others, every three or four hours, according to the severity of the cough ; abstaining at the same time from a stimulating or a too nourishing diet.

" These means will soon remove the cough : though it is often advisable to follow them up for a few nights with a pill of calomel and aloes, a grain of each, in relief of the secondary derangements of the liver and associated organs, which constantly succeed to cold ; and from the neglect of which, though persons often get well of the prominent affections of the chest, they yet remain for a length of time afterwards valetudinary.

**Tests of Pure Water.**—The following practical rules for testing the wholesomeness of water (says Dr. Marcet) may be relied on :—1. The water must be perfectly colourless and transparent, leaving no deposit when allowed to stand undisturbed.—2. It must be quite devoid of smell.—3. When litmus paper is immersed in the water, the colour of the paper must remain unaltered.—4. The water when boiled must not become turbid. 5. About half a tablespoonful of the fluid being evaporated to dryness on the spirit lamp, there must be a slight residue left at the bottom of the spoon not turning black from organic matters.—5. The residue obtained by evaporating to dryness a sample of the water in a porcelain cup upon the tea-urn, must not become black on the addition of a solution of sulphuretted hydrogen.

**Dry-Nursing.**—Wherever it can be, this evil practice should be avoided, as being dangerous to the health of both mother and offspring. For no other reason than that of inability on the part of the mother to suckle her infant should the natural law be departed from. But should a bad state of health require it, and dry-nursing be decided on, it is essential to attend both to the *mode* of administering the food, as well as its kind or quality. Although the fluid food of the infant does not so much require the mixture of *saliva* to assist digestion, yet a degree of mastication, which increases the flow of this fluid, will usually be beneficial. For this good reason, then, the boat should be discarded from the nursery —the mode of feeding with which is most objectionable. The boat is replenished and laid on the tongue of the infant ; the food is poured on those parts of the throat, the irritability of which immediately prompts them, in self-defence, to the act of swallowing.

The most judicious mode, because the nearest approximation to the nipple, is the sucking-bottle. In its use, however, great cleanliness must be observed. The mouth of the bottle should be covered with wash-leather, or the nipple of a young heifer, in which a small piece of sponge is placed, in imitation of the pores of the nipple, to prevent too rapid a flow. The first is more easily kept clean ; but the second is the most acceptable to the child, and, indeed, more eligible, as it brings the necessity of constant cleansing ; it should be removed, and its sponge withdrawn, after each supply to the infant, and kept in rose or distilled water, with a few drops of spirits of wine, and re-applied when it is again used.

Of the species of artificial food, we give preference to the Aylesbury Condensed Milk, a new preparation, but one that is fast supplanting all others in the estimation of nurses and doctors. When this is not attainable, let the following preparation be used, which nearly resembles the milk of the mother:—Fresh cow's milk, two-thirds, spring water, one-third; well sweetened with loaf sugar, which is the least liable to acidify and cloy. One teaspoonful of sugar is the right quantity to sweeten one pint of water, or milk. It is the large proportion of sugar, the bland and nutrient property of which renders the milk of the mare and the ass so nearly resembling that of the mother, for which they are eligible substitutes.

After the first three months, milk with less water, or milk alone, should be given. The milk should not be sweetened until a few minutes before it is given to the baby, or it will turn sour. Neither should it be warmed over a fire; for when milk and water are used, the warm water will make the milk warm enough; when milk is used alone, it can be easily warmed by putting it into the feeding-bottle, and then putting the feeding-bottle into warm water. The milk should never be given more than lukewarm.

**Weaning.**—After the ninth month, if the child has cut three or four of its front teeth, and appears in good health, the process of weaning should not be delayed, the first period of childhood being then past. It is a process, it must be owned, of much importance, as its results are often unfavourable to the child;—it is a renouncement of its earliest habits, and is frequently marked by disordered functions and derangement of general health, the result of mere change of food. The most frequent malady is that protracted relaxation of the bowels termed the Weaning Brash, which appears to be most frequent in summer and autumn; and in the male oftener than in the female infant.

This disorder does not always appear immediately on the commencement of weaning. We have witnessed it five weeks subsequently. It is marked by frequent evacuation from the bowels, and, occasionally, during the nausea, from the stomach of mucous or green fluid, attended with pain. On this ensue loss of appetite, wasting, fever, fretfulness; and, towards the termination, tumefaction of the limbs, stupor, and convulsions. We would advise, if age and all other circumstances are favourable, that weaning should be adopted in the more temperate months—as March, April, May, and October.

**Measles.**—The earliest symptoms, commencing from ten to fourteen days after exposure, are redness and tumefaction, and water running from the eyes; languor, sneezing, head-ache, intolerance of light, dry cough, fever; on the fourth or fifth day the skin is covered with small, slightly raised, red spots, coalescing and forming red patches of a circular form, with often a few purple spots; sometimes bleeding at the nose; on the seventh or eighth day the redness fades, the fever subsides, and the efflorescence terminates in scaly exfoliation of the skin.

In the milder forms a gentle emetic, if there be an accumulation of mucus in the throat, a mild laxative occasionally, acidulated barley-water and other simple fluids, cooling mixture, and a well-regulated temperature of the room of about sixty degrees, are the only essential rules to be observed. Inflammatory symptoms, or severe relaxation of the bowels, require more scientific consideration.

The danger in measles will be in proportion as the fever is severe, or the more important organs, as the lungs, &c., may become affected during or subsequent to the disease.

On sudden recession of the eruption,

the warm bath should be employed; and on the child being disturbed at night by slight cough and simple restlessness, one teaspoonful or more, according to the age, of red-poppy syrup, may be given at bed-time. This is as far as domestic remedies should extend. On recovery, external exercise should be only employed in dry weather, and the child protected from the cold air by flannel.

**Teething.**—The judicious management of dentition is the prevention o a great majority of infantile disorders. One of the first symptoms of it is a heat in the mouth, perceptible while suckling. The child's food should be lessened, and it should be furnished with an increased supply of cold water while dentition is going forward.

It is highly injudicious to treat this disorder by the use of opiates, which many empirical preparations contain; these injure by a direct influence on the brain, in inducing stupor, and indirectly, by totally suppressing that discharge which was, within limits, a natural effort to relieve.

Equally erroneous is it to administer full doses of anodynes for the purpose of lulling to sleep. We do not so decidedly object to the rubbing of the gum with one drop of the soothing syrup; if this be not swallowed, it will sometimes be beneficial.

A coral is not the substance most proper for an infant's gums to press on. A penny square of India rubber, cut in the form of a cross, is the most suitable for the tender gums.

If the bowels are confined, and will not yield to diet, a gentle purgative, as magnesia or castor-oil, must be given without delay. Lancing the gums should always be adopted if they are swollen, red, hot, and painful. The warm-bath will be found an excellent soother, especially where irritation exists.

**Dew.**—Who does not admire the bright crystal drops that in the early morning glisten and sparkle on every leaf and flower, and every blade of grass? Who, in young, careless childhood, has not felt a delight in beholding his face in these countless mirrors of dew, or in bathing his hands in the fresh cool moisture?

The vapour of the air is condensed into dew by coming in contact with substances colder than itself. After sunset the warm earth radiates its heat into the air, and the surrounding vapour becomes chilled by contact with the cold surface, and settles on it in clear liquid drops. This occurs only when the night is fine, and free from clouds; for, at such times, there is nothing to prevent the radiation of heat from the ground, whilst clouds act as an obstruction to the heat; consequently on a cloudy night no dew falls.

Dew is always most plentiful in open situations, where there are no houses, trees, &c., to check the escape of the heated air; while, on the other hand, the ground beneath a tree in full foliage remains dry.

It is a wise adaptation of Providence that those things which require most moisture radiate heat most freely, and collect the largest quantity of dew; grass, vegetables, and the leaves of plants, which are dependent upon it for sustenance, part with their warmth rapidly and abundantly, while polished metal and smooth stones are bad radiators of heat.

In all cultivated ground, also, a large supply of dew is yielded; for loose soil readily throws off its warmth, and the genial moisture sinks down to nourish the seeds and roots lying embosomed in the earth. How little we consider the wise arrangement of these seeming trifles! We pass by, and think not of such trivial things, and yet God heeds them, and forgets not the use of even a drop of dew.

On a gusty night the wind evaporates the dew as it falls, and in the morning the flowers are disappointed of their fresh glittering ornaments.

**The Death Watch.**—A Naturalist tells us, that, " upon going into my bedroom one night I heard what is commonly called the 'Death Watch.' My inquisitiveness being roused, I determined, if possible, to discover, and have a look at, the author of the ticking. I listened, and after some time traced the sound, as I thought, to my empty hat-box on a chest of drawers. I approached gently, and placed my ear close to the box. Yes! there it was indeed! I examined the box on the outside, but saw nothing of life upon it. I lifted the lid, the ticking ceased at once. I examined the inside of the box in every crevice, but found nothing. I shut the lid again and was quiet. Again was commenced the intermittent ticking; I was certain the sound came from the box, and was puzzled. I again opened the lid and made a most minute search; I tore the joinings of the thin wood apart, and looked there, but found nothing. I replaced the lid, and again the ticking commenced. I scrutinised again the outside minutely, and looking very close, I discovered a little insect about the sixteenth of an inch in length, semi-transparent, and of a rich cream colour, rushing hither and thither over and about a slight elevation of the paper covering of the box, apparently greatly excited. Every now and then he came to a full stop, and with the nether part of his tiny body struck the hollow paper ten or twelve taps (which were very distinctly audible); he then set off as fast as his six (I think) legs could carry him.

Whilst he was thus running about I heard another little tapping, apparently proceeding from underneath the small hollow paper hill. My little lively friend also heard it, and at once came to a stand; and setting his hinder parts in motion, gave the requisite number of taps, and was off again.

I was now curious to see beneath the paper, and tearing it open, (in doing which I unfortunately deprived my insect friend of his paper drum,) I found a similar small insect on the inside. I watched the interesting couple for some time and thought I could divine the cause of the tumult. Ex-

ceeding the bounds of prudence, the male, (I presume it to have been,) having discovered from below a pinhole in the paper, had, most indiscreetly, thrust himself through it, and after a ramble on the fine smooth plateau on which he emerged, he, not having taken proper land-marks, was not able again to find his hole of exit. He thereupon sprang his rattle of alarm, and commenced a frantic search for a way of ingress, at which occupation I first discovered him. His deserted mate, doubtless in no less an excited state, answering with the utmost vigour of her latter-end, to call the wandering loved one back.

**Pictures on the Wall.**—If very well chosen, pictures add much to the good appearance of the room, and impart to it an air of completeness, and a home-look, which many people know how to appreciate. To produce this effect, the subjects of the pictures must be such as we can truly sympathise with, something to awaken our admiration, reverence, or love. All the feelings of our nature may be illustrated by pictures. There are some which we seem to make bosom companions of; others have a moral effect, and at times prevent our going astray by their silent monitions.

It is therefore worth while to take pains and choose good subjects, whether in engravings or paintings, and to frame and hang them suitably when chosen.

Gilt frames are most suitable for rather dark paintings, and on a deep coloured wall: while prints look well in a frame of composition, oak, rosewood, or bird's-eye maple, finished with a gilt moulding.

Care should be taken to hang them in a proper light, so as best to bring out all the effects of the pictures, and to place them so that the light shall fall from the same side as represented by the painter.

In picture galleries and great houses, brass rods are fixed all round the room close to the ceiling, from which the pictures are hung but in small rooms it is often best not to show the lines or wires by which the pictures hang. This is done by nailing a strong cord across the back, about two inches below the top, and then suspending it from two nails standing out but a little way from the wall.

When there are several pictures in a room, the ordinary rule is, to have either the upper or lower edge of the frames in a line, on whichever side they may be hung.

**Gruel.**—There are two ways of preparing gruel ; one from the whole grain, whether oat, barley, or rice ; the other from meal. The former is generally preferred as most delicate and secure from adulteration ; the latter is much more convenient when wanted quickly. There is no nicer gruel than that made of whole oats, with merely the husks removed, or once flattened by passing through a mill. The former are called whole groats ; the latter cracked, or Embden groats ; the fresher they are used the better. If kept at all after being cracked it should be in a closely shut vessel, whether glass, earthen, or tin, and in a very dry place.

The Embden groats done up in paper soon become sour. The coarse Scotch oatmeal, and fine oatmeal purchased by measure of an honest meal-man, is far preferable to those called " prepared," and sold in paper packets. Whether it is owing to the " preparation," or the mode of keeping, it is hard to obtain from the latter article good, well-flavoured gruel.

For groat gruel, the whole or cracked groats should be set on with cold water, and a sufficient quantity of it to allow for at least one-third boiling away. It must be frequently stirred, and should not be allowed to boil over. It is not merely the quantity actually spilt that is wasted, but in the early stage of the process the most nourishing part of the grain rises in the form of scum, which afterwards sinks, and then enriches the whole.

A quarter of a pint of groats will make one quart of thick gruel, being set on with three pints of water, and boiled three quarters of an hour ; then strain. The groats may be boiled again with rather more than a pint of water put to them boiling, and will produce nearly another pint of gruel.

For meal gruel, one large spoonful of oatmeal (either Scotch or fine) ; mix it very smoothly with two tablespoonfuls of cold water. Stir into a pint of water boiling on the fire. Let it boil briskly ten or fifteen minutes, then strain.

For either sort of gruel, a bit of fresh butter and a little salt may be stirred in, or a little sugar and nutmeg.

Rice gruel may be made of ground rice just in the same manner.

As it is generally prescribed when the bowels are in a disordered state, it is of special importance that the rice be perfectly pure and in good keeping. Persons who often use ground rice will do well to have a mill, and grind it at home as wanted.

A stick of cinnamon and a few chips of dried Seville orange-peel may be boiled in the gruel for flavour. If rinsed and dried, they will serve two or three times in succession. When strained, sweeten with loaf sugar, and add a grate of nutmeg.

Rice gruel is sometimes ordered to be made with port wine or brandy, and it is possible for a sick person to be in such a state as to render these additions suitable, but they should never be used but in cases of emergency, and under medical direction. In ninety-nine cases out of a hundred they would do no good, but would probably do great harm. We are pleased to observe a growing reluctance on the part of the profession to prescribe alcohol but in most exceptional cases.

Thick gruel, whether of oat, barley, or rice, may be thinned with new milk, and is a very nourishing and agreeable food, when the particular disorder does not render it unsuitable.

**Chest Preservers.**—No portion of the human body requires more protection from cold than the chest. Various chest protectors, as they are termed, have been devised for this purpose, and the most popular of these are made of wash-leather, lined, or of hare or rabbit-skin, also lined. As at present made and used, these are very dangerous contrivances. They keep out the cold, it is true, but they hinder the exhalation so necessary to health constantly going on from the surface of the skin, and to a greater extent in the region of the chest where the lungs are situated. Those who employ them are often in a high state of fever, especially felt when the weather changes suddenly from being cold to a mild temperature ; colds are frequently thus generated, the causes of which are unknown to the sufferers, or believed to arise from other circumstances.

To render chest protectors useful for the purpose of keeping the chest warm, they should be perforated with a number of small holes about the size of a grain of pearl barley, so as to permit the escape of perspiration from the pores of the skin. The prepared thin leather and hare-skin protectors, unless perforated, retain the impurities that are constantly being exuded. The use of flannel for the same purpose is not liable to the same objection, being a porous material. In all cases, persons should have several of them, in order to admit of a frequent change.

Unless the suggestions now pointed out are attended to, these useful articles of clothing, instead of being chest protectors, are most injurious.

**Pillar Roses.**—To ornament a garden, there is no kind of shrub, however beautiful, so well adapted to take various forms as the rose. It can be used as a dwarf to fill the smallest beds, as a bush to plant amongst evergreens, and as a tall standard to form avenues of roses on each side of a walk. In the centre of larger circular beds it is often planted in groups, with half-standards around, and dwarfs in the front, thus forming an amphitheatre of roses, which, when in bloom, is one of the finest sights in the floral garden ; again, as climbers, to ornament the amateur's villa, or the more humble abode of the cottager ; also, to plant against bare walls and palings, forming drooping shrubs, when budded on high standards, waving gracefully their boughs, laden with fragrance and bloom, in the warm gales of summer and autumn. What can be more desirable ? All these forms are certainly very pleasing, and, however elegant their appearance, still none of them show off the beauty and grandeur of the rose so effectively as training it upwards to a pillar.

In the gardens of the gentry of this country, pillars for roses are frequently made of iron rods, with arches of the same, or small chains hung loosely from pillar to pillar, so as to form beautiful festoons of those lovely flowers. These arches and chain festoons of roses on each side a terrace walk have a splendid effect. Sometimes the arch is thrown over the walk only, and the roses trained accordingly. They may either be made of a single upright rod, or with four rods at about nine inches distant from each other, thus forming a square pillar, fastened with cross pieces of strong wire. The rose may be planted in the centre, and the branches as they grow be trained to each corner rod, and the small shoots arranged between them. Bring all the shoots to the outside, and do not allow any to twine round the rods, but tie them to each other with bar matting or small string, as they can then be easily loosened from the pillars whenever they require painting— an operation that must not be neglected, as the iron would soon rust, and thereby injure the plants, and be very unsightly.

Previously to planting the roses the soil should be rendered rich, so that they may grow quickly, flower freely, and cover the pillars, arches, and festoons, as soon as possible.

This rather modern and pleasing mode of culture cannot be too strongly recommended, and for that purpose, if expense be an object, we would suggest that poles, either of oak, ash, hazel, or larch, may be used by fixing them firmly in the ground in a triangular shape, three feet square at the base, the ends being brought together at the top, and tied with some strong tarred cord or stout copper wire, and then three roses of the same variety, or of different kinds, according to taste, to be planted one at the foot of each pole, and trained so that when in full foliage and blossom a handsome tall pyramid will become apparent, formed of the beauteous and odoriferous queen of flowers.

**Perforated Carving and Fret-Cutting**—Ladies will find the art of Fretwork or Perforated Carving one well worthy their attention as an agreeable employment for their hours of leisure. We class this art as the first for utility and beauty amongst the numerous ones specially awarded to their delicate manipulation. There is really no limit to the useful articles that may be made with the aid of this accomplished art. Happily, too, it is easy to acquire, and the tools and apparatus required for its performance are inexpensive to purchase. Mr. W. Bemrose, Junr., in his beautiful volume of designs and instructions in the art has made it so clear to those who choose to pursue it, that there is nothing but perseverance required on the part of the student.

In his introductory remarks, Mr. Bemrose observes :—" Fretwork, or Perforated-Carving, is an agreeable, useful, and ornamental art to practice, and one that can be easily accomplished by a lady ; it has also the further advantage of being an employment for leisure moments, which is neither expensive, nor one that requires a special apartment, as it can be practised in any room, and upon an ordinary table."

The volume which makes this art so easy and accessible to ladies, conducting them, as it were, by a royal road to its acquisition, contains fifty-three exquisite designs and instructions for book slides, brackets, book-rests, table mat, or panel for window plant box,

paper knives, hand mirror, card baskets (four designs), letter rack, corner bracket, blotting book slide, envelope box, thermometer plate, or finger plate for door, ornament for top of wire window blind, picture frame, book side, photograph frame, table easel, key and trinket cupboard, reading desk, with wood hinges, finger plates for doors, hand mirror, flower-pot cover, hanging book shelves, bread and butter platters, dragon-fly bracket, picture, or mirror frame showing carved fretwork, &c. &c.

We give this enumeration of designs contained in Mr. Bemrose's volume, with a view of showing the numerous useful purposes for which this art is capable. Nor need it be restricted to these, which are only to be received as an earnest of a hundred other domestic articles this feminine art may be made available.

Our author says, " simple Fretwork, of good design, is rich and pleasing to the eye, but this effect is greatly increased when the aid of the carving tools is called in, to further embellish it ; and, it being further advisable that the amateur, after having mastered the simple art of Fretwork, should proceed to the more advanced operation of Wood Carving, she must study well the instructions given in the " Manual of Wood Carving," (published by Bemrose and Sons, Paternoster Row), which contains upwards of 130 designs.

Fret-Cutting and Wood-Carving are susceptible of developing manual dexterity and taste to a very considerable extent. These sister-arts, pursued by the simple method pointed out in the volumes referred to, will be found useful in many ways other than those for which instructions and elaborate designs are given. The theory once acquired, the practice of the art can be extended, as we have said before, in innumerable ways to embellish our homes, and convert them into homes of taste.

**Preservation of the Teeth.**—Horace Walpole says in his " Letters,"

" Use a little bit of alum twice or thrice in a week, no bigger than half your nail, till it has all dissolved in your mouth, and then spit it out.   This has fortified my teeth, that they are as strong as the pen of Junius.  I learned it of Mrs. Grosvenor, who had not a speck in her teeth till her death."

Do not let your brushes be too hard, as they are likely to irritate the gums and injure the enamel.

Avoid too frequent use of tooth-powder, and be very cautious what kind you buy, as many are prepared with destructive acids.  Those who brush their teeth carefully and thoroughly with tepid water and a soft brush (cold water should never be used, for it chills and injures the nerves) have no occasion to use powder.

Should any little incrustation (tartar) appear on the sides or at the back of the teeth, which illness and very often the constant eating of sweetmeats, fruit, and made dishes containing acids will cause, put a little magnesia on your brush, and after two or three applications it will remove it.  While treating on the care of the teeth, which is a subject of the highest importance to those who have young families, and in fact every one who wishes to preserve them, we beg to remind our readers that as the period generally occupied by sleep is calculated to be about (at least) six hours out of the twenty-four, it would greatly promote the healthful maintenance of the priceless pearls whose loss or decay so greatly influences our appearance and our comfort if we were to establish a habit of carefully cleaning them with a soft brush before going to bed.  The small particles of food clogging the gums impede circulation, generate tartar and caries, and affect the breath.  Think of an amalgamation of cheese, flesh, sweetmeats, fruit, &c., in a state of decomposition, remaining wedged between our teeth for six or seven hours ; yet how few ever take the trouble to attend to this most certain cause of toothache, discolouration, and decay, entailing the miseries of scaling,

plugging, extraction, and the crowning horror—false teeth.

**Dreams.**—The following are medical signs of dreams, as published in a medical work—

Lively dreams are, in general, a sign of nervous action.

Soft dreams a sign of slight irritation of the brain ; often, in nervous fever, announcing the approach of a favourable crisis.

Frightful dreams are a determination of blood to the head.

Dreams about blood and red objects are signs of inflammatory conditions.

Dreams about rain and water are often signs of deceased mucous membranes and dropsy.

Dreams of distorted forms are frequently a sign of abdominal obstructions and disorder of the liver.

Dreams in which the patient sees any part of the body especially suffering, indicates disease in that part.

The nightmare, with great sensitiveness, is a sign of determination of blood to the chest.

**Rules of Sleep.**—Dr. Forbes Winslow wisely says there is no fact more clearly established in the physiology of man than this, that the brain expends its energies and itself during the hours of wakefulness and that these are recuperated during sleep.  If the recuperation does not equal the expenditure, the brain withers—this is insanity.  Thus it is that, in early English History, persons who were condemned to death by being prevented from sleeping, always died raving maniacs ; thus it is that those who are starved to death become insane—the brain is not nourished, and they cannot sleep.

The practical inferences are the following :—

1st. Those who think most, who do most brain work, require most sleep.

2nd. That time " saved " from necessary sleep is infallibly destructive to mind, body, and estate.

Give your servants, your children, yourself—give all that are under you the fullest amount of sleep they will take, by compelling them to go to bed at some regular hour, and to rise in the morning the moment they awake ; and within a fortnight, nature, with almost the regularity of the rising sun, will unloose the bonds of sleep the moment enough repose has been secured for the wants of the system.

This is the only safe and sufficient rule ; and as to the question how much sleep any one requires, each must be a rule for himself—great nature will never fail to write it out to the observer under the regulations now set down.

**Non-Inflammable Clothing.**—Dr. Odling, of Guy's Hospital, in a letter addressed to a contemporary, on the subject of the dangers arising from the inflammability of ladies' dresses, gives the following valuable information on the effects of certain salts upon fabrics : —The various means proposed for rendering textile fabrics non-inflammable were carefully investigated a short time back by two eminent chemists, Messrs. Versmann and Oppenheim. They undoubtedly demonstrated that linen and cotton goods dried after immersion in a solution of one or other of several salts possessed the property of non-inflammability, and that the best results were obtained with a solution of sulphate of ammonia, or of tungstate of soda, neither of which liquids produced any injurious effect upon the tissue or colour of the fabric. The tungstate of soda solution was found most applicable to laundry purposes, on account of its not interfering in any way with the process of ironing. Muslins, &c., steeped in a seven per cent of sulphate of ammonia, or a twenty per cent solution of tungstate of soda, and then dried, may be held in the flame of a candle or gas lamp without taking fire. That portion of the stuff in contact with the light becomes charred and destroyed, but it does not inflame, and consequently the burning state does not spread to the rest of this material.

**Frumenty.**—We give a receipt for the preparation of this article of diet, although we cannot recommend it as wholesome, especially if made, as it generally is, of new grain :—Boil a quarter of a pint of wheat in water for three or four hours, then drain off the liquid, and add a quart of milk, with which has been previously mixed two tablespoonsful of flour, two eggs, quarter of a pound of currants, a little lemon peel and cinnamon ; boil for about twenty minutes and sweeten ; no doubt this is very nourishing, but it is heavy and difficult of digestion ; if taken at all it should be as a very occasional luxury. The name of the above is commonly corrupted to *Frumity* or *Fermity*.

**Fruit, when to Eat and Avoid.**—There can be no doubt that fruit, both in their fresh and dried state, are extremely wholesome and useful, affording to the blood the saline constituents which it generally needs, cooling the system, and in many cases acting as a gentle aperient ; the best, because the most easily digested kinds, are those which are soft and pulpy, having the seeds enclosed in a pouch, skin, or rind, such as grapes, currants, gooseberries, strawberries, raspberries, blackberries, mulberries, 'among native, and oranges and lemons among imported fruits ; apples, although not soft and pulpy, are very wholesome ; but as much cannot be said for pears and medlars, as, in most kinds of these, decomposition commences directly the ripening process is completed, so that they are seldom eaten in a perfectly sound state.

Stone fruits, such as cherries, plums, apricots, &c., are not so wholesome as those with seeds, although taken in moderation they act beneficially, especially in a cooked state. Melons and pine apples we must pronounce decidedly unwholesome.

With regard to the best time for eating fruit, let us observe that it is digestible in proportion to its perfection, and, therefore, care should be taken to have it perfectly ripe, and yet not in a state of decay. Most juicy fruits are best taken in hot weather, and the drier kinds in the cold seasons. The beet time of day for eating fruits is the morning, none but the more watery kinds should be eaten after midday, and none at all late in the evening. The worst possible time to eat them is just before going to bed.

**Fritters.**—Capital fritters may be made with a kind of paste, which, being allowed to cool, is cut into shapes, which are dipped in butter and fried. Here are several forms of it :—

1. Pass some potatoes through a sieve, stir into them a little melted butter and enough whole eggs to form a stiffish paste ; season with salt, pepper, and a little nutmeg ; form into the shape of little balls, and dip in batter and fry. This may be varied by adding a little cream, also some ham or Bologna sausage finely minced, and some chopped parsley.

2. Have a saucepan with about a pint of boiling water and one ounce of butter ; drop into this gradually with the hand some Indian corn flour, stirring all the time until you get a liquid paste. Take care not to put too much flour, and to put in gradually, else it will form into knots and spoil the dish. Removing the saucepan from the fire, you stir into the paste a good allowance of grated Parmesan cheese, a little salt and pepper, and pour out your paste on a marble slab to cool. When cold, cut it out into any shape and fry. The addition of ham or sausage can also be made to this.

3. Make the paste as above, only with common corn flour ; when half cold stir into it some yolks of eggs, and flavour it with pepper, salt, and nutmeg ; add chopped parsley and minced ham, then treat it as the others ; or you may flavour it with cheese. All the above pastes may be fried without being previously dipped in batter, but it is more difficult to fry them creditably that way.

**Mixing a Salad.**—This is a point of proficiency which it is easy to attain with care. The main point is, to incorporate the several articles required for the sauce, and to serve up at table as fresh as possible. The herbs should be " morning gathered," and they will be much refreshed by laying for two hours in spring water. Careful picking, and washing, and drying in a cloth, are also very important, and the due proportion of each herb requires attention.

The sauce may be thus prepared :— Boil two eggs for ten minutes, and then put them in cold water for three or four minutes, so that the yolks may become quite cold and hard. Rub them through a coarse sieve with a wooden spoon, and mix them with a tablespoonful of cream, and then add two tablespoonsful of fine flask oil, or melted butter ; mix, and add by degrees, a teaspoonful of salt, and the same quantity of mustard ; mix till smooth, when incorporate with the other ingredients about three tablespoonsful of vinegar ; then pour this sauce down the side of the salad bowl, but do not stir up the salad till wanted to be eaten.

Garnish the top of the salad with the white of the eggs cut in slices ; or these may be arranged in such manner as to be ornamental on the table. Some persons may fancy they are able to prepare a salad without previous instruction, but, like everything else, a little knowledge in this case may not be thrown away.

**Care of Linen.**—When linen is well dried and laid by for use, nothing more is necessary than to secure it from damp and insects ; the latter may be provided against by a mixture of aromatic shrubs and flowers, sewed in silken bags, to be interspersed among the drawers and shelves. These may consist of lavender, thyme, roses, cedarshavings, powdered sassafras, cassia, lignea, &c., into which a few drops of otto of roses, or other strong-scented perfume, may be thrown. In all cases it will be found consistent with economy, to examine and repair all washable articles, especially linen, that may stand in need of it, previous to sending it to the laundry. It will also be prudent to have every article carefully numbered, and so arranged, after washing, as to have their regular term and turn in domestic use.

**Dry-Cleaning and Scouring Carpets.**—In London, and indeed all large towns, carpets that require cleaning or renovating are usually sent to the dyer's or scourer's ; but they may be cleansed effectually by washing at home on the floor or on tables. In either case they must be taken up and well swept.

Grease is taken out by rubbing hard soap on the spot, and scrubbing it out with a brush dipped in clean cold water. Each spot must be rubbed dry with a cloth as it is washed. Dissolve a bar of soap in two gallons of water by cutting it into the water and heating it to boil. Lay the carpet on the floor and tack it down. Provide brushes, and any quantity of coarse cotton cloths, flannels, and a large sponge. Take two pails of blood-warm water, put two quarts of the melted soap into one of them to scour the carpet with, and use the other for rinsing. Dip the brush in the soap-suds, and scour a square yard of the carpet at time, using as little water as possible, not to soak it through. When the soap has done its work, rub it well out of the carpet with a flannel or a coarse sponge, sucking up with these all the wet and dirt left by the brush, rinsing the article used in fair water repeatedly. Have ready a pail of clean cold water, with enough sulphuric acid or sharp vinegar in it to taste sour ; dip a clean sponge in this, and squeeze and rub it well into the spot just cleansed. Afterwards wipe dry with coarse cloths, rinsing and hanging them where they will be dry when the next yard is washed. Finish yard after yard in this way, rubbing each clean and dry as you go. Keep a good fire in the room to dry the carpet thoroughly.

This is a tedious but thorough process. Hearth-rugs may be cleaned in the same way, beating and brushing them well, and tacking them on a large board before washing. Scrub one-sixth of it at a time, unless you are expeditious, and dry well with an old sheet. The secret of having carpets look well

is to wash and rinse them thoroughly, without soaking them through. Ingrain, tapestry, Brussels and Turkish carpets are all cleaned in this way. Good authorities recommend a teacupful of ox-gall to a pail of suds for scrubbing carpets, rinsing with fair water.

**Hints on Stocking and Managing an Aquarium.**—Having resided several years at the seaside, writes a Correspondent, and studied those animals most suited to an Aquarium, I think a few hints on the subject might be acceptable. First, in choosing the aquarium ; the best shape is oblong and not too deep, as many of the animals, particularly the common smooth anemone, are amphibious, and live nearly as much out of the water as in. It is therefore advisable to have some of the rocks projecting above the water, on which the animals may crawl whenever they choose.

The aquarium should be placed before a window with a good light, but out of the sun. The great mistake that most beginners make is putting in the animals and seaweeds at the same time, which has the effect of making the water thick and muddy. The seaweed should be arranged in the tanks quite a week before any of the animals are put in. The water will then be perfectly clear, with small bubbles constantly ascending, and ought to last, without being changed, any length of time. At low water it is easy to find many stones of a suitable size, with different kinds of seaweeds attached ; or else a chisel and hammer will quickly knock off some pretty specimens. All loose seaweeds must be taken out of the tank, as they will quickly corrode the water. The smooth anemone is the most healthy of that class, and therefore well suited for the aquarium ; they look, when out of the water, like little lumps of green and red jelly sticking to the rock, having in this state a most uninviting appearance ; by passing the thumb-nail or a pocket-knife under the base they are easily detached, and when placed in the water quickly begin to present a much more charming aspect. They are soon surrounded by a beautiful fringe, and when fully expanded, a row of little blue globules may be seen.

Another anemone well suited for the aquarium, and on some coasts nearly as common as the moss, is the strawberry anemone, so called from its resemblance to the fruit of that name.

The " gem " and the " daisy " anemone are also very hardy little animals, though much more difficult to procure. For though common enough they are less easily seen, and have a way of fixing themselves in small crevices, out of which it is very troublesome to get them.

Of all the anemones the " crass " is the most delicate, but will repay any trouble, as, when fully expanded, it presents a most magnificent appearance. It is only to be found at low water, and then, when left dry by the tide, looks like a dry mass of sand and shells—a very difficult and tedious task it is to procure one without injuring the base. It ought to be placed at the bottom of the tank, as it is accustomed to plenty of water. When a " crass " is not in a healthy state, it begins to puff out striped bladders from its mouth, which gradually get to an enormous size ; when this occurs it is not likely to live long, and had therefore better at once be taken out of the tank. The crass is of an exceedingly voracious nature, and will eat any amount of food. None of the anemones are particular what kind of meat they eat—cooked or raw—beef, mutton, or rabbit. Once a week is quite sufficient to feed them, but they will live months without requiring any, and the less they are fed the prettier they look, as a little food at a time entices them to keep their tentacles extended in search of more.

The anemones do not actually eat their food, they only suck it, and some days after small pieces of white meat will be seen floating on the water, the nourishment having been all extracted. Over the " moss " will often be seen a white film, which ought to be removed with a camel hair brush, and after being released from it they will usually extend their tentacles.

It is as well to have some shell-fish in the aquarium, as some of them, particularly the periwinkle and silver-top are very useful in keeping the sides of the tank clean.

The acorn shells with which many of the rocks are covered, are a decided risk in an aquarium. Though out of water they look most unattractive, no sooner are they put in than they completely change their appearance, extending numerous little feelers like so many feathers, which they wave about most gracefully. Though very pretty at first in an aquarium, they soon get lazy, and cease to put out their feelers, and often die, scenting the water with a most disagreeable smell of gas, which kills all the other inhabitants.

Crabs are most amusing inmates of an aquarium, as they wander over the whole place, often, however, coming to an untimely end, by venturing too near the " crass," which is certain destruction, as its tentacles have a wonderfully tenacious power, and will retain a crab much larger than itself. A hermit crab does not live very well in confinement, but while it does it is most amusing. It has a soft tail, and to shield it lives in any shell it happens to come across, often previously destroying the rightful owner. It is most interesting watching one changing its home ; if an empty shell is put near, it will examine it most minutely, and if satisfied with its appearance, will change shells with great rapidity. It is a peculiar-looking animal, crawling about and dragging its tail behind, as if ashamed of it. It always leaves its shell to die.

Besides being amusing, crabs are very useful, as they are not at all particular as to what they eat—they will search out and devour every dead shell-fish or any of their own tribe. Enough shrimps can easily be caught to stock an aquarium from the little rock pools.

**Archery.**—Archery for ladies, besides being one of the most healthful pastimes, is highly valuable for giving grace to the figure. It is much to be regretted that ladies should have allowed this delightful game to have so much dwindled out of use.

Much importance is properly attached to the attitude assumed by a lady archer. To this end care should be taken to attend to the following instructions: To keep the heels a few inches apart, the neck slightly curved, and the face and side turned towards the target.

*The Aim.*—When the arrow is three parts drawn, the aim is to be taken ; in doing this, the pile of the feather should appear to the right of the mark ; the arrow is then drawn to its head, and immediately loosened. Observe well the distance and the lateral direction in taking aim, for there is no bow that will send an arrow many feet straight without some elevation, though it may be slight ; but when the distanc is many yards, and the bows weak, the elevation would be considerably increased. To meet this unavoidable contingency, the bow should be somewhat raised above the object aimed at. It is impossible to shoot an arrow straight to a point, and, if so shot, will fall below it, for it is subject to the earth's attraction. Therefore much practice is required properly to arrange the elevation, and in this nice matter much will depend of course on the strength of the bow and the distance of the shot.

Again, there is the lateral direction to be considered—by the lateral direction we mean the side to which the bow is directed—which depends very much on the state of the wind, by which the arrow in its flight is materially affected. If the wind blows from the left hand, the bow should incline to the left, and if from the right hand, to the right.

*The Position.*—A glance at our Illustration will at once show this. Stand at right angles with the target, turning the face over the left shoulder. The heels, as we have before observed, must be kept a little apart, while the head should incline slightly forward, but the figure should be kept straight from the waist. Care must be taken not to overdraw the string without an arrow attached ; keep the longer limb of the bow upwards, for it is liable to break if held downwards.

*The Target.*—The face of a target generally contains four circles, with a gold centre ; the inner circle is usually red ; the next, white ; the third, black ; and the outer, white, bordered with green. The mode of counting the hits, is by the following increased scale ; one in the gold, counts nine ; one, red, counts three ; inner white, one as two ; in black, four counts as five ; the outer white, one counts as one. The prize can be computed in this manner by numbers, or, as is sometimes preferred, by the hit nearest the centre of the gold.

*To Draw the Bow.*—The bow should be held with the left hand, placing the arrow on the under side of the string, and the upper side of the bow, until the head of the arrow reaches about three inches beyond the left hand, and there secure it with the fore-finger while the right hand is removed down to the notch, or " nock," as it is more generally termed amongst archers. Then raise the arrow until the dark feather is uppermost ; then pass it down the bow, and fix it on the " nocking" part of the string. Have shooting-gloves on the fingers when drawing the bow. Place a finger on each side of the arrow on the string, and, to steady it, the thumb on the opposite side ; then extend the bow by means of the arrow and the string to the full length of the outstretched left arm, till the right hand reaches beyond the bottom of the left ear ; and thus the arrow is raised or pointed to an exact line with the centre or bull's-eye of the target, when nothing more is required than to speed the arrow on its lightning way to the object aimed at.

*Implements.*—The bow best adapted for the use of ladies is made of lancewood, and should not exceed five feet in length. The resisting power should not be more than twenty-three pounds, and scrupulous regard should be observed when purchasing a bow that it be not above the strength of the fair archer.

Arrows, in their weight, must be duly proportioned to the power of the bow, and preference given to those which

ATTITUDE WHILE TAKING AIM.

taper from the pile to the feathers. The brace, which is made of stout leather, is buckled round the bow arm just above the wrist, to prevent the string from hurting it.

The shooting-glove to protect the fingers, the tassel to wipe the arrows when covered with dirt from striking the ground, and a belt to contain the pouch or quiver, are the other ordinary accessories for following the delightful and healthy pastime of archery.

**Bead Mosaic.**—This elegant art for ladies will well repay the patience required for its due performance. In the following respects it differs from common bead-work, for the beads are fixed by cement to a firm background in the manipulation of this art, which is applicable to many purposes, and has the advantage of being executed with greater rapidity, and possessing more durability than any other kind of bead-work.

of metal or hard wood, while in the ordinary kind of bead-work the beads are sewn upon canvas.

We are indebted to "Cassell's Household Guide" for the following clear and practical instructions

"*Materials.*—All descriptions of glass beads may be used for this very interesting art, except, perhaps, those of extremely large size and of eccentric shapes, the different ordinary sizes and shapes being applicable to different positions and purposes. For such fine and delicate work as is to be placed near to and upon a level with the eye, small beads are most pleasing in effect ; but when the work is to be considerably elevated, or is intended to be seen from a distance only, tolerably large beads are to be preferred. Generally speaking, neatly rounded beads are those most appropriate ; but in some parts of the work, as, for instance, where perfectly straight lines have to be represented, these mere pieces of glass tubing, cut in lengths, and known as ' bugles,' may be found serviceable, and time will be economised by using them. Beads of as many different colours as possible should be provided, and the mosaicist will do well to have a large stock of these to select from ; but those beads which are of mixed colour should be avoided, as they will give more trouble, and not be so good in effect as the self-coloured beads. If gold beads which are thickly gilt with genuine metal can be procured, they will be of great value for enriching the work. Steel beads should be avoided, as being liable to rust.

*Cement.*—There are two or three kinds of cement used in bead mosaic. The most easily prepared is made by moistening isinglass in as much acetic acid as will quite dissolve it ; or (another) by melting best Russian glue and adding to it a small quantity of flake-white. These cements must be applied warm ; but the latter is inapplicable where tracing is necessary, as it will completely obscure it.

*Groundwork*—The groundwork to lay the beads on may be either wood or metal, or in some cases the mosaic may, if desired, be applied to evenly plastered walls. Where panels of wood are employed, it is always desirable that they should be formed of mahogany, that wood being less liable to warp. Whatever substance is used for a background, it will be well, before commencing, to paint it white, in order that the drawing of the design may be seen more plainly, and also that the brilliancy of the beads may be enhanced. It will in all cases be necessary that a rim, as of wood, or a gilt moulding, should surround the space to be filled, to give support to the mosaic, and to prevent its being dislodged by accidents.

*Process.*—Suppose, then, that the design from the well-known fable of the " Fox and the Crow," (p. 17), has been traced on the panel. A quantity of the isinglass cement, which is transparent, should be warmed, and a coat of it spread with a brush over the whole panel ; when this has somewhat dried, a smaller brush should be taken, and a little of the cement applied with it to a portion of the outline of one of the objects in the design, as the back of the fox. To hold the beads while at work, it is well to have a number of little china palettes, or similar shallow receptacles, into which a small number of each of the different coloured beads may be poured. From one of these, with a box-point, finely tapered to enter the holes in their centres, take some of the beads of the required colour, and arrange them side by side in a row within the outline ; carry this round the entire animal, varying the shade as required, and applying more cement from time to time. Inside this line another similar one must be placed in the same manner, and if the object to be represented be of a large size, three or even more of these outline courses will be desirable ; but for small objects two will generally be sufficient. After this the interior has to be filled up, by working across it, in curved lines (according to the direction of the shading) in a rounded object, and in straight lines in a flat one. In a similar manner all the other objects in the design would be worked. Afterwards the background must be filled up, by placing, first, a single row of beads, following the outline of the object with which it comes in contact, and by filling the remainder of the space in straight or curved lines, as may be best suited to its character. Thus, in the example given, the wall in the background would be composed of straight rows of beads, while above and below it the lines might be flowing. As the work proceeds, it should be smoothed and flattened, by pressing it gently with a small and perfectly smooth piece of ivory or box-wood ; and when the whole design is finished—for the purpose of finally correcting any irregularity of surface—a piece of paper should be laid over it, and it should be pressed down with a flat iron, moderately heated.

Finally, linseed oil must be spread over the work, and allowed to run between the beads, and finely-powdered whitening sprinkled upon it, and well worked with the brush into the interstices. This will at the same time thoroughly cleanse the surface from any cement, and by forming a kind of putty between the beads, combine them into a compact mass. The face of the beadwork may be wiped clean with a soft rag. In a few days, when the linseed oil and whitening have become thoroughly dry, and have set, the whole will be so firm that it will bear any reasonable amount of rough usage without injury to the work.

The subjects most easily worked in bead mosaic are those of a flat character, such as geometrical patterns, and the art is admirably adapted to the representation of heraldic devices. Strictly pictorial subjects are more difficult of treatment, especially if they are brought very near to the eye.

Where a rim of dark wood surrounds the mosaic, it will always be well to place next it a border of gold, yellow, or other light beads ; but where the rim is gilded, if there be no suitable dark colour next it in the design, a border of black beads should be placed adjoining it.

**Painting upon Glass with Varnish.**—This method is adapted well for copying pictures on windows. The following colours, specially prepared by Messrs. Barnard and Son, 339, Oxford Street, are nearly all the materials necessary for its due fulfilment :—

Raw and burnt sienna, brown pink, yellow, lake, ultramarine, verdigris, carmine, or crimson lake, gamboge, Prussian blue, and opaque ivory black.

These colours are in fine powder, and, when used, must be mixed with picture copal varnish, diluted, when necessary, with spirits of turpentine.

There were also be required a few sable pencils, a flat camel's-hair brush, some picture copal varnish, and a little spirits of turpentine.

The materials being ready, proceed as follows :—Lay the glass flat on the print or drawing to be copied, and with a very fine sable pencil and ivory black, mixed with varnish, trace all the outlines. When *thoroughly dry*, raise it to a slanting position, by placing it upon a frame with pieces of upright wood upon either side, and a sheet of white paper flat beneath it ; by this means the effect of the colouring, which may at once be proceeded with, will be better seen. One caution is perhaps here necessary ; be careful not to rub up the black in the colouring, as it is liable to smear if much worked over. On this account moist ivory-black is frequently, and with advantage, substituted for putting in the outline. It may be used with a pen most conveniently, fine or coarse at the points, according to the nature of the work. When finished, the painting should be fixed up in the window with the unpainted side outwards.

A few hints as to mixing the colours may be useful. The nearest approximation to scarlet is made by the admixture of gamboge with rose madder, crimson lake, or carmine ; for greens, verdigris is very brilliant, and almost every shade may be made by adding yellow lake, or brown pink, in different proportions. When a flat even tint is required, the camel-hair brush is used, and a dabber (made by simply covering a little cotton wool with fine leather), which is particularly useful for backgrounds in figure subjects, and skies in landscapes, and this applies also to the use of water-colours. When your painting is finished it must be carefully varnished. This pretty art may be executed at small cost.

**Names.**—A great point in the selection of names is, not to give your children such high-sounding names as may in after-life make them appear ludicrous in the eyes of the world when pursuing an ordinary or common occupation. It is perfectly true that Plato recommended to parents to give happy names to their children, and that Pythagoras taught that the minds, actions, and successes of men, were according to their fate, genius, and names; but such a doctrine is wholly untenable by any rational system of philosophy.

We knew a lady (she is dead now) who had in her girlhood been an inveterate reader of plays and novels, from which she had gathered all the long-winded, high-sounding, and chivalrous names which are usually found to belong to the heroes and heroines of such productions. These she unhesitatingly appropriated and treasured in her memory till the happy time would arrive when she should have an opportunity of conferring some of them upon her own offspring. Accordingly this period did arrive, but the novel-reading lady had united herself to a butcher, and she came to stand in the public market selling meat. She had a large family, and these she had designated, to the great horror of her common-place husband, after the Orlandos, Dianas, Desdemonas, and the like. This being the case, on a busy day, she might be heard crying in her shop, " Orlando, Roderigo, Alexander Smith, fetch the cleaver !" Than this there could be nothing more absurd.

**Characters to Servants.**—Masters and mistresses are not bound to give a character; the refusal to do so, however, might not only appear to arise from vindictive feeling, but might even be more prejudicial to a servant than a fair statement of the facts affecting the character, from which the person requesting it would be at liberty to draw his own conclusions, and act upon his or her own judgment. As a general rule, therefore, it is right and proper, and of importance to the public, that characters should readily be given. The servant who applies for the character, and the person for whose information it is given, are equally benefited. Indeed, there is no class to whom it is of so much importance that characters should be freely given as to honest servants.

Masters and mistresses need be under no apprehension of the consequences of making such communications ; for the law very properly treats them as privileged where the occasion is justifiable, and the party makes them honestly and *bona fide*, and with a sincere and conscientious belief that they are true. It is where masters and mistresses wantonly and capriciously volunteer, or from spite and malice make statements injurious to the servant, that they are not protected. Indeed, in one case it was held, where a servant, upon the strength of a character given by her mistress, got a place, and that it was afterwards discovered that the character was undeserved, that the mistress was morally bound to inform the new mistress of the circumstances, and that the communication made concerning them was privileged.

All facts ought to be disclosed which might be supposed fairly to weigh with or influence another in engaging or rejecting a servant ; *for the suppression of the truth is as unjustifiable as an untrue statement.* It is much to be regretted that, through timidity or a mistaken sense of kindness, this important duty of giving true and faithful characters is not oftener observed. If such a duty were the more habitually recognised, the more would servants find it to their interest to conduct themselves with propriety, and to the satisfaction of their masters and mistresses ; and honest servants would not have such frequent reason to complain of characters being given with an unfairness and a want of discrimination which place the bad on a footing of equality with the good.

WRITTEN CHARACTERS.—The principal objections to written characters are the difficulty, if not the impossibility, of verifying the authenticity of the writing, and the identity of the parties, and that they do not afford the same precise information as may be elicited by a personal interview.

**Medical Attendance to Servants.**—Masters and mistresses are not liable for medical attendance, or medicine supplied to their servants, unless expressly or impliedly authorised by them, as by their sending for the doctor, &c. ; but, as stated by a County Court Judge, in a case of the kind tried before him, " it must be left to the humanity of every master to decide whether he will assist his servant according to his capacity or not."

Nor are masters and mistresses responsible to their servants for accidents occurring to them from the carelessness of their fellow-servants or others, unless they have knowingly employed a grossly incompetent person.

**Dismissal of Servants.**—Servants may be dismissed without warning for grossly immoral conduct, for wilful misappropriation of their master's or mistress's property, or for wilful disobedience.

If the instances of such gross misconduct cannot be clearly established by such evidence as would satisfy impartial persons, it will be more proper and prudent to pay the month's wages.

Where a servant was negligent in his conduct, frequently absent when his master wanted him, it was held that his master had a right to discharge him without notice. So where a servant requested leave to absent herself during the night to enable her to visit her mother, who was seriously ill, and her mistress refused such leave, and she nevertheless went, it was held that she was justifiably dismissed.

The latter is an extreme case, and probably arose from the master finding it absolutely necessary, for the convenience of her family, to refuse her servant leave ; but it serves to illustrate the law, that a servant's time is at the master's and mistress's disposal, and that the servant is bound to obey all lawful orders in the regular course of the employment.

**Rouge.**—On no subject connected with a lady's toilet does there exist so much variety of opinion as on the use of artificial paints. We will not attempt to discuss the matter, on which there are strong arguments on both sides, but merely point out such preparations as are most strongly recommended for their innoxious qualities.

The most deleterious sorts of paints are those in which mineral and metallic substances prevail. Great care ought, therefore, to be paid to the nature of such articles, especially when bought ready prepared ; and nothing of this sort should be used without knowing the ingredients of which it is composed. If mineral and metallic substances form their bases, or even if present in considerable quantities, they cannot fail to be injurious, and produce effects much more to be deprecated than those they are employed to conceal. Vegetable preparations, on the contrary, especially if not compounded with vinegar, are little liable to be hurtful when used in moderation. The following preparation will be found free from these objections :—

There is a Brazil wood of a fine golden red, called Pernambouc Brazil wood. Of this take nine ounces, cut it into little bits, and pound them well in a clean iron mortar, with a very heavy pestle, so as to bruise the wood almost to a pulp. Put it into a well-tinned stew-pan, with a quart of the best white-wine vinegar, and let them boil together during half-an-hour over a good fire, keeping the stew-pan well covered ; strain the liquid through linen, pouring out everything that will go through ; put it again into the stew pan, which must previously be well washed and wiped, and place it once more over the fire ; meanwhile dissolve in a pint of the same kind of vinegar four ounces and a half of pounded alum. Mix the two liquids together over the fire, stir them well with a wooden spoon entirely free from grease, and let them gently simmer. A scum will now rise, which, with a very clean skimmer, must be carefully taken off, well drained, and then placed upon sheets of white letter-paper. This scum must be gradually dried in a very slack oven, or on a stove very little heated, or before the fire, taking care that no dust falls upon it. When dry it will form a most beautiful rouge, which will not injure the most sensitive skin.

What is generally used as rouge is, however, merely a preparation of the colour sold in the shops under the name of " pink saucer." It is prepared in a variety of ways to suit the fancies of individuals, some preferring it in powder, others in the form of a pomade, some, *en crepons*, while a fourth class choose to apply it in a liquid form.

When it is preferred in powder, take Briancon chalk. or talc, reduced to a very fine powder, mix with carmine in due proportion, and carefully triturate. The preparation may be applied to the cheeks by means of a little bag or ball of cambric or muslin. A pomade is easily formed, by adding the carmine to a mixture of white wax and soft pomade. This variety is applied by means of the finger, being rubbed on the cheek in small quantities until it ceases to feel greasy.

Rouge *en crepons* are pieces of gauze or silk crape, which have been steeped in rouge, and being rubbed on the cheek, impart their colour to the complexion. Liquid rouge requires to be very carefully applied, from its being so very apt to be administered in undue quantity.

In France they have a preparation of rouge called " Vinaigre de Rouge de Maille," which is applied to the cheek by means of a bit of raw cotton and gentle friction. As it does not colour until it begins to dry, great caution is necessary in its application.

A humorous story is told of a young Englishwoman, who, ignorant of this quality of the vinaigre," applied an over-dose, and in her nervous anxiety to remove it, rubbed her cheeks with a towel and spread it all over her face,

and, in short, so be-rouged herself, that when she appeared in a ball-room, whither she was instantly hurried by the impatience of her companions, who were altogether ignorant of her mishap, every one stared at and shunned her. A report soon spread that she had been suddenly seized with a malignant scarlet fever. She was immediately hurried away ; she had forgotten all about the rouge, and so excited had her feelings become, that she seemed really threatened with the dreaded disease. On reaching home, however. the cause of her strange appearance was explained. The application of the wet towel to the half-dried rouge had streaked her face, so as to give it a most singular look. As this preparation, when it once dries, cannot be removed by any application of soap and water, she was obliged to confine herself to her room for more than a fortnight ; her numerous admirers, in the meantime, suffering unspeakable anxiety from the report that she was dying of a malignant fever.

In order to impart brilliancy to the complexion, white paint is sometimes used, but its use is principally confined to theatrical ladies. As almost the whole of these paints are compounded of metallic substances, they are very injurious. But such objections do not apply to the following recipe for a simple preparation :—

Pound a piece of Briancon chalk, and pass it through a sieve of fine silk into a pint of good distilled vinegar ; shake the liquid several times a-day for about a fortnight : then pour off the vinegar, and fill the vessel with clear filtered water, stirring it well with a wooden spatula ; when the chalk settles to the bottom, pour the water gently off. Repeat this process several times, until the powder attains to the desired softness and whiteness. The water may then be poured off, and the chalk dried so as to be quite free from dust. It may be applied by means of a small piece of raw cotton touched with pomade, to make the powder adhere to the skin.

Now for a word of counsel to our

young and lovely Englishwomen. Be not beguiled by the trumpery, and too often pernicious compounds, which too many tricking perfumers force upon your notice, backed by every imaginable falsehood. Yet there are some honourable exceptions amongst perfumers to those reckless compounders of " villainous stuffs." But your youth, health, and cleanliness, are charms of more potent spell than all the known cosmetics the earth could fabricate. Be content to use that universal soap and water which bathed the delicate skin of your infancy. And, ye " dames of certain age," be not cajoled with the vain hope of emulating the bloom and texture of youthful complexions. No cosmetics can bring you back that which Time with his ruthless hand is stealing from you.

**Treatment of Canaries.**—This pet bird, which has been so long acclimatised in this country, and where his sweet song may be heard from almost every parlour, is a native of the Canary Islands, from which it obviously derives its name.

There are several varieties in colour, owing to the changes of climate, domestication, and breeding it has undergone, but the London bird-fanciers acknowledge but two kinds, the *Jonquil* and the *Mealy*, or, the plain and the variegated. The male should be a dark gray, or grayish brown (the original colour of the bird), a green or very regularly pencilled.

The usual time for pairing canaries for breeding is in April. Great care should be taken in selecting birds for this purpose. Attentive males are difficult to be obtained, and good females as rarely to be met with.

As soon as the brood is hatched, which occupies a period of thirteen days, the male commences his labours, which consist in supplying them with food for another thirteen days, at the end of which period they are enabled to pick alone. During this time the female never leaves the nest but for the purposes of feeding, when her place is supplied by the male. The food for young birds consists of a quarter of hard egg minced fine (white and yolk together), mixed with a little bread steeped in water. This should be pressed and placed in one vessel, while another should contain a small quantity of boiled rape-seed, washed in fresh water. Care must be taken to change the food of young birds every day ; for should the bread turn sour, and they partake of it, it will cause their death. At the end of a month they may be placed in separate cages.

The following is a list of complaints to which canaries are subject, and with the best remedies to be applied :—

*Asthma.*—Give plantain and rapeseed, moistened with water, as their sole food.

*Rupture.*—The usual symptom of this complaint is excessive thinness, and the bird will not eat. It is very common to young birds, and the bird will not eat. It is also common to older birds, and is generally supposed to arise from eating too much ; a rusty nail immersed in the water they drink will be found efficacious.

*Lice.*—Canaries are subject to these insects ; supply them frequently with fresh water for bathing, keep the cage clean, and strew dry sand over the bottom.

*Loss of Voice.*—This frequently happens to the male after moulting. Hang up a piece of rusty bacon for the bird to peck at.

*Epilepsy*, which arises from fright ; and *Sneezing*, produced by an obstruction of the nostrils, to cure which a quill must be inserted ; are some of the most common complaints to which canaries are subject.

It is necessary at certain periods to cut the claws of cage-birds, and in doing so great care should be taken to avoid drawing blood.

**English Christian Names.**—It is probable, from careful calculations, that two-thirds of all the children in England and Wales are called by one of the following twenty-five names, certain that in any 100,000 children they will occur in the following order :—

Mary, 6819. William, 6590. John, 6220. Elizabeth, 4617. Thomas, 3876. George, 3620. Sarah, 3602. James, 3060. Charles, 2323. Henry, 2060. Alice, 1925. Joseph, 1720. Ann, 1718. Jane, 1697. Ellen, 1621. Emily, 1615. Frederick, 1604. Annie, 1580. Margaret, 1546. Emma, 1540. Eliza, 1507. Robert, 1323. Arthur, 1237. Alfred, 1232. Edward, 1170.

Total number of children (out of 100,000) registered under the above 25 names, 65,892.

**Blancmange.**—Get four calves feet ; if possible some that have been scalded, and not skinned. Scrape and clean them well, and boil them in three quarts of water till all the meat drops off the bone. Drain the liquid through a colander or sieve, and skim it well. Let it stand till next morning to congeal. Then clean it well from the sediment, and put it into a tin or bell-metal kettle. Stir it into the cream, sugar, and mace. Boil it hard for five minutes, stirring it several times. Then strain it through a linen cloth or napkin into a large bowl, and add the wine and rose-water. Set it in a cool place for three or four hours, stirring it very frequently with a spoon, to prevent the cream separating from the jelly. The more it is stirred the better. Stir it till it is cool. Wash your moulds, wipe them dry, and then wet them with cold water. When the blancmange becomes very thick— that is, in three or four hours if the weather is not too damp—put it into your moulds. When it has set in them till it is quite firm, loosen it carefully all round with a knife, and turn it out on glass or china plates.

**In-Growing Toe-Nails.**—This is one of the most painful of the diseases of the nails, and is generally caused by the improper manner of cutting them, then wearing a narrow, badly-made shoe —our remarks, of course, apply chiefly to the great toe. The nail beginning to grow too long, and rather wide at the corners, is often trimmed round the corner, which gives temporary relief. But then it begins to grow wider in the side where it was cut off ; and, as the shoe presses against the corner, the nail cuts more and more into the raw flesh, which becomes tender and irritable. If this state continues long the toe becomes more painful and ulcerated, and fungus—proud flesh—sprouts up from the sorest points. Walking greatly increases the suffering, till positive rest becomes indispensable.

*Treatment*—Begin the effort at cure by simple application to the tender part of a small quantity of perchloride of iron. It is found at chemists in a fluid form, though sometimes in powder. There is immediately a moderate sensation of pain, constriction, or burning. In a few minutes the tender surface is felt to be dried up, tanned, mummified, and it ceases to be painful. The patient, who before could not put his foot to the floor, now finds that he can walk upon it without pain. By permitting the hardened, wood-like flesh to remain for two or three weeks, it can be easily removed by soaking the foot in warm water. A new and healthy structure is found, firm and solid, below. If thereafter the nails be no more cut round the corners or sides, but always curved in across the front end, they will in future grow only straight forwards ; and by wearing a shoe of reasonable good size and shape, all further trouble will be avoided.

**Academy Rolls.**—Two quarts of flour, one pint of milk, butter size of an egg, half a cup each of sugar and yeast, and half a teaspoonful of soda. Scald the milk, and when tepid put it with the other ingredients in the centre of the flour, and mix in enough of the flour to make a sponge ; let it rise twelve hours ; if light, knead in the rest of the flour for fifteen minutes, and let it rise till light ; then knead fifteen minutes more, roll out half an inch thick in circles the size of a saucer, spread with butter, double the buttered surfaces together, and let it rise a few hours until light enough to bake. Follow the receipt as here given, and a delicious pudding will be the result.

**How to Choose Meat.**—Ox-BEEF, when it is young, will have a fine open grain, and a good red colour ; the fat should be white, for when it is of a deep yellow colour, the meat is seldom very good. The grain of cow-beef is closer, the fat whiter, and the lean scarcely so red as that of ox-beef. When you see beef, of which the fat is hard and skinny, and the lean of a deep red, you may be pretty sure that it is of an inferior kind ; and when the meat is old you may know it by a line of a horny texture running through the meat of the ribs.

MUTTON must be chosen by the firmness and fineness of the grain, its good colour, and firm white fat. It is not considered prime until the sheep is about five years old.

LAMB will not keep long after it is killed. It can be discovered by the neck end in the fore quarter if it has been killed too long, the veins in the neck being blueish when the meat is fresh, but green when it is stale. In the hind quarter, the same discovery may be made by examining the kidney and the knuckle, for the former has a slight smell, and the knuckle is not firm, when the meat has been killed too long.

PORK should have a thin rind ; and when it is fresh, the meat is smooth and cool ; but, when it looks flabby, and is clammy to the touch, it is not good ; and pork, above all meat, is disagreeable when it is stale. If you perceive many enlarged glands, or, as they are usually termed, kernels, in the fat of pork, you may conclude that the pork cannot be wholesome.

VEAL is generally preferred of a delicate whiteness, but it is more juicy and well-flavoured when of a deeper colour. Butchers bleed calves profusely in order to produce this white meat ; but this practice must certainly deprive the meat of some of its nourishment and flavour. When you choose veal, endeavour to look at the loin, which affords the best means of judging of the veal generally, for if the kidney, which may be found on the under side of one end of the loin, be deeply enveloped in white and firm looking fat, the meat will certainly be good ; and the same appearance will enable you to judge if it has been recently killed. The kidney is the part which changes the first ; and then the suet around it becomes soft, and the meat flabby and spotted.

BACON, like pork, should have a thin rind ; the fat should be firm, and inclined to a reddish colour ; and the lean should firmly adhere to the bone, and have no yellow streaks in it. When you are purchasing a ham, have a knife stuck into it to the bone, which, if the ham be well cured, may be drawn out again without having any of the meat adhering to it, and without your perceiving any disagreeable smell. A short ham is reckoned the best.

**How to Choose Fish.**—TURBOT, which is in season the greater part of the year, should have the underside of a yellowish white, for when it is very transparent, blue, or thin, it is not good ; the whole fish should be thick and firm.

SALMON should have a fine red flesh and gills ; the scales should be bright, and the whole fish firm. Many persons think that salmon is improved by keeping a day or two ; but in London this precaution is unnecessary. That which is caught in the Thames is considered the finest, though there can scarcely be better fish than the Severn salmon.

COD should be judged by the redness of the gills, the whiteness, stiffness, and firmness of the flesh, and the clear freshness of the eyes, these are the infallible proofs of its being good. The whole fish should be thick and firm. It is in season from December to April.

SOLES, when fresh, are cream-coloured on the under part ; but when they are not fresh, their appearance is blueish and flabby. They are a valuable fish, being in season pretty well all the year round, besides being excellent eating. The middle of summer is the period however, in which they are considered to be in the greatest perfection.

WHITINGS may be had good almost throughout the year ; but the time in which they are in their prime is early in the year. The whiting is a light and delicate fish, and in choosing it you must examine whether the fins and flesh be firm.

MACKEREL is almost the worst fish for keeping, or for carrying to any distance. When they look flabby, the colours of the scales faded, and the eyes dull, they are not fresh.

The MULLET, the DORY, and some other fish, too, are so rare, that it is difficult to determine the qualities which characterise their degrees of excellence ; but you will seldom err if you choose them from the firm texture of their flesh, the redness of their gills, and the brilliancy of their colours.

FRESH-WATER FISH may be chosen by similar observations respecting the firmness of the flesh, and the clear appearance of the eyes, as salt-water fish.

CARP and TENCH are in season during the months of July, August, and September. The former should be killed as soon as it is caught, because it will live a considerable time out of water, and when this is permitted it wastes the firmness of its flesh.

EELS caught in the Thames are considered finer than any others which are brought to market, and may be known by their bright silvery underside. Eels caught in pools have generally a strong, rank flavour. They are in season all the year, except for a short time during the winter.

In a LOBSTER lately caught, you may put the claws in motion by pressing the eyes ; but when it has been long caught, the muscular action is not excited. The freshness of boiled lobsters may be determined by the elasticity of the tail, which is flaccid when they have lost any of their wholesomeness. Their goodness, independent of freshness, is determined by their weight.

CRABS, too, must be judged of by their weight, for when they prove light, the flesh is generally found to be wasted and watery. If in perfection, the joints of the legs will be stiff, and the body will have an agreeable smell. The eyes, by a dull appearance, betray that the crab has been long caught.

CRAY-FISH are good when they are heavy and the eye bright, and they have no unpleasant smell.

PRAWNS and SHRIMPS are firm and crisp to the touch when they are good.

In fresh OYSTERS the shell is firmly closed ; if at all opened, the oysters are not fresh. The Milton oysters are the best ; they are small in the shell, but this is completely filled with the fish. Those from Colchester, Purfleet, and Milford, are also in demand for their fine flavour. The rock oyster, which is very large, is coarse in flavour, and fit only for stewing or for sauce.

**How to Choose Poultry.**—In the choice of Poultry, the age of the bird is the chief point to which you should attend. A young TURKEY has a smooth black leg ; in an old one the legs are rough and reddish. If the bird be fresh killed, the eyes will be full and fresh, and the feet moist.

FOWLS, when they are young, the combs and the legs will be smooth, and rough when they are old.

In GEESE, when they are young, the bills and the feet are yellow, and have a few hairs upon them, but they are red if the bird be old. The feet of a goose are pliable when the bird is fresh killed, and dry and stiff when it has been killed some time. Geese are called green till they are two or three months old.

DUCKS should be chosen by the feet, which should be supple ; and they also should have a plump and hard breast. The feet of a tame duck are yellowish, those of a wild one reddish.

PIGEONS should always be eaten while they are fresh ; when they look flabby and discoloured about the under part, they have been kept too long. The feet, like those of poultry, show the age of the bird ; when they are supple, it is young ; when stiff, it is old. Tame pigeons are larger than wild ones.

**How to Choose Game.**—VENISON, when young, will have the fat clear and bright, and this ought also to be of a considerable thickness. When you do not wish to have it in a very high state, a knife plunged into either the haunch or the shoulder, and drawn out, will by the smell enable you to judge if the venison be sufficiently fresh.

With regard to venison, which, as it is not an every-day article of diet, it may be convenient to keep for some time after it has begun to get high or tainted, it is useful to know that animal putrefaction is checked by fresh burnt charcoal; by means of which, therefore, the venison may be prevented from getting worse, although it cannot be restored to its original freshness. The meat should be placed in a hollow dish, and the charcoal powder strewed over it until it covers the joint to the thickness of half an inch.

HARES and RABBITS, when the ears are dry and tough, the haunch thick, and the claws blunt and rugged, they are old. Smooth and sharp claws, ears that readily tear, and a narrow cleft in the lip, are the marks of a young hare. Hares may be kept for some time after they have been killed; indeed, many people think they are not fit for the table until the inside begins to turn a little. Care, however, should be taken to prevent the inside from becoming musty, which would spoil the flavour of the stuffing.

PARTRIDGES have yellow legs and a dark-coloured bill when young. They are not in season till after the first of September.

**To Clean Plate.**—After the plate has been washed with hot water, rub it over with a mixture of levigated hartshorn and spirits of turpentine, which is the best known preparation for cleansing plate and renewing its polish. Remember, that two good-sized leathers are required for cleaning plate, one of which should be kept for rubbing off the hartshorn-powder, and the other for polishing up the silver afterwards. This process should be performed twice a week; but on other days, merely rubbing with the leathers, after washing, will be sufficient. There is nothing in the ingredients mentioned that can in the least injure the silver, which is sometimes the case with the nostrums that servants employ. The only thing to be strictly regarded by the servant who uses it, is to rub it off so well that the plate shall not retain the slightest smell of the turpentine. The turpentine is useful in removing every particle of greasiness from the plate, which mere washing will not do. We have seen some plate cleaned with muriatic acid, which gives a very high polish, but also a deep colour to the plate, almost resembling steel. The hartshorn and turpentine give as good a polish as the acid, without injuring or changing the colour of the silver.

Many people, however, still prefer whiting and water, which cleans tolerably well, but does not renew the polish. When silver has, through neglect, become very dim and dirty-looking, it is necessary to boil it in soap-and-water for some little time, and afterwards the turpentine and hartshorn-powder can be used to great advantage.

**Management of a Piano-Forte.**—Have your piano tuned at least four times in the year by an experienced tuner; if you allow it to go too long without tuning, it usually becomes flat, and troubles a tuner to get it to stay at concert pitch, especially in the country. Never place the instrument against an outside wall, or in a cold, damp room, particularly in a country house; there is no greater enemy to a piano-forte than damp.

Close the instrument immediately after your practice; by leaving it open, dust fixes on the sound-board, and corrodes the movements, and if in a damp room the strings soon rust. Should the piano stand near or opposite to a window, guard, if possible, against it being opened, especially on a wet or damp day; and when the sun is on the window draw the blind down.

Avoid putting metallic or other articles on or in the piano ; such things frequently cause unpleasant vibrations. The more equal the temperature of the room, the better the piano will keep in tune.

**Baths and Bathing.**—The morning ablution—the sitz or sitting-bath—the local steam-bath—the foot-bath—the pail-douche—wet-douche — wet-pack—water-drinking—the hot stupe—the wet bandage, and the Turkish-bath, are appliances that can always be used with advantage in health, as well as in illness.

The *morning ablution* will always depend on the individual case. To the healthy, we should recommend the free use of cold water to the whole person, rubbing with a coarse towel, so as to bring the blood well to the surface, and to produce a healthy glow. It is a great mistake to make this bath a regular washing one. It should only be used as a tonic. Those who do not take the Turkish bath should wash once a week, at night, with hot water and soap.

It should be understood by all, that a bath which does not produce the healthy glow is injurious. Therefore, those whose reaction is weak, should at first be only rubbed in a wet sheet till well warmed, and then dried quickly. If care is taken to get out of bed thoroughly warm, a good reaction will generally be obtained.

Some form of ablution is necessary to all, for independent of the demands of cleanliness, if our pores are not closed after the heat of bed, we are likely to chill on exposing ourselves to the air.

For those with an over-excited nervous system, whose skin is hot and feverish, or who have much tendency of blood to the head, as well as for those of too full habit, *tepid* water is the best and safest ; for their systems require a soothing treatment, while the healthy, and those who are low and chilly in constitution, should use cold applications. Tepid water, ranging from eighty-five to ninety-two degrees, is also best in cutaneous eruptions.

The *Rubbing Sheet*, or *Wet Towel*, is most valuable in illness, and may be used with great advantage after a severe wetting. Experience proves we never suffer from a wetting as long as we are in motion ; on the contrary, the exercise and moisture act on the pores like a wet pack ; it is only when we sit down and *chill* in wet clothes that the mischief is done.

THE SITZ BATH.—Most persons are familiar with the nature of this bath, from the hip-bath now in general use—but this is quite inadequate to perform the duties of the sitz-bath, being a great deal too shallow to cover the person to the necessary depth ; the best size for a sitz-bath (used solely for the purpose) would be as follows :—diameter at bottom, 1 foot 2 inches ; ditto at top, 1 foot 7 inches ; depth, 1 foot ; height at back, 1 foot 9 inches. In putting in water for a bath, allowance must be made for the space occupied by the person.

The benefits of this bath are numerous. It is a tonic and a derivative : strengthening the back, relieving the head, stimulating the digestive organs, increasing the appetite, regulating the bowels, removing congestion from the internal viscera, and producing a variety of other good effects.

A sitz-bath, taken in health or in chronic disease for the purposes named, should be taken cold for twenty minutes, with the person covered with a blanket ; and a quiet walk is useful and necessary before and after it, to secure that all-important point, *reaction*.

THE FOOT-BATH.—This bath is good for all affections of the head and eyes. Putting the feet into cold water up to the ankles, for ten minutes, and rubbing one against the other ; a walk *before* and *after* this is absolutely necessary, which will put the feet in a glow, and keep them so all day.

THE PAIL-DOUCHE is pouring a couple of buckets of water on the head and person, at a temperature of from 85 to 95 degrees, according to the urgency of the case. Invaluable in feverish forms of head attacks. This bath requires **to** be given in the dish-bath, or, if nothing better is within reach, a large tub, in which the patient should sit.

The WET-PACK is a simple and almost certain way of preserving health, and curing disease, where human agency is available. It consists merely in wrapping up the body in a wet sheet, wrung out of cold water, and well covered with two or three blankets so as to exclude the air. It reduces fever and inflammation in a surprisingly short time ; is most deliciously soothing when the mind or body is overtasked and excited, and may be believed, on the authority of those whose every nerve sometimes quivers in undue excitement, to be inexpressible peace.

In acute illness, to reduce fever or relieve the head, short pack of half an hour are given, and frequently repeated. In ordinary cases, three quarters of an hour is the time allotted for this soothing process. The popular idea, that it is intended to produce perspiration, is quite erroneous. But as its effect is to open the pores, it must always be followed by a cold or tepid ablution, over the whole person. The wet pack may be called a universal poultice.

The TURKISH BATH.—If we only apply the single fact, that " waste is more necessary than nutrition," we shall get at least one reason. not only why the bath is serviceable to health, but also why it should be universal in its application. Take, for exemplification, the two extremes—persons above or below the standard of health—we mean those in the former case, whose tendency is to put up too much fat, in itself a fruitful cause of disease, and originating, we may presume, in some want of due activity in the organs of waste. Hence we see how the bath is likely to serve them.

On the delicate and thin its effect is just the reverse ; for it must be remembered that the bath never takes away what is necessary to health, but only the superfluous material. It stimulates into healthy action the digestive and other organs which disease had made torpid, facilitates the absorption of oxygen, increases appetite, fortifies against cold, invigorates the circulation of the body, so as to remove its morbid sensibility to the vicissitudes of climate, and so strengthens the constitution, as to enable it to throw off whatever morbid influences were depressing its vital energy.

For three or four nights before taking the Turkish bath the delicate should take a tepid-bath at bed-time, or rub themselves well with flannel soaked in hot water and soap ; or those who understand it, may take a wet pack so as to soften the dead cuticle, and induce its long unaccustomed circulation of blood to return to the skin.

Many persons take their first bath *because* they feel uncomfortable, and we should prefer to have the feeling of discomfort first removed by the wet bandage, so as to prevent an unfavourable, as well as an unjust, impression of the bath.

But it will never supersede the wet bandage. To those who are wise enough to combine them, the bath *and* the bandage will always be found of inestimable value. For we must remember, that the Turkish bath is only the highest development of the water-cure, acting more fully on the skin than any yet discovered agent.

The beneficial influence of the bath is strikingly shown in the case of the shampooers, who may be said to live in the bath, and not only continue to enjoy perfect health after an experience of four or five years, but may be taken as very models of health and strength.

The Turkish-bath should be taken in health, for then the public would be sure to come to it in illness. In fact. to use it as a preventive to disease, as a means of cleansing and keeping the system up to the standard of health, and as an almost certain guard against colds, epidemics, &c. When the pores are once brought into order. a bath once a week will be quite sufficient for all these purposes.

It is a common question, " Is the

Turkish bath likely to produce congestion of the lungs, brain, &c. ?"  Its effect is exactly the reverse, for it not only equalises the circulation, but, in the words of Dr. Armstrong, " it will bring pounds of blood to the surface, which were suffocating some internal organ."

[We are mainly indebted to an excellent little volume entitled " Simple Questions and Sanitary Facts," for this article on Baths and Bathing.]

**Rhubarb.**—This plant has been for centuries held in the highest estimation on account of its active medicinal properties, few drugs being of more efficacy in various complaints.  It is a mild cathartic, and commonly considered as one of the safest and most innocent of the substances of this class.  Besides its purgative virtue, it has a mild astringent one ; hence it is found to give strength to the stomach, and to be one of the most useful purgatives in all disorders proceeding from a debility and laxity of the fibres.

In addition to the medicinal qualities of the rhubarb, it is allowed by all medical men to make one of the most cooling, wholesome, and delicious tarts sent to table ; many persons prefer it either to green gooseberries or apples. In the early part of the season the stalks of rhubarb are cut up and mixed with these fruits ; with the former before they have obtained their flavour, and with the latter after losing it by long keeping.

As a plant, too, the rhubarb, particularly the *Rheum palmatum*, is highly ornamental in many situations in the pleasure-ground ; its luxuriant foliage, height of growth, and large palmated leaves, render it very striking and beautiful.

The varieties of the Tart Rhubarb, by which name it may be justly designated, form an object of much interest and profit to the market-gardener ; and to the cottager it cannot be too strongly recommended as a most salubrious vegetable for his family, either as tarts, puddings, or when baked whole in a

dish.  It is of the easiest culture, and can be planted in any light soil, either in an open or sheltered situation in any part of his garden.

Few vegetables have made a more rapid progress in their cultivation since its introduction into England, about seventy years ago, than the tart rhubarb ; for not only are large quantities annually forced for the London markets, but many acres are planted for the same supply ; and the wagon-loads of stalks tied up in bundles and sent thither during the season would almost exceed credibility.

RHUBARB TART.—See that the stalks are firm and of a large size, and then, after removing the thin skin, slice them in pieces about four inches long ; place the pieces in a dish, and pour over them a syrup of sugar, thinned with water ; then cover with another dish, and simmer slowly for an hour, upon a hot hearth, or do them in a block-tin saucepan.  Allow it to cool, and then make it into a tart ; the baking the crust will be sufficient when the stalks are tender.

**Rhubarb Fool.**—Scald two quarts of rhubarb, cleanly peeled, which cut into pieces about one inch long, mix it to a pulp, which pass through a sieve, then let it remain to cool.  Then put a quart of new milk into a pan, which flavour with cinnamon, cloves, and lemon-peel, sugar to taste, and let it boil for ten or twelve minutes.  The yolks of four or five eggs well beat up with a little flour, should be stirred into the milk, then, stirring the while, keep it over the fire till it boils, after which remove, and set it to cool.  Mix the milk and rhubarb together, and grate some nutmeg over it.

**Rhubarb Wine.**—To make rhubarb wine in the month of May or June, when rhubarb is green, the stalks of the leaves are used in the following proportions :—Five pounds of the stalks are bruised in a suitable vessel, to which is added one gallon of spring water ; after remaining *in mash* three or four days, the liquor-juice is thrown off ; when to every gallon of this juice three pounds of loaf sugar are added, and allowed to ferment four or five days in a vat. As soon as the fermentation has ceased, the liquor must be drawn off in a cask, and allowed to remain until the month of March, when all fermentation will be over ; it must then be racked off, and more lump sugar added. In the month of August a second crop of rhubarb will be ready to gather for this improved method of making wine. Rhubarb is largely employed in making fictitious champagne ; thus here, as elsewhere, rhubarb has largely usurped the place of the gooseberry.

**Easter-Day.**—A solemn festival in commemoration of the Resurrection of our Lord and Saviour. From " Chambers's Information for the People," we gather that the word used by us is from " *Ostara*, in Anglo-Saxon *Eastre*, the name of a goddess once extensively worshipped by the Teutonic nations, and personifying the light of the rising sun, or the dawn ; it is allied to *east*. In England, before the Reformation, the Catholic observances of Easter were as fully enacted as in any other country. Early in the morning, a sort of theatrical representation of the Resurrection was performed in the churches, the priests coming to the little sepulchre where, on Good Friday, they had deposited the host, which they now brought forth with great rejoicings, as emblematical of the rising of the Saviour. In the course of the day, the clergy had a game at ball in the church, a custom which it is now difficult to believe that it could ever have existed.

" The viands appropriate to Easterday in the old times were, first and above all, eggs, then bacon, tansy-pudding, and bread and cheese. The origin of the connection of eggs with Easter is lost in the mists of remote antiquity. They are as rife at this day in Russia as in England. There it is customary to go about with a quantity, and to give one to each friend one meets, saying, ' Jesus Christ is risen ;' to which the other replies, ' Yes, he is risen ;' or, ' It is so of a truth.'

" The pope formerly blessed eggs, to be distributed throughout the Christian world for use on Easter-day. In Germany, instead of the egg itself, the people offer a print of it, with some lines inscribed.

" At this day, the Easter eggs used in England are boiled hard in water containing a dye, so that they come out coloured. The boys take these eggs and make a kind of game, either by throwing (bowling) them to a distance on the greensward—he who throws oftenest without breaking his eggs being the victor—or hitting them against each other in their respective hands, in which case the owner of the hardest or last surviving egg gains the day.

" It was at one time customary to have a gammon of bacon on this day, and to eat it all up, in signification of abhorrence of Judaism. The tansy seems to have been introduced into Easter-feasts as a successor to the bitter herbs used by the Jews at the Passover. It was usually presented well sugared."

**Dandriff in the Hair.**—Part the hair, and rub the scalp with rum, using a piece of sponge or flannel to apply it. Eau-de Cologne may also be fearlessly used for the same purpose. When the hair becomes greasy and dirty, it ought to be washed with warm (not too warm) soft water and soap ; an operation which is always requisite when pomatums and hair-oils are much used, as they are apt to combine with the scales which are always coming off from the skin, and form a thick crust very detrimental to the loss and beauty of the hair.

Frequent cutting of the hair is of advantage to the eyes, the ears, and, indeed, to the whole body ; in like manner, the daily washing of the head with cold water is an excellent prevention against periodical headaches. In Seryzas, or defluxions of the humours from the head, and in weak eyes, the shaving of the head often affords immediate relief. It is altogether a mistaken idea that there is danger of catching cold from the practice of washing the head, or leaving it exposed to the free air after having been washed. The more frequently the surface is cleansed of scorbutic, and scaly impurities, the more easy and comfortable we feel.

**To Prevent Lamps from Smoking.**—To lessen or prevent the smoking of lamps, the wicks should be well soaked, either in dilute muriatic acid, well washed in water, and dried, or in strong vinegar. Large lamps, that emit much smoke, should be burnt under a funnel to carry it off ; or a large sponge, dipped in water, may be suspended over them ; in all cases the wicks should not be put up too high.

**Floral Ornaments for Windows.**—Nothing amidst all our refinements of home is so much neglected as our windows, which, with a little taste and

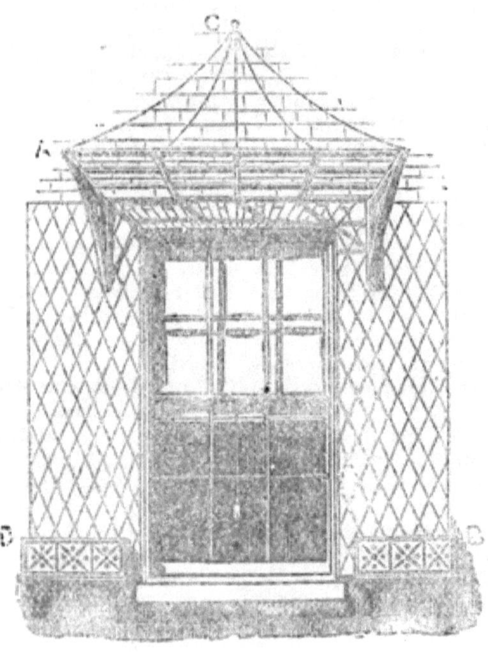

FIG. 1.

expense, are capable of being made very picturesque. In many towns on the Continent, especially in Spain, great attention is paid to this subject, and balconies during the summer are frequently to be seen draped with creeping plants, and some of the very streets festooned with these refreshing summer trophies.

Let us now be practical, and by pictorial illustration help all those who are desirous to beautify their windows, and to convert them into objects of attraction.

Our illustration, Fig. 1, shows how, with a few simple appliances, a window may be at the same time sheltered from the sun and rendered pretty. A is a framework of a few laths nailed together, which by means of rings or staples at its two upper corners may be hung upon hooks, driven into the wall during the summer, and removed before the winter. Its projection should be from eighteen inches to two feet. Two or more brackets, B, B, are fastened on either side of the window sill, to receive flower-pots or boxes, and between these and the framework nails are driven into the wall, so that string can be tied upon them to form a kind of lozenge-shaped trellis-work. The brackets, strings, and framework should all be painted green, and a further improvement can be made by carrying other strings, as at C, from the top of the framework to a hook driven into the wall above. In Fig. 2 we show this as it would appear when covered with evergreens. For cultivation in this instance some of the smaller climbing plants might be used, such as the canary creeper, the major convol-

FIG. 2.

vulus, the sweet pea, &c. The above arrangement can also be adapted to a doorway.

**How to Air your Rooms.**—It is a common mistake to open only the lower part of the windows of an apartment, whereas if the upper part were also opened, the ventilation of the room would be more speedily effected. The air in an apartment is generally heated to a higher temperature than the ex-ternal air, either by the heat supplied by the human body or by lamps, fire, or candles ; this renders the air in the room lighter than the external air, and consequently the external air will rush in at all openings at the lower part of the room, while the warmer and lighter air passes out at the higher openings. If a candle be held in the doorway near the door, it is ten to one that the flame will be blown inward ; but if it be

D

raised near to the top of the doorway it will be blown outward. The warm air in this case flows out at the top, whilst the cold air flows in at the bottom. A current of warm air from the room is generally rushing up the flue of the chimney, even though there be no fire in the grate ; hence the unwholesomeness of using chimney-boards.

**Broken Chilblains, Boils, and Cuts.**—An excellent salve for these may be made in the following manner : Take a quart of sweet oil and a pound of red lead, and gently stir and boil them until they are well mixed, and assume a dull brown colour. Then shake in six ounces of finely powdered resin, and let it continue boiling until the resin is well dissolved and mixed ; then remove the vessel from the fire and add half an ounce of gum elemi ; when that is well blended the salve will be made, and may be poured into vessels for use ; common red earthen jars are suitable for this purpose. It may be kept without injury for many years, and when wanted for use may be spread with a warm knife upon a linen rag. In making it, great care should be taken that not a drop falls or boils over into the fire, as it is very inflammable, and might cause serious mischief. This salve has been found very efficacious in the most obstinate cases.

**The Best Blacking.**—For preserving the leather of boots and shoes, and which will make them perfectly waterproof, blacking made after the following manner is the best known :—Take of yellow wax one ounce and a half, of mutton suet four ounces and a half, horse turpentine half an ounce, ivory black three ounces ; melt first the wax, to which add the suet, and afterwards the horse turpentine ; when the whole is melted, remove it from the fire ; mix in gradually the ivory black, constantly stirring till it is cold. When it is used, it may be rubbed or laid upon a brush, which should be warmed before the fire. When it is wanted in a large quantity, it may be gently melted in a ladle or pot over a chafing-dish with live coals.

**Advice to Wives.**—A wife must learn how to form her husband's happiness ; in what direction the secret of his comfort lies , she must not cherish his weaknesses by working upon them ; she must not rashly run counter to his prejudices. Her motto must be never to irritate. She must study never to draw largely upon the small stock of patience in man's nature, nor to increase his obstinacy by trying to drive him ; never, if possible, to have " scenes." We doubt much if a real quarrel, even if made up, does not loosen the bond between man and wife, and sometimes, unless the affection be very sincere, lastingly. If irritation should occur, a woman must expect to hear from most men a strength and vehemence of language far more than the occasion requires. Mild as well as stern men are prone to this exaggeration of speech ; let not a woman be tempted ever to say anything sarcastic or violent in retaliation. The bitterest repentance must needs follow such an indulgence if she does. Men frequently forget what they themselves have said, but seldom what is uttered by their wives. They are grateful, too, for forbearance in such cases : for, whilst asserting most loudly they are right, they are often conscious they are wrong. Give a little time, as the greatest boon you can bestow, to the irritated feelings of your husband.

**Contrivances and Make-shifts.**—In the most easy and monotonous existence, no woman is exempt from circumstances in which the means and materials they have at their command are, apparently, insufficient to procure them what they very much require, or to deliver them from annoyances from which they continually suffer. And here it is—the power for moulding what we *have* into substitutes for what we *are denied*—the power of producing *good* " make-shifts " where the unwise would bring forward bad ones, and the stupid and indifferent remain in difficulty ; this is in all a valuable accomplishment, and may be reckoned as several hundred pounds in any woman's marriage portion. Of course, nothing that has, originally, a specific and restricted use, can be so entirely satisfactory as the absent desideratum of which it is made to take place ; yet, under the direction of the ingenious and the judicious, many a humble resource will be available to produce comfort, or alleviate inconvenience ; and this is no mean consideration.

As each emergency would require a different expedient, it would be impossible to give *directions* for contrivances ; but, as *specimens* of the application of simple and inexpensive means to promote comfort in a small dwelling, we subjoin the following :—

Instead of Venetian blinds or outer shutters, where the sun is powerful, blinds, or small curtains of white holland, towards the window, and dark silk, or stuff, towards the room ; and again, lined curtains within, to draw close before the sun turns sound, and undraw after it goes off. By this fourfold protection from the summer heat is composed of materials that would otherwise have been " lying-by." By these means shutterless bedrooms may be kept cool and comfortable, whereas, with a single white blind, and the windows open during the heat of the day, they are scarcely habitable.

The great triumph of adaptation is, when that which, in one shape, would be unsightly lumber, is transformed into something comfortable, useful, tidy, or even elegant. Such transformations have we seen affected in regard to certain chests and boxes, which, either hidden under beds, put in some " out-of-the-way," or left in some equally " much-in-the-way " place, but necessary for the stowage of what drawers and chests were insufficient to contain, were, when out of commission, and on half-pay, most ugly and inconvenient. Even such chests and boxes have been introduced to us as very available and respectable-looking pieces of furniture. A little spare damask, and a cushion to match, afforded a seat or settee to the eye as well as use, and the box secured

alike from damp and dust, and easily " got at," gave ample room to many articles of wearing apparel that would have been crushed in drawers, or must otherwise have been dragged out from bandboxes beneath the beds. In various other ways—on landings and in attics, such coverings as the piece-box may easily supply, and ingenuity will advantageously apply, will make lumbering boxes useful and presentable, and at the same time preserve them from mildew and decay ; the space beneath the beds will be left unencumbered, and the house delivered from that look of departure and discomfort which the sight of boxes here and there, or the presence of " things about " that should be put away, is calculated to give.

**Mistletoe.**—The custom of adorning houses and churches with branches of mistletoe, holly, and other winter shrubs and trees, is perhaps of older date than any other Christmas observance. It had its origin with the Druids, who were the priests of the ancient Britons, long previous to the invasion of this country by the Romans, under Julius Cæsar.

It was their wont, at a certain period of the year, to resort to the forests in which grew the largest oak trees, followed by a great concourse of people of all degrees. There, with many ceremonies, they proceeded to cut down a quantity of the branches of the mistletoe growing on the oaks, which, having divided into small pieces, they distributed amongst the religious students and votaries who had accompanied them, and who, considering these branches as so many emblems of good fortune, adorned their dwellings with them.

This Druidical custom appears to have survived the shock attending the incursions of foreign races and the overthrow of the old established religion ; and Christianity, loth to wage war with every ancient usage consented to retain this one as the most innocent of them all. Indeed, green boughs seem to have been almost universally looked upon as emblems of purity.

**The Yule Log.**—The custom of burning the yule log at Christmas time, was, it appears, of Anglo-Saxon origin. That race of people were in the habit of celebrating a feast at the winter solstice, which they called the Juul, or Yule, and on this occasion they were wont to burn a large log of wood, as an emblem of returning light and heat, the sun being then at its furthest point from them. From that feast the burning of the log became transferred to the eve of Christmas Day ; and, as such, was never omitted up to the early part of the present century. It is now rarely met with, and only in very remote rural districts.

The yule-log was the stem of one of the largest trees that could be found on the estate of the proprietor in whose halls it was to raise its cheerful flame. It was hewn down on the Candelmas Day, in the month of February of the same year ; then kindled where it fell, and suffered to burn until sunset, when the fire was extinguished, and the log laid in a proper place until it was required at Christmas.

At the appointed time it was carried into the mansion hall by a number of domestics, amidst much rejoicing, and kindled on the hearth with no little mirth and merry-making.

**The Waits.**—These Christmas bards are a remnant of the old minstrels attached to courts and cities, and who added to their musical offices the more important, though less pleasant duty, of watching and guarding the streets. They perambulate the principal thoroughfares in small parties, crying the hour at each corner, or street, or lane ; and inasmuch as in those remote days —during the 13th and 14th centuries— our cities were not lit up at night by anything like lamps, these waits carried beacons, or large fires, supported upon high poles. Their office appears to have fallen into disuse during the reign of Henry VIII. ; and subsequently, the watchmen, established on a better footing, exercised their musical powers only at Christmas-time ; and hence the prac-tice of bands of nocturnal musicians perambulating our streets at this season, in the " witching hour of night."

**Mince-Pies.**—The origin of these and plum-pudding, objects of such absorbing interest to us at Christmas— indeed whenever they come in our way —is attributed to a practice of the bakers, in primitive times, to make presents to their customers of little images in paste, just as, in the present day, the tallow-chandlers present a few doll's candles to the children of their customers. These presents were called Yule Cakes, and were believed to have been originally designed to represent the infant Jesus.

It was also the custom at Rome to present boxes of sweetmeats to the fathers of the Vatican at Christmas. From these, it is said, come the modern mince-pies and plum-pudding. The former was said to be of a coffin shape, and intended to represent the manger wherein the child was laid.

**Rules for Eating.**—Dr. Hall, on this important subject, gives the following advice :—1. Never sit down to table with an anxious or disturbed mind ; better a hundred times intermit that meal, for there will then be that much more food in the world for hungrier stomachs than yours ; and besides, eating under such circumstances can only, and will always, prolong and aggravate the condition of things.

2. Never sit down to a meal after any intense mental effort, for physical and mental injury are inevitable, and no one has a right to deliberately injure body, mind, or estate.

3. Never go to a full table during bodily exhaustion—designated by some as being worn out, tired to death, used up, done over and the like. The wisest thing to be done under such circumstances is to take a cracker and a cup of warm tea, either black or green, and no more. In ten minutes you will feel a degree of refreshment and liveliness which will be pleasantly surprising to you ; not of the transient kind which a glass of liquor affords, but permanent ;

for the tea gives present stimulus and a little strength, and before it subsides, nutriment begins to draw from the sugar, and cream, and bread, thus allowing the body gradually, and by safe degrees, to regain its usual vigour. Then, in a couple of hours, a full meal may be taken, provided that it does not bring it later than two hours before sundown ; if later, then take nothing for that day in addition to the cracker and tea, and the next day you will feel a freshness and vigour not recently known.

No lady will require to be advised a second time, who will conform to the above rules ; whilst it is a fact of no unusual observation among intelligent physicians, that eating heartily, and under bodily exhaustion, is not unfrequently the cause of alarming and painful illness, and sometimes sudden death. These things being so, let every family make it a point to assemble around the table with kindly feelings—with a cheerful humour and a courteous spirit ; and let that member of it be sent from it in disgrace who presumes to mar the re-union by sullen silence, or impatient look, or angry tone, or complaining tongue. Eat ever in thankful gladness, or away with you to the kitchen, you " ill-tempered thing, that you are." There was good philosophy in the old-time custom of having a buffoon or music at the dinner-table.

**Salmon.**—The life history of the salmon is very interesting, and as we ought to know something more than the gross culinary character of the daily food we consume, both animal and vegetable, we shall briefly give it.

We will begin with the salmon's cradle. This is a groove in the gravelly bed of a river, and is scooped out by one or both of the parents : after this it is the duty of the male salmon to watch over his mate, and to fight any other fish of his own sex and species who may intrude upon their home. The whole process of depositing the numerous eggs occupies, on the average, about ten days, and, after it is accomplished, the parent fish leave the eggs to be hatched by surrounding influences, while they themselves quit the spot, and remain in the river for a short period, while they recover from the exhaustion caused by the process. During this period they are unusually ravenous, and vast quantities of the young of their own kind, which are about that time abundant in the river, fall victims to their insatiable appetite. After a time, and about the months of March and April, they drop down from pool to pool, in any flood which may seem favourable to them, until they reach the sea, where they are supposed to remain from six weeks to three or four months, when they again seek the river, vastly increased in weight, and improved in condition.

While they are occupied in this migration, the abandoned eggs are gradually approaching maturity, under the influence of warmth and the rushing waters, and, after a period, varying according to the temperature of the water, the young salmon bursts through its prison. It is then a tiny and almost transparent creature, hardly to be recognised as a fish ; and, being too feeble to employ the mouth in obtaining subsistence, bears a portion of the egg still adhering to the abdomen, like a transparent amber-coloured sac, flecked with tiny blood-vessels : and, by gradually absorbing this material into the system, preserves its life until its increased dimensions permit it to seize prey with the little mouth, afterwards to be so formidably arrayed with teeth.

In this stage of their existence, the little salmon are called by a great variety of names, and are marked with eight or ten dark patches upon the sides. When the fish are about to depart for the sea, their mottled coat is exchanged for a covering of bright silvery scales, under which, however, the dark patches still exist, and can be seen by holding the fish in certain lights, or by rubbing off the lightly-clinging scales. At this period the fish is called a smolt.

It now prepares itself for an excursion to the sea, and, urged by an irresistible instinct, finds its way down the stream, until it at last emerges into the ocean. What may be the course of its marine life is not known, the fish being lost in the wide expanse of ocean ; but, in the course of the autumn, it returns to the river whence it came, and forces its way up the stream.

The technical name for the fish is now grilse, or salmon peal, and, after its second visit to the sea, it is called a salmon. The perseverance shown by the salmon passing up the stream is really wonderful. No rapid seems too powerful to be overcome, and even falls of a considerable height are surmounted with marvellous force and address, the fish shooting from the bed of the river, and concentrating all its forces into a simultaneous effort, which drives it high into the air.

During their whole lives, salmon continue to migrate to the sea, invariably, if possible, returning to the identical river in which they were born.

The food of the salmon is extremely varied, as must necessarily be the case with a fish that passes its life alternately in fresh and salt water, and is certainly of an animal nature, but the precise creatures that form its sustenance are not generally known ; it is, however, ascertained that it feeds largely on some varieties of the *echinus*, or sea-urchin.

The salmon is one of those fish that must be eaten fresh, in order to preserve the full delicacy of its flavour. If it be cooked within an hour or two after being taken from the water, a fatty substance, termed the "curd," is found between the flakes of flesh. If, however, more than twelve hours have elapsed from the death of the fish, the curd is not to be seen, and the salmon is much deteriorated in the opinion of cooks and epicures.

We will now give some instructions for cooking this favourite fish, which, when in season, (April, May, and June it is in perfection,) no dinner is complete without it :—

To Boil Salmon.—Put the fish into into a kettle with plenty of cold water, and about a handful of salt ; let it boil gently, adding a little vinegar to the water, which will give firmness to the salmon. Four pounds will take one hour to cook, especially if thick. To ascertain whether it is done try it with a skewer ; if the flesh of the fish sticks to the bone it is not done enough, but if the flesh drops off, it is overdone. When cooked, place it on the fish-strainer transversely across the kettle, which will keep the salmon hot while draining. Serve the salmon on a fish-plate, then fold a napkin, lay it upon the plate, and place the fish upon the napkin, garnished with parsley.

To Pickle Salmon.—Scale, split, and divide the fish into well-sized pieces ; scrape away all the blood about the backbone, but do not wash it ; about five or six inches long the salmon should be cut into ; then boil the pieces in a pickle made of equal parts of water and vinegar, with three or four blades of mace, and some cloves, until done ; skim carefully all the time the salmon is boiling in the pickle, and, when done, remove the fish, and pour the liquor into a jar, until both that and the fish become cold, and then put the fish into the liquor, with about one-third more vinegar, and some whole pepper. One pint of vinegar to three quarts of water, with a dozen bay leaves, half that quantity of mace, quarter of an ounce of black pepper, and a good handful of salt, is the pickle salmon should be boiled in. Let the air be kept from the fish, and, if kept for any length of time, it will be found necessary to occasionally drain the liquor from it, and to skim and boil it.

Collared Salmon.—Split sufficient of the salmon to make a substantial roll, which should then be washed and well wiped ; rub the inside and outside thoroughly with white pepper, salt, and mace ; then tightly roll it, and bind it up ; put as much water, and one-third vinegar, as will cover it, adding salt, long pepper, allspice, and two or three bay leaves ; cover it close, and let it simmer till quite done. Drain and boil the liquor quickly, and pour it over the fish when cold ; garnish with fennel. Only the primest part of the salmon should be collared ; when rolled, it should be bandaged with broad tape before it is put into the saucepan. While boiling be sure to keep the lid perfectly closed.

To Dry Salmon.—The fish should be opened, and the whole of the inside removed, even the roe. It should then be scalded, and well rubbed over with salt, and then hang it to drain for about twenty-six hours. Two ounces of bay salt, the same quantity of foot's sugar, and about three ounces of salt-petre, should be well mixed together, and the mixture thoroughly rubbed into the fish ; then place it on a dish, and there let it remain for two days and nights, after which period rub it further with common salt. After this let it remain another day, and it will then be in a fit condition for drying. After drying wipe it thoroughly, then spread it open with two sticks, and hang it in a chimney where a wood fire is kept up.

To Broil Salmon.—Cut it in slices about an inch thick, then season with common pepper and cayenne, adding salt and nutmeg, a little of each. Wrap each slice in white paper, which has been smeared with fresh butter ; each end should be fastened by twisting or tying ; broil over a slow fire for seven or eight minutes ; a coke fire is preferable ; serve in the paper, with melted butter, anchovy, tomato, or lobster-sauce.

**Imitation Carved Ivory.**—For this art is required a wooden box or card-case, or any other article that it is desired to ornament. If they are not made of smooth white wood, use the following composition to cover them : —Half an ounce of isinglass, boiled slowly in half a pint of water, till dissolved ; then strain it, and add flake white, finely powdered, till it is as white as cream. The box, or whatever other article is to be manipulated on, should have three or four coats of this solution, letting each dry before the other is laid on ; then smooth it with a piece of damp rag. When the composition is dry, the imitation ivory figures can be put on. The figures can be made as follows : —Boil half a pound of the best rice in a quart of water, till the grains are soft enough to bruise into a paste ; when cold, mix it with starch-powder till it becomes as stiff as dough ; roll it out to the thickness of a shilling, then cut it into pieces two inches square, and set them to dry before a moderate fire.

When required for use, get a coarse cloth, make it thoroughly wet, then squeeze out the water, and put it on a dish four times double ; place the rice cakes in rows between this cloth, and when sufficiently soft to knead into the consistence of new bread, make it into a small lump ; if too wet, mix with it more starch-powder ; but it must be sufficiently kneaded to lose all appearance of this powder before you take the impression, to do which you must procure some gutta-percha half an inch thick ; cut it into pieces about two inches square, and soften it in hot water ; then get any real carved ivory you can, and take off the impression on the pieces of gutta percha, by pressing it carefully upon the carved ivory till a deep impression is taken.

When the moulds are quite dry and hard, and the paste in a proper state, with a small camel-hair brush lightly touch with sweet oil the inside of the mould you are going to use, and then press the rice paste into it ; if the impression is quite correct, on removing it, take a thin, sharp, small dinner-knife, and cut the paste smoothly, just so as to leave all the impression perfect ; then with a sharp-pointed penknife turn all the rough edges, and with Barnard and Son's Cement place your figures on the box in large or small pieces, just as your own taste directs , the figures adhere better if put on before they are quite dry. Sometimes, from frequent kneading, the paste gets discoloured; these pieces should be set aside and used separately, as they can be painted in water-colours to imitate tortoiseshell or carved oak; this should be done after being stuck to the box. Having completed your work, finish by varnishing it very carefully with ivory varnish, which should be almost colourless. This design so nearly resembles carved ivory, that, when carefully done, it has been mistaken for it; if properly cemented, too, it is very strong, and looks well for boxes, card-cases, &c., either as ivory or tortoiseshell.

From the completeness and readiness with which the materials can be obtained from Barnard & Son, 339, Oxford Street, this is an elegant amusement for any ingenious lady.

**Milk of Roses.**—Take two ounces of blanched almonds, twelve ounces of rose water, two drachms each of white soft soap, or Windsor soap, white wax, and oil of almonds, three ounces of rectified spirits, one drachm of oil of bergamot, fifteen drops oil of lavender, and eight drops otto of roses. Beat the almonds well, and then add the rose-water gradually, so as to form an emulsion; mix the soap, white wax, and oil together, by placing them in a covered jar upon the edge of the fireplace, then rub this mixture in a mortar with the emulsion. Strain the whole through very fine muslin, and add the essential oils, previously mixed with the spirit.

This is an excellent wash for SUN-BURNS and FRECKLES, or for cooling the face and neck, or any part of the skin to which it is applied.

**Stains from the Hands.**—To remove fruit and other stains from the hands, first damp them with water, then rub them with tartaric acid, or salt of lemons, as you would with soap; then rinse them, and rub them dry. Tartaric acid, or salt of lemons, will also quickly remove stains from white muslin or linen. Put less than half a tea-spoonful of the salt or acid into a table-spoonful of water; wet the stain with it, and lay it in the sun for at least an hour; wet the spot once or twice with cold water during the time. If this does not remove the stains, repeat the acid-water, and lay the article again in the sun.

**Sausage Rolls.**—Take equal portions of cold roast veal and ham, or cold fowl and tongue; chop these together very small, season with powdered sweet herbs, salt, and cayenne pepper; mix well together, and put a portion of the chopped and seasoned meat, rolled together, into puff paste to cover it; and bake for half an hour in a brisk oven. These rolls are excellent eating, either hot or cold, and are especially adapted for travelling or pic-nic parties.

**Rissables.**—These are made with veal and ham, chopped very fine, or pounded lightly; add salt, pepper, nutmeg, a few bread crumbs, and a little parsley and lemon peel, or shalot; mix all together with the yolk of eggs, well beaten; either roll them into shape like a flat sausage, or into the shape of pears, sticking a piece of horse-radish in the ends to resemble the stalks; egg each over, and grate bread-crumbs; fry them brown, and serve on crisp-fried parsley.

**To Dress Cold Meat.**—Cut the meat in pieces, and lay them in a mould in layers, well seasoned. Then pour over and fill the mould with some clear soup, nearly cold, which, when left to stand some hours, will turn out to be as firm as isinglass, especially if shank bones were boiled in the soup.

Should the cold meat be poultry or veal, the addition of some small pieces of ham or bacon, and of hard-boiled eggs cut in slices, and put between the layers of meat, is a great improvement.

Another way to dress cold meat is to have it minced very fine, well seasoned, and put in patty-pans, with a thin crust below and above it, and baked in a quick oven. Cold meat, cut in small pieces, and put in a pie-dish, with batter poured over it, and baked until the batter rises, is a third way. Potatoe-pie is another capital method of using cold meat. For this purpose the meat should be cut in pieces and covered with mashed potatoes, then put into the oven to bake until the potatoes are well browned.

**The Art of Cookery.**—Of all the arts upon which the physical well-being of man, in his social state, is dependent none has been more neglected than that of cookery, though none is more important, for it supplies the very foun tain of life. The preparation of human food, so as to make it at once wholesome, nutritive, and agreeable to the palate, has hitherto been beset by imaginary difficulties and strong prejudices.

Many persons associate the idea of wealth with culinary perfection ; others consider unwholesome, as well as expensive, everything that goes beyond the categories of boiling, roasting, and the gridiron. All are aware that wholesome and luxurious cookery is by no means incompatible with limited pecuniary means ; whilst in roasted, boiled, and broiled meats, which constitute what is termed true English fare, much that is nutritive and agreeable is often lost for want of skill in preparing them. Food of every description is wholesome and digestible in proportion as it approaches nearer to the state of complete digestion, or, in other words, to that state termed *chyme,* whence the chyle or milky juice that afterwards forms blood is absorbed, and conveyed to the heart. Now, nothing is further from this state than raw meat and raw vegetables. Fire is therefore necessary to soften them, and thereby begin that elaboration which is consummated in the stomach. This preparatory process, which forms the cook's art, is more or less perfect in proportion as the aliment is softened, without losing any of its juices or flavour—for flavour is not only an agreeable but a necessary accompaniment to wholesome food. Hence it follows, that meat very much under-done, whether roasted or boiled, is not so wholesome as meat well done but retaining all its juices. And here comes the necessity for the cook's skill,

which is so often at fault even in these simple modes of preparing human nourishment.

Pork, veal, lamb, and all young meats, when not thoroughly dressed, are absolute poison to the stomach ; and if half-raw beef or mutton are often eaten with impunity, it must not be inferred that they are wholesome in their semi-crude state, but only less unwholesome than the young meats.

Vegetables, also, half done, which is the state in which they are often sent to table, are productive of great gastric derangement, often of a predisposition to cholera.

A great variety of relishing, nutritive, and even elegant dishes, may be prepared from the most homely materials, which may not only be rendered more nourishing, but be made to go much further in a large family than they usually do. The great secret of all cookery, except in roasting and broiling, is a judicious use of butter, flour, and herbs, and the application of a very slow fire—for good cooking requires only gentle simmering, but no boiling up, which only renders the meat hard. Good roasting can only be acquired by practice ; and the perfection lies in dressing the whole joint thoroughly without drying up the juice of any part of it. This is also the case with broiling ; whilst a joint under process of boiling, as we have said, should be allowed to simmer gently.

With regard to *made-dishes,* as the horrible imitations of French cookery prevalent in England are termed, we must admit that they are very unwholesome. All the juices are boiled out of the meat, which is swimming in a heterogeneous compound, disgusting to the sight, and seasoned so strongly with spice and Cayenne pepper enough to inflame the stomach of an ostrich.

French cookery is generally mild in seasoning, and free from grease ; it is formed upon the above-stated principle of reducing the aliment as near to the state of chyme as possible, without injury to its nutritive qualities, rendering it at once easy of digestion, and pleasant to the taste.

**To Fry Fish.**—The art of frying fish consists in having plenty of grease in the pan, and making it boil to the utmost before putting in the fish, which should have been laid to dry for some time in a cloth, and then rubbed with egg, and dipped in bread crumbs ; the grease should be so hot that it browns the fish, not *burns* it ; the fish should be turned once. Fried fish is not an economical dish, because it requires a great deal of fat to fry it in.

**To Boil Fish.**—For all kinds of fish put two spoonfuls of salt to every quart of water ; put the fish on in cold water ; remove the cover, and only let the water simmer. To ascertain when it is done try it with a skewer ; if the flesh of the fish stick to the bone it is not done enough. A mackarel will take from fifteen to twenty minutes, a haddock a little longer ; as a general rule, a pound of fish takes from fifteen to twenty minutes.

**Sponge Cake.**—Dissolve in half a pint of water three quarters of a pound of lump sugar ; simmer it over a slow fire until it is quite clear ; then pour it into a bowl, adding the grated rind of a lemon, and keep stirring it until it is cold. Then take the yolks of eight eggs, and the whites of two, and beat them together for a quarter of an hour ; mix the eggs and syrup together, and beat the mixture half an hour longer. Just before you put it into the oven, stir in by degrees half a pound of flour. One hour and a quarter will bake it.

**To Wash Lawn and Muslin.**—Delicate lawn and muslin dresses are so frequently spoiled by bad washing, the colours of the fabrics yielding so readily to the action of soap, that it is better to adopt another and a better method of cleaning the finest materials, and imparting to them the appearance of newness. Take two quarts of wheat bran, and boil it for half an hour in soft water. Let it cool, then strain it, and pour the strained liquor into the water in which the dress is to be washed.

Use no soap. One rinsing alone is required, and no starch. The bran water not only removes the dirt, and ensures against change of colour, but gives the fabric a pleasanter stiffness than any preparation of starch. If the folds are drawn from the skirts and sleeves, the dress will iron better, and will appear, when prepared in this way, as fresh as new.

**Receipt for Making Crumpets.**—Set two pounds of flour, with a little salt, before the fire till quite warm ; then mix it with warm milk and water till it is as stiff as it can be stirred , let the milk be as hot as it can be borne with the finger ; put a cupful of this with three eggs well beaten and mixed with three spoonfuls of very thick yeast ; then put this to the batter and beat them all together in a large pan or bowl ; add as much milk and water as will make it into a thick batter ; cover it close, and put it before the fire to rise ; put a bit of butter in a piece of thin muslin, tie it up, and rub it lightly over the iron hearth or frying-pan ; then pour on a sufficient quantity of batter at a time to make one crumpet ; let it do slowly, and it will be very light. Bake them all the same way. They should not be brown, but of a fine yellow colour.

**Pickling.**—Never use brass, copper, or bell-metal kettles for pickling, because the verdigris produced in them by the vinegar is very poisonous. Kettles lined with porcelain are the best ; but if you cannot procure them, blocktin may be substituted. Iron is apt to discolour any acid that is boiled in it. Vinegar for pickles should always be of the best cider kind. In putting away pickles, use stone or glass jars. The lead, which is an ingredient in the glazing of common earthenware, is rendered very pernicious by the action of the vinegar.

Have a large wooden spoon and a fork for the express purpose of taking pickles out of the jar when you want them for the table. See that, while in the jar, they are always completely covered with vinegar. If you discern in them any symptoms of not keeping well, do them over again in fresh vinegar and spice.

The jars should be stopped with large flat corks, fitting closely, and having a leather, or a round piece of oil-cloth, tied over the cork. It is a good rule to have two-thirds of the jar filled with pickles, and one-third with vinegar.

Alum is very useful in extracting the salt from pickles, and in making them firm and crisp. A very small quantity is sufficient, too much will spoil them.

In greening pickles, keep them very closely covered, so that none of the steam may escape, as its retention promotes their greenness, and prevents the flavour from evaporating.

Vinegar and spice for pickles should be boiled but a few minutes ; too much boiling takes away the strength.

**Etiquette of Visiting.**—VISITS OF CEREMONY.—These visits should necessarily be short, and they should on no account be made before the hour of luncheon, nor yet during the time. Persons who intrude themselves at unwonted hours are never welcome ; the lady of the house does not like to be disturbed when she is, perhaps, dining with her children. Ascertain, therefore, which you can do readily, what is the family hour for luncheon, dinner, &c., and act accordingly. Half an hour amply suffices for a visit of ceremony. If the visitor is a lady, she may remove her boa, or any neck covering, but on no account either the bonnet or shawl, even if politely requested to do so by the mistress of the house. If, however, your visit of ceremony is to a particular friend, the case is different ; but even then it is best to wait until you are invited to do so.

A mother when paying a ceremonial visit ought never to be accompanied by young children ; nor are favourite dogs ever welcome visitors in a drawing-room.

MORNING CALLS.—Be very careful not to acquire the character of a " day goblin," which is understood to mean one of those persons who, having plenty of leisure, and a great desire to hear themselves talk, make frequent inroads into their friends' houses. Though perhaps well acquainted with the rules of etiquette, which prescribe the time when the doors of English homes freely admit all who have a right to pass the threshold, they call at the most unseasonable hours. If the habits of the family are early you will find them in the drawing-room at eleven o'clock. It may be that they are agreeable and well-informed people ; but who wishes for calls at such a strange hour ? Most families have their rules and occupations, and it is almost past endurance to have them broken in upon by thoughtless people, who, having gained access, inflicts his or her presence till nearly luncheon time, and then goes off with saying, " Well, I have paid you a long visit," or, " I hope that I have not stayed too long."

VISITS OF CONDOLENCE.—These visits should be paid within a week after the event which occasions them ; but if the acquaintance is slight, immediately after the family appear at public worship. A card should be sent up ; and if your friends are able to receive you, let your manners and conversation be in harmony with the character of your visit. It is courteous to send up a mourning card ; and very soothing for ladies to make their calls in black silk or plain-coloured apparel. It denotes that they sympathise with the afflictions of the family ; and such attentions are always pleasing.

EVENING CALLS.—In some families evening calls are allowed. Should you chance to visit such a family, and find that they have a party, present yourself, and converse for a few minutes with an unembarrassed air ; after which you may retire, unless urged to remain ; a slight invitation, given for the sake of courtesy, ought not to be accepted. Make no apology for your unintentional intrusion, but let it be known, in the course of a few days, that you were not aware that your friends had company.

**Hints on Marketing.**—In the first

place, the housewife ought, where it is possible, to do her marketing herself, and pay ready money for everything she purchases. This is the only way in which she can be sure of getting the best goods at the lowest price. We repeat, that this is the only way compatible with economy ; because, if a servant be entrusted with the buying, she will, if she is not a good judge of the quality of articles, bring home those she can get for the least money (and these are seldom the cheapest) ; and even if she is a good judge, it is ten to one against her taking the trouble to make a careful selection.

When the ready-money system is found inconvenient, and an account is run with a tradesman, the mistress of a house ought to have a pass-book in which she should write down all the orders herself, leaving the tradesman to fill in only the prices. Where this is not done, and the mistress neglects to compare the pass-book with the goods ordered every time they are brought in, it sometimes happens, either by mistake, or the dishonesty of the tradesman, or the servant, that goods are entered which were never ordered, perhaps never had, and that those which were ordered are overcharged ; and if these errors are not detected at the time, they are sure to be difficult of adjustment afterwards. For these and other economic reasons, the housewife should avoid running accounts, and pay ready-money.

Condiments.—The name of condiment is usually given to those substances which are taken with food for the immediate purpose of improving their flavour. But most of them serve other and much more important purposes in the animal economy than that of gratifying the palate. Most of them are, in fact, alimentary substances—the use of which has become habitual to us.

But all the substances used as condiments are not necessary to our existence. This is the case with the aromatic and pungent condiments. The purpose which these substances serve in the animal economy is not very obvious ; they probably act as stimulants, and, in some cases, they may answer to correct the injurious qualities of the food with which they are partaken.

Saline Condiments.—Common salt is considered by most persons as a mere luxury, as if its use were only to gratify the taste, although it is essential to health and life, and is as much an aliment or food as either bread or flesh. It is a constituent of most of our food and drinks, and nature has kindly furnished us with an appetite for it. In many cases of disordered stomach, a teaspoonful of salt is a certain cure. In the violent internal pain, termed *colic*, a teaspoonful of salt, dissolved in a pint of cold water, taken as soon as possible, with a short nap immediately after, is one of the most effectual and speedy remedies known. The same will relieve a person who seems almost dead from receiving a heavy fall. In an apoplectic fit, no time should be lost in pouring down salt water, if sufficient sensibility remains to allow of swallowing ; if not, the head must be sponged with cold water until the sense returns, when the salt will restore the patient from lethargy. In cases of severe bleeding of the lungs, and when other remedies have failed, it has been found that two teaspoonfuls of salt completely stayed the blood.

Acidulous Condiments.—Vinegar, either by accident or design, has been employed by mankind in all ages, in greater or less quantity, as an aliment, or rather substances naturally containing it in small quantities have been employed as food, or it has been artificially formed, to be used and eaten. It is necessary, in one or other form, for the preseravtion of health. The prolonged absence from juicy vegetables or fruits, or their preserved juices, is a cause of scurvy. Vinegar is used as a condiment on account of its agreeable flavour and refreshing odour. It is employed alone or with pickles. When taken in small quantities, it is wholesome ; but, of course, if immoderately used, it will cause trouble. Citric acid is employed, as a substitute for lemon and lime juice, in the preparation of cooling and refreshing beverages. Tartaric acid is employed as a cheap substitute for citric acid or lemon juice. Besides being cheaper, it has another advantage over citric acid ; it is not deliquescent (or does not contract moisture) when exposed to the air. Cream of tartar is used in cooling drinks. There are other acids contained in fruits and vegetables, which are constantly employed and necessarily eaten by all.

OILY CONDIMENTS.—These are oils derived from the seeds of fruit called *vegetable oils*. They are used raw, as in almonds, walnuts, flax-seed, cocoa-nuts, and nutmeg, and other fruits. They are also pressed, as olive oil or sweet oil, oil of almonds, and many volatile or essential oils. The sweet or savoury herbs, such as mint, marjoram, sage, &c., owe their peculiar flavour and odour to volatile oil contained in the leaves. In fact, all fruits and leaves, and some vegetables, as onions, garlic, with the spices, owe their grateful odour and taste to volatile oil. These oils, prepared, sold, and dissolved in spirit of wine, form the essences for flavouring, &c.

*Butter* is employed as a condiment. When rancid by keeping, or when melted by heat, it is injurious to the dyspeptic.

**Furniture.**—It is scarcely possible to lay down a rule with respect to the ordinary furniture of a room, yet there is a general law of propriety which ought as much as possible to be observed. Regard must be had to what is called the "fitness of things," and thereby the avoiding of violent contrasts. For instance, sometimes a showy centre-table is seen in the middle of a room, where the carpet and every other article is out of repair ; or a resplendent looking-glass stands above the chimney-piece, as though to reflect the incongruous taste of its owner. Shabby things always look the shabbier when thus contrasted with what is bright and new. We do not mean to say that new

articles should never be purchased ; we remark only, that in buying furniture, regard should be had to the condition of the room in which it is to be placed. For this reason, second-hand furniture is sometimes preferable to new.

" So many men, so many minds," is an old saying ; and scarcely two people agree in choosing their assortment of furniture. What is convenient for one is inconvenient for another, and that which is considered ornamental by one family, would be thought ugly by their neighbours. There are, however, certain articles suited to most rooms—an ordinary parlour for example. The number of chairs depends on the size of the room ; eight are usually chosen, two of them being elbows. A circular table, with tripod stand, should occupy the centre of the apartment. At one side stands a sofa, a sideboard, a cheffonier, or perhaps a bookcase. Sometimes the cheffonier, with a few shelves fixed to the wall above it, is made to do duty as a bookcase, and it answers the purpose very well. If there be no sofa, there will be probably an easy chair, in a snug corner, not far from the fireplace ; in another corner stands a small work-table, or a light occasional table is placed near the window, to hold a flower-basket, or some other ornamental article. These constitute the furniture most needed in an ordinary parlour ; there are several smaller things, which may be added according to circumstances.

It is one thing to have furniture in a room, and another to know how to arrange it. To do this to the best advantage, requires the exercise of a little thought and judgment. Some people live with their furniture in the most inconvenient positions, because it never occurred to them to shift it from place to place, until they really had found which was the most suitable. Those who are willing to make the attempt, will often find that a room is improved in appearance and convenience by a little change in the place of the furniture.

It is too much the practice to cover the mantel-piece with a number and variety of knick-knacks and monstrosities by way of ornament ; but this is in very bad taste. Three, or, at most, four articles, are all that should be seen in that conspicuous situation. Vases of white porcelain, called " Parian," or of old china, or a statuette, are the most suitable. The forms of some of the white vases now sold at a low price, are so elegant, that it is a real pleasure to look at them.

**Indian Receipt for Curry.**—The following is a *real* Indian receipt by a native cook for the preparation of curry :—Cut a chicken into pieces, saving the bones ; fry them gently in an ounce of fresh butter, strewing over them, after they have been on the fire for a few minutes, one tablespoonful of curry powder. Have ready two large onions cut small into rings, and take care to have them fried without turning. Put the onions with the fried chicken into a stew-pan, and add half a pint of good stock (or, if not to be had, of water) ; cover the pan, and stew the whole gently, until the meat becomes tender. If desired, just before it is served, add the juice of half a small lemon ; salt it to the taste. If made from meat already cooked, it should not be stewed at all.

**Management of the Finger-Nails.** —They should be of an oval figure, transparent, without specks or ridges of any kind ; the semi-lunar fold, or white half-circle, should be fully developed, and the cuticle which forms the configuration around the root of the nails, thin and well-defined, and, when properly arranged, should represent as nearly as possible the shape of a half-filbert. The proper arrangement of the nails is to cut them of an oval shape, corresponding with the form of the fingers ; they should not be allowed to grow too long, as it is difficult to keep them clean ; nor too short, as it allows the ends of the fingers to become flattened and enlarged by being pressed upwards against the nails, and gives them a clumsy appearance.

The epidermis, which forms the semi-circle around, and adheres to the nail, requires particular attention, as it is frequently dragged on with its growth, drawing the skin below the nail so tense as to cause it to crack and separate into what is called agnails. This is easily remedied by carefully separating the skin from the nail by a blunt, half-round instrument.

Many persons are in the habit of continually cutting this pellicle, in consequence of which it becomes exceedingly irregular, and often injurious to the growth of the nail. They also frequently pick under the nails with a pin, penknife, or the point of sharp scissors, with the intention of keeping them clean, by doing which they often loosen them, and occasion considerable injury.

The nails should be cleaned with a brush not too hard, and the semicircular skin should not be cut away, but only loosened, without touching the quick, the fingers being afterwards dipped in tepid water, and the skin pushed back with a towel. This method, which should be practised daily, will keep the nails of a proper shape, prevent agnails, and the pellicles from thickening or becoming rugged. When the nails are naturally rugged or ill-formed, the longitudinal ridges or fibres should be rubbed and scraped with lemon, afterwards rinsed in water, and well dried with a towel ; but if the nails are very thin, no benefit will be derived by scraping ; on the contrary, it might cause them to split. If the nails grow more to one side than the other, they should be cut in such a manner as to make the point come as near as possible in the centre of the end of the finger.

**To Boil New Potatoes.**—These are never good unless freshly dug. Take them of equal size, and rub off the skins with a brush, or a very coarse cloth, wash them clean, and put them, without salt, into boiling, or, at least, quite hot water ; boil softly, and when they are tender enough to serve, pour off the water entirely, strew some fine salt over the potatoes, give them a shake, and let them stand by the fire in the saucepan for a minute, then dish and serve them immediately. Some cooks throw in a small piece of fresh butter with the salt, and toss them gently in it after it is dissolved. This is a good mode, but the more usual one is to send melted butter to table with them, or to pour white sauce over them when they are very young, and served early in the season, as a side or corner dish. Very small potatoes take from ten to fifteen minutes to boil ; moderate sized, fifteen to twenty minutes.

**Mashed Potatoes.**—Boil them perfectly tender quite through, pour off the water, and steam them very dry ; peel them quickly, take out every speck, and while they are still hot, press the potatoes through an earthen colander, or bruise them to a smooth mash, with a strong wooden fork or spoon, but never pound them in a mortar, as that will reduce them to a close heavy paste. Let them be entirely free from *lumps*, for nothing can be more indicative of carelessness or want of skill on the part of the cook, than mashed potatoes sent to table full of lumps. Melt in a clean saucepan a slice of good butter, with a few spoonfuls of milk, or, better still, of cream ; put in the potatoes after having sprinkled some fine salt upon them, and stir the whole over a gentle fire, with a *wooden* spoon, until the ingredients are well mixed, and the whole is very hot. It may then be served directly ; or heaped high in a dish, left rough on the surface, and browned before the fire ; or it may be pressed into a well-buttered mould of handsome form, which has been strewed with the finest bread-crumbs, and shaken free of the loose ones, then turned out, and browned in an oven.

More or less liquid will be required for potatoes of different kinds. For two pounds of potatoes add one teaspoonful of salt, one ounce of butter, and one quarter-pint of milk or sweet cream.

**Potatoe** Omelette.—This may be made with a mashed potatoe or two ounces of potatoe-flour, and four eggs, and seasoned with pepper, salt, and a little nutmeg. It should be made thick, and, being rather substantial, a squeeze of lemon will improve it. Fry a light brown.

**A New Receipt to Boil Old Potatoes.**—Wash, wipe, and pare the potatoes, cover them with cold water, and boil them gently until they are done ; pour off the water, and sprinkle a little fine salt over them ; then take each potatoe separately with a spoon, and lay it in a clean, *warm* cloth, twist this so as to press all the moisture from the vegetable, and render it quite round ; turn it carefully into a dish placed before the fire, throw a cloth over, and when all are done, send them to table quickly. Potatoes dressed in this way are mashed without any trouble ; it is also by far the best method of preparing them for puddings, pies, or cakes.

**To Roast or Bake Potatoes.**—Scrub and wash the potatoes exceedingly clean, and let them be of the same size ; wipe them very dry, and roast them in a dutch oven before the fire, placing them at a distance from it, and keeping them often turned ; or, arrange them in a coarse dish, and bake them in a moderate oven. Dish them neatly in a napkin, and send them very hot to table ; serve cold butter with them. They will take nearly two hours to roast or bake before a moderate fire.

**To Fry Potatoes.**—Dainty dishes of fried potatoes, to set between the principal ones at table, *(entremets,)* may be prepared in the following manner :—After having washed them, wipe and pare some raw potatoes, cut them in slices of equal thickness, or into thin shavings, and put them into a pan with plenty of boiling butter, or very pure clarified dripping. Then fry them of a fine light brown, and very crisp : lift them out with a skimmer, drain them on a soft warm cloth, dish them very hot, and sprinkle fine salt over them. This is an admirable way of dressing old potatoes. When pared round and round to a corkscrew form, in ribbons or shavings of equal width, and served dry and well-fried, lightly piled in a dish, they make a handsome appearance, and are excellent eating. They are sometimes served with a slight sprinkling of Cayenne. If sliced, they should be something less than a quarter of an inch thick.

**To Promote Sleep.**—The means of promoting sound sleep are of great importance to health, as the grand purposes of sleep are more fully effected, the sounder and more perfectly it is enjoyed. The greatest refreshment is derived from the most complete repose of the functions. For this purpose they should have been as generally exercised as possible during the day, both those of body and mind—this exercise, however, should not have proceeded so far as to produce a state of painful fatigue or exhaustion, as nothing is more sure to preclude refreshing sleep—the state of the circulation in the head should not have been excited by deep study, intense thought, tea, coffee, or other stimulant, for some time previous to retiring to rest ; late and copious suppers should be expressly avoided ; the head should not be kept too warm by thick, or flannel night-caps ; the feet and lower extremities should have been brought to a comfortable temperature, if necessary, by artificial means, such as the warm foot-bath, or flesh-brush ; lastly, and above all, the cares of the day should have been put off with the clothes, a habit, which, like every other in connection with the subject of sleep, may be materially influenced by determination. Dr. Priestley enumerates it among the privileges of his particular constitution, for which he expresses gratitude to his Maker, that, however much his mind might have been tried and perplexed through life during the day, as soon as he laid his head on the pillow all his cares were forgotten. He found time enough for all the pursuits of his busy life, without studying in bed—without employing the hours that should be hours of repose in deep meditation and thought.

**Currants and Gooseberries.**—The currant, properly propagated, is the most beautiful shrub growing ; and the same may be said of the gooseberry. Cultivators who pay any attention to the subject, never allow the root to make but one stock, thus forming a beautiful miniature tree. To do this you must take sprouts of last year's growth and cut out all the eyes, or buds, in the wood, leaving only two or three at the top ; then push them about half the length of the cutting, into some mellow ground, where they will root, and run up a single stock, forming a beautiful symmetrical head. If you wish it higher, cut the eyes out again the second year. This places your fruit out of the way of the fowls, and prevents the gooseberry from mildewing, which often happens when the fruit lies near the ground, and is shaded by a superabundance of leaves and sprouts. It changes an unsightly bush, which cumbers and disfigures your garden, into an ornamental dwarf tree. The fruit is larger, and ripens better, and will last on the bushes, by growing in perfection, until late in the fall. The mass of people suppose that the roots make out from the lower buds. It is not so—they start from between the bark and wood, at the place where it was cut from the parent root.

**Modelling in Gutta Percha and Leather.**—Besides being one of the greatest novelties of the present day, these arts combine usefulness and elegance, for by the aid of the beautiful enamel colours, an ordinary white china cup and saucer can be made to represent the old china with its quaintly-raised blossoms, figures, birds, leaves, &c. Old family relics, in the form of quaint vases, Egyptian figures, and all other articles of *vertu*, can be reproduced with wonderful exactness, the only requisite being a slight knowledge of painting, and a little patience and taste.

Pretty card-baskets may be entirely moulded out of the gutta percha ; ancient china frames to hold mirrors, old-fashioned gilt frames which are tarnished, and seemingly only fit for the lumber room, can, by the aid of the white enamel, be made to represent the purest white china, then with a wreath of the passion flower, either scarlet, crimson, blue, or the so-called white, with its rays of purple shading to blue, pressing with their dark green glossy leaves and light green tendrils upon the frame. The white frame fixed upon black velvet with a richly-carved cross, in ivory or gutta percha, which would look quite as well if painted to

represent ivory, placed on the velvet, the latter would be suitable for high church decorations. Elegant brackets formed of flowers, birds, and fruit in gutta percha enamelled white, supporting a crimson velvet stand, suitable for wedding and other gifts, besides many beautiful articles to fill ancient cabinets, and which could be made with taste to look as well as the costly articles so often seen within them, and for a very small sum. Wood, stone, and leather, besides gutta percha, can all be made to represent china in all its varieties, by the aid of the white and beautiful tinted enamels, which can never be displaced from the article painted with it, except by the use of turpentine, and that with great difficulty.

The materials required for the art of gutta percha work are but few, and are as follows :—The purest white gutta percha which is sold in sheets, and by the pound, the thickness of it should be less than a quarter of an inch, and quite smooth on its surface. Barnard and Son's enamel colours in bottles, consisting of white, deep rose, crimson, pale pink, blue, three shades of green, yellow, orange, scarlet, mauve, violet, and two shades of brown ; a pair of sharp pointed scissors, and several wooden moulds for leaves, &c., together with six camel's hair brushes of different large sizes, and six of the sable brushes from the medium to the finest, for veining and tinting tiny blossoms, butterflies, birds, &c.  Three sizes of copper wire, from the fine for stems of leaves and flowers, to the medium thick, for centre stems, stalks of large flowers, &c., where strength is required, and a pair of small pliers.

To soften and mould the gutta percha, a piece of it should be dipped into boiling water and instantly taken out again, and then stretched and moulded with the fingers into a thin smooth surface, and whilst warm and pliable, moulded or pressed on to the article required.

The leaves should be formed from the gutta percha whilst warm, by pressing a leaf upon it, that the impression of it may be obtained upon its surface, and then as quickly cut out with the scissors, and moulded with the fingers into natural form. Another, and equally as good a way, is to get a smooth piece of wood, and after placing the natural leaf or spray of leaves upon its surface, trace with a pencil round the outer edge, then remove the leaf and cut sharply round the edges with a penknife, to the depth of sixteenth of an inch, slicing as it were the piece in the form of the leaf out of the wood, then with a pencil trace the veins of the natural leaf, upon the indented outline which is on the wood, doing it with great care and precision, after which cut the lines out with a knife.

This mode saves much time and trouble, especially to those living in out of the way places where moulds would be difficult to procure ; all that is next to be done is to warm the gutta percha, and whilst wet, press it upon the indented mould, when upon being removed it will be found to bear upon its surface an exact copy of the veins and outline just formed upon the wood. The leaf should then be moulded with the fingers, by bending or crinkling according to the style of the leaf copied.

The flowers are simply formed from the warm gutta percha, after pressing it out to the even thickness of the real flower intended to copy ; each petal should be, as in wax, cut and moulded from nature ; if for a rose, or any other many-petaled flower, the sizes should be cut, moulded and regulated, in their order before making up.

The stems and tendrils are formed of wire covered smoothly with gutta percha.

As an example to which our instructions may be applied, we give an illustration (p. 49), of a Fuschia and Ivy Leaf Vase.  This vase is simply formed of well seasoned wood, and then covered with a thin coating of size, afterwards a coating of Barnard's oak stain should be applied, and then varnished ; between each process an hour or two should pass to let it dry.  The vase is then adorned with a garland, composed of a double branch of fuschias formed in leather, stiffened and oak stained as before described, they should be arranged according to the illustration, with small pins or tacks, taking care they are not seen, by placing a leaf or bud to cover them.  A trail of nicely formed ivy leaves should wreath round the foot and stem of the vase, ending in a graceful tendril to meet the garland of fuschias on each side of the vase.

This design would be equally suitable for gutta percha and enamels on a china cup or vase. If in gutta percha each part of the calyx should be separate as in wax and moulded accordingly.

**To Boil Vegetables.**—When green vegetables are fresh gathered they will not require so much boiling by quite a third of the time, as when stale. To get out the insects carefully shake the cabbages, greens, &c., and take off the outside leaves. Soft water is best for cooking vegetables ; but if only hard water can be obtained, a little soda should be used, (never pearlash,) which will soften the water, and improve the colour of the vegetables. Salt should also be used with them. Green vegetables, which should always be boiled by themselves, take from twenty to thirty minutes fast boiling to make them tender. When they sink they are done, and then, to maintain their flavour, they should be at once taken up and drained. They invariably should be put on in boiling water, in an uncovered saucepan, which will improve their colour.

When thoroughly boiled, all vegetables are both wholesome and nutritious, but the reverse when under done. In boiling them, the chief matter to be careful about is to see that they are soft before they are taken up ; as we have stated before this is usually accomplished in half an hour ; but the time will vary with their freshness, and the season in which they are grown.

To restore frost-bitten vegetables, lay them in cold water one hour before cooking, and when set to boil, put a piece of saltpetre in the water.

CAULIFLOWERS should not be allowed to boil so fast as greens ; they should be boiled in spring water with a little salt in it. In cutting off the stalks leave a little of the green on.

GREEN PEAS should be sent to table green ; this is their charm ; but when they wear a grey or yellow colour they should not be brought to table, for few persons would be tempted to eat them. Let but little time elapse between shelling and cooking, and care should be taken to have them as near of a size as possible. Before boiling, place them in a colander, and let some cold water run through them. Put them in fast boiling water, and, with the saucepan uncovered, let them boil rapidly for a quarter of an hour, or until tender. Put a slice of butter with them in the tureen in which they are to be served, and when it has melted, gently stir the peas, adding pepper and salt.

ASPARAGUS.—This esteemed vegetable should be cooked as soon after it has been cut as possible. Scrape the stalks well, and put them into cold water, and then gather them together and tie them in bundles of equal size ; after they have been put into boiling water, add to them a moderate handful of salt, and then let them boil until the ends of the stalks are tender, which will be in about thirty minutes ; toast a round of bread, which moisten with the water in which the stalks were boiled ; serve them with the white ends of the stalks outwards, and with melted butter.

ARTICHOKES.—After having cut away the outside leaves, and made the stalks even, put them, with a handful of salt, into boiling water, and they will be tender in about twenty-five minutes if they are young, but double that time if they are old. Drain, cut off the points of the leaves, and serve with melted butter.

ANGELICA.—Cut the stalks in lengths of four or five inches, and well boil them in a small quantity of water, keeping on the lid of the saucepan ; then dish them and peel them, and then boil again until a fresh green, then dry the stalks on a cloth, and lay them in an earthenware pan, adding about a pound of sifted sugar to each pound of stalks ; let them thus remain for three or four days, and then boil them again until very green, then place them in a sieve to drain, and powder them with pounded sugar. If the angelica is to be candied, lay it out to dry in the sun.

FRENCH BEANS.—If young the stalks and ends should alone be removed, and the beans should be thrown one by one as they are trimmed into cold water ; they should be put on in boiling water to be cooked, with a handful of salt ; in about twenty minutes they will be tender. They should boil rapidly, but not in too much water, and they should be uncovered. Beans at their maturity should have the ends and strings taken off, and they should be divided lengthwise and across. To preserve their fresh green colour a little soda should be thrown into the pot ; soda imparts a fine colour to all vegetables, and therefore it should never be overlooked by the cook

HARICOT BEANS.—Let about half a pint of beans remain in boiling water until the skins come off ; then put them in cold water for a few minutes, and then put them into a saucepan with some stock, and boil them to a glaze, when add some brown sauce.

WINDSOR BEANS.—These beans, if young, are a welcome addition to bacon or boiled pork, with which they are usually served. They should be boiled in salt and water till tender, and served with parsley and butter.

SPINACH.—Carefully wash, pick, and put into a small saucepan of boiling water, and it will be done in about eight or nine minutes ; cover the saucepan close, and shake it frequently. When the spinach is done, beat it up with a little butter, and squeeze it between two plates, then place it before the fire for the moisture to evaporate before serving.

TURNIPS, TO BOIL AND MASH.—After boiling until tender, drain them on a sieve, and then mash with butter, pepper, and salt, taking care that they are free from lumps.

SEAKALE.—This should be boiled till very white, and, like asparagus, may be served on toast. Seakale cannot be done too much. After trimming it should be tied in bundles, and if intended to be served on toast it should be thoroughly drained. It will take half an hour to boil ; an equal proportion of milk should be used with the water.

SPANISH ONIONS.—These are much improved by being dressed with some lean ham. While cooking three or four together they should not be allowed to touch each other ; cover them close, and place them with the ham on a slow stove, turning them repeatedly until they are done all round, which will be in about two hours. They should be prepared for roasting by taking off two skins, but the stalk or the root should not be much cut away.

Fruit Jars.—For the preservation of all kinds of fruits, use glass bottles or jars. Select those of even thickness, or rather of even thinness, for they are often exposed to considerable heat ; and while they should not be so thin as to break in common handling, or burst from internal pressure caused by fermentation, nor should they be thick, or of pressed glass, when blown-glass jars can be readily obtained. So much for the bottles. Now as to closing them air-tight, we know corks will not do it. The very structure of the substance is against it, unless cork of the most velvety character is obtained, and this is costly. We recommend waxed cloth, tied over the jar, as a substitute at once cheap and effective, and have never found anything superior to it. Prepare the cloth in this way :—melt together some resin, beeswax, and tallow, in equal parts ; tear the cloth in strips four inches wide, or at least sufficiently wide to conveniently tie over the mouth of the jar, and dip these strips into the hot wax, then stripping nearly all the wax off. With cloth thus prepared, after the jar is filled with hot preserves, and while still hot, close the mouth, and bind it on with good linen cord. Then with shears trim off as much of the waxed cloth as is desirable, and then dip it in some melted wax, which should be made with only about half as much tallow. Sealing-wax may be used instead, if desired. The jars should be put where the wax will cool at once, so that the exhaustion caused by the cooling of the preserves, and the condensation of the steam, may not cause the wax to run through the cloth. Nothing can be more thoroughly air-tight than bottles so prepared.

**Brown Sauce.**—Put into a saucepan two pounds of beef, the same quantity of veal, an old fowl, some onions and carrots, and throw over the whole a pint of water; place the saucepan on a strong fire until the sauce begins to glaze; then put the vessel on a slower fire, and when your glaze begins to brown, put to it a little stock, adding some mushrooms, a bunch of parsley, a few cloves, and some bay leaves; skim it, put a little salt, and let it simmer for three hours; then strain the liquor off, and add to it a roux which you have made in a separate vessel, and let it boil again another hour; you have only then to take the fat off and pass it through a sieve, when it is ready for use.

**Economical Pudding.**—Take two tablespoonfuls of rice, put it into a small saucepan with as much water as the rice will absorb. When boiled enough add a pinch of salt, then set it by the fire until the rice is quite soft and dry. Throw it up in a dish, add two ounces of butter, four tablespoonfuls of tapioca, a pint and a half of milk, sugar to the taste, a little grated nutmeg, and two eggs beaten up. Let it all be well stirred together, and baked an hour.

**Bread without Yeast.**—Some years since, when unfermented bread was first becoming known, the following recipe was very successfully tried; and we have since been told that an almost similar method of preparing bread is common in many remote parts of both England and Ireland, where it is almost impossible to procure a constant supply of yeast. Blend well together a teaspoonful of powdered sugar and fifty grains of the purest carbonate of soda: mix a salt-spoonful of salt with a pound of flour, and rub the soda and sugar through a hair-sieve into it. Stir and mingle them well, and make them quickly into a firm but not hard dough,

with sour buttermilk. Bake the loaf well in a thoroughly heated but not fierce oven. In a brick, or in a good iron oven, a few minutes less than an hour would be sufficient to bake a quartern loaf. The buttermilk should be kept till it is quite acid; but it must never be in the slightest degree rancid, or otherwise bad. All unfermented bread, it must be repeated, should be placed in the oven directly it is made, or it will be heavy.

**To Preserve Pears.**—Take small, rich, fair fruit, as soon as the pips are black; set them over the fire in a kettle, with water to cover them; let them simmer until they yield to the pressure of the finger, then with a skimmer take them into cold water; pare them neatly, leaving on a little of the stem, and the blossom end; pierce them at the blossom end to the core, then make a syrup of a pound of sugar to each pound of fruit; when it is boiling hot, pour it over the pears, and let it stand till the next day, when drain it off, make it boiling hot, and again pour it over; after a day or two, put the fruit in the syrup over the fire, and boil it gently until it is clear; then take it into jars or spread it on dishes; boil the syrup thick, then put it and the fruit in jars.

**Cool Rooms.**—In fevers a cool room frequently does as much good as medicine. Blinds coated with the following composition and placed *outside* the window, are both sun and rain-proof; the greatest heat will not affect them:—Boil well together two pounds of turpentine, one pound of litharge in powder, and two or three pounds of linseed oil; the blinds are to be brushed over with this varnish, and dried in the sun. Umbrellas, light linen coats, and covers of hats may be so treated.

**Rules for Ladies.**—Mrs. Jamieson recommends the ladies to observe the following rules:—" In the morning use pure water as a preparatory ablution; after which they must abstain from all sudden gusts of passion, particularly envy, as that gives the skin a sallow paleness. It may seem trifling to speak of temperance, yet this must be attended to, both in eating and drinking, if they would avoid pimples.

Instead of rouge, let them use moderate exercise, which will raise a natural bloom in their cheek, inimitable by art.

Ingenuous candour and unaffected good humour will give an openness to their countenance that will make them universally agreeable. A desire of pleasing will add fire to their eyes, and breathing the air of sunrise will give their lips a vermilion hue.

That amiable vivacity which they now possess may be highly heightened and preserved, if they would avoid late hours and card-playing, as well as novel-reading by candle-light, but not otherwise ; for the first gives the face a drowsy, disagreeable aspect ; the second is the mother of wrinkles ; and the third is a fruitful source of weak eyes and a sallow complexion.

A white hand is a very desirable ornament : and a hand can never be white unless it be kept clean ; nor is this all, for if a young lady excels her companions in this respect, she must keep her hands in constant motion, which will occasion the blood to circulate freely, and have a wonderful effect. The motion recommended is working at her needle, brightening the house, and making herself as useful as possible in the performance of all domestic duties."

Dyeing.—This art is very ancient ; indeed in all ages brilliant colours have excited admiration, and even the uncultivated savage has evinced a passion for the beautiful and bright hues to be found in the feathers of birds and other natural objects. The origin of dyeing, or producing colours by artificial means, is of great antiquity, for Moses speaks of stuffs dyed blue, and purple, and scarlet, and of sheep skins dyed red.

Among the Greeks, dyeing seems not to have been very much practised ; the woollen clothes usually worn by them were of the natural colour of the sheep ; but the wealthy classes preferred co-loured dresses, of which scarlet was much esteemed ; still purple was more highly valued, and was the distinguishing mark of the greatest dignities, being reserved for princes only. The most famous of their purple dyes was that called Tyrian, which is said to have been drawn from a certain shell-fish, a species of murex, common on the shores of the Mediterranean ; but the quantity of purple juice afforded by this animal is exceedingly small, and consequently garments stained with it were of great price. The Romans were equally severe in restricting the use of purple to the highest rank ; and it does not appear that the number of their dyes and dyed colours were considerable, although coloured dresses were not rare among them. The art of dyeing slowly improved in modern times, until the application of chemistry, by throwing on it peculiar light, has of late advanced it to a degree of perfection formerly unknown ; and this has afforded great resources to the ingenuity and industry of man.

" A remarkable circumstance connected with dyeing," (we quote from " Chambers's Information for the People,") " is the different degrees of facility with which animal and vegetable substances imbibe the colouring matters applied to them. Tissues composed of the former, as silk and wool, receive more brilliant colours than those composed of the latter, as cotton and linen. The cause of this difference has not hitherto been discovered.

Although, in the most numerous class of cases, it is easy to impart colour to various tissues, yet when these become exposed to moisture, the dye-stuff is removed. It has therefore been found necessary to employ certain chemical substances which shall have the property of permanently fixing the colour upon the body which is dyed. These substances have obtained the name of *mordants* (from the latin word *mordere*, to bite), because they were supposed at first, figuratively speaking, to bite the dye into the cloth. The action of the mordants in fixing the colour on the cloth is very decided. If a piece of calico be simply soaked with a solution of the colouring-matter of Brazil-wood, and thereafter washed the whole of the dye can be washed out ; but if the calico be first immersed in a solution of acetate of alumina (a mordant), and thereafter treated with Brazil-wood solution, it acquires a permanent red colour, which cannot be washed out.

By varying the mordant, a great variety of shades may be derived from the same colouring-matter. Indeed, the mordant itself, in many instances supplies a colour. For example, in dyeing with cochineal, when the aluminous mordant is employed, the colour produced is crimson ; but when oxide of iron is substituted for the alumina, a black colour is the result. Cloth first treated with a mordant of acetate of alumina, and thereafter with a decoction of madder, Brazil and peach woods, comes up a *red ;* with the same mordant and cochineal, a *pink ;* with the same mordant and madder alone, a *lilac ;* with the same mordant and quercitron and Persian berries, a *yellow.* With a very dilute solution of acetate of iron as a mordant, cloth becomes a *red* with madder ; with stronger solution, a *purple* is produced ; and a still stronger gives a *black. Chocolates* are procured by treating the cloths first with a mixture of the iron and alumina mordants, and thereafter dyeing with madder. *Yellows* are formed by immersing the cloth in solution of acetate of lead, and then in solution of bichromate of potash. *Oranges* are readily produced by taking the cloth already dyed yellow, and boiling it in dilute milk of lime, or even washing soda. *Browns* are formed by heating the cloth in solution of the sulphate of manganese, and passing it through caustic soda, and lastly placing it in solution of bleaching powder.

When parts of the cloth are to remain uncoloured, it is necessary to print on a substance which destroys or throws off the colour."

**Rainbows.**—The rainbow has, from the earliest times, been an object of interest with those who bestowed attention on optical appearances, but the rainbow is much too complicated a phenomenon to be easily explained. In general, however, it was understood to arise from light reflected by drops of rain falling from a cloud opposite the sun. The difficulty seems to be how to account for the colour, which is never produced in white light, such as that of the sun, by mere reflection.

Maurolycus advanced a considerable step, when he supposed that the light enters the drop, and acquires colour by refraction ; but in tracing the course of the ray he was quite bewildered. Others supposed the refraction and the colour to be the effect of one drop, and the refraction of another ; so that two refractions and one reflection were employed, but in such a manner as to be still very remote from the truth.

Antonio de Dominis, Archbishop of Spalatro, had the good fortune to fall upon the true explanation. Having placed a bottle of water opposite to the sun, and a little above his eye, he saw a beam of light issue from the underside of the bottle, which acquired different colours, in the same order and with the same brilliancy as in the rainbow, when the bottle was a little raised or depressed. From comparing all these circumstances, he perceived that the rays had entered the bottle ; and that, after two refractions from the convex part, and a reflection from the concave, they were returned to the eye tinged with different colours, according to the angle at which the ray had entered.

The rays that gave the same colour made the same angle with the surface, and hence all the drops that gave the same colour must be arranged in a circle, the centre of which was the point in the cloud opposite the sun.

**New Year's Gifts.**—The ancients made presents out of respect on the New Year's Day, as a happy augury for the ensuing year, which were called *Strenæ.* Symmachus adds, that the use of them was first introduced by King

Tatius, Romulus's colleague, who received branches of vervain, gathered in the sacred grove of the goddess Strenua, as a happy presage of the beginning of the year. Strenua was a goddess among the Romans, of an opposite character to the goddess Sloth, and who had a temple at Rome. Anciently a pound of gold was given to the emperors every New Year's Day, by way of *Strena*.

To the Romans we owe the ceremony of wishing "a happy new year." "A time," says Lord Chesterfield, "when the kindest and warmest wishes are exchanged, without the least meaning; and the most lying day in the year,"——an assertion the boldness of which is only equalled by its want of truth.

We have been often asked what is the best present to make to a friend at Christmas or on New Year's Day? Our answer has always been a suitable book, for books are imperishable gifts, and ever reminding one of the giver as it is taken up for perusal, and the eye glances at the affectionate inscription to us in the donor's handwriting.

**A Cure for Love.**—Take of spirit of resolution, 14 ounces; syrup of good advice, 12 ounces; spices of employment, 13 ounces; spirit of indifference, 1 ounce; oil of absence, 2 ounces; powder of disdain, 2 grains. Put these ingredients into a saucepan of sound reason, with a good quantity of the best heart's ease. Stir it up with a large quantity of time, and strain it through a long bag of patience. A small portion of this mixture to be taken frequently. Should this recipe ever fail, the patient may be considered *incurable*.

**New Lodgers' Goods Protection Act** (August 16th, 1871.)—*An Act to Protect the Goods of Lodgers against Distresses for Rent due to the Superior Landlord.*—Whereas lodgers are subjected to great loss and injustice by the exercise of the power possessed by the superior landlord to levy a distress on their furniture, goods, and chattels for arrears of rent due to such superior landlord by his immediate lessee or tenant.

Be it enacted by the Queen's most Excellent Majesty, by and with the consent of the Lords Spiritual and Temporal, and Commons, in this present Parliament assembled, and by the authority of the same, as follows (that is to say):—

1. If any superior landlord shall levy or authorise to be levied, a distress on any furniture, goods, or chattels of any lodger for arrears of rent due to such superior landlord by his immediate tenant, such lodger may serve such superior landlord, or the bailiff or other person employed by him to levy such distress, with a declaration in writing made by such lodger, setting forth that such immediate tenant has no right of property or beneficial interest in the furniture, goods, or chattels so distrained or threatened to be distrained upon, and that such furniture, goods, or chattels are the property or in the lawful possession of such lodger; and also setting forth whether any and what rent is due and for what period from such lodger to his immediate landlord; and such lodger may pay to the superior landlord, or to the bailiff or other person employed by him as aforesaid, the rent, if any, so due as last aforesaid, or so much thereof as shall be sufficient to discharge the claim of such superior landlord. And to such declaration shall be annexed a correct inventory, subscribed by the lodger, of the furniture, goods, and chattels referred to in the declaration; and if any lodger shall make or subscribe such declaration and inventory, knowing the same or either of them to be untrue in any material particular, he shall be deemed guilty of a misdemeanour.

2. If any superior landlord, or any bailiff or other person employed by him after being served with the before-mentioned declaration and inventory, and after the lodger shall have paid or tendered to such superior landlord, bailiff, or other person the rent, if any, which by the last preceding section such lodger is authorised to pay, shall levy or proceed with a distress on the furniture,

goods, or chattels of the lodger, such superior landlord, bailiff, or other person shall be deemed guilty of an illegal distress, and the lodger may apply to a justice of the peace for an order for the restoration to him of such goods ; and such application shall be heard before a stipendiary magistrate, or before two justices in places where there is no stipendiary magistrate, and such justices or magistrate shall inquire into the truth of such declaration and inventory, and shall make such order for the recovery of the goods or otherwise as to him or them may seem just, and the superior landlord shall also be liable to an action at law at the suit of the lodger, in which action the truth of the declaration and inventory may likewise be inquired into.

3. Any payment made by any lodger pursuant to the first section of this Act shall be deemed a valid payment on account of any rent due from him to his immediate landlord.

4. This Act shall not extend to Scotland.

| | D. | H. | M. |
|---|---|---|---|
| **The Seasons.**—The SPRING Quarter begins March | 20 | 8 | 10 A. M. |
| The SUMMER Quarter begins June | 21 | 4 | 52 A. M. |
| The AUTUMN Quarter begins September | 22 | 7 | 16 A. M. |
| The WINTER Quarter begins December | 21 | 1 | 3 P. M. |

**Registration of Births.**—Parents should cause their children to be registered within six months after birth, by giving personal notice to the registrar of their district. No fee is payable ; but after forty-two days a sum of 7s. 6d. is chargeable. Registration of birth answers all the purposes of baptism as regards property.

**Sore Throat.**—Sore throat is best relieved by the inhalation of steam from a basin of hot water, around which a towel is thrown enclosing the head, and the application externally of a mustard-plaster, or a liniment of equal parts of spirit of hartshorn and oil on flannel.

Sucking a piece of saltpetre, before swallowing it, and gargling the throat with its solution in the mouth is another useful remedy. When accompanied by fever, after relieving the bowels by a pill or two of calomel and aloes, a saline mixture with antimony should be employed.

Persons subject to sore throat find cayenne a good preventive. In the form of lozenges this may be taken at any time pleasantly, and its use in this way will frequently crush the disease in its first attempt at outbreak.

**Cure for a Cold.**—Dr. Hall says, " A bad cold, like measles and mumps, or other similar ailments, will run its course of about ten days, in spite of what may be done for it, unless remedial means are employed within forty-eight hours of its inception. Many a useful life may be spared, to be increasingly useful, by cutting a cold short off in the following safe and simple manner :—On the first day of taking a cold there is a very unpleasant sensation of chilliness. The moment you observe this you go to your room and stay there ; keep it at such a temperature as will entirely prevent this chilly feeling, even if it requires 100 degrees Fahrenheit. In addition, put your feet in water, half leg deep, as hot as you can bear it, adding hotter water from time to time for a quarter of an hour, so that the water shall be hotter when you take your feet out than when you put them in ; then dry them thoroughly, and put on thick, warm, woollen stockings, even if it be summer ; and for twenty-four hours eat not an atom of food, but drink as largely as you desire of any kind of warm teas, and, at the end of that time, if not sooner, the cold will be effectually broken without any medicine whatever."

**How to Catch Cold.**—When, in the spring or commencement of summer, you throw up the window to enjoy the fresh air, if you feel a delicious coolness blow over the face and neck, you may rest assured that you are taking cold. If you get heated with exercise, and sit down with uncovered head, to enjoy the air from an open door or window, and find a similar sensation of refreshing coolness, be sure again that you are taking cold. If you are fond of gardening—and what lady is not ?—and want to see how the beautiful flowers get on after the rain, or frost, go straight out from the fire just as you are, if you want to catch cold, for you will succeed to a certainty.

**To Avoid Catching Cold.**—Colds are more frequently caught in summer than winter, especially in June, when cold nights follow warm days. We are so much in love with young summer, that we are betrayed into too much abandoning ourselves to his genial influences, and when the cool evening air blows deliciously over us, the next day we have a snuffling in the nose, a blearness in the eyes, and an unpleasant sensation in the throat. Whoever gets heated with summer exercise should put on extra clothing while getting cool.

Another prevalent source of cold indeed more than any other, is cold feet. To get the feet wet will not give cold, provided you do not sit or stand without changing. As long as you keep walking the wet does no harm ; but the moment you have occasion to rest, the circulation will sink, and the damp will do its destructive work. Hence, on arriving home, off with your shoes and stockings, wash your feet in *cold* water, if necessary, and quickly dry them, and put on warm woollen stockings. Thin shoes are to be condemned, as affording insufficient protection, and those who use them in winter should use cork soles. There is an old saying, " keep the head cool, the feet warm, and the bowels open, and you will never want the doctor." We can say this, that the dogma involves the whole theory of the management of health.

Protecting the back with wash-leather or flannel, should be well observed by those who would avoid catching cold. Many persons are not aware that it is quite as necessary to protect the back between the shoulders, and especially under the blade bones, where the lungs come near the surface, from cold and draughts, as it is the chest.

Keep a thermometer outside your bed-room window, and another in your sitting-room. When you rise in the morning, the first one will give you a hint how to dress, and the second how to regulate the fierceness of the fire.

Beware, too, of sudden transitions from hot to cold. In a sitting-room the thermometer ought never to go higher than 63, and never below 50 degrees. Of course we speak here only of the heat under our control, or artificial heat. A temperature of 70 degrees, though very comfortable in winter and spring, is also very weakening, and predisposes the system to take cold on any slight exposure. (*See* Cure for a Cold.)

**Abbreviations.**—A. Alto and Alt in music.

A.A.G. Assistant Adjutant General.

A.B. Bachelor of Arts.

Abp. Archbishop.

A.D. *Anno Domini*, in the year of our Lord.

Admors. Administrators.

Æ. *Ætatis ( Anno)* In the year of his (or her) age.

Affeto. (Music) *Affetuoso*, affectionately.

Affectly Affectionately.

A.G. (Military) Adjutant General.

A.G (Official) Accountant General.

A.G.E. Attorney General of England

Ald. Alderman.

Alexr. Alexander.

Alf. or Alfd. Alfred.

Allo. (Music) *Allegro*, quick and lively.

Alt. Altitude.

A.M. Master of Arts.

A.M. *Anno Mundi*, In the year of the world.

A.M. or a.m. (Time of day) *Ante Meridian*, before midnight—morning.

Ando. (Music) less slow than Andte.

Andte. *Andante*, moderately slow

A.R.A. Associate of the Royal Academy.

**A.R.S.A.** Associate of the Royal Scottish Academy.

**B.A.** Bachelor of Arts.

**Bart.** Baronet.

**B.B.** (Drawing Pencils) Black Black (Blacker than those marked B).

**B.C.** Before Christ.

**B.C.L.** Bachelor of Civil Law.

**B.D.** Bachelor in Divinity.

**Beds.** Bedfordshire.

**Berks.** Berkshire.

**B.I.** British Institution.

**B.L.** Bachelor of Laws.

**B.M.** Bachelor of Medicine.

**Bp.** Bishop.

**Brill.** (Music) *Brillante*, brilliantly.

**Brit.** British, or Britain, or Britannia.

**B.V.** *Bene Vale*, Farewell.

**B.V.** Blessed Virgin.

**C.** (Roman Numeral) *Centum*, a hundred.

**Cap.** *Capitulum*, Chapter.

**Capt.** Captain.

**Cantab.** One educated at Cambridge.

**C.B.** Companion of the Bath.

**CC.** Two Hundred.

**C.C.E.** Committee of Council on Education.

**CCC.** Three Hundred.

**C.C.C.** Corpus Christi College.

**CCCC.** Four Hundred.

**C.E.** Civil Engineer.

**Ch.** Chapter.

**Chron.** Chronology or Chronicle.

**C.J.** Chief Justice.

**Co.** Company and County.

**Col.** Colossians, Colonel, and Colonial.

**Coll.** College, Collection, and Collector.

**Como.** (Music) *Commodo*, in an easy style.

**Compts.** Compliments and Accounts.

**Cont.** (Music) *Contano*, they count [or rest.]

**Cr.** Creditor.

**C.S.** Civil Service.

**Cwt.** A Hundredweight.

**Cor.** Corinthians.

**D.** (Roman Not.) Five Hundred.

**D. or d.** (Money) *Denarius*, a Penny, or *Denarii*, Pence.

**D.C.** Duchy of Cornwall.

**D.C. or d. c.** (Music) *Da Capo*, from the beginning.

**D.D.** Doctor of Divinity.

**Deg.** Degree.

**Deut.** Deuteronomy.

**Do.** *Ditto*, the same.

**Dol.** (Music) *Dolce*, sweet, soft.

**Dox.** Doxology.

**Dr.** Debtor, Doctor, Drachm, and Dear.

**D.V.** *Deo Volente*, God willing.

**Dwt.** Pennyweight.

**Devon.** Devonshire.

**Ec., Eccl., or Eccles.** Ecclesiastes.

**Ed.** Editor.

**E.G. or e. g.** *Exempli Gratia*, for instance (Example.)

**E.H.B.** (Drawing Pencils) Extra Hard Black.

**Eng.** England or English.

**Eph.** Ephesians.

**Epiph.** Epiphany.

**Esq. or Esqre.** Esquire.

**Etc.** (Various) *Et cætera*.

**Etym.** Etymology.

**Eur.** Europe and Euripides.

**Ev., or Evg., or Even.** Evening.

**Ex.** Example.

**Exch.** Exchange and Exchequer.

**Ex. or Exod.** Exodus.

**Exors.** Executors.

**Ez. or Ezek.** Ezekiel.

**F.** (Music) *Forte*, Loud.

**F.A.** Fine Arts.

**Fah.** Fahrenheit.

**F.A.S.** Fellow of the Antiquarian Society.

**Fcp.** Foolscap.

**Feb. or Feby.** February.

**Fem.** Feminine.

**F.E.S.** Fellow of the Ethnological Society.

**FFF. or fff.** (Music) *Fortissimo*, as loud as possible.

**F.G.S.** Fellow of the Geological Society.

**Fid. Def.** *Fidei Defensor*, Defender of the Faith.

**Fig.** Figure.

**Flebe.** (Music) *Flebile*, pensive.

**F.L.S.** Fellow of the Linnæan Society.

F.M. Field Marshal.

Fo. or Fol. Folio.

For. Foreign.

F.R.A.S. Fellow of the Royal Astronomical Society.

F.R.C.S. Fellow of the Royal College of Surgeons.

F.R.S. Fellow of the Royal Society.

F.S.A. Fellow of the Society of Arts.

Ft. Foot or feet.

F.Z.S. Fellow of the Zoological Society.

Gal. Galatians.

Gen. Genesis.

Gent. Gentleman.

G.P.O. General Post Office.

Gs. Guineas.

G.C.B. Grand Cross of the Bath.

Hab. Habakkuk.

Hants. Hampshire.

H.B. (Drawing Pencils) Hard Black.

Heb. Hebrews.

H.H. His (or her) Highness.

Hhd. Hogshead.

H.J. *Hic Jacet*, here lies (interred or entombed here).

H.M. His (or her) Majesty.

H.M.S. His (or her) Majesty's Ship.

Hon. Honourable and Honorary.

H.P.R. *Hic pace Requiescat*, May he rest in peace.

H.R.H. His (or Her) Royal Highness.

H.S.L. *Hic Sitis*, Here rests (or is deposited).

I. (Roman Notation) One.

Ib. or Ibid. *Ibidem*, the same (as before named) in the same place.

I.E. (i.e.) *id est*, that is.

I.H.S. *Jesus Hominum Salvator*, Jesus the Saviour of Men.

I.H.M. *Jesus Hominum Mundi*, Jesus the Saviour of the World.

Imp. Imperial.

In. Inch or Inches.

Incog. *Incognito*, in disguise.

Infra. dig. *Infra dignitatis*, beneath (one's) dignity.

Inst. *Instant*, the present (the current month).

Int. Interest.

IO.U. "I owe you."

J.C. Justice Clerk.

Je. or Jer. or Jerem. Jeremiah.

Jno. John.

Jos. Joseph.

J.P. Justice of the Peace.

Jr. or Junr. Junior.

K.B. Knight of the Bath.

K.C.B. Knight Commander of the Bath.

K.G. Knight of the Garter.

K.T. Knight of the Thistle.

Kt. or Knt. Knight.

K.G.C.B. Knight Grand Cross of the Bath.

L. (Roman Notation) Fifty.

L. *Libra*, Pound (twenty shillings) or pounds.

L. (Music) Left-hand.

Mac. Maccabees.

Maj. Major.

Mal. Malachi.

Mar. Marine and March.

Matt. Matthew.

M.B. Bachelor of Medicine.

M.B. Bachelor of Music.

M.C. Master of the Ceremonies.

M.D. Doctor of Medicine.

Mdlle. *Mademoiselle*, Miss.

Mem. Memorandum.

Messrs. *Messieurs*.

Mf. (Music) *Mem forte*, rather loud.

Mgr. *Monseigneur*, My Lord.

Michs. Michaelmas.

Mon. *Monsieur*, Mr.

Mor. (Music) *Morendo*, dying away.

Mos. Months.

M.P. Member of Parliament.

M.R.G.S. Member of the Royal Geographical Society.

Mr. Mister.

Mrs. Mistress.

MSS. Manuscripts.

N.B. *Nota Bene*, mark well, notice, bear in mind.

N.B. North Britain.

N.E. North East.

Neh. Nehemiah.

Nem. con. *Nemine contradicente*, no one contradicting.

N.L. North Latitude.

N.N.E. North North East.

N.N.W. North North West.

Non compos mentis. Not of sound mind (insane).

Nov. November.
N.W. North West.
Ob. or Obit. He or she died.
Oct. October.
Oct. or 8vo. A sheet of paper folded to form eight leaves.
Ott. (Music) *Ottava*, Octave.
Oz. Ounce.
P. or p. (Music) *Piano*, softly.
P.C. Privy Councillor and Police Court.
Ped. (Music) Pedal or Pedals.
Pet. Peter.
Ph. D. Doctor of Philosophy.
P.M. *Post Meridian*, after mid-day (afternoon).
P.O. Post Office.
P.O.O. Post Office Order.
pp. Pages.
pp. (Music) *Pianessimo*, very softly.
Pro tem. *Pro tempore*, for the time.
Prof. Professor.
Proximo. The coming (next) month.
P.S. *Post scriptum*, Postscript.
Ps. Psalm or Psalms.
Pt. Pint and Part.
Q. Question, Query.
Q.C. Queen's Counsel.
Qrs. Quires.
Qt. Quart.
R. *Regina*, Queen.
R. *Rex*, King.
Sam. Samuel.
S.E. South East.
Sec. Section.
Sec. Secretary.
Sep. or Sept. September.
Serjt. Serjeant.
Servt. Servant.
S.M. Short Metre.
Solr. Solicitor.
Sov. Sovereign.
S.S.E. South South East.
S.S.W. South South West.
Sun. Sunday.
S.W. South West.
Syn. Syntax and Synonym.
Therm. Thermometer.
Thes. Thessalonians.
Tim. Timothy.
Typ. Printer.
Ult. *Ultimo*, the last (month).
U.S. United States.

V. (Roman Notation) 5,
v. *Versus*, against,
v. *Vide*, see.
Ven. Venerable.
Viz. *Videlicit*, namely,
Vis. Viscount.
Vol. Volume.
V.R. *Victoria Regina*, Victoria the Queen.
W. West.
Wed. Wednesday.
W.N.E. West North East.
W.N.W. West North West.
W.O. War Office.
Wm. William.
W.S.E. West South East.
W.S.W. West South West.
X. (Roman Notation) 10.
Xmas. Christmas.
Yd. Yard.
Zec. Zechariah.
Zep. Zephaniah.
Zoo. Zoology.

**Introductions.**—Be very cautious to whom you introduce a friend. A gentleman should never be introduced to a lady, always the latter to the former. Avoid street introductions, except business demands them. Time and place should be studied when you introduce a friend. Permission, too, should always be obtained before you introduce your friends to each other. Should you by chance meet an acquaintance while walking with a friend, merely bow and proceed in your walk.

**Imitation Preserved Ginger.**—In making this ginger, well scrape and split in halves *young* yellow carrots, and cut them into the races or cloves of West Indian ginger, as we see it preserved. Parboil them, taking care that they do not break or lose their shape; drain them thoroughly, and let them lie on the back of a sieve all night. Next day weigh them and put them into a stewpan with their own weight of syrup of ginger, which is to be obtained from any respectable chemist. Let them simmer *very* gently over a *low fire* for four hours. Fill your preserve-pots, taking care to apportion fairly both vegetables and syrup. Tie them down with bladder, and let them stand on the hob three days. This preserve is an excellent substitute for the real West Indian importation, which is reckoned so great a delicacy, and is also so expensive. It improves by keeping.

**Patterdale Pudding.**—Visitors to Ulleswater are well acquainted with this delicious mixture, which is thus made :—One pound of butter worked into a cream, the same weight of well-pounded white sugar, and the yolks of eight eggs, well beaten and well mixed with the butter and sugar. Whisk the whites to a strong froth, and put them to the rest. Then add one pound of flour and one lemon, rind and juice ; blend all thoroughly together, and bake in buttered cups for twenty minutes. Make a sauce of arrow-root, with a little sherry, and pour over the pudding before serving. These puddings, too, are excellent without the trouble of beating the yolks and whites of the eggs separately. Simply take equal weight of eggs, butter, flour, and sugar, and a little lemon-peel grated very finely. If left till cold, and untouched by the sauce, they make very nice pound-cakes.

**Maccaroons.**—Blanch and beat half a pound of sweet almonds in a mortar with a spoonful of water till quite fine, gradually adding the whites of eight eggs whisked or beaten to a froth ; then mix in half a pound of loaf sugar, finely powdered. Spread sheets of white paper on your baking-tin, and over that the proper wafer-paper ; lay the paste on it in pieces about the size of a walnut, and sift fine sugar over. Bake carefully in a moderately hot oven, and, when cold, cut the wafer-paper round. If it is desired, two or three almond strips can be laid on the top of each cake as they begin to bake.

**Light Tea-Buns.**—Take half a teaspoonful of tartaric acid, and the same quantity of bicarbonate of soda, and rub them well into a pound of flour, through a hair sieve, if leisure permit. Then work into the flour two ounces of butter, and add two ounces of crushed and sifted lump sugar, also a quarter of a pound of currants or raisins, and (if liked) a few carraway-seeds. Having mixed these ingredients well together, make a hole in the middle and pour in half a pint of cold new milk ; one egg, well beaten, mixed with the milk, is a great improvement, though the buns will do without any. Mix quickly, and set your dough with a fork on baking tins. The buns will take about twenty minutes to bake. The ingredients enumerated ought to produce a dozen buns.

**Veal Cake.**—This is a pretty tasty dish for supper or breakfast, and uses up any cold veal that you may not care to mince. Take away the brown outside of the cold roast veal, and cut the white meat into thin slices ; have also a few thin slices of cold ham, and two hard-boiled eggs, which also slice, and two dessert spoonfuls of finely-chopped parsley. Take an earthenware mould, and lay veal, ham, eggs, and parsley in alternate layers, with a little pepper between each, and a sprinkling of lemon on the veal. When the mould seems full, fill up with strong stock, and bake for half an hour. Turn it out when cold. If a proper shape be now at hand, the veal-cake looks very pretty made in a plain pie-dish. When it is turned out garnish with a few sprigs of fresh parsley.

**Fig Pudding.**—Procure one pound of good figs, and chop them very fine, and also a quarter of a pound of suet, likewise chopped as fine as possible ; dust them both with a little flour as you proceed—it helps to bind the pudding together ; then take one pound of fine bread crumbs, and three ounces of sugar ; beat two eggs in a teacupful of milk, and mix all well together. Boil four hours. If there is no objection, serve it with wine or brandy sauce, and ornament your pudding with blanched almonds. Simply cooked, however, it is better for children, with whom it is a great favourite. Flavour the pudding with a little allspice or nutmeg ; but the spice should be added before the milk and eggs.

**Common Cement.**—Mix together half a pint of vinegar and half a pint of milk. When they have formed a curd, take the whey only, and mix it with the whites of five eggs, beating the whole very hard. Then sift in gradually sufficient quicklime to convert the whole into a thick paste. This will be found useful for broken bowls, jugs, &c. Rub both the broken edges, and then cover the crack with it, allowing it a fortnight to dry. Another good cement may be made by mixing together equal quantities of melted glue, white of egg, and white lead, and boiling them.

**Woollen Clothing**—It is not generally understood how clothing keeps the body cool in hot weather, and warm in cold weather. Clothes are, generally, composed of some light substance, which does not conduct heat ; but woollen substances are worse conductors than those which are made of cotton and linen. Thus, a flannel shirt more effectually intercepts or keeps out heat than a linen or cotton one ; and whether in warm or cold climates, attains the end of clothing more effectually. The exchange of woollen for cotton undershirts in hot weather, is therefore an error. This is further proved by ice being preserved from melting when it is wrapped in blankets, which retard, for a long time, the approach of heat to it. These considerations show the error of supposing there is a positive warmth in the materials of clothing. The thick cloak which guards the Spaniard against the cold of winter, is also in summer used by him as a protection against the direct rays of the sun ; and while in England flannel is our warmest article of dress, yet we cannot more effectually preserve ice, than by wrapping the vessel containing it in many folds of the softest flannel. Black cloths are known to be very warm in the sun ; but they are far from being so in the shade, especially in cold weather, when the temperature of the air is below that of the surface of the skin. We may thus gather the importance of attention to children's clothing. It is an absurd idea that, to render young limbs hardy, the body should be exposed to the undue influence of our capricious climate.

**To Wash Cotton Bed-Furniture and Printed Calicoes.**—1. Get rid of as much dirt as possible by brushing and shaking.

2. Do not let the dirty things lie about in a damp wash-house, or in any way become damp before they are fairly wetted.

3. On no account use a particle of soda, pearlash, or anything of the kind.

4. Allow plenty of water and plenty of room in the tub.

5. Use soft water, no hotter than would be pleasant for washing the hands.

6. Rub with soap in the ordinary way. Mottled soap is preferable to yellow. If a general wash is about, the water in which flannels a second time have been washed does very well for the first washing of coloured things ; or that in which muslins have been washed a second time, provided that no soda or anything of the kind has been used.

7. When the first washing is completed, have ready another tub with water of the same degree of warmth, into which put each piece, immediately on wringing it out of the first water.

8. Repeat the process of washing in the second liquor, carefully observing that every part is clean.

9. On wringing out of the second water, immediately plunge each piece into cold *spring* water for rinsing.

10. On wringing each piece out of the rinsing water, immediately hang it out, and let it dry as quickly as possible.

11. In hanging up, put any thick double parts next the line, letting the thinner part hang down and blow about. When these are dry, the positions may be changed, and the thick parts hung downwards.

12. If, through unfavourable weather, or any other circumstance, the drying cannot proceed at once, the things had better remain all night in the rinsing water, than be laid about

damp. If they are half dry out of doors, when taken in for the night, let them be hung or spread in a room, and again hung out early next day. If there is no chance of favourable drying abroad, they should be quickly dried before a fire, or round a stove.

13. If starching is required, a sufficient quantity of made starch may be stirred into the rinsing water.

**Everton Toffey.**—Take one pound and a half of brown sugar, three ounces of butter, a teacupful and a half of water, and one lemon. Boil the sugar, butter, water, and half the rind of the lemon together, and when sufficiently done—which will be known by dropping into cold water, when it should be quite crisp—let it stand aside until the boiling has ceased, and then stir in the juice of the lemon. Butter a dish, and pour it in, about a quarter of an inch in thickness. The fire must be quick, and the toffey stirred all the time.

**Bed Clothing.**—Bed-clothes, says Dr. Johnstone, should be just sufficient to enable the patient to sleep. It is better to wake with a sensation which induces an inclination to draw the bed-clothes more closely around the shoulders, than with an oppressive sense of heat, which induces a disposition to throw the clothes back. We should sleep as we should eat, because it is necessary, and not for the sake of the luxurious animal gratification which it yields. The short morning doze, into which one often suffers oneself to fall, after the full complement of the night's sleep is over, merely because it is not time to rise when one wakes, perhaps about five or six o'clock, is injurious.

**Over Eating.**—This is not a common practice with the ladies, and we have but little need to point out to them the numerous evils that flow from the error of eating too much at a meal. Yet there are some ladies to be found amongst those who complain of never being well, who might trace the source of their frequent indisposition to the attractive pleasures of the table.

It is affirmed that thousands eat themselves into fever, throat affections, and other maladies.

"But I never eat more than I want," is the common reply to a remonstrance against the dangers of excessive eating. Every person wants the quantity he is in the habit of eating. If he would digest well two pounds a day, but eats four pounds, he wants the latter quantity. The body, however, is strengthened by what it can digest and assimilate. The large eater is always hungry.

"During many years' practice of my profession," a medical gentleman told us, "I had but little muscular exercise. I ate enormously. An hour's postponement of my dinner was painful. Now I labour very hard several hours a day in my gymnasium. I do not eat more than a third the quantity of former years. Now I can omit a dinner altogether without inconvenience. I have lost twenty pounds in weight, but feel a great deal younger. More than half of the thin people would gain flesh by eating less. I have only one dietetic rule from which I never depart; this rule, kind reader, I commend to you. Always take on your plate, before you begin, everything you are to eat. Thus you avoid the dessert, and are pretty sure not to eat too much.

**How to be Miserable.**—Be constantly afraid lest some one should encroach upon your rights; be watchful against it, and if any one comes near your things snap at him. Contend earnestly for everything that is your own, though it may not be worth a pin; for your "rights" are as much concerned as if it were a pound of gold. Never yield a point.

Be very sensitive, and take everything that is said to you in playfulness in the most serious manner. Be jealous of your friends, lest they should not think enough of you. And if at any time they should seem to neglect you, put the worst construction upon it you can, and conclude that they wish to avoid your acquaintance; and so the next time you meet them, put on a sour look and show a proper resentment. You will soon get rid of them, and cease to be troubled with friends. You will have the pleasure of being shut up in yourself.

Be very touchy and irritable. Cultivate a sour, cross, snappish disposition. Never speak in good-nature if you can help it. Never be satisfied with anything, but always be fretting. Never look at, or admire, anything that is beautiful or good ; but fix your eye on the dark side of everything ; complain of defects in the best of things, and be always on the look-out for whatever is deformed or ugly, or offensive in any way, and turn up your nose at it. If you will do half of these things you will become miserable enough.

**Thunderstorms.**—The safest situation during a thunder-storm is the cellar ; for when a person is below the surface of the earth, the lightning must strike it before it can reach him, and will, of course, in all probability, be expended on it. Dr. Franklin advises all persons apprehensive of lightning to sit in the middle of a room, not under a metal lustre, or any other conductor, and to lay their feet upon another chair. It will be safer still, he adds, to lay two or three beds or mattresses in the middle of the room, and folding them double, to place the chairs upon them. A hammock suspended with silk cord would be an improvement upon this apparatus. Persons in fields should prefer the open part to the vicinity of trees. The distance of a thunder-storm, and consequently the danger, is not difficult to be estimated. As light travels at the rate of 192,000 miles in a second of time, its effects may be considered as instantaneous within any moderate distance. Sound, on the contrary, is transmitted only at the rate of 1,142 feet, or about 380 yards, in a second. By accurately observing, therefore, the time that intervenes between the flash and the noise of the thunder which follows it, a very near calculation may be made of its distance, and there is no better means of removing apprehensions.

**Bran Tea.**—A very cheap and useful drink in colds, fevers, and restless-ness from pain. Put a handful of bran in a pint and a half of cold water, let it boil rather more than half an hour, then strain it, and flavour with sugar and lemon-juice ; but it is a pleasant drink without any addition.

**Rice Glue.**—Mix some rice flour intimately with cold water, and gently simmer over a fire, when it forms a delicate and durable cement, answering all the purposes of common paste, and admirably adapted for joining paper, card, &c., in forming the various ornaments which afford amusement and employment to the ladies. When made of the consistence of plaster or clay, models and busts may be formed ; and the articles, when dry, are susceptible of high polish, and are very durable.

**Water Cress.**—The salutary and grateful qualities of this vegetable are too well known to need description ; but at certain periods of the year, when perhaps the cress is in its best state for the table, it is common for the under part of the leaves to have a white gummy substance adhering to them, which cannot be removed by washing ; and small snails are also fixed on them. It may be useful to many to learn, that if the cresses are put into strong brine, made with salt and water, and suffered to remain there ten minutes, everything of the animal and insect kind will be detached from the leaves, and the cresses can afterwards be washed in clean water and sent to the table. Small salads, cabbages, cauliflowers, brocoli, celery, lettuces, and vegetables of all descriptions, by the same simple method, may be freed from slugs, worms, or insects. If a jar of brine is kept for the purpose, and strained after being used, it will last many weeks.

**To Convert Hard Water into Soft.**—If any are troubled to get soft water for washing, fill a tub or barrel half full of wood ashes, and fill it up with water, so that you may have ley whenever you want it. A gallon of strong ley, put into a kettle of hard water, will make it as soft as rain-water. Some housekeepers use pearlash or potash ; but this costs something, and is very apt to injure the texture of the cloth.

**To Clean Paint that is not Varnished.**—Put upon a plate some of the best whiting ; have ready some clean warm water, and a piece of flannel, which dip into the water and squeeze nearly dry ; then take as much whiting as will adhere to it, apply it to the paint, when a little rubbing will instantly remove any dirt or grease ; wash well off with water, and rub dry with a soft cloth. Paint thus cleaned looks equal to new ; and without doing the least injury to the most delicate colour, it will preserve the paint much longer than if cleaned with soap ; and it does not require more than half the time usually occupied in cleaning.

**Care of the Eyes.**—Most people may preserve good sight through their lives by taking care of it ; and yet it is so often forfeited by neglect. Among the rules for keeping the eyes sound and healthy the following are some of the most important :—

Avoid glaring lights ; avoid abrupt, violent transitions from light to darkness, and from heat to cold, and *vice versa* ; keep the eyes clean ; wash them with lukewarm water. If you suffer from irritation of the eyes, moisten your finger with your fasting saliva, and apply it gently to your eyes. There is great virtue in this. But do not rub or press your eyes at all roughly unless you wish to injure them.

Never allow dust or hairs to remain in your eyes ; but if they get in, fill the eyes with lukewarm water, so as to set the encumbrance afloat, and gently draw your fingers across the eyes in the direction of the nose, until the offending substances slip out at the corners.

Do not put poultices over your eyes, lest in attempting thus to draw out the inflammatory diseases, you draw out eyes and all.

In order to preserve your eyesight, preserve your general health by air, exercise, and temperance in all things. Accustom your eyes to moderate and varied exercise, but never strain them by too long persevering over a work they are weary of.

Weak eyes are more benefited by a green shade, or blue or green spectacles, or railway goggles (made of wire gauze), than by thick bandages.

Avoid reading small print after dinner, and do not read much by any artificial light, nor sew black clothes.

Avoid exposing your eyes to a draught of air, and do not roast them by sitting too much before a bright fire. If your usual position exposes one eye more than another to a glare of light, protect the exposed eye with a green shade.

Use double eyeglasses when you require them, rather than single ones, or even spectacles, and take care that their focus entirely suits your own. Choose apartments that are evenly and well lighted. Accustom your eyes to the natural influence of the atmosphere and solar light ; those who live in close and dark rooms will produce a morbid weakness of the optic nerves.

Beware of strong, reflected lights, especially those from white walls, chalk rocks, &c. ; for white hardly absorbs any ray whatever, whereas the other colours absorb many. Accustom your eyes to view varied objects at near and remote distances, as by this means you will preserve their free play and flexibility ; whereas, if you direct your sight too exclusively to near objects you will become near-sighted.

Let the coloured papers of your rooms be rather mild and soft than brilliant or garish. View objects in oblique lights so as to avoid their direct reflections, which often dazzle the eyes.

The best colour for spectacles is pale blue.

Do not let a glaring light fall on the paper while you read or write.

**Ennui.**—This is a French word, signifying listless fatigue of the mind, resulting chiefly from want of employment of the mental powers. Those affected by *ennui* are generally the idle and thoughtless ; and no better cure for the disease, for such in most cases it really is, can be recommended than active useful employment. We say to persons who are thus afflicted—Why stand ye thus idle when there is so much work to be done ? Why waste the precious time which God has given for your own benefit, and that of your fellow-creatures ? Do something that shall be beneficial to yourself, if not to others ; although the latter ought to be a great aim and object of your existence. Industry like virtue is its own reward ; it conduces to health both of mind and body, but idleness consumes both, as rust doth metal, and one of the most obvious signs of this wasting of the mental powers is *ennui*.

**Rheumatism.**—For this too common disease the application of e'ectricity in the form of galvanism experience has taught us to be the best remedy. Galvanism, so named from its discoverer, Galvani, is usually elicited by the mutual action of various metals and chemical agents upon each other, copper and zinc and sulphuric acid being those most commonly employed.

The principal effects of *Electro-Galvanism*, as applied to disease, appears to be that of a powerful stimulant to the nervous and muscular systems ; but, besides this action, it appears to have the power of allaying pain and irritability in the part to which it is applied.

In Rheumatism, and similar chronic disoaders, galvanism has been proved to be exceedingly efficacious. Among the recent inventions for the application of electricity to the cure of rheumatism and numerous other " ills that flesh is heir to," is the " Electro-Samaritan," a very ingenious appliance which may be worn with comfort, the galvanic plates being enclosed and isolated, so as to prevent irritation of the skin, and also to intensify the power of the current, which is communicated to the body by two open plates or poles—the chain itself being enclosed in gutta percha, and enveloped in cloth or silk. The sensation imparted by the " Electro-Samaritan " is simply one of a comforting stimulus—no shocks, nor other un-

pleasant effects. The prices range from 7s. 6d. to 21s. The central depot is at 113, Strand, London.

**Game.**—Legally the term only includes hares, pheasants, partridges, and the several kinds of grouse and bustards. The snipe, quail, landraii, woodcock and coney, are not game, strictly speaking, although they may not be shot by unlicensed persons. But it is with game as an article of diet that we have here to do, and generally (we quote from " The Family Doctor,") it may be recommended as safe and wholesome, as it contains a smaller proportion of oily and fatty matter than most flesh. It is too commonly, however, eaten in such a state of semi-putrefaction as to render it extremely objectionable ; it may be known to be too " high " for safe eating when air bubbles are observed near the bones, and the meat, on being cut, gives out what can hardly be called a crackling sound, but a sensation, to the carver. This is owing to the evolution of carbonic acid gas, and in this state game sometimes acts as an irritant poison. The best remedy is to give a full dose of castor oil, with about 20 drops of laudanum, as the irritant matter will have passed beyond the stomach before the symptoms show its deleterious nature, and therefore emetics or the stomach pump would be useless. If there are colicky pains after this, give calomel and opium, 1 grain of each, about every quarter of an hour.

To PRESERVE GAME, the best way is to enclose a piece of charcoal in the body, out of which the viscera have been removed, close the skin by sewing, and tie a piece of skin tightly round the neck to exclude the air

**Bee Stings.**—In most cases any one stung by a bee can instantaneously obtain relief by pressing on the point stung with the tube of a key. This will extract the sting and relieve the pain, and the application of aqua ammonia (common spirits of hartshorn) will immediately remove it. The poison being of an acid nature, is at once neutralised by the application of this penetrating and volatile alkali. A small quantity introduced into the wound on the point of a needle or fine-nibbed pen, and applied as soon as possible, will scarcely ever fail.

**Essence of Ginger.**—Take two and a half ounces of unbleached ginger, crush it, but not to powder ; then add one pint of the best brandy, or rum, place them together in a bottle, and shake them now and then for a fortnight ; then strain, and it is ready for use. A few drops of this essence of ginger, taken on a lump of sugar, is an excellent thing for flatulency. A good deal of the essence of ginger of commerce contains Cayenne pepper, and is made of spirits of wine instead of the cordial spirits.

**Salads.**—Salads are composed chiefly of lettuce, endive, radishes, green mustard, land and water-cresses, celery, and young onions. All or any of them should be washed and placed ornamentally in a salad bowl ; the lettuce is generally cut in pieces lengthwise, and stuck round the dish ; the celery, also divided, is placed in the centre ; and the small salads, such as cresses and radishes, are placed between. This is the mode of serving a salad *plain*. When a *dressed* salad is to be served, the whole is cut in small pieces, and mixed in the bowl with a dressing. The dressing is made in the following manner :—For a moderate quantity of salad, boil one egg quite hard ; when cold, take out the yolk and bruise it with the back of a spoon on a plate ; then pour on it about a teaspoonful of cold water, and a teaspoonful of salt. Rub all this together till the egg has become quite smooth like a thick paste. Add a teaspoonful of made mustard, and continue mixing. Next add and mix a tablespoonful of salad oil, or cold melted butter. After this, add and mix a tablespoonful or more of vinegar. The dressing is now made, and may be either mixed with the salad, or put into a glass vessel called an *incorporator*, which is sent to table along with the salad. The top of the salad may be ornamented with small bits of the white of the egg, and pieces of pickled beetroot.

**Perfumed Soap.**—Take four ounces of marshmallow roots skinned, and dried in the shade ; powder them, and add one ounce each of starch and wheaten flour ; six drachms of pine-nut kernels, two ounces of blanched almonds, an ounce and a half of kernels husked, two ounces of oil of tartar, the same of cil of sweet almonds, and thirty grains of musk ; thoroughly incorporate these ingredients, and add to every ounce half an ounce of Florentine orris-root in fine powder ; then steep half a pound of fresh marshmallow roots, bruised in the distilled water of mallows (or orange flowers) for twelve hours, then squeeze out the liquor ; then, with this liquor, and the preceding powders and oils, make a stiff paste, to be dried in the shade, and formed into round balls. This soap is excellent for smoothing the skin, or rendering the hands delicately white.

**"Turncoat."**—The opprobrious appellation of " turncoat," took its rise from one of the first Dukes of Savoy, whose dominions lying open to the incursions of the two contending houses of Spain and France, he was obliged to temporise and fall in with that power that was most likely to distress him, according to the success of their arms against one another. So, being frequently obliged to change sides, he humourously got a coat made that was blue on one side, and white on the other, and might be indifferently worn either side out. While on the Spanish interest he wore the blue side out, and the white side was the badge of the French. From hence he was called the turncoat, by way of distinguishing him from other princes of the same name.

**A Saunterer.**—The words " saunter " and " saunterer " are singular records of mediæval practices and feelings. " Saunterer," derived from " la sainterre," is one who visits the Holy Land. At first a deep and earnest conviction drew thousands thither—drew them to visit—

may be instanced of change in the position of leaves, whilst in flowers there seems to be no limit to variation. The greater number shut the petals at night, the stalks declining on one side ; but there are some which roll their petals back, and curl them up like miniature volutes. When the petals are numerous, they usually form a conical pent-house, as every one must have observed in marigolds and daisies. When there are only three or four, the complicate elaborateness of their interfolding is most beautiful, and baffles all description. Such is the common scarlet poppy of the cornfields, and the less gaudy eschscholitzia of the flower-garden. The corollas of plants, like dead-nettles and snap-dragon, are not formed to open and shut ; but the protection which the internal parts of the former kind derive from their nocturnal closing has here a substitute in the form of the flower. The sleep of such plants is probably unaccompanied by any external change. The same may be said of campanulas, and other bell-shaped flowers. The four petaled flowers of cruciferæ, it should have been observed, are remarkably careless of repose. Their sleep never appears sound, or even constant for many successive nights ; they seem restless ; and in the morning always look dozy and uncomfortable. When flowers are overblown, or the plant, if an annual, is near its decay, the phenomena of sleep are very considerably diminished, partaking, with humanity, the characteristics of old age. In fact, they only sleep in perfection when in the full energy of youth and health.

**To Make Common Pomatum.**—Take four pounds of fresh and white mutton suet, skinned and shredded very fine, which melt in about two quarts of spring water ; and whilst hot, put the whole into a well-glazed earthen pan, small at bottom and wide at top. Let it stand until the fat is quite cold, and all the impurities fall to the bottom, which carefully scrape off. Now break the fat into small pieces, which put into a pan with two gallons of spring water, for a whole day ; stir and wash often. Next day change the water, and when poured off a second time, at the end of twenty-four hours, dry the fat by rubbing on a clean linen cloth. Now put the suet, with one pound and a half of fresh hog's lard, into a large pan, and melt the whole over a gentle fire. When properly combined, put the whole into an earthen pan, and beat it well with a wooden spatula until quite cold. Whilst beating, add six drachms of essence of lemon, and thirty drops of oil of cloves, previously mixed together. Now continue beating until the mixture be perfectly white, and afterwards put it up into small pots. Leave the pots open until the pomatum is quite cold ; when cover them by pieces of bladder, &c. In summer, use more suet, and mix in a cool place ; in winter, use more hog's lard, and make the pomatum in a warm room.

**Picture of Woman.**—" The true woman," says Charles Dickens, " for whose ambition a husband's love and her children's adoration are sufficient, who applies her military instincts to the discipline of her household, and whose legislatives exercise themselves in making laws for her nurse ; whose intellect has field enough for her in communion with her husband, and whose heart asks no other honours than his love and admiration ; a woman who does not think it a weakness to attend to her toilet, and who does not disdain to be beautiful, who believes in the virtue of glossy hair and well-fitting gowns, and who eschews rents and ravelled edges, slip-shod shoes and audacious make-ups ; a woman who speaks low, and does not speak much ; who is patient and gentle, and intellectual and industrious ; who loves more than she reasons, and yet does not love blindly ; who never scolds and never argues, but adjusts with a smile ; such a woman is the wife we have all dreamed of once in our lives, and is the mother we still worship in the backward distance of the past."

**To Restore the Colour of the**

**Teeth.**—Dissolve two ounces of borax in three pints of hot water. Before quite cold, add thereto one teaspoonful of tincture of myrrh, and one table-spoonful of spirits of camphor. Bottle and mix for use. One wine-glassful of the solution, added to half a pint of tepid water, is sufficient for each application. Only a soft brush should be applied to the teeth, as a hard one destroys the enamel.

**English Surnames.**—The Registrar-General estimates that there are nearly 40,000 different surnames in England. Among these there are 53,000 families bearing the name of Smith, and 51,000 the name of Jones. The Smiths and Joneses alone are supposed to include half a million of the population. In an average it seems that 1 person in 73 is a Smith, 1 in 76 a Jones, 1 in 112 a Williams, 1 in 148 a Taylor, 1 in 162 a Davies, and 1 in 174 a Brown. Among the list of peculiar names given, we note the following:—Allbones, Alabaster, Affection, Awkward, Baby, Bolster, By (the shortest English name), Camomile, Corpse, Cakebread, Dagger, Eighteen, Eatwell, Fowls, Fussy, Gin, Hogsflesh, Idle, Jolly, Jelly, Kiss, Lumber, Muddle, Nutbrown, Officer, Pocket, Quince, Rabbit, Sanctuary, Tombs, Unit, Vulgar, Waddle, Yellow, and Zeal.

**Pea Soup.**—Put one quart of split peas to soak overnight in soft water ; the next morning wash them out, and put them into a soup-pot with two carrots, two onions, a stalk of celery, and four quarts of water ; let this boil four or five hours ; have boiling water at hand to add, as the water boils away in pea soup more than any other kind ; strain the soup through a very coarse sieve. Have a piece of salt pork boiled in another pot one hour ; then take it out and skin it ; put the soup and the pork back into the pot, and boil it gently one hour, frequently stirring it with a large spoon. Care should be taken that it does not scorch.

**Make your Children Sing.**—All children can learn to sing if they commence in season. In Germany every child is taught to use its voice while young. In their schools all join in singing, as a regular exercise, and in their churches singing is not confined to the choir, who sit apart from the others, but there is a vast tide of incense going forth to God from every heart that can give utterance to this language from the soul. In addition to the delightful influence singing has upon the character, it has also a marked influence in suppressing pulmonary complaints. Dr. Rush used to say, that the reason why the Germans seldom die of consumption was, that they were always singing.

**Flowers.**—How the universal heart blesses flowers ! They are wreathed round the cradle, the marriage-altar, and the tomb. The Persian in the far east delights in their perfume, and writes his love in nosegays ; while the Indian child of the far west claps his hands with glee as he gathers the abundant blossoms—the illuminated scriptures of the prairies. The Cupid of the ancient Hindoos tipped his arrows with flowers, and orange flowers are a bridal crown with us, a nation of yesterday. Flowers garlanded the Grecian altar, and hung in votive wreaths before the Christian shrine. All these are appropriate uses. Flowers should deck the brow of the youthful bride, for they are in themselves a lovely type of marriage. They should twine round the tomb, for their perpetually-renewed beauty is a symbol of the resurrection. They should festoon the altar, for their fragrance and their beauty ascend in perpetual worship before the Most High.

**Toasted Cheese.**—This is much relished by some persons, but is seldom met with well prepared. The following receipt may be found useful :—Cut the cheese into slices of moderate thickness, and put them into a tinned copper saucepan, with a little butter and cream ; simmer very gently until quite dissolved, then remove it from the fire, allow it to cool a little, and add some yolk of egg, well beaten ; make it into a shape, and brown it before the fire.

**Eating Between Meals.**—Among the many slight causes of impaired digestion is to be reckoned the very general disregard to eating between meals. The powerful digestion of a growing boy makes light of all such irregularities ; but to see adults, and often those by no means in robust health, eating muffins, buttered toast, or bread-and-butter, a couple of hours after a heavy dinner, is a distressing spectacle to the physiologist. It takes at least four hours to digest a dinner ; during that period the stomach should be allowed repose. A little tea or any other liquid is beneficial rather than otherwise, but solid food is a mere encumbrance ; there is no gastric juice ready to digest it. And if any reader having at all a delicate digestion, will attend to her sensations after eating muffins or toast at tea, unless her dinner has had time to digest, she will need no sentences of explanation to convince her of the serious error prevalent in English families of making tea a light meal, quickly succeeding a substantial dinner. Regularity in the hours of eating is far from necessary ; but regularity of intervals is of primary importance. It matters little at what hour you lunch or dine, provided that you allow the proper intervals to elapse between breakfast and luncheon, and between luncheon and dinner. What are those intervals ? This is a question that each lady must settle for herself. Much depends on the amount eaten at a meal, much also on the rapidity with which digestion is carried on. Less than four hours should never be allowed after a heavy meal. But those who dine at six or seven o'clock never need food again till breakfast next day, unless they have been dancing, or exerting themselves in walking ; in which case a light supper is requisite.

**Shin of Beef Soup.**—The cheapest joint sold by butchers is a leg or a shin of beef. This costs from one to two shillings, according to the quantity of meat upon it. Saw the bone into short pieces and put in a covered jar, and fill it up with water and flour in an oven for from five to fifteen hours, according to the heat of the fire, until the flesh falls from the bone. If it is not intended to retain all the meat in the soup, it can be taken out, and made afterwards into potted beef or a pie. The bones, peas, celery, carrots, &c., and whatever else may be fancied, must now be boiled in about five quarts of water until quite soft. The peas will be better boiled separately, and generally require a longer time than the rest. When the whole is sufficiently boiled, add the liquor obtained from stewing the leg, and there will be soup enough for six or seven persons—a good dinner for each.

**How to Choose Eggs.**—In putting the hands round the egg, and presenting to the light the end which is not covered, it should be transparent. If you can detect some tiny spots, it is not newly laid, but may be very good for all ordinary purposes except boiling soft. If you see a large spot near the shell, it is bad, and should not be used on any account. The white of a newly-laid egg boiled soft is like milk ; that of an egg a day old, is like rice boiled in milk ; and that of an old egg, compact, tough, and difficult to digest. A cook ought not to give eggs two or three days old to people who really care for fresh eggs, under the delusion that they will not find any difference ; for an amateur will find it out in a moment, not only by the appearance, but also by the taste.

**Beef Steaks.**—The cooking of steaks everybody imagines they can do to perfection ; but the reverse of this is the case, so common a dish as it is. The following is the method that we recommend :—Steaks should never be covered after they are laid upon a dish ; a cover smothers them, and thus they lose their best flavour. Beef-steaks should be eaten as soon as they are cooked. The best pieces for steak are the sirloin and the rump. The top part of the round, near to the aitchbone, is very juicy, and by pounding it with a mallet, may be made as tender as the rump. The steaks should be cut nearly an inch in thickness. It is not necessary to grease the gridiron before putting on the steak; indeed, the flavour of the meat is much impaired by so doing. Prepare a brisk fire of coals, put your gridiron over it, but do not let the gridiron get hot before you put on the steak. As soon as the sinews become crisped a little, turn the steak. Do not spill the gravy upon the fire. Take up the steak on a hot dish, then turn the steak and replace it upon the gridiron. It will require ten minutes to scald it through and brown the outside. As soon as the steak is cooked, put it upon a dish and serve.

Ironing.—Shirt-fronts are most conveniently ironed upon a deal board about 12 inches long and 8 wide, covered with fine flannel; to be placed between the back and front of the shirt after the back is ironed. The skirts of dresses also may be ironed in a similar manner, using a board as long as the skirt, 26 inches long at one end, and 12 inches at the other. The board should be covered with a blanket, and rest upon a thin block of wood at each end, to keep it from creasing the skirt beneath it.

Coffee as a Disinfectant.—Numerous experiments with roasted coffee prove that it is the most powerful means, not only of rendering animal and vegetable effluvia innocuous, but of actually destroying them. A room in which meat in an advanced degree of decomposition had been kept for some time, was instantly deprived of all smell on an open coffee-roaster being carried through it, containing a pound of coffee newly roasted. In another room, exposed to the effluvium occasioned by the clearing out of a pit in which sulphuretted hydrogen and ammonia could be detected, the stench was removed within half a minute, on the employment of three ounces of fresh-roasted coffee, whilst the other parts of the house were permanently cleared of the same smell by being simply traversed with the coffee-roaster, although the cleansing of the obnoxious pit continued for some hours afterwards. The best mode of using the coffee as a disinfectant is to dry the raw bean, pound it in a mortar, and then roast the powder on a moderately-heated iron plate, until it assumes a dark brown tint, when it is fit for use. Then sprinkle it in sinks or cesspools, or lay it on a plate in the room which you wish to have purified. Coffee acid, or coffee oil, acts more readily in minute quantities.

Godfrey's Cordial.—This nostrum, once so celebrated, and still used by nurses to pacify infants when showing evidence of pain, is compounded of the following ingredients: one ounce each of seeds of coriander, anise, and carraway, and nine ounces of sassafras, simmered in six ounces of water, until reduced to one quart. Then add six pounds of brown sugar or treacle, and boil the whole for ten minutes. When cold, add three ounces of laudanum. [We give the receipt, but we cannot recommend its use.]

To Pack Glass or China.—Procure some soft straw or hay to pack them in; and if they are to be sent a long way, and are heavy, the hay or straw should be a little damp, which will prevent the things slipping about. Let the largest and heaviest articles be always put undermost in the box or hamper. Let there be plenty of straw, and pack the articles tight; but never attempt to pack up glass or china which is of much consequence, till it has been seen done by some experienced person. The expense will be but trifling to have a person to do it who understands it, and the loss may be great, if articles of much value are packed up in an improper manner.

Clandestine Courtships.—The secret engagements between the young of both sexes constitute an evil which should be specially cautioned against. Whatsoever may be read of in romances about the success and happiness of secret love, rest assured that the result of such courtships in real life is very uncertain, and too commonly dishonourable. However pure and sincere the feelings of either party may be, the concealment implies a doubt of the integrity of one of the parties. Either the man is ashamed of the woman, or the woman is ashamed of the man, or somebody interested is ashamed of one or the other of them, or they design to deceive a trusting parent or guardian ; but look at it in any way or light, the proceeding is disreputable.

It may be said that it sometimes occurs that a mutual affection is formed, which, without any reasonable cause, is opposed by the parents, and which cannot be abrogated without violence to the feelings, or it may be urged that love is not to be overcome by mere argument or persuasion. It rarely happens, however, that parents are instigated by any other motive in regulating the conduct of their children than that of an anxious desire for their present and future happiness ; and it must be admitted that they are more likely to be better able to judge the probable results of any act than youth and inexperience can possibly be. It may seem spirited and adventurous to sacrifice everything for what is called "love," but the admiration and enthusiasm which attaches to such an act will be brief and transient ; the realities of life will gather around, and soon prove that reflection and judgment should be exercised and advice listened to in regulating our behaviour and actions, and more especially in affairs of the heart, from the important influence which they exert over the future well-being of the parties concerned.

Besides being morally wrong and unjustifiable, however, a clandestine courtship, especially with respect to the female, is injurious to present prospects and character. The young lady compromises her reputation ; for "people will talk," scandal will originate, and society is prone to be censorious. The man, too, if not restrained by some purity of principle, is ever ready to regard the lady with suspicion. He naturally thinks, that if she deceives her parent,

she will deceive others. So, young ladies, have a care that, in attempting to deceive others, you are not yourselves deceived.

**What is your Daughter Thinking about ?**—You are very careful of her dress ; you attend personally to its purchase and fit. You go with her to see that her foot is nicely booted ; and you give your milliner special instructions as to the style of her bonnets ; but do you ever ask yourself, "What is she thinking about ?" Do you know anything at all of her inner life ? Many who are esteemed most excellent mothers are as ignorant on this all-important point as if they had never looked upon their daughters' faces. They exact respectful obedience ; and if the young creature yields it, and has no need of a physician's immediate services, they consider their duty done. Alas ! what a fatal mistake. These are the mothers who, never having invited the confidence of those young hearts, live to see it bestowed anywhere and everywhere but in accordance with their wishes. Is it, can it be, enough to a mother worthy the name, to be satisfied that her daughter's physical wants are cared for ? What of that yearning soul that is casting about, here and there, for something to satisfy its questionings ? When she sits there by the fire, or by the window, musing, sit down by her, and coax her thoughts out of her. Cast that fatal dignity to the winds which has come between so many young creatures and the heart to which they should lie nearest in these important early years. "Respect" is good in its place ; but when it freezes up your daughter's soul-utterances ; when it sends her for sympathy and companionship to chance guides, what then ? A word, a loving, kind word, at the right moment—no mind can over-estimate its importance. Remember this, when you see the sad wrecks of womanhood about you ; and amid the sweeping waves of life's cares and life's pleasures, what else soever you neglect, do not fail to know what your young daughter is thinking about.

**Cold Fish.**—By the following plan a good dish may be made from any kind of cold fish. Free the fish from all bone, and cut it into small pieces; season them with onions and parsley chopped together, and salt and pepper; mix two eggs well with a tablespoonful of ketchup. Mix the whole together with the fish, and put it in a baking-dish with two or three slices of bacon over it. Bake before the fire in a Dutch oven. Serve with melted butter or oyster sauce.

**Bad Taste.**—We violate the laws of nature when we seek to repair the ravages of time on our complexion by paint; when we substitute false hair for that which age has blanched or thinned, or conceal, by dyeing, our own gray hair; when we pad our dress to conceal that one shoulder is higher than the other. To do either is not only bad taste, but it is a positive breach of sincerity. It is bad taste, because the means we have resorted to are contrary to the law of nature. The application of paint to the skin produces an effect so different from the bloom of youth that it can only deceive an unpractised eye. It is the same with the hair; there is such a want of harmony between false hair and the face which it surrounds, especially when that face bears the marks of age, and the colour of the hair denotes youth, that the effect is unpleasant in the extreme. Deception of this kind, therefore, does not answer the end it had in view; it deceives nobody but the perpetrator of the wouldbe deceit. It is as about a senseless proceeding as that of the goose in the story, who, when pursued by the fox, thrust her head into the hedge, and thought that because she could not see the fox, the fox could not see her. But in a moral point of view, it is worse than silly. It is a false proceeding to all intents and purposes. Zimmerman has an aphorism which is applicable to the case—" Those who conceal their age do not conceal their folly."

**To Scour Boards.**—Mix together one part of lime, three parts of common sand, and two parts of soft soap; lay a little of this on the scrubbing-brush. Afterwards rinse thoroughly, and dry with a clean coarse cloth. This will keep the boards a good colour. It is also useful in keeping away vermin. For that purpose, early in the spring, bedsteads should be taken down, and furniture in general removed and examined; bed-hangings and windowcurtains if not washed should be shaken and brushed; and the joints of bedsteads, the backs of drawers, and, indeed, every part of furniture, except polished mahogany, should be carefully cleaned with the above mixture, or with equal parts of soft soap and lime without any sand. In old houses, where there are any holes in the boards, which often abound with vermin, after scrubbing in as far as the brush can reach, a thick plaster of the above should be spread over the holes and covered with paper. When these things are timely attended to, and combined with general cleanliness, vermin may generally be kept away, even in crowded cities.

**How to Cook an Egg.**—What a wretched thing is a badly-cooked egg! whether it be liquid as a lady's tear, or solid as a Somersetshire dumpling. If you want an egg well cooked, first try the plan recommended by a correspondent of the " Cottage Gardener," who remarks—" An egg should be scalded or coddled. Immerse your egg in, or, which is better, pour boiling water upon your egg. For time, proportion it to the size and number of your eggs, and the collateral accidents. If you cook the eggs upon the breakfast-table more time will be required; but if you station your apparatus on a good hob, where there is a fire, and so the radiation of heat is less positive, shorter time will suffice. The latter way is mine, winter and summer, and the differences of the surrounding circumstances equalise, or nearly so, the time. I keep an egg under water nine minutes; two, nine and a half; three, ten; and four nearly eleven minutes. The yolk first owns the power of the caloric, and will be even firmly set, while the wh it will be milky, or at most tremulously gelatinous.

**Rue.**—The common rue has a strong ungrateful odour, and a bitter, hot, penetrating taste. The leaves are so acrid as to irritate and inflame the skin if they are much handled. Rue was often used by the ancients, who ascribed to it many excellent qualities. It is still employed in some country districts as a tea ; and also externally in various kinds of fomentations. A conserve, made by beating the fresh leaves with thrice their weight of sugar, is the most commodious form for using the herb in substances. It is a powerful astringent, and adapted to phlegmatic habits, or weak and hysterical constitutions. It is a very hardy shrub, and is a native of the south of Europe. It was introduced in England about the year 1540.

**Setting Tea-things.**—Instead of the ever-recurring clatter and loss of time incidental to putting all that is wanting twice a day in most families entirely away, and getting it out again for breakfast and tea, the better plan is to set the necessary articles ready for the next meal, immediately after washing them up from the former. Of course this necessitates the consecration of the tray to cups and saucers, &c., and thus make it advisable to find or provide a shelf wide enough to hold it. But in materially hastening the operations of " bringing tea " fourteen times in every week, it would be worth some contrivance for its comfortable accomplishment in all houses. It might be a curious test of the comparative prevalence of what is by courtesy termed " common sense," to ascertain how many individuals in the different classes of mistresses and servants, in their endeavour to carry out the above method, would *naturally* wash the tray *first*, and how many would begin with the cups and saucers !

**German Paste.**—An excellent food for birds, much better than what is generally sold under this name, may be made as follows :—Take four fresh eggs

and boil very hard, a quarter of a pound of white pease meal, and about a tablespoonful of good salad oil ; if the least rancid it will not do. The eggs must be grated down very fine, and mixed with the meal and olive oil. The whole is then passed through a tin colander, to form it into grains, like small shot ; then placed in a frying-pan, set over a gentle fire, and gradually stirred with a broad knife, till it be partially wasted and dried, the test of which will be its fine yellowish brown colour.

**Shopping.**—Ladies should always bear in mind that a shop is a public resort ; that they are speaking before, and often to, strangers—and therefore a certain degree of reserve should be observed in all they do or say. Never carry on any conversation with your companions on topics that have nothing to do with your shopping, and do not speak or laugh aloud, but despatch your business in a polite and quiet manner, equally removed from haughtiness and familiarity. Sometimes, in pressing you to buy their goods, young shopkeepers will become too talkative and familiar. Silence and seriousness are the best checks to this ; and it should always be met with calm self-possession. If you have good manners you will very rarely meet with impertinence or rudeness. When ladies complain of being frequently annoyed in any such way, it is a sure sign that their own deportment is faulty. Self-possession and self-reliance are the result of a well-disciplined mind and cultivated manners, and a person possessed of them will always be equal to the occasion : their looks alone are sufficient to repress insolence.

**Cold Food for Infants.**—Our best authorities direct that the cow's milk should be given to the child at the same temperature as that of the mother's milk—90 to 95 degrees Fahrenheit— and, when great accuracy is required, a thermometer employed. On reflection, it is obvious that these instructions can never be carried out so that the little one will take all its food at the same temperature ; for during a meal the bottle becomes cold, and there may frequently be considerable difference of temperature between the first and the last milk imbibed by the infant. It is unnecessary to state that very little will upset the feeble powers of the digestive organs in the early days of infantile life ; and this difference in the temperature of the food, I am disposed to believe, is one of the causes of gastric and intestinal disorder which we so often have to deal with among infants brought up by hand. Instead of giving warm milk, I have adopted the plan of giving cold milk entirely—ordering the babe's bottle to be kept standing in iced water in the summer, and in a cold place in winter. This method I have found, from practical experience, to answer remarkably well. If there is any tendency to diarrhœa, I recommend the milk to be heated to 212 deg. Fahr., and afterwards allowed to get quite cold before being used. In private practice, I am of opinion that bottle-fed infants generally have their food given them too warm. They soon like it even better than warm food, and during the teething period cold milk seems especially agreeable to the inflamed gums of the little sufferers.

The above plan for the preparation of food for infants is certainly worthy of trial. We all know the difficulty of having artificial food properly prepared, notwithstanding minute directions are given concerning it and the importance of keeping the nurse-bottle scrupulously clean. Many devices are resorted to by those who have the care of infants to avoid the trouble of freshly preparing the food every time it is wanted, and the temptation is great, particularly at night, to have in readiness a quantity sufficient for several meals. As a consequence come the various disturbances to the system resulting from the ingestion of food which is often sour before it is taken. If it can be given cold without detriment to the child, there seems to be no good reason why the diet should not always be fresh.

**To Pack Fruit.**—Nothing requires so much care as to pack fruit for presents, &c. It is generally done in baskets ; but this should not be, as they are often placed among heavy articles, and the fruit, of course, will become bruised and spoiled. Strong deal boxes have been recommended in lieu of the baskets ; the size of the box, of course, to vary with the quantity of fruit to be arranged for. Follow this plan in packing :—Put a layer of dry moss at the bottom of the box, then some fruit, then another layer of moss, and so on, alternately moss and fruit until the box is so full that the fruit cannot be exposed to friction.

Then make a layer of moss and dry grass, mix well, and place in the bottom of the box ; pack in melons tight between all the rows, and also between the melons in the same row, till the layer is finished ; let the fruit be nearly of a size as possible, and fill up any interstices that may happen with grass and moss.

When the melons are provided for, put a layer of moss and grass over them, upon which place the tin box with the currants, packing it well all round with grass to prevent friction, then place a layer of moss over the box, and pack the pears firmly on that layer, similar to the melons, and the same way with the plums, nectarines, and peaches, and last of all, the grapes, filling up the said box with moss and grass, that the lid may shut down so tight as to prevent any friction among the fruit.

Locks and two keys should be provided to each box, so that the persons who pack and unpack should have a key. In returning the box the moss and grass should always be sent back, which, with a little addition, will serve the whole season, being well aired and shaken up after each journey. The box should be corded firmly, as well as locked. Fruit thus packed may be safely sent to any distance, when it would arrive fresh and sound.

**Head-Dresses.**—For in-door wear we could wish more head-dresses were in vogue. Hair unornamented, when plentiful, and when prettily arranged, is always beautiful, of course ; but there are so many cases where, from the hair not being of a very fine colour, or the complexion being pale or imperfect, some decoration of the head would be a vast improvement. The simple ribbon or snood that many young girls wear, simply passed around the hair and tied, is an extremely good and pretty fashion, and, when the colour is well chosen, often makes a bad coarse brown appear richer, and the face clearer. The net, in vogue some years ago, may be a very beautiful ornament. A gold net, or one netted in colours and beads, especially light blue, is very pretty and appropriate, but the hair requires to be tastefully arranged beneath it. The slovenly habit of just brushing the hair into a tail, and then passing a net over it, so that the net hangs down long and only half-filled, will never do : no hair is sufficiently abundant to fill out a net well without some care in arrangement : at the same time hard and ill-disguised padding is equally out of place. The hair usually requires to be waved, and then gathered up broadly and shortly —the meshes of the net being sufficiently wide to show the colour of the hair within it.

It is a pity that caps are so entirely forgotten by young people.

Caps seem to be considered only fit for servants and great-grandmothers. Even middle-aged ladies fancy that, by assuming a cap, they are renouncing youth ; whereas, by continuing to expose the bald patch on their heads, and the increasing thinness of their locks, they imagine they still retain it. This is a terrible mistake. The bad taste which does not scrupulously conceal such a misfortune as a bald patch cannot be too severely condemned ; at the same time there is no reason why anything so becoming, so coquettish, and so cleanly as some sort of cap, should not be adopted by the young. Fifty years ago, or even thirty, girls were never seen without a cap in the morning, and very

pretty they looked, with the transparent halo around their rosy faces, and a blue ribbon to crown it.

The modern mania for showing off the whole of the hair in season and out of season, in the street and in the house, is of quite recent date, and has many demerits ; and as the greater part of our mighty plaits are false, they are not such a "glory" after all. For full dress, hair-powder is one of the most surprisingly becoming fashions ever invented by a crafty woman to beautify herself, and only uncleanly when the powder is of a kind that clots, and is seldom or never brushed out. The powder used in the last century with such disagreeable results, was a kind of meal, very unfit for our purpose ; modern hair-powders are quite different. Powder is a most appropriate and beautiful ornament. The "bends" of silk, metal, &c., worn in the middle ages across the head, in imitation of the circlets of gold termed *bindæ*, among the Normans, are very pretty, and have been adopted among some of the ladies who admire a pre-Raphaelite style of dress. But, beyond all head-dresses, real flowers are the most perfect and the least appreciated. Their price (in towns) and their fragility are a hindrance to many who love them ; but why, when they are both loved, and within one's means, are they only used at little quiet parties ; while for a formal party, or a large ball, they are condemned in favour of a hideous stiff wreath of artificial ones, gummed and wired into the most unnatural directions ? It has often made us angry to hear it said, "Oh yes, a camellia or a rose in the hair is very pretty to wear at home, but it would not be proper for a good party !" People who say this are unworthy ever to see or to touch real flowers.

**Almond Icing for Bride Cakes.**— The whites of six eggs, a pound and a half of double refined sugar, and one pound of Jordan almonds blanched and pounded with a little rose water, mix together, and whisk it for an hour, lay it over the cake, and put it in the oven.

THE POMEGRANATE.

**Modelling and Making Paper Flowers.**—This art is so elegant, clean, and delicate, that the most refined lady need not scruple to practise it ; it requires only to examine Flora's gifts with exactness, and delicacy in handling the materials, to bring it to perfection.

The following instructions will be found sufficient for the modelling a Pomegranate and Burige's Rose Campion.

THE POMEGRANATE.—This is a beautiful flower to model, and is of a brilliant scarlet, of a peculiar tint, and will amply repay the pupil for the care bestowed in making it. There is another beautiful and delicate variety of this flower, which is white, much more crimped at the edges, and most richly marked with scarlet ; it is rather scarce in this country, but an elegant flower for a vase. This flower requires but two patterns for the petals, and about 35 to 40 form a flower—20 of No 1, and 16 of No. 2. Place the petals No. 1 on a piece of crape, fold them in two, and crimp between the fingers and thumb the upper part of

THE CAMPION ROSE.

the petals. Fold them together lengthways, and bring the upper edges forward. Proceed in the same way with petals No. 2. Then take a piece of middling-sized wire, bend the end a little, and roll round it some paper to the shape and size of a plum-stone, and cover with some scarlet paper; after which, fix the petals No. 1 with some cement and silk in rows of threes and fives together. Then proceed with petals No. 2 in like manner; after which draw on the calyx (which may be purchased ready prepared) of nearly a similar colour to the flower. Finish by preparing the thickest wire by covering it with reddish brown paper for the stem, in imitation of bark (or woody stalks); then cut the stalk of your flower about an inch long, just sufficient to attach it to the stem. This flower grows in trusses of three and four together, with two or three buds above them (which may also be obtained ready prepared), and which will give great effect to its appearance.

BURIGE'S ROSE CAMPION.—This species of flower is a beautiful scarlet, and easy to model. It is a native of Asiatic Russia, an herbaceous perennial, very pretty and ornamental, and displays its rich scarlet flowers in the month of July. This flower is peculiarly graceful on account of its lanceolate leaves: hence it has been selected as a good flower for grouping. This flower requires but one pattern for the petals, namely, to show the size, and has five in number. You must avoid cutting every petal alike, but vary them more or less (as seen in the whole flower in the engraving). After having cut the petals in bright scarlet paper, form fine veins on them, as seen in diagram, with a tint mixed of carmine and indigo, and placed on with a fine sable brush. Con-

G

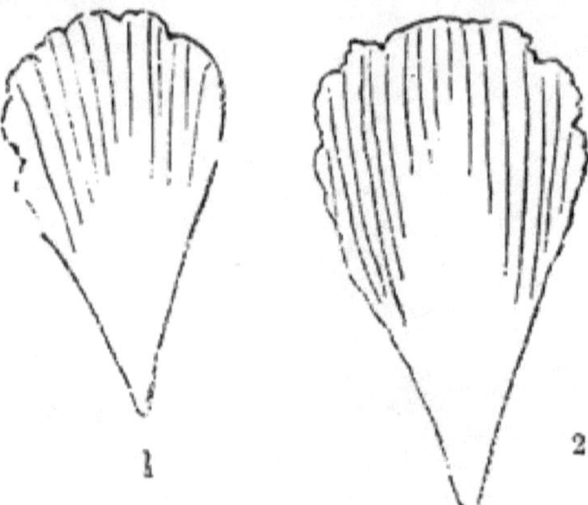



struction : Take a piece of white paper about an inch square, and roll round the end of a smooth penholder so as to form a tube, taking care to cement the edge ; then take the petals one by one, touching the base with a little cement, prepared, and screw the base round the wire and tie with some silk ; then cut five small green leaves, as seen in diagram, for the calyx, which cement round ; roll some green paper round the stalk, and the flower is finished.

and fix them carefully and regularly round the tube ; then take the stamens, the knots at the ends of which must be blue : fix them at the end of a middling-sized wire about five inches long, and pass it through the tube just Books with fuller instructions than our space admits of our giving, as well as the few and inexpensive tools and materials necessary for the due performance of this art, may be obtained from Barnard and Son, 339, Oxford Street.

**Culture of Hollyhocks.**—The hollyhock is not so generally grown as its decorative qualities entitle it to be, says a correspondent in the *Gardener*. When grown amongst shrubs in situations moderately sheltered, few plants produce a finer floral display during the autumn months. The great drawback to its cultivation is the liability of the plants to get broken with the winds ; but if secured when 18 inches high to suitable stakes, this objection is at once got over. At planting time give each plant a few spadefuls of rotten manure, and if possible a little fresh soil ; press the earth firmly round the plants ; and if the ground is dry, give a good watering. In due time, stake each plant, and as the stems advance in growth, secure them thereto with strong ties of matting. If the above simple hints are attended to, the result in most instances will be satisfactory.

When Holyhocks are grown for exhibition, they must have a plot of ground devoted to themselves ; let the situation be as sheltered as possible, but never near to anything that would in the least obstruct the noonday sun or a free circulation of air. To produce spikes such as are seen at some of our horticultural shows requires a rich soil. To secure this, let the ground be trenched in autumn, adding, as the work proceeds, a liberal supply of good manure. When the trenching is complete, give the surface a dressing two or three inches thick of the best manure procurable ; the winter rains will wash the best parts of it into the soil, and when planting-time comes, a slight forking is all that is required to make the bed in readiness to receive the plants. The plants should not be put out until all danger from severe frost is passed, say the end of March or the beginning of April. Let the plants stand three feet apart in the lines, and five feet from line to line."

When finished planting, if the ground is moderately dry (which it should be, as it is a bad plan to plant when the soil is over-wet), make the surface rather firm by giving the whole a gentle treading with the feet. Place at once over each plant some spruce or other evergreen branches, as a protection against frost and cutting winds ; as, if they get frozen to any extent, the spikes are never so fine. As soon as all danger from frost is past, remove the protection, examine each plant, and see that all are firm in the soil.

Let only one stem rise from a plant, and nip all laterals as they appear.

Never allow the plants to suffer for want of water ; and as soon as flower-buds are formed, mulch the beds with rotten manure. I prefer this to giving manure water, as the latter, unless applied with judgment, has a tendency to make the plants grow by fits and starts, thereby causing irregularity in the build of the spikes, a fault which neither length of spike nor size of blooms will compensate for. In most instances, two flower-buds will start from the axil of each leaf ; nip out the smaller of the two ; and in any case of crowding thin to the requisite number. During the three weeks preceding the show, the spikes must be protected from rain and strong sun. This, in the case of the hollyhock, is not so readily accomplished, but it is necessary to the production of clean spikes ; and the cultivator must not neglect, as by doing so he will destroy his chance of attaining the end in view.

**Culture of the Chinese Primrose.**—The large purple and white-fringed varieties of last season being a great improvement both in size and colour, will now more generally commend this favourite flower to the notice of the public. About the middle of March the seeds are sown in a pan of light rich soil, in gentle heat, in a cucumber frame, or in any other warm place, and when plants have obtained their rough leaf, to be removed to the greenhouse, and placed on a shelf or trellis as near the glass as possible, to give them strength and dwarfness. When fit, they are potted off singly into small 60-sized pots. About the end of May they are shifted into large 60-sized pots. using compost of equal portions of turfy leaf-mould, peat, and silver-sand well mixed together in a rough state ; the drainage must be carefully looked to, or most probably, if not well drained, many of the plants will damp off and others grow weakly. They are to be placed again in the greenhouse near the glass, and to have plenty of air and room. About the beginning of July, when the plants will have filled their pots with roots, they are shifted into 48-sized pots, in the same sort of compost as before, with the addition of a little decomposed cow-dung, and if any blooms appear, they are pinched off.

About the middle of August they are shifted in 32-sized pots, in a compost of two-thirds charred turf, one-third rotten cow-dung and silver-sand. When large specimens are required, they are shifted into 24-sized pots, the soil to be made quite firm around the roots, and then to be removed to a shady situation in the open ground until, if the weather is favourable, the first or second week in October, when the best-fringed and coloured flowers are chosen, and removed to shelter under glass, where air can be freely admitted to them in fine weather. By such treatment they will bloom freely from November to May.

**Ventilation** is required in all apartments, but especially in those we sleep in. Various methods have been used for this purpose, the most useful of which is that of Dr. Arnott, which consists in making an aperture opening into the chimney, as near to the ceiling as possible.

The chief points requiring attention in ventilating rooms or houses consist : 1. Of having an inlet for fresh air, and an outlet for vitiated air. 2. The air admitted should be as pure as possible, free from local vitiations, such as drains, smoke, &c. 3. When air is admitted into an apartment it should be at the lowest part, and the aggregate area of admission should be twice as great as that of the outlet.

Where gas or oil is consumed for lighting a room a large amount of carbonic acid and water is generated, and this takes place in every room where we have even candles. Now, the reason is this : the hydrogen of the gas, or oil, or tallow unites with the oxygen of the air, taking eight measures of oxygen to one of itself, to form nine measures of water, which is deposited on the windows and walls if provision is not made for its escape ; then the carbon unites with a portion of the oxygen to form carbonic acid gas.

Each room should have a fireplace, and particularly bedrooms, and when there is not one, some other means of ventilation should be contrived, such as inserting a revolving ventilator in the upper part of the room, over the door. Such a contrivance can be procured and fixed for about sixpence or ninepence, and when the upper sash of the window is let down for about an inch, the room will be rendered quite sweet and wholesome.

Whenever persons have left a room in which they have sat for some time, the window should be opened and the door set ajar ; the same plan should be pursued with bedrooms. Many persons sleep with their windows a little open, and the plan is not objectionable, except in damp weather. In high houses it is advisable to light the staircase by a skylight hung in the centre, so that it will serve for the purpose of ventilation as well.

Dr. Darwin, while addressing an audience of mechanics at Derby, some years ago said : "By your exertions you procure for yourselves and families the necessaries of life ; but if you lose your health, that power of being of use to them must cease. I fear some of you do not understand how health is to be maintained in vigour. This, then, depends upon your breathing uncontaminated air ; for the purity of the air becomes destroyed where many are collected together, effluvia from the body corrupts it. Keep open, then, the windows of your workshops, and as soon as you rise in the morning, open all the windows of your bedrooms. Inattention to this advice, be assured, will bring disease on yourselves and families. Let me again repeat my serious advice—*open your windows to let in the fresh air*, at least once in the day. Remember what I say ; I speak now without a fee, and can have no other interest but your good in this my advice."

**Palpitation of the Heart.**—This is sometimes in the heart or its great vessels, or in all—a remedy for which it is scarcely in the power of medicine to offer, although temperate living (avoiding the excitement of violent exercise or spirituous liquors) and wholesome air, may so far palliate, as to give a chance to the diseased parts, if not to recover their tone, at least to become no worse.

But the disease known by "palpitation of the heart," vulgarly called "a beating about the heart," arises far more frequently from a debilitated state of the nerves, and a vitiated state of the digestive organs. The heart is a muscle, and, like others, is itself liable to nervous tremours. This disease is a frequent attendant on females and those young men who indulge in excesses. To remove it, the patient cannot expect that physic will be competent, although it will most materially assist. All excesses must be left off, and habits of health adopted ; nourishing diet, a small portion of wine. early rising, cold bathing, gentle exercise, and air.

**The Human Temperaments.**— We quote from Mrs. Shimmelpennick, that there are four temperaments : choleric and sanguine, *active ;* phlegmatic and melancholic, *passive ;* sanguine is characterised by activity ; choleric by force ; phlegmatic by inertness ; melancholic by sensibility. In sanguine and choleric the outline is convex ; phlegmatic and melancholic outline with concavities.

SANGUINE.—Convexities united by angles ; features, salient ; complexion, pink ; hair, red and crisped ; light of eyes, sparkling ; colour, blue ; voice, sharp ; movements, agile and with elasticity ; attitudes, with spring, bird-like, constant in motion.

CHOLERIC.—The manner strongly de-

fined ; complexion, bilious ; eyes, dark ; light of the eyes, flashing ; nostrils, well pronounced ; hair, black and curled strongly ; gestures, violent ; voice, deep and harsh ; shaggy eyebrows ; the mouth closes determinately : jaw-bone marked forcibly.

PHLEGMATIC.—The body bears a large proportion to the limbs, and the plane of the face to the features ; complexion, sodden ; features, sunk, not well formed ; hair, hempen and lank ; eyes, open, dull, grey in colour ; eyebrows, an unmeaning arch ; cheeks, pendulous ; lips, thick, without coarse expression ; voice, uninflected and deep ; attitude, without gesticulation ; light of the eyes, tranquil.

MELANCHOLIC.—Features in a concave basis ; cheekbone, flat, without muscular constriction ; white manifest under the iris of the eye ; hair, lank, dark in colour ; voice, unsubstantial, susceptible of modulation ; chest falls in ; limbs long in proportion to their figure ; light of the eyes, sparkling ; attitude, pensive.

The sanguine will be an entertaining companion, not deep.

The choleric a brave champion, not tender.

The melancholic, a warmly-attached friend.

The phlegmatic, ballast, rest.

It is always desirable there should be an active and passive temperament. The character is likely to be poor without this union. If there are only the two passive temperaments the character is without spring, and little able to help itself. If the two active, there is little quiet or rest between the violence of the choleric and the restlessness of the sanguine. The finest characters generally possess all four temperaments.

**Economy of Joints.**—There is a great difference in the economy of certain joints of meat. A leg of mutton, in our opinion, is by far the most economical, while a boiled neck of mutton is the most extravagant. It may be useful for the young housekeeper to know that a roast leg of mutton weighing 10 lb. ought to make from fifteen to eighteen dinners ; a piece of boiling beef will yield the same ; but roasting beef is more extravagant—the bone in a piece of the ribs or sirloin weighs so much. We are convinced, as a rule, we do not make as much soup in our households as we ought to do. All the bones should be saved and stewed for hours. The liquor in which beef, mutton, and even bacon, is boiled, should be kept to make stock for soup ; with an addition now and then of part of a shin of beef, or a shilling's worth of bones from the butcher, you can nearly always have soup for the late dinner where there is a family of eight or ten. The cook should be ordered to preserve all the dripping, which should be clarified before it is set aside, taking care always to keep the beef dripping separate from the rest, as it can be used for making pastry.

**Lobsters.**—These shell-fish are neither wholesome nor digestible, but they have a curious history. Their claws are something more than lines of beauty, or to be associated with mere delicious pickings. Like our metropolitan postmen, they change their coat, and put on a new one once a year, and previous to laying aside the old one it appears sick, languid, and restless. Whether these are a lobster's manifestations of joy, sorrow, or pride, we cannot tell, but such they really are, and it mounts its new coat in a few days. During the change of its habiliments it seeks a very lonely spot, lest the temptation of its uncovered skin should tempt its brethren to devour it in its defenceless condition. " It is hard, however, to conceive," observes Travis, " how lobsters, in casting their shells, are able to draw the flesh of their large claws out, leaving the shell entire and attached to their body, in which state they are constantly found." Fishermen state that the lobster pines before casting its shell, till the flesh of its large claw is no thicker than a goosequill, a circumstance which enables them to draw its parts through the joints and narrow passages near the trunk. The new shell, as at first, quite membraneous, but, by degrees, becomes

hardened. The lobster only grows while the shell is in this soft state.

**Names.**—A great point is, not to give your children such high-sounding names as may in after life make them appear ludicrous in the eyes of the world when pursuing an ordinary or common occupation. For example, we know a lady who had in her girlhood been an inveterate reader of novels and plays, from which she had gathered all the long-winded, high-sounding, and chivalrous names which are usually found to belong to the heroes and heroines of such productions. These she unhesitatingly appropriated and treasured in her memory till the happy time would arrive when she should have an opportunity of conferring some of them upon her own offspring. Accordingly this period did arrive, but the novel and play-reading lady had united herself to a butcher, and she came to stand in the public market selling the meat which her husband had slaughtered. She had a large family, and these she had designated, to the great horror of her husband, after the Orlandos, Dianas, Desdemonas, and the like. This being the case, on a busy day, she might be heard crying at her stall from the one end of the market alley to the other, " Orlando, Roderigo, Alexander Smith, fetch the cleaver !"— Than this, nothing could be more absurd. Custom had familiarized it to the ears of the surrounding butchers, but the auricular organs of a stranger must have been singularly tickled by hearing such an assemblage of dignified appellations being employed in so common an occupation. It is perfectly true that Plato recommended it to parents to give happy names to their children, and that Pythagoras taught that the minds, actions, and successes of men, were according to their names, genius, and fate ; but such a doctrine is wholly untenable by any rational system of philosophy.

**To Cleanse Argand Lamps.**—The management of a table lamp of any kind is rather a difficult business, and one which the mistress should consider as her duty, for servants are not to be entrusted with it. Great care should be taken in the purchase to obtain one from a maker of known reputation, for the cheap ones, particularly those picked up at brokers' shops, are always out of repair.

The principal of the Argand lamp (so named after its inventor, a Frenchman) is, that a free current of air should be drawn through the centre of the flame, and to ensure this, it is necessary to clean the lamp frequently, and remove any dust or impurities from the oil or charcoal of the wick, which collects the small holes in the rim, through which the cold air is drawn. If the lamp is used every night it should be cleaned daily. The methodical mode is this :—

Remove the shade carefully before you soil your hands with the oil. Provide a bottle of warm water (a little above blood heat), and in this first wash the glass chimney, then pour the oil from the fountain, and remove any sediment from about the brass work. Screw up the wick, and if it is not long enough for the time it may probably be required to burn, replace it with a fresh one by means of the stick. Having washed all the brass work, wipe the parts carefully, screw everything in its former position, and take care in replacing the wick that the small notch at the side of the brass enters the groove which is sank to receive it ; turn it up and down once or twice to make sure that it works freely ; then prime it (that is, singe the top), replace the fountain (filled with oil), chimney and shade ; the lamp is now ready for use.

Purchase the best oil—the inferior qualities emit an offensive smell, and produce so much sediment that the delicate works of the lamps are quickly clogged, and the current of air impeded, which causes it to burn dimly.

Occasionally it is necessary to wash the shade, which should be done in clean lukewarm water, with the admixture of a little soda, which removes all stains, and does not injure the appearance of the ground glass. The glass chimneys will sometimes crack with the heat, particu-

larly in frosty weather. This may be prevented by scoring a small notch in the glass at top and bottom.

**Best means of Safety during a Thunder and Lightning Storm.**— The best means of safety in a thunder-storm would be to maintain the horizontal rather than the upright position ; to avoid the contact of metallic substances. If out of doors, not to take shelter under trees, which are equally good conductors of the electric fluid with animal bodies ; to keep the clothes dry ; and to retire into a vaulted cellar, if under the domestic roof, where no conductor is attached to the building ; or to keep in the middle of a room with a boarded floor ; or, which is better, to lie down on a feather bed. The covering of a looking-glass during a storm can add no safety to the house or room. It prevents it reflecting the light given out by the electric discharge, but the covering can produce no other effect. Lightning can only produce an effect upon the human body when it is the object through which the fluid passes to the earth. Thus it is dangerous to stand or sit against a wall, because the body is a better conductor than the substance of the wall, and the electric fluid would therefore pass from the wall through the body, and so to the earth. If the wall was of iron—the iron being the better conductor—no such accident would occur. Houses with lead coverings and metal spouts running to the earth are less dangerous than those covered with tiles or slates, with wooden spouts. On a wide and open heath, where no house shelter can be obtained, the safest plan in case of alarm is to lie down flat upon the earth.

**Vulgarities.**—We often have inward promptings of the vulgarity of our actions ; there is a sort of instinctive propriety in all of us, and whenever we heed these monitions from within, we are almost pretty sure to be in the right. If you have a doubt at any time of the propriety of an action, let instinct guide you, and you are safe. I have observed that it is very common for persons to talk very loud when in conversation with foreigners, as if increase of noise would compensate for difficulties of mutual understanding. In omnibus and railway travelling there is a good deal of bawling, treading on toes, thrusting of elbows into sides, crushing, crowding, and running to and fro. In the midst of all this confusion the gentleman, punctual to time, walks with ease to his place, takes his seat without hurry or noise, and, in securing his own comfort, regards the comfort of others by a spirit of conciliating accommodation. The other day, while riding in an omnibus, I was much annoyed, as were others of the passengers, by two females (I regret I cannot say *ladies*), who sat with heads protruding from the windows, shouting and passing pleasantries to some acquaintance on the pathway. Rudeness of any kind on such occasions causes annoyance to all who witness it.

Avoid all boastings and exaggerations, backbiting, abuse, and evil speaking ; slang phrases and oaths in conversation ; depreciate no man's qualities, and accept hospitalities of the humblest kind in a hearty and appreciative manner ; avoid giving offence, and if you do offend, have the manliness to apologise ; infuse as much elegance as possible into your thoughts as well as your actions ; and as you avoid vulgarities you will increase the enjoyment of life, and grow in the respect of others.

**The Hair of the Head.**—In the 5th verse of the 6th chapter of Numbers, we find permission given to man for the hair to grow long, in the following words, " and shall let the locks of the hair of his head grow." This alludes to a custom among the Nazarites and Persians, to allow the hair to grow until the completion of a vow ; and then, when the term of the vow expired, they shaved the head, or, as it afterwards mentions in the 18th verse of the same chapter, they took " the hair of the head and put it in the fire, which is under the sacrifice."

It was a very ancient custom among the heathen nations to consecrate to the gods the hair when cut off, as well as when growing on the head. The hair was sometimes consumed on the altar, sometimes deposited in the temples, and often suspended upon trees. A famous instance of the consecration of the hair is that of Berenice, the consort of Ptolemy Euergetes. When the king went on his expedition to Syria, she was anxious for his safety, and made a vow to consecrate her hair, which was much admired for its fineness and beauty, to Venus, if he returned safe. He did return safe ; and she offered her hair in the temple at Cyprus. This consecrated hair, being afterwards missing, was fabled to have become a constellation in the heavens, which constellation is called *Coma* Berenices (*the head of Berenice*), to this day. Another remarkable instance is that of Nero, who according to Suetonius, cut off his first beard, put it in a casket of gold set with jewels, and consecrated it to Jupiter Capitolinus. In fact, the hair of the head and beard has been held, more or less, in a sort of mystical respect in most nations. It may be traced in our own country, perhaps, in the reputed use of the human hair in spells and incantations. To this day, the Arabs and other Orientals, treat the hair which falls or is taken from them, with a degree of care which indicates the superstitious feelings which they connect with it. They bury it very carefully, that no one may see it, or employ it to their prejudice."

From the passage in Numbers, it is therefore evident that the hair was worn *long* by men earlier than b. c. 1490. In the year b. c. 1027, we also find that Absalom, the king's son, wore his hair very long ; and that " when he polled his head (for it was at every year's end that he polled it, because the hair was heavy on him, therefore he polled it), he weighed the hair of his head at two hundred shekels after the king's weight." (2 Samuel xiv. 26). There cannot be a doubt that Absalom wore his hair unusually long, because we afterwards find (2 Samuel xviii. 9), that as he was riding a mule, and passing under the thick boughs of an oak, that his head caught hold of the oak, and he was taken up between the heavens and the earth ; and the mule that was under him went away." When we remember that it was the custom at that time to anoint the head with ointments, and then to sprinkle the hair with gold-dust, so that it might look handsome, we may almost account for the great weight of Absalom's hair ; and in this we are somewhat assisted by the passage " after the king's weight," which refers to the lesser shekel in use among the Hebrews at that time. The suspension of Absalom by his hair is a very remarkable proof of the extraordinary strength of the human hair, and calculating at the rate of 10 grains as the weight sustained by every hair, and the number of hairs as 648 to the square inch of his head, we shall find that Absalom's hair was quite capable of sustaining the weight of his body.

In the New Testament we are told that if a man have long hair, it is a shame unto him ; but if a woman have long hair, it is a glory to her, for her hair is given for a covering (1 Cor. xi. 14, 15).

The ancient Egyptian ladies wore their hair long and plaited. The back part was made to consist of a number of strings of hair, reaching to the bottom of the shoulder-blades ; and on each side other strings, of the same length, descended over the breast. The hair was plaited in the triple plait, the ends being left loose ; or, more usually, two or three plaits were fastened together at the extremity, by woollen strings of corresponding colour. Around the head was bound an ornamental fillet, with a lotus bud, by way of *feroniere*, falling over the forehead ; and the strings of hair at the sides were separated and secured with a comb, or a band ornamented in various ways according to the fancy of the wearer, and occasionally a round stud or pin was thrust into them at the front.

The short hair at the side of the face, which the ingenuity of ancient Romans, and modern European ladies has, by the aid of gum, compelled to lie in an immovable curve upon the cheek, was interwoven with several of its longer neighbours ; and these, being bound together at the end with string, fell down before the ear-ring, which they partially concealed. Many of the mummies of women have been found with the hair perfectly preserved, plaited in the manner I have mentioned ; the only alteration in its appearance being the change of its black hue which became reddened by exposure to great heat, during the process of embalming.

Sir G. Wilkinson also tells us that slaves or servants dressed their hair different to the ladies. " They generally bound it at the back part of the head, into a sort of loop, or ranged it one or more long plaits at the back, and eight or nine similar ones were suffered to hang down at either side of the neck and face. Several woodcuts are given to illustrate the various methods of dressing the hair, both by the ancient Egyptian ladies, and their slaves or servants ; and in one of them, we observe that the side hair is confined by a comb, and falls in six plaits down the side of the neck, while the short hair before it is arranged in three separate plaits on the cheek.

The custom of plaiting the hair is referred to in the Bible (1 Peter iii. 3), and we learn from Josephus and other historians, that certain of the Jewish women gained a living by adorning and plaiting the hair of the women of that period. It was not an ordinary mode of plaiting the hair, as we may easily see from the statues in the British Museum, but required great skill and taste.

**Pomegranates.**—Pulpy fruits, are distinguished from others by the softness of the texture in which the seeds lie imbedded. They differ very materially amongst themselves in botanical characters—some being berries, others pulpy receptacles. We will now try to trace the origin of the Pomegranate. It was cultivated in the western countries, on the borders of the Red Sea, and held in great esteem, before the peach, the nectarine, or the apricot had been brought from Persia to the more western countries. The children of Israel murmured for the fruits of Egypt—" It is, they exclaimed, in the wilderness, no place of seed, of figs, or of pomegranates." Moses described the promised land as a " land of wheat, vines, fig-trees, and pomegranates—a land of olive-oil, and honey." Solomon sings of " an orchard of pomegranates with pleasant fruits." The tree possesses considerable historical interest  It is probable that as it differs from stone fruits, it travelled from the West to the East.  Pliny says it is a native of Carthage, as its name (Pumica Granatum) imports ; it is found wild in the botanical regions of Europe, in countries of the same temperature as the northern coasts of Africa. It is a tree partaking of the antiquity of the vine, the fig, and the olive ; and in point of utility is numbered with the grain-bearing plants, and with honey, which constituted the principal food of the nations of antiquity in their first stages of civilisation.  It is still common in Barbary, where Shaw says the fruit often weighs a pound, and is three or four inches in diameter.  It has entered the heathen mythology, for in the isle of Eubrea, there formerly was a statue of Juno, holding in one hand a sceptre, and in the other a pomegranate.  The Jews employ the fruit in their religious ceremonies in the south of France, Italy, and Spain. It being so generally diffused in the climates suited to it, implies that it possesses highly valuable properties.  Its juice is grateful to the palate, and assuages thirst in a degree peculiar to itself ; from its pleasant acid, an acid so soft, that the pomegranate, to use Moore's description of it, " is full of melting sweetness." The tree grows to the height of twenty feet, the branches are thick, and varieties are armed with spines ; the bark was anciently used for dyeing leather.  The yellow Morocco of Tunis is still tinted with it.  The flowers are also used to dye cloth a light red.  The leaves are a beautiful green, and stand opposite each other.  The flowers come out in clusters of three or four at the end of the branches ; their blowing is so irregular, that it often continues for months.  Independent of its fruit, the beauty of the tree has caused it to be planted for ornament in the South of Europe, as also in the East.  The petals are handsome, thick and fleshy.  Russel says, in his account of Aleppo, " The nightingale sings from the pomegranate groves in the day time."  Gerard says he reared plants from the seeds.  It is supposed to have been first cultivated in England in the reign of Henry VIII. It is mentioned as bearing fruit in the orangery of Charles 1.  The tree is highly prized for its beauty as an ornament, the flowers are of a bright scarlet colour, the double ones are very handsome, but the fruit seldom arrives at maturity in England.  The odour of the flower is as fragrant as its colour is bright.  The tree is remarkable for its longevity ; there are specimens at Paris and Versailles which have existed more than two centuries.  It will not even in Paris bear exposure to the open air too early in the spring ; but it is not quite so delicate as the orange, and is generally removed from the houses eight or ten days earlier.

**Sausage Cakes.**—Chop lean pork very finely, having removed all the bone and skin previously, and to every pound of meat add three-quarters of a pound of fat bacon, half an ounce of salt, a pinch of pepper, quarter of a nutmeg grated, six green onions chopped finely, and a little chopped parsley ; when the whole is well chopped and mixed, put it into a mortar and pound well, finishing with three eggs.  Then have ready a pig's caul, cut into pieces large enough to fold a piece of the above preparation of the size of an egg, but rather flattened, and broil gently over a moderate fire. This is a very nice relish for breakfast, luncheon, or supper.

**Care of Linen.**—When linen is well dried and laid by for use, nothing more is necessary than to secure it from damp and insects ; the latter may be provided against by a mixture of aromatic shrubs and flowers, sewed in silken bags to be interspersed among the drawers and shelves.  These may consist of lavender, thyme, roses, cedar-shavings, powdered sassafras, cassia, lignea, &c., into which a few drops of attar of roses, or other strong-scented perfume may be thrown. In all cases, it will be found consistent with economy, to examine and repair washable articles, especially linen, that may stand in need of it, previous to sending it to the laundry. It will also be prudent to have every article carefully numbered, and so arranged, after washing, as to have their regular turn and term in domestic use.

**Becoming Dress.**—A young girl will often wear a rich and heavily-trimmed silk dress which is quite unsuitable to the wearer and to the occasion. The toilette of a French demoiselle at a ball is nearly always spotless white ; the dress of tulle or some such delicate or airy-looking material, adorned by bouquets or a garland of flowers to match those worn in the hair ; a few ornaments are worn, but the effect of the toilette is of exquisite freshness and elegant simplicity. It is a mistake to suppose the most expensive dresses are the most admired or the most effective. To those who are still young, good but inexpensive materials, well made and with few but good trimmings, are far more becoming than over trimmed and costly silks. A lady is well-dressed only when her appearance accords with her position and means ; for all pretension in dress is in bad taste. It is difficult to decide how far the ever-varying changes of fashion should be followed, but to dress in the fashion and never to carry it to excess is the most sensible plan. To wear anything outre, or that attracts attention by its novelty, is in bad taste. Frenchwomen are very careful of their dresses, and this is why they always look so fresh and crisp. We have heard of ladies who, on going to a ball, stood the whole way in their carriages rather than allow the delicate tulle puffings and flowers to be crushed. This is going to the extreme, but there is no doubt that if ladies wish their toilettes to look fresh and charming, they must use care to preserve them so. It is natural and right that every lady should give a certain amount of time and thought to dress ; it is only when this is carried to excess, and absorbs the mind to the exclusion of better things, that it has a bad effect on the character.

**Tapioca.**—This starch is the produce of the roots of the Jatropha Mamihot, a plant which grows in great abundance in the West Indies. The roots in their raw state are called Cassado, and are strong poisons, yet the starch extracted from them is similar in its nutritive qualities to sago, which it resembles in appearance, but is not so high coloured, and is formed into larger grains ; it is prepared in the same manner, only that it does not require to be macerated, or boiled more than half the time. It is much used by invalids and infants. Dr. Christian observes of this food—" no amylaceous substance is so much relished by infants about the time of weaning ; and in them it is less apt to become sour during digestion than any other farinaceous food, even arrowroot not excepted.

**Vinegar.**—Next to salt, this is, perhaps, the most important condiment ; it is very serviceable in aiding the digestion of celery, lettuce, beet-root, and other raw vegetables, and in preventing them from inducing flatulence ; it is equally useful in promoting the digestion of rich and oily substances such as salmon. Lemon-juice has a similar effect when used with goose and wild fowl ; upon the same principle apple sauce is probably, from the malic acid which it contains, eaten with pork. Acetic acid is the volatile acid principle, which, diluted with water, constitutes vinegar. It is prepared from sugar, cyder, malt, and wine, and from the destructive distillation of wood. This condiment is both useful and wholesome, more, however, to some persons than others. But taken immoderately vinegar is decidedly injurious, destroying the digestive powers rather than assisting them, even, indeed, inducing active disease of the stomach. It is sometimes used in large quantities for the reduction of corpulency, which is a very dangerous practice.

Vinegar is a valuable disinfectant ; burnt or sprinkled about a sick room, it becomes both refreshing and agreeable. The colour of the brown vinegar is generally imparted by burnt sugar.

**Frittrers.**—Very nice fritters may be made with a kind of paste, which, being allowed to cool is cut into shapes, which are dipped in batter and fried. Here are several forms of it :  1. Pass some potatoes through a sieve, stir into them a little butter melted and enough yolks of eggs or whole eggs to form a stiffish paste ; season with salt, pepper, a little nutmeg ; form into the shape of little balls, and dip in batter and fry. This may be varied by adding a little cream, also some ham or Bologna sausage finely minced, and some chopped parsley. 2. Have a saucepan with about a pint of boiling water and 1 oz. of butter ; drop into this gradually with the hand some Indian corn flour, stirring all the time until you get a liquid paste. Take care not to put too much flour, and to put it in gradually, else it will form into knots and spoil the dish. Removing the saucepan from the fire, you stir into the paste a good allowance of grated Parmesan cheese, a little salt and pepper, and pour out your paste on a marble slab to cool. When cold, cut it out in any shape you like, and fry. The addition of ham or sausage can also be made to this. 3. Make the paste as above, only with common corn flour ; when half cold stir into it some yolks of egg, and flavour it with pepper, salt, and nutmeg ; add chopped parsley and minced ham, then treat as the others ; or you may flavour it with cheese. All the above pastes may be fried without being previously dipped in batter, but it is more difficult to so fry them creditably.

**Use of Fruit.**—Instead of fear of a generous consumption of ripe fruits, we regard them as positively conducive to health. The maladies commonly assumed to have their origin in the free use of apples, peaches, cherries, melons, and wild berries, have been as prevalent, if not equally destructive, in seasons of scarcity. There are so many erroneous notions entertained of the bad effects of fruit, that it is time a counteracting impression should be promulgated, having its foundation in common sense, and based on the observation of the intelligent. No one ever lived longer, or freer from the paroxysms of disease, by discarding the delicious fruits of the land in which he finds a home. On the contrary, they are necessary to the preservation of health, and are therefore caused to make appearance at the time when the condition of the body, operated upon by deteriorating causes not always understood, requires their grateful, renovating influences.

**Manna.**—Some persons have attempted to trace a connection between the food miraculously rained down from heaven for the sustenance of the Israelites in the wilderness and the substance now known as "manna." Of the composition of the former we know nothing, while we do know that the latter cannot be used as food. The manna now used is obtained chiefly from Sicily and Calabria, and is the concrete juice of several species of ash of the genera ornus and fraxinus The juice exudes in the summer months, either spontaneously or through incisions made for that purpose in the bark, and is collected in leaves placed in cups to receive it ; or it forms incrustations upon twigs, straws, and leaves placed under the trees. The best is of a light yellow or whitish colour, in flakes and tears. It possesses a sweet, somewhat nauseous taste, and is soluble in water and alcohol. It consists of a crystalizable, sweet principle, called "mannite," which sometimes amounts to 75 per cent. of true sugar, and of a yellow nauseous matter, which gives it its value as a purgative medicine. A substance called manna is obtained by the Bedouin Arabs in the form of an exudation from a plant which grows in the country.

**Destroying Crickets.**—On taking charge of my establishment two years ago the place was completely overrun, but by steady perseverance in using phosphoric paste I am almost clear of crickets, cockroaches, beetles, rats and mice. 1 tried it at first alone on bits of slate and glass ; but I find the best plan is to mix it with a little butter or lard, and spread it on small bits of stout grey paper with a thin knife, and then dust a little coarse sugar on the top. Rats and mice carry the paper off to their haunts, and enjoy their feast at leisure. I have proved also that wood-lice will take it with sugar, although 1 have, like others, found hot water the most effective remedy where it can be applied. For ants 1 have used a strong dose of guano-water mixed with helibore powder, poured on their runs and into their castles.

**Raised Cake without Eggs.**—Stir together a large coffee-cupful of light brown or white sugar, and half a cupful of butter ; add to it half a pint of sweet milk and half a pint of warm water. To this mixture stir in flour enough to make a thick batter, and half a cupful of yeast ; set it to rise over night. Next morning stir in a cupful of chopped raisins or currants, and a teaspoonful each of cinnamon, cloves, and nutmeg. Put it into two baking pans ; let it rise until perfectly light, then bake three-quarters of an hour.

**New Treatment of Hydrophobia.**—In a recent coroner's inquest held at Salford, on a groom who died from hydrophobia from the bite of a cat, the coroner said it was very desirable that the public should know what was best to be done in these cases. He had had a case similar to the present one, and the medical man agreed with him that the best method was to suck the wound and spit out the blood, bathe it in warm water, in order to encourage bleeding, and continue this until the wound could be cauterised.

**What the Ladies Say of Themselves.**—Among other things, the present day may be considered the field of coquetry. Never, since the time of the Renaissance, has the genius of womanhood exerted itself more strenuously to render personal appearance piquante and coquettish than it has during the last few years ; and never has the result been more satisfactory, according to the ideas of its originators, if startling to the quiet bystanders. Those of us who are old enough to remember the fashions of the early Victorian era can scarcely believe that we were contented to be so simple, so plain, so absolutely uncoquettish in our attire as we were. And some of us, bitten with the new faith in fuzzy heads, queer hats, and multitudinously frilled shirts, bewail the cruel fate that doomed our best years to Dutch-cut petticoats, corkscrew ringlets, or smooth-banded heads innocent alike of chignons or Gainsborough-fringed foreheads. Our bonnets, too ; do any of our readers remember the " neat straw bonnet " of our own youth ?—the side frills dotted about with loops of narrow ribbon, sometimes ornamented with broad bows, sometimes with rosebuds placed alternately in and out the quilled blonde " whiskers ?" the cross-cut curtains ? the bow at the back with long ends ? if very coquettishly-minded, we put that bow to the side, trembling lest a knot of ribbon not just in the middle of the crown should look too " coming"—which was the slang term thirty years ago for the " fast " of to-day. And then the dresses, utterly devoid of ornamentation, put into thick " box plaits " round the waist ; the bodice fastened with hooks and eyes under a concealing hem, to the eternal cry of " Oh, do come and hook my frock for me !" though some clever girls, who do not " screw in," could manage to do that office for themselves by a series of gymnastic efforts behind their backs—if low, laced with many holes that always came crooked at the end, to the exceeding irritation of the patient operator ; the *berthas*, which required careful pinning to the loose chemisette which was before the fixed lace tucker began, and which had the bad habit of coming up over the shoulder and showing a bare tract of youthful flesh. Well, it was all very simple, inconvenient, not picturesque, and decidedly not coquettish.

But were the young hearts that beat beneath those round-necked, long-waisted, peaked bodices, very different from those which now throb beneath the wonderful creations of millinery skill called "costumes" and "trained skirts?" Does the shape of the dress make much difference to the creature within it? or is not human nature at eighteen much the same whether it dances in a bulbous Dutch-built petticoat which makes "cheeses" as it spins or trails after its long eddying lengths of silk and muslin, for ever under its own feet or its partner's?—a train that becomes a disreputable mass of dirt and rags before the evening is over. There may be, and is, a question of comparative beauty, niceness, and convenience in costumes; but, so far as the human soul is concerned, it is to be hoped it is not so much influenced by externals as might be imagined; else, if it were so, there would not be a girl left in England who was not a thorough coquette, both body and mind. And coquetry, though it has an innocent side, pretty and perfectly harmless, yet has also an ugly tendency to broaden out into utter heartlessness, into selfishness, and something near to sin.

The truth is, we use the term in a double sense; the one means simply the desire to attract admiration by manner, dress, or personal beauty; the other means the desire to attract love which is not returned, and which is wanted only for the public triumph of a pitiful vanity.

**The Importance of Walking Exercise.**—A moderate use of walking, as a means of strengthening the frame, is far too much neglected by us. At some large boarding schools, indeed, more especially where there are one or two German masters who have brought with them the habits and traditions of their own *Gymnasia* and *Turnvereine*, the boys are taken on every fine day for a good long walk; and it is surprising to observe in such cases how rapidly apparently weak lads will grow into proficient pedestrians, and how they will persevere,

long after they have left school, in a form of exercise which yields them health and enjoyment. But, as a general rule, the virtues and uses of walking are not sufficiently impressed upon our English youth of both sexes. Yet it is the one form of exercise which especially commends itself to universal adoption. It costs nothing. The opportunities for practising it are always at hand. It strengthens the constitution as no other exercise does, unless we admit riding as its rival—and riding is the privilege of the few. The habit of taking long walks, which boys and girls may acquire, is an accomplishment which may stand them in good stead in many an emergency of life; and even if no useful results were possible, walking, like virtue, is its own reward.

**The Teeth.**—In the adult there are 32 teeth. They are generally lost for want of due care, and a few from defects, in some families. When we finish a meal it is impossible to avoid leaving some bits of food in the mouth. Should any lodge between the teeth that generally gives us some uneasiness, and we endeavour to pick it out. But the surfaces of the teeth employed for grinding the food (five above and five below on each side) are very uneven, that they may be better suited for bruising it. Small grains of food are liable to remain in these irregular places, on the surface; or, if the gums are not healthy, some will lodge between them and the teeth. In all cases, these bits of food ought to be removed by washing the mouth.

In some European countries they even do this before company, but it does not look well. The teeth should be carefully cleansed with a good brush and water every night before going to bed; as sleeping with uncleaned teeth does them harm, and frequently gives a bad taste in the mouth. A little charcoal toothpowder should be used occasionally, if the teeth will not keep white without it, as foul teeth are so very offensive.

Everything we use for food is subject to decay. It is also a law of matter, that food left in the mouth will decay, and in time, if suffered to remain, may breed insects to eat through the hard enamel of some tooth or teeth, and that this will give us severe pain and cause the loss of those beautiful instruments given us by our benevolent Creator to minister to our comfort, health, and life.

**Toothache.**—Where a tooth is so far gone as to be very troublesome, it is best to have it out. For toothache (which everyone is liable to) the "Family Doctor" recommends creosote, chloroform, and laudanum, either separately or in combination. The mode of application is to saturate a small piece of lint or wadding, and introduce it into the hollow of the tooth, keeping it there as long as may be necessary ; should there be no available hollow, apply it as close as possible to the seat of pain. Other remedies are, inhaling the vapour from henbane seeds put on a hot piece of metal ; chewing a piece of pellitory root, or using the tincture ; putting a piece of sal prunella in the mouth and allowing it to dissolve ; applying a drop or two of the oil of cloves or cinnamon, on lint ; or thrusting into the hollow tooth a piece of wire previously dipped in strong nitric acid ; this application, if properly made, destroys the nerve, but it must be very carefully done, so that the acid does not touch the other teeth or the mouth.

**Tooth-Brushes.**—The habitual, or even occasional, employment of hard tooth-brushes is a great mistake. No specimen of hog's bristles can well be too soft for this use ; and when employed in conjunction with a suitable dentifrice will sufficiently answer the purpose for which tooth-brushes are intended. Even a soft-haired tooth-brush may, in many cases of irritable gums, be advantageously dispensed with in favour of a sponge rubber, an instrument which may be easily prepared by tying a piece of sponge to the handle of a worn-out tooth-brush.

**Stopping Decayed Teeth.**—"So soon," says Dr. Scoffern, in his "Philosophy of Common Life," "as the pain of a carious tooth has been sufficiently alleviated to bear the pain of stopping, recourse should be had to the dentist at once. The sufferer must be content to depend upon the use of one of the many varieties of soft stopping known to dentists. I regard the amalgam of mercury and standard (not pure) silver to be the most eligible material for the purpose, all things considered. When carefully impacked it will last many years, frequently to the end of life."

The **Female Character.**—Of all the charms which twine themselves about the female character, none is more lovely, more touching, more worthy to be honoured and admired than—simplicity—the gentle yet frank open-heartedness of character, which seems to make the soul a place of light and purity, like the mild, sweet radiance of a spring morning, among budding leaves and opening flowers. How exquisitely beautiful, how unspeakably delicate, says a late writer, is the loveliness of a woman unaccustomed to the world ! "Unscathed by the chilling influence of blasted hopes, of wounded affection, her sharply-defined feelings manifest themselves in all their freshness, with a warmth unchecked by the dictates of jealous prudence, or the wary suggestions of calculating, narrow-minded, self-protecting interest. For her to think, is to give utterance to her thoughts ; and to feel is to give expression to her emotions, with a guileless simplicity, unsuspicious of ill-natured misrepresentations, and fearless, because unconscious, of the possibility of misconstruction." Compare this sweet and touching simplicity, which makes the life but the expressive countenance of the soul, with artifice—that hateful weed, which often takes root so vigorously even in early life, hardening and blackening the soil in which it grows, till nothing is seen but smut and stubble. Compare a subtle, contriving, tortuous, snaky thing—with her crafty, satin-spoken words, her quick, furtive glances, her readily changing brow, and her artificial softness of demeanour—the heartless syren of the dance, who lures on her victim with deceitful smiles and clustering ringlets, and jewelled fingers, and the pattering of tiny feet clothed in slippers of the choicest satin—the false-hearted, smooth-face creature, who attunes her shrill voice " by a system of polite solfeggio," and conceals the sharpness of her talons under a feline velvetude of paw—compare the words and looks of such a being with the unconstrained and artless vivacity, the open looks, of fair simplicity—of the guileless being, who knows no restraint but that delicacy which has grown up with her inmost thoughts, shading but not concealing them, like the sheath of sheltering green around the exquisite lily of the valley ! No, no ! simplicity is the very soul of beauty—the sweet spirit of fascination which makes us love what otherwise we could but at the most admire. All artifice or affectation of character, all prettinesses, all exquisite and elaborate contrivances to rivet the enchanted gaze of the beholder—whether displayed in the dress or manners—can never so bewitch us as Nature's self. In female dress, when youth and beauty appear arrayed in simple white, with perhaps a single bouquet reposing on the bosom of innocence, or with a single brilliant diamond sparkling among the light masses of auburn curls which nature herself has entwined, and which fall like fleecy clouds on each full and ripening cheek—how infinitely does such a vision outshine the mere earthen image, tricked out in all the puffs and papillotes, all the dangling bows and tresses, all the glittering ribands and sparkling paste, which wealth or fashion, vanity or folly, can string together !

It is a grand defect of the science of female education in this country that it is too much the science of mere behaviour. Instead of educating the feelings, we are critically didactic as to the mode of their expression—the sentiment and disposition reigning within are not constantly visible in the external deportment. We do not encourage intrepidity and independence of thought,—there is nothing original—nothing fer-

vent—nothing which may prolong the delicate spell of respectful tenderness and admiration, by casting upon the every-day occurrences of life the glow of feeling and the charm of novelty. Some minds there are by nature so strong and elastic, as to rebound from the pressure of education into the beautiful region of natural enthusiasm and innocent true-heartedness, but the mass are so moulded that they are often but pasteboard, buckram, and whalebone things—creatures of puffery and artifice —whose every word, look, and act, everything they do, is but a trick of custom. Education, which should prompt the mind to expand into generous emotion, and teach it to trace with delicate discernment new views of things, seems only to check the earnest expression of natural feeling and lively thought.

**Excellent Fruit Wine.**—Take red and white currants, red and green gooseberries, mulberries, raspberries, and strawberries of different sorts, black and white grapes, cherries of different sorts (except the little black ones). All the fruit must be thoroughly ripe. Take an equal quantity of each and throw them into a mash-tub, bruising them lightly. Take some golden pippins and nonpareils ; chop and bruise them well, and mix them with the others. To every two gallons of fruit put one gallon of spring water ; boil all twice a day for a fortnight ; then press it through a hair bag into a stone vessel. Have ready a wine hogshead, and put into it one hundred raisins with their stalks ; fill it with the strained juice, and lay the cork on lightly till it has done fermenting ; then add one gallon of French brandy, and cork the hogshead close. Let it stand six months ; then tap it, and see if it is clear. If it is, bottle it off ; if it is not, cork it up for six months longer, and then bottle it. The longer it is kept the better it will be. It is necessary to put in with the brandy half a dozen bay leaves.

**How To Keep Fowls.**—No fowls can possibly thrive well, or be profitable to the owners, unless they are plentifully fed, and have a comfortable place to roost in at night and for a shelter in cold or wet weather. Their room or hen-house may be adjoining to some other out-building. It is best to have it facing the east or the south, and it must be perfectly weather-tight. It should have a door and windows, and be very well lighted ; the windows may either be latticed with wood, or netted with iron wire. In the evening, after the fowls have gone to roost, let the door be locked ; seeing that it is opened very early in the morning, unless in bad weather. The hen-house should be frequently cleaned out, and occasionally ; for, if kept dirty, the fowls will be infested with vermin. If this should happen, catch every fowl, even to the smallest chicken, and rub their skins and feathers well with lard or dripping ; then have their house thoroughly cleaned and whitewashed at once ; afterwards fumigating it with burning brimstone. Next, throw some sand or fresh earth on the floor.

If fowls are scantily supplied with water, or if they have access only to that which is dirty or puddled, they will contract a disorder called the pip, which is a thin white scale that grows on the tip of the tongue, and prevents their feeding. Catch them, pull off the scale with your fore-finger nail, and then rub the tongue with salt. When fowls have this or any other disease, they look drooping, their eyes appear dull, and their combs and gills become pale and flabby. When they are sick, feed them with bran that has been mixed to a paste with boiling water.

In wet weather, keep the fowls shut up all day in the hen-house ; also when it is very cold, taking care that they are properly supplied with food and water. They should have in their house a little manger or feeding-trough, which ought never to be empty. If they have plenty of food always by them, they will eat frequently, but only a little at a time, and it is best for them to do so. When their food is given to them scantily and irregularly, they injure themselves by devouring it too fast.

They should have food given to them regularly three times a day. When newly hatched, they may have bread soaked in milk. By way of variety, you may give your fowls, occasionally, buckwheat, barley, rice, and oats.

If always fed there, they will stay chiefly in their house during the winter, and will, in consequence, be more healthy, and in every respect more profitable. They must be well supplied with plenty of clean water, in large shallow pans of tin or earthen-ware, turned bottom upwards, on which the fowls can stand to drink without wetting their feet, which often makes them sick. Recollect always, that dirty water gives them diseases, but a little clean brick-dust thrown occasionally into their drinking pans is good for their digestion.

Their nests should be movable, that whenever she has done sitting they may be taken away, and cleaned out before they are replaced. For the nest, you may place on the floor (not far from the walls, but not against them) old flat baskets, or deep boxes set up on the side, the open or entrance part turned from the light. Fill them with clean dry straw or hay. Place near the boxes lime, for the hens to form their egg-shells. Old rubbish lime, or plaster from old walls, is very proper for this purpose, if well broken up. If you cannot procure this, mix lime and water to a mortar ; let it dry, then break it up and put it into the hen-house. See that the setting hens have plenty of food and water every day, at the time they come off their nests. If they are not supplied at once they will go back to their nests without waiting, and suffer much in consequence.

Their roosts or perches should be contrived as not to be exactly over each other, and some should be placed low enough for the young fowls to reach without difficulty in flying up to them. Let none of the nest-boxes be placed under the roosts.

The hen-house should frequently be cleaned out, whitewashed, fumigated with sulphur, or by burning boughs ; and then strewed with sand.

Wormwood and rue, sowed plentifully every spring about the neighbourhood of the hen-house, will tend to keep away vermin ; and if strewed about the floor in the vicinity of their nests, it will keep off weasels and other such animals that come to suck the eggs.

Bantam fowls are less injurious to a garden than any others, as the feathers about their feet prevent them from scratching up the seeds. If your garden fence has the paling sharp-pointed at the top, the fowls that are outside will find it difficult to get over ; as after flying up to the top, they will have no place to rest their feet on, while preparing to take their flight downward.

**Quince Marmalade.**—The following is the best method. Slice the quinces into a preserving pan, with sufficient water for them to float. Place them on the fire to stew until reduced to a pulp, keeping them stirred occasionally from the bottom to prevent their being burnt ; then pass the pulp through a hair sieve to keep back the skin and seeds. Weigh the pulp, and to each pound add a pound of loaf sugar broken small. Place the whole on the fire, and keep it well stirred from the bottom of the pan with a wooden spoon, until reduced to a marmalade, which may be known by dropping a little on a cold plate, when, if it is of a jelly-like consistence, it is done. Put it into jars or pots while hot, and cover with pieces of paper (cut to the size of the mouths of the jars) that have been saturated with some good sweet oil or olive oil, or with spirit. This should be done when the marmalade is cold. The tops of the jars may be afterwards covered with pieces of bladder or paper, and be tied round the edge.

**Quince or Apple Jelly.**—This is prepared as directed for marmalade, except that when the fruit is reduced to a pulp the clear juice is strained off, and to each pint a pound of loaf sugar is added, and then boiled to a jelly. The residue left on the sieve will serve to make a common marmalade, by using moist sugar instead of loaf, and boiling it as before directed. The apple jelly will be found excellent to pour over fruits that have been preserved in syrup. It is in this way that the fruits termed compotes sold in the shops, packed in small bell glasses, are done.

**Oyster Ketchup.**—Procure some fine fresh oysters, open sufficient to fill a pint measure ; save the liquor, and scald the oysters in it, with a pint of sherry wine. Good cider or pale ale may be substituted for the wine. Strain the oysters, and put them into a mortar with three ounces of salt, a drachm of cayenne pepper, and two drachms of pounded mace. Pound the whole until reduced to a pulp, then add it to the liquor in which they were scalded ; boil it again five minutes, and skim it. Rub the whole through a sieve ; bottle and cork close when cold.

*Another Way.*—Take half a hundred fine large oysters, open them, and save the liquor that runs from them ; add this to a quart of spring water, half-a-pound of bay salt, half-an-ounce of white pepper, and a quarter-of-an-ounce of pounded mace. Boil slowly a quarter-of-an-hour, adding the oysters towards the last, to scald them in it. Strain and pound them well until reduced to a paste ; add them again to the liquor, boil a quarter-of-an-hour, and take off any dark scum that may rise. Rub the whole through a fine sieve ; add two or three spoonfuls of white wine vinegar, bottle and cork close when cold.

**Salad Cream.**—Rub the yolks of hard-boiled eggs smooth, with the back of a table-spoon in a basin, or with a small pestle and mortar. To each yolk of egg add a table-spoonful of good salad oil, some made mustard, a salt-spoonful of salt, and sufficient strong vinegar, with the addition of some Chili vinegar, to make it of the consistence of thin cream, and bottle for use. Some prefer the addition of a little cream, but for bilious persons we consider that it had better be left out.

**Dangerous Diets.**—The failure of the potato-crop is likely, from what we read to bring about an epidemic of scurvy, unless the public can be better informed of the requirements of an antiscorbutic diet. The fact, therefore, cannot be too widely made known that pease-pudding, haricot beans, and boiled rice, which have been suggested in the journals as substitutes for potatoes, will not prevent the occurrence of scurvy. In the absence of the potato—an excellent antiscorbutic—fresh green vegetables or fruits will be requisite, or the health will certainly fail, even though fresh meat be taken. Amongst the vegetable material which may be used, the Lancet states, are the various forms of cabbage, lettuce, oranges, lemons, onions, mustard-and-cress, dandelion, and sorrel. The experience of the crews of vessels on long voyages has shown, over and over again, the uselessness of the pea and bean tribe in preventing scurvy.

**Strychnia for Blindness.**—Professor Nagel of Tubingen has published reports of cases in which he has, by the use of strychnia, restored sight to patients suffering from decay of vision or from blindness. Strychnia, as is well known, is a deadly poison, but it has a wonderful effect in stimulating the nerves, and Professor Nagel found that in diseases of the optic nerve, whether functional or organic, its operation was alike speedy and efficacious. The quantity used is of course exceedingly small —one fortieth of a grain—mixed with water, and this solution is not to be swallowed, but is injected under the skin of one of the arms, which seems to render the result more remarkable. This remedy has also been tried by oculists elsewhere, and with marked success.

**To Make Good Blacking.**—Take four ounces of ivory black, half-an-ounce of Prussian blue, one ounce of sweet oil, two ounces of treacle, one ounce of sulphate of iron (commonly called green vitriol), and a quart of strong vinegar. Mix the first five ingredients well together, then gradually stir in the vinegar, bottle it off, and keep from six to eight weeks before using. Some persons add to the above, half-an-ounce of oil of vitriol (sulphuric acid) ; but this, though we admit that it improves the polish, is very pernicious to the leather and stitches.

**Kid Glove-Making.**—When dried, the skins feel hard and brittle, and have to undergo the process of staking, (the next stage) to render them again elastic. This is done by means of a semi-circular smooth-edged iron plate fixed upright on the top of a stout piece of timber, across which the workman draws the skin, first in one direction and then in the opposite, manipulating it well with his hands until it is made soft and elastic. It is then passed on to the parer, who shaves down all inequalities, making it of a like substance all over ; this he does by fixing one half of the skin under a strong cord round a horizontal ash pole, grasping the loose end with his left hand, and carefully shaving it with his right by means of a circular knife of quoit-like shape and extraordinary keenness ; removing the skin, reversing it on his pole, and shaving the other half in like manner, when, after a little polishing, or stoning off, and padding down, it is finished. We may here remark that at every stage the work is inspected by a competent foreman before it is passed on to that which follows. The skins are now removed to another room, where they are examined and sorted for cutting into such kinds of gloves as they are best fitted for in quality, size, substance, &c. ; they are thence sent to the cutter (in lots, generally, of from four to five dozen) with full instructions for his guidance respecting every skin. The cutter, taking one skin at a time, stretches it to the fullest extent, and cuts it up by measure into plain oblong pieces of the required size, which he submits to be stamped while stretched out, as a proof of his correctness in measuring and marking, before finishing them off in the form he is required to give them. From the cutter these oblong pieces called "tranks," are sent to the puncher, who, taking two or three pairs at a time, and placing them on the knife to which they correspond in size and shape (being so numbered by the cutter), puts them under a press, when the form of the glove is instantaneously produced, with all the necessary slits and openings, button-holes, gussets, &c., for enabling the sewer to put them together. The thumbs, and the forgettes or fourchettes—the pieces put between the fingers—are punched separately. The "tranks" now go to the trimmer, who, with a very fine cutting pair of scissors, removes every roughness that may have been left in the punching, after which they are supposed to be finished, though they have yet to be again closely examined, so as to correct any faults, and prevent any defective pieces being sent out to the sewer. Having passed this examination they are handed to boys, who fold each pair with its complement of thumbs, forgettes, and other pieces inside, and put them up into half-dozen or dozen packets, each packet with full instructions for making, written on the band ; the sewing materials are then added to each packet ; and after being duly entered out they are taken by travelling clerks to the various sewing stations throughout the county of Worcester, and into parts of Warwickshire, Oxford, Hereford, Gloucester, Devon, and Somerset. Each clerk will take out daily the number of dozens required for his particular station, and bring home made goods to a like extent, the quantity varying with the population of the different localities. All these goods when brought in from the makers have yet to receive the last finish, that is, the " topping," button and button-holing, &c., and this is done by hands in the city of Worcester, within easy reach of the manufactory. The gloves are now completed ; but they must still be " dressed," or put into straight and attractive form ; they are then subjected to their final examination by an " expert," and when passed by him have the firm's name stamped inside one glove of each pair ; after which being neatly made up, banded in half-dozens, and put into small boxes or cases, they are labelled and sent off to the London warehouse, whence they are distributed to every part of the kingdom, the colonies, America, &c. Messrs. Dent and Co. now employ nearly seven hundred hands within the walls of their manufactory, and about five thousand sewing people, &c., outside.

**Dancing.**—Dancing is, perhaps, the oldest amusement in the world, remarks a contributor to the Victoira Magazine, and too natural not to outlive all opposition, yet while we often hear it disparaged, we scarcely ever hear it defended for its extreme reasonableness. A small book entitled " Dancing in a Right Spirit," is the only attempt of the kind I have met with, but the author has greatly limited himself by considering the question in one direction only. Whilst very rightly and sensibly reminding us how dancing was a religious pastime among the Jews, and how it is nowhere forbidden, but rather commended, in the Bible, he leaves untouched any consideration apart from the Bible, and much may be said in favour of dancing from an artistic point of view. As beauty of colour to the eye, as sweet sounds to the ear, so is the luxury of quick, easy motion, to the healthy frame. All young things delight to skip and dance. When it hears quick, lively music, the child must dance ; it is an irresistible, spontaneous instinct, as much as to use its young voice and shout and laugh and sing out its merriment. It is the first praise of the child to its Creator. By enjoying the life He gives it, the child unwittingly, unconsciously, praises Him in its bright, swift motion, as hereafter it will do consciously in a maturer form by the life it will lead to His glory. So in the childhood of mankind, men danced before God in the full joy of their hearts. It was a kind of praise to God from these children of the earth's earlier days, and as much the right and natural mode for them to express praise, as it is now the right and natural mode for children to enjoy themselves. Whatever gives us highest enjoyment is most appropriately connected with religion ; and as physical enjoyment comes before mental, dancing formed a part of religious ceremonial before more recondite rituals, or more abstract ideas, superseded it. When that time came dancing slipped out of the religious sphere. And not only that, but in process of time a grim theology, which would banish all cheerfulness from life, did its best to condemn dancing, together with many other innocent and natural amusements. But such gloomy views of things are too unnatural to retain the world in their bondage, so dancing is still an enjoyment to thousands ; and when nature's pre-eminent right of guidance is more and more recognised, dancing will again assume its place amongst the arts which add beauty and joy to our lives, and, though no longer amongst the rites of religion, will, far from being considered hurtful to the religious sentiment, be seen to be a futherance therefore in the same manner as are painting, music, and all other branches of the joyous and beautiful.

**Mixing a Salad.**—This is a point of proficiency which it is easy to attain with care. The main point is, to incorporate the several articles required for the sauce, and to serve up at table as fresh as possible. The herbs should be " morning gathered," and they will be much refreshed by laying an hour or two in spring water. Careful picking, and washing, and drying in a cloth, in the kitchen, are also very important, and the due proportion of each herb requires attention. The sauce may be thus prepared :—Boil two eggs for ten or twelve minutes, and then put them in cold water for a few minutes, so that the yolks may become quite cold and hard. Rub them through a coarse sieve with a wooden spoon, and mix them with a tablespoonful of water or cream, and then add two tablespoonfuls of fine flask oil, or melted butter ; mix till smooth, when incorporate with the other ingredients about three tablespoonfuls of vinegar ; then pour this sauce down the side of the salad-bowl, but do not stir up the salad till wanted to be eaten. Gar-

nish the top of the salad with the white of the eggs cut in slices ; or these may be arranged in such manner as to be ornamental on the table. Some persons may fancy they are able to prepare a salad without previous instruction, but, like everything else, a little knowledge in this case may not be thrown away.

**Vegetables for a small Garden.**—what are the most profitable crops to be grown in a small garden ? The answer must be as follows :—*Broad Beans* should only be grown to a limited extent, and the main-crop varieties only sown. *French Beans* are the most valuable, because of the little space they require, and the great excellence of their produce, and also because they are not soon affected by the drought. *Scarlet Runners* must also be grown rather extensively, as they continue in bearing throughout the season, even in dry summers, if well supplied with water. *Beetroot*, if grown at all, should be cultivated in limited quantities, as it is by no means profitable. *Borecoles* are invaluable ; but *Borecolis* are too precarious, and *Brussels Sprouts* are hardy productive enough to be considered first-rate, although they cannot well be excluded. *Cabbage*, especially the small-growing sorts, is perhaps the most profitable crop that can be grown, as the stumps will, in ordinary seasons, yield a plentiful supply of tender greens after the hearts have been cut. Those who have been accustomed to the monster market cabbage will probably not hold this vegetable in very high esteem, and it is necessary to tell them that there is nearly as much difference between light and darkness as there is between a cabbage cut just as it begins to harden, and sent to table within two or three hours afterwards, and one that is allowed to remain until it shows signs of bursting, then subjected to a slight fermentation for a considerable period, and finished off with lying in a greengrocer's shop for two or three days. *Cauliflowers* are admissible in limited numbers. They can, no doubt, be grown cheaper than they can be purchased, but they are not profitable. *Carrots* for drawing young should be grown, and, where space can be spared, for storing also. *Celery*, unless stable manure is handy and abundant, should not be thought about. *Onions* for drawing during the summer, and a few for storing, will be valuable; but a summer crop only should be grown. *Turnips* take up too much room, and are not so profitable as many other things. Main crops of the best varieties of *Peas* only should be sown, as peas can be purchased so cheap at the time when the ordinary crops come in; therefore, it is a waste of space to grow any but the best marrowfats, which can only be purchased at a high price. *Early Potatoes* only that will come off in time to admit of the ground being planted with winter greens must be selected. A considerable space must be set apart for salading, as it is much better to be able to have *Lettuces*, *Radishes*, and *Cresses* fresh from the garden than to buy them after they have been lying about several days. In addition to the foregoing, a moderate quantity of *Endive* should be planted in August, to take the place of the lettuce in the autumn. Those who love *Spinach* may obtain abundant supplies with very little trouble from a small garden.

**Preserving Eggs.**—The following is an easy mode of keeping eggs in a perfectly edible condition for ten months. Have ready a square deal box, of the size you are likely to require; cover the bottom with a layer of sweet bran, about 3 inches thick; as the eggs are brought in from the fowl-house, wipe them carefully over with a piece of new flannel, well saturated with sweet oil; lay them carefully on the layer of bran, taking care that they do not touch each other; then add another layer of bran, and proceed as before. We are now using eggs which were so treated, and which were laid as long ago as the 4th of last June, and are perfectly good for all kitchen purposes.

**Excellent Ox-Tail Soup.**—Take a couple of ox-tails, and cut them into pieces at the joints; fry them in butter until they are quite brown; put them in a stewpan, with two or three quarts of clear gravy soup, together with some carrots and turnips, cut into fancy shapes with a vegetable cutter, also a few small onions (whole), and a head or two of celery sliced—(partly boil the vegetables first in a little stock). Simmer all together until the vegetables are perfectly boiled, skim off the butter as it rises, and your soup will be perfect. If thick ox-tail is preferred, stir in a thickening of arrowroot or rice flour—or thicken it with *roux*; flavour it strongly with spice, add a little port wine, and serve.

**New Remedy for the Tooth-ache.** —At a meeting of the Medical Society, Dr. Blake, a distinguished practitioner, said he was able to cure the most desperate case of tooth-ache, unless the disease was connected with rheumatism, by the application of the following remedy :— Two drachms of alum reduced to an impalpable powder. Mix, and apply to the tooth.

**Domestic Uses of Ammonia.**— Ammonia is nearly as useful in housekeeping as soap, and its cheapness brings it within the reach of all. For many household purposes it is invaluable; yet its manifold uses are not so generally known as they should be. It is a most refreshing agent at the toilet table; a few drops in a basin of water will make a better bath than pure water, and if the skin is oily, it will remove all glossiness and disagreeable odours. Added to the foot-bath, it entirely absorbs all noxious smells so often arising from the feet in warm weather, and nothing is better for cleansing the hair from dandruff and dust. For the headache it is also a desirable stimulant, and frequent inhaling of its pungent odours will often entirely remove catarrhal cold. For cleansing paint it is very useful. Put a teaspoonful of ammonia to a quart of warm soapsuds, dip in a flannel cloth, and wipe off the dust and fly-specks, grime and smoke, and see for yourselves how much labour it will save you; no scrubbing will be needful. It will cleanse and brighten wonderfully; to a pint of hot suds mix a teaspoonful of the spirits, dip in your silver spoons, forks, &c., rub with a brush, and then polish on chamois skin. For washing mirrors and windows, it is also very desirable ; put a few drops of ammonia upon a piece of newspaper, and you will readily take off every spot or finger-mark on the glass. It will take grease-spots from any fabric ; put on the ammonia nearly clear, lay blotting paper over the place, and press a hot flat iron on it for a few moments. A few drops in water will clean laces and whiten them finely, also muslins. For cleaning hair and nail brushes it is equally good. Put a teaspoonful of ammonia into one pint of warm or cold water and shake the brushes through the water ; when the bristles look white, rinse them in cold water, and put into the sunshine or in a warm place to dry. The dirtiest brushes will come out from this bath white and clean. There is no better remedy for heartburn and dyspepsia, and the aromatic spirit of ammonia is especially prepared for these troubles. Ten drops of it in a wineglass of water are often a great relief. The spirits of ammonia can be taken in the same way, but it is not as palatable a dose. Farmers and chemists are well aware of the beneficial effects of ammonia on all kinds of vegetation ; and if you desire your roses, geraniums, fuchsias, &c., to become more flourishing, you can try it upon them, by adding five or six drops of it to every pint of warm water that you give them ; but don't repeat it lest you stimulate them too highly. Rain-water is impregnated with ammonia, and thus it refreshes and vivifies vegetable life. So be sure and keep a large bottle of ammonia in the house, and have a glass stopper for it, as it is very evanescent, and also injurious to corks, eating them away.

**Corn-Flour Recipes.**—Corn-flour is carefully prepared from the best Galatz Maize, and has all the good properties of the real arrowroot, than which it is, however, more nutritious. For light dishes, puddings, blacmange, cakes, &c., suitable for children and invalids, it stands unrivalled, being wholesome and easy of digestion. Such of our readers as have not tried it should do so. We append for their guidance a few reliable recipes ;—

BLANCMANGE.—Take one quart of milk, and mix it with four ounces or four tablespoonfuls of the flour ; add a little salt, and flavour to taste ; then boil the whole for a few minutes, allow it to cool in a mould, and serve up with milk and jelly, or milk and sugar.

PUDDING.—Prepare as above, adding one or two eggs. To be eaten warm.

BAKED PUDDINGS.—Nearly four tablespoonfuls of the flour (or three and a half ounces), to one quart of milk ; add a little salt ; boil three minutes, stirring it briskly ; allow it to cool, and then thoroughly mix it with two eggs, well beaten with three tablespoonfuls of sugar ; flavour to taste, and bake for half an hour in an oven, or brown it before the fire.

CUSTARD.—One quart of milk, and mix it with three ounces of the flour : one or two eggs well beaten ; and a little butter and salt, and four tablespoonfuls of sugar. Flavour to taste, and boil three or four minutes, then pour it into a pie-dish, and brown it before the fire. This is an exquisite delicacy.

FRUIT PIE.—Bake or stew the fruit with sugar, put it into a pie-dish, then pour over it corn-flour, boiled with milk, in the proportion of four ounces of the flour to one quart of milk, then brown it before the fire or in the oven. This makes a covering lighter and more delicious than pie-crust.

OMELET.—Beat up two eggs, and with them one tablespoonful of the flour, and a teacupful of milk ; add a little pepper and salt, and sugar if preferred : throw the whole on a flat saucepan, previously well heated, and covered with melted butter ; keep the saucepan in motion over the fire, then turn it several times and roll it up, keeping it in motion till it is slightly browned.

SPONGE CAKE.—Half a pound of corn flour, quarter, or half pound of butter, and two teaspoonfuls of baking powder, to be very well mixed together. Take three eggs, and beat the yolks and whites separately for fifteen minutes, then add to them a quarter of a pound bruised white sugar ; mix all together, flavour to taste, and beat for fifteen minutes ; put it into a well-buttered tin, papered all round two inches deeper than the tin, and bake in a quick oven for one hour

It may also be used as arrow-root in every kind of preparation.

**Parlour Pastime.**—The following beautiful chemical experiment may be easily performed by a lady, to the great astonishment of a circle at her tea-table :—Take two or three leaves of red cabbage, cut them into small pieces, put them into a basin, and pour a pint of boiling water upon them ; let it stand an hour, then pour it off into a decanter. It will be a fine blue colour. Then take four wine-glasses ; into one put six drops of strong vinegar ; into another six drops of solution of soda ; into a third a strong solution of alum, and let the fourth remain empty. The glasses may be prepared some time before, and a few drops of colourless liquid that have been placed in them will not be noticed ; fill up the glasses from the decanter, and the liquid poured into the glass containing the acid will become a beautiful red ; the glass containing the soda will become a fine green ; that poured into the empty one will remain unchanged. By adding a little vinegar to the green it will immediately change to red, and on adding a little solution of soda to the red it will assume a fine green, thus showing the action of acids and alkalies on vegetable blues.

**Sick Headache.**—Much sick headache is caused by overloading the stomach—by indigestion. It may be relieved very much by drinking freely of warm water, whether it produces vomiting or not. If the feet are cold, warm them or bathe them in water as hot as you can bear it. Soda or ashes in the water will do good. If the pain is very severe, apply a cloth wrung out of hot water to the head—pack the head, as it were. To prevent it, let plainness, simplicity, and temperance preside at your table. In some cases medicine is necessary ; but if the above is properly carried out, almost immediate relief is experienced.

**Steaming Food.**—If ladies knew the superiority of steaming many articles of food over boiling them, they would be better supplied with conveniences for that purpose. Cooking can be done much quicker, and with less fuel, by steam, than in any other way. Apple dumplings are far superior when steamed, to boiled ones, which are apt to be heavy and water-soaked. Steam till done, then set in the oven a few minutes to dry the moisture. So it is with other puddings, custards, brown bread, vegetables, &c., and for cooking fruits, to preserve or put up in their own juice, it is an excellent way to steam till tender, before putting into syrup. In warm weather, a steamer is valuable indeed, for a very little fire will do.

**Warm Bed-Covering.**—When the nights are cold, and the bed-clothes insufficient, adopt the following very simple plan :—throw off one or two of the top covers from the bed, then get two or three large newspapers—one very large one will do—spread them on the bed, and replace the cover. The result will be a warm and comfortable night, without any perceptible increase in the weight of the bedding. Again, for a cold ride on boat, coach, or a long walk against the wind, spread a newspaper over your chest, and you will not become chilled through. Nothing can be cheaper, and nothing more efficient.

**Tea Cake.**—Rub into a quart of dried flour of the finest kind, a quarter of a pound of butter ; then beat up two eggs with two teaspoonfuls of sifted sugar, and two tablespoonfuls of washed yeast ; pour this liquid mixture into the centre of the flour, and add a pint of warm milk as you mix it ; beat it up with the hand until it comes off without sticking ; set it to rise before the fire, having covered it with a cloth ; after it has remained there an hour, make it up into good-sized cakes an inch thick ; set them in tin plates to rise before the fire for ten minutes, then bake them in a slow oven. These cakes may be split and buttered hot from the oven, or split, toasted, and buttered after they are cold.

**Sponge Biscuits.**—Beat the yolks of twelve eggs for half an hour ; then put in a pound and a half of beaten sifted sugar, and whisk it until it rises in bubbles ; beat the whites to a strong froth, and whisk them well with the sugar and yolks ; work in about fourteen ounces of flour, with the grated rinds of two lemons. Bake them in tin moulds buttered, in a quick oven for an hour ; before they are baked, sift a little fine sugar over them.

**Icing for Cake.**—Beat the white of one egg perfectly light—then add eight teaspoonfuls of loaf sugar, pounded fine and sifted, very gradually, beating it well ; after every spoonful, add one drop of the essence of lemon or rose-water to flavour it. If you wish to colour it pink, stir in a few grains of cochineal powder or rose pink ; if you wish it blue, add a little of what is called powder-blue. Lay the frosting on the cake with a knife, soon after it is taken from the oven ; smooth it over, and let it remain in a cool place till hard. To frost a common-sized half of cake, allow the white of one egg and half of another.

**Crystallised Baskets.**—A pleasant reminiscence of summer may be retained by the manufacture of crystallised flower-baskets. The process is very simple, and can be accomplished by any lady of taste. Construct some baskets of fancy form with pliable copper-wire, and wrap them with gauze. Into these tie to the bottom violets, ferns, geranium leaves—in fact, any flowers except full-blown roses—and sink them in a solution of alum, of one pound to a gallon of water, after the solution has cooled. The colours will then be preserved in their original beauty, and the crystallised alum will hold faster than when from a hot solution. When you have a light covering of crystals that completely covers the articles, remove the basket carefully and allow it to drip for twelve hours. These baskets make a beautiful parlour ornament, and for a long time preserve the freshness of the flowers.

**The Opal.**—This gem comes from Hungary and Mexico. The Hungarian opals are much the superior, and have not the disadvantage of deteriorating with time. For the perfection of an opal, it should exhibit all the colours of the solar spectrum, disposed in small spaces, neither too large nor too small, and with no colour predominating. The opal is sometimes called the *harlequin*, in allusion to the great variety of colours which it displays. The substance of the opal is of a milky hue, and of a pale greenish tint. The milkiness is generally known by the term opalescence. It is the colour of water in which a little soap has been dissolved. In order to explain the brilliant colours of the opal, we may imagine in the stone a great number of isolated fissures, of variable width, but always very narrow. Each fissure, according to its width, gives a peculiar tint similar to the effect produced by pressing two plates of glass together ; we may recognise violet, blue, indigo, red, yellow and green, the last two being exhibited more rarely than the others.

As a proof that the brilliant colours of the opal are due to narrow fissures, similar colours may be produced by partially fracturing, with the blow of a hammer or a mallet, a cube of glass or even a rock crystal. Colours obtained in this way are of the same character as those of flowers, which result from the overlaying of the transparent tissues of which the petals are composed. Herein lies the secret of all their final decay.

Sometimes the opal is coloured only in its substance, and has not so great a play of lights as when it is variously traversed by fissures, and then it is not so much esteemed. The opal is not a very hard stone. In its chemical composition it is only quartz combined with water. Heat, expanding its fissures, varies its colours, and pressure obviously produces the same effect. M. Babinet states that he thus often changed, without permanent alteration, the colours of a beautiful Hungarian harlequin opal. The opal of the Roman senator, Nonius, of the size of a hazel-nut, which he selected from among all his treasures as the companion of his exile, was estimated at about 160,000 pounds. This gem has appropriately been called the " Koh-i-noor of Rome."

**Patchouly.**—It is well known that the real Indian shawls possessed a peculiar and agreeable odour, which was new to European noses as the shawls were to European eyes. This odour pertinaciously clung to the fabric, and a genuine " India" unfailingly advertised it as such by its perfume. The cause of this odour was fully inquired into, and it was found to be given to the shawls by contact with an herb known to the Hindoos as putcha, pat or patchouly, as it is more commonly called. Importation of the dried herb, as an aid to the shawl-maker's enterprise, naturally followed, and this led to its introduction as a perfume.

**Egg Sauce for Fish.**—Boil one or two eggs quite hard. When cold (which you may hasten by throwing them into cold water), chop them quite fine, yolks and whites together. Taste the liquor in which your salt fish and parsnips have been boiled. If not too briny, take some of this, and, with the addition of a little water or milk, make good melted butter with flour and butter. When smooth, throw in your chopped-up eggs, give it one boil up, and transfer it to your sauce-boat.

**Irish Method of Boiling Potatoes.** —In Ireland potatoes are boiled in perfection ; the humblest peasant places his potatoes on his table better cooked than could half the cooks in this country by trying their best. Potatoes shou'd always be boiled in their " jackets ;" peeling a potato before boiling is offering a premium for water to run through it, and go to table waxy and unpalatable. They should be thoroughly washed, and put into cold water. In Ireland they always nick a piece of the skin off before they place them in the pot ; the water is gradually heated, but never allowed to boil ; cold water should be added as soon as the water in the pot commences boiling, and it should thus be checked until the potatoes are done, the skins will not then be broken or cracked, until the potato is thoroughly done ; pour the water off completely, uncover the pot, and let the skins be thoroughly dry before peeling.

**To Extract Marking Ink.**—The following process will be found easy and effectual :—Take the piece of marked linen, and immerse it in a solution of chloride of lime, when in a few minutes the characters will pass from black to white, owing to a new preparation of silver being formed, namely, white chloride of silver, which still remains in the fabric, but owing to its solubility in solution of ammonia, it may be entirely extracted by immersion in that liquid immediately it is removed out of the first, and allowing it to remain in it for a few minutes ; after this it only requires to be well rinsed in clean water, which completes the process.

**Liquid Glue.**—An excellent liquid glue is made by dissolving glue in nitric ether. The ether will only dissolve a certain amount of the glue, consequently the solution cannot be made too thick. The glue thus made is about the consistence of treacle, and is doubly as tenacious as that made with hot water. If a few bits of India-rubber, cut into scraps, be added, and the solution allowed to stand a few days, being stirred frequently, it will be all the better, and will resist damp twice as well as glue made with water.

**Sacredness of Marriage.**—For the man and woman who truly and purely love each other, and are guided by the law of justice, marriage is not a state of bondage. Indeed, it is only when they become, by this outward acknowledgment, publicly avowed lovers, that freedom is realised by them in its full significance. Thereafter, they can be openly devoted to each other's interests, and avowedly chosen and intimate associates and friends. Together they can plan life's battles, and enter upon the path of progress that ends not with life's eventide. Together they can seek the charmed avenues of culture, and, strengthened by each other, can brave the world's frown in the rugged but heaven-lit path of reform. Home, with all that is dearest in the sacred name, is their peaceful and cherished retreat, within whose sanctuary bloom the virtues that make it a temple of beneficence.

**Sweet Words.**—Five of the sweetest words in the English language begin with H, which is only a breath : Heart, Hope, Home, Happiness, and Heaven. Heart is a hope-place, and home is a heart-place, and that man or woman sadly mistaketh who would exchange the happiness of home for anything less than heaven.

**Female Society.**—What is it that makes all those men who associate habitually with women superior to those who do not ? What makes the women who are accustomed to, and at ease in, the society of men, superior to their sex in general ? Solely because they are in the habit of free, graceful, continued conversation with the other sex. Women in this way lose their frivolity, their faculties awaken, their delicacies and peculiarities unfold all their beauty and captivation in the spirit of rivalry. And the men lose their pedantic, rude, declamatory, or sullen manner. The coin of the understanding and the heart changes continually. Their asperities are rubbed off, their natures polished and brightened, and their richness, like gold, is wrought into finer workmanship by the fingers of women, than it could ever be done by those of men.

**Cement for Wood.**—A very superior cement for joining wood may be made by soaking isinglass or gelatine in water until it swells. The water should then be drained off, and spirit poured on it, and the vessel placed in a pan of hot water until the isinglass is dissolved. This cement must then be kept in a well-stoppered bottle.

**Bed Sores.**—Many ladies would be shocked, perhaps, to learn that scores of people die, when long confined to bed, not of the disease or accident, but of sores caused by neglect ; and in numbers of cases neither patient nor nurse has any idea of what is going on. Particularly in acute fevers, the patient's mind is not in a state to complain of a slight pain, therefore they must be sought for by the nurse, and prevented. They generally form about the bottom of the back, and about the hips. The constant pressure of the body causes a slight redness at first, and if attended to then the mischief may be stopped ; but if allowed to go on the part dies, and leaves a sore which too frequently takes away all chance of recovery. Examine carefully every day, bathe the parts with spirits and water, and take off the pressure, first by altering the position, if possible, and secondly, by making little pillows or pads, and placing them so as to bear the weight. Unless you can do this, all treatment you can adopt will be of no avail.

**Widowhood.**—A great vicissitude in a woman's circumstances and situation not unfrequently occurs upon the death of her husband ; and in the higher rank of society this is often peculiarly severe. A widow thus placed has much need for fortitude ; and even those of an inferior rank have their trials and difficulties to support with dignity and composure.

During her temporary seclusion from general society, a widow can hardly employ her time more wisely, than in forming her plans, and arranging her future establishment and mode of living. In doing this she would do well to lay her intentions and wishes before those whom her husband has appointed, with herself, his executors, and the guardians to his children.

It often happens, however, that a widow and her co-executors are at variance ; she, tenacious of her power, jealous of their interference, and suspicious of their negligence in promoting her interests or those of her family ; while they, perhaps, are irritated and troubled by her ignorance in matters of business, and made angry by want of friendly confidence in their intentions.

When a widow is satisfied as to the integrity and prudence of her co-executors, she will only be doing them justice if she confide all matters of business to them. A prudent woman cannot be blind to the advantages which may accrue to her children, from the unanimity she preserves with their other guardians.

When time has healed the wound which her husband's death has inflicted, and when the season has elapsed which decorum has appointed for retirement from public amusements, and from circles of gaiety (supposed to be incompatible with the state of feeling of one recently bereft of the most intimate of human ties), the widow will probably be again seen in the world, and will again mix in her usual societies. She should, now, bear in mind, that, from the circumstance of her being left entirely to her own conduct, many eyes will be upon her ; and, from various motives, many will curiously examine into the circumspection and prudence of her conduct. If the breath of slander ought not to reach her as a wife, it is even more essential to her, that as a widow it should be completely suppressed. She has no longer a protector to shelter her when reproached, nor to sanction with his approbation her future steps. She has to screen the name she bears from the very shadow of disrepute, because, besides belonging to her children, he who owned it and bestowed it upon her can no longer defend and rescue it from calumny and disgrace.

A widowed mother is liable to fall into the error of over-indulgence of her children. To guard against this maternal weakness should be more than ever her earnest aim, since paternal firmness is no longer at hand to counteract its injurious effects  Without regard to puerile wishes for relaxation, she should steadily persevere in the plan of education which she has formed for her children, preserving, with conscientious care, the precious years of their youth from waste and neglect. Thus, the widow who strives to fulfil every obligation to her children has no sinecure ; but, with Heaven's blessing on her endeavours, she will have her day of compensation ; her success will be honoured in the world, and affectionately and dutifully acknowledged by her children, who, with one voice, " will rise up and call her blessed."

**The Monthly Nurse, and her Duties.**—In respect of age, a monthly nurse should not exceed fifty, but it is still better if she be between thirty-five and forty. She should possess bodily strength sufficient to enable her to lift her charge with ease ; she should be a light sleeper, or rather capable of doing with very little sleep ; and as this would be incompatible with the habits of a glutton, or of one fond of ale and porter, we will suppose that she is free from any inclination towards intemperance. She should be gentle, tender, kind and tolerably lively in her manner, and should have great command over her temper, and have so much self-possession, that, under any circumstances, even the most alarming that can occur, she should be able to maintain a cool and collected manner. Above all things she should not be addicted to quackery, nor should she ever presume to prescribe medically either for the mother or the child.

A nurse should be taught the art of emptying the mother's breast by suction when the infant is weakly, and the supply of milk great ; for, then, the breast becomes turgid, and the efforts of the infant are insufficient to draw it, until it has been previously relieved, either by suction or some other means. It is a better plan to have the breasts drawn by the mouth than by any of the various contrivances which are invented for that purpose. Sore nipples, which are so painful, and so disappointing to the young mother, who is generally desirous of fulfilling every part of her maternal duty, are the consequence of this turgidity, which excites inflammation. When, however, the nipple becomes sore, the shield is the best remedy, and a nurse should know how to render this little instrument serviceable, for unless it be properly applied the intention for which it is used will be defeated. All salves and washes are useless without the aid of the shield.

Some ladies, who have never suffered from sore nipples, have attributed their escape to the habit, which they had adopted some weeks previous to their confinement, of washing the nipples with weak brandy and water.

A nurse should not be of an avaricious disposition, otherwise to visit the lying-in room is quite a disgraceful tax upon the friends of the lady. The terms upon which the nurse attends for the month should be settled at the time she is first engaged ; and every lady who has any feelings of delicacy, will explain to her, that she is to expect nothing beyond her just pay ; and that any expectation of receiving money from visitors must be abandoned.

As the moment of confinement approaches everything should be in readiness, so that no hurry or bustle occur. One friend, who possesses some considerable degree of fortitude, the nurse, and the doctor, are the only persons who should be admitted into the room during the labour. Whatever conversation is permitted—the less the better —should be of a cheerful and encouraging description ; all depressing passions, want of confidence in the medical attendant, and alarm of any description, inasmuch as they weaken the powers of the animal economy, and protract the sufferings of labour, also tend to interrupt the natural steps of the process, and cause difficulties which would not otherwise happen. Every female should be previously informed, that, unless some unforeseen difficulty present itself, the child may be born without manual assistance : and, therefore, the less the

doctor interferes, or appears to aid her efforts, the more his skill is to be depended upon.

When the child is born, and the mother is, therefore, in some degree relieved from her state of suffering, she should be restrained from any lively expressions of joy, for they would be dangerous to her at the time in which so much of her strength is exhausted. Many of the fatal occurrences in childbed have been attributed to the want of this precaution. Rest, and, if possible, sleep, should be obtained for two or three hours before the young mother be laid comfortably in bed after delivery. After this has been done, the infant should be brought to her, and then should be applied to the fountain of its natural and only proper food. When medicine is required, the doctor will order it, but on no account should the nurse be allowed to administer it without his orders.

It is a very common practice with monthly nurses to keep an infant from its mother's milk for two or three days after its birth ; this is equally bad for the parent and child. The first milk which the child draws acts as a purgative upon it, whilst its sucking keeps the breast soft and pliable, and brings the milk into the proper channel. For these reasons the infant should be put to the breast three or four hours after its birth, and this should be repeated as often as the mother's strength will permit it. If a lady is to suckle her infant, the sooner it is applied to the breast the less chance there is of the nipples becoming sore ; but in some constitutions this will occur in spite of every precaution, and when it does, the child should be kept from the breast until the milk has been nearly carried off by purgatives and low diet ; then the child being again placed at the breast causes a return of the milk, while the breast and the nipple remain cool. Until the infant can be applied to the mother's breast, its aptitude for sucking should be kept up by placing it at the breast of a temporary wet nurse.

If the strength of the new-made mother permit, after the end of six or seven days she may be removed for an hour or two into another room, provided it be not very remote from her own, and that it be brought to a similar temperature. During the time she is absent from her own room, the nurse should see that it be thoroughly ventilated. This change of air will assist to strengthen the mother ; but there is usually a prejudice, almost unconquerable, in monthly nurses, that ladies should not change their rooms for the first fortnight or three weeks of their confinement, which system has often so weakening an effect, that, at the end of a month, a lady is sometimes as weak and reduced as if she had had a serious illness.

At the end of the month, or even before that time, if the weather and other circumstances permit, gentle exercise is very desirable for the lying-in lady, and particularly if she suckle her baby ; because, whatever tends to give her health and strength, will render her better able to perform that important duty.

**Washing Infants.**—This is a chief duty for mothers or nurses. The experience of the latter enables them to dress and wash an infant with more facility, and with greater gentleness, than others ; but their prejudices are often unconquerable in favour of ignorant and vulgar practices, by which an infant may be tormented, if not seriously inconvenienced ; therefore the young mother should learn what is right to be done, and then be prepared to oppose firmly any contrary modes which her nurse may suggest.

In washing an infant during the month, the water should be tepid, for water either too hot or too cold is alike injurious. The whole body of the infant, with the exception of the head, should be immersed in the water when it is washed. If a nurse be so ignorant as not to know what will take off the white mucous matter which occasionally adheres to the skin of a newly-born infant, the mother should be able to inform her that it is most readily loosened by rubbing the part over with lard or fresh butter, after which a little soap will remove the whole. The same plan is recommended to be pursued again if the skin of the infant does not appear to be thoroughly cleansed after the first washing. Afterwards it is not necessary to wash an infant more than once a day, except locally, as circumstances point out.

The nurse should, in the morning, have in readiness a basin of tepid water, a very soft sponge, and a fine soft towel. On her right hand should stand her basket, in which should be laid her dust bag, containing powdered starch, a clean flannel band, and, in proper order beneath, all the other articles she will require in dressing the baby. The nurse herself should wear a flannel apron, upon which she should lay the child while gently extricating him from the clothes which are about to be changed. The head, face, and throat, are then to be washed with the sponge, and to be dried with a soft linen towel. Remember how very delicate and tender the skin of an infant is, and do not suffer it to be rubbed but in the most gentle manner ; indeed, an infant should rather be gently pressed than rubbed with the towel, and particularly under the joints ; the hands, arms, and thighs should next be washed, and when perfectly dry, the starch powder may be used in those parts which appear at all tender or likely to become chafed ; but unless this be the case, it is better to use no powder of any kind. Drying the skin well, when it has been wetted, is the best mode to prevent soreness. The infant should not be kept longer undressed than can be avoided ; but if it do not appear to be chilled, the nurse may gently rub its back, head, and limbs with her hand, until there is a general appearance of circulation. As soon as the clothes have been put on, the nurse should dip the end of a soft piece of cambric into warm water, and cleanse the tongue with it. Some nurses employ sugar and water for this purpose ; but unless there be any disease in the mouth, plain water is the best ; and the friction on the tongue should be so gentle as not to occasion the infant to cry out.

When there is hair on the head of an infant, great care should be taken to dry it well after washing ; for, to put a cap on with the hair damp, would be to incur the danger of cold and inflammation in the eyes, or of ear-ache and deafness. A careful nurse will endeavour to guard the organs of sense from any injury, such as exposing the eyes to a strong glare of light, or the ears uncovered to currents of air.

**Nursing an Infant.**—An infant should not be nursed in an upright position for the first two months of its life. It is painful to see the bent back and weak neck of a young child compelled to support a weight to which it is rarely equal. Some ladies, however, err in the other extreme, and, by keeping their infants too long in a reclining position, have prevented that gradual supply of strength which might have been acquired by a gentle and timely use of the muscles and bones of the back and neck ; and when infants have been brought to this state, it has been difficult to ascertain whether it had been caused by the disuse of the parts, or was the effect of disease. An infant should rarely be taken out of doors for the first month of its life, unless the weather be peculiarly favourable. The extremes of heat or of cold are alike injurious to it, and damp weather is peculiarly so.

An infant should never be left to sleep alone. Frightful accidents have occurred from negligence in this respect ; and, indeed, for the first few days of its life, an infant should not be in its bed for half an hour at a time without being looked at ; for, if it should chance to roll on its face, it has no power to turn itself again, and were it left for any length of time in this situation, with its face against the blanket or pillow, it would be in great danger of being smo-

thered. Infants are also liable to return from their stomachs any surplus of milk they have received ; and when this occurs while they are sleeping, they should be gently lifted up, so that what they vomit may be entirely emptied from the mouth.

The cry of an infant ought never to be disregarded, as it is Nature's voice, which speaks of some pain or suffering. Cries, however, are of different kinds : for example, that of hunger may be known ; it is short and wrangling ; but when the cry is a continued one, and the legs are drawn up, there must be pain. In such a case as this, the breast must not be administered until the pain be removed. Warm bathing, gentle friction on the bowels, examination of the clothes to ascertain whether any ligature is drawn too tight, should be first tried, and if the infant still appear to be in pain, a gentle aperient medicine, or an injection, should be administered. Powerful medicines should be given only by the advice of the medical attendant.

**To Secure Photographs in Albums.**—From starch is made a preparation known as dextrine ; it is in the form of a powder, and this made into a rather stiff paste with cold water, is the best material for fixing photographs in albums. Keep the dextrine very clean, and proceed as follows : cover the whole back part of the photograph lightly with the paste, then place it on the page of the album, with a sheet of white blotting paper on the other side of the album page. Then gently smooth over the face of the picture with a handkerchief. Thick starch will also answer the purpose.

**Seasonings for Soups.**—Spices always should be put in whole into soups. Allspice is one of the best, though it is not so highly esteemed as it deserves. Seville-orange juice has a finer acid than lemon-juice, but both should be used with caution. Sweet herbs for soups or broths consist of knotted marjoram, thyme and parsley—a sprig of each tied together. The older and drier onions

DESIGN FOR A CHURCH WINDOW IN VITREMANIE. See page 115.

DESIGN FOR A STAIRCASE WINDOW IN VITREMANIE.

are, the stronger their flavour ; in dry seasons also they are very strong ; the quantity should be proportioned accordingly Although celery may generally be obtained for soup throughout the year, it may be useful to know that dried celery-seed is an excellent substitute. It is so strongly flavoured that a drachm of whole seed will enrich half a gallon of soup as much as will two heads of celery. Mushrooms are much used, and when they cannot be obtained fresh, mushroom ketchup will answer the purpose ; but it should be used very sparingly, as nothing is more difficult to remove than an over-flavouring of ketchup. A piece of butter in proportion to the liquid, mixed with flour, and added to the soup, when boiling, will enrich and thicken it. The finer flavouring articles, as ketchup, spices, wines, juice, &c , should not be added till the soup is nearly done. Wine should be added late in the making, as it evaporates quickly in boiling. A teaspoonful of sugar is a good addition in flavouring soups.

Pea-Fowl.—This gorgeous bird is a native of India, being found in great numbers in the extensive plains of that country, in the neighbourhood of the ganges, and in the kingdom of Siam. It has long been naturalised in Europe, but in the country it is now kept more for ornament than use. The male bird —the well-known peacock—is one of the most beautiful of the feathered creation. It is elegantly shaped, its length, from the tip of the bill to that of the tail, being about four feet. The head, neck, and breast are of a brilliant blue, shaded with gold ; the back and upper part of the wings are bright ash, mixed with black stripes ; the ground of the feathers of its splendid fan-like train is black ; but they are studded with what are popularly called "eyes ;" lovely spots, of a round form, diversified with the most attractive colours, and sparkling with the radiance of the brightest gems. The neck and head are gracefully formed ; and from the crown springs a tuft of twenty-four feathers, which have long slender shafts, terminating in a web of the most exquisite green edged with gold. The tail consists of eighteen feathers, of a grey-brown colour, and assists in supporting the train, when it is expanded, and assumes its fan-like form. The pea-hen is rather smaller than the male bird, and her colour is more subdued and homely. The legs of both male and female are of a grey-brown. That of the former displays a strong spur, and the feet are clumsy, at striking variance with the grace and elegance of his general form. The voice is also harsh and dissonant.

Management of the Pea-Fowl.— It would be idle to think of domesticating these birds in the ordinary poultry-house or yard. Their habits are of the most rambling description, and they cannot be confined to one spot, though they may be so accustomed to it that they will make it their home, to which they will constantly return.

They are very destructive birds in gardens ; therefore, they should never be kept, except where there are extensive lawns or parks and shrubberies for them to disport in. They require no shelter at night, for they love to roost on trees, frequenting the very highest branches ; and when they cannot find a tree, they will perch upon a hay-stack or the roof of a house.

After they have passed what may be called the age of infancy, they require very little food, providing chiefly for themselves ; but where you wish to attach them to yourself, and to train them to come back to a particular locality, you must feed and pet them, giving them the same food as turkeys. By feeding and kindness, he will come for his meal as punctually as a human being. They know the voice of their keeper. If she calls them, they will come to her, and eat out of her hand. The hen is more timid than the male, and cannot be brought to show such confidence in her keeper.

They do not pair. The peacock requires four or five hens, who generally make their nests on the bare ground, amongst nettles or loose weeds ; it is often placed under the shading boughs of the fir-tree, and consists merely of a few sticks and twigs, put together with dried leaves. She lays from five to six, or ten eggs. She is partial to sitting, and goes through the duties of incubation with great assiduity. She sits from twenty-seven to twenty-nine days, and begins about her third summer. She endeavours to conceal her nest from the knowledge of the male, as he will destroy the eggs.

If the eggs are taken away she lays a second time during the summer. They are sometimes taken from the nest, and kept as you keep those of the fowl or turkey, till the time for hatching, and then placed under a common hen, or a turkey-hen—the latter proving the best foster-mother. Thus you can have two broods in one year.

The peacock, both in its natural and domestic state, destroys numerous insects which would be very destructive ; and they will keep a place clear of frogs, lizards, and similar reptiles. If they are killed, when poults, about nine months old, they make an excellent dish. The old birds, when they are getting to maturity, are not wholesome food. But they are excellent food at a much more advanced age than the nine months.

They should be well fed, but not put up to fatten ; be killed at any period except the moulting season, and then hung in the larder some time before cooking. They live eighteen or twenty years.

**Hints for Wives.**—Don't imagine when you have obtained a husband, that your attention to personal neatness and deportment may be relaxed. Now, in reality, is the time for you to exhibit superior taste and excellence in the cultivation of your address, and the becoming elegance of your appearance. If it required some little care to foster the admiration of a lover, how much more is requisite to keep yourself lovely in the eyes of him to whom there is now no privacy or disguise—your hourly companion ? And if it was due to your lover that you should always present to him, who proposed to wed and cherish you, a neat and ladylike aspect, how much more is he entitled to a similar mark of respect who has kept his promise with honourable fidelity, and linked all his hopes of future happiness with yours ? If you can manage these matters without appearing to study them, so much the better. Some husbands are impatient of the routine of the toilette, and not unreasonably so ; they possess active and energetic spirits, sorely disturbed by any waste of time. Some wives have discovered an admirable facility in dealing with this difficulty, and it is a secret which, having been discovered by some, may be known to all, and is well worth the finding out.

**Asparagus for the Lungs.**—The frequent use of asparagus is strongly recommended in affections of the lungs and chest ; in fact, asparagus is one of the most wholesome as well as agreeable vegetables we possess.

**American Remedy for Diarrhœa.** —Take one teaspoonful of salt, the same of good vinegar, and a tablespoonful of water ; mix and drink. It is said to act like a charm on the system, and even one dose will generally cure obstinate cases of diarrhœa or the first stages of cholera. If the first dose does not bring complete relief, repeat the dose, as it is quite harmless. The patient should keep perfectly quiet, a reclining posture being the best. In severe cases soak the feet thoroughly in very warm water, chafing them well. Flannel wet with pretty warm vinegar and salt (especially in warm weather) and placed around the loins, wrapping warm flannel over it, is an excellent aid to recovery. Any and everybody can apply these remedies without a physician, running no risk, and will be astonished at the beneficial result.

**An Excellent Tonic.**—Hops, six ounces, boiling water, one pint ; soak for four hours. Dose, half a wine-glassful.

**On Furnishing.**—The great point in furnishing is to study well the aspect, the general style of the house, and to make all our efforts harmonise with it : for incongruity is a great offence against good taste. There is a fitness in things which should never be lost sight of, if we desire success. We know of an instance where, in an old-fashioned house, abounding in mullioned windows which run high up into the ceiling, the present possessor has hung all the rooms with Chinese papers, and fitted them up with light-coloured ultra-modern furniture, as inconsistently as if you were to decorate Westminster Abbey like the Italian Opera House. It would not be difficult to multiply instances where furniture has been transplanted from one house to another without the smallest reference to its appropriateness. Our theory is that no one thing should catch the eye. There should be harmony throughout : and we recommend that great attention be paid to the colour of the walls. If they, the ceiling, and the carpet, are well selected, all other points of detail are like the finishing touches of a picture. The right tone having been attained, the rest is comparatively easy. We have found greys, light greens, and pale mauve, to work up well ; and the less pattern there is in the paper the better, unless, for some special reason, a chintz paper is desired. If the room faces the south, a cool grey or mauve is good ; and for a north room we have seen a yellowish green answer admirably, imparting to the room an appearance of sunshine. As a rule, we have found it best to avoid reds, especially dark reds, which are offensively dingy. Blue is a dangerous colour to use ; it is so apt either to make a room gaudy or cold ; though we have seen it effectually used with pink to give it a Pompadour look. For carpets we incline to small inoffensive patterns, and generally avoid those which are flowery, as being in theory and effect bad.

**Female Occupation.**—Women in the middle rank are brought up with the idea that if they engage in some occupations they shall lose their position in society. Suppose it to be so ; surely it is wiser to quit a position we cannot honestly maintain than to live dependent upon the bounty and caprice of others ; better to labour with our hands than to eat the bread of idleness : or submit to feel that we must not give utterance to our real opinions, or express our honest indignation at being required to act a base or unworthy part. And in all cases, however situated, every female ought to learn how all household affairs are managed, were it only for the purpose of being able to direct others. There cannot be any disgrace in learning how to make the bread we eat, to cook our dinners, to mend our clothes, or even to clean the house. Better to be found busily engaged in removing the dust from the furniture than to let it accumulate there until a visitor leaves palpable traces where his hat or his arm have been laid upon a table.

**To Manage a Husband.**—"Husbands in the main are very harmless animals if properly managed," remarks Fanny Fern. "There is, perhaps, no animal in existence that requires so much skill and tact in the management as a husband ; for these lords of creation become quite obstreperous and unmanageable as soon as they begin to suspect any design to control them. They have a particular aversion to the sway of woman—that is, when it becomes apparent. Intimate, for instance, that they are under woman's control, and they will bristle up indignantly, as though it were an insult to their manhood. They are docile enough so long as there is no appearance of control, but once show them the reins of government and they will resist you with all the obstinacy of their nature. The woman who would live in harmony with her spouse must study his nature and disposition. She must not cross his temper, nor assume authority, and presume to dictate, for there is nothing so exasperates the spirit of a man *that is a man* as any attempt to trespass upon his prerogative. She must gracefully concede his lordship, and pay it all due respect and reverence ; then, if she possess the magnet of his affections, she may lead him whichsoever way she wills. Woman's power lies in her affections ; and love, when judiciously exercised, the husband cannot resist—except, perchance, he partake of the nature of a bear, and is as impervious to the influence of the tender passion. Another chief requisite in the management of a husband is a genial, cheerful nature ; for, if we have not sunshine in his home, he will be a gloomy fellow—cross and surly beyond endurance. In order to make him a pleasing object of contemplation, or companionship, he must be kept in good humour by the enlivening influence of a cheerful home. His physical wants must also be studied. One of the best receipts for a good-natured husband is digestible food ; sour nature is oftentimes the result of bad digestion. Keep the digestive apparatus in a healthy condition, and you may be pretty sure of a pleasant face and a kindly greeting. Give a man a miserable breakfast, and you will be quite sure to have a miserable companion for the day. It is most astonishing how much cheer there is in a good cup of coffee and a nice bit of toast ! A man may live on love for a long time, but he soon finds it rather an insipid article of diet, if not combined with something more substantial. Depend upon it, wholesome food and a well ordered house lie at the foundation of domestic felicity. Show me the man that can be ill-natured when he comes home to a cheerful fireside, where the smiling wife awaits his arrival with a comfortable dinner, and I will show you a genuine specimen of a bear. Another hint I would suggest to wives is, that they look well to the condition of their husbands' shirt buttons. No man can keep his temper over a buttonless shirt ; he can bear the loss of a fortune with better grace than the loss of a shirt button. Men cannot bear petty vexations and inconveniences ; they have not patience and endurance ; therefore I would counsel all wedded ladies who would live in comfort with their liege lords, to avoid unnecessary occasions of irritation and dissatisfaction.''

**Character and Treatment of Pulmonary Consumption.**—Dr. Searle, in his excellent book, " The Blood in its Relations to Life, Health, and Disease," describes Consumption as a " disease specific in character, dependent upon some general cause of derangement of the nutritive and healthy condition of the system. A disease, connected with some depraved or altered condition of the blood, in relation to its elements derived from without," thus described, " as food, air, or beverage, or of defect in their assimilation ; or in the purification and secretive, or in the nutritive processes of the system—whereby there ensues a deposition from the blood of small granular albuminous bodies in the substance of the lungs ; though not in the lungs exclusively, the same granular bodies or tubercles, as they are called, being not unfrequently deposited in the peritoneum and bowels also, and often conjointly so with the lungs. Scrofula is a disease of a similar character, affecting more particularly the absorbent glands, and occasioning a deposition in their substance, with enlargement and subsequent inflammation and abscess in those parts. These tubercles often exist in the lungs without occasioning any very sensible inconvenience ; but the lungs so affected, under the influence of cold, become more amenable to inflammation ; and under a low and insidious form of it these tubercles increase in size, and then, compressing and occupying the space of the air-tubes, become a permanent source of irritation to these tubes, and of extended inflammation : hence cough, expectoration, febrile commotion, &c., ensue. The tubercles increasing in size, and the parts surrounding them being involved in one common inflammation, they coalesce, and either in distinct clusters, or severally, soften, and become the seat of abscess ; the contents of which communicating with the air-tubes, are now in part expectorated; a portion being also absorbed into the blood, and thus contaminating the vital stream—hectic fever, diarrhœa, and numerous secondary derangements follow; from the exhaustion of which, and the destruction of the organisation, death necessarily closes the scene.

"I have detailed thus much, with a view of showing that there can be no specific remedy for this disease—which, like scrofula, is an affection of the general system, and that all treatment must bear reference to the stage of affection. In the early stages it must be sought in the causes which gave rise to the tubercles; attention must not be directed alone to the relief of the cough, and the symptoms of inflammatory irritation, but to the condition, so to speak, of the blood, or the depravation that may exist, of whatever kind, of the assimilative and nutritive processes, and of the general health and strength of the system. Strict attention to diet, air, exercise, warmth, clothing, and the like expedients of renovation, are evidently the remedies. And seeing that these bodies (the existence of which may be determined by auscultation and percussion of the chest—that is to say, tapping the outside, and noticing the sound imparted of vacuity or consolidation, and of the air's murmur within) are soluble in an alkali, as Dr. Campbell proved by experiment; an alkali may very probably be taken with advantage, as he has recommended. And an occasional vapour-bath, or rather the lamp-bath, may be employed to secure a more active state of the functions of the skin, and prevent at the same time the development of inflammation. Sponging the chest every morning with salt water, and the daily use of the flesh brush, are also useful expedients, and it is now a well-authenticated fact, that cod-liver oil has often proved itself to be a most valuable auxiliary.

"A young lady, the subject it was said of consumption, having been sent to an hydropathic establishment, the lamp-bath for half an hour, followed by the wet sheet, was prescribed for her daily use; from which she experienced such sensible relief, that unknown to her professional adviser, she was induced to take two baths every day, and so great was the benefit that in less than six months she had not only got rid of all her ailment, but had become quite strong and stout."

**Shoulder of Mutton Boned.**—The joint to be operated on should not be too fat; remove the bone as far as the first joint from the knuckle, sprinkling the incision with pepper and salt. Make a stuffing the same as for veal, with half a pound of bread-crumbs, four ounces beef suet chopped fine, a little onion minced, salt and pepper, also a little grated nutmeg, and one egg; place the stuffing into the incision, fold over the meat into its former place, and tie it up tightly with string. Shoulder of mutton done in this way may be roasted, but should properly be braised—that is, first fried of a golden colour in oil or clarified butter, and then put into a stewpan with a pint and a half of stock, and any trimming of vegetables at hand; four or five cloves, six peppercorns, salt, thyme, parsley, and bay-leaf. Leave it to boil gently for two hours, strain off the stock, remove the fat, let it reduce on the fire until it becomes like glaze, pour over the mutton, and serve.

**To take Impressions of Leaves and Plants.**—Take half a sheet of fine wove paper and oil it well with sweet oil; after it has stood a minute or two, to let it soak through, rub off the superfluous oil with a piece of paper, and let it hang in the air to dry; after the oil is pretty well dried in, take a lighted candle and move the paper over it, in a horizontal direction, so as to touch the flame, till it is perfectly black. When you wish to take off any impressions of plants, lay your plant carefully on the oiled paper, lay a clean piece of paper over it, and rub it with your finger equally in all parts for half a minute, then take up your plant and be careful not to disturb the order of the leaves, and place it on the paper on which you wish to have the impression ; then cover it with a piece of blotting-paper, and rub it with your finger for a short time, and you will have an impression superior to the finest engraving. The same piece of black paper will serve to take off a number of impressions. The principal excellence of this method is, that the paper receives the impression of the most minute veins and hairs, so that you obtain the general character of most flowers. The impressions may afterwards be coloured.

**Vitremanie.**—This is the name given by Messrs. Barnard and Son of 339, Oxford Street, for a much improved process of Diaphanie, and which the new art supersedes. The great success of Diaphanie—(no less than 250,000 sheets of designs having been sold in England alone)—is well known to every lady, as are its great defects, the chief of which was that, the sheets being applied with transfer varnish, bubbles of air sometimes remained between the design and the glass, which, in the subsequent process of rubbing off the paper resulted in holes ; this rubbing off, moreover, required much time, patience, and care, and was rarely perfectly performed. These defects are entirely obviated by Vitremanie. By this method the designs, after being covered with Glucine, may be applied to the glass with water only, and the paper removed entire, a few minutes sufficing for the operation, and nothing being left upon the glass but the design in colours of unclouded brilliancy and transparency.

The materials required are as follows · The printed designs, three brushes— two of camel's hair and one of hog's hair,—a bottle of each Glucine and enamel varnish, a roller, a sponge, a little blotting paper, and a pair of scissors.

The instructions are as simple as the materials, designs, &c., are inexpensive. With the camel-hair brush pass a coating of Glucine over the coloured face of the designs that are proposed to be used, care being taken that the Glucine does not touch the plain side of the paper ; the sheets of the designs should be laid flat to dry, they should be left two or three days before being used, and they will remain good for three months, or even longer.

To apply the design to the glass, it should be wetted with water on both sides, the glass should also be wetted ; lay the design on the glass, and roll well down—all air bubbles will be easily removed by this means—keep the plain side of the paper wet for a few minutes, then, with the point of a knife, carefully raise a corner of the paper, and pull it gently off ; the work is now to be washed with a camel-hair brush, and water, and afterwards dried by placing a piece of blotting paper over the work, and rolling it ; leave it now for a few hours, then coat it with enamel varnish, and the work is finished. In removing the paper, it is sometimes better, particularly when the design is large, to carefully scratch a hole in the paper, and tear it off in pieces from the centre. The work is more easily performed on free glass, cut to the proper sizes, and afterwards fixed over the glass already in the window, by means of a bead ; it may, however, be done upon the window as it stands.

The designs may be arranged to fit any window, strips of lead foil applied with gum being used for the purpose of covering the edges of the groundings, borders, &c., where they join. For circles and other shapes the strips of lead may be stretched with the thumb and fingers to any pattern desired, the creases being smoothed by the handle of a knife or paper-cutter, slightly wetted.

It is needless to state that for private residences, where the private look-out is not inviting, this art should always be called into requisition. It has, too, been most successfully adopted by many churches, and if some 250,000 sheets of designs for Diaphanie have been disposed of in England alone, it is certain with this improvement in the manipulation of the process, a much more extensive patronage may be counted on.

**The Best Way to Wash.**—First look out all your fine white things in one parcel, and your coarse things in another, throw them into two separate pans, with the quantities of soap and washing-powder, and *cold* water, according to the instructions on the packets. Leave them to soak all night, and the next day give the wristbands and collars of shirts a slight rubbing with soap in *cold* water, and then boil the fine things first, according to the printed instructions, then the coarse things, and proceed in the usual way till the whole is completed. By adopting this method it will be found that the labour of washing is reduced almost to nothing ; the clothes have a most perfect whiteness, and the whole may be got out of the way as fast as you can dry them.

**Porridge.**—To make porridge you must have what is called round meal, which consists of crushed (not ground) oats, the saucepan must be placed on the fire with the necessary quantity of boiling water in it, and then, with a wooden spoon in one hand, and a handful of meal in the other, sprinkle in the meal and stir it round till it is as thick as you want it. It should boil for at least ten minutes, and should then stand before the fire for some time before it is eaten. If of a good thickness, it may be eaten with cold milk and sugar, and will give health and strength to all who partake of it. Many first-class Scotch families make oatmeal-porridge their staple food for breakfast ; it is highly healthful and economical. A little experience will soon render a person efficient in its preparation.

**Art of Tea-making.**—To make a fragrant and refreshing cup of tea proceed as follows :—Use soft water, and be sure it boils. If you are compelled to use hard water, throw into the kettle a pinch of carbonate of soda ; but the latter should never be used unless the water requires correction, and then very moderately, for it is apt to destroy the roughness of the flavour. After the tea has been put into the pot place it before the fire, or on the hob, or, better still, on the hot plate of an oven, till the tea is well heated, but, of course, not burnt ; then pour upon it the boiling water, and a fragrant infusion of good strength is instantly produced.

VIRTUES OF TEA.—A cup of good tea is one of the best material blessings ; it will refresh both head and heart, and help the rest of the fatigued body ; it will cure almost any minor ailment, from headache to cholera ; and do more to cement the bonds of friendship than a thousand congratulatory epistles or a wagon-load of presents. We have faith in the ladies who love tea, who make it skilfully, and elegantly serve it. The poorest woman should aim at having a complete tea-table, and should even give way to extravagance in securing the choicest herb and the most fragrant infusion of it.

But extravagance is not necessary, for tea is in itself positively beneficial, and at the present day within the reach of those of most humble means. Whatever you may tolerate in shabby crockery for breakfast and dinner, bring on your best at tea-time ; and if your best is not so good as you would like, seize the first opportunity to substitute for it better.

**Dinner Etiquette.**—Never let your guests sit down to table without acquainting them beforehand with the bill of fare, that is, if the dinner be a ceremonious one ; because the great variety of dishes placed on the table is to give a choice to the different tastes of the company.

By selecting a few favourite dishes, digestion is rendered more easy, as it is then aided by the fancy of each individual ; but should you be helped to a dish which does not meet with your approval, though, at the same time, you feel yourself constrained by politeness to eat of it, your dinner is spoiled, and you do no justice to the bountiful supply of your Amphitryon.

When you help at table never give more than two or three slices of meat, cut thin. Carve everything a little in a slanting direction, that is, a leg of mutton or lamb, shoulder of ditto, neck, ribs, sirloin of beef ; the last ought never to be carved without giving the thin part, that is, the fat as well as the lean, or your joint will soon be disfigured. A good carver ought never to ask if any person likes their meat well-done or under-done, as you disfigure the joint at once ; such fancies cannot be tolerated, except at the table of the wealthy ; for the million it is a waste of many pounds annually.

Have your vegetables, no matter how plainly dressed, but always well done ; the crudity of such aliments is unwholesome, and apt to destroy the most delicate part of the digestive organs. Be also contented with one sort of vegetable on your plate at once, potatoes excepted. We have often witnessed on one plate, with salt beef, carrots, greens, peas, and potatoes.

The greatest compliment a guest can pay his host is to be asked to be served a second time of the same dish, though not above half the quantity first served should be given.

Never cut up a joint, or any kind of birds, at once, without knowing how many persons are going to partake of it. The proper manner is to ask each person, and then to help them separately.

Never remove any dish which has been placed by a servant, however awkwardly it has been set. It is not your business to serve at your own table, unless your servant pleads ignorance.

Never press any one to take more food or wine than they wish ; it annoys your guest, while you make yourself too cheap, and your dinner too common.

Never place more than one wine-glass before each guest at the commencement of dinner ; have the others ready, and place them as required ; it saves confusion, and often relieves a person from great distress, who, by chance, may not be acquainted with the different glasses which each sort of wine requires.

**Beef-Tea for Convalescents.**—The following is M. Soyer's receipt for this preparation :—Cut into small slices one pound of lean beef, add one ounce of fresh or salt butter, two ounces each of onions and carrots ; put the whole into a stew-pan holding a little more than two quarts, set it on a brisk fire, then add half an ounce of salt, a teaspoonful of sugar, and three cloves ; stir continually for a few minutes, until the meat gets a little dry, then fill with two quarts of boiling water, set it on the corner of the fire to boil gently for one hour, skim until there remains no fat on the surface, pass through a thin cloth, and it is fit for use. A little tapioca, semolina, or vermicelli, may be added for convalescents, after it has been passed through a cloth, and set afresh on the fire in another stew-pan, until either is done. The vegetables are a very great improvement in flavour, and cannot be in the least injurious to a patient ; but, if objected to by the medical gentleman, they may be omitted ; also the cloves and half the salt. The meat, if dressed with a sharp sauce, well seasoned, makes a very excellent dish.

**Hotch Potch.**—Make the stock of sweet fresh mutton. Grate the zest of two or three large carrots, slice down also young turnips, young onions, lettuce and parsley. Have a full quart of these things when sliced, and another of green peas, and sprays of cauliflower. Put in the vegetables, withholding half the peas till near the end of the process. Cut down four pounds of ribs of lamb into small chops, trimming off superfluous fat, and put them into the soup. Boil well, and skim carefully ; add the remaining peas, white pepper and salt, and when thick enough serve the chops in the tureen with the hotch potch.

N.B.—As parsley loses its colour in boiling, it should be chopped very fine, and be put in just before dishing, which gives a delightful freshness.

**Winter Soup.**—Make a good brown stock of a small shin of beef, with vegetables, carrots, turnips, onions and celery ; when sufficiently boiled the vegetables must be taken out *whole*, and the soup seasoned with pepper and salt and a little cayenne to taste ; also a little Harvey's sauce and ketchup ; then fry some mutton cutlets, the quantity required for the number, a pale brown, add them to the soup with the vegetables cut up small.

**Salmon Curry.**—Have two slices of salmon weighing about a pound each, which cut into pieces of the size of walnuts ; cut up two middling-sized onions, which put into a stew-pan with an ounce of butter and a clove of garlic cut in thin slices ; stir over the fire till becoming rather yellowish, then add a teaspoonful of curry powder, and half that quantity of curry paste ; mix all well together with a pint of good broth, beat up and pass through a tammy into a stew-pan, put in the salmon, which stew about half-an-hour, pour off as much of the oil as possible ; if too dry, moisten with a little more broth, mixing it gently and serve as usual with rice separate. Salmon curry may also be made with the remains left from a previous dinner, in which case reduce the curry sauce until rather thick before putting in the salmon, which only requires to be made hot in it. The remains of a turbot may also be carried in the same way, and also any kind of fish.

**Influence of Female Society.**—It is better for you, says Thackeray, to pass an evening once or twice a week in a lady's drawing-room, even though the conversation is slow, and you know the girl's song by heart, than in a club, tavern, or the pit of a theatre. All the amusements of youth to which virtuous women are not admitted, rely on it, are deleterious in their nature. All men who avoid female society, have dull perceptions, and are stupid, or who have gross tastes, and revolt against what is pure. Your club swaggerers, who are sucking the butts of billiard cues all night, call female society insipid. Poetry is insipid to a yokel ; beauty has no charms for a blind man ; music does not please a poor beast who does not know one tune from another. I protest I can sit a whole night talking to a well-regulated, kindly woman about her girl coming out, or her boy at Eton, and like the evening's entertainment.

One of the great benefits a man may receive from a woman's society is, that he is bound to be respectful to them. The habit is of great good to your moral men, depend upon it. Our education makes us the most eminently selfish men in the world. We fight for ourselves, we push for ourselves, we yawn for ourselves, we light our pipes, and say we won't go out ; we prefer ourselves and our ease ; and the greatest good that comes to a man from a woman's society is, that he has to think of somebody beside himself—somebody to whom he is bound to be constantly attentive and respectful.

**Earache.**—No lady who suffers with this painful malady should be without a bottle of arnica. It is indispensable in cuts, burns, and bruises, and in earache it is an infallible remedy. As soon as any soreness is felt in the ear—which feeling almost always precedes the regular " ache,"—let three or four drops of arnica be poured in, and then the orifice filled with a little cotton to exclude the air, and in a short time the uneasiness is forgotten. If the arnica is not resorted to until there is actual pain, the cure may not be so speedy, but it is just as certain. If one application of the arnica does not effect a cure, it will be necessary to repeat it, it may be several times. It is a sure preventative for gathering in the ear, which is the usual cause of earache. We have never yet known any harm or serious inconvenience to attend this use of arnica ; though if the spirits with which it is made are very strong, it may be diluted with a little water, as the spirits—not the arnica—will sometimes cause a dizziness of the head, which is unpleasant.

**Mushroom Ketchup.**—To every peck of mushrooms half a pound of salt is required. To each quart of mushroom liquor, two blades of pounded mace, half ounce each ginger and allspice, and quarter of an ounce cayenne pepper. The mushrooms should be full grown, and fresh gathered in dry weather. Put a layer of them into a deep pan, sprinkle salt over them, and then another layer of mushrooms, and so on alternately. After they have remained a few hours break them up with the hand; put them in a cool place for three days, occasionally stirring and mashing them so as to extract from them as much juice as possible. Measure the quantity of liquor without straining, and to each quart allow the above proportion of spices, &c. Put all into a stone jar, cover it up closely, put it into a saucepan of boiling water, set it over the fire, and let it boil for three hours. Then turn the contents of the jar into a clean stew-pan, and let the whole simmer *gently* for half an hour; pour it into a jug, and let it stand in a cool place until the next day. Then pour off into another jug, and strain into dry bottles. Be careful not to squeeze the mushrooms. Cork well, so as perfectly to exclude the air.

**To Roast Ducks.**—Be careful to clear the skin entirely from the stumps of the feathers; take off the heads and necks, but leave the feet on, and hold the feet for a few minutes in boiling water to loosen the skin, which must be peeled off. Wash the insides of the birds by pouring water through them. Put into the bodies a seasoning of boiled onions, mixed with minced sage, salt, pepper, and a slice of butter. Cut off the pinions at the first joint from the bodies, truss the feet behind the backs, and roast the birds at a brisk fire, but do not place them sufficiently near to be scorched; baste them constantly, and when the breasts are well plumped, and the steam from them draws towards the fire, dish, and serve them quickly, with a little good brown gravy poured round them, and some also in a tureen. Young ducks should be roasted half an hour; large ones, about an hour, but that is the extreme time for roasting a full-grown bird.

**White Wine Whey.**—Boil half a pint of new milk: as soon as it boils up, pour in as much white wine as will turn, and make it look clear; boil it up, set the saucepan aside till the curd subsides, and do not stir it. Pour the whey off, and add to it half a pint of boiling water, and a bit of white sugar. The whey will thus be cleared of milky particles, and may be made as weak as you choose. Cheese whey is a very wholesome drink, particularly if the cows have fresh herbage. Whey may be made of vinegar or lemon; and when clear, diluted with boiling water and a little sugar. This is less heating than wine, and if required to excite perspiration, answers quite as well.

**Giblet Soup.**—The giblets should be well washed in warm water two or three times, the bones broken, the neck and gizzards cut into convenient pieces; the head also should be split in two. If goose-giblets are used, a couple of sets should be dressed; but if duck giblets are cooked, four sets will be wanted; a pint of water is to be allowed to each set. Put them into cold water, let them boil up gradually, take off the scum, and when they boil, add some sweet herbs, pepper and salt, mace, and an onion. Let the whole stew for about two hours, until the gizzards are tender: take out the giblets, strain the soup, and thicken it with a little flour and a bit of butter; and flavour it with a little ketchup. Serve up the giblets and the soup together.

**Care and Management of the Hair.**—Perfect cleanliness is indispensable for the preservation of the health, beauty, and colour of the hair, as well as its duration; this is attained by frequently washing it in tepid soft water, using those soaps which have the smallest portion of alkali in their composition, as this substance renders the hair too dry, and by depriving it of its moist colouring matter, impairs at once its strength and beauty. After washing the hair should be immediately and thoroughly dried ; and when the towel has ceased to imbibe moisture, brushed constantly in the sun or before the fire until its lightness and elasticity are fully restored ; and in dressing it, a little marrow pomatum, bears' grease, or fragrant oil should be used.

The belief that washing the hair induces headache, or catarrh, or injures the hair, is erroneous ; as the application of water to the skin is the most natural and effectual method of cleansing it, and of keeping open the pores through which the perspiration must pass, in order to ensure its healthy condition ; besides, scales naturally form around the roots of the hair of the most cleanly person ; and these can only be completely detached by the use of soap. The constant and persevering use of the brush, is a great means of beautifying the hair, rendering it glossy and elastic, and encouraging a disposition to curl. The brush produces further advantages, in propelling and calling into action the contents of the numerous vessels and pores which are interspersed over the whole surface of the head, and furnish vigour and nourishment to the hair ; five minutes, at least, every morning and evening, should be devoted to this purpose. If these rules be abided by, there will be no scurf in the hair.

The only true mode of managing the hair is to dress it in a style consistent with the character of the face. Young ladies ought never to wear many flowers in their hair, or many leaves, whatever be the fashion. If a bud, it should just peep out now and then, while the lovely wearer, with a light laugh, sweetly waves her ringlets to some pleasant whisper ; if a full-blown rose, let it— as ye hope to be happily married—be a white one ; white for the hair, but a " blush " for the bosom.

**To Make Rose Perfume.**—The manufacturers of rose perfume, when they wish to preserve rose-leaves fresh until they have got a sufficient quantity to distil, or use in other ways, are in the habit of separating the leaves from the stalks, and mixing them into a paste with salt, in proportion of six pounds of leaves to one of common salt. This, put in jars, will keep any length of time. Packing alternate layers of salt and fresh rose-leaves away in jars is a first-rate, simple way of getting a fine essence of rose. Let the jars remain covered in the cellar for a month or two, then put the pulp into a crape, and press the moisture from it. Bottle this essence, and let it stand out, well corked, in the sun and dew until it is quite clear. One part of this essence, one part of spirits of wine, and ten parts of spring water, will give you a fine-flavoured rose-water. A good tincture of rose-leaves may be made by simply digesting them in strong spirits ; while three parts of leaves of just-opened roses to four parts of sweet olive-oil, pounded in a mortar, kept still for a week, and then expressed, will give you an excellent oil of roses.

**To Preserve Flowers.**—Procure some river sand, and let it be sifted through a fine sieve, then wash it well to remove all particles of dirt that may remain. Take a jar or a box, large enough to contain the flowers you wish to preserve ; place a bed or layer of sand in it, and stick the stem of the flower in the sand, so that it may stand in a perpendicular position ; then (from the sieve) shake the fine sand you have prepared gently on the flowers, taking care to spread out and arrange the leaves in their natural position, and see that the sand penetrates and lies well between the interstices of the blooms, which should be gathered in dry weather. Continue shaking on the sand till it has reached the height of about an inch above the flower. Shake the box gently during the above process, to ensure the requisite penetration of the sand into the open parts of the flower. If the plant be small, and of a dry nature, it will be sufficient to expose the jar containing it to the heat of the sun during a few of the hottest days of summer ; but if it be large it must be placed in an oven after the bread has been withdrawn. Practice alone will enable any one to judge exactly how long it may be necessary to leave it in the oven —say two or three hours. After the drying, the sand must be gently poured off, and if the degree of heat has not been too strong, the flower preserves for two or three years its primitive beauty. Some kinds of flowers demand more particular attention to secure their perfect preservation; thus, before burying tulips in the sand, it is necessary to take out their pistil, otherwise the petals would often be separated from the stem. The calyxes of pinks and carnations should be pierced in several places with a pin; it is well to use the same precaution with all double flowers. Should the leaves and stems have lost their verdure, it may be restored by exposing the plant to the gas arising from a mixture of steel filings and sulphuric acid diluted with water.

**Proposal of Marriage.**—A lady's conduct at this particular time must be governed by the estimate she has been able to form, by a frequent intercourse, of the sincerity of the gentleman's attachment to her; and, it is presupposed that she is perfectly satisfied with his moral character and social position by her previously having accepted him as a lover. When gentlemen marry, they can afford to disregard circumstances somewhat; but a lady must not do so, we do not mean through any sordid motive, but as a security against a life of future misery and degradation. Never trifle with a proposal of marriage; delays are dangerous; at once refer the offer to your elders in the household, and if their decision be favourable, and the gentleman is perfectly in accordance with your own wishes, then there can be scarcely any objection to a speedy union.

Should, however, a proposal be made to you not be agreeable with such an alliance as you desire to consummate, then your wisest plan is to refer the gentleman to your parents, at the same time acquainting them with the obstacles which you think are very unfavourable to an union, and he will receive his answer from them, written of course in as friendly a spirit as the delicacy of the subject permits of.

On no account whatever must you delay sending a reply to a proposal of marriage. Think of the suspense of an individual who has thrown himself, as it were, upon your kindness, enter into his feelings if you can, and consider if you do not act uprightly towards him, and as becomes a lady, your own good name will be compromised, and his feelings will either be lacerated, or, which would be most deserving, he would regard you with a cold contempt, and would not feel himself bound to conceal the particulars of the case from any one. Let him have a reply from you, and there is no opening then for his revealing anything derogatory to your character as a lady.

We have said that in the event of a refusal it should be written by your parents or guardians; this is the *law* of etiquette; but if your *love* for sparing pain be at all strong, and you have any fear that your parents are not qualified to send a refusal in a proper tone, then sit down yourself to break the law by writing him a letter of condolence, acknowledging your obligation of the honour he intended you, and promising him your friendship, if he be worthy of it, as a mark of your appreciation of him in many particulars; but let him unmistakably know that you can *never* be his wife.

If your parents determine to reply as well as yourself, and you are conscious that their reply will not be tempered with kindness, then a letter from you in addition, in a consoling tone, will be as an oasis in the deserted heart of the gentleman, and will only leave in him regrets and not chagrin that he has not secured a prize as one who has a heart can feel for others' woes.

**Short and Long Courtships.**—Those courtships of seven years' duration, which formerly were so common, are now almost reckoned amongst the things that were, and we do not think that society is any loser by the change,

When such periods had to elapse before a prudent union could be effected, there were many contingencies which might intervene to set aside the most sincerely pledged vows, and then the respective parties found themselves perhaps considered as out of date by the world.

Such courtships are now so infrequent that the people who were engaged in them would be considered as rarities.

On the other hand, short courtships, though not always fatal to happiness, ought, for many reasons, to be discouraged. It is no argument in defence of them to single out many instances in substantiation of the fact that they have been successful. Many cases of marriages at sight we have known to have resulted in happiness. But we must look at the mass of the people, and note down what a larger view affords. A thorough knowledge of character is not to be acquired by an exterior impression. Conversation and observation of habits, for at least twelve or eighteen months, is necessary for most courtships. If the respective persons have resided in the same town for the whole of their lives, and have been previously acquainted, the period of courtship may, without danger, be diminished. The caution which we have suggested as necessary is not called into use in a case of this kind ; it is only requisite where there is an imperfect knowledge of the habits and principles. Time's all-trying ordeal is necessary to discover whether the core is as worthy of admiration as the beautiful exterior.

When a young lady and gentleman enter upon the field of love, they place themselves open to remark ; and should they be hasty in running to the altar, or long and weary in their amours, they will be equally a topic of censure or approval. When an engagement has been made, the most judicious course is to let both circles of friends and acquaintances know of it, in order that no gentleman may be pining in solitude for the lady whose love he knows not is bespoke. So long as we do not adjourn to the prairies of America or the wilds of Siberia, we must conform to the usages of society. There are many ridiculous rules which may be overlooked, but in main points we must give way to prevalent customs or be regarded with feelings not very conducive to our peace.

While we are on the subject of long and short courtships it will not be out of place to touch upon those courtships which, though very short, are nevertheless very often productive of acute pain. A gentleman, we will suppose, makes a proposal to a lady, and the answer he receives is, that she will consider about it and let him know after she has taken the advice of her parents. She is so unfeeling, and we think ungrateful, as never to think of the man who has paid her the highest compliment which can be paid by a gentleman to a lady ; and, to darken the picture, represents to her friends that Mr. So-and-So had made her an offer and she had rejected him, and that when she consulted her parents they were very much annoyed at an offer having been made to their daughter from any such quarter. Such heartless conduct, the product of excessive vanity, cannot be too highly censured, and if her friends calmly listen to such a breach of all the rules of good faith, they may be deservedly classed with the individual who has, with their silent sanction, violated the laws of society.

**Leaving Company.**—French leave is the fashion now-a-days in good society, and we should hope will continue so. By this method you slip out, shake hands quietly and unobserved with the host and hostess, and the party goes on undisturbed ; otherwise the movement of the one is the signal for the movement of another, and the party is broken up prematurely. We have seen, in homely assemblies, a sedate matron retire to dress, and reappear with bonnet and shawl on to shake hands with the whole company. Nothing can be more vulgar or detrimental to the life of a party, however unpretending its character.

**Economy the Basis of Comfort.**—Let it be your first aim to make the most of everything, and thank God that you have so much. If your income is ample, guard against extravagance and study economy that you may avoid debt, and enjoy the pleasures of life free from pressing anxieties. It is too much the fashion for ladies to ignore their husbands' pecuniary affairs, and to profess ignorance of money matters, and to encourage themselves in the idea that their wishes at least must be gratified —with the rest they have nothing to do. Now the affectation of this is bad enough, but the actual practice is worse —many a ruined house, many a bankruptcy springs out of it—many a domestic circle is broken up, and the pride which led to the ruin humbled to the dust as a reward. Make the best of everything, and keep within your income, and if your means be ever so limited, you will now find that care and economy will place you in the enjoyment of as much comfort and respectability as is enjoyed by many who have greater resources than yourself. The matter of first importance in the economic management of a household is skilful marketing.

**To Keep Jam.**—Ordinary jam, it has been discovered—fruit and sugar that have been boiled together for some time—keeps better, if the pots into which it is poured are tied up while hot. The reason for this will be perfectly obvious from the following simple explanation. If the pot of jam or preserve be allowed to cool before it is tied down, little germs will fall upon it from the air, and they will retain their vitality, because they fall upon a cool substance ; they will be shut in by the paper, and will soon fall to work decomposing the fruit. If another pot, perfectly similar, be filled with a boiling hot mixture, and immediately covered over, though, of course, some of the outside air must be shut in, any germs which are floating in it will be scalded, and in all probability destroyed, so that no decomposition whatever can take place. We are sure that the important reasons cited for tying up the jam hot will induce every one to do so.

**Influence of Marriage on the Duration of Life.**—M. Bertillon lately read before the Academy of Medicine a paper on the relative influence of marriage and celibacy, based on statistical returns derived from France, Belgium, and Holland. In France, taking the ten years 1857—66, he found that the 1,000 persons aged from 25 to 30, 4 deaths occurred in the married, 10·4 in the unmarried, and 22 in widowers ; in females at the same age the mortality among the married and unmarried was the same—9 per 1,000, while in widows it was 17. In persons aged from 30 to 35, the mortality among men was, for the married 11 per 1,000, for the unmarried 5, and for widowers 19 per 1,000 ; among women, for the married, 5, for the unmarried 10, and for widows 15 per 1,000. There appears to be a general agreement of these results of marriage in Belgium and Holland, as well as in France and Paris.

**A Certain Recipe to Remove Fruit Stains from Table Linen.**—Tie up some cream of tartar in the stained part, and then put the linen into a lather of soap and cold water, and boil it awhile. Then transfer it wet to some lukewarm suds, wash and rinse it well, and dry and iron it. The stains of either fruit or wine will be extracted during the process. They may be also removed by rubbing them while wet with common salt. A third plan is to mix in equal quantities, soft soap, pearlash, and slacked lime. Rub the stains with this preparation, and expose the linen to the sun, with the mixture plastered on it. If necessary, repeat the application. As soon as the stain has disappeared, wash out the linen immediately, as it will be injured if the mixture is left in it.

**Leaves for Garnishing the Dessert.**—A rare old leaf is the ivy, green, or golden, and yet its smell is anything but sweet, its taste is rank and poisonous, and it leaves somewhat of both on the fruit it adorns. Therefore, beautiful as the ivy is, it ought not to be brought into contact with fruit. The Portugal, or common laurels, are much better. Unless bruised, they give out little odour and no taste. Their size is suitable, and their bright glossy surface cleanly. The colour, especially of the Portugal variety, is a rich dark green, and the forms of both are well adapted for association with dished-up fruit. Hollies, especially the plainer-leaved varieties, form beautiful garniture for desserts, and give out neither smell nor taste. Even the pricklier varieties, both green and variegated, may be turned to useful purpose by using terminal tufts instead of single leaves. These can be handled better, and the little rosettes, set off with prickles as defensive armour, guard the fruit from danger, and force us to handle it with care. Ancuba leaves are very handsome, but they smell rather strong, and many of them are too large, even were we prepared to pluck the leaves of the finer sorts. The common Ajaponica is the best for this purpose, and, setting aside its smell, is very pretty. The Berbius aquifolium, and other species, afford the most useful of all leaves for garnishing the dessert. They yield so many leaves of different sizes and colours, as to furnish a rich variety ; they are also clean and scentless, and fit in well with most fruits. Rhododendron leaves are bright and glossy, and look well either singly or in terminal branchlets. Laurustinus is clear, bright, shapely, and has a good effect. The Arbutus is also clean and pretty, in terminal bunches or single file ; and sweet bay leaves are light, glossy, and sweet, without, however, flavouring the fruits that rest upon them.

Notwithstanding this wide range of choice, many ladies, however, elect to cushion their fruit on variegated or green kale. It is pretty enough, but both the sight and the smell are suggestive (often highly so) of cabbage, which is a somewhat incongruous association with a luscious dessert. All leaves from the outside should be washed and well dried before being used. Frozen leaves will lower the quality of most fruits that touch them, and nothing can be more displeasing than the adorning of choice fruits with imperfect or unclean leaves. Therefore, gather your leaves for the garniture of the dessert early in the morning, sponge them perfectly clean, if not already so, and lay them aside in a temperature of 10 degrees or more above freezing, but not in sunshine ; they will then be in a proper state for using when wanted.

Those who grow stove or greenhouse plants in quantity—especially climbers —or force early fruit and flowers, will hardly ever be scarce of choice leaves for the garnishing of their desserts. And yet it is by no means every pretty or fine leaf that is suitable for this purpose. For instance, the whole family of pelargoniums must be set aside, from their excess of perfume. There are other beautiful leaves, again, that are too thin to go creditably through a dinner without shrivelling up into useless encumbrances of the dessert. Such is to a great extent the case with abutilons of all varieties—very fresh and beautiful, but fragile. The leaves of the variegated and the common form of cobæa scandens have the same failing. Again, there are some of the passion flowers that give out a disagreeable odour, and some of them, like P. quadrangularis, are too large ; and kermesina, in a young state, is almost too tender. Still, this noble family is rich in leaves for garnishing. P. alata, edulis, and racemosa, being among the very best species, are also rich in beautiful leaves ; but some are fragile, and those that are suitable have more or less scent. Camellia leaves are models of smooth, glossy beauty, but no one cares to gather them for fruit garnishing ; while those of oranges, lemons, &c., are too highly perfumed. Stephanotises are too leathery, were one inclined to pick them off. The early forcer of fruit and flowers can seldom, however, be at a loss for choice foliage for garnishing desserts. Even common leaves out of season acquire an uncommon beauty. Of course, those who have vine leaves, need no other ; nothing can supersede or equal them. They are the best of all, from the time the tender leaflets will barely pass through the dinner, till the winter leaves of many colours crumple into a handful of dust in our fingers. Early fig-leaves are also admirable. Later in the season they seem too rough and common for choice fruit ; but the early leaves have a soft freshness that is most pleasing. Even early peach, plum, pear, apple, and cherry leaves are admirable ; while the leaves of forced roses have a cleanly beauty that is seldom seen on those out of doors. The lily of the valley leaf, with a flower or two here and there, gives one of the choicest, sweetest finishes to a dessert, without flavouring the fruit. A fine Czar violet and leaves of the common primrose are by no means to be despised. That most useful of all plants for cutting, the astilbe japonica, yields a harvest of exquisite leaves for the adorning of the dessert. Again, forced lilacs, especially all the varieties of the Persian, are invaluable. Doubtless a considerable proportion of the charm arises from the fact of the leaves being out of season ; but they are likewise more beautiful, that is, more fresh and green, when produced under the shelter of glass. It is astonishing how much variety of garniture adds to the interest and beauty of the dessert. And this reminds us of another set of leaves which we have not named that are amongst the most useful and beautiful of all—those of the strawberry. This fruit never looks so well as when nestling upon its own leaves ; and doubtless desserts generally would be far more interesting and beautiful than they are, if, as far as practicable, early fruit were adorned with leaves or branchlets of its kind.

[We must make our acknowledgments to "The Garden" for this lucid and practical article.]

**New Cure for Bee-Stings.**—There are a number of well-known antidotes to the sting of the honey-bee, and, were it not for the fact that they are seldom available when required, it would be unnecessary to direct attention to an additional cure. But the antidote we now submit and recommend is everywhere available, for it is nothing more nor less than an application of common soil to the wound. A friend of ours had the misfortune to be stung by a bee in her garden, and as none of the usual antidotes were then available, she drew the sting from the wound and applied a little common soil, after wetting it sufficiently to admit of its being worked into the consistency of thick cream. The pain previous to the application of the soil was most intense ; but in a few seconds after it was reduced to a dull ache, and nothing more was felt afterwards beyond a slight stiffness in the joints of the thumb. The same remedy has been often tested, and with the same degree of success. As the stings of bees and wasps affect some persons more than others, it is proper to observe that the remedy of soil is applicable to all, and may be implicitly relied on.

**Keeping Fish Fresh with Sugar.** —A method adopted in Portugal for preserving fish consists in removing the viscera, and sprinkling sugar over the interior, keeping the fish in a horizontal position, so that the sugar may penetrate as much as possible. Fish prepared in this way can be kept completely fresh for a long time, the flavour being as perfect as if recently caught. One tablespoonful of sugar is sufficient for a five-pound fish.

**Sick-room Disinfectant.**—When a solution of chloride of lime is used to sprinkle the floors of sick rooms, it leaves insoluble stains of carbonate of lime. These may be removed by vinegar, but chloride of soda, sometimes called from the name of its discoverer, "Labarraque's Disinfecting Fluid," is far better, as the resulting carbonate can be removed by a wet cloth. By breathing fumes of chlorine from this compound, Mr. Roberts was enabled to traverse the sewer of the Bastile, which had been closed for thirty-seven years, and was full of sulphuretted hydrogen.

**Charcoal as a Tooth Powder.—** Charcoal, for the service of the teeth, as usually sold in boxes, is useless. It is an excellent tooth-powder, as it corrects the fetor of the mouth. It should be strongly ignited in a fire or crucible, and quickly rubbed to powder in a mortar. It must then be immediately transferred to stoppered bottles, which should be opened as little as possible; for, like spongy platinum, charcoal loses its efficacy by exposure to air, but regains it when heated red hot, even after use, as the organic matters and gases absorbed are either volatilised or decomposed.

**Bezique Chinoise.—** The following rules and instructions to play this new game are from *The Queen* newspaper:—

The game is played with four packs of cards, and only two persons can play. The ordinary score is 3000, but we find this makes the game too short, so have altered it to 6000. Cutting is the same as at ordinary bezique, the player winning the cut giving himself and opponent three cards at a time, till they have nine each. No trump card is turned up, but whoever can first proclaim a marriage after winning a trick makes that marriage trumps. It scores 40. The players then continue as at ordinary bezique, till one can proclaim a combination; take for instance four aces. Should he happen to have a fifth ace in his hand, or to take one in while he has four on the table, he plays away one of the aces proclaimed, and putting down the other ace scores 100 again, provided he wins the trick; if not he must wait. This may be continued through all the sixteen aces, should the player be so fortunate as to get them. Marriages may be scored almost any number of times, as for example, suppose the player has a queen of trumps, or any other suit, and has three kings of the same suit in his hand, he can put one king down with

the queen and proclaim the marriage. He then wins the trick, perhaps, with a small trump, lays the second king down, and scores another marriage. The third king is exposed in the same way. He will then have a queen and three k'ngs on the table; should he get another queen of the same suit, he can marry her to all the kings in the same way, but he must win a trick between each. Should he get a fourth king of any suit, he can then declare four kings, playing them away and replacing them as with the aces. Queens and knaves are played in the same manner.

The great rule in this game is to play for a sequence, and not to think too much of smaller scores. A royal sequence is the same as at ordinary bezique, but scores 500; but when the player has scored once he must be careful not to break it, as each time he takes a sequence card into his hand he plays away the corresponding card proclaimed, puts the undeclared one down, and scores 500 again.

We are convinced the best play (unless the player has a very strong hand for treble bezique, such as three queens of spades, or two knaves and a queen of bezique cards, at quite the commencement of the game) is to go in for a royal sequence and four aces, as they bring in large returns.

On the subject of bezique, suppose the player declares single bezique, he of course scores 40; he takes in another queen, and lays her down alongside the knave, still retaining the other queen, and can score 40 once more. Supposing he then gets a second knave of diamonds, it is double bezique, which scores 500. Should the player then think he has a fair chance of treble bezique, let him sacrifice everything for it, as it gives 1,500.

We were once watching a most exciting game, when a gentleman got double bezique first, then treble; he then played away a queen of spades, took in the fourth, declared treble bezique again, making a score in four proclamations of 4000. But this is very seldom done. It is important to keep in mind all the combinations and the principal cards declared and shown. We trust we have explained the game clearly.

We now give a list of the scores which differ from those of ordinary bezique :

Double bezique, 500 each time.

Treble bezique, 1500 each time.

Royal sequence, 500 each time.

Common sequence of any suit (not of much use unless the player has only 200 or 300 to win the game) 250 each time.

The sevens of trumps do not count, or winning the last trick. The last eight cards are played like the ordinary game, and the brisques—viz., the tens and aces—amount in all to 320. The best way of scoring is to procure four bezique markers, two for each player, and to make one marker score the tens and hundreds, and the other the thousands.

**Ivy as an Ornament for Drawing-Room Fireplaces.**—The following is a new and successful utilisation of ivy. Procure several boxes of the same length as the width of the fireplace ; to these boxes flat and rather stout wire trellises (just large enough to cover the grate) should be fixed, by fastening the uprights to the back of the boxes by means of screws. The boxes should then be filled with a composition consisting of turfy loam three parts, leaf-mould one part, and decayed manure one part. Previous to filling with soil, three six-inch pots should be put in each, one in the centre, and one at each end, for the purpose of receiving pots of a smaller size, containing ferns or flowering plants, when the boxes are placed in the drawing-room. The best ivy to use is that known as the common Irish, although, probably, any of the strong-growing green-leaved ivies would do equally well for the purpose. To prevent loss of time, strong plants in five-inch pots ought to be procured, and three plants put in each box, and the shoots trained regularly over the trellis. If this is done early in the spring of the previous year the trellis will be densely covered with healthy deep green foliage. To keep the ivy within bounds it will be simply necessary to prune, early in the spring, all straggling shoots. There is practically no limit to the plants that may be placed in the receptacles provided in the boxes, as bright flowers with the ivy, and the appearance of ferns is very cool and refreshing in hot weather, and the hardy varieties are equally desirable as the choicest of the exotic species. When the plants in pots require water they are simply lifted out of their places, and taken where the superfluous moisture running from the pots will do no harm, but when the soil in the boxes becomes dry it is necessary to take them outside, which can be readily done by two persons, one at each end. Of course the bright part of the stoves should be removed and packed away carefully, as they will be hidden by the ivy. Possibly one of the variegated ivies would be useful for the same purpose.

**Semolina Pudding.**—Drop lightly into a pint and a half of milk, two tablespoonfuls of semolina, and stir all together for seven or eight minutes : then throw in two ounces of butter, three and a half ounces of sifted sugar, with the grated rind of a lemon, and while the semolina is still hot, beat with it gradually and briskly four eggs. Bake for half an hour in a moderate oven.

**To Fry Soles.**—Skin and clean your fish carefully ; slip a knife down the spine, and loosen the flesh from the bones for about three-fourths of the length of the fish. Put the fish into milk for ten minutes or a quarter of an hour ; then take out and flour all over. Have your frying-pan with sufficient melted lard or fat to cover the fish, but not absolutely boiling ; put in the fish and fry until of a golden brown. Take the fish out : pat it lightly on both sides with a perfectly clean cloth ; powder with a little salt, and serve with fried parsley and a lemon cut into slices. Do *not* be persuaded to serve the fish on paper.

**Comparative Health of Water-**

ing Places.—The Registrar-General gives in his Quarterly Return the usual statement of the (annual) rate of mortality in the second quarter of the year 1872 in the districts or sub-districts of England, comprising and approximately representing the watering places :—In Ramsgate the rate of mortality was as low as 11·7 per 1ooo living : Leamington, 11·9 ; Eastbourne, 12·8 ; Folkestone, 12·9 ; Hove, 13·9 ; Lowestoft, 13·9 ; Worthing and Littlehampton, 14·6 ; Sidmouth, 14·8 ; Dawlish and Teignmouth, 15·2 ; Hastings and St. Leonards, 15·5 ; Tenby, 15·6 ; Weymouth, 15·8 ; Southend, 16·1 ; Cheltenham, 16·3 ; Isle of Wight, 16·4 ; Torquay, 16·5 ; Clifton (with part of Bristol), 16·5 ; Tunbridge Wells, 16·7 ; New Brighton, 16·9 ; Harrogate, 17·6 ; Buxton, 17·7 ; Brighton, 17·8 ; Ilfracombe, 17·8 ; Yarmouth, 18·1 ; Bangor, and Beaumaris, 18·1 ; Scarborough, 18·5 ; Blackpool, 19·1 ; Aberystwith, 19·1 ; Exmouth, 19·5 ; Weston-super-Mare, 20·2 ; Penzance, Marizion, and St. Ives, 20·6 ; Malvern, 20·9 ; Llandudno, 21·1 ; Rhyl, 21·2 ; Bath, 21·4 ; Margate, 22·5 ; Herne Bay, 22·6 ; Southport, 23·7 ; Matlock, 24·3 ; Whitby, 24·3 ; Anglesea, 22·5 ; Dover, 35·6.

**Syrup of Coffee for Travellers.**—This preparation is of great use to those who have long journeys to make. Take half a pound of the best ground coffee ; put it into a saucepan containing three pints of water, and boil it down to one pint. Cool the liquor, put it into another saucepan, well scoured, and boil it again. As it boils add white sugar enough to give it the consistency of syrup, Take it from the fire, and when it is cold put it into a bottle, and seal. When travelling, if you wish for a cup of good coffee, you have only to put two teaspoonfuls of the syrup into an ordinary coffee-pot, and fill with boiling water. Add milk to taste.

**Caution to Sea-side Visitors.**—The most important clause of the new Sanitary Act, and one that will be invaluable to travellers of all conditions, whether on business or pleasure, or who seek health at popular watering-places, is to this effect : If any person knowingly lets any house, room, or part of a house, which any person suffering from a contagious or infectious disease has inhabited, without having such house, room, or part of house, and all articles therein liable to retain infection, disinfected to the satisfaction of a qualified medical practitioner, as testified by a certificate given by him, such person shall be liable to a penalty not exceeding twenty pounds. If the authorities of watering-places do not enforce observance of this clause, they will deserve a severer punishment than the law provides for neglectful lodging-house keepers. Infectious diseases are frequently left behind by visitors, and unhappy persons following them, who have gone out for pleasure and recreation, become miserable victims to a lifelong disease.

**Australian Meat.**—On the nutritive qualities of this meat, the " Food Journal" says—

" This subject was brought before the British Association, by Dr. Edward Smith, who read a paper on the economic and nutritive value of the three principal preserved foods, namely—preserved milk, preserved meat, and Liebig's extract of meat. Dr. Smith's estimate of the value of preserved milk and Liebig's extract is certainly very low indeed ; and it can scarcely be said that his opinion of the economic value of Australian preserved meat is relatively much higher ; at the same time he adds his testimony to that of all other scientific men in favour of this meat as being perfectly wholesome and containing all the elements of nutrition in the same proportions as English meat.

" Dr. Smith says that the saving by its use in institutions now supplied with fresh meat at 7d. per pound would not be great. That there should be any saving at all, say one halfpenny a pound, in such extreme cases, is a fact of importance ; but other persons very capable of forming a true opinion, and placed in favourable circumstances for so doing, regard the matter in a very different light. They say that a pound of poor meat loses from 20 to 30 per cent. in the cooking, and as Dr. Smith admits that the Australian meat contains all the nutritive elements of fresh meat, it is difficult to escape the conclusion that he underrates the economy of the preserved meat, even when compared with meat at 7d. per pound. If this be the case, as we firmly believe it to be, what must be the saving caused by using tinned meat as compared with fresh meat at a shilling a pound !

"One of the great obstacles to the general adoption of Australian meat is that unless eaten cold—when it is excellent—it requires some little knowledge of cookery to manage it properly. It cannot be roasted, or baked, or boiled, like a fresh joint. Now, with rare exceptions, the wives and servants of England scarcely know how to produce eatable soups or stews, except at lavish cost. An ordinary French cook-maid will produce a more palatable and more succulent *entrée* with the scraps pared off a joint than nineteen-twentieths of our so-called cooks can with the most expensive meats. Those who wish to get variety, to make the most of Australian meat, must take the trouble to learn to cook it."

From a pamphlet issued from the office of the "Anti-Adulteration Review," we extract the following hints and recipes for the Best Methods of Cooking Australian Meat :—

Cut off the lid of the tin evenly and cleanly ; invert it, and should the contents not readily slip out, slightly warm the tin by immersing it two-thirds in warm water, when they will be found to slip out in a solid block.

This being done, carefully remove, with a spoon, the jelly and superfluous fat that will be found surrounding the meat. Carefully preserve these for use.

In cutting the meat be careful to use a sharp knife, and cut cleanly. A blunt knife will necessarily give a broken and ragged appearance to the grain of the meat.

After opening the tin, and removing the meat, place it for a short time before use in a cool place, with free circulation of air.

The meat need not be all consumed at once, or necessarily in a hurry, or to waste. It will keep as long as cooked meat generally.

Being cooked when newly killed, and without any salt or other condiment or preparation, it necessarily requires a flavouring or accompanying appetiser. Pickles, hot vinegar, &c., will do, but a good sauce is preferable.

ROAST AUSTRALIAN BEEF.—A lady gives the following :—Carefully scraping off with a wooden spoon all the fat and gravy from the block of beef, which seemed, as far as I could make it out, to be the undercut of a large sirloin, I tied it tightly round with string, putting a piece of solid fat in the centre, much in the same manner as rolled beef is tied, only I tied it very tight. I then hung it as though it were a fresh joint, to be roasted before a clear and bright fire, giving it a slight sprinkling of flour all over after it was hung. Separating, as well as I could, the congealed gravy from the mass of grease that surrounded the meat, I placed it in the dripping-pan, and, at intervals of a few minutes, basted with it the turning joint. In less than twenty minutes the savoury smell that filled the kitchen convinced me that, so far, my experiment was succeeding. In half an hour, the meat having become well browned by the brisk heat, I took it down. Pouring off the dripping out of the pan, I made a rich brown gravy in the ordinary way, by the addition of a little flour and water to what remained, and sat down to dinner. Expectantly I watched the first slice cut off ; the knife passed through the meat cleanly and easily, and a second, third, and fourth satisfied me that one fault had been cured—the meat was no longer stringy, but firm and compact. Tasting what I had on my plate, I found it all I could desire ;

it was tasteful, agreeable, and even rich, almost melting in the mouth, and in all respects equal, if not superior, to second-rate English beef.

BEEF.—A very savoury dish with Australian beef is to be produced as follows :—Put some of the fat from the tin into a frying-pan, and in it some sliced onions, till browned. Mix a teaspoonful of curry with two tablespoonfuls of flour, and mix together in a paste. Boil about a quart of water in a stew-pan, well stirring in the paste and onions. Add your meat sliced. Simmer for a few minutes, and season. You can boil some rice and serve with it.

IRISH STEW OF AUSTRALIAN MUTTON. —Boil your potatoes, onions, and if you think proper, a turnip or two, till sufficiently done ; then add your Australian mutton, cut in suitable slices, and with a fair proportion of the fat and jelly. Let this simmer for a few minutes. Season with pepper and salt, and skim. Serve hot.

TOAD-IN-THE-HOLE OF AUSTRALIAN BEEF.—Mix some good batter ; season it well. Pour some into a dish, previously well greased, and place in oven. When well set, place on it a slice or slices of beef, about two inches thick, then add remainder of the batter, which should cover the meat. Bake, and when done, turn it out on a dish, bottom upwards.

To CURRY AUSTRALIAN MUTTON.— Thoroughly boil some turnips, onions, and a head of celery, with a clove of garlic. When perfectly pulped, strain if preferred. To this liquor add the meat cut in slices, with curry-powder to taste, boiled in water and thickened with flour, and seasoned. Have ready some rice slowly simmered, one part rice to three of water, with a lump of butter, but not stirred. Put this on a dish, pour on curry, and serve.

Pea Pods.—The pods of peas are commonly thrown away as refuse after shelling, or used only for feeding cattle or pigs ; but when young and tender they are an excellent vegetable, very fit for being used in soups. There is a kind of pea called the sugar pea, the pods of which have only a thin pellicle as an internal lining, instead of the hard lining found in other kinds, and peas of this kind are boiled in the pod, and used like kidney beans. The pods of the ordinary garden varieties are, however, of equally delicate flavour, and the only, but insuperable objection to their use as a boiled vegetable is, the hard and unmasticable interior lining. They may, however, be used in soups, being, in the first place, boiled in a separate vessel, until they can be easily rubbed to pieces. This is done by means of a wooden spoon, or similar implement, and the pea shells are then placed in a drainer having wide holes, with the water in which they were boiled, when the eatable part passes through the drainer with the water, and forms an excellent addition to soups : or a good soup may be made by merely adding to it a proper quantity of extract of meat, or of Australian cooked meat, and beating it a little. The strips and hard linings of the pods remain upon the drainer.

**Nutritive Properties of Macaroni.**—This, the national fare of Italy, deserves much more popularity than it enjoys among ourselves. Weight for weight, macaroni contains from two to three times as much flesh-forming material as good household bread. This is the opinion of eminent analytical chemists both at home and abroad ; while Dr. Hassall claims for it far more nutrient power than any of the cereals employed as food in this country. Now that butchers' meat has become so high in price, the use of macaroni, as a substitute, twice or thrice a week, deserves consideration from those who have to practice economy. It is susceptible of varied culinary treatment, and is not only palatable and appetising, but of high nitrogenous value when cooked with cheese.

The finest qualities of macaroni (from the Italian *maccare*, to bruise or crush) are those which are whitest in colour, and do not burst or break up in boiling ; it should swell considerably and become quite soft ; but if it does not retain its form when boiled, it has not been made of the best wheat. Some makers flavour and colour it with turmeric, to suit tastes ; but this is limited to very few. Only hard kinds of wheat are applicable to the manufacture of macaroni, as they contain a large percentage of gluten. The following is the method of preparation :—The wheat is first ground into a coarse meal, from which the bran is removed—in that state it is called semolina ; while the grinding is going forward, it is necessary to employ both heat and humidity to ensure a good semolina. This is worked up into a dough with water, and for macaroni it is forced through piped-shaped gauges. Strictly speaking, indeed, the name macaroni implies exclusively to wheaten paste in the form of pipes, varying in diameter from the size of an ordinary quill pen to an inch. There is no essential difference between vermicelli and macaroni.

To Cook Macaroni.—There is no better way of cooking this wholesome food than the following :—Put as much of the pipe to soak in water as may be required ; then boil it in milk and water till quite tender, with a small onion ; when done, strain off the milk and add a piece of butter about the size of a plum, and a little nutmeg ; some prefer a little salt and cayenne to the nutmeg. Mix thoroughly together and put it into a dish, then cover with grated Cheshire cheese ; put it into the oven or before the fire to be lightly browned, and serve hot with mustard.

Another method is :—Put in an iron pot or stew-pan two quarts of water ; let it boil ; add two teaspoonfuls of salt, one ounce of butter ; then add one pound of macaroni ; boil till tender ; let it be rather firm to the touch : it is then ready for use, either for soup, pudding, or to be dressed with cheese. Drain it in a colander ; put it back in the pan, add four ounces of cheese or more, a little butter, salt, and pepper ;

toss it well together and serve. It will be found light and nutritious, and well worthy the notice of vegetarians.

To Make Macaroni Soup.—Boil a pound of good macaroni in a quart of the best stock till it is very tender ; then take out half, and place it in another saucepan. To the remainder add more stock, and boil it until you can pulp all the macaroni through a fine sieve. Then put it to the two liquors, adding a pint or more of boiling hot cream, the macaroni that was first taken out, and half-a-pound of grated Parmesan cheese ; make it hot, but it should not be allowed to boil ; serve it with French roll crusts, cut into small pieces.

**Ferns as Basket Plants for Room Decoration.**—It is impossible to imagine a more beautiful object for imparting grace and elegance to rooms, corridors, &c., than a well-grown basket of ferns, either suspended from the ceiling or from ornamental brackets in the walls. During the hot summer months the various shades of green in their arching, feathery fronds, imparts an elegant and cool appearance ; and when two or more sets of plants are grown for the purpose, so as to admit of frequent changes, the interesting features of this mode of room decoration are considerably enhanced. Amongst the best strong-growing ferns for very large rooms are Polypodium aureum, Woodwardia radicans, and Aspidium exaltatum. Their long arching fronds have a grand appearance, especially when the rooms are artificially lighted ; but the bottom of the basket should be covered with a few trailing sprays of Cissus discolor, hanging about in apparent negligence. This Cissus does well in baskets ; short pieces of the old wood strike freely in early spring if taken off before growth commences. If the cuttings are put in in February, the growth of this plant is so rapid that nice young plants will be ready for filling baskets in April.

Almost all the hardier kinds of stove and greenhouse ferns do well in baskets

—not only those whose mode of growth naturally fits them for suspending, but many of the erect growers also ; but the bottom of the basket should in all cases be covered with creeping or trailing plants, such as Panicum variegatum, Tradescantia zebrina, Isolepis gracilis, Lycopodiums, &c.  The object should be to hide every wire of the basket, which should be made as plain and simple as possible.  Highly elaborate and ornamental baskets are not required ; they are more difficult to fill satisfactorily, and the projecting ornamental work seems out of place.

" Some time ago," says a correspondent of *The Field*, " I made an observation to the above effect ; but the dealer remarked that every man liked to bring into prominence his own handiwork.  A plainly-made basket, simple in shape, lined with green moss, and one or more plants planted in it according to the size, the bottom covered with creeping or trailing plants, which should be pegged in till the basket is covered, and then allowed to hang down negligently—this, according to my ideas, fulfils the conditions required in a tasteful basket of plants.  Our baskets are home-made, and are generally circular in shape.  A handy man, after a little practice, will make half-a-dozen to begin with in a few hours, and will soon be able to impart a certain amount of neatness to his work.  As the wires are intended to be hid with moss and foliage, fine workmanship is unnecessary.  We use two kinds of wire.  A stout wire forms the framework of the basket, and is lashed together with a smaller wire ; when finished, the whole is painted two coats, to keep the wire from rusting.  A file and a pair of pliers are all the tools required, and such work could be done on wet days.  It is always best to fill a few new baskets every spring ; there is thus always a lot of fresh young specimens coming on."

**Origin of Cards.**—Cards were invented about the year 1390, to divert the melancholy of Charles VI. of France. The inventor proposed by the figures of the four suits to represent the four classes of men in the kingdom.

By the *cœurs* (hearts) are meant the *gens de chœurs*, choir men, or ecclesiastics ; and therefore the Spaniards, who learnt the use of cards from the French, have *copas*, or chalices, instead of hearts.

The nobility, or prime military part of the kingdom, are represented by the ends or points of lances ; and our ignorance of the meaning or resemblance of the figure induced us to call them spades.  The Spaniards have *espados*, swords, in lieu of pikes, which are of similar import.

By diamonds are designed the order of citizens, merchants, or tradesmen, *carreaux*, square stones, tiles, or the like.

*Trefle*, the trefoil leaf, or clover grass, corruptly called clubs, alludes to the husbandmen and peasants.  The Spaniards have *bastos* (stones or clubs) instead of the trefoil.  It is probable that we give the Spanish signification to the French figure.

The names of the four kings were David, Alexander, Cæsar, and Charles. These names are still used by the French, and represent the four monarchies of the Jews, Greeks, Romans and Franks under Charlemagne.

By the queens are meant Argine (anagram of *regina*), Esther, Judith, and Pallas, representing truth, piety, fortitude, and wisdom.  The knaves were designed as servants to the four knights.

To whatever nation belongs the credit of inventing cards, they seem to have designed them in accordance with the phenomena of the year ; the two colours represent the two great divisions of the year ; the number of suits represent the four seasons ; the number of cards in each suit is equal to the number of weeks in each quarter ; and the number in the pack is equal to the number of weeks in the year.  The number of pips on the cards, counting the court cards, according to their value, as eleven, twelve, and thirteen, is 364, within one of the number of days in the solar year.

**Whist.**—Whatever may be the antiquity of this game, it is certain that whist as it is now played was not understood till early in the eighteenth century. It was not till the time of Hoyle that it became a game of science. He gave instructions in the game at a guinea a lesson, and was the first to throw together the results of experience, and his work has been the corner stone of all that has since been published on the subject. The learned Doctor Johnson, in his explanation of the word, says it is derived from the verb whist, because it is a game requiring you to keep silence. All the lexicographers have followed in his train, and some, in accordance with the remarks of a lively Frenchman, who said that, " Etymologists considered consonants of little consequence, and vowels of none at all," derive it from the word hush. Silence, at all events, is markedly observed by whist players.

Laws of the Game.—I. In cutting for partners, the two highest and the two lowest go together ; the ace is counted lowest.

2. Every player has the right to shuffle the cards, but the dealer may shuffle last. The pack must be cut by his right hand adversary.

3. If a card be turned up in dealing, a new deal may be called ; if any card be faced, there must be a new deal.

4. Should the dealer drop two cards to one heap, and continue beyond that heap, it is a misdeal.

5. No one may touch the cards whilst they are being dealt ; should a misdeal arise in consequence, the cards to be redealt.

6. The dealer should leave the last card on the table till he has played, after which, no one may ask what was the card turned up ; but any one may ask which is the trump suit.

7. Should the dealer not turn up the last card, the deal is lost.

8. Should any player have but twelve cards, while the rest have thirteen, the deal is good, provided the pack was perfect ; should any one have fourteen, the deal is lost.

9. If any one omit playing to a trick, and, consequently, have one card more than the rest, the adversaries may call a new deal.

10. If any one play out of his turn, the adversary may call a suit, or call the card so shown at any time during that deal.

11. If any player show a card the penalty is the same.

12. A card once played cannot be taken up again.

13. Cards thrown down, under the supposition that the game is lost, may be called by the adversaries in any order they like : provided they do not make the player revoke.

14. Every one may ask, before a trick is taken up, who played a particular card.

15. Honours cannot be called after you have played.

16. Any one calling honours before they have scored eight, the adversaries may consult and demand a new deal.

17. If any one revoke, he loses three tricks—these may either be taken from the score of those revoking, or added to the adversaries' ; and though there still remain a sufficient number of tricks to win the game for the party revoking, they must remain at nine.

18. A revoke cannot be claimed before the trick is turned, or the person who revoked, or his partner, has played again ; nor after the cards are cut for a new deal.

19. The game is ten up. Five points save a double game—one point saves a treble game. Honours do not count at nine.

Technical Terms used in Whist. —*Double.*—Gaining ten points before your adversary scores five in the long game, and five before your adversary scores three in the short game.

*Finessing*—Is when holding the best and third best of a suit, you put your third best on your adversary's card, and risk the left hand adversary having second best.  If he has it not you win two tricks.

*Forcing.*—Playing a card that compels your adversary or partner to put on a trump.

*Long Trump.*—The last trump.

*Loose Card.*—A card of no value for winning a trick, or for returning your partner's lead.

*Points.*—The numbers scored either for points or honours.  Ten make the game, and five save a double in Long Whist.  In Short Whist, five make the game, and three save the double.—Five points of the game count as one point of the rubber.

*Quart.*—A sequence of any four cards.  Quart-major—a sequence of ace, king, queen, knave.

*Quint.*—A sequence of five.  Quint-major—a sequence of ace, king, queen, knave, ten.

*Ruffing or Trumping.*—Playing a trump upon any other suit.

*Renounce.*—Not holding a card of a particular suit.

*See-saw.*—Partners trumping each a suit, and playing to each other for that purpose.

*Sequence.*—Two or more cards of a suit following each other.

*Slam.*—One party winning every trick.

*Tenace.*—Holding first and third best of any suit, and having to play after the person who holds the intermediate one.

*Terce.*—A sequence of three cards.—Terce-major—a sequence of ace, king, queen.

*Rubber.*—Winning two games out of three, or winning two before the adversaries win one.

**A New Dish.**—When quaint old Tusser wrote his Five Hundred Points of Good Husbandrie, he could scarcely have been aware of a dish which, for simplicity, economy, and savoury taste, may be said to have no rival.  Whilst the materials are both homely and popular, the combination comes to us from the lovely tropical island of Mauritius, and is as follows :—Select a large, mature, and firm cabbage, from which the coarse outer leaves have been detached, and the stalk chopped off; scoop out the heart, fill up with minced meat, bread crumbs, onions and seasoning; fasten up in a cloth, plunge into boiling water, and boil for half an hour.  A savoury viand of nature's own suggesting (for it is indebted to no culinary legerdemain), such a dish, if properly cooked, ought to recommend itself to the poor man equally with the epicure.

**Frozen Water-Pipes.**—This accident is caused by the expansion of water in freezing.  When pipes or taps are frozen, the best way to thaw them is to let warm water gradually flow over their surface; remembering, at the same time, that if the water is used too hot or too quickly, the thaw will be too sudden, and broken pipes will be the result.  The precaution of throwing a bit of woollen covering over taps and pipes in frosty weather, or binding them round with a straw band, would often save both inconvenience and expense.

**Hints for Sea-Voyages.**—On shipboard is no place for fine dressing, and those who attempt it must do so, not only at the expense of personal comfort, but to the destruction of good clothing.  A dress worn three or four days at sea will never be in condition to wear on land again ; hence those who have had any experience in ocean travel always take an old woollen dress, and keep their trunks locked.

Ladies will find a shoe-bag, with a half-dozen pockets, an admirable article of state-room luxury.  In it can be dropped breast-pins, watch, hair-pins, tooth-brushes, combs, &c., and all the small articles that would otherwise be sliding about the floor before morning.  A well-corked bottle of cologne or bottles of medicine, are always safe from breakage, and handy, in this receptacle.  It would also be well to take a few small brass screw-hooks to serve as extra hangers for the shoe-bag, and articles of wardrobe which two ladies in a small state-room will find it necessary and convenient to suspend. There are but two hooks for each passenger, which is sufficient for men, but lamentably deficient for ladies. A small gimlet to make holes in which to screw the hooks will be desirable.

**Weight of the Body at Night and Morning.**—If two persons are to occupy a bed-room during the night, let them step on a weighing scale as they retire, and then again in the morning. Frequently, there will be a loss of two or more pounds, and the average loss throughout the year will be a pound of matter, which has gone off from their bodies, partly from the lungs, and partly through the pores of the skin. The escaped matter is carbonic acid and decayed animal matter or poisonous exhalation. This is diffused through the air in part, and part absorbed by the bed-clothes. If a single ounce of wood cotton be burned in a room, it will so completely saturate the air with smoke that one can hardly breathe, though there can only be one ounce of foreign matter in the air. If an ounce of cotton be burned every half-hour during the night, the air will be kept continually saturated with smoke, unless there be an open window or door for it to escape. Now the sixteen ounces of smoke thus formed is far less poisonous than the sixteen of exhalations from the lungs and bodies of two persons who have lost a pound in weight during the eight hours of sleeping ; for, while the dry smoke is mainly taken into the lungs, the damp odours from the body are absorbed both into the lungs and into the pores of the whole body. Need more be said to show the importance of having bed-rooms well ventilated, and of thoroughly airing the sheets, coverlids, and mattresses in the morning, before packing them up in a neatly-made bed ?

**Quinsey.**—Those who suffer from quinsey, or ulcerated sore throat, will be thankful to hear of a simple and efficacious mode of relief, namely, an onion poultice. Bake or roast three or four large onions, or half a dozen smaller ones, till soft. Peel them quickly, and beat them flat with a rolling-pin or glass bottle. Then put them directly into a thin muslin bag that will reach from ear to ear, and about three inches deep. Apply it speedily, and as warm as possible, to the throat. Keep it on day and night, changing it when the strength of the onions appears to be exhausted, and substituting fresh ones. Flannel must be worn round the neck after the poultice is removed.

**The Jewels of the Months.**—In Poland, according to a superstitious belief, each month of the year is under the influence of some precious stone, which influence is attached to the destiny of persons born during the course of the month. It is, in consequence, customary among friends, and more particularly between lovers, to make, on birthdays, reciprocal presents, consisting of some jewel ornamented with the tutelar stone. It is generally believed that this prediction of happiness, or rather, of the future destiny, will be realised according to the wishes expressed on the occasion :—

JANUARY.—The stone of January is the Jacinth, or Garnet, which denotes constancy and fidelity in any sort of engagement.

FEBRUARY.—The Amethyst, a preservative against violent passions, and an assurance of peace of mind and sincerity.

MARCH.—The Bloodstone is the stone of courage and wisdom in perilous undertakings, and firmness in affection.

APRIL.—The Sapphire, or Diamond, is the stone of magnificence, and kindliness of disposition.

MAY.—The Emerald. This stone signifies happiness in love and domestic felicity.

JUNE.—The Agate is the stone of long life, health, and prosperity.

JULY.—The Ruby, or Cornelian, denotes forgetfulness of, and exemption from, the vexations caused by friendship and love.

AUGUST.—The Sardonyx. This stone denotes happiness in conjugal felicity.

SEPTEMBER.—The Chrysolite is the stone which preserves and cures madness and despair.

OCTOBER.—The Aqua-Marine, or Opal signifies distress and hope.

NOVEMBER.—The Topaz signifies fidelity and friendship.

DECEMBER.—The Turquoise is the stone which expresses great sureness and prosperity in love, and in all the circumstances of life.

**Croquets.**—Chop very finely any sort of cold meats with bacon or cold ham, rub a teaspoonful of summer savoury very fine, pound twelve allspice finely ; boil one egg hard, and chop it very fine, and one onion minced fine ; mix all this together, then grate a lemon, and add a little salt ; when well mixed, moisten it with walnut ketchup, form it into pear-shaped balls, and dredge well with flour ; at the bottom ends stick in a whole clove. Then have boiling fat or dripping in the pan, dredge each croquet again well with flour, lay them in the boiling fat, and fry a nice brown ; then take them out and lay on a soft cloth in a hot place to drain. Serve hot.

**Junket.**—Put three pints of milk into a saucepan, with lump-sugar to taste. When slightly warm, add three large teaspoonfuls of essence of rennet, stir well, then add a large wine-glassful of brandy or rum ; stir again, then pour the mixture into your junket-bowls, and leave it undisturbed for two hours and a half. Before serving, grate a little nutmeg over the top. In Devonshire it is customary to cover it with clotted cream. This is, of course, a great improvement, but not absolutely necessary.

**The Lady's Garden.**—There is nothing better for wives and daughters physically than to have the care of a garden ; a flower-pot, if nothing more. What is pleasanter than to spend a portion of every passing day in working among plants and watching the growth of shrubs and trees, and to observe the opening of flowers, from week to week as the season advances? Then how much it adds to the enjoyment to know that your own hands have planted and tilled them, and have pruned and trained them ? This is a pleasure that requires neither great riches nor profound knowledge. The wife or daughter who loves home, and would seek ever to make it the best place for husband and brother, is willing to forego some gossiping morning calls for the sake of having leisure for the cultivation of plants, shrubs and flowers. The advantages which women personally derive from stirring the soil and snuffing the morning air are freshness and beauty of cheek and brightness of eye, cheerfulness of temper, vigour of mind, and purity of heart. Consequently she is more cheerful and lovely as a daughter, more dignified and womanly as a sister, and more attractive and confiding as a wife.

**Length of Woman's Hair.**—Dr. Benjamin Godfrey says that a woman's hair may grow to the length of six feet, and that a young lady of Massachusetts refused two hundred pounds for her cranial covering, which was only an inch short of this measurement. Four hundred hairs of average thickness would cover an inch of space. The blonde belle has about 140,000 filaments to comb and brush, while the red-haired beauty has to be satisfied with 88,000 ; the brown-haired damsel may have 109,000 ; the black-haired but 102,000. Few ladies consider that they carry some forty or fifty miles of hair on their head ; the fair-haired may even have to dress seventy miles of threads of gold every morning. A German experimentalist has proved that a single hair will suspend four ounces without breaking, stretching under the process and contracting again. But the hair thus heavily weighted must be dark brown, for blondes' hair breaks down under two ounces and a half.

**Egg Baskets.**—Boil hard half a dozen eggs, or more, according to the size of the family. When done, throw into cold water immediately. (This should always be done with hard-boiled eggs, else the yolk will turn black). Cut the eggs in half, after taking from the cold water. Rub the yolks in a marble or wedgwood mortar, or with a silver or wooden spoon, with some melted butter, pepper and salt, to a smooth paste; and, if you know it will be agreeable to all, add a very little made mustard. Pound the meat of a cold fowl, finely-minced, or grind some cold tongue or ham, and, having made it smooth, mix with the egg paste, moistening, as you proceed, with a little gravy, or, if you have none to spare, with melted butter. Cut a thin slice from the bottom of the white of the egg, so that it will stand, and fill each of the hard whites with this paste. Place close together on a flat dish, and pour over the gravy left from the roast fowl yesterday, heated boiling hot, into which a few spoonfuls of cream or rich milk have been stirred. Cover closely with a hot cover, and let them stand a few minutes before sending to table. If liked, a little parsley, chopped fine, be added to the paste.

**Plant Odours.**—As a general rule, those flowers which are most brilliant or decided in colour are, in like degree, less fragrant, the degree of fragrancy decreasing from white to yellow, then red, followed by blue, violet, green and orange. It is also noted that, among flowers of the same colour, certain types of scent are prevalent. In the white, the odour of honey is often found, though greatly varying in strength, or partially neutralized by some scent. The odour of prussic acid, so decided in the flowering almond and hawthorn, is also often met with in white flowers. Among yellow blossoms the scent of the orange prevails in a greater or less degree, while in those of a purple or a violet hue the odour of vanilla is common, the heliotrope and lilac being readily recognised as members of this group.

**Instinct in Plants.**—The root constitutes the plant's mouth. It terminates in a little sponge. The sponge drinks up the moisture from the sur-

rounding earth. Every boy has seen in the woods the root of some tree, planted by the birds or the winds in the crevices of a rock, wandering down the sides of a boulder in search of nourishment. In one case, a horse-chesnut tree, growing on a flat stone, sent out its roots thus to forage for food. They passed seven feet up a contiguous wall, turned at the top, and, passing down seven feet upon the other side, found the needed nourishment there which their own barren home denied them. A yet more singular instance of this search for food is related. A seed had been dropped by one of Nature's husbandmen, a bird, in the decaying trunk of an old tree. It sprouted, put forth roots, branches, and a little stem. But its roots in vain sought nourishment at the breast of its dying foster-mother. At length, abandoning all hope of support from her, they pushed out from home to seek a living. They dropped to the ground, a distance of sixty or seventy feet, and, fastening there, succeeded in securing an independent living. As time passed on, the old trunk died, decayed, and disappeared. The new tree remained suspended, as it were, in mid-air, the roots proceeding downward, and the branches upward, from a point about equi-distant between the two.

**To Roast a Turkey.**—Make a veal stuffing, and fill the breast at the crop. Cover the turkey with buttered paper, and roast it at a distance of about seventeen inches from a quick fire, and frequently baste. Three hours for a turkey weighing twelve pounds. Remove the paper when the bird is done, sprinkle it with salt, dredge on a little flour, and froth it well with fresh butter. Serve with a good gravy and fried sausages round.

**To Boil a Turkey.**—Stuff the breast with two pounds of sausage-meat; put it into sufficient hot water to cover it, and let it boil gently for an hour and a half. This is sufficient time for an eight pound turkey. Dish up, and serve with oyster sauce over.

**Oyster Sauce.**—Take two dozen oysters; blanch and **remove the beards.** Put three ounces of butter into a stewpan with two ounces of flour, add the beards and liquor with a pint and a half of milk, a teaspoonful of salt, a pinch of cayenne, two cloves, and half a blade of mace. Place over the fire. Keep stirring, letting it boil ten minutes; then add a teaspoonful of essence of anchovy and one of Harvey's sauce. Pass it through a sieve into another stewpan, add the oysters, and make very hot, but do not let it boil. A less quantity may, of course, be made, using less proportions.

**Charlotte Russe.**—Take eighteen Savoy biscuits, brush the edges of them with white of egg (care must be taken not to put too much egg upon them, or they will stick to the mould), and line a plain mould with them, arranging them in a star-like shape at the bottom, and in an upright position round the side. Place them closely together, so that the egg connects them firmly. Then put it in the oven for about five minutes just to dry the egg. Now whisk to a stiff froth a pint of cream with a tablespoonful of pounded sugar, half an ounce of melted isinglass, and any flavouring that may be preferred, a tablespoonful of liqueur of any kind, or a wine-glassful of wine will be sufficient. Fill the mould with it and cover it with a slice of sponge-cake cut to the shape of the mould. Place it in ice until ready for table. Great care must be observed in turning it out that the cream does not burst the case.

**Salutations.**—They should always be suited to the parties saluted. It is a much disputed point upon whom the obligation of the first salute lies, when persons of different age or condition meet. The best rule is for the younger to salute the senior, as was the custom with the Romans. When a lady meets a gentleman she salutes first, or no recognition takes place. Salutations should always be hearty, but softened by politeness. When a gentleman shakes **hands** with a lady, he should not grasp the whole palm as he might with a bosom friend of his own sex, but let the fingers only meet, and be immediately withdrawn.

**Baby's Wardrobe.**—Every article of dress, for a new-born infant should be white. The materials must differ, according to the fortune of the wearer; but those we suggest are such as would be suitable for any family of the middle classes. For night-dresses and petticoats, fine long cloth; for morning gowns, striped, or other fancy muslin, or what is called hair-cord muslin; for shirts, very fine linen; and the same for night-caps. Some articles are always cheaper if bought ready-made, than by purchasing the articles and making them at home with the aid of a sewing-machine. Among these hoods may be reckoned, as the stuff for a single one cuts very much to waste.

Every mother wishes that her first baby clothes should be as pretty as possible; but she frequently lays out a great deal of money unnecessarily in trimmings, on the plea that they are so cheap. It is very true she may get them for a moderate sum; but nice crochet and knitting, which she can generally do herself, would be far more durable than cheap embroidery, and quite as handsome. The question in the young mother's mind should be this: is it my business to *earn* money, or is it only in my power to save it? If the latter, every shilling saved by employing remnants of time in doing the little necessary decorations, is of consequence, besides affording a pleasant occupation for leisure hours. The trimmings that can be readily made at home, are edgings and insertions in crochet, knitting, and tatting. Each piece should be made of the length required, with a slight allowance for shrinking; thus, the pieces for the top, epaulettes, and sleeves of a little frock should all be made separately.

THE FITTINGS OF THE WORKBOX.—Before beginning any such a lengthened occupation, as preparing a baby's wardrobe, every implement necessary should be procured. We consider the following as quite essential :—Large, small, and button-hole scissors, thimble, a round and a flat bodkin, good needles (from 5 to 11), stiletto, bodkin, cotton cord of various sizes ; tapes, stay-binding, flannel-binding ; white silk ; fine knitting cotton, sewing cottons of various sizes ; Mecklenburg thread, and linen and pearl buttons of medium and very small sizes. The pincushion should also be well stocked with pins, and a few fine headless needles, with sealing-wax tops, are very useful in all fine work. Cotton and linen or Mecklenburg thread may be used ; the former for cotton work, the latter for linen and French cambric.

**Cod Liver Oil.**—In all diseases connected with a scrofulous habit of the constitution, this oil has been used with great advantage ; in general debility, its decidedly nutritive properties render it extremely valuable.

The Best Methods of Administering the Oil.—The common dose of cod liver oil for an adult is one table-spoonful, two or three times a day ; sometimes double this quantity is given, but it is always advisable to begin with a small dose, and gradually increase. With regard to the best vehicle for its administration, this must depend generally upon individual taste ; but milk, orange wine, ale, or some bitter infusion, cinnamon, or other aromatic water : and cold coffee may be mentioned as among the best ; for children it may be made into an emulsion with yolk of egg and sugar, or disguised in well-sweetened cocoa, in which state it is sometimes taken unknowingly ; raspberry vinegar is not a bad vehicle. An hour before a meal is the best time for taking this oil ; it is then less likely to cause nausea, and more likely to become assimilated with the food. Patients, who have become accustomed to it, experience a sensation of sinking and faintness when the usual dose is omitted, which fully bears out its character as a nutrient ; with some it acts slightly as a laxative, and with others causes a

difficulty of breathing, and a feeling of fulness in the chest and head, and even spitting of blood ; but these effects are quite exceptional.

Medical practitioners are by no means agreed as to whether the pale or the dark oils are the best ; the former appears to contain the largest quantity of iodine, bromine, phosphorus, and salts of lime, soda, and magnesia ; and the latter to be richest in the component parts of bile, butyric, and acetic acids ; the pale is less likely to cause nausea, if it is really fresh and pure, and for this reason mostly preferred.

**Castor Oil.**—This very safe and common aperient is an oily substance secreted by the beaver. We obtain it from both America and Russia, but that imported from the latter country is esteemed the best. Without doubt it is the mildest, safest, and most certain cathartic known, seldom griping, or causing flatulency ; it may therefore be administered in irritable conditions of the system to persons suffering from debility, and young children ; also after childbirth, dysentery, and where there is any inflammatory disease. With most purgatives the immediate effect is followed by a constipating tendency : it is not so with castor oil, the dose of which, after repetition, may be generally decreased.

The usual quantity required, is for children from one to two drachms ; for adults, from one to an ounce and a half. The best mediums for its administration for those who cannot take it in its pure state, are tea, coffee, gruel, spirits and water, or peppermint ; those to whom its oily flavour is especially nauseous, will do well to chew a piece of fresh orange or lemon peel just previously to taking it ; this renders less acute the nerves of taste. It is sometimes made into an emulsion as follows : Put into a clean mortar the yolk of an egg, add to this six drachms of castor oil, and well mix by trituration ; then add gradually, to the extent of six ounces, cinnamon, or some other aromatic water.

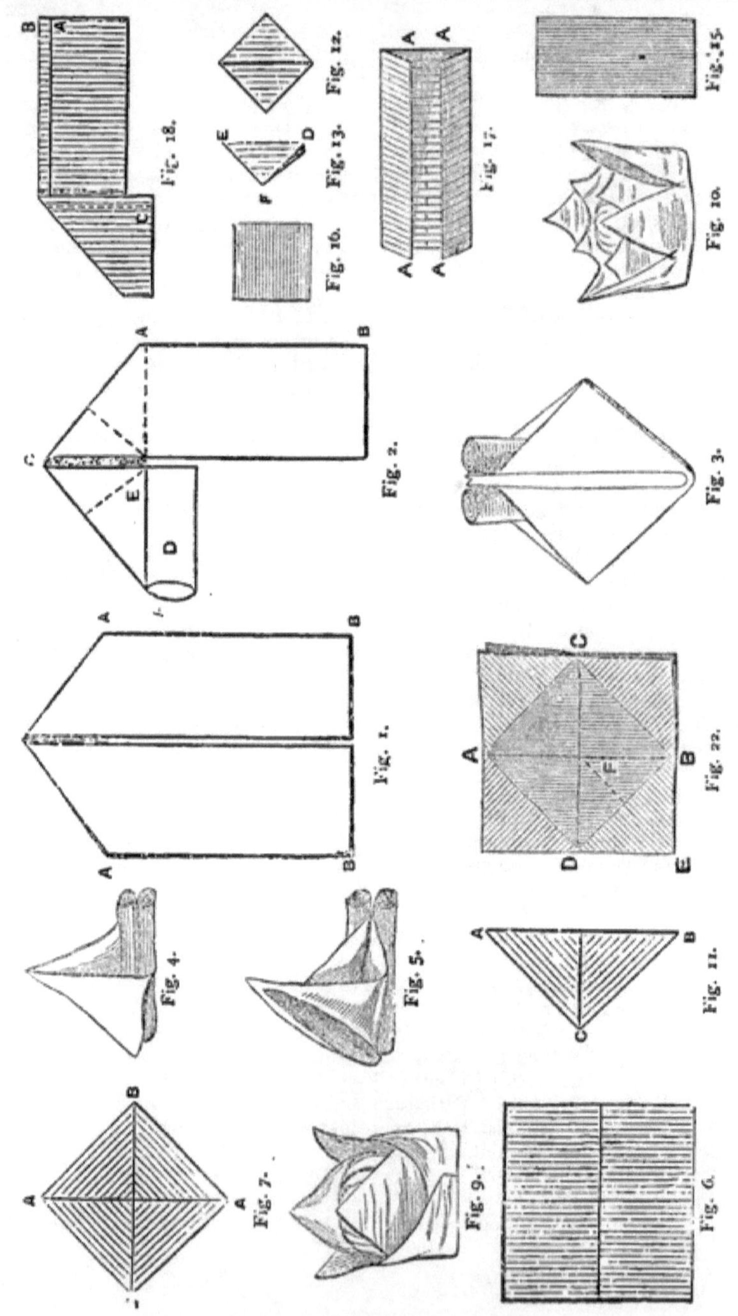


SERVIETTES OR TABLE-NAPKINS.

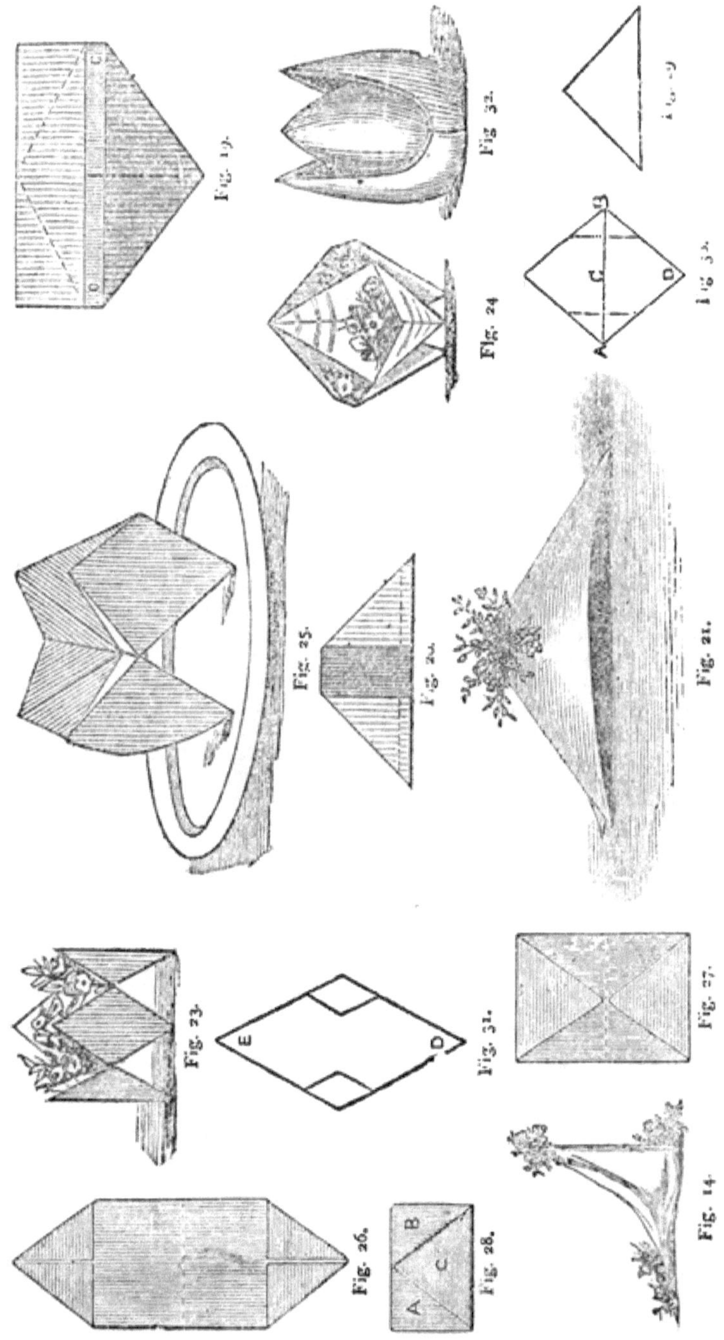



SERVIETTES OR TABLE-NAPKINS.

**Serviettes, or Table Napkins.—** We are indebted to "Cassell's Household Guide," for the following instructions on folding table-napkins, and the illustrated designs which accompany them:—"Almost any amount of fancy or ingenuity can be displayed in folding table-napkins, or as they are commonly called, adopting the French name, *serviettes*. To make them look well, serviettes are required very fine, exactly square, not too large, to be starched, and folded quite damp, every fold creased in place with a clean hot iron. A box-iron is the best for this purpose, and it should be a small one easily used.

1. One of the simplest styles is to fold the napkin in four, lengthways; then, like Fig. 1, keeping the whole of the fold at the top and the edges at A A and B B; roll up the ends at B to A, one at a time, as in Fig 2, but roll them the reverse way to Fig. 2—that is, over, not under. When both ends are rolled up as close as E, with a twist of the hand bring the ends of the rolls, D, to the point C, like Fig. 3. Then lay the part shown in Fig 3 flat on the table, and set up the diamond-shaped fold at the top with the hands; slip the dinner roll or slice of bread into the hollow. Before the bread is put in, Fig. 4 represents the form of the folded serviette.

2. This varies a little from No. 1 in appearance. First fold it four times, lengthways, and then like Fig. 1, as already described, keeping the hemmed edges at A A and B B; then roll it up precisely like Fig. 2, the rolls as there shown, outside. When both are close as E, take the points of the rolls at E between the thumb and finger of each hand, and bring them together *underneath* at C. By this means the point C will stand perfectly upright. Press the whole properly into place. The difference between No. 5 and No. 4 is this: in Fig. 2, No. 4 is rolled under; No. 5, over. In Fig. 3, the part where the fold meets, which is shown by Fig. 4, is under or next the rolls which form No. 5. To form No. 5 this fold is outside.

Fig. 5 displays the folds of No. 2. No. 5 stands more upright than No. 4, and is a little less simple in appearance.

3. CROWN PATTERN.—This requires the damask to be very stiff. Halve and quarter it each way, like Fig. 6; bring all the corners exactly to the centre, like Fig. 7; bring the four corners of Fig. 7 also to the centre, and smooth them at the crease; then form it into the crown by folding the corners at A A in Fig. 7, and slipping them into similar folds at B B, bringing the napkin round and upright in the form of a crown (Fig. 9).

4. THE FLOWER.—To make this way of folding resemble a flower, copy Fig. 6 and then Fig. 7; bring all the corners of Fig. 7 nearly, but not quite, to the centre for the second fold; finish it as before, and then curl up the four centre points like Fig. 10.

5. The CORNUCOPIA looks very pretty down a long dinner-table. Fold the serviette in a half, lengthways; then fold it like Fig. 11, the hems at the broad end. Take the corners, A and B, bring them back again to the corner C, like Fig. 12. Double Fig. 12 together down the centre. This represents Fig. 13. At D, in Fig. 13, three folds exist, two outer and one inner. Set Fig. 13 upright, over the dinner roll with three of these folds to one side. Shape it nicely, keeping the space from E to F close. A flower at the point E has a very pretty effect, especially if it be a scarlet geranium, which contrasts well with the white damask, and gives a brighter look to the table. To carry out the idea of the cornucopia, a few flowers and leaves may be placed in the manner shown in Fig. 14, the stalks slipped under the edge, but must not be done too profusely.

6. THE COCKED HAT is made by folding the serviette first in half one way, and then in half the other way and once more in half, lengthways, in the way illustrated by Figs. 15 and 16, the dotted lines showing in each diagram where the next fold is made. Then make a fold still lengthways, turning one one

way and one the other, not quite to the top. This fold is shown by A A A A in Fig. 17. The serviette is supposed in this diagram to be laid flat on the table, the dotted line in the centre marking the fold, which is shown in Fig. 18 by the line at B. The lines in Fig. 17, from A to A and A to A, are the folds to be made lengthways, not quite meeting the top, with the hemmed edges upwards where the lines are marked. The napkin is supposed to be doubled in half again in Fig. 18, with the hems outside at the line A, on each side of it ; then fold as in Fig. 18, first one side and then the other, and iron down the crease ; then partly unfold one side, as shown in Fig. 19. The dotted lines mark the creases in the unfolded part, and C and C show how the piece marked C, in Fig. 18, is turned down. The piece raised is now folded down again, the dotted line, creased, passed over the other side, and the ends tucked in and crossed down flat. The serviette now resembles Fig. 20. Arch it nicely over the dinner roll, and put a spray of flowers at the top to resemble the feather in a cocked hat, in the manner shown in Fig. 21.

7. THE BASKET.—Fold a serviette twice, like Figs. 15 and 16, once longways, and the second time across. This is to reduce its size. Fold the four points to the centre, like Fig. 7 ; turn it over on the other side, and again fold the four points to the centre ; again turn it face downwards, and with the other side up, turn back the four corners, Fig. 22 ; fold it from A to B, Fig. 22, and C to D, both folds to be made keeping the part uppermost outwards. Open the last fold from C to D, and bring the shoulder B to the shoulder D by a fold at the dotted line between E. Repeat the same fold as that at E all round. The napkin will now stand on end as a basket, by standing it on its legs at E and the other three corners, and opening it back at F, in the way shown at Fig. 25. Fill the spaces with a few flowers, or cut the roll in four, put a portion in each, and just a flower

or two. This pattern placed the reverse way on the plate also looks well, the dinner roll in the centre outside, Fig. 24 ; it requires the napkin to be very stiff, and exact in the folding. In Fig. 25 the bread is to be placed underneath.

8. TO FOLD A SERVIETTE AS A DAHLIA.—Make it very stiff ; fold the four corners to the centre as in Fig. 7. Repeat the process by folding the four corners now existing to the centre, and still repeat it a third time ; form it round by pleating the edge, one pleat in the centre of every side, and one pleat to every corner. When placed upright over the bread, the flower should open to the heart and display every petal.

9. THE MITRE is not difficult to fold, and always looks well. First fold the napkin in half ; then fold down the corners as shown in Fig. 26 ; turn these corners down again to meet in the middle, which is indicated by a dotted line. The napkin now looks like Fig. 27. Fold this in half at the dotted line in the centre, bringing the two points back to back, for the fold is made outwards. Fig. 28 is the result. Fold over the two ends A and B, and produce Fig. 29. Let down the point C in Fig. 28, and fold the corners inside it ; fold back C in its place again, turn the napkin over, and let down the point like C on the other side. The napkin now resembles Fig. 30. Fold it down at the dotted lines, turning the points A and B towards C. Fig. 31 is the figure now represented. D is the point let down ; turn it up again to E ; slip the hand inside the hollow underneath the napkin, and shape the mitre nicely, and then place it over the dinner roll like Fig. 32.

**Deserted Wife.**—If a wife is deserted by her husband, he remains liable for her necessaries, just as though she lived with him, but especially if they are known to be living apart, the expression " necessaries " will be very severely interpreted in case of proceedings ; it has been laid down that if a shopkeeper *will* sell goods to every one that comes, it lies on him to make good his claim on the husband.

**Mince Pies.**—Put a pound of flour upon your pastry slab, with two ounces of butter ; rub well together with your hands ; make a hole in the centre, in which put a pinch of salt, the yolk of an egg, the juice of a lemon, and a wine-glassful of water. Knead it into a soft, flexible paste ; roll it out into a thin sheet, lay half a pound of butter in the centre, fold the paste over. Roll and fold again twice over. Lay it in a cold place a quarter of an hour. Give another roll. It is ready for use ; cover the patty pans with paste, fill them with mincemeat, and cover. Slightly butter your patty-pans before covering them with the paste.

**Mincemeat.**—Chop very finely two pounds beef-suet, quarter of a pound each candied lemon, orange peel, and citron, one pound lean cooked beef, two pound of apples, two pound of currants, washed and picked, one and a half pound of raisins, stoned and chopped fine, one ounce of mixed spice, one pound of sugar, the juice of four lemons, half a pint of brandy, and a teaspoonful of salt. Mix all well together, put it in jars, and tie down until it is ready for use, which will be in a few days.

**Hand-Rubbing.**—There is no doubt that hand-rubbing is an art. It is so useful an art and so excellent a remedy that more people ought to learn it. It has nothing to do with *surface rubbing*. That is better done with a Turkish towel, or a hair-glove on the hand. The hand-rubbing used for stiffness, painful joints, disabled limbs, &c., should begin by taking the course of the muscles. It is simply surprising to what extent the force and power of the rubber may reach, without any roughness, and with distinct gratification to the patient. After a time, enlargement and swelling will be rubbed away, and then little "kernels" may be often felt by the fingers, like deep-seated hard grains fastened to joints and muscles. When these are rubbed away, as they soon will be by an experienced hand, the stiffness is gone, and the cure completed.

**Brush-Rubbing.**—For rheumatism, or other affections, when brush-rubbing is resorted to, it should be done at first as lightly as possible ; this is the best mode of treatment for all *pains not arising from sprains.* Gradually increase speed and pressure, but never rub *very* fast. A child's hair-brush, which is soft, or a soft clothes-brush, may be used very effectually, if you have no hair-glove. Aching backs, children's "growing pains," face-aches, as well as rheumatism, are comforted, if not cured, by brush-rubbing.

**Throat Steam-Bath.**—In cases of sore throat and quinsy this is an admirable bath, and one the nurse and patient may safely use. A tea-pot must be filled with boiling water, just so far as not to cover the aperture into the spout. Choose a tea-pot of such a shape as shall give room for the largest surface of water. If the spout is put into the mouth, and the breath drawn back, the steam will reach the throat, and a perfect bath will be accomplished. Act carefully, and draw the breath gently at first, or the throat may be scalded. This may be used many times a day when there is inside swelling and inflammation.

**Laying a Table.**—This is so well understood by all good English servants that few need instruction on this point : but for those ladies who have not experienced servants, we propose to submit a few leading rules. First, then :— The table having the oil-skin cover, with the woollen cloth or common table cover over it, should have a fair white damask table-cloth, and the creases made in the folding of the cloth should be so arranged as to go from head to foot directly in the centre of the table. The cloth should be smoothed down to the table as much as possible ; over this should be placed what the French call a napron, or smaller table-cloth of the same pattern. To each guest should be laid a table-napkin, folded according to taste. In France, they fold every other napkin like a fan, and put it in the long champagne glass, and the other one made to stand up in the plate, so that one plate is without a napkin, and one plate with ; but we recommend all the napkins to be folded alike. In the napkin should be placed a small roll, and to each place should be laid a plate and a soup plate, and the napkin put on the plate. On the right-hand should be placed a knife and spoon ; on the left-hand side should be placed the fork ; on the right-hand side the cooler, wine-glass, hock and champagne glasses, and the caraffe and tumbler. At the centre and four corners should be placed salt-cellars and salt-spoons, and to each salt-cellar, or rather at the side, two ordinary table-spoons. In France the centre of the table is always adorned with a plateau, either in silver or ormolu, the interior of which is of looking-glass, and on this plateau is laid the dessert. This has been tried in England, but is not much followed. The ice-pails or wine-coolers, when used, should be placed one near the top, that is, sufficiently near to admit of the dish being placed before it, and the other at the same distance from the bottom of the table. If there is an epergne, it may be placed in the centre of the table to hold salad ; but we do not admire flowers being placed in the epergne, because we do not eat flowers, and we think that all things used at a dinner-table should be used for holding things to eat or drink. Bottle-stands should be placed near to the salt-cellars, to hold your small decanters filled with sherry ; light wines should be in your ice-pails, as likewise champagne, if any. Now, if you have not these things you are not obliged to get them ; but then do not attempt a great dinner ; by that we mean, only give a plain dinner to a few friends, and then let your arrangements be as near our directions as possible, or as circumstances will permit. We have given these instructions upon the presumption that you have the things we mention ; but if you have other and better things, we do not say they should not be used, nor do we say that you should not receive friends unless you have all the things named.

Perfumes.—Paris, says Mr. Rimmel, in his interesting "Book of Perfumes," is the great centre of the manufacture of perfumery, which forms an important item of what are called "articles des Paris" There are in that capital 120 working perfumers, employing about 3000 men and women.

Next to Hungary-water, the most ancient perfume now in use is eau-de-Cologne, or Cologne-water, which was invented in the last century by an apothecary residing in that city. It can, however, be made quite as well anywhere else, as all the ingredients entering into its composition come from the South of France and Italy. Its perfume is extracted principally from the flowers, leaves, and rind of the fruit of the bitter orange, and other trees of the *Citrus* species, which blend well together, and form an harmonious compound,

Toilet vinegar is a sort of improvement on eau-de-Cologne, containing balsams and vinegar in addition. Lavender-water was formerly distilled with alcohol from fresh flowers, but is now prepared by simply digesting the essential oil in spirits, which produces the same result at a much less cost. The finest is made with English oil, and the common with French, which is considerably cheaper, but is easily distinguished by its coarse flavour.

PERFUMES FOR THE HANDKERCHIEF are composed in various ways ; the best are made by infusing in alcohol the pomades or oils obtained by the processes I have previously described. This alcoholate possesses the true scent of the flowers entirely free from the empyreumatic smell inherent in all essential oils ; as, however, there are but six or seven flowers which yields pomades and oils, the perfumer has to combine these together to imitate all other flowers. This may truly be called the artistic part of perfumery, for it is done by studying resemblances and affinities, and blending the shades of scent as a painter does the colours on his palette. Thus, for instance, no perfume is extracted from the heliotrope ; but it has a strong vanilla flavour, by using the latter as a basis, with other ingredients to give it freshness, a perfect imitation is produced ; and so on with many others.

TOILET SOAPS.—The most important branch of the perfumer's art is the manufacture of toilet soaps. They are generally prepared from the best tallow soaps, which are remelted, purified, and scented. They can also be made by what is called the cold process, which consists in combining grease with a fixed dose of lees.

English toilet soaps are the very best that are made : the French come next, but, as they are not remelted, they never acquire the softness of ours. The German soaps are the very worst that are manufactured ; the cocoa-nut oil, which invariably forms their basis, leaves a strong fœtid smell on the hands, and their very cheapness is a deception, for as cocoa-nut oil takes up twice as much alkali as any other fatty substance, the soap produced with it wastes away in a very short time.

SELECTION OF PERFUMES.—The selection of a perfume is entirely a matter of taste, and I should no more presume to dictate to a lady which scent she should choose, than I would to an epicure what wine he is to drink ; yet I would say to the nervous, use simple extract of flowers, which can never hurt you, in preference to compounds, which generally contain musk and other ingredients likely to affect the head. Above all, avoid strong, coarse perfumes ; and remember, that if a woman's temper may be told from her handwriting, her good taste and good breeding may as easily be ascertained by the perfume she uses. Whilst a *lady* charms us with the delicate ethereal fragrance she sheds around her, aspiring vulgarity will as surely betray itself by a *mouchoir* redolent of common perfumes.

HAIR PREPARATIONS are like medicines, and must be varied according to the consumer. For some pomatum is preferable, for others oil, whilst some,

again, require neither, and should use hair-washes or lotions. A mixture of lime-juice and glycerine has been introduced, and has met with great success, for it clears the hair from pellicles, the usual cause of premature baldness. For all these things, however, personal experience is the best guide.

TOOTH-POWDERS are far preferable to tooth-pastes. The latter may be pleasanter to use, but the former are certainly more beneficial.

LOTIONS FOR THE COMPLEXION require of all other cosmetics to be carefully prepared. Some are composed with mineral poisons, which render them dangerous to use, although they may be effectual in curing certain skin diseases. There ought to be always a distinction made between those that are intended for healthy skins, and those that are to be used for cutaneous imperfections ; besides, the latter may be easily removed without having recourse to any violent remedies.

PAINTS FOR THE FACE I cannot conscientiously recommend. Rouge is innocuous in itself, being made of cochineal and safflower ; but whites are often made of deadly poisons. The best white ought to be made of mother-of-pearl, but it is not often so prepared. To professional people, who cannot dispense with these, I must only recommend great care in their selection ; but to others I would say, cold water, fresh air, and exercise, are the best recipes for health and beauty ; for no borrowed charms can equal those of " A woman's face, with Nature's own hand painted."

[We quite endorse Mr. Rimmel's outspoken advice, which, coming from this chief amongst perfumers, should be seriously considered by our fair readers.]

Musk.—Still quoting from Mr. Rimmel's delightful volume, we find that musk is a secretion found in a pocket or pod under the belly of the musk-deer, a ruminant which inhabits the higher mountain ranges of Tonquin, China, and Thibet. " It is a pretty grey animal," says Dr. Hooker, " the size of a roebuck, and somewhat resembling it, with coarse fur, short horns, two projecting teeth from the upper jaw, said to be used in rooting up the aromatic herbs from which the Bhoteas believe that it derives its odour." The male alone yields the celebrated perfume, the best thing which comes from Tonquin.

Musk is an unctuous substance of a reddish-brown colour, which soon becomes black by exposure to the air. It is so powerful that, according to Chardin's authority, the hunter of the animal is obliged to have his mouth and nose stopped with folds of linen when he cuts off the bag from the animal, as otherwise the pungent smell would cause hæmorrhage, sometimes ending in death. As, however, the natives take good care to adulterate the musk before they send it to Europe, we are not exposed to such accidents.

Musk is, without any exception, the *strongest* and *most durable* of all known perfumes, and it is, in consequence, largely used in compounds, its presence, when not too perceptible, producing a very agreeable effect. Musk is also to be found, though in a less degree, in other animals, such as the musk-ox, the musk-rat, the musk-duck, &c.

**Civet.**—This is the glandular secretion of an animal of the feline tribe, which is found in Africa and India. When properly diluted and combined with other scents, it produces a very pleasing effect, and possesses a much more *floral* fragrance than musk ; indeed, it would be impossible to imitate some flowers without it. Its price varies from 20*s.* to 30*s.* per ounce, according to quality.

**Ambergris.**—This scent for a long time puzzled the *savans*, who were at a loss to account for its origin, and thought it at first to be of the same nature as yellow amber, whence it derived its name of *grey amber (ambre gris)*. It is now ascertained beyond a doubt to be generated by the large-headed spermaceti whale, and is the result of a diseased state of the animal, which either throws up the morbific substance, or dies of the malady, and is eaten up by other fishes. In either case, the ambergris becomes loose, and is picked up floating on the sea, or is washed ashore. It is found principally on the coasts of Greenland, Brazil, India, China, Japan, &c.

Ambergris is not agreeable by itself, having a somewhat earthy or mouldy flavour, but blended with other perfumes it imparts to them an ethereal fragrance unattainable by any other means. Its price varies very much, according to the quantity to be found in the market.

**Floral Perfumes.**—The floral series includes all flowers available for perfumery purposes, which hitherto have been limited to eight—viz., jasmine, rose, orange, tuberose, cassie, violet, jonquil and narcissus.

JASMINE is one of the most agreeable and useful odours employed by perfumers, and highly valuable are the fragrant treasures which they obtain

" From timid jasmine buds, that keep
    Their odours to themselves all day,
    But, when the sunlight dies away,
    Let their delicious secret out."

It was introduced by the Arabs, who called it Yasmyn, hence its present name. It grows in the shape of a bush from three to four feet high, and requires to be in a fresh open soil, well sheltered from north winds. The flowering season is from July to October. The flowers open every morning at six o'clock with great regularity, and are culled after sunrise, as the morning dew would injure their flavour. Each tree yields about twenfy-four ounces of flowers.

THE ROSE—the queen of flowers. And well does the perfumer turn their delicious fragrance to account ; for he compels the lovely flower to yield its aroma to him in every shape, and he obtains from it an essential oil, a distilled water, a perfumed oil, and a pomade. Even its withered leaves are rendered available to form the ground of sachet-powder, for they retain their scent for a considerable time.

The species used for perfumery is the hundred-leaved rose. It is extensively used in Turkey, near Adrianople, whence comes the far-famed otto of roses ; and in the south of France, where pomades and oils are made.

Rose trees are planted in a cool ground, and may be exposed to the north wind without any injury. They bear about eight ounces of flowers in the second year, and twelve ounces in the following ones. The flowering season is in May, and the flowers, which generally open in the night, must be gathered before sunrise, as after that time they lose half their fragrance.

THE ORANGE PERFUME.—The orange-blossoms used for perfumery are those of the bigarrade or bitter orange-tree. They yield by distillation an essential oil which forms one of the chief ingredients in eau-de-Cologne ; a pomade and an oil are also obtained from them by maceration. The largest bigarrade-tree plantations are those to be found in the south of France, in Calabria, and in Sicily. A full-grown tree yields on an average from fifty to sixty pounds of blossoms. The flowering season is in May, and the flowers are gathered two or three times a week after sunrise.

THE TUBEROSE is a native of the East Indies where it grows wild, in Java and Ceylon. It springs from a bulb which is planted in the autumn and bears flowers every year. It was first brought to Europe by a Spanish physician in 1594.

CASSIE is a shrub of the acacia tribe, which only grows in southern latitudes. All those who have travelled on the coast in Genoa, in the months of October and November, will no doubt remember what charming bouquets and garlands are made of the cassie intermixed with other flowers. To perfumers it is a most valuable assistant, possessing in the highest degree a fresh floral fragrance, which renders it highly useful in compounds. It bears some resemblance to the violet, and, being much stronger, is often used to fortify that scent, which is naturally weak.

The cassie requires a very dry soil, well exposed to the sun's rays. The tree does not bear flowers until it is five or six years old. The yield varies from one to twenty pounds for every tree, according to age and position. The blossoms are gathered three times a week after sunrise ; a very strong oil and pomade is obtained from them by maceration. In Africa, and principally in Tunis, an essential oil of cassie is made, which is sold at about 4£ per ounce ; but French and Italian flowers are not sufficiently powerful to yield an essence.

THE VIOLET is one of the most charming odours in nature. It is a scent which pleases all, even the most delicate and nervous, and it is no wonder that it should be in such universal request. The largest and almost only violet plantations have hitherto been at Nice, its exceptional position rendering it the most available spot for them. The species used is the double Parma violet. It flowers from the beginning of February to the middle of April, and each plant yields but a few ounces of blossoms, which are culled twice a week after sunrise.

THE JONQUIL AND NARCISSUS are two bulbous plants which are also cultivated for perfumery purposes, but in much smaller quantities than any of those already mentioned, their peculiar aroma rendering their use limited. Mignonette, lilac, and hawthorn are also sometimes worked into pomades, but on such a small scale that they are not worth mentioning. The extracts named after these flowers are generally produced by combination.

HERBAL PERFUMES.—This series comprises all aromatic plants, such as lavender, spike, peppermint, rosemary, thyme, marjoram, geranium, patchouly, and wintergreen, which yield essential oils by distillation.

LAVENDER is a nice, *clean* scent, and an old and deserving favourite. The best lavender is grown at Mitcham, in Surrey, and at Hitchin in Hertfordshire. It is produced by slips, which are planted in the autumn, and yield flowers the next year and the two following ones, when they are renewed.

SPIKE is a coarser kind of lavender, which is principally used for mixing with the other, or for scenting common soaps.

PEPPERMINT is more used by confectioners than perfumers, yet the latter find it useful in washes and tooth-powders. It is, like lavender, best grown in England, the foreign being very inferior.

ROSEMARY is another plant of the labiate order, which yields a powerful essence, used chiefly for scenting soap. The resemblance of its flavour to that of camphor is very remarkable.

THE ROSE-GERANIUM yields an essence which is greatly prized by perfumers on account of its powerful aroma, by means of which they impart a *rosy fragrance* to common articles at a much less cost than by using otto of roses, which is worth six times as much. It is cultivated in the south of France, Algeria, and Spain.

PATCHOULI comes from India, where it is known under the name of *puchaput*. It has a most peculiar flavour, which is as offensive to some as it is agreeable to others.

WINTERGREEN we receive from North America. This essence is exceedingly powerful, and requires to be used with great caution to produce a pleasing effect. Well blended with others in soap, it imparts to it a rich floral fragrance.

**Hasty Pudding.**—We give two receipts for making this favourite dish :—Into a pint of boiling milk stir about a tablespoonful of flour, previously rubbed down with a little cold milk ; sweeten with sugar, and serve hot : a little nutmeg may be added, if agreeable, or a few currants. For a BAKED PUDDING :—Into a pint of cold milk stir half a pound of flour, and boil, stirring it the while ; let it stand until cold, then add two eggs previously beaten up ; mix well with sugar to sweeten, and any desirable spice, and put into cups and bake. There are good nou-

rishing puddings, and not expensive ; but they are too heavy for persons with weak digestive organs.

**The Wholesomeness of Fruit.**—There can be no doubt that, both in their fresh and dried state, they are extremely useful, affording to the blood the saline constituents which it generally needs, cooling the system, and in many cases acting as a gentle aperient ; the best, because the most easily digested kinds, are those which are soft and pulpy, having the seeds enclosed in a pouch, skin, or rind, such as grapes, gooseberries, Mulberries, strawberries, Raspberries, blackberries, and currants, among native, and oranges and lemons among imported fruits ; apples also, although not soft and pulpy, are very wholesome ; but as much cannot be said for pears and medlars, as, in most kinds of these, decomposition commences directly the ripening process is completed, so that they are seldom eaten in a perfectly sound state. Stone fruits, such as cherries, plums, apricots, &c., are not so wholesome as those with seeds, although taken in moderation they act beneficially, especially in a cooked state. Melons and pine-apples we must pronounce decidedly unwholesome.

BEST TIMES FOR EATING FRUIT —It may be observed that fruit is digestible in proportion to its perfection, and, therefore, care should be taken to have it perfectly ripe, and yet not in a state of decay. Most juicy fruits are best taken in hot weather, and the drier kinds in the cold seasons. The best time of day for eating fruits is the morning, none but the more watery kinds should be eaten after midday, and none at all late in the evening. The worst possible time to eat them is just before going to bed.

**Roast Goose.**—Peel and cut in small pieces six onions, and put them in a stewpan with two ounces of butter, half a teaspoonful of salt, a quarter of a teaspoonful of pepper, a little grated nutmeg and sugar, and six leaves of fresh sage chopped fine ; put over the fire, and stir with a wooden spoon till the ingredients come to a pulp. Stuff the goose with this while hot, and roast for two hours before a moderate fire, frequently basting. Serve with a good brown gravy on the dish, and apple sauce in a boat.

**Apple Sauce.**—Pare, quarter, and core six large apples, and throw them into cold water to preserve their whiteness. Put them into a stewpan with a little water to moisten them, and boil them to a pulp. Beat them up, adding sugar and a small piece of butter.

**Christmas Plum Pudding.**—Stone and chop one pound of raisins ; wash, pick, and dry one pound of currants ; blanch and chop fine two ounces sweet, and one ounce bitter, almonds ; quarter of an ounce mixed spice, and the rind of a lemon, grated. Pour over them two glassfuls of brandy, and let it stand four hours. Soak one pound of bread crumbs in milk, then squeeze dry. Take one pound of flour, one pound of beef-suet, chopped fine, three-quarters of a pound of moist sugar, six ounces candied peel, and a full teaspoonful of salt. Mix these with the bread-crumbs to the other ingredients ; then well beat eight eggs, add them to the pudding with sufficient milk to make it quite stiff. Boil for eight hours.

**Economy of Fuel.**—The person laying a fire should fill the grate up to the top bar with coals, putting larger pieces at the bottom and smaller over them ; then, upon these, paper enough to light the sticks, which should be laid *upon*, and not *under*, the coal. Cover the sticks with the cinders remaining from the previous day's fire ; these will soon become red hot ; the coal below will be warmed sufficiently to make it throw off gas ; this, passing through the hot cinders, will be kindled, and will burn with a bright flame, instead of going up the chimney in smoke, as it does when the coals are laid on the top. The fire thus laid will require no poking, and will burn clear and bright from six to eight hours without the necessity for more coals to be thrown on.

**Burns and Scalds.**—From a useful little manual showing us how to proceed in emergencies " Till the Doctor Comes,"—which is its title—we extract the following sound counsel :—Burns and scalds are constantly occurring, not only in poor families, but in every class of society. The number of children who die from these causes is dreadful ; but when we consider the love of playing with fire common to children, the dress swelled out with crinoline when cooking or doing anything near a fire, the careless manner in which lucifer matches are carried loose in pockets and dropped on to floors, or the way in which hot liquids are placed in the way of children, the wonder is that they do not happen more frequently.

PUTTING OUT THE FIRE.—Take this case, a description of what is unfortunately happening every day :—A female's clothes takes fire ; she is wrapped in flames ; her arms and hands, her neck and face, are scorched with the heat ; her hair is in a blaze ; the smoke is suffocating her. She becomes utterly confused, and rushes to and fro, so creating a current of air which increases the fire. The best thing she could have done would have been instantly to roll upon the floor. But how few would have presence of mind to do this ! The more need for a friend to do it for her. Seize her by the hand, or by some part of the dress which is not burning, and throw her on the ground. Slip off a coat or shawl, a bit of carpet, anything you can snatch up quickly, hold this before you, clasp her tightly with it, which will protect your hands. As quickly as possible fetch plenty of water ; make everything thoroughly wet, for though the flame is out, there is still the hot cinder and the half-burnt clothing eating into the flesh ; carry her carefully into a warm room, lay her on a table or on a carpet on the floor— *not the bed*—give her some warm stimulating drink, send for the doctor, and proceed to the next operation—

REMOVING THE CLOTHES.—Perhaps in the whole course of accidents there is not one which requires so much care and gentleness as this. We want only three people in the room—one on each side of the patient, and one to wait upon them. Oh, for a good pair of scissors or a really sharp knife! What misery you will inflict upon the sufferer by *sawing* through strings, &c., with a rough-edged blunt knife. There must be no dragging or pulling off; do not let the hope of saving anything influence you. Let everything be so completely cut loose that it will fall off; but if any part stick to the body let it remain, and be careful not to burst any blisters.

TREATMENT.—The treatment of burns or scalds in the first stage consists of wet, warm, but not sour applications, and excluding the air.

Get out the old linen or calico ; wet a piece of this well with linseed-oil and lime-water, and as soon as an injured part is exposed, put this on ; cover it with another dry rag or flannel, and secure it with a bandage. If you have not got the mixture of oil and lime-water, get a pint of hot water and milk (equal parts), with a small teaspoonful of carbonate of soda in it. If you have no milk at hand, use warm water with plenty of common soap in it ; or if you have no soap, use plain water with the carbonate of soda, or a little morsel of common washing soda, not more than the size of a small hazel-nut, to a pint of water, dissolved in it ; but whatever you use, keep the parts thoroughly wet and well covered. If you have a waterproof sheet or coat, a piece of oil-cloth, lay this over the mattress, and then a blanket over it. As soon as you have removed all the clothing, and applied the dressings, lift her gently into bed, and cover her as warmly as possible. In after-dressings large surfaces must not be exposed to the air ; either leave a thin covering and wet it with the lotion, or if you are using an ointment, remove only a small portion of the dressing at a time, have everything in readiness, and cover again as quickly as possible.

If there be much pain and fretfulness, you may safely give to an adult thirty drops of laudanum in a little water, and repeat this in an hour, and even a third time if needful. To a child ten years of age give in like manner only three drops, but beware of giving any to an infant.

You must not attempt to manage this case further by yourselves. You have now done your best for her till the doctor comes.

Those of us who are accustomed to see these accidents know well that when the surface injured is sufficiently large to cause death, there is not much suffering, the person seems to die from the shock. Friends are constantly deceived by this, and suppose because there is not much pain, and the patient appears calm and comfortable, there cannot be much danger, whereas it is really the absence of pain, or more truly the want of power to feel pain, which constitutes the danger. Especially is this the case with a child, if the burn be large, particularly on the chest, and the little one remains perfectly quiet, utters no complaint, sighs deeply, and asks frequently for cold water, it is almost certain that life is fast drawing to a close.

SMALL BURNS.—For smaller burns use the same remedies till the inflammation has subsided, or as people say, till the fire is out ; then spread some Turner's cerate on the *woolly* side of lint, and dress the sores with it. They will generally get well without much trouble. You can make a capital ointment yourself of common whiting— (which you use for polishing tins)—and lard without any salt. If the burn be small, and the person can stay indoors, try the following

RECIPE FOR SMALL BURNS.—Take chalk (whiting) and linseed or common olive oil, and mix them to the consistency of honey, then add vinegar so as to reduce it to the thickness of treacle ; apply with a soft brush or feather, and renew the application from time to time. Each renewal brings fresh relief and a most grateful coolness. But if the patient is compelled to go about, you can use the ointment at once, or dust the part thickly over with flour, kept on with rag and bandage; but I am greatly in favour of wet applications, as they do not stick to the raw surface, which is most painfully sensitive. Unless the burn or scald be very small you will almost always find warm dressings much more grateful to the patient than cold.

**To Make Lime-Water.**—Put a piece of unslacked lime the size of a very large walnut into a common-sized wine-bottle full of cold water, shake it up a few times, then let it settle. You need not fear making it too strong; the water will take up only a certain quantity of the lime, however much you put into it.

**Cold Meat.**—If made into an aspic is a delicious way of using the last of a joint, especially in summer time. Cut the meat in pieces, and lay them in a mould in layers, well seasoned. Then pour over and fill the mould with some clear soup nearly cold, which, when let to stand some hours, will turn out and be as firm as isinglass, especially if shank-bones were boiled in the soup. Should the cold meat be veal or poultry, the addition of some small pieces of ham or bacon, and of hard-boiled eggs cut in slices and put between the layers of meat, is a great improvement.

**Wrinkled Silk.**—It may be rendered nearly as beautiful as when new by sponging the surface with a weak solution of gum arabic, strained, or white glue; then iron on the wrong side.

**Rabbit Pie.**—Skin two rabbits, wash them thoroughly, and cut them into small joints. Have ready some lean bacon, and a pound and a half of rump steak; cut both into small pieces, place them all on a large dish, or on a chopping-board, sprinkle them with salt, pepper, chopped parsley and thyme, mix all well together, and put them into the pie-dish, adding force-meat balls, or the yolks of hard-boiled eggs.

Fill the dish with water, cover the whole with a light paste, beat up an egg with a pinch of salt, glaze the pie with it, and bake in a moderate oven two hours.

**Springing out of Bed.**—Dr. Hall disapproves of the doctrine that everyone should spring out of bed the instant they wake in the morning. "Up to eighteen," says Dr. Hall, "every child should be allowed ten hours' sleep, but time should be allowed to rest in bed, after the sleep is over, until they feel as if they had rather get up than not. It is a very great mistake for persons, old or young—especially children and feeble or sedentary persons—to bounce out of bed the moment they wake up; all our instincts shrink from it, and fiercely kick against it. Fifteen or twenty minutes spent in gradually waking up, after the eyes are opened, and in turning over and stretching the limbs, do as much good as sound sleep, because the operations set the blood in motion by degrees, tending to equalise the circulation: for during sleep the blood tends to stagnation, the heart beats feebly and slowly, and to shock the system by bouncing up in an instant and sending the blood in overwhelming quantities to the heart, causing it to assume a gallop, where the instant before it was in a creep, is the greatest absurdity. This instantaneous bouncing out of bed as soon as the eyes are open will be followed by weariness long before noon.

**Lucifer Matches.**—Although friction matches are so common, a very small proportion of those who use them understand the principle on which they operate. It is, in fact, a very simple affair. The tip of the match is a combination of sulphur and phosphorus. The phosphorus ignites at the heat of 150 degrees, which a slight friction will produce, and this in turn ignites the sulphur, which requires 450 or 500 degrees. The flame of the sulphur sets fire to the pine wood, of which the match is composed, and which ignites at about 600 degrees. The combination is necessary, because the phosphorus alone would not kindle the match, while the sulphur alone would not ignite with the ordinary friction.

**Secret Marriages.**—Every now and then the public is startled by the exposure of some domestic or social villainy based on a secret marriage. Some confiding young lady has been induced to marry her lover secretly, and to keep the marriage secret for months, and perhaps for years. Of course a man who wishes to keep his marriage a secret is always actuated by selfish, and usually by base, motives. He is acting a part, playing a game ; and his confiding wife is pretty sure, in the end, to find herself the victim of his treachery and baseness. A woman should never consent to any such arrangement. Her marriage should be solemnised in the light of publicity, and not in the shadow of concealment. She should distrust a man who has any reason for shrouding in darkness the act which, in his estimation, at least, should be the crowning glory of his life. The man who always has some plot on hand—who naturally takes to trickery and concealment, and is never ready to have his actions brought out into the clear light of day, is apt to be so constitutionally base, that he seldom, even by accident, deviates into the path of honour and virtue. No woman who values her domestic happiness should ever listen to the suggestions of such a man in favour of a secret marriage.

**Importance of Salt.**—To every person whose diet consists largely of bread or its equivalents, common salt is a positive necessity. It is a universal constituent of animal bodies, so universal that unless an animal can acquire it in one way or another that animal cannot live. Widely diffused all over the world, it is taken up, too, by the roots of vegetables, and may also be found in their ashes. Dietetically regarded, salt is by no means in the same category with mustard, pepper, vinegar, and other condiments. These are not to be found in blood or muscle. Salt is. In one

way or another, it is, in fact, the very essence of existence.

**A Nice White Soup.**—Break up a shin of veal, and let it soak in cold water for two hours ; then put it to boil in four quarts of water, with an onion, a little mace, pepper, and salt ; let it simmer for five hours. Strain it through a sieve, and set away to cool until the next day. Then take off all fat, wiping with a cloth ; put it to boil. When quite hot, if not well seasoned, add whatever may be required ; mix two spoonfuls of ground rice with water ; stir it until it boils, then add a pint of good sweet milk, and give it one boil.

**Brown, Black, and Blue Eyes.**—That the colour of eyes should effect their strength may seem strange ; yet that such is the case need not at this time of day be proved ; and those whose eyes are brown or dark coloured should be informed that they are weaker and more susceptible of injury, from various causes, than gray or blue eyes. Light blue eyes are generally the most powerful, and next to those are gray. The lighter the pupil, the greater and longer continued is the degree of tension which the eye can sustain.

**Marriage.**—Men and women, and especially young people, do not know that it takes years to marry completely two hearts, even of the most loving and well assorted ; but nature allows no sudden change. We ascend very gradually from the cradle to the summit of life. Marriage is gradual—a fraction of us at a time. A happy wedlock is a long falling in love. I know young persons think that love belongs only to the brown hair, and plump, round, crimson cheeks. So it does for its beginning. But the golden marriage is a part of love which the bridal day knows nothing of. Youth is the tassel and silken flower of love, age is the full corn, ripe and solid in the ear. Beautiful is the morning of love, with its prophetic crimson, violet, purple, and gold, with its hopes of days that are to come. Beautiful also is the evening of love, with its glad remembrances, and its rainbow side turned towards heaven as well as earth. Young people marry their opposites in temper and general character, and such a marriage is commonly a good match. They do it instinctively. The young man does not say, " My black eyes require to be wed with blue, and my over-vehemence requires to be a little modified with somewhat of dulness and reserve." When these opposites come together to be wed they do not know it ; each thinks the other just like itself.

Old people never marry their opposites ; they marry their similars, and from calculation. Each of these two arrangements is very proper. In their long journey, these two young opposites will fall out by the way a great many times, and both get out of the road ; but each will charm the other back again, and by and by they will be agreed as to the place they will go to, and the road they will go by, and become reconciled. The man will be nobler and larger for being associated with so much humanity unlike himself, and she will be a nobler woman for having manhood beside her that seeks to correct her deficiencies and supply her with what she lacks, if the diversity be not too great, and there be real piety and love in their hearts to begin with. The old bridegroom, having a much shorter journey to make, must associate himself with one like himself. A perfect and complete marriage is, perhaps, as rare as perfect personal beauty. Men and women are married fractionally ; now a small fraction, then a large one. Very few are married totally, and they only, I think, after some forty or fifty years of gradual approach and experiment. Such a large and sweet fruit is a complete marriage that it needs a very long summer to ripen in, and then a long winter to mellow and season it. But a real, happy marriage of love and judgment between a noble man and woman, is one of the things so lovely that if the sun were, as the Greek poets fabled, a god, he might stop the world in order to feast his eyes on so rare a spectacle.

**To Remove Grease from Carpets, and Silk and Woollen Fabrics.—**The following recipe for this purpose will be found reliable :—Carbonate of magnesia, saturated with benzole, and spread upon the grease spot, to the extent of about a third of an inch in thickness, is the best known remedy. A sheet of porous paper should be spread upon the benzonated magnesia, and a flat-iron, moderately warm, put upon the top of all. The heat of the iron passes through and softens the grease, which is then absorbed by the porous magnesia. The iron may be removed in an hour, and the magnesia dust brushed off. Soapstone dust may be used in the same manner, but does not answer quite so well.

**Bread-and-Butter Pudding.—**Let your pie-dish be well buttered, and strew the bottom with currants and candied peel ; then place alternate layers of bread and butter in rather thin slices, and the peel and currants, until the dish is nearly full, observing to have currants at the top ; then pour over, slowly and equally, a custard of sweetened milk and two or three eggs, flavoured to taste, and bake in a moderate oven for twenty minutes.

**To Pickle a Tongue.—**Wash it well ; then salt it in common salt for three days ; then mix a quarter of a pound of the coarsest brown sugar, and half an ounce of saltpetre, well pounded, and rub it well into the tongue. Then return the tongue into the first pickle, and keep it in it, close covered, for three weeks, turning it every other day.

**Good-Bye.—**There is hardly any greater perversion of the meaning of a phrase in the English language than is contained in the words " good-bye "— which in themselves have no meaning whatever. In olden times it was customary among pious people, when parting from those they loved or respected, to commend them to the protection of God. The phrase in French was *a Dieu*, to God.—*Anglice*, " adieu," and now used by thousands without a knowledge of its meaning. The old English form of expression, " God be with you," (a most beautiful expression when taking leave of a friend) is, by corruption, shortened into " good-bye."

**Lace.**—During the fifteenth century the nuns in Italy became famous for the exquisitely-manipulated point or pillow-lace. The origin of this famous lace is quite romantic. The story is, that a sailor brought to his lady-love a splendid bunch of " mermaid's lace," which is generally called " coralline." The girl was a lace-maker, and exceedingly artistic in taste. She greatly admired the delicate beauty of the coralline, and studied to imitate in lace the beautiful lines of the sea-weed. This kind of lace is made entirely upon a pillow or cushion, which the workwoman holds on her lap. Over the pillow is placed a piece of parchment ; upon this the pattern is pricked. The threads are carefully wound upon several bobbins. The process requires nimble and skilful fingers, and a great deal of patience. The groundworks are various, and contain the flower. There are several laces that are not worked upon a ground. Valenciennes and Mechlin laces have the designs and ground made together, finished with either the pearl or picot edge.

At one period guipures were the mode. During the reign of Henry VIII., this lace was so extensively worn, that the costumes of pages were covered with this costly garniture ; and at the coronation of Henry II. the church was richly trimmed with guipure lace.

About the beginning of the fifteenth century, Brussels lace was first introduced to the *beau monde.* The manufacture of this lace is a sort of jobbing affair. The manipulation of it is very complicated, every part being made separately. The thread is exceedingly fine ; from one pound of flax there can be manufactured lace to the value of 700£ sterling. Valenciennes became known in the seventeenth century. The finest qualities are from Ypres. It re-

quires great patience to make Valenciennes. The work is very slow. A good lace-maker, working twelve hours a-day, can only make one-third of an inch a-week.

Alencon, the queen of laces, is the only lace in France that is made on a pillow. This lace has great strength, and is not injured by washing. The French revolution was the destroyer of lace-manufactures, but under the First Napoleon, Alencon was again received with favour. The Emperor purchased a dress of this costly lace for 70,000 francs, and gave it to the Empress.

Honiton lace was introduced into England by Flemish refugees. This style of *dentelle* owes its great reputation to its sprigs, which are applique work on a costly and beautiful ground. Queen Adelaide first patronised the Honiton lace-makers. The Queen gave an order for a lace dress, and that the flowers should be all copied from nature. The skirt was adorned with wreaths of flowers, the initial of each sprig forming the name of her Majesty—Amaranth, Daphne, Eglantine, Lilac, Auricula, Ivy, Dahlia, Eglantine. Queen Victoria's bridal dress was made of Honiton lace, and cost one thousand pounds.

**Damson Jelly.**—To four pound of damsons put four pound of loaf-sugar and half a pint of water ; boil them for half an hour over a gentle fire, till the skins break, then take them off, and set them by for an hour ; place them over the fire again for half an hour more ; then set them by again ; repeat for a third time. While they stand by the fire put a weight upon them to keep down the syrup. The last boiling must be continued till they appear of a very high colour in the part where the skin is broken ; then take them off, set them by to cool, and when they are cold drain off the syrup. Boil a dozen good-flavoured apples to a pulp, and some peach or plum kernels with them, add the apples to the damson syrup ; boil together twenty minutes, and put into glasses or pots.

**To Loosen Glass Stoppers.**—A very common source of trouble and vexation is the fixed stopper of a smelling-bottle, or of a decanter ; and as in the case of all frequent evils many methods have been devised for its remedy. Some of these methods (we quote from " *Cassell's Household Guide*), we shall enumerate :—

1. Hold the bottle or decanter firmly in the hand, or between the knees, and gently tap the stopper on alternate sides, using for the purpose a small piece of wood, and directing the strokes upward. .

2. Plunge the neck of the vessel into hot water, taking care that the water is not hot enough to split the glass. If after some immersion the stopper is still fixed, recur to the first process.

3. Pass a piece of list round the neck of the vessel, which must be held fast while two persons draw the list backwards and forwards. This will warm the glass, and often enable the hand to turn the stopper.

4. Warm the neck of the vessel before the fire, and when it is nearly hot, the stopper can be generally moved.

5. Put a few drops of oil round the stopper where it enters the glass vessel, which may then be warmed before the fire. Next take the decanter or bottle, and employ the process No. 1, described above. If it continues fixed, add another drop of oil to the stopper, and place the vessel again before the fire. Then repeat the tapping with the wood. If the stopper continues still immovable, give it more oil, warm it afresh, and rub it anew, until it gives way, which it is almost sure to do in the end.

6. Take a steel pen or a needle, and run it round the top of the stopper in the angle formed by it and the bottle. Then hold the vessel in your left hand, and give it a steady twist towards you with the right, and it will very often be effectual, as the adhesion is frequently caused by the solidification of matter only at the point nearest the air. If this does not succeed, try process No. 5, which will be facilitated by it. By combining the two methods numbered 5 and 6, we have extracted stoppers which have been long fixed, and given up in despair after trying the usual plans. Broken stoppers are best left to professional hands.

**To Choose Eggs.**—The safest way is to hold them to the light, forming a focus with your hand. Should the shell be covered with small dark spots, they are doubtful, and should be broken separately in a cup. If, however, in looking at them, you see no transparency in the shells, you may be sure they are only fit to be thrown away. The most certain way is to look at them by the light of a candle. If quite fresh, there are no spots upon the shells, and they have a brilliant yellow tint. New-laid eggs should not be used until they have been laid about eight or ten hours ; for the part which constitutes the white is not properly set before that time, and does not obtain its delicate flavour. Three minutes are quite sufficient to boil a full-sized egg ; but if below the average size, two minutes and a half will suffice. Never boil eggs for salads, sauces, or any other purpose, more than ten minutes ; and, when done, place them in a basin of cold water for five minutes to cool. Nothing is more indigestible than an egg boiled too hard.

**Rice Pudding.**—Put two tablespoonfuls of the best rice in a pie-dish ; wash it well ; mix two tablespoonfuls of sugar with it. Pour on a pint of milk, and bake very slowly for two hours. A few shavings of butter laid on the top of the milk, or a small quantity of finely-minced beef-suet will help to keep the milk from burning ; but the oven should never be hot enough for this. Rice boiled in milk, sweetened, poured into a mould, and eaten cold with jam is very good ; and tapioca, after having been soaked in water for some time, may be boiled in milk (which has been flavoured with lemon-peel) till perfectly tender, sweetened, poured into a mould, and turned out when cold. It should be made very stiff if it is to retain its shape. This is very nourishing, and much nicer to many tastes than tapioca-pudding made with eggs. Always use good milk, never skimmed milk, if you would have pudding nourishing and digestible.

**Ball-Room Etiquette.**—A month at least should elapse before the ball is given after the invitations have been sent out. As the company is generally numerous at balls, it is neither necessary, nor is it expected, to be so select as at smaller parties. On these occasions the rooms may be well filled, although too great a crowd should be avoided. The majority ought, of course, to be juvenile, and the number of gentlemen should be equal to, or even exceed, that of the ladies.

Be beforehand in all the necessary preparations for parties of every kind. Early in the day, the sofas, chairs, and tables should be removed, as well as every other piece of furniture which is likely either to be in the way or to be injured ; forms should be placed round the walls of the room, as occupying less space than chairs, and accommodating more persons with seats.

A chalked floor, besides being ornamental, is useful in disguising for the time an old or ill-coloured floor, which would otherwise form a miserable contrast to the well-dressed ladies and gentlemen. When the season will allow it, we must not forget to fill the fireplace with flowers and plants, which, indeed, form an appropriate and pleasing ornament on the landing-places, and in other parts of the house through which the guests may have to pass.

In consulting the beauty of the fair visitants, those flowers should be selected which reflect colours in harmony with the human complexion ; as, for example, the rose, the early white azalea, the white and pink hyacinth, and other flowers of similar tints. There should not be an undue proportion of green ; for, as this colour reflects the blue and yellow rays, it is by no means favourable to the feeble complexion ; and still worse are yellow and orange-coloured groups, whether of natural or artificial flowers. In some degree, however, the flowers should be chosen to harmonise also with the colour of the paper, or the walls of the ball-room.

The lady of the house, who is expected to appear in rather conspicuous full dress, should be in readiness to receive her guests in good time ; allowing herself a few minutes' leisure to survey her rooms, to ascertain that everything is in proper order, and that nothing is defective in any of her arrangements. The arrival of the guests will be between eight and nine.

A retiring room should be in readiness for ladies who may wish to disburthen themselves of shawls and cloaks ; and here a female should be in attendance to receive them, and to perform any little office of neatness which a lady's dress may accidentally require. Tea and coffee may also be presented in this room, if any be deemed necessary ; but of late the custom of introducing these refreshments at balls has been nearly abolished.

The mistress of the house should be as near the entrance of the ball-room as possible, that her friends may not have to search for her to whom, of course, they wish first to pay their respects, and from whom they expect their welcome.

As soon as a sufficient number of dancers are arrived, the young people should be introduced to partners, that they may not, by any unreasonable delay of their expected amusement, lose their self-complacency, and cast the reflection of dulness on the party.

When the lady of the house is a dancer, she generally commences the dance ; but when this is not the case, her husband should lead out the greatest stranger, or lady of highest rank present ; and while one dance is proceeding, the mistress of the ball should be preparing another set of dancers to take the place of those upon the floor as soon as they have finished.

Nothing displays more want of management and method, than a dead pause after a dance ; while the lady, all confusion at so disagreeable a circumstance, is begging those to take their places who have, perhaps, never been introduced to partners. There should be no monopoly of this delightful recreation, but all the dancers in the party should enjoy it in regular succession.

REFRESHMENTS—such as ices, lemonade, wine, and small rout cakes—should be handed round between every two or three dances, unless a room be appropriated for such refreshments. Supper should be announced at twelve, and each gentleman should then be requested to take charge of a lady to the supper-room. Both with regard to the pleasure of her company, and her own comfort, the mistress would do well to discountenance the habit, which is sometimes sanctioned, of the gentlemen remaining long in the supper-room after the ladies have retired.

When the gentlemen remain in the supper-room, it frequently causes a formal party of silent and listless fair ones, who seem to consider this temporary suspension of their amusement as an evil of sufficient magnitude to rob their countenances of the smiles of cheerfulness and good-humour, which they had worn during the preceding part of the evening. As our gentle islanders lose half their charms when they lose their good-humour, it is charitable to them to prevent, if possible, this half-hour of discomfiture.

THE SUPPER.—The variety of little delicacies of which suppers generally consist, makes them rather expensive. The table is often crowded with dishes, which, however, contain nothing of a more solid nature than chickens, collared eels, tongue, prawns, lobsters, jellies, trifles, blancmange, whips, fruit, cake, ornamental confectionery, &c.

As it would be scarcely possible to seat a very large party at once at a supper-table, it is advisable to keep one part of the company dancing in the ball-room, whilst another is at supper; and, even in this case, the gentlemen need not be seated nor sup until the ladies have retired. Very little apparent exertion is necessary in the lady of the house, yet should she contrive to speak to most of her guests some time during the evening, and to the greatest strangers she should pay more marked attention.

**Conversaziones.**—These are understood to be select meetings both in respect to the number and the characters of the individuals who are invited. To routs the invitations are general and unlimited; to conversaziones they are limited, and the individuals are, at least, supposed to possess a taste for information, whether obtained from books or from conversation.

This description of evening amusement is not, however, general, but is confined either to literary circles, or to those persons of rank and fortune who wish to patronise literature. When you wish to give a conversazione, the party should be selected with some care; and although persons of the same pursuits should be brought together, yet individuals of the most opposite characters and acquirements should also be invited, to give variety and interest to the conversation, which is the object of the assembly. The tables should be spread with the newest publications, prints, and drawings; shells, fossils, and other natural productions should also be introduced, to excite attention and promote remark.

Card parties may be united with conversaziones. The introduction of cards takes off the air of pedantry which is supposed to pervade a pure conversazione, and sets aside the character of gaming, which might attach to a party met solely for the purposes of play. Many of our ablest men of science and in literature, are fond of whist, and would willingly go to such a mixed party, although they would hesitate to attend one purely conversational, or convened solely for card-playing.

**Qualifications of a Housekeeper.**—Trust-worthiness is an essential quality in a housekeeper; but, if she be not as vigilant as she is honest, she cannot discharge her duty well. As she is the deputy of her mistress, she should endeavour to regard everything around her with the keenness and interest and regard of a principal, rather than with the indifference of a servant. She should be constantly on the alert in observing and detecting anything wrong in the conduct of those under her. It is a part of her duty to see that each fulfils his or her share of the household employments, without appealing to the heads of the family ; unless she find her authority insufficient to keep the whole in order.

She should be a good accountant ; having books in which she may note down strictly all expenses of the house, and which should be cast up weekly, in order to show them to her lady, and have them settled at a time convenient to her. She should have a book, also, in which those articles of housekeeping that are brought into the house and not immediately paid for should be entered. It is a satisfaction to her master and mistress that this book should be ready to compare with the accounts sent by the tradesmen.

It is the province of the housekeeper to have the charge of the store-room, with the preserves, pickles, and confectionery, and to see that no waste takes place in anything entrusted to her. A clever housekeeper will be able to judge of the consumption which, from the size of the family she superintends, will necessarily take place in each article ; and when that quantity is exceeded, she will instantly try to discover the cause and to rectify it, if it proceed from any waste or carelessness of those under her superintendence.

It is absolutely necessary that she should understand the art of cooking, and everything connected with it. It is true, there are many houses in which professed cooks are kept ; but where this is not the case, it is necessary that the housekeeper should be well qualified to superintend the whole business of the kitchen. In most domestic establishments the housekeeper has to prepare the confectionery ; and how far she may be required to take an active part in the cooking, must depend on the qualifications of the cook under her. The housemaids, laundress, and dairymaid, should also be under her eye, so that each should feel aware that her conduct is observed.

Even if you should be perfectly satisfied that your housekeeper is a woman of great integrity, you will still find it desirable to fix your eye constantly upon her, that her vigilance and integrity may not relax for want of this incitement. Symptoms of neglect on her part should never be overlooked, as they would tend to throw the whole house into confusion.

**To Wash Glass.**—Decanters, in which the wine has stood some time, may be cleaned by putting a few drops of muriatic acid into them, and afterwards washing them well with cold water. Muriatic acid, put into the water in which the glass is washed, removes any discolouration from wine, and certainly improves the polish of the glass. Egg-shells pounded small, and put with some water into decanters, will have the same effect. Much of the brilliancy of glass depends on drying it with great care, immediately after it is washed, and rubbing it for some time after it is dry. You must remember in purchasing glass-cloths to buy them tolerably fine, because, from fine linen, there is but little lint ; when these cloths give much lint to the glass, it occasions great trouble to the servant to remove it entirely. A brush is necessary for polishing cut-glass after it has been wiped dry. Glass should be washed in cold water, and china in as hot as can be used. Some people think it better to wash glass in water just warmed, but we do not think it looks so clear afterwards as it does when washed in cold water ; besides, servants are sometimes hasty in their proceedings, and we have seen them plunge glass into hot instead of warm water, by the effect of which there has been an instant loss of one or more articles. In frosty weather, glasses are very liable to crack, if hot water be put suddenly into them. This circumstance is owing to the sudden expansion of the inside of the glass, while the outside remains contracted ; for as glass is a very bad conductor of heat, the heat does not permeate the side of the vessel sufficiently quick to expand it equally throughout. Glass lamps and lustres should be washed in cold water with soap, put on with a sponge or a piece of flannel.

**How to Mix Mustard.**—Mustard should be mixed with water that has been boiled and allowed to cool ; hot water destroys its essential qualities, and raw cold water might cause it to ferment. Put the mustard in a cup, with a small pinch of salt, and mix with it, very gradually, sufficient boiling water to make it drop from the spoon without being watery. Stir and mix well, and rub the lumps well down with the back of a spoon, as mustard properly mixed should be perfectly free from these. The mustard-pot should not be more than half full, or rather less, if it would not be used for a day or two, as the mustard is so much better when fresh made.

**Glove Flirtation.**—When you wish to be acquainted, carry your gloves with the finger-tips downward ; if you wish to say, Introduce me to your company, use them as a fan ; for saying, Be contented, hold them loose in the right hand ; I wish to get rid of you very soon, bite the finger-tips ; Yes, drop one of them ; No, clench them rolled up in the right hand ; I am indifferent, draw one glove half way on the left hand ; Get rid of your company, fold them up carefully ; Follow me, strike them over the left shoulder ; I love another, tap your chin with them ; I am engaged, toss them up gently ; Be careful, somebody is watching us, twirl them round the fingers ; I hate you, turn them inside out ; I am satisfied, hold them loose in the left hand ; I wish I were with you, smooth them out gently ; I am displeased, strike them over the hand ; I am vexed, put them away ; Do you love me ? put one on the left hand, with thumb exposed ; I love you, drop both of them.

**How to Judge Furs.**—In purchasing furs, a sure test of what dealers call a prime fur is the length and density of the down next the skin ; this can be readily determined by blowing a brisk current of air from the mouth against the set of the fur. If the fibre opens readily, exposing the skin to the view, reject the article ; but if the down is so dense that the breath cannot penetrate it, or at most shows but a small portion of skin, the article may be accepted.

**The Lips.**—Leigh Hunt remarks, " I have observed that lips become more or less contracted in the course of years, in proportion as they are accustomed to express good humour and generosity, or peevishness and a contracted mind. Remark the effect which a moment of ill-temper or grudgingness has upon the lips, and judge what may be expected for an habitual series of such moments. Remark the reverse, and make it a similar judgment. The mouth is the frankest part of the face ; it can't in the least conceal its sensations. We can neither hide ill temper with it, nor good ; we may affect what we please, but affectation will not help us. In a wrong cause it will only make our observers resent the endeavour to impose upon them. The mouth is the seat of one class of emotions, as the eyes are of another ; or, rather, it expresses the same emotions, but in greater detail, and with a more irrepressible tendency to be in emotion. It is the region of smiles and dimples, and of a trembling tenderness ; of a sharp sorrow, or a full-breathing joy ; of candour, of reserve, of anxious care, or liberal sympathy. The mouth, out of its many sensibilities, may be fancied throwing up one great expression in the eye—as many lights in a city reflect a broad lustre into the heaven."

**The Eye.**—The little sphere, of an inch or so in diameter, which forms the eyeball, is a camera, essentially like the one used by the photographer to throw the image of external objects upon the surface prepared to receive it and placed within the apparatus.

The mere forming of this picture inside the eye is not, however, *seeing*. The picture might as well be anywhere else, if there were not some means of making the mind aware of its existence.

The optic nerve answers this purpose —a branch of the brain which enters the eye through a small hole in the rear, and spreads out a delicate network over the surface whereon the picture is formed.

The impression is made by the rays of light upon the network of nerves, is telegraphed to the mind, which then *sees* the object, or rather, from seeing its image in the eye, comes to recognise the existence of the object itself outside of the eye.

If the optic nerve should be severed, the picture in the eye might be as perfect as before, but we would, nevertheless, be blind to it.

If any portion of the network of nerves just mentioned should be paralysed, we would cease to see part of the picture formed on the portion of the eye's inner surface. If the entire image of some small object should fall upon that insensible spot, we could no more see it, though looking straight at it, than if we had no eyes, or kept them shut.

**Cheerful Activity.**—If a lady desires to retain the possession of a healthy organisation, she must not remain inert and idle three-fourths of her time. She who sits down by the fire to keep quiet and pore over novels, while the physical health grows delicate day by day, and the mind morbid from lack of exercise and occupation, are more to be pitied than the overworked women of the land, who rise early in the morning, refreshed after sweet sound sleep, and with glowing cheeks, quick step, and strong muscle, begin the task of the day The workers live longer and enjoy more than the idlers. Women expect men to exert themselves, and, rain or shine, to go forth to arduous labour, and encourage them not to waste their time and strength by praising what they accomplish. Why not adopt the same plan in reference to themselves? That it would work well there can be little doubt, for health and happiness can surely be attained by cheerful activity.

**Julienne Soup.**—Three each carrots, turnips, and the white parts of three heads of celery, with the same number of leeks and onions, which should all be cut into thin shreds of an inch long. With about two ounces of butter, a tea spoonful of sugar, and a little salt. Simmer them over a slow fire until they are slightly brown. Add three quarts of good stock. Let the soup boil. As the butter rises to the surface skim it off. Add the leaves of two cabbage-lettuces when the vegetables are done, and a handful of sorrel ; shred fine like the other vegetables, adding a few leaves of tarragon and chervil. Boil them for twelve minutes longer, and serve hot.

**Rose-tinted Curtains.**—By dissolving magenta in water, white muslin curtains can readily be tinted of a beautiful rose colour. A shilling's worth of magenta-powder, dissolved in barely as much water as to steep the curtains in completely, and then wrung out, tinted two large pairs of window-curtains after being starched, and another pair after these were done. The tint fades were much exposed to the sun, but it can be readily renewed, where faded, by a soft brush, or by dipping anew. There are various applications of it—for example, to toilet-covers, &c.

**Economy in Coal.**—The most practical suggestion yet made towards economy of coal seems to be the use of solid bottoms in ordinary fire-grates. It is asserted, and even proved, that in any fireplace not exceedingly small, a plate of iron placed upon the grate will halve the consumption of coal, reduce the smoke, and leave a cheerful, free-burning fire. Quite sufficient air enters through the bars, no poking is necessary, and the fire never goes out till the coals are consumed. There is no ash and no dust, every particle being consumed. Any housekeeper can try this experiment, and, at the cost of a shilling, reduce the expense of coals at least thirty per cent.

**Names of the Months.**—JANUARY is the given name of the first month of the year, according to the computation now in legal and ordinary use. The word is derived from the latin *Januarius*—a name given it by the Romans, from *Janus*, one of their divinities, to whom they attributed two faces ; because, on the one side, the first of January looked towards the new year, and on the other towards the old. The Christians heretofore fasted on the first day of January, by way of opposition to the superstition of the heathens, who in honour of *Janus* observed this day with feastings, dancings, masquerades, and other ignorant manifestations.

FEBRUARY.—This month is so called from *Februa*, a feast held in the second month of the Roman chronology. In the first ages of Rome, February was the last month of the year, and preceded January till the Decemviri made an order that February should be the second month of the year, and come after January.

MARCH.—According to the common way of computing, March is the third month of the year. Among the Romans March was the first month ; and in some ecclesiastical computations that order is still preserved, as particularly in reckoning the number of years from the incarnation of our Saviour, which is done from the 25th of March. In England, before the alteration of the style, March, properly speaking, was the first month in order, the New Year commencing from the 25th : though in complaisance to the customs of our neighbours, we usually ranked it as the third, but in this respect we spoke one way and wrote another. It was Romulus who divided the year into months, to the first of which he gave the name of his supposed father, *Mars*. The month of March was always under the protection of Minerva, and always consisted of thirty-one days. The ancients held it an unhappy month for marriage, as well as the month of May.

APRIL.—This is the fourth month of the year according to the common computation, but the second according to that of the astronomers. The word is derived from *Aprilis*, of *aperio*, *I open ;* because the earth in this month begins to open her bosom for the production of vegetables.

MAY.—This flowery month was called *Maius* by Romulus, in respect to the senators and nobles of his city, who were named *Majores ;* though some will have it to have been thus called from *Maia* the mother of Mercury, to whom they offered sacrifice on the first day of this month. In May the sun enters Gemini, and the plants of the earth in general begin to flower.

JUNE.—The word comes from the Latin *Junius*, which some derive from *Junone*. Others derive it from *junioribus*, this being for young people, as the month of May was for old ones. In this month is the summer solstice.

JULY—This word is derived from the Latin *Julius*, the surname of C. Cæsar, the dictator, who was born in it. Mark Antony first gave the name of July, which was called *Quintilis*, as being the fifth month of the year in the old Roman Calendar, established by Romulus, which began in the month of March. For the same reason August was called *Sextilis*, and September, October, November, and December, still retain the name of their first rank. On the third day of this month the dog-days are commonly supposed to begin, and to end on the eleventh day of August.

AUGUST.—This is the eighth month of the Julian year. This was called in the ancient Roman Calendar *Sextilis*, as being the sixth from March, from which the Romans began their computation. The Emperor Augustus changed the name, and gave it his own ; not that it was the month in which he was born, but because it had been fortunate to him, by several victories which he had

meric gives the transparent yellow crystals ; logwood, purple, &c.

**Tonics.**—Iron is the best of tonics, and may be taken with advantage by weakly persons of pale complexion, or in any case where symptoms of febrile or intermittent disease are present. The best form is that of the muriated tincture—dose eight or ten drops in water, gradually increased to fifteen or twenty drops. This medicine, and, indeed, tonics generally, should not be used for more than a fortnight at a time, and a long interval should elapse between such periods of taking them. Iron taken in conjunction with Peruvian bark or quinine will soon restore the colour to the cheek, and the strength to the frame of the dilapidated valetudinarian. Bark steeped in port wine forms an agreeable tonic draught, but the cheapest, most easily obtainable, and by no means the least efficacious tonic, is made by throwing a clean iron nail into a bottle of ripe old ale, and after a week drinking the liquor in regular doses.

Gentian, camomile, and other popular bitters, are valuable tonics, many of which would be found more rapidly corrective of the system than laxative medicines—always, indeed, where illness resulted from weakness of the digestive organs. Rhubarb root is also a valuable tonic when used in *small* doses, when used in large doses it is a purgative.

**The Invalid's Calendar.**—
Bitter is the wind in March ;
April winds your frame will search ;
Go out most cautiously in May ;
In June, you'll go out every day ;
July—you are free at length ?
August air will give you strength ;
September—now begin to mind ;
October is not often kind ;
November—now you close shut up :
December—patiently receive your
    cup ;
January—watch and wait ;
February—think upon your state,
And thank God every month and
    year
That He still doth leave you here ;

Yet willingly prepare to go,
If your Father wills it so.
Nor be impatient to be gone,
Be content to linger on
If that should be your Father's will,
He forgets not you are ill.
You must not murmur at delay,
That lands you in such glorious day,
And keeps you there with him for
    aye ;
Only patient—watch and pray !

**The Dangers of New Houses.**—One of the many errors which people who build houses are apt to commit is that of living in them, or rather dying in them, before they are sufficiently dry for occupation. It not unfrequently happens that a man, disgusted with the defective sanitary arrangements of the generality of houses, ancient and modern, builds a dwelling for himself and his family, constructed with all the latest improvements, and, in his extreme anxiety to commence a career of longevity, rushes into it almost before the workmen are out of it, and while the walls are still saturated with moisture. The consequence is, as might have been expected, in addition to the architect's charges, the rash owner is called upon to pay within the first few months a further bill to the doctor, and too often to the undertaker also. A house agent not long ago, being asked why the house agency business was so commonly combined with that of the undertaker, grimly replied that the two went together ; and on being asked for a further explanation stated that he had observed, as an almost invariable rule, that, when as a house agent he found a tenant for a newly-built house, he was applied to as an undertaker on behalf of that tenant or some member of his family within a twelvemonth from the date of occupation. He added that he would be sorry to live in any house " that had not been baked by six summer suns." Whether this amount of baking is absolutely required is a question for doctors and architects to decide ; but there can be no doubt whatever that a want of caution in this respect leads occasionally to the most lamentable consequences.

**Origin of Clans and Tartans.—** Clans were Highland families, all members of which bear the same surname, and are supposed to be descended from a common ancestor, of which the chief of the clan is the lineal representative.

Most of the Highland noblemen and gentlemen have designations peculiar to them as chiefs of their clans, which, in their own country, no feudal titles or distinctions, however exalted, are allowed to efface. These names were usually patronymic, expressive of descent from the founder of a family. Thus, the Duke of Argyll is called Mac-Cullum More, or son of Colin the Great. Each clan is distinguished by the pattern of its tartan, and the rank of the wearer by the number of its colours. For instance, royalty wore seven colours. viz., red, blue, purple, brown, yellow, white, and green ; the Oldhams, or men of learning, six ; the nobility, five ; gentlemen who entertained strangers at their table, four ; commanding officers in the army, three ; soldiers, two ; and the peasantry, one. This, perhaps, is the origin of the tartan. Another curious account is given of the origin of tartan plaids. It is said that they are in commemoration of the coat of many colours that Jacob prepared for his son, adopted by the Celts in Scotland and in the North of Ireland, in honour of Joseph, it being asserted that the Israelites of the tribe of Joseph came over from Egypt and settled in Scotland, some of whom, in course of time, passed over to Ireland, and introduced the tartan into Ulster. It is a disputed matter whether the Israelites at first settled in Scotland or Ireland ; but we must leave the Irish and Scotch to settle the affair amongst themselves in the best possible way. But there is one thing certain, that if the Israelites had been adventurers on the Western seas, the natives of Scotland seem to have made the most of it in commemorating their memory by adhering to the tartan for many ages.

**New Modes of Safety during a Lightning Storm.—** In commenting on an interesting case of lightning-stroke, Mr. Lane, in a clinical lecture delivered at St. Mary's Hospital, remarked that there is no doubt that the safest place for shelter is in the interior of a dwelling-house or other enclosed building, at a distance from windows and street-doors ; and in a cellar, perhaps, for choice, not only is the chance of being struck infinitely less, but the risk of serious injury is also much diminished. The popular notion that it is imprudent to take shelter under a tree appears well founded, especially if the tree be isolated, or standing alone. A low tree, or a hedge with several high trees near, is less objectionable, as the lightning will generally be attracted by preference to the most prominent objects. Trees standing together in a wood are seldom struck ; the electric cloud coming within the attraction of a mass of trees possibly discharges itself insensibly through the innumerable points of foliage. A wood, therefore, is not an unsafe place, though even there it may be well to keep away from a tree which is higher than its neighbours. Many persons have been killed while standing under a hay or corn-rick ; these, therefore, should be avoided. From their dryness they are worse conductors than the human body, so that the current passes from them to the latter, as the readiest channel by which it can reach the ground. But is it safer to remain in the middle of a large open space ? This is a doubtful question ; for a man in the erect position, though less prominent than a tree, still offers a dangerous point of attraction when no other object is near, and if struck, the whole force of the stroke will pass through his body, entering probably by his head ; whereas under the tree the current is likely to be divided and split up, so that though the chance of being struck may perhaps be greater, the risk of fatal injury is considerably less. It appears to be pretty generally agreed that the safest plan, supposing shelter within a house to be unattainable, is to remain near some prominent object, such as a tree, but on the side opposite to that from which the storm is proceeding, and at a distance sufficient (say 20 to 30 yards) to avoid the risk of the electricity being attracted from the tree to the person. Under any circumstances, the recumbent is undoubtedly safer than the erect position ; elevated and prominent situations being, of course, carefully avoided. Additional security may also be obtained by depositing watch and chain, money, or other metallic substances which attract electricity, at a safe distance. Wet clothes are not without a compensating advantage—they are all the better conductors of electricity ; and, if they do not convey safely the whole of the current, they will transmit a much larger proportion of it, so that there will be all the less risk of personal injury. It is unwise to walk along an exposed road under an umbrella, especially.one with metallic stem and framework.

**Statistics of Life.**—Half of all who live die before 17. Only one person in 10,C00 lives to be 100 years old, and but one in a hundred reaches 60. The married live longer than the single ; and out of every 1,000 born, only 95 weddings take place. Of 1,000 persons who have reached 70, there are of clergymen, orators, and public speakers, 43 ; farmers, 40 ; workmen, 33 ; soldiers, 32 ; lawyers, 29 ; professors, 27 ; doctors, 24. Farmers and workmen do not arrive at a good old age as often as clergymen and others, who perform no manual labour ; but this is owing to the neglect of the laws of health, inattention to proper habits of life in eating, drinking, sleeping, dress, and the proper care of themselves after the work of the day is done.

**Chilblains.**—To those especially liable to these tiresome and painful affections we recommend, as a preventive, wearing kid-skin gloves lined with wool, which not only keep out the cold, but absorb any moisture that may be upon the hands ; and to rub over the hands before washing a small quantity of glycerine, which should be allowed to dry or become absorbed to a partial extent. When chilblains do manifest themselves, the best remedy for not only preventing them ulcerating, but overcoming the tingling, itching pain, and stimulating the circulation of the part to healthy action, is the liniment of belladonna, two drachms ; the liniment of aconite, one drachm ; carbolic acid, two drops ; and collodion flexible, one ounce, painted with a camel-hair pencil over their surface. When the chilblains vesicate, ulcerate, or slough, it is better to omit the aconite and apply the other components of the liniment without it. The collodion flexible forms a coating or protecting film, which excludes the air, whilst the sedative liniments allay the irritation, generally of no trivial character.

For CHAPPED HANDS e advise the free use of glycerine and good olive oil, in proportion to two parts of the former to four of the latter ; after this has been well rubbed into the hands, and allowed to remain for a little time, and the hands subsequently washed with Castile soap and tepid water, we recommend the belladonna and collodion flexible to be painted, and the protecting film allowed to permanently remain. These complaints not unfrequently invade persons of languid circulation and relaxed habit, who should be put on a generous regimen and treated with ferruginous tonics. Chapped lips are also benefited by the stimulating form of application here advocated, but the aconite must not be allowed to get on the lips, or a disagreeable tingling results.

**Process of Enamelling the Face.** —All the materials for the operation being at hand, the operator begins to overlay the skin of his patient with a skin of his own composing. He applies the enamel to her face, and then to her bust. This enamel consists chiefly of white lead or arsenic, made into a semiliquid paste. It requires a good deal of skill to lay it on, so that it shall be smooth, and not wrinkled ; and two or three hours, and sometimes a much longer time, are consumed in making a good job of it. This being done, there yet remains the finishing touches and adjuncts of head and cheek-gear ! So down she sits again, and he, with his pigment of Indian ink and pencil of camel-hair, paints her eyebrows divinely. Then her cheeks are inlaid with " plumpers," which she brings with her, and which cost her £5. They are made into pads, and composed of a hard substance, which combines various chemical materials. After the cheeks are thus made to look like a girl's cheek, they are carmined with a vegetable liquid rouge, laid on with a hare's foot. The finale of the make-up is the adjustment of the teeth, which, when properly set, give the mouth a lustre as of opals. The lady then goes away with a chuckle of deep satisfaction as she thinks of the conquests she will make in the evening, in the glare of the lamps, wax candles, and gas. She has a bust as white as alabaster, with shoulders and arms to match, and warranted to stand for six months.

Strange facts these, but such fantastic tricks, thank Heaven ! are not at all common in England, however they may obtain amongst the ladies of America. At the same time we fear that our women are not wholly *sans reproche* in the matter.

**To Preserve Milk.**—A teaspoonful of fine salt or of horse-radish in a pan of milk will keep it sweet for several days. Milk can be kept a year or more as sweet as when taken from the cow, by the following method :—Procure bottles, and as they are filled immediately cork them well, and fasten the cord with packthread or wire. Then spread a little straw in the bottom of a boiler, on which place the bottles with straw between them until the boiler contains a sufficient quantity. Fill it up with cold water, and as soon as it begins to boil draw the fire and let the whole gradually cool. When quite cold take out the bottles and pack them in sawdust in hampers, and stow them away in the very coolest part of the house.

**Facts from the Marriage Law.**—Persons under the age of twenty-one may not marry without the consent of their parents or guardians ; but a marriage without such consent is good, and the issue of it will be legitimate, unless the publication of the banns was rendered void by the parent or guardian openly dissenting, or unless the registrar's certificate was issued in spite of its being forbidden by one whose consent is necessary ; but minors marrying without the required assent are liable to certain penalties, such as being indicted for perjury, where the licence was procured by a false oath, or forfeiting all property which would otherwise accrue from the marriage.

A marriage cannot be set aside on the ground that the parties had not resided in the parish or district a certain number of days prescribed by law, or that the marriage did not take place between the hours of eight and twelve in the forenoon. The marriage is absolutely null and void, if the parents were within the prohibited degrees of consanguinity or affinity, that is, persons in the ascending and descending line *ad infinitum*, and collaterals to the third degree inclusive.

The marriage is void where one or both of the parties are already married : but if one of the parties has been absent, and not heard of for seven years, and is still living, though the second marriage of the other party is void, yet there can be no prosecution for bigamy in such a case. And, with reference to bigamy, if the first marriage is valid, it is bigamy to marry again, though the marriage be void on another ground besides that of its being bigamous ; but the converse of this is not law, so that if the first marriage is void, a second marriage may be contracted without fear of a prosecution.

Although it is unlawful for a person under age to marry without the consent of parent or guardian, where he or she has any ; and though no person can be married (unless by special licence), except within the parish or chapelry where one of the parties has resided fifteen days ; and though the guilty parties, and the minister who colludes with him or them, are subject to certain penalties for disobedience to this law, yet, when in either of these cases the marriage has been once celebrated, it remains a valid marriage, and not only is no evidence of consent, or of residence necessary to prove the validity of the marriage, if disputed, but the party disputing the marriage will not even be allowed to show that there was *no* residence, or *no* parental sanction.

**The Voice.**—It may be vastly improved in its tone and modulations by the practice of reading aloud. Confidence gives the voice fulness and clearness ; and trepidation is generally accompanied with a huskiness of utterance that has a most unpleasing effect. The modulation and proper management of the voice should be made a great point of by young ladies, for a fine and melodious voice is a " joy forever." This can only be done by a certain degree of confidence and a total absence of affectation ; for uncertainty, agitation, and striving for effect, are always ruinous to the voice of the speaker, which is constantly running against breakers or getting upon flats. Temper and disposition are more perfectly marked by voice and manner of speaking than we are willing to allow.

**Relative Nutriment of Different Food.**—The time taken to digest any kind of food does not show the proportion of nutriment it gives to the body. A pound of rice would give far less strength to the body than a pound of raw eggs, though both digest in about an hour. Farinaceous food is the most nutritive, and forms the substantial aliment of mankind. Cheese-like and mucilaginous food are also very nutritious when they agree well with the stomach, as are also albuminous and gelatinous food, only they stimulate as well as nourish the body. Fibrinous food is the most stimulating ; but the best

chemists unite in telling us that a pound of it, eaten by man, adds much less to his own body than a pound of eggs, or peas, or beans, or even good bread would have done Fatty or oily food is only fit for stomachs possessing very strong digestive powers. Acidulous and saccharine food are not only nourishing, but are naturally adapted to, and furnished at the right time for, allaying man's thirst. Millions of labouring people enjoy excellent health and vigour, and live very long, who never eat any flesh food, nor does any strong working animal eat it. No animal willingly eats the flesh of a flesh-eating animal. They like flesh made from vegetables best.

**To Preserve Eggs.**—The following experiments with pure oil will show their value :—Ten eggs were rubbed with the finger dipped in flax-seed oil, just lightly covered with the oil, which dried in a few days ; ten other eggs were oiled in the same manner with the oil of the French poppy, to ascertain the comparative effect of the two oils ; ten eggs were not oiled, and received no preparation : the thirty eggs were placed side by side, but not in contact, in a vessel, the bottom of which was covered with sand enough to keep them standing upright, three-fourths of each egg being exposed ; they remained thus for six months ; they were weighed when first put into the tub, and weighed in six months after. The following will show the result :— First, the eggs not prepared lost 18 per cent. of the primitive weight, were half empty, and exhaled an odour of corruption ; the eggs rubbed with oil of poppy lost 4 per cent., were full, without odour or bad taste ; the eggs rubbed with flax-seed oil lost 3 per cent. of their primitive weight, and had the odour and taste of an egg perfectly fresh. Hence, flax-seed oil may be deemed preferable for preserving eggs.

There are several other modes for preserving eggs, but there can be no doubt now that flax-seed oil will be the popular method, since it is proved to be the most reliable.

Fig. 1.

**D'Oyleys, Anti-Macassars, &c., from Natural Foliage.**—To young ladies desirous of making prssents to friends, by whom the work of their own hands is more likely to be appreciated than the most expensive article merely bought in a shop, or to those at a loss what to contribute to bazaars or fancy fairs, we would suggest the beautiful and ingenious method of arranging ferns, or other gracefully-shaped leaves, as centres of a set of d'oyleys, where

Fig. 2.

Fig. 3.

each can have a varied design, according to fancy or skill. The material should be of the finest jean, cut into circles, either with a cheese-plate or in any other simple way. The ferns or leaves selected should be flattened, by leaving them several days under pressure. The kinds which will be found most suitable, and have the best effect, are those of an open character, that is, very much pierced or perforated, such as the fern, wild geranium, oak, very young sprigs of vine, jessamine, or rose-leaves ; also the airy stems of grasses and harebells ; these can easily be had in the country, and seaside visitors can obtain the same results with sea-weed. Many will find it most convenient to begin their work

N

upon a drawing-board, as it gives greater facilities for being laid aside in the intervals of the process. Having arranged the leaves tastefully in one of the cut circles, they may be held in their place by some very small pins, standing perpendicularly. The next thing to be done is to rub down a sufficient quantity of good Indian ink, or neutral tint, with water into a saucer. It is better when not too thin. Then by dipping an old tooth-brush into it, and drawing it backwards and forwards with great care across the teeth of a small tooth-comb, or a small steel instrument sold for this purpose, the d'oyley is covered all over with the finest spray, which produces the effect of a delicate granular ground, as fine as a highly-finished lithograph, or even a photograph. Continue the process until it is of the required shade ; never hurrying over it, or taking too much ink on the brush, for fear of blots ; nor even allowing the dots to be coarser at one time than another.

Fig. 1 is simple, but appropriate in design, consisting merely of a few young vine leaves, *apparently* laid over grasses, but in reality the grasses are laid over the vine ; for the darkest leaves in the d'oyley are the first removed, the pure white always remaining till the ground is finished, which has generally the best effect when graduated or vignetted from the centre outwards. When satisfactorily concluded, it must be left a short time to dry ; care also should be taken to allow it to be sufficiently dry between the removal of each layer of leaves. Then proceed with a pen, dipped in the same ink, to draw in the veins, &c., taken from the originals ; the whole to be finished by a rose-coloured silk fringe round the edge ; or, by way of greater variety, each might have a different-coloured fringe.

Fig. 2 is a design which is capable of extensive adaptation to a great variety of tastes and requirements, inasmuch as, instead of the monogram here introduced, anyone may substitute their crest, armorial bearings, or a scroll with motto or name. This monogram was traced on paper, afterwards cut out with the scissors, and placed on first, the leaves arranged as in Fig. 1. The whole effect of this d'oyley could be reversed, by keeping it darker towards the outer edge, leaving the monogram upon a light ground in white, which could be tinted with colour or gold at pleasure.

Having completed the d'oyleys, we give directions for the anti-macassar in Fig. 3. Its average size is about one yard in length by three-quarters wide. As this involves more labour and material (though nothing in comparison to the time demanded by crochet, knitting, or tatting), we would advise that it should be done with marking ink, as it then admits of being washed. A larger kind of leaf may be selected to suit the proportion. The group of Cupids chosen for the centre of Fig. 3 was traced, cut out, and placed in the same way as the monogram, and the details finished afterwards with the pen from the original. If the drawing should prove too difficult for the artistic powers of the operator, and the engraving selected be not too valuable, an easier method is to cut it out, and paste it on, after the dark ground is finished ; it has only to be carefully steeped in cold water to be taken off before the anti-macassar is washed, and can then be replaced as before. The corners should be composed of leaves a size less than those used for the centre, and the four connected by a trailing border of convolvulus, vetch, speedwell, ragged robin, or ivy. Another application of this process is the decoration of lamp-shades and fire-screens, where the green ground, generally preferred, suits admirably as the natural colour of the foliage, and it may also be used for the decoration of bedroom and other furniture, made of light-coloured woods, and afterwards varnished.

We will only add that this fascinating combination of nature and art affords great scope for the display of good taste and decorative arrangement.

This delightful art is worth the careful study of every lady.

**To Preserve Gold Fish.**—A correspondent in the *Queen* gives us the following hints on how to preserve gold fish in good health. He says—" In the first place let me dissuade any one from keeping gold fish in a bowl with water only ; this involves constant trouble in changing the water, the neglect of which causes disease and death to the fish, is anything but pretty, and can offer little interest to the owner. Most people are alarmed at the name of an aquarium, but, in reality, the aquarium is far less trouble than the usual water globe. Those who have not the former can utilise the latter as an aquarium with very little difficulty. Put about an inch depth of coarse, pebbly sand at the bottom of your globe ; procure a few weeds from a dealer in aquaria (who will tell you which are the best sorts), sink these by means of a stone attached to the roots in the sand, otherwise the movements of the fish may uproot them, then pour in the water ; the sand should be well washed before being used. In a few days (generally less than a week) the weeds will begin to thrive ; this will be recognised by their giving out little air bubbles, which rise to the surface or cling to the leaves. Then only, and not before, is the time for putting in the fish. Of these, the smallest are the best ; the large ones are only suited for the large aquaria. The usual mistake is, the overstocking of the globes. For the average-sized ones, three, or at most four, small fish, about three inches in length, are sufficient. Fish require a certain quantity of air ; this is supplied by the bubbles emanating from the plants. It is therefore evident that if more fish are put in than the plants can supply air for, the balance will be destroyed, the fish will perish, and the whole result will be a failure. The usual mistake is, putting in the fish before the plants are ready for them, and then putting in too many. Never allow the bowl to remain long in the blaze of a strong sunshine. The best position is on a stand or table between two windows, or in a window not too much exposed to the sunshine. Following these instructions, the water never requires changing, a cupful being occasionally added to supply the loss by evaporation only. All the trouble of changing the water and feeding the fish is thus avoided, and the bowl and contents may be left to themselves. Avoid giving the fish bread, which is injurious. They require no food ; but a thread of vermecelli crumbled small may be given them from time to time as a treat, if desired. A bit of wash-leather, tied to a stick, should be used occasionally to clean the inside of the glass, and to remove the minute vegetation growing thereon. Some allow this to grow on the side turned to the light, to which it forms a natural screen and modification. A few water-snails will assist in keeping the interior clean. A freshwater mussel may be added, and, if desired, one or two small water-beetles, procuring those only which are harmless to the fish. In my bowl I have neither changed the water nor fed the fish for two years, and they are in excellent condition. A little care at first will ensure success and prevent all trouble afterwards, except the occasional cleaning of the glass and the addition of a little more water, as before stated."

**Wear Flannel.**—If your constitution is delicate, wear flannel next the skin during summer, and be particularly careful that your children wear it also. It is the sudden changes and alterations of the weather—the ordinary effects of which may be warded off by wearing flannel next the skin—which produce those fatal colds, and those bowel complaints which are generally ascribed to too great an indulgence in summer fruits. We have heard an eminent physician say, that a very large proportion of the deaths by cholera could have been prevented by the simple precaution of wearing flannel next the skin.

**Lungs and Stays.**—The fatal consequences of pressure upon the lungs cannot be too much impressed upon women. They ought, in health, to measure from 27 to 29 inches round the waist ; but most females do not permit themselves to grow beyond twenty-four —thousands are laced down to twenty-two, some to less than twenty inches ; and, by means of wood, whalebone, and steel, the chest is often reduced to one half its proper size. A physician says, " I hold it a positive fact, that *pressure* is the exciting cause of consumption ; if the chest be not sufficiently expanded, the lungs themselves cannot undergo the natural distension."

**The Secret of Warm Feet.**—Many of the colds which people are said to catch commence at their feet. To keep these extremities warm, therefore, is to effect an assurance against the almost interminable list of serious disorders which spring out of a " slight cold." First, never be tightly shod. Boots or shoes when they fit closely, press against the foot, and prevent the free circulation of the blood. When, on the contrary, they do not embrace the foot too tightly the blood gets fair play, and the space left between the leather and the stocking is filled with a comfortable supply of warm air. The second rule is, never sit in damp shoes. It is often imagined, that unless they are positively wet, it is not necessary to change them while the feet are at rest. This is a fallacy : for, when the least dampness is absorbed into the sole, it is attracted farther to the foot itself by its own heat, and thus perspiration is dangerously checked. Any person may prove this by trying the experiment of neglecting the rule, and his or her feet will become cold and damp after a few moments, although, on taking off the shoe and examining it, it will appear quite dry.

**Orchids as Ornaments for the Hair.**—It is now a common practice amongst ladies to fasten their hair with pins, upon the head of which is an imitation, in silver or gilt, of a butterfly with its wings expanded, the insect being placed upon a piece of fine wire twisted like a corkscrew, so that the least movement of the wearer causes the insect to oscillate in a more or less life-like manner. When the three larg-est species of Phalanopsis are coming into bloom, we would suggest the use of single flowers of these lovely moth-like orchids in a similar manner. They can be procured from florists in Covent Garden Market for a shilling a bloom : they are not at all difficult to mount on a hair-pin, and with care will last well for two or three evenings. Ladies who have worn them once are not likely to care about artificial butterflies while these orchids can be had in their place.

**Jet and Jet Ornaments.**—It would excite surprise in the minds of many a lady adorned with what are known as jet ornaments, were she told that she is wearing only a species of coal, and that the sparkling material made by the hand of the artistic workman into a thing of beauty, once formed the branch of a stately tree, whereon the birds of the air rested, and under which the beasts of the field reposed ; yet geologists assure us such is really the fact. They describe it as a variety of coal which occurs sometimes in elongated uniform masses, and sometimes in the form of branches, with a woody structure. It is, in its natural state, soft and brittle, of a velvet black colour, and lustrous. It is found in large quantities in Saxony, and also in Prussian amber mines in detached fragments, and, being exceedingly resinous, the coarser kinds are used for fuel, burning with a greenish flame and a strong bituminous smell, leaving an ash also of a greenish colour. Jet is likewise found in England, on the Yorkshire coast.

**Hastings as a Winter Sea-side Resort for Invalids.**—" As autumn advances the question naturally arises to the head of the family and the invalid," writes Dr. Garrett, a physician and a resident of Hastings, " as to whither they shall go for the winter. Enough has been written respecting foreign climates, and the means that should be employed in certain foreign localities for the recruital of health ; but little has been said, and far less has been investigated, as to the natural attributes of our own insular regions. I lay aside the fact of our geological protection from north and north-east winds, and deal with a subject in reference to a quality that has been assigned against it, that the air of this place is 'relaxing,' and I think I shall be able to show how this misconception has arisen.

It is well known that the beneficial effects of sea air are partially due to its purity, the equability of its temperature, and to certain marine emanations, but more especially to its ozone, which is, amongst other things, a powerful constitutional invigorant, or, as Dr. Tanner says, ' a stimulant to all the vital functions.

Ozone is generated in increased quantity by the churning action of the waves, and the nearer you approach the surface of the sea by a shore only a few feet above its high-water mark, the more abundant must be its supply of ozone. Now, an invalid coming to this climate, at once feels the influence of this invigorating ingredient of the atmosphere. He takes a deep, refreshing inhalation which he may not have experienced before for some time. His appetite is immensely improved, and he becomes aware of a marked and considerable change in his respiratory and digestive functions. Now, the probability is, that this pulmonary patient, or dyspeptic, continues his full animal diet, consumes his liberal quantum of stimulants (spirits, wine, and bitter ales), and takes his customary doses of iron, bark, and mineral acids, to the full extent that his system will tolerate. He forgets that he is sipping a tonic atmosphere all day long, ' a stimulant to the vital functions,' and what takes place? The pneumogastric nerves become unduly excited, the breathing becomes less full and free, the appetite diminishes, and a lassitude is the sure and inevitable result. Hence, the over-tonicised patient forfeits his benefits, loses his confidence, and at once pronounces the climate 're-laxing.'

I might speak of several other attributes appertaining to this littoral lo-cality, such as the absence of land-damp, from the fact that the S. and S.W. winds (which are those which usually bring rains) sprinkle us with their showers and then pass inland, leaving us no accumulated terrestrial moisture in the direction from which they have come, nor thus creating, to our windward on land, a moist atmosphere which would give solution or suspension to the carbonic acid generated by decomposing vegetable matter at the season of " the fall of the leaf.' "

**To Prevent Pitting in Small-Pox.**—Dr. Revillod, of Geneva, has studied the various means applied to prevent the variolic pustules in the face. He discards collodion, because it cracks the skin, and causes so much pain ; the sublimate, because it sometimes produces ulcers ; tincture of iodine, because it does not prevent pustulation. The doctor recommends glycerine, which, through its exosmotic action, diminishes the intensity of the eruption. His favourite formula is, soap, ten parts ; glycerine, four parts ; triturate, and add mercurial ointment twenty parts. This ointment does not prevent swelling of the face, causes no pain, and prevents pustulation. It should be applied before the pustules have been transformed into vesicles.

**Spices.**—CLOVES are the dried blossoms of a tree which is a native of the Molucca Islands, particularly of Amboyna. It grows to the height of the laurel tree, and no verdure is ever seen under it. From the extremities of the branches grow quantities of flowers, which are first white, then green, and at last red, and hard, in which state they are properly cloves. When they become drier they assume a yellow cast, which ends in a dark brown. Cloves are stimulating aromatics, and yield abundance of oil.

CINNAMON is the inner bark of a species of bay tree, which grows scarcely anywhere but in Ceylon.

NUTMEGS and MACE are the produce of a tree which grows in the Moluccas ;

the nut is covered with three rinds; when the nut is ripe, the first falls off itself; then the second appears, which is very thin and fine. It is taken off the fresh nut with a great deal of care, and exposed to the sun to dry; this is the Mace. The nut is taken out of the shell, and put into lime-water for several days, and is then prepared and fit to send abroad.

PEPPER is the fruit of a shrub, the stem of which requires a prop to support it; the wood of it is knotty, like the vine, to which it bears a near resemblance. It produces white flowers, whence the fruit grows in bunches, like gooseberries, and each fruit bears twenty or thirty peppercorns.

**Collecting and Laying out Sea-Weeds.**—It must be borne in mind, that if exposed to the sun or rain, the plants, as a general rule, soon change colour. The gleaner should, therefore, always seek for them at low tide, in pools among the rocks, where the finest specimens may be found. It should be noticed whether they were found growing from or attached to the rocks, or whether they were accidentally left there by the falling tide. Specimens which are found attached to the rocks will almost invariably be the most perfect; and care should be taken to obtain the entire plant, raising with it the tendrils by which it holds to the stone. When gathered, the sooner they are laid out the better. Miss Gifford—a high authority on the subject—gives the following explicit instructions:—

"First wash the sea-weed in fresh water; then take a plate or dish (the larger the better); cut your paper to the size required, place it in the plate with fresh water, and spread out the plant with a good-sized camel-hair pencil in a natural form (picking out with a pin gives the sea-weed an unnatural appearance, and destroys the characteristic fall of the branches, which should be carefully avoided); then gently raise the paper with the specimen out of the water, placing it in a slanting position for a few moments, so as to allow the superabundant water to run off; after which place it in the press. The press is made with either three pieces of board or pasteboard. Lay on the first board two sheets of blotting-paper; on that lay your specimens; place straight and smooth over them a piece of old muslin, fine cambric, or linen; then some more blotting-paper, and place another board on the top of that, and continue in the same way. The blotting-paper and the muslin should be carefully removed and dried every day, and then replaced; at the same time those specimens that are sufficiently dried may be taken away. Nothing now remains but to write on each the name, date, and locality. You can either gum the specimens in a scrap-book, or fix them in, as drawings are often fastened, by making four slits in the page, and inserting each corner. This is by far the best plan, as it admits of their removal without injury to the page, at any future period, if it is required either to insert better specimens or intermediate species.

"Some of the larger algæ will not adhere to the paper, and consequently require gumming. The following method of gumming them will be found one of the best:—After well cleaning and pressing, brush the coarser kinds of algæ over with spirits of turpentine, in which two or three small lumps of gum-mastic have been dissolved, by shaking in a warm place; two-thirds of a small phial is the proper proportion, and this will make the specimens retain a fresh appearance.

**To Neutralise the Smell of Paint.**—Place a vessel full of lighted charcoal in the middle of the room, and throw on it two or three handfuls of juniper berries, shut the windows, the chimney, and the door close; twenty-four hours afterwards the room may be opened, when it will be found that the sickly, unwholesome smell will be entirely gone. The smoke of the juniper berry possesses this advantage, that should anything be left in the room, such as tapestry, &c., none of it will be spoiled.

**About Enigmas.**—The earliesr enigma on record is probably that propounded by Sampson, and which was so prematurely divulged by his wife. (Perhaps it was this circumstance that gave rise to the unjust doubts as to the power of a lady to keep a secret.) The next enigma of ancient date that occurs to us is the famous one which we are told was put forth by the Sphinx, and solved by Œdipus. It was in these terms, "What animal is that which goes on four legs in the morning, on two at noon, and on three in the evening ?" The answer to the enigma was, "Man, who in infancy crawls on all fours, in his prime walks erectly, and in old age props himself with a staff."

Cleobulus, one of the seven wise men of Greece, is said to be the author of the following riddle :—"There is a father with twelve sons , each son has thirty daughters, who are parti-coloured, having one cheek black and the other white ; who never see each other's faces, nor live above twenty-four hours." An allegorical enigma of such construction hardly requires the skill of an Œdipus for its solution. Whatever number of riddles, however, the ancients composed, but few have been handed down to us, so we must pass at once to those of more recent times.

With regard to the different species of enigmatical compositions, some little confusion appears to exist, as the distinguishing names are frequently misapplied. It may not then be amiss to describe the different forms of enigmas in general use. The word enigma is a comprehensive term that may be applied to any riddle, of whatever nature it may be. A CHARADE is an enigma composed on a word that may be syllabilically divided into other words, which are severally described as first, second, third and fourth, as the case may be ; while all together are called the whole.

A REBUS is strictly a pictorial enigma, but this word is now very frequently used to designate all those irregular forms of enigma that are supposed to require a separate name.

An ANAGRAM consists of a word trans-posed into other words. A LOGOGRIPH is a riddle formed on a similar plan, but on a larger scale. A TRANSPOSITION is the same as an anagram. Many distinguished writers, and even poets of eminence, have occasionally amused themselves with the composition of these trifles.

Lord Byron's celebrated enigma on the letter H is doubtless well known to our readers. Cowper, Bernard Barton, and Lord Macaulay, have also contributed to our amusement in this way. Canning, the statesman, writes the following :—

A noun there is of plural number,
Foe to peace and tranquil slumber.
Now any other noun you take
By adding *s* you plural make ;
But if you add an *s* to this,
Strange is the metamorphosis.
Plural is plural now no more,
And sweet what bitter was before.

Perhaps one of the most happy of enigmatists was the late Winthrop Mackworth Praed, who wrote many enigmas and charades that charm the ear by their musical cadence, and, in fact, possess poetical merit for which we may often search in vain in many compositions of a more ambitious aim. As puzzles they are, perhaps, very easy of solution, with the exception of one or two which have never been quite satisfactorily answered. That commencing "Sir Hilary," has recently been introduced into a popular magazine. Many words have been suggested for its solution ; but the best answer, with the exception of "good-night," is presented by the word "rest-rain." Both answers are faulty ; the former being a *phrase*, the latter being unsyllabically divided. Another enigma of Praed's, beginning "Sir Gregory sat in his cushioned chair," has, we believe, as yet defied all attempts at solution. It is too long to quote here. Here is a riddle attributed to Professor Whewell—

A handless man had a letter to write,
He who read it had lost his sight ;

The dumb repeated it word for word,
And deaf was he who listened and
   heard.

We will, by way of conclusion, present our readers with an enigma, the author and answer of which are alike unknown—

I'm the sweetest of voices in orchestra heard,
  And yet in an orchestra never have been ;
I'm a bird of bright plumage, and less like a bird,
  Nothing in nature has ever been seen.
Touching earth I expire, in water I die,
In air I lose life, yet I run, swim, and fly,
Darkness destroys me, and light is my death,
You can't keep me alive but by stopping my breath,
If my name can't be guessed by a boy or a man,
By a girl or a woman it easily can.

**Arranging Flowers.**—In arranging flowers in tasteful bouquets, the more loosely and confusedly they are arranged, the better. Crowding is especially to be avoided, and to accomplish this a good base of green of different varieties is needed to keep the flowers apart. This filling up is a very important part in all bouquet-making, and the neglect of it is the greatest stumbling-block to the uninitiated. Spiked and drooping flowers, with branches and sprays of delicate green, are of absolute necessity in giving grace and beauty to a vase-bouquet.

Flowers of a similar size, form, and colour, ought never to be massed together. Large flowers, with green leaves or branches, may be used to advantage alone, but a judicious contrast of form is most effective. Avoid anything like formality or stiffness. A bright tendril or spray of vine can be used with good effect, if allowed to wander over and around the vase as it will. Certain flowers assort well only in families, and are injured by mixing. Of these are balsams, hollyhocks, sweet pea, &c. The former produce a very pretty effect if placed upon a shallow oval dish upon the centre-table.

No ornament is so appropriate for the dinner-table or mantle as a vase of flowers ; and if you expect visitors, by all means cut the finest bouquet your garden will produce, and place it in the room they are to occupy. It will tell of your regard and affectionate thoughtfulness in a more forcible and appropriate manner than you could find words to express. If a small quantity of spirits of camphor is placed in the water contained in the vase, the colour and freshness of the flowers will remain for a much longer period. Thus prepared, we have known flowers to keep a week, and at the end to look quite fresh and bright.

**A Wise Proverb.**—The Spanish proverb which says, " When you cannot get what you want, it is best to want what you can get," embodies a cool wisdom for the want of which the lives of half the world are shipwrecked. To love the beautiful is a good thing ; but to be wretched because circumstances make it impossible for you to surround yourself at home with the fine pictures and graceful statues and silken hangings you see elsewhere, is as unwise as it would be to refuse to enjoy the roses of summer because December is in the year. If you cannot have good paintings, you may perhaps buy some good engravings—or if those are too dear, there are left chromos and photographs ; and if all the rest fail, Nature, lavish colourist, paints still the sunset sky with gold and crimson, and veils the distant hills with soft mists or gleaming snows. To have the thing you like is the best—but shall the thing you have be turned out of doors ? Get what you like, by all means, if you can —but to like what you can get is by far are important to your happiness.

**To Pickle Onions.**—Well cover the

pickling onions with vinegar. To each quart of vinegar allow two teaspoonfuls of allspice, two of black pepper, and one of mustard-seed. Have the onions gathered when quite dry and ripe ; take off the outside skin, then with a silver knife (steel would spoil the colour of the onions) remove the inner skin ; pierce the onions with a silver fork, and as fast as they are prepared put them into very dry bottles or jars. Pour over sufficient vinegar to cover them, with the spice, &c., mixed in the above proportions  Tie down with bladder, and put them in a dry place. In a fortnight they will be ready for use.

**Oxtail Soup.**—Cut two tails into pieces, and with an ounce of butter and two small onions, lay them in a stewpan and brown them, Cover them with boiling water, and add a couple of stems of celery, some thyme, a carrot and a turnip, a little parsley, four cloves and four peppercorns, and a little allspice ; for about four hours let it all gently boil. Then prepare half a pint of button onions, and a carrot and a turnip cut into small balls, which boil in water with a little salt. Take the pieces of tail carefully out, strain the liquor, and skim off the fat. Mix in a stewpan two ounces of flour and an ounce of butter ; when mixed, add it to the liquor, with a teaspoonful of salt and the prepared vegetables ; let all boil together. Add a glass of port, and serve hot.

**To Roast Sucking Pig.**—After the little porker has been prepared for the spit, make the following stuffing :—slice four onions, fry them in a little butter, chop a few sage-leaves, and salt, pepper, four ounces of bread-crumbs, five ounces of stoned raisins, three eggs, and three dessert-spoonfuls of melted butter. Mix all well together, and fill the pig with the same, after which sew up the pig, and rub it with butter, and roast for nearly three hours. Serve with rich gravy, adding the brains and sage-leaves, chopped small, together with a little melted butter.

**To Jug a Hare.**—Mix together a quarter of a pound of butter and half a pound of flour in a stewpan, and keep it stirring over the fire a few minutes, then add twelve ounces of bacon cut into small pieces. The hare should be ready cut up, then put it into the stewpan and stir it for ten minutes. Then add half a pint of port, and sufficient beef broth to cover it ; add a couple of bay-leaves, three cloves, and, when the hare is half done, a pint of button onions and a little brown sugar, and let it simmer until it is well done, when dish it up. It will take about four hours to jug.

**To Clean Black Marble.**—Equal parts of soft-soap and pearlash ; with soft flannel rub it over the marble, and let it remain a few minutes ; then wash off with warm water, and a second time with cold spring water ; and when quite dry polish with paraffine oil.

**Qualities of Cocoa.**—When mixed with water, as it is usually drunk, it is more properly to be compared with milk than infusions of little direct nutritive value, like those of tea and coffee ; and, on the other hand, it has the great advantage over milk, and over beef-tea, and other similar beverages, that it contains the substance theobromine, and a volatile empyreumatic oil ; thus it unites in itself the exhilirating qualities of tea, with the body-sustaining and strengthening qualities of milk.

Its analogy to theine leads to the belief that it exercises a similar exhilirating, soothing, hunger-stilling, and waste-retarding effect. But it has the advantages over tea and coffee of being eminently nutritious. It is rich in all the important principles which are found to co exist in the most valued kinds of food.

The finest qualities of  cocoa are found not in Mexico, but in the isthmus of Central America, Venezuela, and some of the West Ind a Islands. The cocoa plant is an evergreen, which grows to the height of fifteen or twenty feet, with drooping bright green leaves, in shape oblong, eight or nine inches long, three inches broad, and pointed at the ends. The flowers and fruit bear at all seasons of the year.

**Common Politeness.**—There is nothing that costs so little as common politeness, and yet it is a commodity that few possess or take pains to enrich themselves with. Rudeness and ill-manners are so prevalent that, when we come in contact with a polite person, we are apt to be astonished. With some persons this polish is innate, also hereditary, for there is more good and evil inherited than is generally credited, and in others it is developed by proper home training and refined associations.

True politeness springs from goodness of heart; a person who is sympathetic, who looks upon his fellow-creatures from a personal stand-point, cannot fail to be polite, for feeling prompts generosity. The contrast visible between dress and mental culture is curious to a student of human nature. The genuine jewel shines forth the brighter in proportion as the setting is dull; the patched coat or humble dress often fails to conceal the true nobility of character within.

To those desirous of impressing this subject upon their friends, we would refer to railway travel, which from day to day affords opportunities of judging what is due to those with whom we come in contact. We have heard a poor person say "Thank you" when offered a seat; and have seen elegantly-dressed ladies, whose position in society is supposed to afford advantages for acquiring good manners, take a seat under similar circumstances, without a word of recognition, as if conferring a favour. Ah! the simple "Thank you;" how it warms the heart, kindling pure emotion, strengthening one's faith in humanity, and carrying joy to secret places!

Those of us who possess the advantages which good society affords should surely be careful not to lower ourselves below the humble classes, whose surroundings all tend to rudeness and vulgarity. According to our action so is our reward. If we grudge the simple "Thank you," the appreciative glance, we openly acknowledge our inferiority to men and women in whom the omission would be excusable.

"I have never found anything else so cheap and so useful as politeness," said an old traveller to us once. He then went on to state that, early in life, finding how useful it was, frequently, to strangers, to give them some information of which they were in search, and which he possessed, he had adopted the rule always to help everybody he could in such little opportunities as were constantly offering in his travels. The result was, that out of the merest trifles of assistance, rendered in this way, had grown some of the pleasantest and most valuable acquaintances that he had ever formed.

**To Make Good Bitters.**—According to the flavour desired, take either of rum, brandy, or whisky, one pint; gentian and quassia root, of each three ounces: dried orange peel, four ounces; cardamon seeds, half an ounce; allow the whole to steep for a week or fortnight. Finally strain through muslin, and it is ready for use. If agreeable to the taste, half an ounce of cinnamon or nutmeg may be added to the above ingredients.

**Domestic Uses of Ammonia.**—Ammonia is nearly as useful in housekeeping as soap, and its cheapness brings it within the reach of all. For many household purposes it is invaluable; yet its manifold uses are not so generally known as they should be. It is a most refreshing agent at the toilet table; a few drops in a basin of water will make a better bath than pure water, and if the skin is oily it will remove all glossiness and disagreeable odours. Added to the foot-bath, it entirely absorbs all noxious smell so often arising from the feet in warm weather, and nothing is better for cleansing the hair from dandruff and dust.

For the headache it is also a desirable stimulant, and frequent inhaling of its pungent odours will often entirely remove catarrhal cold.

For cleansing paint it is very useful. Put a teaspoonful of ammonia to a quart of warm soapsuds, dip in a flannel cloth, and wipe off the dust and fly-specks, grime and smoke, and see for yourselves how much labour it will save you : no scrubbing will be needful.

It will cleanse and brighten silver wonderfully ; to a pint of hot suds mix a teaspoonful of the spirits, dip in your silver spoons, forks, &c., rub with a brush, and then polish on chamois skin.

For washing mirrors and windows it is also very desirable ; put a few drops of ammonia upon a piece of newspaper and you will readily take off every spot or finger-mark on the glass.

It will take out grease-spots from any fabric ; put on the ammonia nearly clear, lay blotting-paper over the place, and press a hot flat-iron on it for a few moments.

A few drops in water will clean laces and whiten them finely, also muslins.

For cleansing hair and nail brushes it is equally good. Put a teaspoonful of ammonia into one pint of warm or cold water and shake the brushes through the water ; when the bristles look white, rinse them in cold water, and put them into the sunshine or in a warm place to dry. The dirtiest brushes will come out from this bath white and clean.

There is no better remedy for heartburn and dyspepsia, and the aromatic spirit of ammonia is especially prepared for these troubles. Ten drops of it in a wineglass of water are often a great relief. The spirits of ammonia can be taken in the same way, but it is not as palatable a dose. Farmers and chemists are well aware of the beneficial effects of ammonia on all kinds of vegetation ; and if you desire your roses, geraniums, fuschsias, &c., to become more flourishing, you can try it upon them, by adding five or six drops of it to every pint of warm water that you give them ; but do not repeat the dose oftener than five or six days, lest you stimulate them too highly. Rain-water is impregnated with ammonia, and thus it refreshes and vivifies vegetable life. So be sure and keep a large bottle of ammonia in the house, and have a glass stopper for it, as it is very evanescent, and also injurious to corks, eating them away.

**Who is an Heiress?**—After speaking of lords who owe much of their greatness to having married richly-endowed heiresses, Sir Bernard Burke, in his Rise of Great Families, says, " These few instances, chosen out of many which readily present themselves, show the influence heiresses have had on the rise of our great houses. In the cases cited, the heiresses carried with them not only the heraldic inheritance, but the much more substantial succession to the family estates. But it must not be taken for granted that all ladies who succeed to property are heiresses. Generally, this may be the fact, but not always. " There's often an heiress without a penny," is an Irish proverb. Many ladies who succeed to extensive estates or large property (as Lady Burdett Coutts) are not heiresses, and many ladies who succeed to none, are. The true definition of an heiress or co-heiress is this— a lady who is representative or co-representative in blood of her father. This representation, which depends on her having no brother, or on her brother or brothers having died without issue, entitles her descendants to quarter her arms forever In right of his descent from heiresses, the present Duke of Athole has a shield of more than a thousand quarterings. His Grace is not only the senior representative in blood of the Nevills, Lords Latimer, but also of the Stanleys, Earls of Derby, the De Veres, Earls of Oxford, and the Percys, Earls of Northumberland. Yet he does not inherit Knowsley, Hedingham, or Alnwick. As a set-off against this accumulation of heiresses combined in the possessor of one Scotch dukedom, it is a curious circumstance that another Scotch duke, Montrose, is representative of ancestors quite as illustrious— courtiers and cavaliers, *par excellence*— not one of whom, from their first appearance in history, found favour with an heiress. Consequently the Graham shield has no quartering."

**Pouring Out Tea and Coffee.**—There is more to be learned about pouring out tea and coffee than most ladies are willing to believe. If those decoctions are made at the table, which is by far the best way, they require experience, judgment, and exactness ; if they are brought on the table ready made, it still requires judgment so to apportion them that they shall prove sufficient in quantity for the family party, and that the older members present shall have the stronger cups. We have often seen persons pour out tea, who, not being aware that the first cup is the weakest, and that the tea grows stronger as you proceed, have bestowed the weakest cup upon the greatest stranger, and given the strongest to a very young member of the family, who would have been better without any. Where several cups of equal strength are wanted, you should pour a little into each, and then go back, inverting the order as you fill them up, and then the strength will be apportioned properly. You should learn every one's taste in the matter of sugar and milk, too, in order to suit them in that respect. But why not let each individual sweeten his own tea to his own liking ? A far more convenient fashion this would be, than the present one, where the hostess has to be asking with every cup she pours out for her guest, " Is your tea to your liking ?" &c. Besides, this plan would save the president of the tea-table a world of trouble and anxiety about the tastes of her visitors, and fears that she might have put too much sugar in somebody's cup, and too little in somebody else's.

Delicacy and neatness may be shown in the manner of handling and rinsing the cups, of helping persons to sugar, and using the cream-pot without letting the cream run down from the lip. There are a thousand little niceties which will occur to you, if you give due attention to the business, and resolve to do it with the thrift of a good housekeeper, and

the ease and dignity of a refined lady. When you have once acquired good habits in this department, it will require less attention, and you will always do it in the best way without thinking much about it.

**Rules for Obtaining Good Singing Canaries.**—The following are the best rules for obtaining and preserving good singers. The most essential is to choose from among the young that which promises a fine tone, and to seclude it from all other birds, that it may learn and remember nothing bad. The same precaution is necessary during the first and second moulting ; for being likely to relearn its song, it would introduce into it with equal ease foreign parts. It must be observed whether the bird likes to sing alone or in company with others, for there are some which appear to have such whims, liking to hear only themselves, and which pout for whole years if they are not humoured on this point. Others sing faintly, and display their powers only when they can try their strength against a rival. It is very important to distribute regularly to singing birds the simple allowance of fresh food which is intended for the day. By this means they will sing every day equally, because they will eat uniformly, and not pick the best one day and be obliged to put up with the refuse the next.

**Non-Medicated Hair Oils and Pomatums.**—Perhaps the best hair-oils are those which hold castor-oil as the basis. Castor-oil alone, however, is rather too glutinous, requiring to be diluted with oil of olives, or, what is still better, spirits of wine, which latter has the property of uniting with castor-oil. As regards the perfume wherewith hair-oil is to be scented, this is a matter of taste, and the perfume which will be liked by one person will be disagreeable to another.

Essence of bergamot furnishes an odorous matter very commonly used for the scenting of pomatum, and which is, perhaps, more generally agreeable than any other class of perfumed pomatum ; however, various other odoriferous agents will be mentioned. Occasionally hair-oils are tinted delicately red. There is no positive advantage in this ; but those who wish to produce the tint may readily do so by heating or steeping the oil with alkanet root, the red colouring matter of which has the property of dissolving in fixed oily substances. Besides pomatums for the hair, there are compounds of almost similar composition for application to chaps, broken lips, &c. ; to these the term pomade is generally applied. We shall now subjoin a few approved recipes for the preparation of pomades and pomatums ;—

POMADES FOR HEALING CHAPS.—1. Spermaceti, two drachms ; white wax, one and a half drachms ; oil of almonds, sweet, half an ounce ; Florence oil of olives, half an ounce ; oil of poppies, half an ounce ; liquid balsam of Peru, four drops. All the ingredients, except the last, are to be heated together over a water-bath, and the balsam of Peru will incorporate with the melted compound by heating with a whisk.

2. White wax, two drachms ; spermaceti, four ounces ; oil of sweet almonds, four ounces. Melt the three together over a water-bath, and add three fluid ounces of water—about six tablespoonfuls. Rub all together in a marble or Wedgewood mortar, adding a few drops of Mecca balsam and rosewater towards the end of the operation.

3. Rub together, in a mortar, equal parts of purified lard, fresh butter, and honey ; finally, add half a portion of Mecca balsam, and a minute quantity of otto of roses.

**The Art of Eating Oranges.**—The Brazilians, on whose plantations grow some of the finest oranges in the world, make an art of eating that delicious fruit. To enjoy an orange thoroughly, you should eat it in Brazilian fashion ; you slice a segment of the flower end deep enough to go completely through the skin ; then replacing the segment, thrust a fork through it to the very centre of the orange. Holding the fork in your left hand, peel the orange with a very sharp small table-knife, slicing all the skin off, the segment at the base of the fork being in this operation a shield to prevent any danger of cutting the left thumb. Now, with two cuts of the knife, dissect out the pulp of one pocket, and convey it to the mouth. Follow this up, pocket by pocket, and the skins of the pocket remain on the fork, like the leaves of a book upon which the covers touch.

**Crystallised Baskets.**—A pleasant reminiscence of summer may be retained by the manufacture of crystallised flower-baskets. The process is very simple, and can be accomplished by any lady of taste. Construct some baskets of fancy form with pliable copper wire, and wrap them with gauze. In these, tie to the bottom violets, ferns, geranium leaves—in fact, any flowers except full-blown roses—and sink them into a solution of alum, of one pound to a gallon of water, after the solution has cooled. The colours will then be preserved in their original beauty, and the crystallised alum will hold faster than when from a hot solution. When you have a light covering of crystals that completely covers the articles, remove the basket carefully and allow it to drip for twelve hours. These baskets make a beautiful parlour ornament, and for a long time preserve the freshness of the flowers.

**Fish in Season, and How to Choose it.**—COD is in season from October to February, and in best condition for table about Christmas, when most of the females will be found in roe.

HADDOCKS are in season from November, or perhaps earlier, to February, which is about their spawning time.

WHITING are in condition nearly all the year round, except, perhaps, the first quarter ; they spawn about January.

FLOUNDERS are best late in the autumn and early in the winter.

TURBOT and BRILL may be found in condition all the year round, and out of condition, too ; when in condition, the flesh of these fish is firm and elastic to the touch, when out of condition, soft and flabby ; but both of these fish, as well as HALIBUT, are generally best during the spring months.

With regard to the SKATE, we cannot say when it is in best condition for eating, but this we can say, that for one that is good twenty are inferior, and in purchasing skate for table, reliance must be placed on the judgment of the fishmonger. More than half the skate sent to market is only fit for manure.

Concerning LING, also, we would say it is necessary to trust to the judgment of some one who understands from its appearance the condition of the fish ; for all the year round a large proportion of the ling sent to market may be found out of condition, and it is necessary that any purchaser should know how to select ling, or leave the selection to a fishmonger who can be trusted. A ling that stiffens when dead is in prime condition, as also is one the liver of which is of an opaque creamish cast, approaching almost to whiteness, the paler the better ; a dark or reddish tint in the liver is a sure sign of ill condition.

MACKEREL, of one kind or another are in season nearly throughout the year. The east coast fish from April to June, the south coast and Cornish from February to April, and Norway and Ireland during the rest of the year. At the same time, there is very much difference in the quality of these mackerel. The east coast fish, though the smallest, are undoubtedly the best as regards flavour ; next in order we would place the Cornish, then the south coast, next the Irish, and, lastly, those from Norway, the two last being very inferior fish to all the others, but they are much larger, and the purchaser obtains quantity if not quality for his money. We have also eaten delicious small mackerel caught off the coast of Wales in August. The goodness and freshness of mackerel are displayed when the beautiful rainbow tints which this fish possesses are of the brightest description.

Irish HERRINGS are in season from August to March.

PILCHARDS, from July to Christmas.

SPRATS, in mid-winter.

WHITEBAIT, from May to September.

RED MULLET from July to February or March.

CRABS from May to October.

LOBSTERS are in best condition from April to October, but are to be found good in all the months. We would advise purchasers always to buy live lobsters, as it is more easy then to discover that they have not died a natural death. A lobster that is lively is sure to be full of meat when boiled ; but too many are sold ready boiled, which have no meat, or but little, inside the shell, on account of having died from a kind of consumption. We do not know why it is, but lobsters that die after having been removed from their natural element are always, when boiled, almost worthless, the flesh being soft and watery, and, moreover, there is very little of it. Can they, under such circumstances, prolong life by existing on themselves, that is, by consuming their own vital juices ?

MUSSELS and COCKLES, we apprehend, are in season all the year round ; they should be full in the shell, and look clean and free from mud. If taken from a muddy ground they should be kept for three or four days in clear sea water, or salt and water. Mussels that are of a deep colour, and sharp at the edges, are best ; those of a slate colour, with shells rough and worn at the edges, are generally hard and tough. Cockles should have as white shells as possible, and should always be kept for some days in clear salt water to free them from sand.

**To Teach a Parrot to Talk.**—Mr. Shirley Hibberd recommends that you should begin with very short sentences. "Pretty Polly" will no doubt be the first lesson for a parrot as long as the world lasts—and a very good one it is.

The best times to teach a parrot are early in the morning and late in the evening, when the bird is in a quiet attentive mood. At dusk put the cage on a table, and remove from the room anything that may distract the bird's attention, such as a living creature of any kind, or anything in motion. Then, with the door ajar, repeat the lesson over and over again just outside the room, and in a few days it will be echoed back to you clearly and distinctly, to give you heart to try another. This is the chief pleasure in keeping a parrot ; its first efforts are so comical, its perseverance so charming. Poll will screw herself into all sorts of shapes in her efforts to respond, and when all is quiet will go over the lesson in an undertone till she knows it perfectly. Until she can accomplish one speech well, it would only perplex her to begin another. Special precautions, however, are not indispensable ; the same sentence repeated again and again will soon be learnt ; but as you find the bird make progress in new lessons, go over all her old ones, or she may discard her first teachings in admiration of the last. Harsh consonants are easily uttered by parrots. You will find that poll can roll the *r* as well as any Hibernian in such a sentence as " Scr-r-r-r-r-atch her poll." When she has accomplished a few lessons, you may teach her according to your fancy ; but it would be folly to attempt sentences of any length until the bird has had at least six months' training ; by that time you will know its capabilities, and may act accordingly. In teaching, it should not be forgotten that parrots have considerable musical powers ; they learn the best notes of the thrush and blackbird quickly ; gray parrots especially have a voice of considerable compass, and execute portions of simple tunes with very rich modulations. By whistling one or two bars at a time when poll is in a quiet listening mood, she will soon pick them up, and in repeating them will frequently treat you to some good original variations of her own. This teach-

ing of song is good for another reason ; it cures the bird of screaming, and supplants those wild harsh cries which belong to them in their wild state. I have had a parrot make considerable progress in the song of the canary, and execute some sweet and simple passages admirably. My famous old Poll whistles the gamut up and down to perfection ; it is really glorious to hear her.

One necessary part of the teaching of a parrot is that of accustoming it to be fondled. If poked at with sticks and fingers, the bird soon learns to snap at every stranger, and occasionally draws blood from the fingers of master or mistress ; but if guarded against such mischievous tricks, there is no animal that becomes more safely familiar. I like to see an old family parrot strut over the carpet, climb the chairs, mount the table and survey the tea-things, to steal a lump of sugar or a strawberry, and then climb on its mistress's shoulder, and chuckle.

**How to Treat Parrots.**—We are also indebted to Mr. Shirley Hibberd for the following instructions in the general treatment of parrots, as their health, diet, &c. :—

A parrot should never be kept a close prisoner. Its health is sure to suffer unless allowed out of the cage pretty frequently ; and as Poll invariably flutters her wings well when she first comes out, it is necessary to give her parole before any meals are served, because of the scurf which is shaken out from the roots of the feathers, the getting rid of which keeps the skin healthy, and preserves the strength of the bird.

So managed, parrots are rarely affected with any disease. They should go out of doors regularly all the summer long, but not be exposed to a burning sun. If anything ails them a little change of diet will generally set them right ; a few green radish-pods, the green seeds of the nasturtium, a green capsicum, or any pungent vegetable in common table use, acts as a corrective, and is much relished. If they get relaxed, give a little more hemp-seed and some yolk of hard-boiled egg, and let the bread-and-milk be nearly dry. If troubled with costiveness, make the bread-and-milk in the usual way, but use cold milk instead of boiling it ; and give a stalk from a grape vine, a few radish-pods, grapes, or fruits of any kind ; in fact, their diet should be varied with such occasional treats, but beware of over-feeding at any time.

DIET.—In putting Poll upon her proper diet, it will be best to give her a meal of hemp the first thing in the morning, and another in the evening just before dark ; a tablespoonful is quite sufficient, for it is very fattening, and they will, if indulged, eat it to excess. The food must be carefully prepared. Cut a slice from a stale loaf, remove the crust entirely, and on the crummy portion pour boiling water. Before the bread goes to pap pour off the water, and squeeze the bread as dry as possible, so that it forms a tough, semi-glutinous mass. It is then quite soaked through, but not too moist, and will absorb milk readily. The milk should be boiled, and as much poured over as the bread will take up. Give it in a porcelain vessel twice a-day, and never allow any in the cage to get sour. Fed in this way, with nuts and fruits, a modicum of bread-and-butter, or biscuit, dipped in milk or beer, all the parrot tribe do well ; but if fed excessively with seed, or much indulged with meat, and especially bacon and ham, they are sure to get diseased, and rapidly lose their feathers. Always be on your guard that no one but yourself, or some one that understands them as well, has anything to do with feeding your parrots. I have lately seen a splendid bird ruined by being sent down to meals with the children, where it [ate of everything, became naked in a month, and died in convulsions ; though it was previously as fine a bird as was ever petted into beauty and cleverness.

BATHING.—In summer and autumn the sooner you can get the bird to bathe the better. Have a proper porcelain bath to attach to the cage where the door opens, and get Poll to take her bath in her own way ; but if she refuses compel her to it for her own good. A favourite gray parrot of my own, now getting delightfully garrulous and full of queer ways, will never take a bath of her own accord ; but she gets a periodical ducking nevertheless. Three or four times a week we let her out, and after she has well fluttered her wings and explored the room, I take a towel well wetted and doubled several times, grasp her with it in my hand so as to hold her across the back, and then plump her into a pan of water ; she then goes to her cage. If the sun shines, she gets dry out of doors ; but if the weather is chilly, she enjoys the fire for an hour ; for, as parrots come from warm climates, they are tender, and must not be exposed rashly to cold. If a bird learns to take a bath of its own accord, let it have one every morning in warm weather, and once a week at least all through the winter ; when the water should be tepid, and there should be a good fire in the room to prevent the bird taking cold.

Now the bathing and feeding, as we have advised them, are of especial importance in more than one respect. Parrots are subject to violent fits of irritability, and these are invariable indications that their health is in some way disordered. Gouty feet and falling off of the feathers are other very common calamities ; and a parrot carelessly treated is sure to get affected with one or all of such complaints sooner or later. Indeed, when once they get the habit of picking off their feathers, and of manifesting strong passion, they are in a very bad state, and need the greatest care and patience to restore them, or they may die suddenly in convulsions. But if properly cared for, this common habit of picking off the feathers may be wholly prevented ; and the means are—first, plenty of fresh water for drinking, and a bath regularly ; sweet wholesome food ; seed only twice a day, and then in small quantities ;

and, above all, means of amusement. This last item is of more importance than may appear at first sight. A parrot fed with exciting food, kept without water, or left to mope in a dull room with no one to talk to or to talk to it, will surely begin to dig away at its own flesh; off comes a feather from the wing, or a whole bunch from the bosom; and, horrible to relate, when once the bird draws blood with its beak, it will peck itself with redoubled vigour, and literally hack itself to death. Keep your bird amused, then, and it will soon repay all your attentions. The wire swing which is usually attached inside a parrot-cage is very useful at first in aiding to tame the bird; but after a-while that should come away, for they get into a habit of swinging themselves stupid, and, from love of the undulating motion, spend all their time dozing in it. Take away the swing when Poll is beginning to get on well, and she will exercise herself about the cage, and be better for it. This last point, however, is not to be enforced too strictly; let the habits of the bird decide.

HINTS IN PURCHASING A PARROT.— In purchasing a parrot, it is always best to procure a young *untaught* bird, if possible; for one that has been taught will also have formed strong attachments; and in passing into strange hands will probably mope, and refuse at first to utter a word in the hearing of its new possessor. This, however, is not a serious matter; kind treatment and frequent attention will soon win its affections. But there is another risk; you may not know all that it has been taught. Parrots bought of sailors sometimes say strange things, and it is very difficult, if not impossible, to eradicate their early lessons. A man given to oaths may be reformed, but for a swearing parrot there is little hope indeed.

DIET.—In the case of a young half-wild bird—which is the best in spite of the extra trouble it occasions—first of all endeavour to win the bird's confidence by kindly attentions, but at the same time beware of your fingers. Give the bird a common bell-shaped roomy cage, with a swing for its amusement. Let it have for the first week nothing but hemp-seed for its staple food, with occasionally a biscuit dipped in milk, a raisin, fig, or any fresh fruit from the fingers, and plenty of clean water and coarse sand. It will scream, yell, fight, and threaten, but never mind; take care it has all it requires, and time will work wonders with it. Above all things, let the person who intends to teach it minister to its wants from the first; let no servants interfere with it; and if visitors tease it, carry the bird away at once, as a quiet reproach to them. Parrots often have their tempers ruined forever by servants and visitors poking at them with sticks, or for presenting their fingers for Poll to snap it. Never allow any one to tempt your bird in that way; for the trick of snapping and pecking is an acquired one; a well-taught parrot never attacks anybody. After a week or ten days the bird will be quieter, more contented, and will begin to know you; then alter its diet, giving less hemp-seed and more fruit, biscuit, and nuts. Their best staple diet is bread-and-milk; but they will not eat it until they are somewhat tamed, and at first must be pressed to it by hunger. If kept wholly on hemp, they get feverish, cast their feathers, begin to peck themselves, and indulge in terrible fits of temper; and animal food, except in minute quantities, has a similar effect upon them.

**Canaries.**—Mr. Kidd, a great authority with bird-keepers, observes, that if you want a good songster, you will sometimes have to dispense with beauty. The brightest colours are frequently the most delicate. Never choose a bird whose feathers are rough, or eyes dim. If the bird be trim and joyous, he may be regarded as in good health. While making your selection, take plenty of time for decision. Exercise your taste, and you may become possessed of a really musical bird. There is, of course, a great difference in the powers of the various performers. Some are shrill and noisy ; others sing *piano*, and rejoice in dulcet notes of harmony.

Your bird selected, and placed in a nice handsome cage, enrol him immediately as one of the family, and ever after consider him as such. He will then be " yours for ever."

Hang your bird low and in a cheerful situation, always protecting him from heat, cold, and draught. If you have more birds than one, suspend them *above* each other. They may hear, but should not be permitted to see each other. Maintain the strictest cleanliness in their cages, and always supply them with the best of seed—canary, flax, and rape, mixed ; the first in excess. Give them clean water *twice* daily, and let their perches be cleansed at least once a week. Provide them, too, with plenty of coarse red gravel, changed every other day, and let some well-bruised *old* mortar be mixed with it.

Now for " luxuries." These consist of hard-boiled yolk of egg, a morsel of sweet cake or mealy potato, and crumb of bread moistened in the mouth with brown sugar. Let them *see* you preparing this, and then watch their movements. Add an occasional hempseed. Lettuce, shepherds'-purse, groundsel, plantain, chickweed, and water-cress,— these are the salads in which they delight.

Always present some one, or all of the above, lovingly with the finger and thumb. At the same time make a gracious bow by way of courtesy. The effect of that bow is magical. It possesses a rare charm, as is fully verified in my own pets. Try it ; and mark the droll result,

PAIRING, BREEDING, REARING, &c.— If your birds be not already paired, no time should be lost in bringing them together. Select handsome *jonque* male-birds ; and let the hens be of a pale yellow, or mealy colour. Both birds should be at least a year old ; strong, healthy, and vigorous. Place them, first, in separate cages near each other ;

gradually diminish the distance, and in two or three days they will be 'mated.'

The next step will be to procure a breeding-cage. These are to be had of any dealer in birds. As regards the size, the larger the better. You cannot give your birds too much space, nor admit too much air. All must, however, depend on the height of the room in which they are to be kept ; for the cage is to be suspended at least six feet from the floor.

See that the cage be provided with nest-boxes, water-glasses, tin pans, &c., &c., all complete ; and having procured two nest-bags, scald them thoroughly to destroy the indwelling vermin. When quite dry, hang them (externally) on the front wires of the cage.

The birds may now be turned into their new habitation ; and they will perfectly comprehend the nature of the provision that has been made for them and their future offspring. Hang them in a quiet corner ; repress all prying curiosity ; and you will very soon be rewarded by seeing her little ladyship commence ' sitting.'

Never attempt to peep into the nest, either while it is in the course of construction, or when there are eggs in it. Nature hates any interference of this kind. Only be patient, and wait thirteen days ; you will then have a new part to play.

On the morning of the thirteenth day after sitting, you must have ready some scalded rape-seed, a piece of stale French roll dipped in cold water, and afterwards well squeezed, and some yolk of a fresh egg, boiled hard. This should be well mixed, and formed into a moderately-soft paste. Supply it in a small saucer. It should be made fresh twice daily. If allowed to be in the slightest degree sour, it would kill all the nestlings.

Sometimes the mother feeds the young ; but more generally this tender task is undertaken by the papa, who considers it a pleasing duty.

Should any eggs remain unhatched after the hen has sat fourteen days, they may be at once removed. No doubt they are unfruitful.

Be very careful to supply the inmates of the cage, during incubation, with ripe chickweed, groundsel, &c. ; also with plenty of small pebbly gravel, mixed with old (bruised) mortar. Clean water, too, should be given twice daily, and occasionally bread and egg.

Sometimes the parents will neglect their children, and refuse to feed them. In such cases *you* must interfere ; removing them in the nest, and feeding them by hand. This is easily managed by the aid of a short pointed stick, at the end of which place some of the food, and drop it into the birds' open mouths. This should be done every hour, assuming that the nestlings are about a week old when they are removed. Administer water, by letting it drip from the end of your little finger.

To encourage them to feed themselves, present the end of the stick to them with the food on it. They will prove very apt scholars, and quickly ' learn the way to their mouths.'

Never remove any young birds from their parents (when they are fed by them) until they are five weeks old ; and take special care not to change their food too soon. Continue to feed with egg and bread, in addition to seed, till they are two months old.

Cage them off separately at this age, and let their dwelling be light and cheerful. They will soon ' record ' their song, and amply repay you for all your past trouble. Give them each a bath daily, also a flight in a spare room if practicable.

By putting up birds of different colours, some very pretty varieties may be obtained. The colour in no way interferes with the song.

**Habit in Eating and Sleeping.—** The quantity of food is so much a matter of habit, that two persons of equal weight, and mental and bodily activity, will consume widely different quantities of food—one eating four times as much as the other, the surplus being of no possible advantage, but the reverse.

So habit makes five meals a day seem necessary to some persons ; while others live equally well—perhaps, far better—on two meals a day. It is a matter of habit whether a man sleep six hours or nine hours a day : and three hours a day is one-eighth of life. It is, therefore, of great importance that we form simple, natural, and healthful habits, and in all ways order our lives to the highest uses.

**Dry Friction.—** Dry friction over the whole surface of the body once a day, or once in two days, is often of more service than the application of water. The reply of the centenarian to the inquiry, to what habit of life he attributed his good health and extreme longevity, that he believed it due to " rubbing himself all over with a cob every night," is significant of an important truth. If invalids and persons of low vitality would use dry friction every day for a considerable period, we are confident they would often be greatly benefited. Cleanliness is next to godliness, no doubt, and a proper and judicious use of water is to be commended ; but human beings are not amphibious. Nature indicates that the functions of the skin should be kept in order mainly by muscular exercise, by exciting natural perspiration by labour ; and delicious as is the bath, and healthful under proper regulations, it is no substitute for that exercise of the body without which all the functions become abnormal.

**Marrow Pudding.—** Take a ripe vegetable marrow, cut out a round at the flower end, scoop out the seeds, and fill the hollow with meat cut into small pieces as for a meat pudding, mixed with pepper and salt and a little cold gravy. Replace the round end and tie it up in a cloth. Put it into fast boiling water, and let it boil three or four hours, according to the size. Those who are fond of a beef kidney will find it cook very nicely in this manner.

**Ginger Pop.—** Put a very clean pot containing a gallon of water to boil on the fire. As soon as it begins to boil add twelve ounces of brown sugar, one ounce of bruised ginger, and two ounces of cream of tartar; stir all well together. Now pour the whole into an earthen pan, cover it with a cloth, and let it get cold. Then stir in half a gill of fresh yeast; stir it well, so as to be perfectly well mixed; cover it again with the cloth, and leave it to work up; this will be in from six to eight hours' time. Remove the scum very carefully, so as not to disturb the clearness of the beer. Take it out with a jug, and pour it into clear bottles. Cork down tightly with a string across the cork, and put away in a cool place, lying down. In four days this pleasant drink will be ready.

Very many add to it scraped dandelion roots and some herbs, which they boil up with it, which makes it a pleasant bitter, and makes it highly beneficial to the health.

**The Best Medicine.**—Dr Hall says the best medicine in the world, more efficient than all the potations of the materia medica, are warmth, rest, cleanliness, and pure air. Some persons make it a virtue to brave disease, " to keep up " as long as they can move a foot or wiggle a finger, and it sometimes succeeds; but in others the powers of life are thereby so completely exhausted that the system has lost all ability to recuperate, and slow and typhoid fever sets in and carries the patient to a premature grave. Whenever walking or work is an effort, a warm bed and cool room are the very indispensables to a sure and speedy recovery. Instinct leads all beasts and birds to quietude and rest the very moment disease or wounds assail the system.

**Intoxicating Drinks.**—Sir Henry Thompson, the eminent physician, has put forth a positive declaration as to the injurious effects of intoxicating drinks, that must excite the earnest attention of thinking men and women. Sir Henry says he has long been of opinion that there is no greater cause of evil, moral and physical, in this country, than the use of alcoholic beverages. He explains that by this he does not mean actual drunkenness, but the habitual use of stimulants far short of what is necessary to produce that condition; and this, he says, injures the body and diminishes the mental power to an extent which he thinks few people are aware of. To this indulgence he attributes a large proportion of some of the most painful and dangerous maladies which come under his notice.

**Whitlow.**—Though in itself a small affair, there are few things which cause such suffering, and which are so neglected and allowed to have their own way. Surgeons are constantly meeting with people who have lost bones of the finger or thumb, and have stiff joints from this cause. At the commencement great relief is sometimes obtained by soaking the part in the following mixture: take half a gill of strong vinegar, and dissolve in it a tablespoonful of carbonate of potash. Let it be used as hot as can be borne, and repeat as often as the pain returns, but if matter be formed there are two ways of treating it; one by allowing the matter to destroy the parts and find its own way out, generally around the nail; this takes from two to six weeks of severe suffering; the other is by making a small opening down to the bone to allow the matter to escape, which takes one moment to do, gives relief in an hour, and can be done without giving any pain. It is a great pity for any one so to fear the very slight operation as to lose the use of a thumb for life, and if near a surgeon or a public institution there is in the present day no excuse. In either case a poultice must be constantly applied.

**Influenza.**—" I do not know any complaint which produces such depression of spirits as this," says Dr. Hope, in his " Till the Doctor Comes." " I have had strong, able men, such as ' navvies,' who work out in all weathers, come and ask me if they were likely to die soon, they felt so ' down.' Any one attacked with influenza should give up at once, remain in bed, and encourage perspiration by every means in his power. If it can be had, the Dover's powder should be taken, as in common colds, and repeated if needful, and either with or without this, I have found the two following preparations of milk very useful. The first is called wine-whey, made by putting two wine-glassfuls of white wine and one tea-spoonful of vinegar to a pint of milk ; simmer it very gently so as not to break the curd, then strain and sweeten. The other is, scald a pint of buttermilk, strain it, and then add one wineglass-ful of rum and one of treacle, or as much sugar as the patient likes. If you are in the country, get the whey direct from the dairy. If you are not able to get wine, use rum in the sweet milk. There is no objection to the use of a little spice to give an agreeable flavour. Either of these may be given in divided quantities very frequently, and are ge nerally very pleasant to the patient.

**Æolian Harp.**—This musical instrument, named after Æolus, god of the winds in the old mythology, emits soft and harmonious notes merely from a current of air passing over its strings. It is made as follows :—Let a box be made of well-seasoned deal, not more than one-fourth of an inch thick ; in length exactly the width of the window in which it is to be placed ; in depth four inches, and in width six inches. Glue on the top of this box, at its two ends, two pieces of wainscot, half inch high and quarter of an inch thick, to serve as bridges for the strings ; inside the box, at each end, glue two pieces of beech wood, about one inch square, and of length equal to the width of the box. Into this beech wood holes must be bored, into which holes the pegs of the strings are to pass. The strings must be of catgut, the size of the first string of a violin, and they are fastened round pegs like those of the violin, and the pegs inserted in the holes at the opposite ends of the box. The strings should be parallel, not drawn tight, and tuned in unison. To procure a proper passage for the wind, a thin board, supported at each corner, is placed over

the strings at about four inches from the top of the box. The instrument must be placed before the opening made by raising the lower sash of the window to about a level with the strings. To increase the current of air an opposite window or door may be opened. When the wind blows the strings emit sound in unison, and, in proportion to its force, change variously through the notes of the diatonic scale, often forming most pleasing harmonic combinations.

**Anchovy.**—This fish is about the size of the middle finger, bluish brown on the back, and silvery white on the belly. It abounds in the Mediterranean along the shores of Spain, Italy, and Greece ; and in the Atlantic on the coasts of France and Portugal. Con siderable anchovy fisheries have been established along the coasts of Provence and Catalonia, but the most productive is at Gorgona, a small island near Leghorn. They are caught only during the night, being attracted near the boats by charcoal fires burning in them. If when the barrels are opened the fish are found to be small, firm, and round backed, with a silvery skin, red flesh, and plump, compact form, they are probably true anchovies. If, on the contrary, they taper much towards the tail, are dark brown on the outside, and the flesh is pale and flabby, they are probably sardines, another Mediterranean species, and much inferior.

**Anchovy Omelet.**—Wash the salt from a dozen anchovies, and lay them in cold water for a quarter of an hour : cut them in slips, and place them on thin slices of bread fried in oil ; beat up a dozen eggs, and season them well ; put some olive oil in a frying-pan, and, when it begins to boil, put in half the eggs to form the omelet. When done, place it on a dish, and lay the anchovy toast on it : then form the second omelet with the rest of the eggs, and put it over the toast. Serve with any sauce you please.

**Anchovy Sauce.**—Pound three an chovies in a mortar with a little bit of butter ; rub the whole through a double hair-sieve with the back of a wooden spoon, and stir what comes through into half a pint of melted butter ; or stir in a tablespoonful of essence of anchovy. To the above many cooks add lemon-juice and Cayenne.  Serve very hot.

**Aniseed Water.**—Take eight ounces of new aniseed ; sift it well to free it from the dust, and then infuse in six pints of water, with the juice of three lemons, and half an ounce of cinnamon. In a week's time distil it over a moderate fire ; put one pint of water into the still ; dissolve three pounds of sugar in three pints of water.  As the anise contains an acid salt, which renders this liquor milky, the following proceeding is necessary :—Reserve one pint of water from that in which you dissolved the sugar, and mix it with the white of three or four eggs, well whipped, and, while the syrup is hot, put to it this egg-water and the aniseed water ; stir it over the fire until the whole is hot, without boiling ; then put it into a glass jar, cork it well, and let it stand ; the next day filter and bottle.

**Anodyne.**—Any medicine capable of allaying pain is called an anodyne. Some are taken internally, and others are applied externally for this purpose. Pain either arises from blood stagnating at a particular spot, causing inflammation, or from a deficient circulation of the blood, which causes similarly local exhaustion  Administering anodynes requires great caution, for they usually operate upon the brain, causing sleep ; and let it always be borne in mind that the frequent use of anodynes increases the necessity for using them. Opium is an anodyne, and any one who indulges in taking that seductive drug may remove pain, but gives birth to a craving as beset with horrors, and terminating in death.  If an anodyne causes sleep, it is called a SOPORIFIC ; and if it rapidly diminishes the circulation, it is called a SEDATIVE.

**Apple Dumpling.**—Make paste the same as for apple pudding ; divide it into as many pieces as you want dumplings ; peel the apples, and core them ; then roll out your paste large enough, and put in the apples . close them all round, and tie them in pudding-cloths very tight.  One hour will boil them, and when you take them up just dip them in cold water, and put them in a cup the size of the dumpling when you untie them, and then they will turn out without breaking.

**Apple Jelly.**—Pare, core, and quarter any quantity of good apples ; cover them well with water, and let them boil till soft ; drain them through a sieve into a pan, and in the meantime have ready a syrup made by boiling the rinds and cores in water ; strain it off, and boil it with a sufficient quantity of sugar to make it rich.  Take as much of this as of the juice which passes through the sieve, and thoroughly boil it ; then add the jelly, and boil all together eight or ten minutes.  This jelly should be kept covered with paper dipped in brandy, like all others made of fruit.

**Apple Pie.**—Take eight apples ; pare, core, and cut not smaller than quarters , place them as close together in a pie-dish as possible, with four cloves ; rub in a mortar some lemon-peel with a quarter of a pound of good moist sugar, and, if agreeable, add some quince-jam ; cover it with puff-paste ; bake it an hour and a quarter.  Clotted cream is a delicious addition to this pie.

**Apple Pudding.**—Chop four ounces of beef suet, very fine, or two ounces of butter, lard, or dripping—but the suet makes the lightest crust—put it on the paste-board, with eight ounces of flour, and a pinch of salt ; mix it well together with your hands, and then put it all of a heap, and make a hole in the middle ; break one egg in it, stir it well together with your finger, and by degrees infuse as much water as will make it of a stiff paste ; roll it out two or three times with the rolling-pin, and roll it large enough to receive about one pound of pared and cored apples.  It should be boiled in a basin, well buttered, which is preferable to a cloth ; boil it an hour and three quarters ; but the surest way is to stew the apples first in a stewpan with a wine-glassful of water, and then one hour will boil it. Some people like it flavoured with cloves and lemon-peel, and sweeten it with two ounces of sugar.

**How to Air Rooms.**—It is a common mistake to open only the lower part of the windows of an apartment, whereas if the upper part were also opened, the ventilation of the room would be more speedily effected. The air in an apartment is generally heated to a higher temperature than the external air, either by the heat supplied by the human body, or by lamps, gas, or fire; this renders the air in the room lighter than the external air, and consequently the external air will rush in at all openings at the lower part of the room, while the warmer and lighter air passes out at the higher openings. If a candle be held in the doorway near the door, it will be found that the flame will be blown inward; but if it be raised near to the top of the doorway it will be blown outward. The warm air in this case flows out at the top, whilst the cold air flows in at the bottom. A current of warm air from the room is generally rushing up the flue of the chimney, even though there be no fire in the grate; hence the unwholesomeness of using chimney-boards.

**Sea-Bathing.**—To have the greatest benefit from sea-bathing, it is proper but to remain a very short time in the water—not exceeding two or three minutes. If longer, the body should be kept immersed under the surface the whole time, and in constant motion, in order to promote the circulation of the blood, from the centre to the extremities. It is much better to remain completely immersed in deep, than to take repeated plunges in shallow, water. On coming out, the body should be rubbed dry with a rough cloth, and the ordinary dress resumed as quickly as possible. It is more necessary to replace the usual vestments quickly, than to be extremely anxious that the surface of the skin is perfectly dry, as any wetness from salt water is not likely to be prejudicial. After bathing use moderate exercise to promote the return of the heat of the body, taking care that it is not too long continued. If chilliness occasionally ensues, breakfast soon after bathing in the morning; or in the forenoon, some warm soup or broth may be taken; and remember, that if immersion, instead of being succeeded by a glow on the surface of the skin, is followed by chilliness, languor, or headache, bathing in the sea should by no means be persisted in.

**Red Currant Jelly.**—Rub the fruit through a sieve, and afterwards squeeze it through a fine linen cloth; put it into a preserving pan, with three quarters of a pound of white sugar to every pint of juice; place it over a brisk fire, stirring it occasionally with a skimmer. Keep it well skimmed; when it is done, it will fall from the skimmer in sheets; then take it up, pour it into pots, and cover them closely. Made in this way, it is used for sauce for game, &c., but if required for other uses, a little raspberry juice will improve it.

**"Welcome."**—This word is derived from the Saxon *wilcuma*; the meaning of which is, "Your coming pleases me." They knew the word right well, did our Saxon forefathers; their hospitality was proverbial. They knew how to welcome a guest; a stranger, no matter whence he came had no cause to complain of a Saxon's good cheer. Rude though they were, as compared with the luxurious Norman, they were at least honest and sincere—qualities of which the wily Norman robber were sadly deficient. "Let welcome make amends for hard cheer," cries Cedric, the Saxon, in Sir Walter Scott's "Ivanhoe," when Prior Aymer and Brian de Bois-Guilbert are announced. "Well, it is but for one night, they shall be welcome. Oswald, broach the oldest wine cask. Place the best mead, the mightiest ale, the richest morat, the most sparkling cider, the most odoriferous pigments upon the board; fill the largest horns. Let welcome make amends for hard fare."

**Mustard Poultices.**—Make a bag the size required of book muslin, and, after mixing equal quantities of mustard and linseed meal, (or a larger proportion of the former, should the case require it) in a basin, with boiling water of a proper consistency, fill the bag, and, sewing it up, apply it to the part affected, covering it with a handkerchief or a piece of linen. The patient will find this a very clean and comfortable plan. After it has been kept on as long as desired, it only remains to remove it, and lay on a piece of old cambric handkerchief, no rubbing or washing being required. The poultice is perfectly efficacious, and all that is necessary afterwards is to dust it with hair powder for a day or two.

**Soda Water.**—Dissolve six drachms of dried carbonate of soda in a quart bottle of water, and four drachms and a half of tartaric acid in another bottle of the same size ; pour out a wine-glassful from each bottle, and throw them at the same time into a tumbler, when it will immediately effervesce ; it should be drunk in this state. This is a good soda-water, and a dozen glasses thus prepared will not cost more than eighteenpence. If ten drops of the muriated tincture of iron be previously put into the tumbler, an excellent and pleasant tonic mineral water is made.

**Artificial Teeth.**—The loss of our teeth is the loss of some of our best friends, and, like our best friends, their true value is only discovered by their absence. Have they not from our childhood materially helped us to sustain the life God gave us ? Could we have assimilated our food without their laborious help ? Have they not done the rough part of preparation by masticating and grinding our daily food for the more delicate offices of the digestive organs ? But for their generous work, our daily food would have been swallowed in indigestible lumps, and remain in the stomach only to torture us, instead of contributing to the life-blood of the body. Is it not to the teeth, too, that we owe our perfect articulation ? But

for them, the young and middle-aged would stammer in the uncertain treble of those in the decline of life. But alas ! by ill-usage or accident they have bereft us, or remain with us only to be perpetual torments and an unsightly exhibition. In the interests of our health, and a due regard to our personal appearance, we fly for succour to the surgeon-dentist, whose skill and ingenuity has at hand remedies for the numerous diseases to which teeth are subject. The skill now shown in the preparation and adjustment of artificial teeth by Mr. Farnham, Essex Road, Islington, has reduced the loss of our teeth to the merest minimum of inconvenience, and the public are much indebted to him for the efficient substitutes he has provided for our offence against those that nature gave us. The artificial teeth referred to perform the good offices of those we have lost in the mastication of food, and the clearness of articulation. Dental surgery has, no doubt, generally made great progress towards perfection, and the art has at length developed itself into one of certainty, still it is more prudent to place our requirements in the hands of those that we know can give us help, than risk getting into unskilful ones—but more prudent still, to take scrupulous care of those beneficently given into our keeping by Nature.

**Argand Lamp.**—This lamp is so named after the inventor, a Frenchman. The wick being cylindrical admits air to both sides of a very thin sheet of flame, and, consequently, renders the combustion, or burning of the oil much more complete than where a common solid wick is employed, and the air can only reach the outside of the flame. The wick of the moderator lamp is like that of the Argand lamp, and differs from it chiefly in having the oil forced up to the wick, whereas, in the Argand lamp, the oil reaches the wick only by its own gravity. The management of a lamp of any kind is rather a difficult business, therefore great care should be taken in the purchase to obtain one from a maker of known reputation, for the cheap ones, particularly those picked up as bargains in brokers' shops, are always out of repair. The principle of the Argand lamp is, that a free current of air should be drawn through the centre of the flame, and to ensure this, it is necessary to clean the lamp frequently, and remove any dust or impurities from the oil or charcoal of the wick, which collects round the small holes in the rim, through which the cold air is drawn. If the lamp is used every night it should be cleaned daily. The methodical mode is this :—Remove the shade carefully before you soil your hands with the oil. Provide a basin of warm water (a little above blood heat), and in this first wash the glass chimney, then pour the oil from the fountain, and remove any sediment from about the brass work. Screw up the wick, and if it is not long enough for the time it may probably be required to burn, replace it with a fresh one by means of the stick. Having washed all the brass work, wipe the parts carefully, screw everything in its former position, and take care in replacing the wick that the small notch at the side of the brass enters the groove which is sunk to receive it ; turn it up and down once or twice to make sure that it works freely ; then prime it (that is, singe the top), replace the fountain (filled with oil), chimney and shade ; the lamp is then ready for use. Purchase the best oil—the inferior qualities emit an offensive smell, and produce so much sediment that the delicate work of the lamp is quickly clogged, and the current of air impeded, which causes it to burn dimly. Occasionally it is necessary to wash the shade, which should be done in clean water, lukewarm, with the admixture of a little soda, which removes all stains, and does not injure the appearance of the ground glass. The glass chimneys will sometimes crack with the heat, particularly in frosty weather. This may be prevented by scoring a small notch in the glass at top and bottom.

**Arrowroot.**—This starch is manufactured from the root of a plant cultivated in gardens in the East and West Indies. As an article of diet it is invaluable, especially in bowel complaints. The purest sort is the Bermuda.

The jelly it forms with boiling water continues firm for three or four days, and does not become sour for several days.

To Prepare Arrowroot.—Mix with two or three tablespoonfuls of arrowroot half a pint of cold water : let it stand for nearly a quarter of an hour ; pour off the water, and stir in some pounded sugar ; boil one pint of milk, and pour it gradually upon the arrowroot, stirring it one way all the time. Or it may be made with water in which lemon-peel has been boiled, and then a glass of port or sherry and a little nutmeg stirred into it.

**Arrowroot Blancmange.**—Take a teacupful of arrowroot to a pint of milk : boil the milk with twelve sweet and six bitter almonds, blanched and pounded ; sweeten with loaf sugar, and strain it : break the arrowroot with a little of the milk as smooth as possible ; pour the boiling milk on it by degrees, stirring all the while ; put it back into the pan ; let it boil a few minutes still stirring ; dip the shape in cold water before you put it in, and turn it out when cold.

**To Make Walnut Ketchup.**—Take the green outside shells from walnuts that are perfectly ripe, put them into a jar with as much strong vinegar as will perfectly cover them, and tie them up securely for twelve months. Then strain them, and press the juice out through a strong sieve, and for every gallon of liquor take—sardines, chopped small, six ounces ; three heads of peeled garlic ; Jamaica pepper, one ounce ; mace, three quarters of an ounce ; black pepper, one ounce ; ginger, sliced, one ounce ; port wine lees, one quart. Let the ketchup boil up, and then simmer ten minutes ; skim it well, and put it away for twenty-four hours ; then boil it until reduced one half. When cold, bottle it for store, and cork and wax it well.

**Choking.**—Persons are frequently in danger of suffocation from fish-bones, pins, &c., which stick in the throat. The moment an accident of this kind occurs, desire the patient to be perfectly still ; open his mouth, and look into it. If you see the obstruction, endeavour to seize it with your finger and thumb, or a long, slender pair of pincers. If it cannot be got up, and is not of a nature to do any injury in the stomach, push it down with the handle of a spoon, or a flexible, round piece of whalebone, the end of which is neatly covered with a roll of linen, or anything that may be at hand. If you can neither get it up nor down, place six grains of tartar emetic in the patient's mouth. As it dissolves it will make him excessively sick, and in consequence of the relaxation, the bone, or whatever it may be, will descend into the stomach, or be ejected from the mouth. If a pin, button, or other metallic or pointed body has been swallowed or pushed into the stomach, make the patient eat plentifully of thick rice pudding, or some other farinaceous substance.

**A Rain-Glass.**—The following may be depended upon as a rain-glass ; a friend of ours says, " I have used it for months. Get a common pickle bottle, such as is sold at every Italian warehouse ; fill it with any kind of water, to within two or three inches of the top ; plunge the neck of an empty Florence oil-flask into the pickle bottle. Before rain, the water will rise two or three inches in the neck of the inverted flask—often in three or four hours. If the weather is settled for fair, the water will remain not more than half an inch high, for days, in the neck of the flask. It never fails to foretell rain. It may stand in or out of doors, in sun or shade, and the water never needs changing so long as it can be seen through. Mine is now green through long standing. The oil-flask must be cleansed before the neck is plunged in the water, and warm water will clear it of oil.

**Economy in Candles.**—If you require to burn a candle all night, unless you use the precaution, it is most sure that an ordinary candle will gutter away in an hour or two, sometimes to the endangering the safety of the house. This may be avoided by the placing as much common salt, finely powdered, as will reach from the tallow to the bottom of the black part of the wick of a partly-burnt candle, when, if the same be lit, it will burn very slowly, yet yielding sufficient light for a bedchamber ; the salt will gradually sink as the tallow is consumed, the melted tallow being drawn through the salt, and consumed in the wick.

**How to Eat an Egg.**—There is an old saying, taken from the Italian,—" Teach your grandmother how to suck eggs." This appears an unnecessary piece of information, as people do not suck eggs as they do oranges ; but as we believe there are few who know how to eat one properly, we shall give the secret. By the usual mode of introducing the salt, it will not mix or incorporate with the egg ; the result is, you either get a quantity of salt without egg, or egg without salt. Put in a drop or two of water, tea, coffee, or other liquid you may have on the table at the time, then add the salt, and stir. The result is far more agreeable, the drop of liquid is not tasted.

**Umbrellas.**—If an umbrella is wet, do not unfurl it for the purpose of drying it more rapidly. If you do, the whalebones acquire a particular set, which it is almost impossible to obviate ; they become permanently bent, in consequence of the shrinking of the cloth while drying, and give the umbrella when furled a bulging and unseemly appearance.

**Rules for Young Wives.**—1. Obey your husband cheerfully, even though you think him in error ; it is better that he should do wrong in what he commands, than that you should do wrong in objecting to it.

2. If he flatters you, do not forget that it is but flattery ; think lowly of yourself and highly of him, or at least make him think so.

3. If you see any imperfections in your husband (which there may be), do not pride yourself on your penetration in discovering them, but on your forbearance in not pointing them out ; strive to show no superiority but in good temper.

4. Bear in mind continually, that you are weak and dependent ; and even if you are beautiful, that it adds to your weakness and dependence.

5. If you displease him, be the first to conciliate and to mend : there is no degradation in seeking peace, or in showing that you love your husband better than your triumph.

6. If misfortunes assail you, remember that you ought to sustain your share of the burden : imitate your husband's fortitude, or show your own for his imitation.

7. When you rise in the morning, resolve to be cheerful for the day ; let your smiles dispel his frowns.

8. Take pride in concealing your husband's infirmities from others, rather than in proclaiming them ; you will only be laughed at by all his acquaintances if you tell his faults to one.

**English Stew.**—This is the name given to the following excellent preparation of cold meat. Cut the meat in slices : pepper, salt, and flour them, and lay them in a dish. Take a few pickles of any kind, or a small quantity of pickled cabbage, and sprinkle over the meat. Then take a teacup half full of water ; add to it a small quantity of the vinegar belonging to the pickles, a small quantity of ketchup, if approved of, and any gravy that may be set by for use. Stir all together and pour over the meat. Set the meat before the fire with a tin behind it, or put it in a Dutch-oven, or in the oven of the kitchen range, as may be most convenient, for about half an hour before dinner-time. This is a very nice way of dressing cold meat, which is well deserving of attention. It is palatable, cheap, and simple.

**To Test Flour.**—To judge if flour be pure and good, take a little in the hand, and squeeze it for half a minute ; if good, it can be put out of the hand in a lump, retaining the form given to it by the hand ; if adulterated, it will fall apart as soon as it leaves the hand of the operator.

**To Keep Suet.**—If chopped suet be spread on a dish, and a little salt sprinkled over, it will keep much better than without this precaution. No salt will be required in making the puddings. In hot weather the suet should be put into strong salt and water, to be changed every few days.

**Tincture for the Teeth.**—Take of Florentine iris-root eight ounces, cloves, bruised, one ounce, ambergris, one scruple. Bruise the root, and put the whole ingredients into a glass bottle, with a quart of rectified spirits of wine. Cork close, and agitate it once a day for a fortnight, keeping it in a warm place. About a teaspoonful is sufficient at a time ; in this a soft tooth-brush should be dipped, and then worked into a lather on the teeth and gums. It cleanses the teeth, strengthens the gums, and sweetens the breath. Apply the tincture in the morning, and before retiring to rest.

**Hair Oils.**—When used moderately, oil tends to strengthen the hair, especially when it is naturally dry. When used in excess, however, they clog the pores, prevent the escape of the natural secretions, and cause the hair to wither and fall off. The varieties of " oils," " greases," " ointments," rivalling each other in their high-sounding pretensions, which are daily imposed upon public credulity, are interminable. We deem the following the best, and certainly the simplest to prepare :—

For an excellent HAIR-OIL, boil together half a pint of port wine, one pint and a half of sweet oil, and half a pound of green southernwood. Strain the mixture several times through a linen rag, adding, at the last operation, two ounces of bear's grease. If fresh southernwood is added each time it passes through the linen. the composition will be improved.

For THICKENING THE HAIR.—To one ounce of Palma Christi oil add a sufficient quantity of bergamot or lavender to scent it. Apply it to the parts where it is most needed, brushing it well into the hair.

OINTMENT FOR THE HAIR.—Mix two ounces of bear's grease, half an ounce of honey, one drachm of laudanum, three drachms of the powder of southernwood, three drachms of the balsam of Peru, one and a half drachms of the ashes of the roots of bulrushes, and a small quantity of the oil of sweet almonds.

CLEANSING THE HAIR.—Nothing but good can be derived from a due attention to cleaning the hair. Once a week is perhaps desirable, but this will depend upon the individual ; persons with light, thin, and dry hair, will require it more seldom than those with thick, greasy hair, or who perspire very freely. Nothing is better than soap and water. The soap should be mild and plentifully rubbed in the hair.

Aspic.—Take a knuckle of veal, a knuckle of ham, a thick slice of beef, and, if these will not make your jelly stiff enough, add two calves' feet, or some swards of bacon, rasped ; put them into a saucepan with one pint of rich stock, and sweat it over a stove till reduced to a glaze : then moisten it with stock, boil and skim it well. Put to it two onions, two carrots, salt, parsley, scallions, four cloves, one clove of garlic, and two bay leaves ; let the whole stew for seven hours, then strain off the liquor. Break four eggs into a stewpan, and put to them the liquor when cold, the juice of two lemons, and two tablespoonfuls of tarragon, and beat it with a whisk over the fire till near boiling, and when it does so remove your stewpan to a smaller fire, and place fire on the lid for half an hour ; then pass it through a wet double napkin. If the jelly is not sufficiently clear clarify it a second time.

Put a layer of this jelly, about half an inch thick, at the bottom of an aspic mould ; garnish it with truffles, whites of eggs, sprigs of parsley, &c., according to your taste ; pour in another half inch of the jelly, while liquid, with great care, so as not to discompose your garnish ; then put either calves' brains, breasts of fowls, veal, sweetbreads, kidneys, cockscombs, fat livers, or game. Be sure to lay whatever you use as smooth and equal as possible ; then fill up your mould with jelly and let it stand till set. When wanted dip the mould in hot water an instant, place your dish on the top, and turn it over at once.

Apparel.—Let it always be borne in mind that to buy good clothing is the cheapest whatever the price may be ; that to be too warmly clad is far safer than to be too thinly clad.

Clothing ought to be suited to the climate. Custom has, no doubt, a very great influence in the matter of dress ; but no custom can ever change the nature of things so far as to render the same clothing fit for an inhabitant of Nova Zembla and the island of Jamaica.

In youth, while the blood is hot and the perspiration free, it is less necessary to cover the body with a great quantity of clothes ; but in the middle and decline of life, when the skin becomes rigid and the humours more cool, the clothing should be increased.

The clothing ought likewise to be suited to the period of the year. Clothing may be warm enough for summer which is by no means sufficient for winter. The greatest caution, however, is necessary in making these changes. We ought neither to put off our winter clothes too soon, nor to wear our summer ones too long. It would likewise be prudent not to make the change all at once, but to do it gradually. Every person of discernment will perceive that most of the colds which prove so destructive to the inhabitants of Britain are owing to their imprudence in changing clothes.

Clothes often become hurtful to the wearer by their being made subservient to the purposes of pride or vanity. Even the human shape is often attempted to be mended by dress. All attempts of this nature are highly pernicious. The most destructive of them amongst ladies is that of depressing the waist into unnatural dimensions. By this practice (not so much observed, we are happy to say, as formerly) the action of the stomach and bowels, the motion of the heart and lungs, and almost all the vital functions are obstructed. Hence proceed indigestion, syncopes, fainting fits, coughs, consumption of the lungs, and other complaints so common among females.

The feet likewise too often suffer by pressure. How a small foot not of Nature's making, came to be considered genteel we will not pretend to say ; but certain it is that this notion has made many persons lame. Corns are universal, and this painful excrescence is seldom occasioned but by tight boots or shoes. Corns are not only very troublesome, but by rendering people unable to walk, they may likewise be considered as the remote cause of other diseases.

The size and figure of the shoe ought certainly to be adapted to the foot. In children the feet are as well shaped as the hands, and the motion of the toes as free and easy as that of the fingers ; yet few persons in an advanced period of life are able to make any use of their toes ; they are generally squeezed all of a heap by narrow shoes, and often laid one over another in such a manner as to be rendered altogether incapable of motion. Nor is the high heel less hurtful than the narrow toe. A lady may seem taller for walking on her tiptoes, but she will never walk well in this manner. It strains her joints, distorts her limbs, makes her stoop, and utterly destroys all her ease and gracefulness of motion. It is entirely owing to shoes with high heels and narrow toes that not one female in ten can be said to walk well.

Children should from the birth be habituated to light clothing, not only by day but in bed, for nothing contributes more to form the constitution.

Infants and children are less apt to have their perspiration checked than persons who are more advanced in life, and, therefore, less apt to catch cold. From the change of childhood to the thirty-fifth year, the strength of the vital powers, and a brisk circulation, tend very much to keep up an equal perspiration ; but, after that period, the force of the circulation being lessened, the clothing by day, and the covering by night, should be gradually increased, for many of the diseases of advanced life are produced or exasperated by obstructed perspiration.

Upon the whole, however, after the age of thirty-five, it may be better to exceed rather than be deficient in clothing. Habit or custom always merits great attention. If persons have been accustomed to warm clothing, there will always be hazard in sudden changes of every kind.

Persons of delicate and irritable constitutions, whose powers are weak and circulation languid and unsteady, are apt to have the perspiration checked by very slight causes. This also happens to invalids, whose complaints are thereby much increased. Until the constitution, therefore, has been permanently strengthened, and, indeed, hardened, by being gradually habituated to air and exercise, they ought rather to exceed than be deficient in the quantity of clothing.

Such addition to the clothing ought to be made to it in cold and damp weather as to protect the body against the sudden and severe impressions of either. Invalids should have clothing accommodated to different seasons and changes of weather—those particularly who are subject to coughs, those whose nerves are weak or irritable, and those who are subject to fits of languor or depression.

**Apricot Marmalade.**—Take some fine apricots, and choose from amongst them those that are of the deepest yellow and ripe, but not too ripe. Peel them, and take out the stones ; weigh twelve pounds of the flesh of the fruit, which cut small, and put in a preserving pan with nine pounds of powdered sugar. Place the pan over a quick fire, and keep the preparation constantly stirred with a wooden spoon. To discover when the marmalade is sufficiently done, let a few drops fall into a glass of cold water, and if they do not spread, the marmalade is ready to put into pots. Another method of ascertaining when marmalade is done, is by taking some on the end of the finger and thumb, and rubbing them together. If on separating them the marmalade forms a thread, it is quite done.

**Chromo-Photography.**—This is so simple an accomplishment, that any one ignorant of art may easily practise it.

The colours, &c., are not expensive, and the work is permanent. The smallest miniature, and the life-size portrait, can be done with little trouble and cost. The few articles required are to be obtained at Messrs. Barnard and Son's fine-art depository, 339, Oxford Street, as well as the necessary directions.

The photograph is not to be mounted on card-board, but thrown into warm water, to soak out as much of the size as possible. Afterwards it is to be thoroughly dried, and laid on a sheet of glass, face downwards. It then receives a coat of the varnish, or several coats, until it be perfectly transparent. When the varnish is quite dry, proceed to colour the photograph, always working on the back. You may, if you like, lay on the varnish before you put the photograph on the glass ; but whichever way you adopt, it will be necessary to place a slip of gummed paper over the edges of the photograph, so that it may remain steadfast on the glass while you are at work.

The photograph to be painted must, by all means, be a good sharp impression ; if it be not you should make it up with water colour *before* you varnish it, and *after* it has been soaked. Indian ink and lake, or lake and sepia, mixed to the colour of the photograph, must be used. Enlargements—that is, copies of small photographs brought up to life-size—are generally very rotten and feeble in the shadows, and they must be made good ere you apply any local colour to them.

You will observe that it—the local colour—is seen *under* the photograph, so if the latter be not tolerably sharp and decided, your labour will be thrown away ; for all the colour you put on the photograph will not make good any imperfections in it.

Indeed, it is advisable to sharpen up the generality of photographs with sepia and lake, ere you lay on the flesh and carnations ; because these colours materially reduce the strength of the photograph, and after they are laid on it is too late to sharpen up. It is therefore advisable to put in a few spirited touches in the eyes, eyebrows, nostrils, mouth, and hair at first, before you proceed to the COLOURING, which is thus accomplished :—

We suppose your picture to be transparent and quite dry, and *ready* therefore for the application of the colours. Unscrew the cup, and squeeze from the bottom of the tube a small quantity of the tints you require on to the palette, and mix with them a little of the Medium ; of the latter use only sufficient to make them work agreeably, for they must not be too thin ; do not mix much more than you require, for the colours, after some hours, will dry and become useless. For the sake of clearness we will suppose that it is a portrait of moderate size you propose to colour. First apply the appropriate colour (pink) to the lips and cheeks very sparingly, softening the latter with a dry brush. In order to see the effect of your work reverse the picture, without removing it from the glass, and place a piece of white paper behind it ; if not sufficiently softened at the edges of the colour use the dry brush again. Next will come the high lights, small touches of white to the eyes, and to the prominent parts of the objects (particularly polished ones) upon which the light strikes.

Then paint in the brightest coloured objects, such as gold, flowers, ribbons, and any other small bright object that may be prominent in your picture. Allow the colours on the face, &c., to dry, then paint over them the flesh tint, which will give solidity to your work.

You may, however, after applying the pink or scarlet on the cheeks, &c., work the flesh-tint into the carnations while wet. This is a quicker method, and sometimes better; the plan you prefer, when you have tried both, you will adopt. Where a bright rosy tint is desired, the flesh-tint must not be worked much into the pink or scarlet. It is, too, important that each colour be kept within its proper boundary.

In ordinary painting there is frequently, in amateur work, too much brightness of colour. In this process no such risk is run, for the painting is seen through the photograph, which softens and blends the colours. We are consequently obliged to use the brightest pigments that can be obtained, to avoid a dull and unpleasant result:—thus bright scarlet used upon a dark photograph, produces almost a brick colour, or if very dark and warm, a maroon; while if the photograph is very pale, it remains scarlet. Again, bright yellow, seen through the photograph, is the appropriate colour for flaxen hair. Except the cheeks, as a rule, paint brighter than the required tint. A little judgment and practice will soon enable you to hit upon the appropriate colours. You may, when you doubt the effect of a colour, try it upon your picture (keeping it as far as possible from the other colours); and if it does not satisfy you, take a piece of linen, damped with the spirit, and remove it, and try again.

The colours may be mixed with each other, and it will be frequently necessary to add white to them,—thus, for the sky, the blue must be mixed with the white; for water, blue, green, and white; and so on.

When the colouring is finished and perfectly dry, pass a penknife round the edges to remove it from the glass, and mount with clear glue, or some similar cement, upon cardboard. In the event of the diaphonous varnish getting upon the face of the picture, it is sometimes desirable to pass a coating of varnish over the whole after the painting is finished.

Barnard's colours may be purchased separately from the manufacturers, as well as in boxes.

**Hydropathy.**—This is a mode of curing disease by means of the application of water. There are in this country a number of large hydropathic establishments. Without claiming for the system all that its votaries demand, there can be no doubt that it is of the greatest benefit in a great number of cases. Particularly is it of service in cases of indigestion, nervousness, an impaired constitution, or a too full habit. The system of dietary and exercise that is kept up at these establishments is, perhaps, not less conducive to a cure than the baths, which are very various. Besides the shower and ordinary bath, one of the most common is the douche bath, in which a single jet of water, varying in size from the thickness of a quill pen to that of a man's arm, is projected with great force, either from above, below, or one side, upon a particular part of the body. The sitz bath is taken sitting; besides which there are the foot-bath, hand-bath, &c. Sometimes, when the patient is sitting in a warm or tepid-bath, cold water is poured over the head and upper part of the person. Pieces of coarse linen, saturated with cold water, are also applied to the skin, and covered over with dry cloths, and re-moistened several times a day. The wet sheet packing is one of the characteristics of the system. It consists in the patient being closely enveloped in a sheet, wrung out of cold water, and then covered over with dry blankets. The great importance of hydropathy consists in the healthy stimulus which it gives to the nerves, bracing them, and acting as a tonic and soother to the whole system.

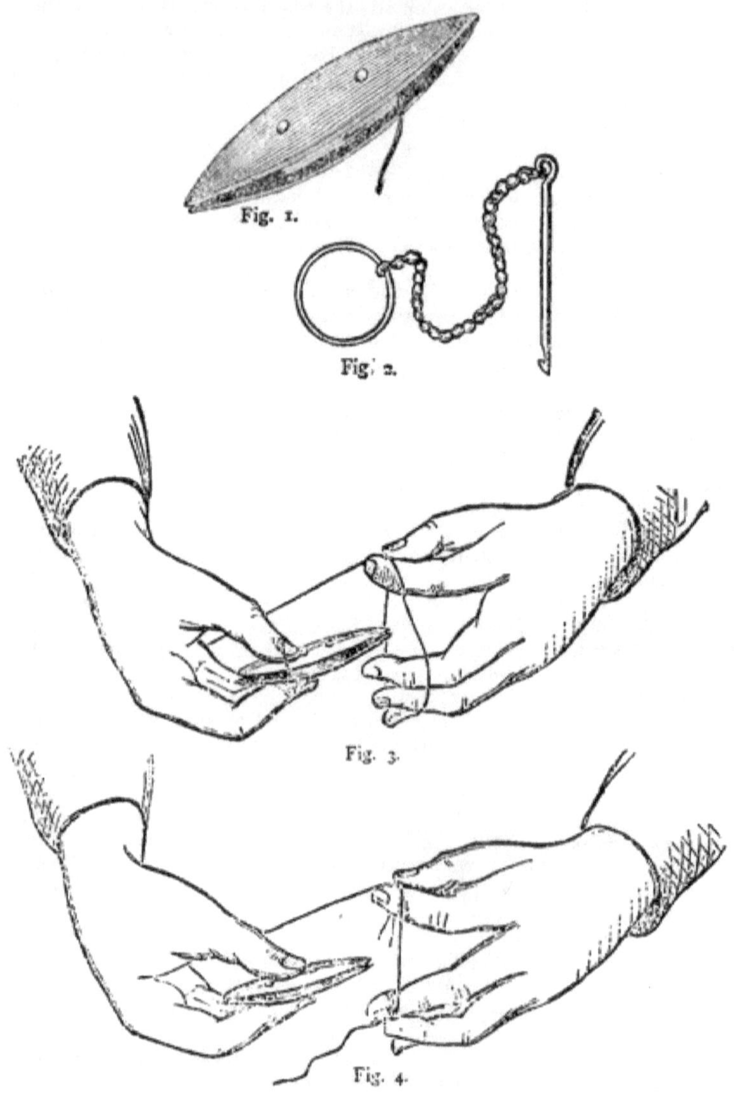

Fig. 1.

Fig. 2.

Fig. 3.

Fig. 4.

**Tatting.**—This branch of needle-work, although it may be considered of recent introduction in modern times, is merely a revival of an art practised by our grandmothers. It has, however, been considerably extended in its pro-cesses, and rendered of more general utility by the manner in which it is now practised. The old tatting, although performed in the same stitch, was al-ways worked with one thread only; and although in modern practice this still

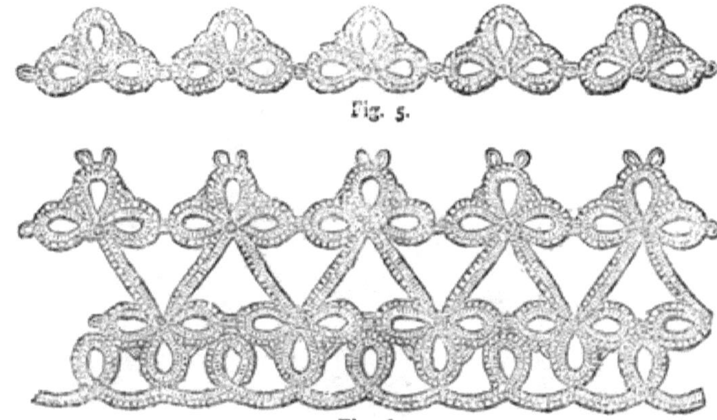

Fig. 5.

Fig. 6.

applies to simple patterns, a great advance has been made by the introduction of two threads for more complicated designs. A new element of variety has also been secured by the introduction of " purls," or loops.

As a description of work which can be conveniently carried in a very small compass, tatting is almost unrivalled ; and it has another advantage in the extreme cheapness of its materials, while the work done in it is capable of being applied to a great number of purposes, such as, in white cotton, to edgings and insertions for trimming under-clothing and baby-linen, for making caps, for trimming aprons of black silk or satin, and summer dresses in any washing material, for anti-macassars, d'oyleys, toilette-covers, &c. ; and, in black, or a mixture of black and white, for parasol covers instead of lace, for trimming bonnets, &c.  For these latter uses, tatting is sometimes worked in silk,

Fig. 7.

but, in our opinion, less successfully than in cotton.

The chief implement used in tatting is the shuttle (Fig. 1), in selecting which care should be taken to choose one that is long and not too thick, as it is easily refilled and the cotton joined by a knot, whilst it is difficult to pass a thick and clumsy shuttle through the loops. The ring and pin (Fig. 2) is used by most tatters, and is undoubtedly useful in coarse work ; but its place may be supplied by an ordinary pin of a large size, and for fine work the latter is in our opinion preferable.  A shuttle in ivory costs sixpence, and they may be bought o higher prices, one in tortoiseshell costing two shillings.  Rings and pins

Fig. 2.

also vary in price, according to material ; a good one in silk brass may be bought for sixpence.

About the best kind of white cotton that can be used is the " Boar's Head ;" and for ordinary tatting, for insertion, edging, &c., 18 is the best size. For coarse work, such as anti-macassars, 16 should be used ; for caps, &c., 20 and 30 will be found most suitable ; for very delicate work, 40 may be used. Any good unglazed sewing cotton of proper size may be made use of for black work. The " Boar's Head " cottons cost three-pence-halfpenny per reel of 200 yards.

In proceeding to work, the end of the cotton is passed through the hole in the shuttle, and the shuttle is filled with cotton to about level with the sides, but not fuller, as that would have a tendency to force the ends open. The ring is placed over the left thumb, and the pin allowed to hang down. The tatting-stitch consists of two parts ; first, the cotton is taken between the thumb and forefinger of the left hand, passed round the first joints of all the fingers, as shown in Fig. 3, and brought back to between the thumb and fore-finger. The shuttle is then passed under the cotton, between the fore and middle fingers (as is also shown), and back again over it, without turning the shuttle round, and leading the cotton which flows from it to the right. This will form a half-stitch in the circle of cotton upon that which flows from the shuttle ; and this latter must be kept tight, or there will be danger, in beginning, of forming the stitch in it upon the cotton of the circle, which would make a knot, and prevent the cotton of the circle being drawn up when required.

The second part of the stitch resembles the first, except that instead of passing the shuttle first under and then over the cotton, it has, in this instance, to be passed first over and back under. By this double action, a number of stitches, varying according to the pattern, have to be formed in succession, which are then to be drawn into a ring by releasing the circle of cotton from the fingers. This, in the old tatting, comprised the whole process, and the rings had afterwards to be sewn together to form the pattern ; but in modern tatting the necessity for sewing together is obviated by the use of loops or " purls," which are made by introducing the pin through the first half of a stitch, and leaving it there till the cotton is secured by making the second half, when the pin may be removed. By hooking the cotton through the loop thus formed while making the next ring, the two are firmly joined.

In tatting with two threads, the end of the cotton on the shuttle and the end of the cotton on the reel have to be tied together in a firm knot. This knot has to be held between the thumb and forefinger of the left hand ; and instead of forming a circle of cotton upon the fingers, that thread which is attached to the reel is twisted several times round the middle finger, as shown in Fig. 4. From this the stitches and loops are made upon the cotton in the shuttle in the same manner as before. Tatting with two threads thus admits of making lines either straight or curved, whilst with the single thread rings only can be formed, and for any elaborate pattern a combination of the two methods is necessary.

In Fig. 5 is shown a simple pattern, suitable for use as edging, to be worked in one thread only. This might well form a first lesson for a beginner. The cotton being taken upon the fingers, as shown in Fig. 3, eight stitches have to be formed, then a purl, then four stitches and a purl, then four more stitches, and draw the ring together. In the second ring, four stitches are made, and the cotton is hooked by means of the pin through the purl on the last ring ; then eight stitches and a purl, then four stitches, and draw the ring together.

For the third leaf of the trefoil, make four stitches, and join as before ; then four and a purl, then eight, and draw together. Before making the next trefoil, carry along the cotton for the length of the last ; then begin and proceed as before.

Fig. 6 is edging worked with two threads. This has to be made at two operations ; first, the double row of trefoils with the connecting stems, the rings being worked upon the thread of the shuttle, the stems upon that of the reel. When the length of this is completed, the line at the bottom by which it is to be sewn to the linen, with the small connecting rings, are added ; the former being worked on the thread of the reel, the latter on that of the shuttle.

Fig. 7 is a pattern which, as we have shown it, is best adapted for laying on dresses, aprons, &c., as a trimming, or, if the squares be brought side to side instead of corner to corner, it will make a good insertion pattern. The stems and rings are of course worked on two threads, as in the last. When one square is completed, the cotton must be broken off and the joining made, as shown, by the purl.

Fig. 8 is a round pattern, suited for an anti-macassar, by simply repeating it till the desired size is reached, or for a d'oyley, by surrounding it with circles of rings and lines like the two outermost, but of proportionately larger size in their details. In working this the four rings in the centre are made with one thread ; the cotton is then broken off, and all the successive circles afterwards are made with two threads. The cotton must be broken off at the completion of each circle.

Tatting is a description of work for which no great number of patterns is required ; its elements are so simple that, by merely introducing well-arranged repetitions, it is easy to produce a variety of pleasing and original designs, and one of its peculiar advantages is, that any pattern can readily be altered to suit the shapes and requirements of a variety of purposes; unlike most kinds of work, therefore, it never requires to be cut. The designs used for white work are also equally applicable for grey or black cotton.

The work, when finished, is invariably dirty from contact with the hands, and it is not always easy, owing to the closeness of the stitches and the hardness of the thread, to clean it. The better plan is to soak it in clean spring water for twenty-four hours before washing.

Tatting work should be starched with very thin starch only, and every loop should be picked out with a pin before ironing, which should be done with a very cool iron. Exceedingly fine tatting should be got up without the use of any starch whatever.

**Pie-Making.**—There is no article of cookery more worthy of admiration, or more appetising, than a well-made pie. It is always in season, and a general favourite. Some are best eaten when cold, and in that case suet should not be mixed with the forcemeat; should the pie be made of meat that requires more dressing to make it tender than the baking of the crust will allow, or should you wish to send it up in a raised pie form, follow these instructions;—Take three pounds of a veiny piece of beef that has fat and lean, wash it, place it in a stewpan, season it with pepper, salt, ground mace, and allspice, and stand it on a very slow fire; let a piece of butter be put at the bottom of the stewpan, which should only just hold it, and cover it over; keep it simmering in its own gravy until it begins to sink down in the stewpan, then add a little more seasoning, some forcemeat, and hard-boiled eggs; if it is intended for a pie-dish, add a little gravy in the dish, but not if it is to be in a raised crust; but when cold, and your stock of a strong jelly, put the forcemeat at the bottom, and top, and middle. Heating the oven properly is of great consequence in baking. Puff paste requires a quick oven, but then if too quick, it will catch and not rise, and if too slow,

it will be soddened, not rise, and want colour.

**Soups for the Poor.**—Charitable ladies, those who are concerned for the welfare of the poor, are often at a loss for a receipt for a cheap nutritious soup to distribute amongst them during the inclement part of the year. The two following will be found useful for the purpose:—

1. Take about two pounds of shin of beef, five or six ounces of barley, a bit of parsley, two or three sliced onions, with salt and pepper; cut the meat into small pieces, and having broken the bone, place it in a pot with four quarts of water; potatoes, cabbage, indeed any vegetable on hand, or left the day before, may be added. Boil gently for four or five hours.

2. Soak a quart of split peas for a day in cold water, and then put them into a boiler with five quarts of water, and two pounds of boiled potatoes, cold, and mashed, with herbs, three small onions sliced, pepper and salt to taste. Cover close, and gently boil for four or five hours, or until reduced to six quarts of water.

**Danger from Eating Nuts.**—Medical men advise that salt should be taken with nuts, especially when eaten at night. "One time," says a writer, "while enjoying a visit from a friend, hickory nuts were served in the evening, when my friend called for salt, stating that he knew the case of a woman eating heartily of nuts in the evening, who was taken violently ill. The celebrated Dr. Abernethy was sent for, but it was after he had become too fond of his cup, and he was not in a condition to go; he muttered, "Salt, salt," of which no notice was taken. Next morning he went to this place, and she was a corpse. He said if they had given her salt it would have relieved her; if they would allow him to make an examination he would convince them. On opening the stomach the nuts were found in a mass. He sprinkled salt on this, and immediately it dissolved." Nuts should never be indulged in; they are unwholesome.

**Birds in their Natural Feathers.** —To produce pictures of birds with their natural feathers is a very delightful and instructive employment. Take a thin board or panel of deal and very smoothly paste on it two or three layers of white paper. When the paper is quite dry, get any bird you wish to represent, and draw its figure as exactly as possible on the papered panel ; then paint what tree or ground-work you intend to set your bird upon, also its bill and legs, leaving the rest of the body to be covered with its own feathers. Next prepare that part to be feathered by laying on thick gum arabic, dissolved in water. Two or three coats of gum are necessary in order to produce a good body on the paper. When your design is so far produced, take the feathers off the bird as you use them, beginning at the tail and points of the wings, and working upward to the head, observing to cover that part of the draught with the feathers taken from the same part of the bird, letting them fall over one another in their natural order. You must prepare your feathers by cutting off the downy parts that are about their stems, and the large feathers must have the insides of their shafts shaved off with a sharp knife, to make them lie flat ; the quills of the wings must have their inner webs clipped off, so that in laying them the gum may hold them by their shafts. When you begin to lay them, take a pair of steel pliers to hold the feathers in, and have some gum-water, not too thin, and a large pencil ready to moisten the ground-work by little and little, as you work it : then lay your feathers on the moistened parts, which must not be waterish, but only clammy, to hold the feathers. You must have prepared several leaden weights, which you may form in the shape of sugar-loaves by means of a stick, by casting the lead in sand.

These weights will be necessary to set on the feathers when you have merely laid them on, in order to press them into the gum till they are fixed ; but you must be cautious lest the gum comes through and smears the feathers. Be cautious not to have your coat of gum too moist or wet. When you have wholly covered your bird with its feathers, you must, with a little thick gum, stick on a piece of paper, cut round, of the size of an eye, which you must paint like the eye of the bird ; glass eyes, however, may be purchased at the naturalist's shops. When the whole is dry, dress the feathers all round the outline, and rectify the defects in every other part. Then lay it on a sheet of clean paper, and a heavy weight, such as a book, to press it ; after which it may be preserved in a glass frame, and then it forms a very pretty ornament.

**Chilblain Liniment.**—One ounce of camphorated spirit of wine, half an ounce of liquid subacetate of lead ; mix and apply in the usual way three or four times a day. Some persons use vinegar as a preventive ; its efficacy may be increased by the addition to the vinegar of one-fourth of its quantity of camphorated spirit.

**Window Plants.**—During January and February the summer flowering window plants such as geraniums, fuchsias, &c., should be kept as nearly dormant as possible, allowing just enough water to prevent flagging, and all the light that can be spared from the more interesting division of winter bloomers, of the latter class such things as China-roses, cinerarias, hyacinths, and other bulbs, will now be in an active state, some of them flowering, and others about to do so, these must be liberally treated with water. Mignonette, however, must be excepted. Above everything keep the leaves clean, they are few in number, and feeble in action, but they have yet an important function to perform, and without they are kept as healthy as possible, the plant cannot begin a new growth with the vigour it is desirable it should possess. The pots should be occasionally scrubbed with clean water, but do not paint or otherwise fill up their pores, for air is as essential to the roots as to the foliage, and no inconsiderable quantity finds its way to them through the sides of a clean pot ; with the same view the surface of the soil should be frequently stirred ; the process keeps it open, prevents the growth of moss and weeds, and imparts a better appearance. The water given should always be rather warmer than the atmosphere of the room, and rain water slightly heated is the best.

In February the whole of these plants will be benefited by re-potting. Geraniums and fuchsias delight in light rich earth ; calceolarias (lady's slipper,) roses, the chimney campanula, and others which grow as freely, should have a large proportion of loam ; whatever manure is added for either must be thoroughly decayed. The pots should be thoroughly clean inside and out ; take care to have each properly drained with pieces of slate or potsherds, in size and number proportionate to the pot, the larger ones require from one to three inches of this drainage. In removing the plants take off the matted fibres with a knife, loosen the soil moderately, and when in its place press the new earth tightly round it ; give a gentle watering, and keep them rather warm for a few days ; afterwards they should have plenty of air on fine days, and water as they become dry ; station each where they may receive the direct light, and pay particular attention to keeping the leaves clean.

On the attention given to window plants through the month of April, most of the success for the season will depend. The plants are now, or ought to be, in very active growth, which must be encouraged by moderate and regular supplies of water and air. Pinch out the points of the growing shoots of such plants as are required to become bushy. This, with such plants as geraniums, fuchsias, myrtles, and others of similar habit, is very necessary. Cactuses must have a sunny position, and plenty of water. Mignonette in pots and boxes will require thinning so as to leave the plant about three inches apart. The several kinds of China-roses form beau-

tiful window ornaments, and occasion but little trouble, at this time they are coming rapidly into bloom. Look for, and destroy insects of all sorts every few days, they multiply so fast, that without constant attention, the plants are soon overrun. The leaves must be kept clear of dust.

From May forward till the middle of September, plants in pots may be placed out of doors ; they are, in fact, better in the open air, than in the heated atmosphere of a room. Except in stormy seasons they may stand out night and day, in some slightly sheltered spot. As a precaution against the effects of strong sunlight, it is advisable to place the pots in which the plants grow, into others a size or two larger, and fill the space between them with moss ; for many plants, having fibrous slender roots, are easily injured by the heat of the sun scorching them through the pot. Such as stand upon the ground should have a thick layer of ashes spread for them, to prevent worms from creeping in ; wash their leaves frequently with clean water, and remove insects. When any portion of the collection is kept indoors, a window facing the north or west is to be preferred, and plenty of air must be admitted. As soon as geraniums have done flowering, they should be cut down, repotted, and the tops struck to form plants for next year. This is a good time to propagate nearly all kinds of pot-plants ; most of them strike with freedom on a warm border in a sandy soil, covered with a glass, and kept moderately watered. Myrtles, and some other hard-wooded plants, may be struck by placing the cuttings for about half their length, into a phial filled with water. Seeds must be sown in light earth as soon as they are tolerably light.

In July, fuchsias in a growing state should receive a final potting ; place them in large perfectly clean pots, using a mixture of turfy loam and peat, or leaf mould ; train the shoots, and water liberally ; geraniums that have done flowering should be repotted ; they require a lighter soil, such as one part turfy loam, two parts leafy mould, and the remainder sand ; cut down the tops to within two or three joints of their base, and set the plants in a warm sheltered place to induce them to grow again ; the cuttings may be struck in a frame or a hand-glass, and will form nice plants by next season. Cactuses should be kept in a sunny situation, and have plenty of water. Camellias which have made their season's growth, may be set out of doors to ripen. China-roses may be repotted if requisite, and are easily propagated now, in the same manner as geraniums. Separate and pot violets for early spring flowering ; keep them and similar plants, as the cyclamen, &c., in the most shaded place out of doors. The whole tribe of lilies are handsome window plants, and some of the dwarf Japan kinds peculiarly adapted for the purpose ; they are just beginning to bloom and should have plenty of air and water. The Chinese primrose may be sown in pots of light rich earth, and if covered with a piece of glass, will vegetate quickly, and form nice plants by the autumn. Propagation of such plants as myrtles, sweet-scented verbenas, or lemon plant, chimney campanulas, &c., is now easy, and should be attended to without loss of time. Water all the plants with regularity, and in quantities proportionate to their size and the state of the weather ; but particularly keep the leaves clean by frequent sprinklings of water and sponging ; the essential points in the culture of every plant is to allow the functions of both roots and leaves to be carried on in a proper manner, the first by placing them in suitable soil, and the latter by clearing them of all impurities.

During August window plants need only a continuance of the attention recommended last month ; let them have plenty of air, light, and water, with a slight protection from the mid-day sun ; propagation may still be carried on successfully. Pot the Guernsey lilies and belladonna to flower in autumn, and the young plants of the Chinese primrose should be placed three or four together, in pots of rich light earth, and nursed to forward their growth as far as possible.

In September the geraniums cut down in July will be pushing forth a number of young shoots ; these must be encouraged as much as possible, by keeping the plants in a sheltered place, and duly supplying them with moisture. When the shoots have grown two or three joints they should be stopped by picking out the points in order to render them bushy. The cuttings made at the same period will now be fit for potting ; put each one separately into a small pot, and treat them as the older plants. Young plants of myrtles, and indeed all others that are properly rooted, should receive similar treatment. Cinerarias are among the most useful of spring-flowering plants, and if a few seedlings can be obtained now (September) they will make nice plants, with the treatment recommended for geraniums. Cyclamen, Guernsey, or belladonna lilies, and lachenalias, should be repotted ; the first and last are very handsome spring flowering-plants, and the lilies are very beautiful through October and November ; all of them are of reasonable price, and well worth adding to the usual stock of window-plants. Fill a few pots with fibrous loam, and sprinkle them over with mignonette, nemophilla insignis, and intermediate stocks : leave the pots in the open air, and thin the plants to about three or four of the strongest as soon as they can be handled. Pot off China-primroses, putting one plant into each 3-inch pot. Encourage the chrysanthemums in pots with alternate applications of manure water, repot the strongest, and allow them all plenty of room, or the leaves are liable to injury. Set all plants as they go out of flower in the sun to ripen their wood, but do not let them suffer from drought.

During October all endeavours must be directed towards getting them into a state of rest ; water very cautiously ·

give air whenever the weather will permit, and at all times let them enjoy whatever sunshine occurs, and uninterrupted light. Now that the respiring power of the leaves becomes lessened, it is most essential that every particle of dust be carefully removed; the surface of the soil in which they grow should be occasionally stirred to keep it clean and porous, and even the outsides of the pots should be washed for the same end. If it be necessary to stand the pots in saucers when the plants are watered, the waste which runs through should be regularly emptied away, as much mischief ensues from allowing the roots to remain in the water.

The directions given for the month of October should be carefully followed throughout the remainder of the year. The great object being to keep the majority of the plants in a resting condition, that they may start the more vigorously on the return of genial weather. Winter, or early spring flowering plants, such as China primroses, violets, cyclamen, and roses, are, however, to be excepted from this rule; they are now in an active state, and must be encouraged accordingly. As soon as hyacinths and other bulbs, placed in pots last month, have become pretty well rooted, they may be brought into the window, and being placed near the light will grow rapidly; those in glasses should have the water changed once or twice a week. Chrysanthemums in pots require plenty of water while in bloom, and when their beauty declines, the plants should be taken to a warm part of the garden, or placed in a light shed to complete their maturity.

During December, if the geraniums or other plants taken from the borders in autumn, exhibit signs of rottenness, remove the decaying parts, and dust the wounds with quicklime or sulphur, keep them comparatively dry, and as much exposed to the sun as possible; air is essential whenever it can be admitted. Water sparingly, keep the leaves clean, and wait patiently. Flow-

ering plants must still form the exception as mentioned last month.

**Excellent and Cheap Biscuits.—** Flour, two pounds, and a large tablespoonful of arrowroot; carbonate of ammonia, a small teaspoonful finely powdered; butter, one ounce; new milk, half a pint, and rather less than a quarter of a pint of boiling water. Rub the arrowroot and the ammonia into the flour dry; dissolve the butter in the hot water, then add the milk, and gradually mix the whole with the flour. Well beat the dough till it is thoroughly mingled and tough. Roll out very thin; cut out in rounds, and stab with a docker. A docker is a hoop of tin or brass, in which is set a frame of points something like a harrow; so it serves at once to cut the dough in rounds and mark the biscuits. Those who have not such an article, may cut with a glass or canister lid, and pierce with a fork. A few minutes in an oven the proper heat for bread, will bake sufficiently. If desired, six ounces of loaf sugar finely powdered, and one ounce of caraway seeds, may be mixed with the dry flour. In that case, allow rather less liquid, as the sugar dissolving adds to the moisture. The above will make a large quantity of biscuits.

**Very Nice Little Cakes.—**The following mixture make cakes equal to maccaroons sold in the shops:—Fine flour dried, quarter of a pound; loaf sugar, finely pounded, three ounces; carbonate of ammonia, two drachms; almond flavouring or essence of lemon, eight drops; two eggs; well beat the eggs, sugar, and flavouring, then add the flour and ammonia, and thoroughly mix the whole. Drop on buttered tins, leaving plenty of space between, as the cakes will expand in baking. Thus, if the drop be the size of a shilling, allow it the space of a half-crown. Bake in a quick oven a very short time. An American oven in front of a clear fire bakes these cakes very nicely

**Rice Cakes.—**Ground rice and loaf sugar pounded, of each, half a pound; essence of almonds, eight drops; four or five eggs, well beaten up; may be dropped on buttered tins as the above article, or may be baked in one deep tin as a whole cake. The tin must be previously buttered and dusted with loaf sugar; also lay at top a piece of white paper buttered.

**Rice Froth.**—A cheap and ornamental dish. For one-third of a pound of rice, allow one quart of new milk, the whites of three eggs, three ounces of loaf sugar finely pounded, a stick of cinnamon, or eight or ten drops of almond flavouring, and a quarter of a pound of raspberry jam. Boil the rice in a pint, or rather less, of water; when the water is absorbed, add the milk, and let it go on boiling till quite tender, keeping it stirred to prevent burning. If cinnamon or laurel leaves are used, boil them with the milk, and remove them when the rice is sufficiently done; if essence of almonds be used for flavouring, it may be dropped among the sugar; when the rice milk is cold, put it in a glass dish or china bowl. Beat up the egg whites and sugar to a froth, cover the rice with it, and stick bits of raspberry jam over the top.

**Hard and Soft Corns.**—When a corn has once been produced on a part, the part goes on producing it, so that when you pare a corn, if shoes be discontinued entirely, it grows again. The part is said to have acquired a habit. The fact is, that the vascular part of the skin which forms or throws out the scarf-skin, becomes adapted to grow too much of this. So then, when a person once has a corn, it is found troublesome and difficult to get rid of. The first thing to be done with this object is to begin with what would have been sufficient to prevent the corn, wearing well-fitting and easy shoes. By this means simply, corns will at least be less troublesome, and will sometimes, after a while, disappear.

There can be no objection to paring, scraping, rasping, or picking corns. But these methods of relief, though perfectly necessary to one's comfort now and then, are all of merely a make-shift

kind, they are insufficient for a permanent cure, and afford but temporary relief.

By painstaking, however, corns may be got rid of. Corns are occasionally *picked out* in such a manner that, by avoiding the cause of their production, namely, tight boots or shoes, they do not return; a skilful hand, by means of a strong finger-nail, or a pointed, but not a cutting instrument, wears out and tears away the substance from its hold. This kind of treatment answers very well for round hard corns; but some corns are flat and considerably spread out, and they cannot be pulled out in such a manner. When corns are removed in this way, ever so skilfully, they are still apt to form again, in the same or in some degree, though, as has been said, they sometimes disappear. The method is usually followed by considerable relief.

Corns are often done away with by wetting them, once in two days, with concentrated acetic acid, and from time to time scraping away what is possible with the thumb or finger-nail. This plan is frequently tried without a successful result, merely because the acid obtained is of insufficient strength. Acetic acid, when strong, which may be said to be concentrated vinegar, is adapted to effect a gradual removal of corns, without making a sore place. Strong mineral acids burn the skin.

In the hands of a surgeon, caustic, or strong acids, are applied for the radical cure of corns with the desired effect. When a corn is effectually picked out in the manner above described, or when it is reduced by the continued application of acetic acid, the surgeon, by the continued application of caustic, or a mineral acid, may destroy what he calls the matrix, or secreting surface, so as to prevent further reproduction.

There are soft corns and hard corns, and this difference puzzles people. We have hitherto been talking about hard corns. Soft corns are soaked corns; they are corns which grow between the toes, when these rub against their fellows, and which become soft in the condensed and accumulated perspiration of people who do not regularly and methodically keep their feet clean, and sometimes even in the cases of those who, in spite of washing, are troubled with hot perspiring feet in summer. For soft corns apply a mixture of equal parts of alum and white of egg. A piece of soft dry lint, or a very thin slice of sponge, interposed between the toes, is often all that is necessary for comfort. To prevent these corns wash your feet daily, rubbing well with the towel between the toes.

Mechanical contrivances, to take off the pressure, both in hard and soft corns, when irritable, are obvious, and frequently very useful means of relief. Circular plasters, with a hole in the middle, are perhaps the most common and the most appropriate of such appliances to corns and bunions.

It may be mentioned that some people are far more prone to the action of the skin which produces corns than others are. The treatment in their case must be the same : they must just be more careful and more persevering in it. Most persons have a corn on the outside of the little toe. This small object is not duly considered in the formation of shoes, and makes us, in consequence, in time experience its importance. Boots are usually made too narrow across the fore part, the little toe is unable to get far enough forward, its back is crooked up, hence the corn.

Every evil, however, appears to have its advantages. Corns prognosticate change of weather. An incredulous reader—one of the happy few without corns—smiles at the assertion that corns are barometers. In certain conditions of the atmosphere, as when much loaded with vapour, the skin, and in fact the whole system, is overcharged with fluids, which otherwise, as in a dry bracing air, would have passed off easily ; the foot, like other parts, becomes turgid and swollen, the print of the stocking is left on the foot, and the poor corn is pushed up in a narrower corner. Besides, the skin in certain states of the air is more irritable than usual, and has an inflammatory tendency where it happens to be chafed or bruised as by a corn.

By-and-by, when shoemaking is better understood, there will be no corns, that is to say, ladies will not be foolish enough to encourage fashions that cause them.

**Wasps.**—It is not generally known that the large wasps which are seen flying about in the months of April and May, are queen wasps, and that, therefore, the destruction of them is the prevention of the birth of myriads of wasps. Those ladies who keep honey-bees ought to know that wasps are their great enemies, and therefore during the months mentioned are eagerly sought after by bee keepers, by whom they are mercilessly destroyed. A noble earl of the present day gives a shilling for each queen wasp brought to him, dead or alive, in the months of April or May ; his lordship pays nine or ten pounds a year in this way to persons on his estate, which he considers a very profitable expenditure as regards the protection of his fruit and honey-bees.

**To Detach Insects from Vegetables.**—At certain periods of the year, when watercress, salads, celery and lettuces are in their best state for the table, it may be useful to many housekeepers to learn that if they are put into strong salt and water for about ten minutes everything of the insect kind will be detached from the leaves, and afterwards washed in pure water and sent to table. Every description of vegetable, by the same simple method, may be freed from slugs, worms, or insects. Watercress, and some other table vegetables, it is common for the under part of their leaves to have a white gummy substance adhering to them, which cannot be removed by ordinary washing ; small snails, too, are also fixed on them. If a jar of brine is kept for the purpose, and strained after being used, it will last many weeks, and the expense, of course, not worth consideration.

**Polishing Paste for Britannia Me-**

**tal, Tins, Brasses, and Coppers.**—This excellent paste is composed of rotten stone, soft soap, and oil of turpentine. The stone must be powdered and sifted through a muslin or hair sieve; mix with it as much soft soap as will bring it to the stiffness of putty; to about half a pound of this, add two ounces of oil of turpentine. It may be made up in balls, or put in pots; it will soon become hard, and will keep any length of time. The following is the method of using:—The articles to be polished should be perfectly freed from grease and dirt. Moisten a little of the paste with water, smear it over the article to be polished, then rub briskly with dry rag or wash-leather, and it will soon bear a beautiful polish.

**Eggs in Cakes.**—In making cakes, whatever eggs are to be used, should be added after all the other ingredients are thoroughly mixed. By observing this rule, two eggs will be found to go as far in enriching the cake and making it light, as three would do, if added at an earlier stage of the preparation.

**Nutritious Beef-Tea.**—The most tender and juicy parts of the animal should be chosen; there is no part equal to the meat which runs lengthways along the bones of the loins. The process of preparing should be completed quickly, *not* carried on by slow simmering. A good moderate broth is made in the proportion of a quart of water to a pound of meat. When very rich tea is required for invalids in a state of great weakness, who perhaps can receive but a spoonful or two at a time, the weight of meat should equal that of water, a pound to a pint. The weight allowed should be of lean meat, perfectly free from skin, bone, and fat. Chop the meat as fine as sausage meat. Pour over it the quantity required of *boiling* water, and set it on the fire when it boils up, throw in a little salt, and a piece of bread slowly toasted, not burnt; let it boil briskly from twenty minutes to half an hour, which should not be exceeded; do not take off the scum, but stir it down as it rises. When done

strain through a sieve. Flavour with an onion, and pepper and salt.

This is not given as the most economical method of preparing beef-tea, or broth, for common family purposes, but as the best, when it is wanted as a restorative in illness, or for the food of young children.

**Black Currant Lozenges.**—Boil or bake the fruit in a jar stopped close. When the juice separates, strain through a coarse sieve. Measure the juice, and boil briskly for half an hour. The more the juice has evaporated before adding the sugar, the better. For every full quart of juice (as measured into the pan, not reduced by boiling) allow—Fine loaf sugar, three ounces, best gum arabic, finely powdered, three drachms, cream of tartar, three drachms. The gum must be mixed in a cup or basin with a very small quantity of the boiling juice, stirred briskly to it till quite smooth, then stir it to the whole. Boil the mass till it is very stiff and candies on the sides of the pan. Pour it on dishes or plates turned upside down; the thickness should not exceed one-eighth of an inch. Dry in the sun or in an American oven, placed in front of a fire, but at a considerable distance. When one side begins to harden, carefully turn on other plates of the same size. When quite hard and dry cut out in lozenges. For this purpose, a sharp tin cutter is the best instrument. The form should be either square, diamond, or hexagonal, that the pieces may be cut one close to another without waste. Shake among the lozenges a little magnesia to prevent sticking. Keep them in a wide-mouthed bottle, with a glass stopper; or in tin boxes, between layers of white paper, in a very dry place. These lozenges may be made with the entire fruit. Proceed exactly as above directed, except omitting to strain after the baking or first boiling.

**Damson or Black Currant Cheese.**—These are sometimes made with the whole skins and pulp of the fruit, sometimes with the pulp only. In either case, the fruit is to be first baked or boiled in a stone jar till perfectly tender, and the juice runs freely ; if damsons, the stones separate. If the skins are to be retained, there is only to remove the damson stones with a silver spoon. Measure the pulp into a preserving pan, brass skillet, or enamelled saucepan ; set it over a clear, brisk fire, and let it boil briskly till the liquid has evaporated and the fruit become dry. Then add powdered loaf sugar, in the proportion of half a pound to one quart of pulp, as measured into the vessel. Stir it well. Let it go on boiling till the jam candies to the sides of the pan. Pour into shallow vessels, such as potting jars, saucers, &c. In a day or two turn them down on a clean dry shelf.

**Good and Bad Meat.**—Dr. Letheby states the following characteristics by which good and bad meat may be distinguished. Good meat is neither of a pale pinkish colour, nor of a deep purple tint. The former is indicative of disease, and the latter a sign that the animal has died from natural causes. Good meat has also a marble appearance from the ramifications of little veins of intercellular fat ; and the fat, especially of the interior organs, is hardy and suety, and is never wet ; whereas that of diseased meat is soft and watery, often like jelly or soddened parchment. Again, the touch or feel of healthy meat is firm and elastic, and it hardly moistens the fingers ; whereas that of diseased meat is often soft and wet—in fact it is often so soft and wet that serum runs from it, and then it is technically called wet. Good meat has but little odour, and this is not disagreeable ; whereas bad meat smells faint and cadaverous, and it often has the odour of medicine. This is best observed by cutting it and smelling the knife, or by pouring a little warm water upon it. Good meat will bear cooking without shrinking, and without losing very much in weight ; but bad meat shrivels up, and it often boils to pieces.

**The Sun Causing Curtains to Rot.** —It is commonly believed that a silk, woollen, or cotton article, not much worn, cannot easily be injured. This is quite correct ; but there is an agent by which it may very quickly be injured, if ladies are not careful ; namely, the rays of the sun through glass windows. Dr. Ure says : " To the same cause (the sun and glass) must be ascribed the decay remarked in stuffs themselves by the action of light. I might adduce several examples of this fact ; among others I might mention a curtain of fugitive crimson taffeta, which had remained long stretched behind a window ; all the parts which were opposite the panes of glass were entirely deprived of colour, whilst those which corresponded to the wood of the casement were much less faded, and, further, the silk itself was almost destroyed in the discoloured parts, where the curtains could be torn with the slightest effort, while it retained elsewhere its usual strength. The injury to the curtains could in great measure, be remedied by having the blinds down when the sun is out.

**Flavouring for Puddings.**—When the hawthorn is in blossom, gather the buds, which are like little white peas, and put them into wine bottles ; let each bottle be three parts full, and then fill it up with British brandy. In two months it is fit for use. This is used for plum pudding, custards, &c., and is delightful as a flavouring.

**Cure for Wasp Stings.**—It is a fact worth knowing at the season of the year when wasps are troublesome with their stings, that no application will afford such instantaneous relief as a drop of liquor of potassæ, (potash-water) ; indeed its effects are so unfailing, that it may be termed a specific cure. It operates by neutralising the injected poison, which is undoubtedly of an acrid nature. Families and persons who have the care of children, will do well to have always at hand a small quantity of this solution, which should be kept in a stoppered phial. It is not an expensive application ; a quarter of an ounce will be quite sufficient to order at once, and a single drop placed on the wound, which should be first slightly opened, is all that is required.

**To Mount Prints or Maps.**—Upon a table, floor, or board, stretch a piece of calico or smooth canvas, by first fixing it with tacks along one side, then straining it tightly with one hand, and driving the tacks with the other: nail the remaining edges, leaving no wrinkles on the surface. Paste the back of the map or print, fold it together, and let it remain until the paper is *soaked*, then open it, and place it evenly on the canvas, cover it with a sheet of clean paper, and, beginning in the middle, rub it down carefully with the hand, going from the centre all round to the edges, until all the air is excluded, and the paper adheres closely to the canvas. When quite dry, with a large camel's hair brush lay on a coating of parchment size, repeating this when dry; then carefully varnish with mastic varnish. Parchment size is made by boiling parchment cuttings in water, until it forms a jelly when cold. Mastic varnish can be procured at oil and colour-shops.

**Vermecelli Pudding.**—When anything is wanted in a hurry it is well to know how it may be most quickly done. The following simple and speedily-prepared pudding has been much admired: New milk a pint, and four eggs well beaten: loaf sugar, powdered, three ounces; almond flavouring, or pure essence of lemon, eight drops; vermecelli, from two to three ounces; butter, from one to two ounces. Butter a deep dish, into which put the milk, eggs, sugar, butter, and flavourings, well mixed—lay the vermecelli at top, and grate nutmeg over; bake for half an hour; a few thin silces of bread and butter, with currants strewed at top, make an agreeable variety.

**Vine Leaf Vinegar.**—Fresh gathered vine leaves with their foot stalks, and any vine shoots of the season, that have not at all become woody—of these drop into the cask intended to be used as many as will fill it lightly; these should not be gathered till the liquor is ready to add to them, prepared as follows:—For every gallon of water allow two pounds of the coarsest moist sugar, boil it half an hour, skim over a sieve, so that what runs through may be restored. The addition of shells and whites of eggs, or shells only, will assist the leaves; boil them in the sugar and water and strain off when done. Cool quickly and work with yeast. When the working begins to subside the liquor sinks, and the froth draws together in a sort of flat cake; skim it, and put the liquor to the vine leaves in the cask—bung it down, and leave it in a cellar or other convenient place for a month or six weeks—then draw off the liquor clear, empty the cask of the vine leaves—soak, scald, and thoroughly dry it; return the liquor and with it one pint of ordinary vinegar, a handful of chervil, and two ounces of raisins to every gallon.

Excellent vinegar, too, may be made from the lees of wine, or from the refuse of raisin or indeed any fruit wine. To any quantity of fruit pulp, add half its weight of coarse sugar or fresh raisins, stirring them well together. When the mixture begins to ferment, for every two pounds, pour over a gallon of boiling spring water; let it steep for two days, stirring it frequently; then strain and work with yeast, as the foregoing articles—adding when the work subsides, vinegar, raisins, and put the whole into the cask. The vinegar will be fit for use in one month, then tighten the bung.

**Dried Flowers.**—Many ladies living in towns are in the habit of taking occasional walks in the country. It would add much to the pleasure of these walks to carefully gather all the wild flowers they can discover, for they will be looked at with pleasure by those sisters who for the want of health or opportunity have not been able to get abroad where the wild flowers grow, and if dried will make a nice collection of specimens. The sheets containing these specimens are called an herbarium. The best way to make one is as follows: when the flower is gathered and before it begins to wither, it must be spread very smooth and flat between some old newspapers, so that all the blossoms may be fairly open. A moderate pressure of books or large weights can be applied. After a few days it will be sufficiently dry to remove. Sheets of writing or wrapping paper may then be used. Cut very neatly narrow strips and make two or more incisions or slits in the sheet on each side of the dried plant, through which put the strips.

**Physical Herbs.**—The following is a list of such plants as are generally denominated physical herbs, and which are found to be more or less wanted in most families, although they are not so much in common use as formerly. We however, will give a short description of them, and the purposes for which they are medicinally used.

These plants, or herbs, may, in most instances, be very easily cultivated ; the soil for growing the greater part should be light and dry, but that of a poorer description is more suitable for some, as lavender, rosemary, rue, sage, wormwood, and a few others ; and if planted in a rich moist soil, much of their aromatic quality flies off, and they are rendered less capable of withstanding any severe weather

1. ANGELICA.—This herb is propagated from its seeds, which are to be sown as soon as gathered in August, in a moist situation ; and when the plants are about six inches high, they must be transplanted to a similar soil, about three feet apart. The flowering stems should be cut down when a few inches high.

The stalks of Angelica were formerly blanched, and eaten as celery, but they are now only used as a sweetmeat, when candied, by the confectioners. The Laplanders extol the utility of this herb for coughs and other disorders of the chest, but in this country it is seldom employed for that purpose, as many other simples surpass it in aromatic and carminative powers.

2. ANISE-SEED.—It was first culti-vated here in 1551, but our summers are seldom warm enough to bring it to perfection. The seeds are annually imported from Malta and Spain. The plant is annual, and propagated by sowing the seed in a light dry soil in the spring.

Anise-seeds have a warm aromatic smell, and a pleasant warm taste, accompanied with a degree of sweetness ; they have been esteemed useful in numerous complaints, but in none more so than flatulent colics and obstructions of the breast, in diarrhœas, and for strengthening the tone of the stomach in general.

3. BALM.—So called from the Greek word signifying honey, because of the abundant and excellent honey of its flowers, for which bees frequent it.

The garden balm is a perennial, and may be easily propagated by parting the roots in spring or autumn, and planting them in beds of common garden mould.

The herb, in its recent state, has a weak, roughish, aromatic taste, and a pleasant smell, somewhat of the lemon kind. Balm was formerly esteemed of great use in all complaints supposed to proceed from a disordered state of the nervous system. As tea, however, it makes a grateful diluent drink in fevers, and in this way it is commonly used, either by itself or acidulated with lemons.

4. BLESSED THISTLE.—This annual is propagated from seed sown in autumn. It obtained the name of *benedictus*, or blessed, from its supposed extraordinary medicinal virtues. It has an intensely bitter taste, and disagreeable smell. It was formerly employed to assist the operation of emetics ; but the flowers of camomile are now substituted for it with equal advantage. It was also thought, when taken internally, to be peculiarly efficacious in malignant fevers. In loss of appetite, its good effects have been frequently experienced. It has now lost much of its reputation, and does not seem essentially different from other simple bitters.

5. BORAGE.—This herb is a hardy annual, and easily cultivated, from sowing the seeds in April, which come up without any care.

Borage was formerly cultivated in our gardens on account of the supposed cordial virtues of its flowers ; but they have long lost their reputation. In Italy its young and tender leaves are in common use, both as a pot-herb and a salad. In France its flowers, with those of nasturtium, are put into salads as an ornament. In England it is now nearly neglected ; but the flowers and upper leaves are sometimes used as an ingredient in that summer beverage composed of wine, water, lemon-juice, and sugar, called a cool tankard, to which they seem to give an additional coolness.

6. CARAWAY.—This herb is biennial, and propagated by sowing the seeds in spring.

The seeds of this plant are well known to have a pleasant spicy smell, and a warm aromatic taste ; and on that account they are much used as a common ingredient in cakes, and are encrusted in sugar for comfits : they are also distilled with spirituous liquors to improve their flavour. The tender leaves in the spring are also boiled in soups.

7. CAMOMILE.—This popular medical herb grows wild in many parts of England. It is a hardy perennial, and by parting the roots early in spring it is easily propagated.

Both the flowers and leaves of the camomile have a strong though not ungrateful smell, and a very bitter nauseous taste. The flowers possess the stomachic and tonic qualities usually ascribed to simple bitters. A watery infusion of them is frequently used for the purpose of promoting the operation of emetics. They are very generally used in emollient decoctions, to assuage pain, and externally as fomentations, and for both purposes held in much esteem.

8. CLARY.—This herb has been long known in English gardens, where it is a hardy biennial. It is easily raised from seed, which should be sown in March, in any bed or border of common earth.

Clary was at one time much used in cookery, but it is not now in much repute.

9. CORIANDER.—This is a hardy annual, and propagated from seeds sown in autumn, in an open situation, on a bed of good fresh earth.

The dried seeds of coriander have a tolerably grateful smell, with a moderately warm and slightly pungent taste. They are carminative (soothing or softening) and stomachic ; and are commonly sold by the confectioners encrusted with sugar.

10 CUMIN.—The seeds have an aromatic, warm, and bitterish taste, with a strong, but not disagreeable smell, and contain a large quantity of essential oil, and are supposed to possess a carminative and stomachic power. In England this herb is a hardy annual, and but little cultivated for use. The seeds reach us from Sicily and Malta.

11. DILL.—Dill may be produced by sowing the seeds soon after they are ripe, in any '' soil.

The seeds of dill have a moderately warm pungent taste, and an aromatic smell, but not of the most agreeable kind ; they are not much now used in medicine, but are sometimes put into pickles to heighten the flavour, particularly of cucumbers.

11. FEVERFEW.—The plants of this biennial are raised from seeds, which should be sown about March, upon a bed of light earth, and afterwards transplanted to some distance apart.

Feverfew has long been employed for medical purposes ; its virtues are stomachic and tonic. It has been successfully given in hysteria, and is a medicine of considerable activity.

13. HOREHOUND.—This herb is common in various parts of England, on waste ground and among rubbish, in hot, dry, and dusty situations. The plant is annual, and may be raised by sowing the seeds in any of the spring months.

The leaves have a moderately strong smell of the aromatic kind, but not agreeable; their taste is very bitter, penetrating, and durable in the mouth. It has been chiefly employed in asthmas, obstinate coughs, and pulmonary consumptions. Its use is also said to be beneficial in affections of the liver. Lozenges, made of the juice of this herb and sugar, are esteemed good for colds. Though horehound possesses some share of medicinal power, its virtues do not appear to be clearly ascertained, and it is now very rarely prescribed by physicians.

14. HYSSOP.—This plant being perennial, is easily propagated by sowing the seeds in a border of light mould, in the spring season, or by slips, and cutting and parting the roots.

The whole plant has a strong aromatic scent, and the leaves and flowers are of a warm pungent taste; they are sometimes reduced to powder, and used with cold salad herbs. Hyssop has the general virtues ascribed to aromatics, and is recommended in asthmas, coughs, and other disorders of the lungs.

The young leafy shoots and flower-spikes are usually employed, being cut as they are wanted. The flower-stems may be cut during the summer, and tied up in bunches for use.

15. LAVENDER.—This is a very hardy plant. It may be readily increased by planting slips or cuttings of the young shoots in the spring.

The fragrant smell of the flower is well known, and to most persons very agreeable; to the taste it is bitterish, warm, and somewhat pungent; the leaves are weaker, and less grateful. The flowers are commonly employed as a perfume, and medicinally as mild stimulants and corroborants, in several complaints, both internally and externally. They are also sometimes used in the form of a conserve.

16. MARSH-MALLOW.—So called from its many excellent qualities. It grows plentifully in salt marshes, and on the banks of rivers and ditches in several counties in England, or near the coast of Cornwall, Holland, France, and other countries. It is perennial, and may be easily propagated by parting the roots in autumn.

Marsh-mallow abounds with a glutinous juice, with scarcely any smell or peculiar taste. The dry roots, boiled in water, give out half their weight of gummy matter. The leaves afford scarcely one fourth, and the flowers and seeds still less. The mucilaginous matter is the medicinal part of the plant, and it is commonly employed for its emollient and demulcent qualities. It was formerly in great repute in many complaints; but is now only principally employed in the form of a syrup.

**Laying Out a Kitchen Garden.**—Scarcely a day passes away without our being reminded of the utility of a kitchen garden by the many varieties of nutritious and wholesome vegetables with which our tables are supplied. Nor can it be disputed that next in importance to the actual possession of such a garden must be the knowledge of its most profitable management, for it is the fact, that for want of this knowledge many gardens are quite unworthy of the name, and prove a source of vexation than a means of pleasure and profit.

That gardening is a healthy occupation for both men and women no one, we presume, will deny; and that, while it bestows health on the body, it is calculated to give serenity to the mind. It has afforded in all ages a pleasing relief from the troubles and anxieties of the world to some of the busiest actors on the stage of life, to whom the pursuit of gardening has become the chief attraction of retirement, and in numerous instances has gilded the evening of life with the blessings of health and contentment.

In kitchen gardens the method of preparing and laying out requires much consideration; since, next to a badly designed, ill-placed house, a misplaced, ill-arranged, and unproductive kitchen garden is the greatest evil of a suburban or country residence.

The SITUATION most suitable for the purpose should, if practicable, have a gentle declination towards the south, so that it may at all times have the full advantage of the sun ; as much as possible it should be well sheltered by plantations, but by no means shaded or confined ; nor should the trees be planted too near the wall or boundary fence, as the roots are apt to run into the garden, thereby impoverishing the soil.

In selecting the ground, it is of considerable importance to have the soil of a good and healthy quality, being sufficiently dry, mellow, and capable of being easily worked with the spade ; the best is that of a rich, friable, and dark loamy texture ; the worst, that of a light, sandy, and stiff clayey description.

In forming a new kitchen garden, the first thing is to have the land well trenched to the depth of two feet and a half—indeed, with proper management, a depth of eighteen inches has been found sufficient.

As to the shape or figure of the garden, this is a point of little consequence —though the square, or that approaching nearest to it, is certainly the best and most convenient.

With regard to the size of the garden, that, of course, must vary according to circumstances.

Too much ground should not be taken up with walks ; these are generally about three feet wide, quite straight, and placed at equal distances, and composed of fine red binding gravel.

But little attention should be paid to ornament in a kitchen garden, but utility should everywhere predominate.

The succession of crops is a matter of considerable importance in culinary gardening, as the growth of wholesome and healthy vegetables in a great measure depends upon it.

We must caution those ladies who have the taste and inclination to engage in kitchen gardening, with a view of always having at hand a bountiful supply of fresh and wholesome vege-tables, against allowing the garden to get overrun with weeds ; thereby occasioning not only much unnecessary labour, but great exhaustion to the soil. It is by neatness, cleanliness, and assiduity in every department connected with the kitchen garden, that it can be rendered alike a source of pleasure and advantage to themselves, and an object of just admiration to others.

We will now submit the mode of operation for each month of the year, beginning with—

JANUARY.—Having very carefully prepared your garden ground commence your operations by sowing early peas. Mazagan beans should be sown in the second week of this month. In open weather sow onions on a light, rich, loamy soil. Sow radish on a warm border, also lettuce in every variety in warm borders or under hand-glasses, to transplant when of sufficient growth. Sow early carrots in a warm border, to be ready for use in April. Raise small salad, on a slight hot-bed, in pots or boxes. Transplant cauliflower plants from small to large pots and keep them in a cool frame. Put out cabbage plants to succeed the autumn-planted crop. Plant potato-onions in shallow drills, and earth them up as they grow. All cool esculents may be sown. Pot strawberries and they will come early. If the weather prove frosty leave most things alone ; if it turn out damp and muggy you may have your hands as busy as bees in looking after the slugs, &c. Plant the hardy kinds of evergreens, and water them at the roots as soon as planted.

FEBRUARY.—In the beginning of the month sow onions for the principal crop. Sow peas to gather early in June, in rows eighteen or twenty inches apart. Sow parsley in drills. Plant the early kind of potatoes under a south wall. Sow parsnips in drills at ten inches apart. Sow radishes and lettuces in warm situations. Sow spinach for an early crop. Sow turnips. Sow cucumber seeds in hot-beds ; they must have air occasionally, and the heat of the beds must be kept up. Transplant such cabbages as you desire seed from. Plant bits of horse-radish. Make asparagus beds and sow seeds. Continue forcing to the end of March. Sow brocoli in a warm situation. Sow beans fo. gathering in June. Sow celery on a slight hot-bed, or in boxes. Sow cauliflowers, either under a frame, hand-glass, or warm situation, to have plants to succeed the autumn sown ones—at the end of the month plant out under a hand-glass for early cutting, four under each. Sow carrots in open weather for an early crop. Cabbage plants should be planted out. Sow seed for cutting in July and August. Continue successive sowings of kidney beans.

MARCH.—In the early part of this month the ground should be dug for the main crop of potatoes. Plant out cabbage, green and red, and sow early Dutch turnip seed. Lettuces now sown will produce plants that will be fit for blanching by the end of May, or the beginning of June. Sow turnips the first of the month. Dress asparagus beds. Such cauliflower plants as have been protected during winter should be planted off in warm situations under hand-glasses for very early use. Plant rhubarb and sea-kale roots in a well-trenched, rich deep soil. Parsley now sown will be fit to gather in August. Sow vegetable-marrow immediately.

APRIL.—Plant Jerusalem artichokes. Sow angelica, and sow, plant, and force asparagus. Plant and hoe beans, and sow and prick out seedling brocoli. Plant cabbages, sow, weed, and thin out carrots, as well as sow and earth up celery. Sow, prick out, and ridge cucumbers, plant horse-radish, sow and plant kale, and plant lettuce out in frames, and tie up those of advanced growth. Sow mustard and cress and onions, and plant potatoes. Sow parsnips; hand-weed advancing crops. Sow and hoe peas; sow radishes, and thin advancing crops. Tomatoes, vegetable marrows, and the whole gourd tribe, may be sown in pots, not more than two in a pot, for after planting out.

MAY.—A busy month is May for the kitchen-gardener, who should be active. Sow more broad beans, take off the tops of those in flower, and draw the earth around those advancing. Sow peas every fortnight or three weeks throughout the season in small quantities, and sow more radishes. The March sown celery will be large enough to prick out, three or four inches apart, on rich ground; sow more seed. Hoe and thin onions, and transplant spring-sown cabbage, as well as earth more, and earth up those advancing. Cauliflowers under hand-glasses show flower, break in one or two leaves to shelter from the wet and sun. Sow brocoli seeds, fortnight between. Plant kidney beans for principal crop. Transplant the strongest lettuce plants. Sow small salad as before. Sow carrots, and parsnips, and thin out. Sow French beans the first week. Attend to cucumbers, and those intended for pickling sow on the common ground. If your onions are thick, take them out by the handful. This is the month for watering, if the weather proves dry; but whenever you do water, do it well.

JUNE.—Prick out cauliflowers into a piece of rich ground, three or four inches apart, to grow stronger before planting. Sow turnips for a principal crop, thin, if required. Sow scarlet beans; earth up those advancing. Sow another crop of kidney beans; and sow peas, and stick those that need it. Tie up lettuce. Transplant Brussels sprouts, sprouting brocoli and cabbage, after a shower, or well watering. Plant out the strongest celery plants. Give air to melons and cucumbers, and regulate them with care for spreading equally over the beds. Plant the latest crop of potatoes, plant leeks, and gather herbs, which should be dried in the shade. Sow carrots, onions, spinach, &c. June is the best month for planting out cucumbers. Too much haste is seldom good speed, and it is quite time enough to transplant upon such beds as we have recommended.

JULY.—This month is equally as good as June for sowing turnips in the garden. Sow radishes; their success will depend entirely on the weather. Top beans in flower and earth up others. Plant a main crop of celery, in trenches twelve to eighteen inches wide, and twelve inches deep, four feet apart. Train the shoots of cucumbers and melons along the surface, to be out of each other's way. Transplant leeks, and sow lettuces and salads. Sow peas once a week for chance crops, and earth up potatoes. Put sticks to scarlet beans, and plant winter greens, Brussels sprouts, Savoys, &c., after wet weather. Sow winter spinach, and carrots to draw young in a month or two, as well as to stand for spring use. Gather cucumbers for pickling if they have been planted out into the frame.

AUGUST.—This month furnishes the kitchen gardener plenty to do in looking after the insects. The green fly may be banished by burning tobacco. Look at your potato crop, and spare no expense to destroy the willow weed there; potatoes will smother most weeds, but the willow weed is too tall and vigorous for them. Sow salads and winter spinach. Take off the useless shoots of cucumbers, pull off dead leaves, and protect from cold winds. Sow cabbage seed for spring and winter crops; sow after a wet day. Sow cauliflower seed from the 20th to the end of the month. Plant out brocoli from seed beds. Hoe between all kinds of crops, clear weeds, stir the ground, and earth up. Top beans in bloom, and earth those that are up. Plant out winter greens and lettuces, and sow turnips after rain.

SEPTEMBER.—Take up potatoes that are ripe, and store them in a dark cellar covered over with straw. Earth up celery on a dry day, and bruise the lumps of soil small. Draw onions as they ripen; dry them on the ground for a day or two; let them be stored very dry and cool, and where they have free air. Prick out the August sown cauliflowers; choose the warmest place in the garden for them, if they are only to be protected in the ground, but if you have a common garden frame and

light to spare, dig up a space the size it will cover, and plant them three or four inches apart all over it. Hoe winter spinach, removing them where too thick, and leaving them six or eight inches apart. Sow salads as usual every month. Take carrots and parsnips up as required, until the leaves have turned yellow, when they may all be taken up and stored. Plant out cabbage plants six inches apart, and in rows fifteen inches apart, in the beds where they are to stand through the winter. Do not wait for one to die after another. For, this reason leave a moderate sprinkling of plants in the seed-bed, for fear you should want them. Asparagus is recommended by most professional gardeners to be cut down this month; those who do not wish to exhaust their beds should perform this operation at least two months earlier. Sow radish seed; your success will depend a great deal upon the sort you sow. The farther the year advances, let the radish be short-topped, or you get a quantity of leaf without any root.

OCTOBER.—Plant out lettuces in warm situations, or where they can be protected. Take up full grown carrots and parsnips for storing, also potatoes if they are still out. Earth celery as it grows up; it is only the covered portion that is eatable. Plant out for spring use the August-sown cabbages twice as thickly as they are wanted, that when every other one or two out of every three are drawn for greens during the winter, the others may be left to form cabbages.

NOVEMBER.—Put cabbage plants in; earth up celery from time to time; plant whole sets of potatoes, six inches deep, in a dry quarter. Look well to your store of onions, not only keeping them thinly spread, but continually turning them, and taking away every one that throws out the least hint of rotting or growing. Plant beans and peas in warm and sheltered situations, and sow a few carrots and radishes under like circumstances.

DECEMBER.—Plant potato onions in

deep drills in a light, rich soil, about one foot apart, any time during this month when the ground is dry. Keep all winter crops free from dead leaves, by gathering them often, and digging them in when preparing any ground. Put your future hot-beds into a course of preparation if you intend to begin your work early in spring.

**Modelling with Rice-Paper.**—To the formation of groups of flowers rice-paper is principally applied, either on card-board, or affixed to small vases, baskets, &c., in festoons and clusters. The rice-paper may be procured in various colours, and intermediate tints may be made by colouring the white. Several pieces of rice-paper are laid on each other upon a tablet of lead, and the leaves and component parts of flowers are cut out with small steel punches, which may be procured at the fancy tool warehouses. A sufficient quantity of the different leaves having been thus formed, and placed on separate trays, each leaf is to be held by a delicate pair of tweezers, and its end affixed, with stiff gum-water, to the article to be ornamented. Thus, the heads of roses and thick clusters of flowers, are formed, and fine delicate parts may be drawn in colours afterwards. Water-colour drawings are sometimes made on leaves of rice-paper, for scrap-books screens, &c. The effect of the colours, if properly managed, on this material is very soft and delicate.

**Crimped Paper Hand Screens.**— The paper commonly used for making these hand-screens, is glazed and coloured on both sides. Divide a sheet into three parts or equal strips, of two of which the screen is to be formed ; join them into one length, crimp them with the machine, and run a thread through completely one of the edges, first putting on the other edge, which will be the margin of the screen, a narrow border of gold paper. Having fastened one end of the thread, begin to draw the crimped paper into a circular form ; when the lower part is drawn by the thread into the shape of the

upper part, fasten the two ends firmly together. The handles may be purchased at any fancy repository, either black or white, according to taste. The taper end, which is the part to be fastened to the screen, should be covered with paper of the same colour as the screen. Gum the handle firmly on, taking care that it covers the part where the paper is joined : it should extend, for the sake of strength, to some distance beyond the centre. For the purpose of entirely concealing the junction on the centre, gum a star, or some other pretty and appropriate ornament, on each side of the screen ; one or two bows of narrow ribbon may be put on different parts of the handle, by way of finish. The two ends of the paper should be so contrived, that the handle, being neatly and firmly gummed on one of them, the other may wrap securely over, without showing where they are joined.

**Transparent Screens.**—Draw on a thin piece of drawing-paper any kind of figure, animal, or small composition ; for instance—a boy holding a mouse in a trap, with a dog jumping up towards it. The design should be sketched very lightly, without any dark shadows. Trace it exactly on another piece of paper, line for line ; then, by adding a frock, bonnet, curls, bracelets, &c., the boy may be changed to a girl, particular care being taken to keep the entire outline of the boy on the folds, &c., of the girl's frock ; or the mouse-trap may be converted into a cage by lengthening the bottom ; the mouse into a bird by the addition of plumage ; and the dog into a cat, by putting a longer tail, rounder head, &c. Again, should the first drawing be a boy blowing bubbles, by the addition of an old hat, longer skirts to the coat, a little beard and a few wrinkles, and blending the bubbles into a little cloud, an old man smoking his pipe may be produced. When the second drawing is finished, cut it out neatly, and paste it at the back of the first, with great care, so that the lines of the original, and the copy which has received the additions, may be exactly opposite each other. At the back of these, paper is to be pasted on, and the production may then be used as the interior, or centre ornament of a screen. When it lies flat on the table, or if placed against the wall over the chimney-piece, with the front exhibited, the first picture only is seen : when held against the light, or the fire, it changes into the second. The taste and ingenuity of the artist will, doubtless, suggest a variety of designs, which will be more elegant in the original, and more amusing in the change, than those we have mentioned. Handles may be added to the screens, similar to those described in " Crimped Paper Hand Screens." To strengthen the paper part of the screen, a thin piece of wire, covered with gold paper, should be fixed round its edges.

**Landscapes, &c., on Transparent Screens.**—Landscapes, that will appear like beautiful sepia drawings, for the embellishment of screens, may be made in the following manner :—Draw, and then cut in paper, any kind of building, taking care to keep it in good perspective. On the parts where the shadows fall, paste pieces of paper, varying in thickness according to the depth of the shadows, from coarse brown paper to thin post. Round the mouldings of the windows, &c., paste narrow slips ; and, if the requisite depth of shade should not be produced, paste other slips, of equal or less thickness, until the part is deepened to the proper tone. Foliage, water, and clouds, may be very effectively indicated by the same means ; the shape of their shadows being cut out and pasted on as above directed ; and where these shadows may become deeper, other pieces of paper of a less size are to be cut out and pasted on as before ; thus, not only the mere masses, but all the variations of light and shade may be produced ; as, also, the nice gradations and soft blending of one into another, as well as the abrupt projections. A moonlight view produces the best effect when the shadows are sufficiently strong, which may be ascertained by holding the work opposite a good light. Paste it between thin paper, and at the corner from whence the light proceeds, put a round spot of oil or varnish to imitate the moon. The landscape may also be improved by putting a little varnish round the edges of the lightest parts with a camel's-hair pencil. It may be formed into screens, and decorated and strengthened in the manner described under the head of " Transparent Screens," p. 228. It is scarcely necessary to observe, that the landscape can only be seen when the screen is held up between a light and the spectator ; nothing, however, must be drawn or fixed to its surface ; but the edges may be elegantly embellished.

**Embossing on Card.**—Various devices of flowers, leaves, wreaths, &c., may be embossed on card-board, for the purpose of forming ornamental borders, groups of flowers, and centres of hand-screens, by raising the design on the surface of the card with a penknife. The subject should not be sketched in pencil, as it would be difficult to rub out the outline afterwards without destroying the embossing ; but the blunt point of a tracing-needle may be employed for this purpose. The penknife should be held in a sloping, or nearly flat position, with the edge towards you ; and the flowers are formed by making a series of slanting incisions in an oblique direction, so as to raise the face of the card a little. A stalk may be formed by cutting a series of waving lines ; small rosettes, or flowers of a star shape, are made by small circular incisions ; leaves, like those of the fern, are composed of one long incision down the middle, and a succession of short ones up the sides. In cutting rosettes it is better to hold the knife still and move the card round ; an infinite variety of forms may be produced by varying the length and shape of the incisions. Care should be taken not to cut through to the back of the card, and the penknife must be of that kind which is called sabre-pointed.

**Charade Flowers.**—Cut a piece of any coloured paper in an oblong form. Rule a very light pencil line along the middle of it, lengthwise, and, taking the centres in that line, describe segments of circles completely across the paper ; fix the compasses again at the opposite side of each segment, and join the two extremities ; the segments on one side of the paper must then be neatly cut out and the whole piece creased by the hand. Run a thread through the part not cut out, draw it into a circle, and thus the form of a flower will be obtained. Make a handle of wire, and fasten it to the flower, co-vering the seam which will be in the centre, with a piece of paper represent-ing the central filaments of the flower. The wire should be covered with thin green paper, or gauze, twisted into the shape of a stalk ; at intervals, introduce a leaf or two, formed likewise of green paper, with a thin piece of wire up the centre to preserve the shape and re-semble the stem. Before creasing the flower, charades, enigmas, &c., should be written on each of the imitative pe-tals. The artist may carry her repre-sentation of flowers, on the above prin-ciple, to a very considerable extent. She may use double, or even treble paper, placing one piece behind another ; and, by a judicious selection of colours, may copy, not merely the shape, but the va-rious tints of the flowers. She will show her good taste by imitating, as closely as possible, the colours of her original ; instead of substituting red for lilac, blue for green, or yellow for vermilion, &c.

An immense variety of other elegant and useful articles may be constructed of pasteboard and paper ; indeed, the application of the art is so extensive, that it would be impossible for us to afford space for describing an hundredth part of the various works in those ma-terials which have fallen beneath our notice. The elementary principles of the art may be sufficiently acquired by constructing the articles we have de-scribed, to enable the young artist to copy others, or to fabricate and embel-lish novelties of her own invention. Working in pasteboard is by no means restricted to trifling productions ; very elaborate and exquisitely-finished archi-tectural subjects, ingenious models of the most delicate works, grottos, trees, &c., and even views on an extensive scale, may be admirably executed in parchment or paper, either in a plain state, or coloured to imitate the objects represented. The attempt to describe the mode of constructing such a class of works would be fruitless ; proficiency in this amusing, and we may venture to say instructive art, is only to be at-tained by practice, taste, and natural ingenuity.

**Good Home-Made Bread.**—Three pounds and a half of coarse or fine flour, a tablespoonful of solid brewer's or one ounce of German yeast, with a pint and a half of warm milk and water, and a little salt. Mix these ingredients thus. Put the flour into a large, dry, earthen pan, and mix it with a teaspoonful of salt ; make a hole in the centre of the flour, leaving some at the bottom ; mix the yeast quite smoothly with the luke-warm milk and water ; stir half of this mixture into the hole in the flour till it forms a thin batter ; cover it thickly with flour broken down from the sides ; cover the pan with a cloth or board, and set it in a warm place, but not too near the fire. In three quarters of an hour the batter will be sufficiently raised, then add to it the remaining liquid, and work up the whole into a moderately stiff paste. Pay strict at-tention to work the dough up very tho-roughly. Replace the dough, cover as before ; in three quarters of an hour it ought to have risen well. Now knead it thoroughly, put it on your board, cut to the sizes you intend, or bake it in one loaf. If baked in one loaf, it will require two hours ; if divided, one hour and a quarter. When tins are used, warm them, and, while warm, rub them thoroughly with well-greased paper, so that while they will part easily from the loaf, they may not make the crust greasy  It is a good plan, where iron ovens are used, to place clean bricks on the bottom to bake the bread on. All bread, when taken from the oven should be turned upside down to cool. A clean wooden shelf in a dry place is the best for keeping bread on. Bread should never be cut under at least one day old.

**Infants' Beds.**—These should be so contrived that the heat is equalised over their bodies, and the head kept cool. This latter is effected by the horsehair pillow. It is better for a baby to lie upon woollen than linen ; a top sheet is sufficient, and that is only required to prevent the flannel irritating the face. A child should never be so covered up as to perspire. The mother should always calculate the warmth of the under, as well as the upper, clothing of the bed, and avoid excessive heat as much as a debilitating cold. A thick mattress and a bed give great under-warmth, and a bed so made requires lighter over-covering than where only a thin mattress, or perhaps a blanket folded to serve for one, is used. An instance of the evil of the latter mode presents itself in a recent workhouse report, during severe cold, the children had to sleep on canvas-bottomed beds, with only a single fold of blanket for mattress. They were amply covered over, but for want of under-warmth most of them became seriously diseased.

**Alamode Beef.**—Take three pounds of beef ; the sticking piece answers very well. Cut the meat into small pieces, and roll them in flour. Slice an onion very thin, and fry it of a light brown, with two ounces of dripping in a stew-pan ; put in the meat, shake it, and lightly brown it ; add twelve berries of allspice, the same of whole black pepper, two bay leaves, a quarter of a tea-spoonful ground pepper, and one of salt ; then add by degrees two quarts of water, stirring all the time. Let the stew simmer gently, closely covered for three hours, or till the meat is quite tender. Take out the bay leaves, and serve hot. The gravy should be of the consistence of cream, and of a rich brown colour.

**Colours of Dresses.**—This is a department of dress that should be regarded from an artist's point of view ; and where the natural taste for colour is deficient, the blending or contrasting of them, as shown in good pictures, should be studied, as well as certain definite laws, such as—yellow, red, and blue are contrasts in all their shades, and the harmonising tints are discovered by the union of two of them. Blue is cold, yellow illuminates, and red warms. Grey and black are contrasts to white ; greens with reds. Light blue contrasts with orange, and harmonises with deep blue. Crimson has its contrast in deep green, and its harmony in violet.

The influence of day and artificial light has also to be regarded. Crimson is very handsome at night ; in the day-time, the finest complexion would be destroyed by it. Pale yellow, often very handsome by day, at night appears dirty, and tarnishes the complexion to which, in the daytime, it added lustre. By these elementary principles, we discover the reasons for effects that surround us daily in the form of unbecoming and bizarre dresses.

We must not arrange colour in dress as the natural colouring of birds and flowers is arranged, because birds and flowers are surrounded by a peculiar atmosphere. Nor must the colours in a painting be always thus used, because the painter has the advantage of a fixed shade in the background.

The rule for colour in dress must be harmony with the tints of the complexion. Thus, for fair complexions, the purest white, and light and brilliant colours, such as rose, azure, light yellow, &c., are becoming. To dark complexions, these colours would impart a black, dull, and tanned hue. These, therefore, should adopt such colours as green, violet, puce and purple ; such colours will give animation and liveliness, bringing out the charms of the dark features, making them vie with and often surpass those of their fair sisters. In short, fair women should correct the paleness of their complexions by light colours, and brunettes their yellow tints by strong colours.

The *form* of a costume is almost of equal importance to colour in artistic dressing. A lady of low stature should not wear her skirts trimmed horizontally, and should avoid *moire antique*, as well as striped materials, unless the stripes are perpendicular. A stout figure should not indulge in tight-fitting costumes, unless she wishes to appear stouter than she really is. The tall, graceful figures have a wider range; nature has so favoured them in respect to form that they, we think, may rest satisfied with merely consulting the rules for colour, although, probably, the reverse of the advice we give to their shorter and less graceful sisters may be with advantage acted upon by them.

**Allspice Baskets.**—The berries of allspice should be steeped in brandy for some time, in order to soften them, and then perforated with a small borer. The berries are strung on a slender wire, sufficient to form the circumference of the bottom of the basket, and the ends are neatly twisted together with a pair of pliers, and then formed into a round or an oval at discretion. Wrought gilt beads strung between the berries, very much improve the general effect of the basket. The interior of the bottom is composed of wires strung with the berries, and crossing each other so as to form diamonds, or any more fanciful shape. The first row, for the sides, consists of a series of small arches, fixed at their bases to the bottom circle, by twisting one wire round the other. The second row consists of another series of arches, the bases of which are fixed in a similar way on the summits of the first row; a third row, in the same manner, completes the height of the basket. A series of semicircles, or bows of wire, is then fixed to the top row, so as to project over the sides of the basket; from the extremities of these are hung festoons of the berries, strung on silk.

The handle is made of two wires, strung as the others, and crossing each other so as to form a succession of diamonds. It is proper to string the berries as the bending of the wires proceeds, and where the wires cross each other, or appear to do so, a larger gilt bead should be introduced. The interior of the basket if lined with doubled satin, gathered at top and bottom, and pulled in puffs through the arches in the sides. The whole is ornamented with ribbons and bows, according to fancy.

**Mock-China Scent Jars.**—Take a common vase, similar in shape to one of foreign china, or a grape jar, and cover it entirely with widow's lawn, which may be fixed on by paste. Cut flowers, &c., out of chintz that has a good Indian pattern, and ornament the jar with them, arranging them tastefully in groups. Procure from a turner a lid and stand to match the jar, and cover and ornament them precisely in the same manner. The jar, cover, and stand, are then to be varnished by a painter.

**Gold-Thread Purses and Reticules.**—The thread is to be procured at the gold-lace shops; a small loop is formed at the end of it; then, with a tambour-needle passed through that loop, the thread is drawn up again into another loop, and thus, in succession, until such a length has been woven as, the two ends being joined, will form the circumference of the purse. The joining is effected by passing the needle through the two end loops, and drawing the thread up through both; then five loops are to be formed on the continuation of the thread; after which, the needle is passed through the third loop from the join, on the completed circle, and the thread drawn through; five more loops are then formed on the perfected round, as before, and so on, in the same manner, until the circle is finished. The succeeding rows are then formed by weaving, as before, five loops at a time, and then passing the thread through the thread, or centre loop, of the row last finished; the rounds are still continued until the desired size is obtained. The bottom is completed by drawing the loops together with gold thread, and affixing a gold-bullion tassel. The top is finished by a straight row of running loops, sewn with gold thread to a spring clasp. The lining should be of satin, and rather smaller than the net.

**Piercing Costumes on Paper.—** Turkish or other Oriental costume or draperies, are produced by a combination of water-colour painting, for the features, with a series of small punctures made with needles of various sizes, for the dresses. The face, hands, and feet being first drawn and coloured, the outline and folds of the drapery are marked with a tracing-needle, the paper is then laid on a piece of smooth cloth, or a few sheets of blotting-paper, and the punctures inserted in the folds of the dress, from the back to the front of the paper. It sometimes affords a pleasing variety, if the costume be wholly or partially coloured, as it relieves the monotony of the white. Needles of various sizes should be used at discretion, and the whole of the back-ground or body of the paper painted in some sober opaque colour, to throw up the figure.

**Chinese Painting.—** A variety of articles, such as work-boxes and baskets, screens, and small ornamental tables, may be procured at the fancy repositories or bazaars, made of a beautiful white wood, quite plain, for the purpose of being ornamented by ladies in the Chinese style. The subjects generally represented are Chinese figures and landscapes, Indian flowers or grotesque ornaments. Patterns on paper, and the colour, which is black, used in the operation, are also supplied at the same places.

Tracing paper is to be laid over the pattern, and the outline drawn with a pencil. The tracing is then placed with the pencilled side downwards on the wood, and the pattern, which will plainly appear through, is then rubbed with the handle of an ivory folder, or a penknife, so as to transfer the pencil lines to the wood. This outline must then be sketched in with a pen dipped in the black colour to be used for the ground. All the shades and lines in the design should be correctly finished by the pen after the manner of line engraving; and the whole of the ground, or space surrounding the outline of the figures, must be covered with the black colour laid on with a camel's-hair pencil. When the painting is dry, the whole article should be finished with a transparent varnish; to perform which, however, it should be observed, that a thin coat of isinglass size is to be passed over the wood previously to the tracing. The varnish to be used is Barnard's white mastic. The general effect is very pleasing, and resembles ebony inlaid with ivory. It is also an art very easy of attainment, and requiring but little proficiency in drawing.

**Poonah Work, or Oriental Tinting.—** Flowers, fruits, butterflies, &c., from original pictures, may be executed in a very brilliant manner in Poonah painting, or Oriental tinting.

A piece of tracing-paper, of a peculiar manufacture, which is sold as Poonah-paper, is laid on the subject to be copied, and all the parts of one colour are marked in outline on it with a steel point; the interior of the outline is then cut out, either with a sharp-pointed penknife, or with little instruments, made for the purpose, and which may be procured at Barnard and Son's, 339, Oxford Street. Another piece of tracing-paper is then laid on for the purpose of marking and cutting out all the compartments of another colour; and so on, until a series of frames, or formules, is obtained, each of them having apertures, through which the whole of some one colour can be laid on the paper. The principal formule is to be placed on a piece of London drawing-board, and the colour applied with a flat Poonah brush, held perpendicularly; the parts are then to be shaded from the edge as may be requisite: the colour being first nearly all rubbed out of the brush on a piece of waste-paper. Each colour is to be laid on, in the same way, through the apertures of its own formule. The wings or bodies of beautiful insects are sometimes ornamented with touches of gold or ruby bronze. A little gum water, mixed with a small quantity of the gold or bronze, is laid on the paper with a brush ; dry gold, or bronze, is then applied with another brush to the same part, and rubbed until it becomes smooth and polished. A small light spot is obtained by laying a drop of water on any part previously coloured, and absorbing the colour from it with blotting-paper. The rich dark specks on the wings of some insects are produced by lamp-black, laid on with a pencil. To produce a regular series of streaks, or bars, the edge of a piece of Poonah tracing-paper, cut in a proper shape, should be used as a guide to the brush. It is necessary to wash the frames, or formules, with a sponge after having used them ; and separate Poonah brushes should be provided for the different colours, as well as for the various shades of each ; about two dozen will be found sufficient ; but a few camel's-hair pencils are also necessary to finish such parts as cannot be completed by means of the patterns in the tracing-paper,—such as small spots, minute streaks, the delicate antennæ of insects, &c. The formules for the various colours may be cut out of one piece of tracing-paper when the subject is small. The colours are the same as those in the common style of water-colours. Chromes are used for yellows ; neutral tint for the dark shades, and smalt and carmine for purples ; a brilliant scarlet is indispensable. A very good effect may be produced by colouring the wings of a butterfly on both sides, cutting it out neatly, gumming its body to a bouquet of flowers, in Poonah-work, and raising the wings a little from the surface. For this purpose an incision must be made in the under side of the drawing-paper with a knife, where the wings are joined to the body. In the choice of colours, the young artist should follow Nature as

closely as circumstances will permit ; otherwise her productions in Oriental tinting will prove offensive, rather than pleasing, to persons of taste.

Treatment of Window Plants.—The following hints will prove useful to those ladies who cultivate window plants in pots :—

1. It is highly necessary that at the outset the plants be young and healthy. Diseased and debilitated plants will bring disappointment, and the labour expended on their culture will be to a great extent, labour lost.

2. Plants should be early potted, that is to say, good soil should be used—something that will supply the plant with the necessary food for its sustenance. There should also be ample drainage ; pieces of broken flower-pots are used for this purpose, and the plants should, as a rule, be firmly potted,—the mould should be well pressed about the roots.

3. The plants should never be allowed to get dry, and, on the other hand, the soil should not be drenched too heavily. It is always best that the water given to the plants be allowed to pass freely from the bottom of the pots ; thus, to keep water standing in the saucers occupied by the plants is generally a bad practice, as it will often so sodden the roots that they will rot, and the plant become unhealthy, if it does not die outright.

4. Air must circulate freely amongst the plants if they are to be made healthy and to thrive well ; therefore, sash windows are always best for flowers, as a supply of air invariably finds its way in from without, even when the sashes are closed. Plenty of light is as indispensable as plenty of air, and the undue crowding of the plants should be altogether avoided. Window gardeners are often what may be termed greedy in this respect. They so crowd their windows that the inevitable result is the plants are all badly grown, whereas a few could be managed with the best possible results. The cultivator of window plants is always open to one pest,

generally denominated the "green fly." When this appears, some soap and water should be applied, either by the use of a soft brush or by the hand, carefully washing off the fly in the act.

**To Keep Flies from Meat.**—In hot summer weather it is almost impossible to procure meat that is neither tough nor tainted. In such seasons the greatest care is needful, and meat should be carefully examined to guard against flies. If it has been touched by them, cut off the part, and wash the joint with vinegar and water. The best way to prevent the flies touching raw flesh or fish is to pepper it well with common black pepper. This is easily removed before dressing, and its use will often make it possible to preserve meat fresh long enough to become tender even in sultry weather.

**To Prevent and Remove Taint.**—It is the best way to remove from meat the parts liable to taint easily, such as the pipe running along the bone of loins of meat, and kernels from the fat of beef or suet. If you have not succeeded in preserving meat from taint, wash it with Condy's crimson fluid diluted, according to directions This is a perfectly harmless disinfectant. It is good always to keep small pieces of charcoal lying about in the meat safe during summer time.

In purchasing meat care should be exercised to have it free from bruises. The rump and aitchbone of beef and legs of mutton, are more likely than other parts to be thus spoilt.

**How to Use Very Stale Bread.**—Very stale bread can be grated into coarse powder and preserved in jars. It must be kept in a dry place well covered up. It will thus keep sound for a long time, and be found useful in the preparation of stuffings, puddings, &c.

**To Cook Fish.**—CLEANING.—Fish should be carefully cleaned, but all soaking in water except in the case of fresh-water fish should be avoided, as it deprives fish of flavour.

BOILING.—Put a little salt and vinegar into the water in which fish is to be boiled; it gives firmness. Never put fish into hot or warm water, but into cold; bring it to the boil gently and keep the fish simmering till done.

WATCHING.—Fish requires very careful watching while boiling; draw up the strainer and try the fish by withdrawing a bone from the fin; when this separates easily the fish is done. If it has to be kept hot, take it on the strainer out of the water, and set it crosswise over the kettle. Place a clean soft cloth over the fish, and above that a piece of folded flannel; by this means you still keep the heat in, without spoiling the colour of the fish.

FRYING AND BROILING.—Fish to be fried or broiled should be cleansed and wrapped in a soft cloth, and thus rendered thoroughly dry. In most cases of frying, egg and bread crumbs are to be used. The best material to fry fish in is oil; the worst, butter; the most economical, clarified lard or dripping, either of which should boil at the time the fish is put into them. Place fried fish on white blotting-paper to absorb the grease. Fish to be broiled should be seasoned previous to dressing; great care is required for this mode of cooking.

**Hands and Face.**—When hot wash in very warm water, and it will remove from the face the unpleasant redness and heat in a comparatively short time, and produce a refreshing sensation. Never apply in these cases cold water, as it is very injurious to the skin, and productive of redness and eruptions which are seldom if ever removed.

**Skylarks.**—These birds are the most eminent of our British song-birds, and are great household favourites. Rising almost perpendicularly from his lowly nest, the lark ascends, by a succession of springs, to an immense height, singing all the while to cheer his brooding mate, whom he continually keeps in view; and, should she attract him, he drops like a stone from his elevation, as it were, to attend her bidding: on other occasions his descent is made in an oblique direction. They usually pass their time on the wing, or on the ground ; the peculiar construction of their hinder claws preventing them from perching, like many other birds of a similar size, on twigs : those even which alight on trees, venture only on the larger branches, which, from their convenient breadth, afford nearly as secure a footing as the surface of the earth. On the ground, also, the larks build their nests, the principal material of which is dried grass. The eggs are usually four or five in number ; those of the skylark are of a greyish brown : those of the woodlark, dusky, spotted with brown ; those of the titlark, closely speckled with the same colour. The woodlark occasionally sings during the night, and, like the titlark, perches upon trees. The three varieties of larks we have mentioned, are very common in this country ; and are frequently kept, particularly the skylark and woodlark, as song-birds. The skylark will sing freely for eight or nine months in the year ; he is very hardy, long-lived, and, if he can be kept from hearing, and, consequently, imitating inferior birds, his song is beautiful.

A fresh turf should be placed as often as possible in the cage we have imprisoned him ; and he may be fed on egg boiled hard, chopped small, and mixed with about half its quantity of bruised hemp-seed : this food is also proper for the other larks ; to the woodlark a little meat, either boiled or raw, but not salted, may occasionally be given with advantage. The woodlark will sing quite as long, and his notes are nearly as beautiful—indeed, in the opinion of many, rather superior to those of the skylark.

**Nightingales.**—Some of our poets differ strangely as to " the humour of their song." Milton deems it " most musical—most melancholy." " Forlorn Philomel " is a poetical expression, which has been long hacknied, in prose and verse ; while another serious poet describes its song thus :—

" 'Tis the merry nightingale
That crowds, and hurries, and precipitates,

With fast thick warble, his delicious notes."

The hen entirely performs the task of incubation ; the male bird brings her food during the day, and, at night, from some adjacent spray, sings his sweet carol, doubtless to solace and delight her. With him it is a season of joy, and why, therefore, should he make his mate melancholy by songs of sorrow ? The associations of time and place when and where the nightingale's song is heard, have given it in the imagination and memory of many persons, a sadness, which neither the song itself possesses, nor would be attributed to it, were the nightingale, like the lark, to carol his lay when the sun is rising in glory above the hill-top, and the leaves flutter in the morning breeze, and the floweret, refreshed by the dew-drop, again lifts its fair face to heaven, and all nature looks jocund.

Caged nightingales are usually fed with egg boiled hard, grated, and mixed with boiled sheep's-heart ; a mixture of bruised hemp-seed and bread is sometimes substituted for the egg. The food must be made fresh every day, and clean water, in which the bird may bathe, should frequently be placed in a little pan on the floor of the cage ; meal-worms and ants' larvæ should, occasionally, be given, as a treat ; particularly the latter, if they can be conveniently procured. Nightingales must not be kept in any of the ordinary bird-cages ; the proper cages for these birds, are dark on their sides ; the perches are padded, and a piece of green baize is stretched across the top, an inch or two below the roof ; these precautions are taken to prevent the bird from hurting itself, which it would otherwise be in danger of doing. When kept in a room, or an aviary out of doors, they are furnished, at the mating season, which is about the end of April, with slender roots, dry grass, twigs, oak-leaves, hair, down, and other fine and warm substances, with which they may build their nests. The female lays four or five eggs of a greenish brown colour ; and, in a wild state, produces two, and sometimes three, broods in a year.

**Thrushes.**—The rich-toned throstle, called by one of our poets the mellow mavis ; the fieldfare ; and that brilliant songster, the blackbird—are the most common birds of the thrush genus in this country. All the birds of the thrush kind have a little notch on each side at the end of the bill, which is rather straight, and slightly bent towards the tip ; the nostrils are oval and naked. The size, shape, and plumage of the thrush and blackbird, or black ouzel, are too well known to require any particular description. The throstle begins his song early in the spring, and continues it during part of the summer. The female lays five or six eggs of a light blue colour, marked with dusky spots. The nest of the throstle is generally built in bushes, and made of dry grass, clay, and rotten wood. These birds feed on insects, and the berries of holly, misletoe, &c. When kept in cages, their usual food, as well as that of the blackbird, is raw or parboiled meat, sopped bread, stale bun, scalded fig-dust, or bruised hemp-seed and chopped egg mixed with crumbs of bread.

**Blackbirds.**—The blackbird sings as soon as the thrush, and continues to enliven the woods with his full, melodious notes for four or five months. The nest of the blackbird is built in a low bush, generally a holly ; the female lays four or five eggs, regularly marked with spots of a dusky hue on a bluish ground. Blackbirds cannot be kept in avaries, on account of their quarrelsome dispositions. They are excellent song-birds for the cage : and, if brought up from the nest, may be taught to whistle tunes very correctly ; the practice, however, in our opinion, is a bad one ; we look upon it as a great waste of time, tending to no good purpose : the native notes of the blackbird are excellent, and it seems a pity to spoil a good song-bird, by making him a middling musician. Netted blackbirds are, generally, worthless in a cage ; those only which are reared from the nest, and have never known the sweets of liberty, become good songsters in a state of captivity. They are so addicted to mocking whatever sounds they hear, that a blackbird, brought up in the metropolis, has often been known, not only to imitate the notes of the birds near him, but even the cries of those persons who carry various sorts of wares for sale about the streets. To obtain a good blackbird, rich in his native note, we must go into some retired village, and there we may probably discover a fine black ouzel, in a plain wicker cage, beneath the eaves of a labourer's cot, chaunting the notes which he has heard his free sire singing from the holly-tree top in the adjacent wood. Blackbirds should be fed on the same food as thrushes, which *see*.

**Goldfinches and Linnets.**—To enter into any description of these birds would be superfluous ; nor is it even necessary to dwell on the mode of treatment most congenial to their habits when kept as song-birds ; for who does not know that these gay little warblers delight in being placed, during the merry spring-time of the year, where the sunbeam may gild their plumage with a richer glow ?—in the sultry season, abroad, but in the shade ?—and, while their feathers are falling, and throughout the winter, in some choice location, which is at once sheltered but not solitary ?—or, that they live on seeds, and require to be regularly provided with food and water, for which, in return, the little captives make their little mansions merry with their melody ?

The goldfinch, when kept in a cage, loses, in moulting, the freshness and beauty of its plumage : those which are purchased in autumn, possess the livery they wore in the woods ; and it is never again equalled, while the birds remain in a state of captivity. The proper time for purchasing these birds is when the young ones flock, at the latter end of summer ; those which are taken in spring, frequently pine, and rarely prove good songsters in the cage. The gold-finch builds a very beautiful nest of moss, and other soft materials, and lays five or six eggs which are white, and marked at the end with purple spots.

The Linnet has a great number of admirers, and, when rich in song, is deemed valuable. Young birds are often brought up under an old linnet of reputation as a songster ; and from being kept in the same room long enough to acquire the variety of notes and execution of its master, the little pupils are reckoned worth two or three guineas each, or even more, if they exhibit any unusual powers of voice. The nest of the linnet is usually built in a white thorn, or furze-bush ; it is composed of bents, moss, &c., and lined with fine down, and sometimes horsehair ; the hen lays four or five whitish eggs.

**Gold-Thread Embroidery.**—Not a long time ago this art was very popular with ladies, and is still practised by a great number. In splendour and richness it far exceeds every other species of embroidery, and is principally used in court dresses and for the ball-room. It is practised on crape, India muslin, or silk ; and, principally, in large and bold designs. The gold-thread should be fine, and it may be worked with nearly the same facility as any other thread. Where the material is sufficiently transparent, a paper pattern is placed underneath ; the outline is run in white thread ; and the subject is then worked with gold thread, in satin-stitch. For a thin stalk to a flower, the running-thread should be omitted, and gold thread laid on the material, and sewn slightly over with another gold thread, thus giving the stalk a very pretty spiral appearance. In embroidering a thick material, the design is to be sketched with a pencil, if the ground be light, or with a white-chalk pencil if dark. The pattern is frequently varied by the introduction of short pieces of fine gold bullion ; sometimes two or three of them coming out of the cup of a flower ; the stitch passes lengthwise through the twist of the bullion, thus confining it flat. The centre of a flower may be also finished with bullion ; in that case, the stitch taken should be shorter than the piece of bullion, the under-side of which will, therefore, be compressed, and the upper side expanded, so as to give it prominence.

Gold spangles may be occasionally introduced, and they should be secured by bringing the thread from beneath, passing it through the spangle, then through a very short bit of bullion, and back through the hole in the centre of the spangle ; this is better than sewing the spangle on with a thread across its face.

**Gauze Screens.**—These screens are made of gauze, stretched over a frame of wire, and ornamented with figures, which are usually cut out of chintz. The handles, as well as the shapes, are merely of wire, bent and fastened in various modes. The gauze must be doubled, stretched lightly over on one side of the wire frame, and neatly sewed at the edges, which should be bound with gold or coloured paper. The ornaments, such as flowers, birds, &c., cut out of chintz, are to be gummed on the front of the screens ; but should a difficulty occur in procuring a variety from chintz, an engraving, rather gaudily coloured, will answer the purpose. Artificial butterflies, and other insects, look well, if fastened to the gauze by their bodies, with their wings extended. Flowers, also, gummed by their calyces and stems, with their petals free, produce an equally good effect. The handles are bound over with ribbon, and decorated with bows.

**Old Maids.**—Being an old maid implies decision of character ; neither sham nor show, nor courtly manners, nor splendid person, have won them over ; nor fair promises, nor shallow tears. They looked beyond the manner and the dress, and finding no cheering indication of depth of mind and sterling principles, they gave up the specious present for the chance of a more solid future, and determined in hope and resignation to " bide their time."

**Puff Paste.**—Mrs. Beeton, in her "Household Management," gives the following recipe for making good puff paste :—" Ingredients ; to every pound of flour allow one pound of butter, and not quite half a pint of water. Mode of mixing :—Carefully weigh the flour and butter, and have the exact proportion ; squeeze the butter well, to extract the water from it, and afterwards wring it in a clean cloth, that no moisture may remain. Sift the flour ; see that it is perfectly dry, and proceed in the following manner to make the paste, using a very clean pasteboard and rolling-pin : —Supposing the quantity to be one pound of flour, work the whole into a smooth paste, with not quite half a pint of water, using a knife to mix it with ; the proportion of this latter ingredient must be regulated by the discretion of the cook ; if too much be added, the paste, when baked, will be tough. Roll it out until it is of an equal thickness of about an inch ; break four ounces of the butter into small pieces ; place these on the paste, sift over it a little flour, fold it over, roll out again, and put another four ounces of butter. Repeat the rolling and buttering until the paste has been rolled out four times, or equal quantities of flour and butter have been used. Do not omit, every time the paste is rolled out, to dredge a little flour over that and the rolling-pin, to prevent both from sticking. Handle the paste as lightly as possible, and do not press heavily upon it with the rolling-pin. The next thing to be considered is the oven, as the baking of pastry requires particular attention. Do not put it into the oven until it is sufficiently hot to raise the paste ; for the best-prepared paste, if not properly baked, will be good for nothing. Brushing the paste as often as rolled out, and the pieces of butter placed thereon, with the white of an egg, assists it to rise in leaves or flakes. As this is the great beauty of puff-paste, it is as well to try this method.

**Suet Crust for Pies or Puddings.** —To every pound of flour allow six ounces of beef suet, and half a pint of water. Free the suet from skin and shreds ; chop it extremely fine, and rub it well into the flour ; work the whole into a smooth paste with half a pint of water ; roll it out, and it is ready for use. This crust is quite rich enough for ordinary purposes, but when a better one is desired, use three quarters of a pound of suet to every pound of flour. Some cooks, for rich crusts, pound the suet in a mortar, with a small quantity of butter. It should then be laid on the paste in small pieces, the same as for puff-crust, and will be found exceedingly nice for hot tarts. This quantity of suet to every pound of flour will make a very good crust ; and four ounces will be found sufficient for children, or for stomachs that do not like rich pastry.

**Management of Table Lamps.**— If the wick be turned too much, the oil will not rise readily ; nor should it be too loose, or it will cause the capillary attracting power to raise too much oil. Lamps require constant attention to the wick, otherwise the light will be unequal. Trim your lamps daily. The wick should be cut perfectly level with scissors ; any ragged bits on the edge of the wick cause the flame to burn unevenly, and to smoke.

**To Wash Phials.**—In most families are gradually collected a number of phials that have been used for medicine. It is well to have a basket purposely to keep them in, and occasionally to wash them. Put into a wash-kettle some sifted ashes, and pour on it a sufficiency of cold water. Then put in the phials (without corks,) place the kettle over the fire, and let it gradually come to a boil. After it has boiled awhile, take it off, and set it aside, letting the phials remain in it till cold. Then take them out, rinse, drain them, and wipe the outsides. You may wash black bottles in the same manner. If you have occasion to wash a single phial or bottle, pour into it through a small funnel some lye, or some lukewarm water in which a little pearlash has been dissolved.

MODEL PATTERN FOR AN INFANT'S HOOD.

**An Infant's Hood.**—An elegant hood, of white pique, embroidered with satin stitch and white braid, trimmed with fringe, and bows of white ribbon. A quilted ruche of lace and muslin surrounds the face.

**White Frieze Ironing-Cloth.**—To make suitable for ironing fine laces and muslins—to the two pieces of white frieze 25 inches long, and 13 inches wide. Cut them into scollops round the edge, and sew on scarlet braid according to illustration No. 1, filling up each scollop with an eyelet hole over each half round, and ornamented with point russe stitches in scarlet crewel. Then lay the two pieces on each other, the wrong side inside, and join them together by working a row of crochet on the star braid, one double on each

No. 1.—IRONING CLOTH.

point of the braid, 5 chains, observing to pass the needle through both braids. On this row work 6 double on each chain scollop. Illustration No. 2 shows the pattern in full size.

This cloth will be found by any lady who is disposed to make it, very durable, useful, and ornamental to the laundry-table.

In a subsequent part of our volume we shall give pattern of a cover for a polished box-iron.

No. 2.—FULL PATTERN IRONING CLOTH.

**Sugar as Food.**—In alluding to the uses of sugar in assisting assimilation, Mr. Bridges Adams says :—" I know by experience, the difference in nutritious effect produced by the flesh of tired cattle on a march, and those slain in a condition arising from abundant food and healthy exercise. In the former case any amount might be eaten without the satisfaction of hunger, while in the latter a smaller amount removed hunger. But I discovered that certain other food, of a different quality, such as grape-sugar and fruit, would help the tired meat to assimilate, and thus remove hunger."

Puddings and fruit tarts are not, therefore, simple flatteries of the palate, but digestive agents, provided always they are not themselves of rebelliously indigestible materials, which, in English cookery, is too frequently the case. We may allude to the fondness of artisans for confectionery, and of patients, just discharged from the hospital, asking for " sweets," in preference to good substantial food, as examples of a correct instinct. There is no doubt that in children, in whom the requirements of growth call for a rapid and efficient transformation of food into tissue, the desire for sweets is very imperious, and parents should understand that the jam-pot will diminish the butcher's bill and increase the amount of nutrition extracted from beef and mutton.

**How to Choose a Carpet.**—Brussels carpet, although estimated by the beauty of design and richness of colour, ought also to possess durability. This chiefly arises from the quantity and quality of worsted on the surface than from the ordinary operations of the weaver. In the best qualities the worsted warp-threads usually appear on the surface, in sets of threes, each set occupying the space between the linen warp-threads or chain, of which threads there are about seven to the inch. This close arrangement maintains the loops of worsted nearly upright, giving thereby greater elasticity, with a well-sustained resistance to the effects of pressure and wear. Inferior carpets usually have a reduction in the quantity of surface worsted, produced by dropping loops. The quality of worsted is not less important than the quantity ; indeed, a carpet made of good worsted, in a smaller quantity, is to be preferred to one crowded with an inferior material. Good worsted is bright, evenly twisted, free from loose, hairy fibre, soft and elastic to the touch. Scarlet and crimson are very durable colours ; greens are sound ; and brown, buff, and fawn colours, somewhat less permanent.

**Lace-Paper Cuttings.**—For fire-paper and stove ornaments, lace-paper cuttings serve much better than the ordinary paper or willow-shavings. The tissue-paper should be in folds two or three inches wide. Mark the outside of the fold over in diamonds with pencil and ruler ; then sketch with the pencil any pattern in agreement with your taste. Between the figures cut out all the diamonds, but be careful not to cut them in the figures. Three or four leaves, arranged in a circle, and cut in some pretty pattern, form tasteful ornaments for candlesticks. The beauty of cut-paper flowers and lace-paper cuttings depends very much upon the taste and ingenuity of the designer.

**To Make Melted Butter.**—Mix the butter and flour smoothly together on a plate ; put it into a lined saucepan, and then pour in about half a pint of milk. Keep stirring it *one* way over a sharp fire ; let it boil quickly for a minute or two, and it is ready to serve. It will only take ten minutes altogether. This is a very good foundation for onion, lobster, or oyster-sauce, and is the melted butter we recommend in preference to any other ; using milk instead of water makes the preparation look so much whiter and more delicate. Another method is to make it without the milk, thus :—mix half a pint of water and a dessertspoonful of flour, to a batter, which put into a saucepan ; add two ounces of butter and a seasoning of salt ; keep stirring one way till all the ingredients are melted and smooth.

**The Art of Salting Meat.**—This consists in rubbing in the salt evenly and thoroughly, dividing the salt in two equal portions, rubbing in the first half, and after a day or two the remainder.

Bay salt is the best kind to use for curing meat, as the flavour is better.

Brown sugar, in the proportion of half an ounce to a pound of salt, is an ingredient that adds greatly to the flavour of the meat. One way of applying it is to rub it well into the meat before salting. Meat should be kept *covered* with brine, and turned and rubbed daily. In *winter* meat should be hung till tender, before salting; in *summer* it cannot be salted too soon.

Frozen Meat will not take the salt properly; indeed, in very cold weather, it is a good plan to rub in the salt warm, as it is more certain, by this method, to penetrate the meat. The pipes in meat and the kernels of fat should be carefully removed, and the holes stuffed with salt.

**Treatment of Hams.**—To preserve hams through the summer, make a number of cotton bags, a little larger than the hams. After the hams are well smoked, place them in the bags, and get the best kinds of sweet, well made hay; cut it with a knife, and with your hands press it well around the hams in the bags; tie the bags with strings, put on a card of the year, to show the age of the hams, and hang them up in a garret or some dry room, and they will last five years, and will be better for boiling than on the day you hung them up. This method costs little, and the bags will last forty years. No flies or bugs will trouble hams if the hay is well pressed around them; the sweating of the hams will be taken up by the hay, and it will impart a fine flavour to the hams. The hams should be treated in this way before the hot weather sets in.

**Isinglass.**—Boil one ounce of isinglass shavings, forty Jamaica peppers, and a bit of brown crust of bread, in a quart of water to a pint, and strain it. This makes a pleasant jelly to keep in the house; of which a large spoonful may be taken in milk, tea, soup, or any way most agreeable.

**Boiled Flour for Infants.**—Make a bag of cheap white calico, say a quarter of a yard square, or smaller if you like. Stuff it quite full of flour till it is quite hard, and the flour does not come out. Tie it very tightly at the top, and put it in a saucepan of boiling water. Let it boil hard for four hours, filling up with boiling water as the water wastes. Then take it up; peel off the skin; chop or break up the ball of flour into pieces; roll it with a rolling-pin on a clean board until no lumps remain; when cold put it into a dry tin. This is far better than arrowroot; indeed, it is one of the very best things for invalids or babies.

**Slatternly Women.**—We cannot believe in the industry, ability, or good qualities of slatternly women. Neat and agreeable dressing is indispensable for them. The influence over a household of a neat mistress is very great. The children also are neat; the servants follow suit and are neat; the house is orderly and well arranged. A woman may be plain, and no longer young; but if her attire is clean and tidy, she may be very pleasant to look upon—pleasanter by far than her beautiful young neighbour always in a slatternly *deshabille*, save when she is got up for the occasion. Her husband is glad to return home and contemplate the home picture. Unconsciously, perhaps, he finds repose in the well-ordered establishment. On the contrary, a slatternly woman, surrounded by unkempt, noisy children, and a disorderly household, gradually drives her husband to feel less comfort at home than elsewhere, and she sits down at last to bewail in vain the fate she has brought upon herself.

Nor is this the whole extent of the evil. Children of a slatternly mother fall under the ban of society; they are either slighted or shunned altogether. Though free from the same error, they have difficulty to make their way in the world. There is a prejudice against them that "like produces like," as it often does.

**Scotch Scones.**—Take two pounds of flour, and rub well into it four ounces of butter and a pinch of salt, with a sufficient quantity of sour butter-milk in a jug to mix the flour into a paste, but not too stiff ; mix in a teacup with cold water until dissolved a large tea-spoonful of carbonate of soda. When well mixed throw it into the butter-milk, which must be sour, stir it up quickly until it effervesces, mix the flour with the milk in its effervescent state ; roll the paste to about a quarter of an inch in thickness, stamp it out in small round cakes, and bake them on a girdle over a nice clear fire.

**A New Hanging-Garden.**—Take a white sponge of large size, and sow it full of rice, oats, or wheat. Then place it for a week or ten days in a shallow dish, and as the sponge will absorb the moisture, the seeds will begin to sprout before many days. When this has fairly taken place the sponge may be suspended by means of cords from a hook at the top of the window where a little sun will enter. It will thus become like a mass of green, and can be kept wet by merely immersing it in a bowl of water.

**Cherry Brandy.**—To every pound of cherries allow half a pound of white powdered sugar, with brandy enough to cover them. Select plump, ripe fruit, free from bruises ; cut off the stalks quite short, and half fill a wide-mouthed bottle ; add sugar in the above proportions, and fill up the same with pure French brandy ; cork and seal the bottles, and place them on a tray, turn-ing them head downward every twelve hours, for twelve days ; the brandy will be ready for use in about two or three months.

**A Happy Home.**—It is possible to make home so attractive that children should have no disposition to wander from it or prefer any other place ; it is practicable to make it so attractive that it shall not only firmly hold its own loved ones, but shall draw others into its peaceful circle. Let the house always be the scene of pleasant looks, cheerful words, kind and affectionate acts : let the table be the happy meeting-place of a merry group, and not a dull one, where a silent, if not sullen, company of animals come to feed ; let the meal be the time when a cheerful laugh is heard, and good things are said ; let the evening meeting in the sitting-room, be a smiling company settling themselves to books or games till the round of good-night kisses are in order ; let there be some music in the household—music not kept like silks and satins, to show to company, but music in which every member of the home may join ; let the young companions be welcomed, and made for the time a part of the group, so that daughters shall not deem it ne-cessary to seek the obscurity of the back parlours with intimate friends, or to drive father and mother to other apart-ments ; finally, let the home be sur-rounded with an air of cozy and cheer-ful goodwill ; then children need not be exhorted to love it—you will not be able to tempt them away from it.

**Mouth Wash to Sweeten the Breath.**—Take a quarter of an ounce each of dried mint, thyme, and lemon-thyme ; half an ounce of cloves, crushed ; half a nutmeg, grated ; pour on to these ingredients half a pint of any spirit, and let the mixture stand together for two or three days ; then strain off the tincture formed, and add ten drops of oil of peppermint ; it is then ready for use. Some people use it by pouring a few drops on the tooth-brush, and clean-ing the teeth with it in the ordinary manner ; but it answers equally well if mixed with an equal quantity of water, and applied as a gargle to rinse the mouth.

**Hair-Dressing Fluid.**—An excel-lent preparation is the following for dressing the hair, and rendering it soft and glossy :—Melt a quarter of an ounce of the best white wax, in four ounces of either almond or olive oil : when nearly cold add any perfume that is preferred, such as a mixture of fifteen drops of oil of cloves, ten drops of essence of almonds, and thirty drops of essence of lemons, which makes a very sweet odour ; but the scent used may be entirely at the option of the maker. If the oil and wax are very good and sweet, some ladies prefer it without any scent.

**Freckles and Sunburns.**—These discolourations are, in persons of light complexion, the result of the sun's influence acting chemically on the peculiar composition of the colouring principle of the skin ; in such cases the spots fade, and become invisible during winter and dark weather, and are therefore termed "summer freckles." Those, on the contrary, which do not depend on light or heat, being equally vivid in winter as in summer, may be regarded as constitutional, and are called " cold freckles." They vary in colour, being sometimes yellow, and sometimes green, and are not, like summer freckles, peculiar to persons of light complexion. Saffron spots, sulphur spots, and liver spots, are all discolourations of the same nature as freckles, though not always permanent, being often referable to some disarrangement of the system, and disappearing with the cause which created them.

Turn we now for a remedy to Mr. Erasmus Wilson, who has so long and so successfully made skin diseases his study. He prescribes :—Elder-flower ointment one ounce, sulphate of zinc twenty grains. Mix well, and rub into the affected skin at night. In the morning wash it off with plenty of soap, and when the grease is completely removed, apply the following lotion :— Infusion of rose petals half a pint, citric acid thirty grains. All local discolourations will disappear under this treatment, and if the freckles do not entirely yield, they will, in most instances, be greatly ameliorated. Should any unpleasant irritation or roughness of the skin follow the application, a lotion composed of half a pint of almond mixture, and half a drachm of Goulard's

extract, will afford immediate relief. If any constitutional disturbance be associated with discolouration of the skin, the advice of a medical man will be required.

**Phrenological Divisions of the Brain.**—1. LOVE OF LIFE.—This propensity is found at the base of the middle lobe of the brain, and is united with Alimentativeness, Philoprogenitiveness, Amativeness, Combativeness, and Destructiveness.

2. ALIMENTATIVENESS.—This organ is situated at the base of the brain, and gives a swell to the head at the temporal arches ; it is situated in front of, and a little above the ear. It is, however, often mistaken for a high cheek bone. This propensity produces a desire for indulgence in food, gluttony, drunkenness, and appetite. If large and unguided, it becomes a fearful source of intemperance.

3. AMATIVENESS.—This propensity is situated on the lower and posterior portion of the brain, and gives a fulness to the back part of the neck between the ears. A small neck at the back implies a small development of this organ. This animal feeling, put into our nature by an all-wise Providence for temperate gratification and for the progress of creation, causes man to sink below the brute, if it acts by itself without being guided by the higher sentiments.

4. PHILOPROGENITIVENESS.—This propensity is the love of children and tender beings, and extends outwards towards the ear, and gives a drooping appearance to the back of the head. This organ is that of a peculiar sentiment given to man, in order that he may have an instinctive love for children, and that he may be willing and ready to make any sacrifice which the care and education of those little ones may call for. When this organ is over-balancing the others, the individual so constituted is particularly fond of children, sometimes weakly indulgent to them, and allowing them to give way to their ill-tempers and obstinacy.

5 CONCENTRATIVENESS.—This organ

is immediately above the last organ, and not seldom acting strongly in combination with it. It produces great love of home and national pride. This organ helps man to concentrate his impressions and feelings systematically on one point ; and if large, raises great aversion to living abroad. It often occurs that this propensity, if nourished too much, produces in young people eccentric and fantastic manners ; on the other hand, if the organ is small in a child, it will show great tendency to travel, love of geography, or instability, proneness to change, combined with want of firmness, and will create a very unstable character if not timely counteracted by prudence and caution.

6. ADHESIVENESS.—This organ is on each side of Concentrativeness, and a little higher than Philoprogenitiveness. It is largest in woman. This organ of Friendship, Fidelity, and Affection, renders man a social being, and binds him to his family, friends, and country. If this sentiment is strong in a child, his parents should not fail timely to select for him fit and suitable companions.

7. COMBATIVENESS.—The organ of opposition is situated at the side of each ear, and gives the power necessary to meet those obstacles which life so often presents. If these obstacles are great and dangerous, then this propensity is called courage. If this organ is very large, its possessor may become truly courageous ; or he may be quarrelsome and fond of fighting and opposition. If combativeness is small, the individual is deficient in the necessary qualification to meet danger, or the attacks of others. Combativeness if early displayed in the character of a boy, ought not to be too much counteracted, but rather regulated. With regard to a girl it is quite different. This sentiment ought only to be nourished in order to lead her to take up the defence of right and virtue.

8. DESTRUCTIVENESS.—The propensity to destroy gives a fulness to the head, above the upper part of each ear, sometimes causing it to project. In a child this propensity is one of the first visible, and one, too, which most speedily will spread its entangling tendrils.

9. SECRETIVENESS.—This organ lies immediately above the last propensity. It shows itself in a thousand different ways, and is a power very difficult to discern, especially if it has become deeply rooted in the individual. It is also of immense consequence, and not seldom attended with deplorable circumstances. The marks for noting the development of Secretiveness are, generally (because in the child the nobler sentiments still slumber), an inclination to conceal emotions and plans ; secresy in words and deeds ; a beginning of cunningness.

10. ACQUISITIVENESS.—It is at the anterior inferior angle of the parietal bone that this organ has its situation. It is usually large, of an oval appearance, and gives a fulness to that part of the head. Acquisitiveness gives a power to possess, to acquire, to collect and provide for future wants. This propensity, if very predominant, leads to avarice.

11. CONSTRUCTIVENESS.—This organ is situated on the temples, in front of and below Acquisitiveness, and causes a desire to build and construct in general.

12. SELF ESTEEM.—This organ is situated at, and gives an elevation to, that part of the head forming the curve or turn from the back to the top of the head. It bears selfishness in its name and essence. It is, in short, the love and esteem of ourselves.

13. LOVE OF APPROBATION.—This is situated at each side of the preceding organ, at the posterior lateral part of the head. While the foregoing sentiment produces esteem of self, this leads to a desire for the esteem and appreciation of others.

14. CAUTION.—This propensity is situated above Secretiveness, at each side of the head, near the middle of each parietal bone. From this sentiment arises the instinct which leads us to apprehend and shun danger.

15. BENEVOLENCE.—Lies at the upper and middle part of the forehead, which it makes full and round. It gives an elevation to the frontal bone in the coronal aspect. Its very name implies and tells us the method of its activity. It is the key which opens the human heart.

16. VENERATION.—Sometimes this is called the organ of religion, has its seat in the upper part of the head, in the centre of the sentimental organs, close to Benevolence. It is of a rather round form, and gives the feeling of dependence with regard to God.

17. FIRMNESS.—This organ is situated between Veneration and Self-esteem at the very summit of the head, to which it gives a towering appearance. It produces constancy and perseverance in the various actions of the other organs, and enables men to conquer difficulties in science, art, and business.

18. CONSCIENTIOUSNESS.—This organ is situated on each side of Firmness, and disposes a man to look for and desire justice ; to respect the rights of his fellow-creatures ; to love truth, and to be open to conviction.

19. HOPE.—This sentiment, situated on each side of Veneration, induces us to believe in the realisation of the desires of the other faculties. With love of life, it creates a belief in immortality, and is the basis of faith.

20. WONDER.—This is situated on each side of Imitation, and gives origin to general curiosity, desire for novelty, to see or hear interesting or striking things ; it also causes belief in presentiments, in secret inspirations, in phantoms, dreams—in short, anything supernatural.

21. IDEALITY.—Is of an elongated form, and situated on the side of the head above the temples. It is the talent of poetry, and produces a desire for anything that is lovely and sublime.

22. WIT.—This organ is situated on the upper and lateral part of the forehead, and gives an inclination for comical things, and to laugh and jest.

23. IMITATION.—Is situated on the front of the head, on each side of Benevolence, and gives the talent for imitating and mimicking the voices, manners, gestures, and peculiarities, of others.

24. INDIVIDUALITY.—This organ gives a fulness and breadth between the eyebrows immediately above the nose ; it produces the talent for remembering objects, and is the great element in observation. With Imitation, this power makes the artist.

25. EVENTUALITY.—It is situated in the middle of the forehead, above Individuality. This organ is the medium by which history is learnt : for, through the same, man possesses the power to remember facts.

26. FORM.—Between the eye and the nose this is situated, giving an appearance of width. From this organ results the talent of perceiving definite forms, substances, &c.

27. SIZE.—This organ is seated at the inner corner of the arch of the eyebrow, and enables man to form an estimate of size, to judge of perspective, and gives an idea of space, dimensions, distance.

28. LOCALITY.—This organ actuates the traveller, landscape painter, geographer, chess player, geometrician, and voyager. It is situated above and on each side of the nose. It also enables its possessor to find out and remember places.

29. COLOUR.—This gives an arched appearance on the middle of the eyebrow. It sometimes only projects, without being large. This faculty gives taste and judgment in the harmony of colours. It constitutes the chief element in the talent of a painter.

30. TIME.—Above the middle of the eyebrow this organ is situated, and gives the power to calculate and judge accurately. It helps greatly to elegant composition, and also to tact in dancing, and is a most important element in true musical talent.

31. LANGUAGE.—It is situated at the back of the orbit, and gives promi-

nence to the eye. It is the power of inventing and recollecting signs, and of remembering words ; it also gives great fluency in the use of words as the medium for the expression of thought.

32. COMPARISON.—This organ is situated in the middle of the upper part of the forehead, and gives a fulness to that part. It produces the power of perception, comprehension, comparison. In short, it forms the general talent of learning and understanding.

33. CAUSALITY.—This organ is situated at each side of comparison, and enables us to trace the cause and effects of any phenomenon.

[This outline of the names, situation, and characteristics of the phrenological divisions of the brain, we have extracted from an excellent little book, entitled " Children's Gifts and Mothers' Duties," by Elise Von Lersner. This work is full of sound advice to mothers on the moral training of their children, and cannot be too highly commended, apart from all phrenological theories, on which the author's deductions are based.]

**Game.**—All kinds of game may be made fit for eating when it appears to be spoiled by cleaning it and washing it with vinegar and water. Birds that are not likely to keep, should be drawn, cropped, and picked, then wash in two or three waters, and rub them with salt ; have ready a saucepan of boiling water, and plunge them into it one by one, drawing them up and down by the legs, so that the water may pass through them. Let them stay for about ten minutes, then hang them up in a cold place ; when they are completely and thoroughly drained, well salt and pepper the insides, and well wash them before roasting.

**Luncheons.**—The luncheon is laid out in two ways , one way is to bring in a butler's tray with let-down sides, on which it is previously arranged upon a tray-cloth. and letting down the sides and spreading the cloth upon the dining-table, to distribute the things as required. The other way is to lay the cloth as for dinner, with the pickle-

stand and cruets opposite each other ; and, if in season, a small vase of flowers in the centre : if not, a water-jug and tumblers, which may be placed on a side-table at other times. The sides of the table are occupied by the requisites for each guest, namely, two plates, a large and small fork and knives, and dessert-spoon. A folded napkin, concealing the bread, should be placed upon the plate of each guest.

The dishes served for luncheons are the remains of cold meat neatly trimmed and garnished ; cold game, hashed or plain ; curries, minced meats, cold pies, savoury, fruit, or plain ; plainly-cooked cutlets, steaks, and chops ; omelettes, bacon, eggs, devilled and grilled bones, potatoes, sweetmeats, butter, pickles, cheese, salad. In fact, almost anything does for lunch, whether of fish flesh, fowl, pastry, fruit, or vegetables. Ale, stout and sherry are generally served, with biscuits and ripe fruit.

**Breakfasts.**—The table, of course, as for every meal, should be covered with a clean white cloth ; the cups and saucers arranged at one end, if for tea, and at both ends if for tea and coffee ; or the coffee-cups and saucers may be arranged at the right-hand side of one end of the table, and the tea-cups and saucers at the left ; the tea-pot and coffee-pot occupying the space between in front, and the urn that at the back. The slop-bason and milk-jug should be placed to the left, and the cream and hot milk to the right. The remainder of the table should be occupied in the centre by the various dishes to be partaken of, while at the sides must be ranged a plate for meat, &c., and a smaller one for toast, rolls, &c., with a knife and fork for each person, the carving-knife and fork being placed point to handle ; the bread-and-butter knives to the right of their respective dishes, which should occupy the centre part, and spoons in front of the hot dishes with gravy. Salt-cellars should occupy the four corners, and, if required, the cruets should be placed in the centre of the table. Dry toast should never be prepared longer than five minutes before serving, as it becomes tough, and the buttered, soppy and greasy, if too long prepared. Hot rolls should be brought to table covered with a napkin. The dishes usually set upon the table are selected from hot, cold, and cured meats.

**To Remove Black Stains from the Skin.**—Ladies that wear mourning in warm weather are much incommoded by the blackness it leaves on the arms and neck, and which cannot easily be removed, even by soap and warm water. To have a remedy always at hand, keep in the drawer of your wash-stand a box, containing a mixture in equal portions of cream of tartar, and oxalic acid (POISON). Get at a druggist's half an ounce of each of these articles, and have them mixed and pounded together in a mortar. Put some of this mixture in a cup that has a cover, and if, afterwards, it becomes hard, you may keep it slightly moistened with water. Be sure that it is always closely covered. To use it wet the black stains on your skin with the corner of a towel, dipped in warm water; then, with your finger, rub on a little of the mixture. Then immediately wash it off with water, and afterwards with soap and water, and the black stains will be visible no longer. This mixture will also remove ink, and all other stains from the fingers, and from *white* clothes. It is more speedy in its effects if applied with warm water. No lady should be without this mixture, but care must be taken to keep it out of the way of young children, as, if swallowed, it is poisonous.

**Packing Household Articles.**—In packing for the removal of a family to a distant place, let all the trunks and boxes be numbered, and the numbers put down in a book; let some one who overlooks the whole of the packing, set down every article, denoting the exact box or trunk in which it is placed, and the order in which the things are put in, beginning with those at the bottom. By this means, after arriving at the place of destination, you will know, by consulting your book, where to find whatever you want, and which of the boxes it will be best to open first. Also, in a long sea-voyage, if there is occasion to have a trunk brought from the hold to get out of it any particular article, your book will tell exactly in which of your trunks that article is. For want of such an inventory, we have seen, in crossing the Atlantic, three or four trunks brought up belonging to one family, opened, and searched, before the right one could be found.

**Ice Cream.**—Put the cream into a broad pan; then stir in the sugar by degrees, and when all is well mixed, strain it through a sieve. Put it into a tin that has a close cover, and set it in a tub. Fill the tub with ice broken into very small pieces, and strew among the ice a large quantity of salt, taking care that none of the salt gets into the cream. Scrape the cream down with a spoon as it freezes round the edges of the tin. While the cream is freezing, stir in gradually the lemon-juice, or the juice of a pint of mashed strawberries or raspberries. When it is all frozen, dip the tin into lukewarm water; take out the cream, and fill your glasses, but not till a few minutes before you want to use it, as it will very soon melt. You may heighten the colour of the red fruit by a little cochineal. If you wish to have it in moulds, put the cream into them as soon as it has frozen in the tin. Set the moulds in a tub of ice and salt. Just before you want to use the cream, take the mould out of the tub, wipe or wash the salt carefully from the outside, dip the moulds in lukewarm water, and turn out the cream. You may flavour a quart of ice cream with two ounces of sweet almonds and one ounce of bitter almonds, blanched and beaten in a mortar with a little rose water to a smooth paste. Stir in the almonds gradually while the cream is freezing.

**Rules for Making Cakes and Pastry.**—In making cakes or pastry, always commence by weighing out the ingredients, sifting the flour, pounding and sifting the sugar and spice, preparing the fruit, and washing the butter. Loaf sugar can be powdered by pounding it in a large mortar, or by rolling it on a paste-board with a rolling-pin. It should be made very fine, and always sifted. All sorts of spice should be pounded in a mortar, except nutmeg, which it is better to grate  If spice is wanted in large quantities, it may be ground in a mill.  The butter should always be fresh and good in quality, and it should be washed in cold water before using it, and then made into hard lumps with your hands, squeezing the water well out.  If the butter and sugar are to be stirred together, always do that before the eggs are beaten, as, unless they are kept too warm, the butter and sugar will not be injured by standing awhile. For stirring them nothing is so convenient as a round hard stick, about a foot and a half long, and somewhat flattened at one end.  The eggs should not be beaten till all the other ingredients are ready, as they will fall very soon.  If the whites and yolks are to be beaten separately, beat the whites first, as they will stand longer.  Eggs should be beaten in a broad shallow pan, spreading wide at the top.  Butter and sugar should be stirred in a deep pan with straight sides.  Break every egg by itself, in a saucer, before you put it into the pan, that in case there should be any bad ones, they may not spoil the others.  Eggs are beaten most expeditiously with whisks.  A small quantity of white of egg may be beaten with a knife, or a three-pronged fork.

**Monthly List of Food in Season.** —JANUARY.—*Meats.*—Beef, veal, mutton, pork, house-lamb.

*Game and Poultry.*—Pheasants, partridges, woodcocks, snipes, turkeys, rabbits, hares, pullets, capons, fowls and pigeons.

*Fish.*—Tench, carp, sturgeon, skate, turbot, whitings, flounders, oysters, lobsters, prawns, crabs, cray-fish, thornback, flounders, perch and smelts.

*Vegetables.*—Sprouts, sorrel, cabbage, spinach, endive, turnips, brocoli, celery, beet-root, potatoes, turnips, parsnips, shalots, lettuces, cresses, cucumbers, scorzanera, and asparagus ; mushrooms throughout the year.

*Fruits.*—Apples, pears, nuts, grapes, medlars and walnuts.

FEBRUARY and MARCH.—All meats, poultry, and game, with the addition of ducklings and chickens, as in January.

*Fish.*—Same as preceding month, excepting cod, which goes out till July.

*Vegetables.*—Same as January, with the addition of kidney beans.

*Fruits.*—Apples and pears, and forced strawberries.

APRIL, MAY, and JUNE.—*Meats.*— Beef, mutton, veal, lamb, with the addition of venison in June.

*Poultry.*—Fowls, pullets, chickens, rabbits, leverets, pigeons, and ducklings.

*Vegetables* as before, only in May early potatoes, peas, French beans, radishes, early cabbages, carrots and turnips, cauliflowers, artichokes, asparagus, and all kinds of salad, but this is forced.

*Fruits.*—In June, strawberries, cherries, melons, apricots, currants and gooseberries.

*Fish.*—Carp, soles, tench, smelts, eels, trout, turbot, lobsters, chub, salmon, herrings, mackerel, crabs, prawns, and shrimps.

JULY, AUGUST, and SEPTEMBER.— *Meats.*—These are the same as the preceding months, except pork, which commences in September.

*Poultry.*—Fowls, chickens, pullets, rabbits, pigeons, and green geese, leverets, poults, turkeys, the two former months ; geese in September.

*Fish.*—Cod, flounders, haddocks, mullet, thornback, pike, carp, eels ; mackerel in July.

*Vegetables.*—All as the past months ; peas and beans.

*Fruits.*—Strawberries, plums of all kinds, gooseberries, cherries, apricots, raspberries, damsons, red and white currants, pears, apples, peaches, grapes, and nectarines.

OCTOBER.—*Meats* do not differ ; this is the month for prime venison.

*Poultry and Game.*—Fowls of all kinds as the former months, partridges, larks, pheasants, hares, wild ducks, teal, snipes, widgeon, and grouse.

NOVEMBER.—*Meats.*—Beef, mutton, veal, pork, house lamb and venison.

All other foods same as the last month.

DECEMBER.—*Meats* as in October.

*Poultry and Game.*—Pheasants, geese, turkeys, pullets, pigeons, pullets, larks, woodcocks, snipes, sea-fowls, Guinea fowls, wild ducks, widgeon, grouse, capons, fowls, rabbits, and hares.

*Vegetables* same as last month.

*Fish.*—Carp, sturgeon, soles, gudgeon, eels, shell fish of all kinds, dories and turbot.

**Saline Drinks.**—These wholesome and pleasant summer drinks now enter largely into domestic medicine, and are found to be no unimportant remedies in cholera, diarrhœa, fevers, gout, bile, heartburn, exhaustion, blotches on the face, and various other diseases arising from altered conditions of the blood. Hence the cause of saline drinks having become so popular. They partake of the qualities of salt, which is the chief constituent of the blood and the body generally, and we find that where salt is deficient in the system, the digestive powers are weakened, and the general tone of the system is impaired. To the condition of the blood may be traced both health and disease. "The life of the flesh is in the blood," we read in Leviticus. Now if upwards of half of the composition of the vital fluid is salt, how important must it be that due supplies of this ingredient should be made to the body for the waste of it that takes place through the functions of the skin and kidneys. Hence the demand that has sprung up for the "Pyretic Saline," which of all others can be recommended for those numerous ailments already referred to, as well as the *ennui* and depression that the heat of summer and an undue amount of electric atmosphere, afflicts us with. We can speak freely of the Pyretic Saline, for we daily are made to feel its refreshing and invigorating power as a dinner beverage. Besides its great curative qualities, and a refreshing summer drink for the fevered and thirsty, we have found it an important agent in preventing disease. We are no advocates for "every man becoming his own doctor," but for the treatment of many of those every-day ailments we are confident that the Pyretic Saline will be found adequate to the occasion.

**Origin of the Forget-me-not.**—The popular tradition which tells how the name came to be applied to the plant which now bears it throughout Europe is not generally known. It is said that a knight and a lady were walking by the side of the Danube, interchanging vows of devotion and affection, when the latter saw on the other side of the stream the bright blue flowers of the myosotis, and expressed a desire for them. The knight, eager to gratify her, plunged into the river, and, reaching the opposite bank, gathered a bunch of flowers. On his return, however, the current proved too strong for him, and, after many efforts to reach the land, he was borne away. With a last effort he flung the fatal blossoms upon the bank, exclaiming as he did so, "Forget-me-not!"

And the lady fair of the knight so true
  Still remembered his hapless lot ;
And she cherished the flower of brilliant
    hue,
And she braided her hair with the blossoms blue,
    And she called it "Forget-me-not."

**Chemistry of the Kettle.**—A kettle is an important and interesting instrument, whether it be an every-day, ugly, black, kitchen kettle, or a bright-lidded copper kettle, or a highly-polished electro-plate or silver kettle for the drawing-room—whichever of the three it may happen to be, experience has taught us to follow the true laws of natural philosophy in their constitution, their shape, and even in their mode of being cleaned.

A heated body throws off or radiates

heat in straight lines, in the same way that the flame of a lamp throws off or radiates light. Those substances which reflect *light* best, radiate and absorb *heat* the worst. Therefore, highly-polished vessels retain their heat the longest.

The kitchen kettle, black and dingy, is always on the hob and continually absorbing heat. It is, therefore, constantly ready to be raised to the boiling point at a moment's notice.

The copper parlour-kettle is always bright on the lid and front part ; but mark—it is never cleaned underneath, nor on the sides, where the soot is deposited. By this means the parts turned towards the fire absorb heat, while the parts turned from it retain the heat which the others gain.

The silver drawing-room kettle presents a highly-reflecting surface all over, since by that means it retains the heat by preventing radiation.

For the same reasons, a bright metal teapot is used where three or four people take tea together ; but old cottagers or people living alone use cosy little black teapots, which they set upon the hob. In both cases the laws of natural philosophy are carried out.

**Breaking Glass to any required Figure.**—Make a small notch by means of a file on the edge of a piece of glass, trace with French chalk the figure required, then make the end of a tobacco-pipe, or the end of a rod of iron of the same size, red-hot : apply the hot iron to the notch, and draw it slowly along the tracing on the glass ; a crack will follow the direction of the iron, and the pieces of glass may be separated.

**Glossy Starch.**—Put about two ounces of white gum-arabic powder into a pitcher, and pour on the same a pint of boiling water, according to the degree of strength you desire, and then, having covered it, let it stand all night. In the morning pour it carefully from the dregs into a clear bottle, and keep it for use. A tablespoonful of gum-water stirred into a pint of starch that has been made in the usual manner, will give black or printed lawns a look of newness, when nothing else can restore them after washing. When much diluted, it is also good for thin white muslin and bobinet.

**To Clean Silk.**—White silk is best cleaned by dissolving curd-soap in water as hot as the hand can bear, and passing the silk through and through, handling it gently, and rubbing any spots till they disappear. The silks should then be rinsed in luke-warm water, and stretched by pins to dry. Flowered white silk is best cleaned by bread crumbs rubbed on by the hands. Black silk is best cleaned by some ox-gall, put into boiling water ; the silk should be laid out on a table, and both sides sponged with the gall-liquor, then rinsed with clear water. A very little gum-arabic or gelatine may be dissolved in water, and passed over the wrong side of the silk, which should then be stretched out on pins to dry.

**Origin of the Word " Husband."** —The word " husband " is derived from the Anglo-Saxon words " hus " and " bond," which signify " the bond of the house ;" and it was anciently spelled " house-bond," and continued to be thus spelt in some editions of the Scriptures after the introduction of printing. A husband then is a house-bond ; the bond of a house ; that which engirdles the family into the union of strength, and the oneness of love. Wife and children, and the " stranger that is within thy gates "—all their interests and all their happiness—are encircled in the house-bond's embrace, the objects of his protection and of his special care.

**Muffling the Throat.**—What is the best mode for protecting the throat from colds where a person is very susceptible of them ? The common way of protecting the throat is to bundle and wrap it up closely, thus overheating and rendering it tender and sensitive, and more liable to colds and inflammation than before. This practice is all wrong, and results in much evil. Especially is this the case with children ; and when, in addition to muffling the throat, the extremities are insufficiently clad, as is often the case, the best possible conditions are presented for the production of sore throats, coughs, croup, and all kinds of throat affections. If the neck is kept overheated a portion of the time, when it is exposed some form of disarrangement of the throat will be apt to occur. The rule in regard to clothing the neck should be to keep it as cool as comfort will allow. In doing so you will suffer much less from throat ailment than if you are always fearful of having a little cold air come in contact with your neck. Those who have been accustomed to the muffling of the throat should be careful to leave off gradually, and not all at once.

**To Restore Colours Taken Out by Acids.**—Hartshorn rubbed on a silk or woollen garment will restore the colour without injuring it. Spirits of turpentine is good to take grease or drops of paint out of cloth ; apply it till the paint can be scraped off. Rub French chalk or magnesia on silk or ribbon that has been greased, and hold near the fire ; this will absorb the grease so that it may be brushed off.

**To Settle Coffee and Secure its Aroma.**—The following method will be found an excellent one for these purposes : For a pound of coffee take an egg and beat it well. When the coffee is nicely browned, and cool enough not to cook the egg, pour the egg over it, stirring it until every kernel is coated with a varnish, and let it stand a few minutes till it dries. This will prevent the escape of all aroma. It is not affected by moisture, and the egg helps the coffee to settle when it is ground and steeped.

**A Parlour Ornament.**—Suspend an acorn by a thread so as to nearly touch the water in any glass vessel, set it upon the mantel, and let it remain there for two months, without being interfered with, except to supply fresh water, and the acorn will burst, and as it throws a root down into the water, a sprout or stem will be sent upward, throwing out beautiful green leaves, thus giving you an oak tree in full health within your parlour.

**Onion Sauce.**—Peel a dozen onions, and put them in a little cold water to whiten ; let them remain about twenty minutes ; then put them into a saucepan, cover them with water, and boil them well ; if the onions are very strong, change the water ; they will require about an hour to boil. When tender, drain them thoroughly and rub them through a sieve. Make a pint of melted butter as follows :—A dessert-spoonful of flour, two ounces of butter, three quarters of a pint of milk ; mix and stir it until it boils ; add the onions, and stir till the sauce simmers, when it is quite ready for the table.

**To Work Devices in Hair.**—This is the most difficult branch in weaving or plaiting hair ornaments. No small degree of artistic taste is requisite to ensure success. Landscapes require as fine shading, and as delicate touches, as when drawn with the pencil. Patience, lightness of hand, good eyesight, and some knowledge of the principles of drawing, are the attributes most likely to conduce to success ; but practice, judgment, and perseverance will alone produce perfection.

It is very difficult, too, to give verbal instructions for this branch of hairwork, which is eminently artistic, and not mechanical. However, we will endeavour to lay down some fundamental directions, which, we trust, the taste of our readers will enable them to carry into practice, and which will guide them towards achieving skill in the art.

Hair of any length above an inch and a half may be used for devices.

The first article we require for this work is ivory, such as is used by miniature painters ; this can be obtained at any ivory-turners ; it must be polished, of a good colour, and flat and even, not warped. Next a clear solution of gumdragon, of about the consistence of cream, must be prepared by soaking a piece of this gum, of about the size of a nut, in three parts of a wine-glassful of cold water ; the gum will take six or eight hours to dissolve.

For implements, a fine-pointed, sharp pair of small scissors, a keen-edged penknife, a palette and ivory knife, one or two fine camel-hair pencils, another with fuller and firmer hair, a hard black-lead pencil, some thread, and a long fine-pointed steel pin, with a small smooth head, are all that will be needed.

There are three preparations of hair used for devices—the *curled*, the *waved, or rippled.* and the *ribbon* hair.

For the *curled* preparation, take a small tress, measuring not less than three inches in length ; arrange all the hairs evenly at one end, and tie them. Damp it, curl it closely as for a " flat-curl," put it in paper, and then set it to press under an iron sufficiently warm to thoroughly dry it without scorching, or rendering it harsh ; put it aside for use in a book. This preparation is chiefly used for feathers.

The *waved* hair is prepared by plaiting hair not less than two inches in length in fine plaits, damping it, enveloping it in paper, and pressing it as we have just directed. When required for use, the plait must be carefully and patiently picked out with a pin, and the hair will be found to be rippled in the manner required. Or, if a larger wave is needed, the hair may be damped, and wound tightly in and out a fine hair-pin, and dried as before. These preparations are chiefly adapted to trees, or to the touches indicating grass, or turf, or the ground.

The *ribbon* hair is formed by taking a tress, not too thick, and measuring three or more inches, and, having previously arranged all the hairs evenly, tying it at one end. Then a few drops of the gum-water must be let fall on the palette, so as to form a straight line ; on this the hair is to be laid down, and held in its place by the tied end, and then smoothed out with the ivory knife in one direction, namely, from the tied end, towards the opposite extremity, until it assumes the form of a flat rib-

bon, or united surface of hair, semi-transparent, and without divisions or interstices. Enough of the gum-water should be used fairly to moisten the hair and unite it, but no more. It must be left on the palette until quite dry, and then carefully raised by means of the tied end, and the edge of a penknife. If it comes off without splitting, it is fit for use ; should it split it must again be moistened with gum, and smoothed out as before. When not required for immediate use, it should be put into a book, for hair is so susceptible of the action of the atmosphere, that it does not do to expose it to those influ-ences.

From this preparation, leaves, petals, or flowers, corns of a wheat-ear, and such like, are cut out, either with the scissors, or by laying the hair on the palette and using the penknife ; and when the ribbon is brittle this latter mode is to be preferred. At first it will be best to cut out the requisite portions from patterns previously prepared ; but after awhile skill and practice will enable it to be done by the eye.

Besides the preparations of hair which we have thus enumerated, it will always be necessary to have an unprepared tress of hair, tied at both ends, to keep it smooth, as from this the hairs for stems, outlines, shading, tendrils, &c., will have to be drawn as they are required.

The device which is intended to be worked, must be traced on the ivory with a hard, fine-pointed pencil. We will suppose that the device to be a tomb with a willow tree drooping over it, and a group of trees and the sky at the back of the picture to be reproduced on the ivory. For this the *ribbon* hair, the *rippled* hair, and some unprepared hair, will be needed ; also a piece of ivory. and a thickish solution of gum-dragon. For the tree stem, or trunk, about twenty hairs must be drawn from the tress, and passed between the finger and thumb after they have been moistened with gum-water : the ends must be cut to shape on the ivory with the penknife. The foliage of the tree is composed of the rippled hair.

We will, however, commence with the tomb. With a fine camel-hair pencil, moistened in gum-water, go over the outlines ; then take two or three hairs from the tress, and passing them between a moistened thumb and finger, lay them down on the outline, cutting off the ends with the point of the penknife, arranging them with the point of the pin, and passing the head of the pin over to smooth and fix them there. With these hairs outline and shade the tomb. Then, for the group of trees at back and the sky, gum the outlines as before, and all the ivory there that is to be worked on ; take some twenty or more hairs from the tress, press their extremities down on the cloud lines, and let them cover that spot, and then shade them out with the point of the pin, as one would throw in pencil shading. Then lay the tress down on the upright trees in the background, and with the penknife cut off the short lengths requisite to form all those up-strokes, and afterwards arrange them all evenly with the pin's point. Make a stem by passing four or six hairs between the thumb and finger, moistened with gum, and press it into its place with the head of the pin, cutting off any superfluous length. Now take the willow tree in front, drooping over the tomb, and having gummed all that portion of the ivory, lay down the trunk, made as above directed, and then form the foliage with *rippled* hair, shading and arranging it by means of the point of the pin, and the larger and firmer brush before described. If reeds and flowers are introduced into the device, the former are made like the stems, and cut into shape with the knife, and the small flowers are cut out from *ribbon* hair, and laid on the gummed surface.

For groups of flowers, the leaves, petals, &c., must first be cut out ; and then—the ivory having been outlined—the spray we intend to work first must be gummed, and each leaf raised separately with the tip of a moist camel-hair pencil, and brought to its place, adjusted there with the point of the pin, and then pressed down with its head. When all the leaves are placed, the stem must be made as above directed, and laid down so as to cover the lower extremities of the leaves, and make them appear to spring from it.

For most flowers, a circle of thread, varying in size from a pin's head to a fourpenny piece, must be gummed on, and the centre of it moistened with gum, and then the petals of the flower made to spring from the centre, and rest on that thread. For double flowers, a second and smaller circle of thread is put in after the first row of petals have been fixed in their places and are dry.

It is always advisable to wait until one portion of the work is dry, before a second portion, or one that overlaps it, is added.

Wheat-ears are composed of corns cut either separately, or in a single piece, from *ribbon* hair, and with single hairs projecting between each corn.

Feathers are made by gumming a portion of the surface of one side of the feather, and laying an end of *curled* hair down on it, and cutting off the tress close to the stem of the feather ; and then with pin and large brush, arranging the bit laid on gracefully and naturally. This is to be repeated until the whole feathery portion on either side is covered. The stem is then made in the same way as flower stems, and laid on so as to cover the ends : and the bands, or ribbons, formed in like manner, and adjusted to their places.

Devices must, of course, always be protected by glass or crystal, as their delicate structure will admit of no rough usage.

**How to Make Wool Flowers.**—There are several ways of making wool flowers, but the one we are about to describe is to be commended for its simplicity and its charming effect. The materials required are wooden or bone meshes of various sizes, single Berlin wool of various colours, and a reel of fine flower, with a skein of fine white

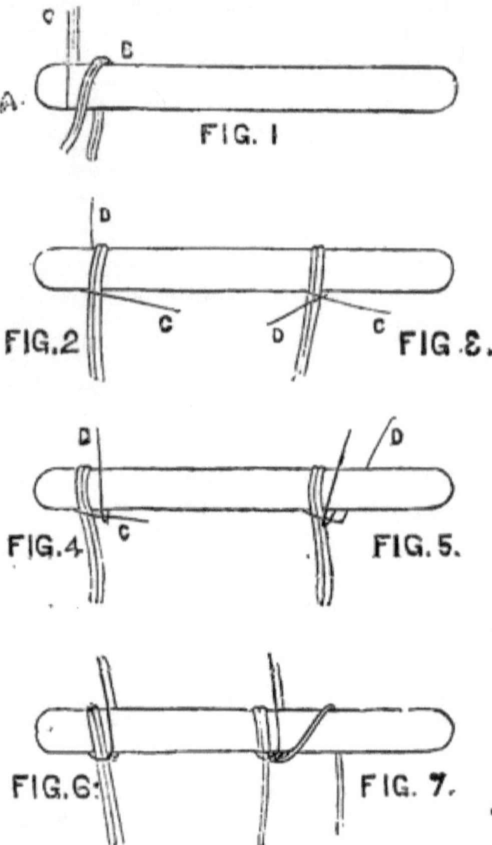


silk. For the moss a pair of steel knitting needles of moderate size.

We will commence by describing a dahlia. Take an inch mesh, cut off about six inches of wire, and place it across the mesh, as shown at A in Fig. 1. Take the wool double, and fold it across the mesh the reverse way, at B. Draw it down tight and close to the wire, holding the hole at the lower end of the mesh by the thumb and finger of the left hand. Then take the end of wire C, Fig. 1, and bring it down across the wool, as shown at C, Fig. 2, keeping it under the thumb and finger. Then take the end D, Fig. 2, and place it like D, Fig. 3. The end D is under the end C. Pull them into as close a tie and as close to the mesh as possible. Take the end C in Fig. 4, and carry it behind the mesh as D in Fig. 5, pulling it up straight and tight, like Fig. 6. Then take the double end of wool and twist it round the mesh, like Fig. 7, drawing the loop close to the previous one. Work this with the wire in the same way. The number of loops required may vary with the size of the flower ; but fifty is a good number. When these are completed slip them off the mesh, and with white silk sew the tops of every two together. Place the silk twice round with the needle, tie the ends together, and cut them off short. A section of this is shown in Fig. 8. Then curl the work into a small

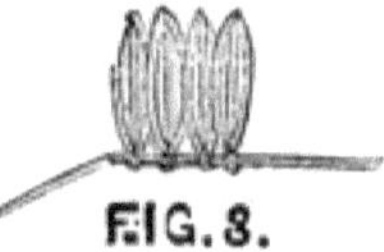

FIG. 8.

circle scarcely the size of a threepenny piece (Fig. 9), and go on winding two more rows behind this to form the re-

FIG. 9.

semblance of a flower, Fig. 13. Cut off the superfluous wire. To make the centre, take a half-inch mesh, lay a wire among it from A to B, Fig. 10, and with

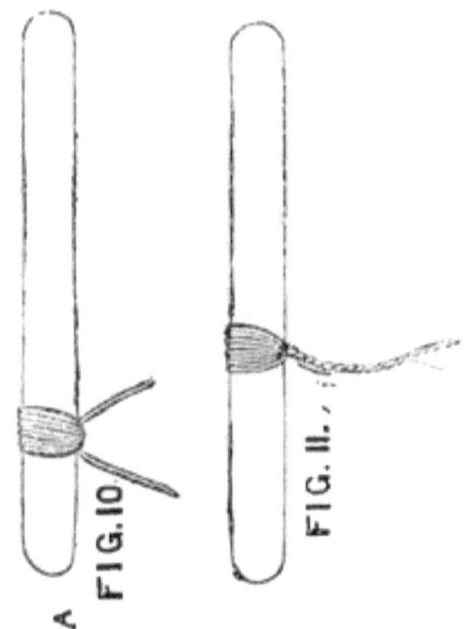



yellow wool double wind it over and over till you have a little thick, lumpy

bunch of it. Then pull down the ends of wire A, B, Fig. 10, draw them as tight as possible to the wool and twist the ends (see Fig. 11.) Now tie the wool a little way above the wire (see Fig. 12), and cut it straight across with

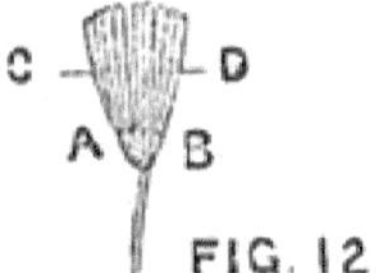



FIG. 12.

a pair of scissors at the dotted line A to B. Plant it in the hole of the dahlia seen in Fig 13, and tack it in place. The flower is now completed.

FIG. 13.

To Make the Moss.—Walker's Steel Knitting Needles No. 64. First wind the wool double, cast on thirty stitches, knit a quarter of a yard according to size required. When finished soak it in boiling water for five minutes, then stretch it whilst wet and dry quickly. Then cut it up the middle, and then fray it by using a smaller mesh, various colours, and forming a flower of fewer knots. For instance a crocus, violet, white, or yellow, can be made on the inch mesh, four knots or tufts to each flower and no heart. A heartsease, by two purple and three yellow knots, and so on. These smaller flowers need to be set in groups.

The moss is made of green wool of all shades, not too bright, plenty of dead sad greens, and a little antique brick dust should be mingled.

Take a round of cardboard, cover it with dark green calico, and ornament the edges about three inches deep. In this moss plant the dahlias of various colours, as one white, one pink, and two shades of red.

Many other flowers besides dahlias

can be made in this wool work, or green shaded wool may be used.

**Expand the Chest.**—Those ladies of leisure, or those who pursue sedentary, indoor employment, use their lungs but very little, breathe but little air into the chest, and thus, independent of position, contract a wretchedly small chest, and lay the foundation for the loss of health and beauty. All this can be perfectly obviated by a little attention to the manner of breathing. Remember that the lungs are like a bladder in their construction, and can be stretched open to double their size with perfect safety, giving a well-formed chest and a perfect immunity from consumption. The agent, and the only agent we require, is the common air we breathe; supposing, however, that no obstacle exists, such as tying it round with stays, or having the shoulders laying upon it. On arising from your bed in the morning, place yourself in an erect position, the shoulders thrown off the chest; now inhale all you can, so that no more can be got in; now hold your breath, and throw your arms off behind, holding your breath as long as possible. Repeat these long breaths as much as you please. Done in a cold room is much better, because the air is much denser, and will act much more powerfully in expanding the chest. Exercising the chest in this manner will enlarge the capability and size of the lungs.

**Gardening Maxims.**—Grow nothing carelessly; whatever is worth growing at all, is worth growing well.

Many kinds of garden-seeds lose their vegetative power if kept over the first year; be sure, therefore, to sow none but new seeds.

Melons, cucumbers, and other plants of the gourd tribe, form an exception to this rule: their seeds should not be sown until they are several years old, for they will then produce plants with scanty foliage, but abundant fruit.

The seeds of most weeds will retain their vegetative power for an unlimited number of years; take care, therefore, that all weeds are burnt, or at all events that they are not thrown on piles, from which they are liable to be brought back to the garden.

The first leaves which appear in the seed-bed (called the seed-leaves) are the sole nourishment of the young plant until it has acquired roots; therefore, if they be destroyed, or seriously injured, the young plant must die.

Seeds will not vegetate unless within the influence of moisture, air, and heat; be careful, therefore, not to sow your seeds too deep, or they will never come up.

Little good is obtained by saving your own seed from common annuals and vegetables: your ground is worth more to you for other purposes than the cost of the quantity of seed which you will require; besides which, you will have a better crop from seed raised in a different soil.

The roots of very young plants are not strong enough to bear removal; the best time for transplanting seedlings is when they have made from four to six proper leaves; for by this time the roots will be able to perform their proper functions.

Plants when exposed to the action of light, transmit moisture copiously through their leaves; transplanted seedlings, therefore, and cuttings, should be shaded from the sun till their roots are strong enough to supply moisture as rapidly as it is thrown off.

Roots require that air should be admitted to them: the surface of a clayey soil should therefore be disturbed as often as it begins to cake.

Let unoccupied ground be left in as rough a state as possible during the winter, in order that a large surface may be exposed to the frost, and the soil become thoroughly loosened.

Frost takes effect more thoroughly on roots that have been dug up than on those which have been left in the ground; therefore, either give your store roots complete protection, or let them stay in the ground.

All plants absorb from the ground

different juices : a constant variation of crops is therefore indispensable

Leaves absorb and give out moisture, and inhale and exhale air ; they are consequently the most important organs of a plant, and, as before observed, if they are destroyed or injured the whole plant suffers.

The pores in the leaves of the plants, by which they transmit moisture and air, are exceedingly minute, and liable to be choked by exposure to dust, and especially soot ; delicate plants should therefore be placed out of the reach of smoke, and if their leaves became soiled they should be washed.

The branches and leaves of plants rarely touch one another while in a growing state ; learn from this not to crowd plants too much in your beds ; air and light are as necessary to them as earth and water.

The throwing off of its leaves by a newly-planted cutting is a sign that growth has commenced ; on the contrary, when leaves wither on the stem, it is a sign that the plant has not strength to perform the natural functions of throwing them off.

When shrubs produce an abundance of foliage but no flowers, either move them to a poorer soil, or cut through some of the principal roots.

Dry east winds are injurious, by absorbing moisture from the leaves of plants more rapidly than they are prepared to give it out ; weather of this kind requires to be guarded against more than the severest frost.

If a grass-plot becomes overrun with moss, manure the surface, and the grass will gain strength so as to overcome the intruder.

In all cases of pruning, cut towards you, beginning a little below a bud, but on the opposite side, and ending just above the bud ; by this means the wood will be kept alive by the bud, and no water will be able to settle and rot on it.

Leaves shaded from the light do not acquire depth of colour or strength of flavour ; gardeners take advantage of this fact, tying up lettuces and earthing celery, that they may be white and mild.

Light is necessary to flowers, that they may acquire their proper hues ; therefore, when kept in rooms, their place should be as near as possible to the window.

All plants have a season of rest ; discover what season is peculiar to each, and choose that season for transplanting.

Plants are in their most active state of growth while in flower ; avoid transplanting them at this period, for in all probability they will suffer from the check.

On the contrary, choose this period in preference to any other, for taking cuttings, as they are then most active in forming roots.

Plants when in bloom have all their juices in the most perfect state ; choose, therefore, the period of their beginning to flower for cutting all aromatic and medicinal herbs.

Profuse flowering soon exhausts the strength of plants ; therefore remove flower-buds before they expand from all newly-rooted cuttings and sickly plants.

No plants can bear sudden contrasts of temperature, therefore bring nothing direct from the hot-house to the open air ; warm weather even should be chosen for bringing out plants from a greenhouse.

Remove all dead flowers from perennials, unless you wish to save seed ; the plants will thus be prevented from exhausting themselves.

To procure a succession of roses, prune down to three eyes on all the branches of some trees, as soon as the buds begin to expand ; defer the same operations with others, until the leaves are expanding ; in the former case the three buds will bear early flowers ; in the latter they will not begin to expand until the others are in full foliage, and will bloom proportionally later.

By choking the growth of plants, you throw strength into the flowers and fruit , this is the reason why gardeners nip off the terminal shoots of beans and other such vegetables ; on this principle, too, is founded the valuable art of pruning.

Generally speaking, the smaller the quantity of fruit on a tree, the higher the flavour : therefore, thin all fruits in moderation, but avoid excess ; a single gooseberry on a tree, or a single bunch of grapes on a vine, no matter how fine it may be, is a disgrace to good gardening.

Fruit should always be gathered in dry weather, and carefully placed in baskets, not dropped in ; the slightest bruise will cause fruit to decay.

All bulbs and tubers should be placed in the ground before they begin to shoot ; if suffered to form leaves and roots in the air, they waste strength.

Never remove the leaves from bulbs after flowering until they are quite dead ; as long as the leaves retain life, they are employed in preparing nourishment and transmitting it to the roots.

Vegetables that are valued for their juiciness and mild flavour should be grown quickly ; the reverse should be the case when a strong flavour is required.

Though rapid growth is desirable in succulent vegetables, this is not the case with most flowering shrubs, which form bushy and therefore handsomer plants when grown slowly.

Few plants thrive in stagnant water ; potted plants should, therefore, always have a thorough drainage of broken pots or brick, and should not be allowed to stand in deep saucers : they require but little water during the winter ; but when they begin to grow they should be liberally supplied.

Plants in pots are more liable to be injured by frost than plants in the ground which are exposed to the same temperature, because the fibres of their roots cling to the sides of the pots and are soon affected ; if they are kept out of doors during the winter, bury the pots in the ground.

All garden hedges should be kept clear of weeds, or when the latter run to seed, they will supply your garden with a stock against next season.

Finally, whether you sow seeds, water the young plants, or reap the produce, remember that you are dependent for all on God's blessing.

**Care of Carpets.**—When carpets are taken up, be careful in removing the tin tacks, so that the edges of the carpet are not torn, then roll up the carpets with the upper part inside, and send them away to be beaten. As soon as the carpets are removed, throw a few tea-leaves, not too wet, over the floor, sweep the room out, and afterwards wash the boards with a flannel, but be careful not to throw too much water about, as it is liable to injure the ceilings of the rooms below. While the floor is drying, beat the carpets, by hanging them over a stout line and beating them, first on one side and then on the other, with a long, smooth stick. After the carpet is beaten, it may be dragged over a lawn, or else brushed on both sides with a carpet broom. If faded or greasy in many parts, an ox-gall mixed with a pailful of cold water, or a little grated raw potato and cold water mixed together, and sponged over the places, and then wiped dry with soft cloths, will make them look clean and bright.

**Pot-Herbs.**—PARSLEY.—This herb is most in use, indeed in constant demand, both for garnishing and cookery. There are two sorts, the plain-leaved and the curly. The latter should always be preferred, being more beautiful, whether growing, or on the dish, and easily distinguished from the *Œthusa*, or fool's parsley—a species of hemlock, which is poisonous. The best mode of cultivation is by seed, sowing where it is to remain, any time between the beginning of March and the middle of June ; and if the stalks are cut down occasionally to prevent their seeding, it will last for several years. The seed, which should be buried about an inch deep, is a long time vegetating, the plant not appearing above ground for five or six weeks. Parsley may be cultivated by transplanting some young roots, the younger the better, watering and shading until they have taken root, and hold their heads up. Many pot-herbs are as good for use dry as green ; but this is not the case with parsley, which is infinitely better for all purposes when fresh. By covering it over with some loose haulm in the winter, the young leaves will be sheltered, and it might be gathered as wanted, all the year round.

MINT is best propagated by cuttings, or by dividing the roots of an old plant. February is the proper season for this ; but it may be done at any time in cloudy weather by shading and watering Those ladies who have conservatories or frames should keep a root or two of mint in pots, as it is in demand for lamb very early in the year, and before it puts forth its young leaves in the open ground.

SAGE.—This herb is indispensable in the stuffing of geese, ducks, or pork, so by all means nourish a few roots of it, which is propagated by planting the young shoots about the month of June. Take some robust shoots, about six inches long, remove all but the top leaves, and insert them in dippled holes, quite up to the leaves, squeezing the earth at the bottom of the shoot, but pressing it lightly towards the top. Shade and water, and when the plants spindle and show an inclination to flower, cut them down, so as to induce the growth of side shoots. Or you may divide the whole root, which is best affected in spring or autumn. If produced from seed, it must be sown in a rich border in April, thinned out when the plants are three inches high, and removed to its final station in the autumn or the following spring. Sage requires a dry soil and sheltered situation.

THYME will grow anywhere, but it prefers a dry poor soil ; if the ground is rich, the plant will become too luxuriant and lose its aromatic qualities. There are several varieties, that preferred for culinary purposes is the lemon-scented, it is also the handsomest in appearance. It is propagated by seeds or slips. Sowing should be performed from the middle of March to the middle of May ; slips should be set out in the spring. It may also be propagated by layers, like carnations. Although a perennial, it becomes stunted after two or three years, and to insure it in perfection, the seed should be sown annually.

There are other pot-herbs, such as marjoram, savory, tarragon, basil, &c., all which may be cultivated in small patches for general use. The sweet marjoram is produced from seeds and so is the basil ; but the common marjoram, savory, and tarragon, may be grown from cuttings or roots, like those already described.

Some corners should be devoted to fennel and horse-radish, esculents in constant use. The first is shy of moving, and unless the plants are very young, it can scarcely ever be done successfully after April.

**Little Presents.**—Life is made up of little things ; every now and then— and every now and then only—is it that we are startled from the usual routine of small events by some great thing happening to us. Small grains make great mountains, and there is a value in little things to which many large ones can never attain. How cheering to the downcast mind is even the bright smile, or the passing sunbeam, and just such cheerful visitants are little presents. We have a great value and regard for them ; it is not the worth of the thing, but the spirit that induced the gift, that we prize. We are all travellers along a road more or less weary to every one : life's journey presents us with many trials, crosses, and cares ; we need to drink at the fountain, for the way is dusty ; to rest by the roadside, for the journey is toilsome : and we like to receive the word of hearty cheer from the fellow-traveller who is bound for the same destination. Many a time have we been thus helped on by a little present. Listless and weary, we had risen from unrefreshing sleep, lo ! the postman's knock sent into our heart a sudden thrill ; if we were hard borne with the small harassings of genteel poverty, others were basking in a glowing sunshine and a sumptuous ease, and some gleam from that bright but distant world might come to us—a ray, yes ! in the shape of a little present. The letter is thick and bulky, we feel it, we wonder, then we break the seal ; something more than a letter springs to sight—some small but useful thing, and we have rejoiced over our little present. Nor is the pleasure evanescent —we feel, all day long, that something pleasant has happened to us ; we have been remembered by a distant friend, and little troubles sink before the rising of the beams shed by our little present.

Let us then give our little presents, called forth by the feeling of love and kindness. Long after we had given and forgotten the gifts, little presents have come up and looked at us again ; we had not remembered the queer old drawing, the work of our childhood ; or the little letter that accompanied it, full of all manner of good wishes ; the only marker, so badly worked that now we are ashamed of it ; yet there they meet us, between the leaves of that old Bible, utterly forgotten by the giver, but oh ! treasured by the recipient— treasured in the greatest treasury of all, the little gifts of love thought worthy of a place between those leaves. They look at us, they remind us of days long past, but surely they were links in a friendship which is not yet severed, some of the little things that yet abide, and, like the small seed, sinking into the ground, containing the germ of great results. We have never valued great and costly gifts as we have little presents. Once we were tempted to ridicule an ornament from its want of taste and fitness, we were stopped by the wearer's words—" It was the present of a friend !" the article at once assumed another aspect, it became the representation of a precious bond, one we take upon us too lightly, and throw off too easily—the bond of friendship.

As far as your means will permit,

give little presents. You will not always meet with a grateful return, never mind ! do you think you will ever repent of a good action ? Let them speak for you when you are absent, and if they do not call forth answering beams of love, and joy, and thankfulness, let them at least glow as the hot burning coals upon the heads of the ungrateful.

" Yes, I love you, little presents,
   In your small array ;
Stars of kindness, mildly beaming
   Light upon my way.

" Oh ! I value little presents,
   They have potent sway
Over care, and grief, and sorrow,
   Driving all away."

**The Art of Bird-Stuffing.**—Beginners should never attempt to stuff any bird smaller than a blackbird ; the larger the bird the easier it is to stuff. First put a small quantity of wool down the throat in order to prevent any moisture escaping from the stomach ; this is highly important, and must never be omitted ; then break the bones of the wings close to the body ; divide the feathers from the breast-bone to the vent ; divide the skin in like manner. Great care must be taken not to puncture the abdomen ; raise the skin with the point of a penknife until you can take hold of it with your finger and thumb ; hold the skin tight and press on the body with the knife as the skin parts from it, putting the knife farther under until you reach the thigh ; break the thigh-bone close to the top joint, and push it gently up until you can take hold of the flesh ; now take the bone that is attached to the leg and pull it gently out, turning the skin of the leg inside out : cut the flesh off close to the knee and skin as far down to the back as you can. Do the same with the other side of the bird ; if any wet escapes from the flesh, dry it up with fresh bran. With a small pair of scissors, put the skin on both sides out of your way as much as possible ; push the body up (the tail of the bird being held in your hand) ; cut through as close to the tail as possible (this is done inside the skin) ; then take the bird by the back-bone, and gently push the skin down by the thumb-nail till you come to the wings : take as much flesh from the wing joints as you can, and go on skinning till you reach the ears ; take hold of them close to the skull and pull them out. Take the eyes out, and be careful not to burst them, holding the skin with one thumb and finger, while you pull the eye out of the skin with the other ; after taking the eyes out, put as much cotton in the sockets as will nicely fill them. Skin down to the beak very gently, cut the neck away from the skull, and also a piece of the skull to take the brains out ; anoint the skin with arsenicated soap, put a little tow round the thigh bones to form the thigh, and gently turn the skin back again : if care has been taken, the loss of the body will make but little difference in the size of the bird. Get three wires, one as long again as the bird, the other two twice the length of the legs, file them sharp at one end, bend the blunt end of the long wire, put some tow on the bend and squeeze it tight to fasten it, then twist the tow until it is about the size of the body ; do it as tight as possible. Have some tow cut up small, get a strong wire, rough one point, and turn the other into a bow to hold in your hand ; take hold of some of the tow with the rough end, and push it up the neck ; this requires but a small portion of tow ; put some in the chest, and a little all over the inside of the skin. Put the body wire up the neck, and bring it out through the skull at the top of the head ; draw the body into the skin and be careful not to stretch the neck, then put the other wires through the centre of the feet up the legs, being careful not to break the skin ; put enough wire inside the skin to push into the body to fasten the legs : cut off a piece of the wire that has gone through the head, put it through the tail into the body (under

the tail, of course) ; open the eyelids, and put in the eyes (patience is required in young beginners to do this) ; mount the bird on a perch fastened to a small board, bend the legs so that it will seem to stand in a proper position ; be careful not to loosen the leg wires from the body, bring the feathers nicely together between the legs, bend the neck, and put the head in the shape you think proper, then run a pin or a piece of wire through the butt of the wing and into the body, to keep it in its proper place. Should the bird be out of shape in places, raise the skin gently with a needle, put the feathers as straight as you can, put a pin in the breast, back, and under each wing near to the top of the thigh, fasten the end of the cotton to one of the pins, and gently wind it round the bird from one pin to the other ; put up the bird when you see that it is right. You had better let the specimen dry of itself, then bake it, keep it free from dust, and it will dry in a fortnight. Spread the tail in a natural position, and when it is dry, unwind the cotton ; cut the pins close to the butt of the wing and the head ; take out the others, and the bird is finished.

This art, though somewhat unpleasant in its operations for fair fingers, is, when accomplished, an interesting parlour ornament, especially when it is a representation and a memento of some favourite pet.

**Electricity from a Black Cat.**—To receive the electrical shock from a black cat, place the left hand under the throat, with the middle finger or the thumb slightly pressing the bones of the animal's shoulder ; then, on gently passing the right hand along the back, sensible electric shocks will be felt in the left hand. Very distinct discharges may be obtained, too, by touching the tips of the ears after applying friction to the back of the cat. It will be hardly necessary to hint how requisite it is that a good understanding should exist between the experimenter and the cat.

**Pocket-Handkerchief.**—The component parts of this familiar term are four, namely, *pocket, hand, ker,* cur or cover, from *couvre; chief,* from *chef,* head; that is, pocket-hand-cover-head, or pocket-hand-head-cover. Hence the transitions that have taken place in the use of that article of dress; first worn on the head, then carried in the hand, and lastly in the pocket. The word *mouchoir* is not the translation of it, unless *de poche* be added; for the French have *mouchoir de tete, mouchoir de cou,* as well as *mouchoir de poche.* In fact *mouchoir* has, like the other, deviated from its original meaning. First confined to the use of the nose, as the verb *moucher* implies; it has passed from that organ to the head, from the head to the neck, and from the neck to the pocket.

**Illegal Marriages.**—A woman may not marry her grandfather; grandmother's husband; husband's grandfather; father's brother; mother's brother; father's sister's husband; mother's sister's husband; husband's father's brother; husband's mother's brother; father; step-father; husband's father; son; husband's son; daughter's husband; brother; husband's brother; sister's husband; son's son; daughter's son; son's daughter's husband; daughter's daughter's husband; husband's son's son; husband's daughter's son; brother's son; sister's son; brother's daughter's husband; sister's daughter's husband; husband's brother's son; husband's sister's son.

It may be observed in this long list of prohibited kindred marriages, there is no reference to such a relationship as that of cousins; therefore cousins in the first and nearest degree are permitted to marry without let or hindrance. Though the law is elaborate in its denunciations of marriages between certain parties concerning whom there can be neither physiological nor moral objection—a husband's brother, or a sister's husband—yet the law permits marriages between grandchildren of the same parents, who may be living evidences of undoubted blood-relationship, the union of which is almost universally repugnant to the moral sense, and believed to be physiologically pernicious.

**Divorce.**—In the event of a marriage being annulled by divorce, the parties so divorced cannot legally marry again until three months have elapsed after the absolute dissolution of the former marriage.

**Legal Modes of Marriage.**—Upon some one of the following modes only is marriage valid in England:—

1. BY BANNS.—The term "banns" applies to a series of public announcements in a church, giving notice of an intended marriage. Notice by one of the parties who have decided thus to be married must be given to the clergyman or the clerk of the church of the parish where the parties reside; or if the parties reside in different parishes, then notice must be given in each parish. There is no accredited form of notice of banns, as it is very rare that a written notice is required, the usual custom being for the parish clerk to enter in his book all particulars of the parties as they are told to him, and this entry in the official book of the church is held to be undoubted evidence of the notice.

On notice of banns being given, declaration must be made that there is no impediment to the marriage, nor any consent wanting to authorise the parties to contract marriage.

After seven days' notice, the clergyman of the parish is bound to publish the banns on the three successive Sundays after the second lesson of both morning and afternoon service.

Should the clergyman, however, receive notice from the parents or guardians of either of the contracting parties that they forbid the banns, the clergyman is then legally bound to abstain from publishing the banns.

Any person may, immediately after the publication of banns, protest against the marriage to the clergyman after the service, and if the protest can be legally sustained, the proceedings are put an end to.

Should there be no prohibition, after

the banns have been duly published the marriage may be solemnised at either of the churches where the banns were published, within three calendar months after such publication, but not elsewhere, nor after the end of the three months.

2. MARRIAGE BY LICENCE.—A marriage licence may be obtained from a surrogate, who is a bishop's representative for the purpose of granting marriage licences. Where there is only one church in a parish, the incumbent is usually a surrogate. Where there are more than one, certain of the incumbents are selected by the bishop to act as surrogates.

In the metropolitan district, marriage licences may be procured either of a local surrogate or in Doctor's Commons.

One of the parties about to be married must make application for a licence, and he or she will thereupon be required to make the following declaration :—

·January 1, 1874.

Diocese of London,

Appeared personally,

William Robinson, of the parish of Fulham, in the County of Middlesex, and prayed a licence for the solemnisation of matrimony in the parish church of Wandsworth, in the County of Surrey, between him and Mary Smith, of the parish of Fulham, in the County of Middlesex——and made oath that he believeth that there is no impediment of kindred or alliance, or of any other lawful cause, nor any suit commenced in any ecclesiastical court to bar or hinder the proceeding of the said marriage, according to the tenor of such licence

And he further made oath that she the said Mary Smith hath had her usual place of abode within the said parish of Fulham, for the space of fifteen days last past

(Signed)     WILLIAM ROBINSON.

Sworn before me :

[Signature of the surrogate.]

If either of the parties is under 21 years of age, then the declaration must affirm the consent of the parents or guardians of such parties.

False declarations, if known to both parties, has the effect of making the marriage void as against the children thereof, according to the strict letter of the law.

The practical effect of a marriage by licence is, that immediately after the declaration is made, the marriage may take place forthwith, or any legal time within three months afterwards, in the church or chapel specified in the licence, but not afterwards, nor elsewhere.

3. MARRIAGE BY SPECIAL LICENCE.—Special licences vary only from ordinary ones that they do not specify any particular church or place where the marriage is to take place, nor do they require the previous residence of either of the parties in any particular parish or district. Like the other licences, they are only available for the space of three months.

MARRIAGE BY CERTIFICATE OF A SUPERINTENDENT REGISTRAR.—Persons desirous of availing themselves of authority to marry by certificate, must conform to the following provisions :—

One of the persons must give notice to the superintendent registrar of the district in which they both reside ; or if they reside in separate districts, then one of the persons must give notice to the superintendent registrar of each district respectively.

[Printed forms of declaration for signature may be had of the registrar.]

The superintendent registrar is required officially to read such notice at the next meeting of the board of guardians, but his omission to do so in no wise affects the progress of the other proceedings or the validity of the marriage. Such notice must be entered in the notice book of the district, or in each district respectively, and a true copy placed conspicuously in the district office or offices. If not notified to the contrary, twenty one days after such notice has been so placed, the superintendent registrar will, when requested to do so by or on behalf of the party to whom the notice is given, issue a certificate, which certificate will be void unless the marriage be solemnised within three calendar months after the date of the entry of notice.

A registrar's certificate of notice of marriage may be used, and will effectually stand, instead of the publication of banns ; and the clergyman of the church or chapel designated is bound to marry the parties in like manner as after the publication of banns. Or a registrar's certificate of marriage is available for the purpose in any building registered under the Act, providing such building is duly entered and notified in the certificate.

Marriages in a registered building may be solemnised according to any form or ceremony which may be customary in such building for such occasions. But every marriage in a registered building must be in the presence of a registrar.

Marriages authorised by certificate or licence of any superintendent registrar may, if desired by the parties, be solemnised by the registrar in his office.

MARRIAGES OF JEWS AND QUAKERS. —When both of the parties are Jews or Quakers a certificate having been first duly obtained, the marriage may take place in any building, whether registered or not, or whether set apart for religious worship or not, and it is not compulsory that the solemnisation shall be between the hours of eight and twelve in the forenoon. All other marriages must be solemnised between those hours.

**Court Plaster.**—This useful article is very easily made, and as home-made plaster is better than what can be purchased, the process of making ought to be generally known. Soak bruised isinglass in a little warm water for twenty-four hours, then evaporate nearly all the water by gentle heat ; dissolve the residue in a little proof spirits of wine, and strain the whole through a piece of open linen. The strained mass should be a stiff jelly when cool. Now extend a piece of silk on a wooden frame, and fix it tight with tacks or pack-thread. Melt the jelly, and apply it to the silk, thinly and evenly, with a badger-hair brush. A second coating must be applied when the first has dried. When both are dry, cover the whole surface with coatings of balsam of Peru, applied in the same way. Court plaster thus made is very pliable, and seldom breaks.

**The Carat.**—Many people, especially the fair purchasers of jewellery, have speculated upon the precise meaning of the word " carat." It is an imaginary weight, that expresses the fineness of gold, or the proportions of pure gold in a mass of metal. Thus, an ounce of gold twenty-two carats fine, is gold of which twenty-two parts out of twenty-four are pure, the other two parts being silver, copper, or other metal. The weight of four grains, used by the jeweller in weighing precious stones and pearls, is sometimes called diamond-weight—the carat consisting of four nominal grains, a little lighter than four grains troy, or seventy-four and one-sixteenth carat grains being equal to seventy-two grains troy. The term of weighing carat derives its name from a bean, the fruit of an Abyssinian tree called kuara. The bean, from the time of its being gathered, varies very little in its weight, and seems to have been, from a very remote period, used as a weight for gold in Africa. In India, also, the bean is used as a weight for gems and pearls.

**Gall Soap.**—Gall soap, for the washing of fine silken cloths and ribbons, is prepared in the following manner :— In a vessel of copper one pound of cocoa-nut oil is heated to 60 degrees Fah., whereupon half-a-pound of caustic soda is added, with constant stirring. In another vessel half-a-pound of white Venetian turpentine is heated, and when quite hot stirred into the copper kettle. This kettle is then covered and left for four hours, being gently heated, after which the fire is increased until the contents are perfectly clear, whereupon one pound of ox-gall is added. After this enough of good, perfectly dry Castile soap is stirred into the mixture to cause the whole to yield but little under the pressure of the finger ; for which purpose from one to two pounds of soap are required for the above quality. After cooling, the soap is cut into pieces. It is excellent, and will not injure the finest colours.

**Hints to Convalescents.**—Convalescence is neither health nor disease, it is an intermediate state. Wasted energies are to be recruited, and the organs are to be prepared to encounter influences from which they have for a longer or a shorter time, been withdrawn—influences of society, friends, noise, heat, light, visits, cold, food, bodily labour, and mental toil.

Intellectual toil or exertion is to be avoided by convalescents, unless only in so far as it is advisable to afford distraction, as is the case frequently with hypochondriacs. But, as a general rule, its effects on the brain, and on associated organs, are too exciting, too disturbing, too apt to rekindle quenched irritations, and to produce relapses of departed diseases. It is a great advantage of watering-places, and other places of invalid resort, that the patient's affairs are left behind. The perfect calm of the passions is included in this advice. Moral emotions of an anxious or exciting character exercise a much more potent and baneful influence on the weak than on the strong.

To invalids who cannot bear much walking, riding is, of all exercises, the most beneficial. It brings into play the greatest number of muscles, and yields to the body the strongest concussions. But if possible, horse exercise should always be alternated with a corresponding amount of walking. In this way it is pre-eminently useful in all nervous, hypochondriacal, and dyspeptic affections. In certain diseases of the heart and lungs, gentle riding is an invaluable resource.

As epidemic influences are found from time to time to prevail, it is well to be provided with the means of defence, and to know their conditions of attack. Everything that materially deranges the health may become the occasion or exciting cause of the prevalent complaint. When the constitution has been deteriorated by any cause, especially by bad diet, by fatigue, by misery, by depression, then it is most liable to be impressed with the noxious influences. Hence the necessity of adopting every means of increasing vigour. A fit of passion, " catching cold," an overdose of physic, an indigestion, a fright, a wound, anxiety, are all causes of individual attacks of reigning epidemics, cholera, typhus, dysentery.

**The Effects of Different Atmospheres on the Health.**—Variation in the qualities of the air we breathe, is a fertile source of disease, and an efficacious means of cure. The effects of a hot and dry atmosphere are muscular weakness, copious perspirations, frequent thirst, disinclination for animal food, and a relish for vegetables, acid fruits, and cooling drinks ; weakened appetite and digestive powers , inaptitude for intellectual as well as bodily exertion ; sleepiness during day, and sleeplessness at night. It induces cerebral affections ; gastric, bilious, and intestinal diseases. It aggravates hysteria, epilepsy and hypochondriasis. It is unsuitable for the lymphatic, the scrofulous, and the rheumatic ; but adapted to dry and bilious temperaments.

A hot and humid atmosphere is still more unhealthy and debilitating than the last. Respiration is more difficult. The energy of the nervous and muscular systems is depressed. This state of the air is the precise condition most favourable to the decomposition of animal and vegetable substances, and to the uprising of putrescent emanations. Hence the prevalence, under these circumstances, of epidemic, intermittent, and typhoid fevers. It is uncongenial to the lymphatic temperament.

A cold and dry air is pre-eminently healthy. An abundant oxygen is supplied to the lungs ; muscular energy is augmented; the appetite is increased; digestion invigorated; perspiration is less. Its benefits, however, depend on sufficient exercise being taken to make the organs react energetically. On the other hand it is uncongenial to those who cannot take active exercise, as persons debilitated by age or sickness, those of lymphatic temperament, and new-born infants. The interior congestions, determined by cold inadequately resisted, predispose to inflammations and bæmorrhages.

A cold and moist atmosphere is very unhealthful It determines powerful abstraction of heat; repels perspiration; produces rheumatisms, inflammation of the mucous membranes of the lungs, and gastro-intestinal canal. The very strong and bilious are often benefited by this kind of weather.

**Cold Water Drinking.**—This fluid is the best adapted for the drink of mankind. It is indispensable to the existence of organic matter—water constituting seven-eighths of the entire weight of the body. The same proportion of the solid food we eat is pure water. Being free from all irritating, corrosive, or corruptible ingredients, it does not injure the most delicate structures which it permeates or saturates. It separates, attenuates, dissolves all other substances: as such it becomes the grand vehicle of nutrition—carrying into the circulation the new materials of growth or repair; while it is, at the same time, a menstruum to carry off the wasted, useless, or dead particles of the frame. It confers upon the tissues that elasticity, expansion, and movement, which their functions require. Hence it is manifest how much of this bland, limpid fluid is necessary for the wants of the economy—to repair the waste constantly taking place, and to replenish all the parts that would otherwise become dry and shrunk from want of moisture. Besides this, there is every reason to believe that, in the elaborate chemistry of the living body, it is in part decomposed—its elements form new combinations; and all go to carry

on the mysterious processes of life. Hence those who are dying of starvation, if they can procure water, protract existence.

The free drinking of cold water increases the appetite, improves digestion, braces the nerves, invigorates the muscles, hardens the entire frame, augments the animal spirits, clears the intellect, calms the passions.

Cold water on an empty stomach excites reaction; so that the blood is immediately determined to that organ in greater abundance, and with a more healthy circulation. The juices peculiar to it are secreted more largely. This reaction is communicated, by sympathy, to other parts of the body; all the secretions are increased. For the same reason, absorption is more rapid. The necessary result of this state of things is a keener sensation of hunger—a greater demand for, and ability to dispose of food. The change of matter is more rapid; waste and supply are more equable and proportionate. The used-up particles are duly carried out of the system. The repair of waste is more perfect. In short, the body is better nourished. The free drinking of cold water sometimes incommodes beginners. But it is only a temporary inconvenience, and passes off by perseverance.

**Alcoholic Beverages.**—All alcoholic drinks and fermented liquors, as well as medicinal stimulants of all kinds, should only be had recourse to on extremely rare occasions, and under circumstances of great exhaustion, when life appears sinking. They can never be taken with impunity in a state of health. The nutritious ingredients in any, of even the best, of the liquors in question, are almost an infinitesimal element compared with the noxious principle they contain. The temporary stimulus of organic activity, and the transient exhilaration of animal feeling they produce, is mistaken for the acquisition of strength and nourishment. To counsel alcoholic drinks to feeble suckling mothers, and dyspeptic invalids, is inexcusable. They may, indeed, temporarily counteract exhaustion, stimulate vascular action, and rouse torpid nervous energy—producing a glow in the stomach, or a draught in the bosom ; but they will fail to impart available nourishment. This counterfeit of strength is soon succeeded by increased weakness, and a more imperious demand for a repetition of the stimulant. The mischief does not rest here ; for, the ordinary dose failing to produce its wonted effect, a deeper and a deeper draught becomes necessary, and at last merges into a habit. In other cases, where the administration of wine or spirits is commonly supposed to be justifiable, in persons exhausted by inordinate fatigue, it is better to allow the system to wait and want, till an interval of repose gives time for the stomach to resume its activity, to utter the voice, and to take upon itself the supply, of the organic demands.

The greatest, and longest continued efforts, both of body and mind, are those made on simple diet, and unstimulating beverages.

**Vaccination Act.**—Since January, 1868, it is the duty of every registrar of births and deaths to give notice of the requirements of the law respecting vaccination to the person responsible for the charge of each infant in his district ; and the law *compels* vaccination, and the notice thereof should include the name and address of the public vaccinator appointed for the district. For purposes of the Vaccination Act, the persons who are responsible for the vaccination of a child are expressly defined, namely—the father (when living), if the child is legitimate : the mother, if the child is that of a widow or unmarried woman ; or the person authoritatively in charge of an orphan ; or the person in accidental charge of the child during a protracted absence of any of the aforesaid persons respectively

When the authorised person (whether the public vaccinator or not) to whom a child is submitted for vaccination is of opinion that the child is not in a fit state of health for the operation, he may give a certificate to that effect, extending the time for two months, which may be repeated as many times as the vaccinator may think desirable, and any such certificate absolves the holder thereof for the two months, but no longer.

**Pin-Money.**—When a marriage settlement of a large family estate is effected, it is upon trustees to the use of the husband, his heirs and assigns, until the marriage, and thenceforth subject to an annuity payable by the husband to the wife for her separate use. The annuity thus payable is what is popularly known as " pin-money " ; or, the provision of pin-money may be by means of a capital sum set apart by the husband or father, or other friend of the wife, and vested in a trustee or trustees, whereby the wife obtains periodical payments.

The real intention of pin-money is to secure the wife in the certainty of pocket-money, and the means wherewith to obtain clothing, and other personal requisites consistent with her social position, without placing her under the necessity of applying to her husband, or of relying upon his caprice.

The institution of pin-money is equivalent to saying, " you, the wife, shall not be reduced to the somewhat humiliating necessity of disclosing to your husband every want of a pound to keep in your pocket ; or of seeking his pleasure and obtaining his consent every time you want to go to the milliner's shop, or for a little charity ; but that you shall have so much, consistent with your husband's income, and your own dignity, which you shall retain apart from him and exempt from his control."

Arrears of pin-money, as a rule, cannot be recovered for more than a year back, unless the husband and wife are advisedly living apart ; but persistent claims for unpaid pin-money, if claimed each time within the year, are held to make the payment binding for any period of arrears.

A wife's unfaithfulness bars her claim to any arrears or future payment of pin-money ; but if the wife leaves the husband at his suggestion or with his consent, then the claim for pin-money remains good.

It is expressly decided that savings of pin-money are separate estate to all intents and purposes, and they may be willed as such.

If the wife suffers her husband systematically to pay for her clothing and personal requirements for any length of time, that is held to be a tacit relinquishment of pin-money, and it has been decided that in such a case it cannot be afterwards claimed, unless its payment has meanwhile been continued or resumed.

**Caution to Unmarried Ladies with Property.**—Eligible ladies with fortunes should refrain from appeals to mercenary suitors by a display or disclosure of their wealth, unless they are willing to part with that wealth ; because, if a lady communicates, or causes to be communicated, to her suitor the existence of her wealth, the communication will be an effectual bar to any secret settlement she may subsequently feel disposed to make prior to marriage , as, when a lady expressly makes known to her suitor the existence of her wealth, and afterwards sees occasion to settle it before her marriage, her husband may afterwards plead that the disclosure of the wealth was purposely made to him as an inducement to propose, and that the settlement is consequently an unqualified fraud.

[We are indebted to Beeton's Hand-Book of the Law Relating to Women and Children," for this paragraph, as well as those on " Pin-money," " Caution to Unmarried Ladies," and " Legal Modes of Marriage." To those of our readers who are desirous of further information on these and kindred subjects, we earnestly recommend this cheap and exhaustive volume.]

**Wakefulness after a Few Hours' Sleep.**—For the benefit of those persons who fall asleep perhaps soon after they get into bed, but wake some two or three hours afterwards, and cannot sleep again, is a condition which may in general be remedied by getting up and eating some bread-and-butter—thus engaging the nervous power in digestion and the nutritive processes, and returning afterwards to a cool bed. (

**Tea and Coffee.**—Dr. Searle observes—" The infusion of these grateful exhilarants in boiling water as ordinarily practised, in moderation there is no great objection to, provided they are not taken too hot or too frequently. They should in a general way be confined to the breakfast-table and to persons of an adult age. The young require no excitants of any kind ; milk to them is more suitable, abounding as it does in nourishment, which is a quality that neither tea nor coffee possesses. I have observed that tea or coffee in a general way should be confined to the breakfast-table, though a cup of one or the other may, without any great objection, be taken by most persons in the evening. I mean by this reservation to say, that I believe there are many who would sleep better, and enjoy much better health, were they not to do so. The exciting qualities of tea upon the nervous system are rendered very apparent by the sleepless nights induced to those unaccustomed to its use in the evening ; and coffee in most cases will produce the same effects. To persons, therefore, who are the subjects of any spasmodic or nervous affection, although sleeplessness may not be induced, they are nevertheless clearly prohibited. And to the dyspeptic—another large class of persons—the sugar, and hot water in which they are infused, render them equally objectionable ; whereas cold water, saturated as it is with atmospheric-air, possesses positively beneficial virtues in many such cases.

**Cautions to be Observed after Exposure to the Cold.**—The secretion eliminated by the skin is in general acid, as is evinced not only by the taste, but by the fact of its so often discharging or staining the colour of ladies' dresses, as may be observed about their arms. And this, without doubt, is the ordinary effect of a healthy condition or active state of the skin's function ; and if so, may well explain how gout, rheumatism, and some other affections, are so often developed by changes in the weather restraining the cutaneous function and this acid secretion from the system. Exposure to a cold or damp state of the atmosphere, or to partial currents of air, is very liable to check, torpify, or arrest this function, and should therefore be guardedly avoided, as well as all unnecessary exposure to cold. And it must be constantly borne in mind, that after any such exposure, warmth must be gradually and cautiously imparted, or inflammation or fever may become developed, as we see exemplified in the chilblains which succeed to cold in the extremities, or cough and catarrhal affections, which are of like inflammatory character, and are often induced in this way—by entering too warm a room on coming out of the external cold air ; the cutaneous surface, it will be remembered, extending along the air-passages into the lungs.

**Elder Sisters.**—Fortunate is a family that possesses an elder sister. The mother confides in her, the father takes pride in her ability to aid and cheer the household, and the younger ones lean upon her as a mother. By her counsels, her example, her influence, she may do quite as much as the parents to give tone to the family life. She is at once companion and counsellor for the junior members, since, separated by only a brief interval from the sports of childhood, she can sympathise easily with the little wants and griefs that fill the child's heart to overflowing, and show it how to compass its desires and forget its sorrows. A short girlhood is usually the allotment of the eldest daughter ; but this is made up to her in the long and delightful companionship she has with her mother, in the sense she is made to have of her own importance in the family, and in the unusual capacity she is obliged by the force of circumstances to acquire and display. It is in some respects unfortunate to be born an eldest daughter, to be kept at home from school on busy days to help mother, and be compelled to take care of the baby from year's end to year's end, to see the younger daughters free and easy, at liberty to come and go as they will, while she sighs in vain for the like freedom from restraint. The oldest daughter grows up adding her daily might of help to build up the family fortunes by saving servants' wages ; and when ease and competence smile on the family circle, her parents are apt to forget that she should enjoy the fruits of her labour and share equally with the younger children in the varied accomplishments that young ladies prize so highly.

**Origin of " Britannia."**—At Lethington Castle, in East Lothian, is a full-length portrait, by Sir Peter Lely, of Frances Theresa Stuart, Duchess of Lennox, the most admired beauty of the court of Charles II. It is stated by Grammont that the king caused this lady to be represented as the emblematical figure *Britannia* on the coin of the realm. The portrait represents a tall woman, with that voluptuous fulness of feature and person which seems, perhaps from the taste of the painter, to characterise the beauties of this reign. She leans upon the base of a pillar, and has an aspect of the utmost sweetness. Her luxuriant hair falls upon her fair white shoulders and her half-seen bosom. She is magnificently attired in purple, and a profuse robe of green, falling away from her shoulders, comes round her limbs, and draws the purple garment nearer to her figure.

**The Flesh-Brush.**—Persons whose circulation is languid, and system generally weak, do well to use the flesh-brush frequently, especially on coming out of the bath, when it is desirable that a healthy glow should be felt through the frame ; the friction, however, has been found too powerful for delicate skins, and it has given place to a better contrivance, the hair-glove.

SILK FAN, EMBROIDERED IN POINT RUSSE.

ORNAMENTAL FRAME FOR A MATCH-STAND.

**Silk Fan Embroidered in Point Russe.**—As an elegant fan is a very expensive article, our fair friends will be glad to learn how to make one for themselves, using for it old mountings or new ones at pleasure. The mounting of the one given in our illustration is covered with white glacé silk, and embroidered with fine black silk in point russe. The materials must be taken double; each part is, of course, embroidered separately, and the divisions of the mounting must lie between both pieces of material. The fan is completed at the upper end with a narrow strip of Chantilly lace. A white silk cord and tassell are fastened on the fan from illustration; a circle, consisting of a plait of white silk gimp cord, is fastened on the cord; the circle is placed on the fan so as to prevent its opening when not in use. Coloured silk may, of course, be used instead of white.

**Ornamental Frame for a Match Stand.**—*Materials :* fine penelope canvas, red floss silk, black ditto, gilt beads; ornaments of gilt metal. An infinite variety of patterns are now prepared in gilt or silvered metal, finely carved for ornamenting articles of fancy work. In our present pattern, the bird's nest which serves as a match-stand is formed of a light trellis-work of iron, the branch, and leaves, and the mother-bird, who, with open wings, seems to consider in despair the nest emptied of her young ones, are of gilt metal. A flight of little birds (those, no doubt, who have deserted the nest) are placed upon the outer border. These little birds are also of gilt metal; they are sewn on with gold-coloured silk over the border, which is worked in common cross-stitch, with black floss-silk, and edged on either side with a row of gilt beads. The centre is filled up with red floss-silk in slanting stitches, forming squares over 8 stitches of the canvas. The metal stand and ornaments are sewn over the centre. The frame is 12 inches long, 9 inches wide. To mount it, fold back the edges of the canvas, and stretch it over a piece of cardboard of the same size, lined with red-glazed calico. Firmly sew together the canvas and lining, and hide the seam under an edge of red gimp cord. Add a metal ring at the top to hang up the frame.

**Cheap Floral Decoration.**—The introduction of natural ornaments into our houses is of comparatively recent date. Fashion, in her changing moods, has willed it, and the conventional and artificial have had their day. Rustic baskets of trailing ivy, stands of gaily-tinted growing flowers, mimic ponds teeming with finny life, and vases of autumnal leaves and grasses, have replaced the cumbersome china or queer old ornaments of buhl and marqueterie; and even in art, the graceful negligence of nature is imitated in the decoration of our modern dwellings, in showy contrast to the geometrical embellishments and prim finery of the houses of half a century ago. And this is true alike in public as well as in private edifices.

Like all fashionable articles, however, and especially in cities, the question of the expense of such decorations is by no means an unimportant one, and doubtless many of our country readers would hesitate at the prices demanded by florists for baskets of the commonest wild grasses and ferns, even as which flourish in abundance on every brook side. The more elaborate devices, which include bowls of gold fish, or cages of birds, with, perhaps, a few exotic plants, bring sums which are beyond the reach of ordinary purses. Paying these prices is, however, not at all necessary, if one has a little mechanical ingenuity, and a fair share of taste. We have made beautiful baskets from old wooden chopping trays that have survived their turn of usefulness in the kitchen, though, perhaps, clean new ones would be better. All the materials needed, are some sticks of red cedar with the bark on, or, if this variety of wood cannot be obtained, almost any kind can be pressed into the service; a few bits of rattan, some gnarled roots, a paper of brads, and a little varnish, complete the requirements. A good plan is to cut the cedar sticks into pieces, say three inches long, split them, sharpen both ends, and nail these neatly around and outside the upper edge of the bowl. Then fasten bits of root or twine the rattan around beneath and finish with an irregular knob below. For handles, select three strong pieces of rattan, and secure them firmly to the bowl, letting them extend about two feet above the same and meet in a neat loop. The bowl should not be less than six inches deep, in order to give the roots of the plants plenty of room to grow downward. After the construction of the basket is finished, give it a coat of varnish and the work is done. Dried walnut skins, acorns, chestnut burrs, may be used as ornaments instead of pieces of root. We have also seen some very neat arrangements made entirely of the shells of English walnuts, which had been carefully removed. In filling the basket first place some broken stone or bits of china at the bottom to serve for drainage, and above add loose earth made of two-thirds garden soil and one third sand. As regards plants, unless the basket be large, or a stand (which, by the way, can be made of a soap box, lined with zinc, and mounted on feet) be used, we do not believe in any large variety of flowers in a single receptacle. It is nonsense to mix exotics with wild ferns and grasses, because the nature of soil which suits one is not generally beneficial to the other; and very often the warm uniform temperature, necessary for delicate plants, is fatal to the more hardy varieties from woods and pastures. Fill a basket entirely with ivy, and a luxuriant growth can be obtained, particularly if too many shoots be not set in. Florists aim to cram as much as possible into their baskets, and are totally regardless about the broad leaves of the begonias shading the stems and roots of the more delicate creeping vines. In first setting in the plants, however, place them for a few days in a cold room until new shoots appear. Remember, also, that plants, and especially ivy, will not grow without light, particularly in the house. Place

a pot of ivy, after it has begun growing for a time in the shady part of a room, and the young shoots will speedily turn white, while the older leaves will begin to drop off. There is another fact that amateur house-gardeners forget, and that is that the roots of a plant need plenty of air; and hence pretty pots of painted china or majolica ware will not answer to contain the earth for their reception. If such vessels, however, should be used, the common earthenware pot must be set inside of them, with plenty of intermediate spaces between; while care should be taken that the higher edges of the outer pot do not shade the base of the plant. Weak vegetation may be rejuvenated with a little ammonia, but it must be used with care as too much kills. About two drops in a teacupful of water, given once a week, we have found to be plenty for a good-sized plant.

A very pretty adornment for picture frames is German ivy, a common trailing vine which grows with great luxuriance. All the old medicine phials which infest out of the way closets may be utilised for this purpose. These should be filled with water, and hung behind the pictures, and a slip of the ivy inserted. The vine is quite hardy. We have seen a single slip, in a pint bottle, grow until it ran along the entire length of a moderate-sized room. A sponge moistened and with fine seed scattered in its pores, soon becomes a mass of living verdure, though a prettier ornament we think can be made of a large pine burr, similarly prepared and hung, like the acorn, over water. Fine grass seed is the best to use. Wardian cases are very easily made. A shallow box lined with zinc, with some holes on the sides to ventilate the soil, and a large glass shade, easily obtained for a small sum, answer the purpose. The plants take care of themselves, the water which they evaporate condensing on the glass and running back to the soil, so that a species of circulation is constantly maintained. Insect fanciers can combine animal and vegetable life in one **case**.

**Bleeding from the Nose.**—There is nothing serious in this unless it is too often ; in some cases, indeed, it may save from fatal diseases ; but when it requires to be stopped, let the person sit upright, bathe the neck and face with cold water, and dissolve a little alum in the water, and squirt it up the nostrils. If this fails, send for the doctor. Do not plug the nostrils, for unless it be done properly you may think the bleeding has ceased, whereas it is only finding its way to the top of the throat, and being swallowed.

**Diarrhœa**—Every summer brings with it this unwelcome visitor to young and old, and is frequently fatal to the former. " Because it is common at the same time of the year that fruit is," says Dr. Hope, " it is generally thought that eating fruit is the cause of it. It is said to come in with the plum season : so it does, but not because of the plums, or infants at the breast would not so frequently die of it. Ripe, sound fruit, in its proper season, does no harm, but great good ; but sour, unripe, or half-decayed fruit or vegetables is little better than poison ; so I would say eat of the fruit of every tree which is good for the use of man, but have patience till it is ripe, and do not use any part which is decayed or rotting. When this complaint appears, it should be attended to, not always stopped immediately, for it is often an effort of nature to throw off something which is better away; but if allowed to run on it becomes serious.

For a young child you will generally find this sufficient. Two tablespoonfuls of warm water, a little sugar, half a teaspoonful of carbonate of soda, and one teaspoonful of paregoric ; mix all together and give a teaspoonful every three hours till the purging stops. To an infant three or four months old, half a teaspoonful will be sufficient, increasing the dose according to the age. For grown-up people and children above seven years of age, I now give you an excellent receipt, which you should keep ready in the house :—

Confection of opium, aromatic confection, powder for compound chalk mixture, of each two drachms ; carbonate of ammonia half a drachm ; oil of peppermint, fifteen drops ; mix thoroughly, and keep in a bottle well corked.

This quantity will make six full doses. To a person above fourteen years of age give one teaspoonful stirred in a little water every three hours till better. Under fourteen years of age give half a teaspoonful. If there is pain in the bowels, apply heat as follows :—Make a common dinner plate or small dish quite hot, lay on some folds of flannel wrung out of hot water, place the hot plate over this, taking care that the edges do not extend beyond the flannel ; then cover with a dry towel. By having two plates, one at the fire while the other is in use, you can change them in a moment, and get any amount of heat you require without the weight of a large poultice.

Now comes the important question—How to know when to stop the action of the bowels, and when to assist them ? You may take this as a good general rule. If what passes from the bowels be very offensive, or if they have not been sufficiently acted upon for some days, then clear them out with a dose of castor-oil before you commence the other medicine."

**The Countenance.**—The " Family Doctor " informs us that " tolerably clear indications of a person's state of health may generally be read in the countenance : where there is great anxiety depicted on this dial plate of the internal organs, there is likely to be organic or functional disease of the heart, pneumonia, bronchitis, croup, chronic consumption, dropsy of the chest, causing a sense of oppression and impeded respiration. In fevers, and other acute forms of disease which shorten life, there is also this anxious expression.

When the countenance is livid and tinged with blood, there is impeded respiration and circulation, probably congestion of the brain : this is the case in apoplexy, disease of the heart, effusion of the lungs, &c. A pale countenance is a sign of fainting and hæmorrhage, external or internal. When the expression is violent and excited, there is probably the delirium of fever, inflammation of the brain, mania, or delirium tremens. In paralysis, convulsions, epilepsy, hysteria, and chorea, we have a distorted countenance ; and a flushed one is symptomatic of fever in general. Sometimes, in the latter stage of an incurable disease, the face becomes what nurses call ' struck with death,' and to this hopeless corpse-like expression has been applied the term *Facies Hippocratica*, because it has been vividly pictured by Hippocrates himself ; here is his picture : ' The forehead wrinkled and dry, the eye sunken, the nose pointed and bordered with a dark or violet circle ; the temples sunken, hollow, and retired ; the ears sticking up, the lips hanging down, the cheeks sunken, the chin wrinkled and hard, the colour of the skin leaden or violet ; the eyelashes sprinkled with a yellowish white dust.' "

**Puddings for Invalids.**—All fat or greasy ingredients should be excluded from these puddings, which should be made of some farinaceous material, and well and carefully cooked ; they will then be found to be excellent articles of diet for invalids. Simple rice, sago, tapioca, and boiled bread puddings, are those best suited for the sick room, or a composition of light egg and flour. To make them very nutritious, and at the same time light, it is best first to bake or boil the farinaceous ingredient thoroughly in milk, and while it is hot to stir in the egg, previously beaten up with a little warm milk ; then set aside to cool ; the egg is thus sufficiently cooked, without having its albumen hardened and rendered indigestible.

**Sea-side Visitors.**—One fact should be borne in mind by those who resort to the sea-side, for the sake of the purer and more bracing atmosphere which prevails there, namely, that invalids are likely to derive more benefit from the fresh sea breezes at the distance of about a quarter of a mile from the sea than close to it. The residence of such should be on a hill sloping down to the shore. On the same level as the sea, the air is rendered somewhat impure by the decaying animal and vegetable matter which is left by each receding tide.

**Newly-Painted Houses.**—Most serious effects have very often arisen from breathing the atmosphere of newly-painted houses ; that the headache, sickness, and other uneasy feelings that arise from this will pass away, and leave no after ill-effects, is the belief of most people, but cases have been known in which the poison, though slight, has worked upon the system, and materially affected the health through life. That it is a poison which is thus inhaled, there is sufficient evidence in the circumstance that on the delicate lungs of a bird it acts as such, causing death very rapidly ; whether the pernicious effects are produced by the fumes of the turpentine used in oil-paints, or to the subtle emanations of the lead, we cannot affirm ; but we would warn our readers to avoid, by all means, living or sleeping in newly-painted houses ; or, if they are obliged to do this, to admit as much fresh air as possible, and to be out of doors as much as circumstances will admit ; children, especially, should be kept away from this morbific influence.

**Moral Government of Children.**—The following admirable rules on this very important subject, we extract from Chambers' " Infant Treatment :"—

Anticipate and prevent fretfulness and ill-temper by keeping the child in good health, ease, and comfort. Never quiet with giving to eat, or by bribing in any way, still less by opiates.

For the first few months avoid loud and harsh sounds in the hearing of children, or violent lights in their sight ; address them in soft tones ; do nothing to frighten them ; and never jerk or roughly handle them.

Avoid angry words and violence both

to a child and in its presence ; by which means a naturally violent child will be trained to gentleness.

Moderate any propensity of a child, such as anger, violence, greediness for food, cunning, &c., which appears too active. Show him no example of these.

Let the mother be, and let her select servants such as she wishes the child to be. The youngest child is affected by the conduct of those in whose arms he lives.

Cultivate and express benevolence and cheerfulness ; in such an atmosphere, a child must become benevolent and cheerful.

Let a mother feel as she ought, and she will look as she feels. Much of a child's earliest moral training is by looks and gestures.

When necessary, exhibit firmness and authority, always with perfect temper, composure, and self-possession.

Never give the child that which it cries for ; and avoid being too ready in answering children's demands, else they become impatient of refusal, and selfish.

When the child is most violent, the mother should be most calm and silent. Out-screaming a screaming child is as useless as it is mischievous. Steady denial of the object screamed for is the best cure for screaming.

In such contests, witnesses should withdraw, and leave mother and child alone. A child is very ready to look round and attract the aid of foreign sympathy in its little rebellions.

Never promise to give when the child leaves off crying. Let the crying be the reason for *not* giving.

Constant warnings, reproofs, threats, and entreaties—as, " let that alone," " be quiet," " how naughty you are," &c., all uttered in haste and irritation, are most pernicious. No fixed or definite moral improvement, but the reverse, results from this too common practice.

Watch destructiveness, manifested in fly and insect killing, and smashing and breaking, quarrelling, striking, &c.

Never encourage revenge. Never allow a child to witness killing animals.

Counterwork secretiveness by exposing its manœuvres. Regulate notions of property—one's own and another's.

Never strike a child, and never teach it to strike again. Never tell a child to beat or threaten any animal or object. Corporal correction may be avoided by judicious substitutes.

Set an example of cleanliness, order, punctuality, delicacy, politeness, and proper ease of manner. This is better than " teaching manners," as it is called.

Inculcate early, and manifest in yourself, a delicate regard for the rights of others and their feelings, in contrast with selfish vanity, arrogance, and exclusive attention to one's own ease, comfort, and gratification.

Prevent all indelicacies and slovenly habits at table—touching the utensils, stretching for what is wanted, sitting awkwardly, &c.

Study early to gain a child's confidence by judicious sympathy in its joys and sorrows. Have no concealment with it.

Govern by love, and not by fear ; the contrast between children governed by the one and the other is truly instructive. Never forget that kindness is power with man and beast. The Arab never strikes his horse.

Cultivate truth, justice, and candour in the child, and manifest them in yourself.

With a child whose firmness is apt to run into obstinacy, never contend : in doing so, you aggravate the feeling by manifesting the same feeling in yourself ; and by further showing your combativeness, exciting the child's opposition. Divert the child from the object, and put in activity its benevolence, justice, and reason.

Never frighten to obtain a child's obedience ; threats of hobgoblins, and all false terrors, are now universally exploded, as atrocities towards the young ; death, fits, idiotcy insanity, have been the consequences. They are, besides, soon discovered to be falsehoods, and operate most immorally."

This excellent counsel we supplement by a word or two upon books for those of tender years. Too much care cannot be given to this subject. Many a false impression has been instilled into a child's mind by an artist or author who had no higher care than to amuse the young mind regardless of its moral welfare. Often and often has a funny narrative, adorned with funny pictures, although they have provoked a laugh, left very unfavourable impressions in the child. Certainly there is much more care now shown by the caterers of books and pictures for the young than in the past. The pens of the best religious writers, and the pencils of artists who rank among the highest in their profession, are now largely engaged on books and magazines for the young —even for infants. "Chatterbox," edited by the Rev. Erskine Clark, is, perhaps, the most popular amongst children's books, and in many respects the best. It may be regarded as a representative book amongst juvenile literature, and we are pleased to observe that its pure tone and cheerful spirit is reflected in most of the other periodicals that appeal to the minds of the young.

**Earliest Intellectual Education.—** Cultivate by exercise the five senses of seeing, hearing, touching, smelling, tasting.

Teach the child to observe forms, sizes, weights, colours, arrangements, and numbers.

Practise all a child's knowing faculties on objects—feathers, shells, ribbons, buttons, pictures of animals, &c.

Practise distinct articulation. If at four years of age a child has any defect, it ought to be systematically taught to pronounce correctly.

Let a child put its toy to another than the intended use, if it does not destroy it. This exercises invention.

Encourage construction, and furnish the materials, leaving ingenuity to work.

Accustom the child to find its own amusement. It is the most unprofitable slavery to be constantly finding amusement for it.

Remember that children love stories —the simpler the better; and delight to have them told again and again. Always give them a moral turn and character.

Be sparing of the marvellous; exclude the terrible and horrible: and utterly proscribe all ghost and witch stories.

Accustom children to reptiles, insects, &c.; and prevent the foolish fears of these creatures which is often found in adults, and leads to the constant and most unnecessary destruction of them.

Induce a child to give attention, by presenting objects, and giving narratives which interest it. Do not tell it that it must give attention.

Avoid employing female servants as nurses who possess coarse habits and sentiments, or whose mode of speaking is coarse or indelicate.

No difference need at first be made between the rearing and training of male and female infants. Allow female children as they grow up to amuse themselves with dolls, and in a similar manner encourage and regulate the amusements of boys.

**Baking Pastry.—** Regulate the heat of the oven according to the article to be baked. Make those things first which will suit the heat of the oven. Light paste requires a moderately quick oven; for if the oven is too hot, the paste will be coloured before it is properly baked; and if it is then taken out of the oven it will fall, and become flat. A cool oven will prevent pastry from rising sufficiently: and puff-paste baked in an oven with anything that causes much steam, will not be so light as otherwise. Iced tarts or puffs should be baked in a cooler oven than those that are not iced; the door should be left a little open if the oven is too hot. Small articles of pastry require to be baked in a fiercer oven than large ones. All pastry should be baked in clean tins or patty-pans, without being buttered. Pastry, when baked sufficiently, may be easily slid about on the tin, or pan, while hot ; and puffs, patties, or small pies, may be lifted from the tin, without breaking, by putting your fingers round the edges and carefully lifting them, which cannot be done unless they are sufficiently baked.

**To Neutralise the Acid in Fruit Pies and Puddings.**—A large quantity of the free acid which exists in rhubarb, gooseberries, currants, and other fruits, may be judiciously corrected by the use of a small quantity of carbonate of soda, without the least affecting their flavour, so long as too much soda is not added. To an ordinary sized pie or pudding, as much soda may be added as, piled up, will cover a shilling. or even twice such a quantity, if the fruit is very sour. If this little hint is attended to, many a stomach-ache will be prevented, and a vast quantity of sugar saved. because, when the acid is neutralised by the soda, it will not require so much sugar to render the tart sweet.

**To Boil a Ham.**—Hams which are bought from a cheesemonger have usually been long hung, and are very dirty ; if such should be the case, the ham should be soaked about twelve hours, then wrapped in a clean cloth, and laid upon stone flags for two days, the cloth being kept moistened with clean soft water, this will render it tender when cooked : let it be thoroughly scraped and cleaned, and placed in the copper, which in small families will be found the most convenient way of cooking it ; it should be put in sufficient water to cover it, which water, when the ham is cooked, will be found of the greatest service in making stock for soups ; the time it will take to boil will depend upon the weight of the ham, a small one three hours and a half, which may progress, according to the weight, to six hours ; when it is done, remove the skin if possible without breaking it, as it prevents the ham when cold becoming dry ; spread over the ham bread

raspings, and garnish the dish with sliced boiled carrots.

**Irish Stew.**—Cut a neck of mutton as for the haricot ; blanch the chops in water, then put them into another stewpan with four onions cut in slices, put to it a little of your second stock, and let it boil a quarter of an hour : pare three pounds of potatoes, cut them into thick slices, put them into a stewpan with a quart of water, two or three carrots, turnips or onions may be added, salt and pepper the mutton when added to the gravy, let it boil or simmer very gently for two hours, and serve smoking hot.

**Calf's Head.**—Let the head be well cleaned, the tongue and brains be taken out, then boil the head in a cloth to keep it white. It is as well to soak the head for two or three hours previously to boiling, it helps to improve the colour. Wash, blanch, and soak the brains, then boil them, scald some sage, chop it fine, add pepper and salt, and a little milk, mix it with the brains ; the tongue, which should be soaked in salt and water for twenty-four hours, should be boiled, peeled, and served on a separate dish. The head should boil until tender. and if intended to be sent plainly to table should be served as taken up, with melted butter and parsley ; if otherwise, when the head is boiled sufficiently tender, take it up, spread over a coat of the yolk of egg well beaten up, powder with bread crumbs, and brown before the fire in a Dutch oven.

**Forcemeat.**—This should be made to cut with a knife, but not dry or heavy, no one flavour should predominate ; according to what it is wanted for a choice may be made from the following list :—Be careful to use the least of those articles that are most pungent ; cold fowl, veal, or ham, fat bacon, scraped, beef suet, crumbs of bread, parsley, white pepper, salt, nutmeg, yolks and whites of eggs beaten to bind the mixture, which makes excellent forcemeat. Any of the following articles may be used to alter the taste :—oysters, anchovies, marjoram, tarragon, thyme, yolks of hard eggs, endive, cayenne, or two or three cloves.

**A Durable Paste.**—Four parts, by weight, of glue are allowed to soften in fifteen parts of cold water for some hours, and are then moderately heated till the solution becomes clear ; sixty-five parts of boiling water are now added, while stirring. In another vessel thirty parts of starch paste are stirred up with twenty parts of cold water, so that the milky fluid is obtained without lumps. Into this some boiling glue solution is poured, and the whole kept at boiling temperature. After cooling, ten drops of carbolic acid are added to the paste. This paste is of extraordinary adhesive power, and may be used for leather, paper, or cardboard, with great success. It should be preserved in close bottles, when it will keep for years.

**French Mayonnaise.**—For a small dish, take a cold chicken, roasted or boiled, and carve it very neatly into joints, skinning it carefully. Take only the two first joints of the wings, the thighs (leaving out the drum-sticks), the neck and side bones, and the merry-thought. Lay these all tidily on the dish in a sloping pile, adding delicate slices from the breast over all ; then grate over a thick shower of well-flavoured, smoked, and cooked ham, with a couple of clean-scraped anchovies, and cut them in the slenderest fillets possible, and stripe them tastefully up the pile of cold chicken. Then take the hearts of three small cabbage-lettuces well washed and dried, cut long ways in quarters, and dispose them tastefully round the bottom of your chicken pyramid. Boil three eggs quite hard, shell them, and when cold, cut two of them in slices, with which garnish the dish at the bottom. Cut the white of the third egg in long strips, and lay it on the upper part between your anchovy fillets. Crown the tops with a bunch of young cress, well washed and dried, placing the yolk of the last egg on the top. The following sauce can be either carefully poured over it, or served with

it :—Put the yolks of one or two new eggs into an earthenware bowl, and beat them well ; add a pinch of salt and a mustard spoonful of made mustard *little* by *little*. Then add, a few drops at a time, two tablespoonfuls of the purest salad oil, continually stirring it, and one tablespoonful of cream. Beat these all well together, and then add a tablespoonful of white-wine vinegar ; add it by drops like the oil, and stir till it is a smooth cream.

**To Boil Rice.**—Very few persons know how to boil rice properly. It is usually so boiled as to become a heavy dough, so tenacious and solid as to be almost impenetrable to the digestive fluids secreted by the mouth and the stomach, which are necessary to dissolve it and to effect its digestion and distribution, as innocent nourishing food. It should be so cooked that the grains shall remain separate and distinct, but not hard, and the whole be in some degree loose and porous. To boil rice properly, it should soak for seven hours in cold water and salt. Have a stewpan ready, containing boiling water, into which put the soaked rice, and boil it briskly for ten minutes. Then pour it into a colander, set it by the fire awhile, and serve it up. The grains will be separate, and will be very large.

**Flannels.**—All flannels should be soaked before they are made up ; first in cold, then in hot water, in order to shrink them. Welsh flannel is the softest, and should be preferred, if it is to be worn next the skin : but Lancashire flannel looks finer, lasts longer, and should, therefore, be selected when it is not to be worn next the skin. Under flannel garments should be frequently changed, because they imbibe perspiration, which is liable to be absorbed again into the system, and this is injurious. All flannel vestments that are made full, should be gathered, not plaited ; because in the latter case they become thick, and matted by washing ; and in the event of their being turned from top to bottom in order to alter the wear, the part that had been plaited will be found to be so drawn and injured, that two or three inches of it must be cut off.

**Pimples.**—A weak solution of sugar of lead or sulphate of zinc may be used as a wash ; if not effective, try two drachms of camphorated spirit, corrosive sublimate of mercury one grain, rose-water or almond-water half a pint, to be applied night and morning. When there is great irritability of the skin, a decoction of the woody nightshade may be used instead of the rose or almond-water. If pimples arise from the condition of the blood, then cooling purgatives should be taken. A Plummer's pill at night, and a teaspoonful of decoction of sarsaparilla twice a-day, with a black draught once a-week, are excellent medicines.

**Bread-and-Water Poultice.**—The great Abernethy used to say that poultices were blessings or curses, as they were made ; we cannot, therefore, give a more useful recipe than that of the distinguished surgeon's for an evaporating poultice, as follows :—Scald out a basin, for you can never make a good poultice unless you have perfectly boiling water ; then having put some into the basin, throw in coarsely-crumbled bread, and cover it with a plate. When the bread has soaked up as much of the water as it will imbibe, drain off the remaining water, and there will be left a light pulp. Spread it a third of an inch thick on folded linen, and apply it when of the temperature of a warm bath. It may be said that this poultice will be very inconvenient if there be no lard in it, for it will soon get dry ; but this is the very thing you want, and it can be easily moistened by dropping water on it, whilst a greasy poultice will be moist, but not wet.

A poultice thus made is, to the surgeon, what well-made stock is to the cook, a foundation to be seasoned or medicined with laudanum or poppy-water, with carrot or horse-radish juice, or with decoctions of herbs, with which the patient or the doctor may be inclined to medicate it, instead of loading an already irritable and very sensitive part with a heap of hard poppy-shells, or scraped carrots, or horse-radish, called poppy, carrot, and horse-radish poultices, but which increase rather than allay the sufferer's pains.

When vegetables are used to medicate poultices, they should be bruised, put into a pot, covered with water, and simmered for about half an hour. The liquid is then to be strained off, and mixed with bread-and-water or linseed to the consistence of a poultice.

**Barometer.**—This instrument (we quote from " Beeton's Medical Dictionary) is for measuring the weight or pressure of the atmosphere. It may be said to be the invention of Torricelli, who first demonstrated the existence of the atmospheric pressure by means of a column of mercury contained in a glass tube, but the practical application of this, as the means of determining the weight of the atmosphere, is more particularly owing to Pascal. The principle of the barometer is very simple. It consists of a glass tube about 34 inches in length, sealed at one end, and filled with mercury. This is inverted in a cistern containing the same fluid, when the mercury in the tube falls so as to correspond with the amount of atmospheric pressure on the metal in the cistern, and rises or falls in proportion to the degree of this pressure. This siphon barometer has in place of the cistern the open end of the tube bent upwards and exposed to atmospheric pressure. For indicating good and bad weather, the wheel barometer, invented by Hook, has long been used, but it is a very imperfect instrument. It is merely a siphon instrument connected with a needle, which moves round a graduated circle. In the shorter leg of the siphon a float is placed, which rises and falls with the mercury. A string attached to this float passes round a pulley, to which the needle is fixed, and at the other end there is a small weight, somewhat lighter than the float. When the pressure varies, the float sinks or rises, and moves the needle round to the corresponding points on the scale. The words rain, fine, variable, &c., generally appear on the graduated circle ; but they do not always afford reliable indications of the weather. As a rule, a falling barometer prognosticates rain ; a rising barometer fair weather. When the column of mercury is unsteady, it indicates an unsettled condition of the atmosphere ; a steady barometer indicates that the weather at the time will last. If the mercury be low, the weather will remain bad ; if the mercury be high, the weather will continue fair. A sudden falling of the barometer almost invariably presages a storm. The connection between the variations of the weather and the pressure of the atmosphere is, however, a subject ill understood. For determining altitude, the barometer is an invaluable instrument. In ascending mountains the mercury is found to sink about the tenth of an inch in 90 feet ; so that, if the mercury fall an inch, we have ascended nearly 900 feet ; but this is subject to variations through change of temperature and other causes, which render various corrections necessary. There are many forms of the mercurial barometer, but they are all modifications of the siphon or the cistern. The aneroid barometer is an instrument used for determining the variations of atmospheric pressure, without the aid of a liquid, as in ordinary barometers. Its action depends on the principle, that if a very thin metallic tube be coiled, any internal pressure on its sides tends to uncoil it, and any external pressure to coil it still more. The instrument essentially consists of a thin metallic tube, curved so as to form seven-eighths of a circle. This tube, being exhausted of air and hermetically closed, is fixed by its middle, so that whenever the atmospheric pressure diminishes, it uncoils ; and, on the other hand, whenever the pressure increases, it contracts.

**Thermometer.**—An instrument for determining the degree of active heat existing in the atmosphere or other bodies ; there are several kinds, but the one commonly used is Fahrenheit's. A Thermoscope is the name of a particular kind of thermometer which shows or exhibits the changes of heat to the eye ; and a Thermostat is a self acting apparatus for regulating temperature, constructed on the principle of the unequal expansiveness of metals.

**To Prepare Oatmeal.**—Scotch oatmeal is by far the best ; to prepare it the grain is first kiln-dried, stripped of its outer skin or husk, and then coarsely ground. Made into porridge, it constitutes, perhaps, the best breakfast diet for the young. It should be prepared thus :—Put into a saucepan as much water as will make the desired quantity —say a pint ; let it boil, then take a handful of the meal, in the left hand, and while letting it fall gradually and gently into the water, stir the mixture quickly round with a wooden spoon, held in the right hand ; continue doing this until the mixture assumes the consistency of thick gruel ; then add a little salt, and let it boil gently for ten minutes, keeping it stirred all the time ; add a little more water, and again boil for another five minutes, still stirring ; it will then be smooth and digestible, to make it which is the object of the lengthened boiling : to make it more nourishing and pleasant, some milk may be added, and, if preferred, a little sugar ; this hides the slight bitter taste of the meal, which is objectionable to many. Scottish children never tire of porridge, but take it morning and night regularly until they grow up, and often afterwards. It would be well if this practice were more followed south of the Tweed than it is.

The kernels or grain of the oat, when deprived of their husks, are called Groats ; they were formerly much used in the thickening of soups and broths, but are now generally superseded by pearl barley, and their chief use at present is for gruels and decoctions for demulcent purposes.

In the process of shelling there is obtained from the grains of oat a kind of thin pellicle or minor scale, which has the technical name of " seeds,' and from which is prepared a peculiar jelly-like food, very good and nourishing for invalids ; it is called in Scotland *sowens*. Either the groats or oatmeal may be employed in the preparation of gruel.

**Moles.**—To remove moles apply a stick of nitrate of silver to it once or twice. Moisten the stick very slightly, touch the mole once, and it will turn black. Do not interfere with it while sore ; it will dry up and fall off. If it does not come off clean enough the first time, repeat the operation.

**A Maiden's Psalm of Life.**—Life is real, life is earnest, single blessedness a fib ; " Man thou art, to man return-est," has been spoken of the rib. Not enjoyment, and not sorrow, is our des tined end or way, but to act that each to-morrow finds us nearer marriage-day. Life is long, and youth is fleeting, and our hearts though light and gay, still like pleasant drums are beating wedding marches all the way. In the world's broad field of battle, in the bi-vouac of life, be not like dumb driven cattle, be a heroine—a wife. Lives of married folks remind us, we can live our lives as well, and departing leave behind us such examples as shall " tell." Let us then be up and doing, with a heart on triumph set, still contriving, still pursuing, and each one a husband get.

**Love of the Beautiful.**—Place a young girl under the care of a kind-hearted woman, and she, unconsciously to herself, grows into a graceful lady. Place a boy in the establishment of a thorough-going, straightforward busi-ness man, and the boy becomes a self-reliant, practical, business man. Chil-dren are susceptible creatures, and cir-cumstances, scenes and actions always impress. As you influence them, not by arbitrary rules, nor by stern example alone, but a thousand other ways that speak through beautiful forms, pretty pictures, &c., so they will grow. Teach your children, then, to love the beau-tiful. Give them a corner in the gar-den for flowers ; encourage them to put it in the shape of hanging bask    ;

show them where they can best view the sunset ; rouse them in the morning, not with the stern "time to wake," but with the enthusiastic " See the beauti-ful sun rise !" Buy for them pretty books with pretty pictures ; and en-courage them to decorate their rooms in his or her childish way. Give them an inch, and they will go a mile. Allow them the privilege, and they will make your home beautiful.

**Ironmould in Linen.**—Wash the spots in a strong solution of cream of tartar and water. Repeat if necessary, and dry in the sun.

Or,—Rub the spots with a little pow-dered oxalic acid, or salts of lemon and warm water. Let it remain a few minutes, and then rinse well in clean water.

**Law of Breach of Promise of Marriage.**—The law requires that promises and agreements in considera-tion of marriage shall be in writing, duly signed ; but with regard to pro-mises to marry there is a very great distinction ; and a verbal promise, if proved, is binding and operative.

Nothing is better established now than that a verbal promise to marry, or even a message to that effect, if duly proved, is binding as completely as a written promise.

Before breach of promise can be alleged, the acceptance of the promise must be proved by the other party, upon the principle that in all contracts both parties must be bound or neither.

Custom has established that though a promise to marry, to be valid, must be in writing, or in unqualified spoken words, yet the acceptance of a promise need not be in words, but may be taken for granted if nothing indicating the contrary be done. It is considered that this distinction is necessary in consider-ation of the modest reserve of the fe-male, who is usually, though not inva-riably, the acceptor.

As a general rule, if the promiser has not married another, nothing in law can be done till an ample " reasonable time" has elapsed, and the other party has distinctly challenged the promiser to redeem the promise, and the challenge must be accompanied by an unqualified expression of willingness also.

A challenge to fulfil a promise may be effectually undertaken by a third party—by the father, mother, or any confidential friend.

An answer to a challenge may be an effectual bar to proceedings if it truly alleges an insufficient lapse of " reasonable time," but there appears to be no other possible bar, provided that the challenger is chaste and in good health.

Bad health will in some cases be a justification for breach, especially if the blemish be in the man.

A woman in most instances is necessarily placed in a position of dependence upon her husband, both as regards herself and her children, and she has a peculiar right to require the fullest candour in reference to anything which may imperil her material interests so seriously as a physical defect, which may, more or less, prevent her husband from obtaining livelihood.

Candour with regard to maladies on either side, though required by law in cases of manifest importance, is not to be supposed obligatory with regard to every little personal peculiarity. The obligation must be considered in the light of what is reasonable, having regard to the circumstances and the permanency of the marriage tie.

Minority on the part of the person deceived, is no bar to proceedings by that party. It was formerly doubted whether a minor could bring an action for breach of promise, but the question is considered settled by a case in which it was decided that though a minor cannot be sued for breach of promise, yet the minor may sue for breach if the other party be of age at the time of the promise.

Effectual defence may be set up against an action by a minor if there is any evidence that the parents or guardians refused their consent, or were so tardy in according it as to amount to a non-acceptance of the promise.—"*Beeton's Hand-Book of the Law Relating to Women and Children.*"

**Separation of Parents.**—In case of the separation of married parents, unless there be some agreement or special intervention of law, the mother has sole right over all her children till they are seven years old; after that age the right is transferred to the father.

**Different Breeds of Fowls.**—The Dorking, so called from the town in Surrey, where they were first bred, is one of the most important breeds. It has the peculiarity of *five* toes, three in front and two behind; the colour is usually a pure white, which sometimes merges into a grey or grizzled and speckled plumage; and they are considered the most delicate of all the varieties for the table. The eggs are of good size and well flavoured.

The Spanish fowl is very frequent about London. It is of large size; the plumage black; the cheek white; and comb and wattles singularly large. The hens are capital layers; their eggs are larger than those of the Dorking breed; and they are, like those of that fowl, of an excellent flavour. The Spanish fowls are also very delicious table-birds.

The MALAY fowls are so named from the peninsula of Malay, the southern point of the continent of India, from whence they were brought. They are very large and strong birds, the colour of the feathers generally black, or of a very dark brown, with yellow stripes; and the legs are large and coarse. The eggs are large, and so rich, that two of them are equal to three of those of ordinary fowls.

There are the POLISH and the HAMBURG breeds—the former a noble and very beautiful bird, and an excellent layer. Their colours are blue and black, and some are speckled; and they have a tufted, feathery crest, which overshadows the beak. The hen has a rose comb, pure white neck and breast, and the rest of the body most exquisitely pencilled with bluish slate-colour and white ; legs light blue. The cock has the back and neck greyish white, breast and wings slightly spotted, tail nearly black, and a fine double comb. They are small and neatly made ; the eggs are also small, and of a French white, and tapering at one end. The chicks are white, except a dark streak on the head, and down the nape of the neck, a curious fact, as when full grown, this is the only part without dark markings. There are gold and silver-spangled Hamburgs ; the former being termed Bolton Bays, the latter Bolton Greys.

The BANTAM family is derived from the Bankiva fowls, a native of Java. The full-bred Bantam cock should have a bright rose comb, a well-feathered tail, full hacklers, a proud lively carriage, and ought not to weigh more than a pound. There are nankeen, black, and white-coloured bantams, the former being the most highly prized. All the bantam cocks are very pugnacious, but the hens are good layers, and good mothers to their own chickens, though they will attack any stranger with fury.

All these various fowls, with ducks, geese, guinea-fowls, and turkeys, are known under the common name of POULTRY, which is derived from the French *poulet*, a chick, or chicken.

Management of Poultry.—Fowls are sometimes kept in large open sheds, roosting upon any projection they can find. Sometimes they are sheltered in out-houses and stables : to say nothing of those in London, and other large towns, that are frequently stowed away in cellars. But, whether fowls are kept for pleasure or profit, there should be a fowl-house for their reception. They cannot thrive properly in the confined unhealthy places in which they are frequently kept.

The fowl-house should front the east or south ; and if it can be erected at the back of a stove-house, or brewery, or stable, so much the better.

Though an extreme heat should be avoided, a genial warmth conduces to the health of the fowls, and greatly improves the faculty of laying.

A piece of gravelly soil should be selected for the house, if possible ; the site should be well drained, lie on a slight declivity, and it would be well if there were trees near to afford shade from the sun, and shelter from the wind. The house should be high enough to allow a man to enter and walk about with ease, in order that there may be no difficulty in cleaning it ; if there be, the chances are that it will be neglected. A fowl-house tolerably lofty is more conducive to the health of the fowls than a low-roofed one, and the perches may be placed more out of the way of vermin, should any find their way in.

Brick and mortar are the best materials for the construction of the house, as the walls should be impervious to vermin. Lath and plaster are sometimes used for the walls ; and a very ornamental house may be made of posts and rails, the interstices filled with faggots. The roof may be made warm and ornamental with thatch, but it harbours vermin : therefore a slated or tiled roof is best. There should, with slates or tiles, be a ceiling of lath and plaster, to prevent currents of air, or drippings of water, both of which are injurious to fowls. Asphalted felt, nailed close, is a good substitute for the ceiling, and affords as safe a protection.

For Ventilation, there should be a small lathed window at each end, which can be opened or shut at pleasure. Or a Venetian blind fitted in the frame answers the purpose, perhaps, better. The door should have a hole at the bottom, with a sliding panel, which should be pulled up during the day, and closed at night. Should there be no windows, then loose movable boards should be used in the door to admit air. Sometimes the hole for the admission of fowls is placed at the top of the door ; and then a slanting piece of wood, with slips nailed across, is placed to enable the fowls to reach it.

The perches should be arranged in the shape of a broad double ladder, the perches being placed so that the fowls do not overhang one another. That the fowls may ascend to the higher perches, steps in the wall should be placed so that the birds can jump from one to the other.

Sometimes perches are suspended across the fowl-house ; and then there should be hen ladders placed close to them, because heavy fowls ascend to their perches with difficulty if they have to fly up to them, and are apt to break their breast-bones by falling to the ground in attempting to fly down.

Perches are best made with rough poles, two or three inches in diameter, with the bark left on. It should be recollected that the feet of fowls are not constructed to clasp smooth poles.

Nests, or laying-places, should be provided in the fowl-house, by fixing wooden boxes to the wall, or placing shallow hampers, or baskets, of wicker-work, and these make the best nests, for they are cooler in summer, and can be easier taken down, well washed, and filled with clean, fresh straw. If fixed nests are used, they should be thoroughly whitewashed, inside and out, at least once a month. If the nests are made of wood, there should be a small ledge, to prevent the eggs from rolling out, and they should not be too large ; if they are, two fowls would be apt to try to sit together in the same nest. About a foot square is a good size for them. They should be placed in tiers, the lowest being about three feet from the ground ; and it is best to reserve this for fowls which are rearing broods, as they can then enter and leave them with more ease, and without danger of disturbing the eggs.

Wheat or rye straw, dried heath, or dried fern leaves, are the best materials for the beds of the nests, while the floor of the house should be hard and dry, and kept covered with clean gravel or sand. To prevent bad smells, which are injurious to fowls, it would be well to keep a basket of slaked lime or cold mortar in a corner, with a shovel, so that some may be shaken over any dirt or impurities.

The poultry house should be cleaned out every day, and the floor washed at least once a week, and the walls frequently whitewashed. The windows should be kept open in summer.

ASSORTING THE FLOCKS.—It is necessary that both cocks and hens should be kept, for though hens kept by themselves will lay eggs, they will be of a very inferior quality. About one cock to seven or eight hens will do. The former should not be less than a year, nor more than two years old, and should be removed when he is four years old.

FEEDING POULTRY.—Having erected your poultry-house, laid out your poultry-yard, and got around you a stock of fowls, the next thing necessary is to attend to their food. Now fowls will eat almost everything in the shape of grain or vegetables, and they will pick bones as clean as a dog. Animal food they will eat cooked or raw, the flesh of their own species as well as any other. They are particularly fond of worms and snails, but slugs they do not like. When they are in the fields they find the insects for themselves, but when kept in poultry-yards, they must be found for them. They require a variety of food, green and hard. Of green food, they will eat almost anything ; cabbage and beet-leaves, lettuces, leeks, radish and turnip-tops, and any kind of herb. The best plan is to fasten heads of cabbages, lettuce, rape, or other green herbs, to some fixture, by means of the roots, and to let the fowls peck for themselves. This practice not merely prevents waste, but is, in consequence of the amusement it affords, decidedly conducive to health.

Of the six kinds of grain—wheat, barley, oats, rye, buckwheat, and Indian corn—they become soonest tired of rye, and eat the least of it ; but it is impossible to say which of the other grains they like best, as they evidently differ in their tastes, and will eat one day what they had previously rejected. About a quarter of a pint of either of the grains will be sufficient each day for an ordinary-sized fowl ; but a large one, or one with a more voracious appetite than ordinary, will require one-third of a pint. Some poultry-keepers recommend boiling the grain , barley and wheat should always be boiled.

Fowls should have grain given to them at least twice, in the morning and afternoon ; and during the day have green food—meat, fish, or insects to peck at, and eat as they please.

LAYING EGGS AND HATCHING.—The care of the poultry-keeper is particularly required in attending to the hens when laying and sitting. It is in this department of her labours that she will have to display much acuteness and activity, as well as patience and good temper.

The best male and female birds that can be found should be selected for breeding. They should have no defects ; but if the male be defective in any point—a hen defective in the same point should not be suffered to make one of his flock. If you wish to ensure purity of breed, and a fine stock, it is best to select a handsome bold male, and about six of the handsomest hens, and put them in a separate enclosure.

When the eggs are laid, they should be collected before noon ; and on those intended for breeding, mark the date, and the name of the hen, that you may know what breed they belong to. They should then be placed in bran, the large end uppermost. Those intended for the table should be handed over to the cook, who will know the best way for preserving those for which she has not an immediate use.

Some hens lay every day, others will lay every other day, and some not more than one egg in three days. Spring and summer are the most general seasons for laying, though some hens will lay for nine months together. The moulting season, when she is renewing her feathers, is the usual time for her to cease laying. It is very easy to make them lay in the winter, by keeping them warm, and giving them rich and stimulating food. Or, by having an early brood of chickens hatched in April

or May, the pullets will begin to lay their eggs about Christmas.

Eggs that you wish the hen to sit upon should not be kept more than a month ; the shorter time they are kept the better. Neither the largest nor the smallest should be taken for sitting ; those of a medium size are preferable ; and those should be selected which are larger at one end than at the other. An egg equally thick at both ends is likely to have two yolks, and, instead of yielding two chickens, as might be supposed, if hatched at all, it will merely produce some monstrosity.

As many eggs should be put under the hen as she can conveniently cover, generally from nine to eleven. When a hen wishes to sit, she becomes very restless, wanders about, hangs her wings, utters an indistinct cluck, runs searching into holes and corners, and if she finds any eggs will sit upon them.

She sits about twenty-one days, and during this time a proper supply of food and water should be placed near her, but not within reach, for it is better that she should get off her nest now and then and refresh herself.

During incubation, take care that no strangers go near them. The less they are interfered with the better. Do not turn the eggs, the hen will do that. About the twelfth day, take the opportunity, when the hen is off the nest, of looking at them. If there is a waving shadow seen, on holding an egg up in the sun, the process of hatching is going on ; if not, you may throw it away, as no chicken is formed. The chicken extricates itself from the shell without the assistance of the hen ; it has a hard horny scale at the upper tip of the bill, with which, after the twenty-first day, it begins breaking its shell. Some will extricate themselves in an hour—others two or three ; and sometimes they are a day and a night, or even two days ; but about twelve hours is the average time.

The chickens should be removed one by one, as they are hatched, and laid in a basket, covered with flannel, and put them in a warm place. As the chickens develope themselves the shells should be carefully removed.

When the hen is exhausted from sitting, which is usually the case, she should be fed on crumbs of bread soaked in port wine.

CARE OF THE YOUNG CHICKENS.— For twenty four hours they require nothing but warmth. Whilst hatching, the yolk forms their nourishment, and they take the remaining part of this before leaving the shell, which will sustain them for the day. The second day they should be put in a basket, lined with tow, and with the mother placed in a coop, or long box, with bars in front, which will permit the chickens to run in and out. While the hen is cooped up with her brood she must be supplied with food and water ; and the coop should, if possible, be placed on a grass plat where it gets the sun.

Chickens hatched in winter require to be comfortably housed ; and if the weather is very cold, they must have artificial warmth. Chickens will thrive in cold weather where the hen has the run of the kitchen.

The best food for young chickens is crumbs of bread soaked in milk ; these may be mixed with boiled rice, and the yolk of an egg boiled hard, and chopped up. Meat, under-done, and chopped very fine, is nourishing ; and after two or three days, curds, grits, or oat cake cut very small, may be given them. Fresh water, in a very shallow dish, must be set for them every day, or oftener, should they empty it.

Chickens should be fed for five or six days on the food we have described ; after that time they should have boiled barley, groats, or bruised barley. In a fortnight or three weeks they may go into the poultry-yard with the hen, who will bestow her motherly care on them till they are fully feathered, and no longer require her watchfulness, when she will beat them off if they do not leave her, or are not taken away, and will begin to lay again.

One hen will bring up two or more broods, if they are of the same age, and placed under her care. The advantage of this is that the other hens can be sent back to sit again, or to lay.

FATTENING FOWLS.—The best food for fattening is potatoes and grains, with rice boiled dry as for curry. Bread and milk, barley meal, or oatmeal and milk, with boiled potatoes, mixed with barley-meal, are all excellent fattening diets, and better than greasy, impure mixtures.

Unless they are barn-door fowls, they should be put up in a coop or close room for a fortnight or three weeks, before they are required for table : and if the barn-door fowls have had access to a stable, they require also to be put up. They cannot have anything better than barley meal, boiled in milk ; with a supply of good clean water

KILLING FOWLS.—The most humane way is to take a blunt stick, tolerably heavy, having a bevilled edge, something like a boy's cricket bat, and strike the fowl sharply on the back of the neck, about the third joint from the head. This causes instant death.

This is a much better mode, and the fowl suffers less, than the poulterer's common practice of dislocating the vertebræ of the neck, by a strain or a sudden twist. The straining operation is very cruel, as it must give the fowl great pain ; and the latter requires much dexterity. If done suddenly and effectually it is as merciful as using the bat.

COCHIN CHINA FOWLS.—The management of this breed does not differ much from that of the domestic fowl. Their house should be dry, sheltered, and warm ; they should have the run of a good yard, and the perch for roosting should be placed near the ground. It is better still not to let them roost at all. Give them a bed of straw, which may be placed on a raised platform, or in a basket large enough for them to lay down without injuring their plumage. The straw should be turned over and cleaned every day ; and renewed once a week.

DISEASES OF POULTRY.—The diseases of poultry are numerous, and till of late they have received little attention, probably because an individual fowl is of small value, and it is considered more economical to kill it, than to waste time and money in attempting a cure.

The common disorders of fowls are apoplexy, the pip or thrush, roup, the gapes, moulting, asthma, consumption, corns, diarrhœa, and constipation.

The symptoms of apoplexy are staggering, shaking of the head, and a sort of tipsy aspect. Limit the supply of food, and apply leeches to the back of the neck.

Diarrhœa may be generally cured by a change of diet, and a little chalk administered in gruel; as constipation may by small doses of castor oil, and a diet upon oatmeal porridge, and green vegetables.

The pip is a very painful disease, to which young fowl are peculiarly liable. The symptoms are a thickening of the membrane of the tongue, especially towards the pip, which makes the bird gasp for breath, whilst his plumage becomes ruffled, he mopes, and pines, and if relief cannot be afforded, dies. The part should be anointed with fresh butter or cream. A teaspoonful of castor oil, or thereabouts, according to age or strength, should be administered. It should have an allowance of fresh vegetable food, mixed with potatoes, and a little oatmeal, and a plentiful supply of water.

The croup or roup is caused by cold, moisture, and uncleanness, the symptoms of which are difficult and noisy breathing, swelling of the eyes, discharge from the nostrils and mouth, and loss of appetite. The common remedies are, rather less than a teaspoonful of salt dissolved in water, or rue and garlic beaten up into a mass with butter, and crammed down the fowl's throat.

Gapes may be detected by running at the nostrils, watery eyes, alteration of voice, and loss of appetite and spirits. If the bird dies, and is opened, the trachea, or windpipe, is found full of narrow worms. The best remedy is a grain of calomel, or two or three grains of Plummer's pill; after which flour of sulphur and a little ginger should be administered in barley meal; and the mouth and beak washed with a weak solution of chloride of lime. The bird should be kept in a warm shed or room apart from the rest of the fowls.

When fowls are moulting, they require warmth and shelter, and a diet of a somewhat more stimulating and nutritious character than usual. Sometimes, however, the feathers fall off when the bird is not moulting. This is a disease, and a change of diet should be made, with good air, cleanliness, and a dusting place, or what some call a dust-bath, are essential. Some, however, recommend small quantities of sulphur and nitre mixed with fresh butter, to be given daily.

Corns may be extracted with the point of a penknife. If ulcerated, as will often occur, touch them with lunar caustic.

Indigestion amongst fowls is caused by over-feeding and want of exercise. This is cured by turning the fowl into an open walk, and giving it some powdered gentian and cayenne in its food.

Asthma is a very painful disorder. It is characterised by gaping, panting, and difficulty of breathing. To effect a cure, warmth, with small repeated doses of hippo powder and sulphur mixed with butter are necessary. The addition of cayenne pepper will be an improvement.

Consumption is also a disorder of fowls. If anything can do good it is change of air and warmth.

With regard to diseases the poultry-keeper should always bear in mind that prevention is better than cure. If fowls are well housed, well fed, and kept perfectly clean, with a due attention to their warmth, they will rarely become diseased; and if they should, the attack will be slight, and the cure more simple. The other diseases are chiefly modifications of those enumerated.

Catarrh—or the effusion of water or mucus from the nostrils, with the loss of the sense of smell and sneezing is often relieved by the frequent use of the smelling bottle of ammoniacal salts; and when unaccompanied with fever, this with a pill of calomel and aloes, and immersing the feet in hot water at bed time, will in general be all that is requisite. But when fever exists, or there is much pain in the forehead, inhaling the steam of hot water from a basin, placing a towel at the same time around it to exclude the air and include the head, is another excellent expedient, conjoined with the use of the pills of calomel and aloes, and the saline mixture with antimony every three or four hours.

**Clothing the Poor.**—The charitable institutions, which abound in every district, afford the means to do extensive good at a trifling expense. The lying-in charities, and the societies for providing the poor with change of linen during illness, are excellent institutions, and extend relief from one end of the kingdom to another, without being too heavy an expense for any one. But we are not great admirers of those societies which are formed for clothing the poor. We think much greater benefits would be conferred by teaching them, or at least their children, how to cut out and make their own clothes. These arts are becoming almost unknown among the lower orders; and this, though it may chiefly be caused by the females being engaged in working at manufactories, has been increased by the ease with which they have procured from the charitable ready supplies of every article of clothing. The object of charity should be to relieve and comfort those who labour under sickness and the infirmities of old age. A woman who is compelled to make and repair the clothes of her family will be much more careful of them than one who imagines that she can draw upon the treasury of benevolence for all her wants. To increase the knowledge of the poor, in every respect, is of important-

ance; for, although it be not easy to enlighten the individual who has journeyed through half her course of existence, in a state of ignorance, or to change the habits which years have strengthened and confirmed, yet, occasionally an instance may occur, in which instruction proves a blessing of far greater value than alms, producing such effects upon the welfare and habits of a family, as would result from no other cause; and this should stimulate the benevolent in the good work, although they may meet with unconquerable difficulties in ninety-nine cases out of a hundred.

There is abundance of zeal displayed in every rank and circle of society, and it is only to be regretted that so virtuous an impulse is not always properly directed, and comfort and relief bestowed in a proportion equal to the time and money expended. Charity without judgment is like scattering seed in the ocean, where it sinks or is dissipated on the waves: but, with judgment, it is like seed sown in a friendly and fertile soil, which springs up in due season, and produces a thousand fold in return. In the first case it is the ruin of individual independence, and of that honest pride which seeks to oppose industry and frugality to the pressure of necessity; while, in the other, it is the blessing of Heaven, and the salvation of sinking virtue in the hour of adversity; and presents the sublimest trait in the human character.

**Fomentations.**—These are, generally, decoctions of mucilaginous or narcotic vegetables. But as the best of these, when externally applied, have very little medicinal virtue, flannels wrung out of boiling water, are of equal, if not of superior use to any of them. The flannels should be about two yards long, and sewed together at the ends, so that by means of two sticks, turned in opposite directions, they may be wrung perfectly dry from the boiling water. They should be applied lightly over the part to be fomented, which thus becomes involved in an atmosphere of hot vapour, without the bed or linen of the patient being wetted. As soon as one flannel begins to cool, another should be wrung dry from the water, and be applied to the part, on the instant the other is withdrawn from it.

**General Conduct when Visiting.** —Impropriety of manner in company, though it does not bespeak a very correct mind, may be attendant on an innocent one. A woman may have too much levity of manner ;—may laugh and talk too loud ; give herself many fantastic airs ; be too familiar with some of her acquaintance, and too haughty to others ; and yet she may mean nothing wrong to any one ; and, perhaps, her sole view may be to attract momentary notice, or to endeavour to render herself a person of consequence in the eyes of others. These are weak, but not criminal motives ; and yet they render her liable to derision, and to just censure, even from the lenient in judgment.

Propriety is to a woman what action is to an orator, the first, and second, and third essential ; that propriety is the centre in which the lines of duty and amiability meet ; and is to the character what proportion is to the figure, and grace to the attitude. Propriety thus characterised, is the union of every desirable quality in woman, by which her conduct and manners are influenced under every circumstance. Propriety never desires a deviation from any of the laws of good society, and neither seek notice nor admiration, which, from their natures, would be incompatible with its own characteristics. Improper familiarities, haughtiness, intrusive forwardness to superiors, and insolence to inferiors ; the indulgence of any whim, by which our conduct to others may be influenced, are all equally unknown to propriety.

Unless a woman desire it, she seems but little called upon in public to bring herself and her actions into a prominent point of view, or to render herself a mark for sarcasm and ridicule. At home,

when entertaining guests, she cannot pass altogether so unobtrusively, although the manners of the present period allow of more ease and latitude of deportment than formerly was deemed correct in a lady hostess, whose time and thoughts were condemned to the strictest attention to the comforts and pleasures of her visitors, often to the entire destruction of both.

Ease of manner in a woman is very pleasing, when the self-possession which gives it is unaccompanied by masculine courage, or by an undue value for herself. In general, the manners will be free from any painful degree of constraint, when the mind is not engaged upon self, or occupied with the idea of exciting attention and admiration from those around. Affectation has its origin from these sources ; and this, besides being a symptom of a weak mind, is entirely destructive of good manners. Good sense and simplicity of manners are generally companions, forming a natural gentility, which is far preferable to any artificial politeness, inasmuch as the one is a part of the individual herself, and the other only a garb worn when occasion calls for it. However, those who possess this natural gentility may, by mixing in good society, have the additional polish given to it, which afterwards distinguishes it as the perfection of good manners.

Young ladies should not be brought early into society ; their time should be chiefly devoted to study, and to the application essential to the acquisition of any accomplishment either mental or practical. Instruction will avail little if the thoughts are withdrawn from it by the attractions of society, which even older people often find incompatible with strict attention to their duties, or to serious occupation ; the effect upon the young and lively must be still greater, in rendering application irksome to them, and in diminishing their zeal and interest in the acquisition of knowledge.

The manners of young ladies will be insensibly formed during the progress of their education, and at this period of life, they will derive more advantage from the example afforded them, in the correct and amiable deportment of those amongst whom they live, than could be obtained from an occasional mixture in more general society. To home they should be indebted for the first impression of good manners ;—to the world for the finishing touches only. The consequences of too early an initiation into the supposed delights of routs and balls are, often, an unfinished education, and from late hours, ruined health ; sufficient evils to render parents cautious of yielding, when urged by the solicitations of their daughters, to introduce them early into those scenes of promised delight. Even when the proper season arrives for the indulgence of these natural wishes, moderation in their enjoyment should be strictly observed. This a regard for health requires, and it is, also, a precaution, by which the zest for such pleasures may be kept alive. Satiety is the mortal foe to enjoyment.

On the score of appearances, too, it is by no means desirable for young people to frequent too commonly the haunts of pleasure. It might lead to an unfavourable inference alike as to the inclination and power of a young lady to discharge the obligations of a wife or a mother, and thus obscure her prospects of engaging the notice and approbation of the sensible and reflecting part of the other sex. This remark must be perfectly familiar to the prudent and wary mother, as well as the truism, that what we behold every day we regard with indifference, or rarely notice. The florist covets scarce and choice plants, and not the flowers that are common to his soil and country, and of which he may easily obtain possession.

We do not think that even the manners of a young person are improved by too great a familiarity with the world. It gives a hardness to them, marking the features of the face with symptoms of effrontery, and the whole person with an undaunted air, resulting from self-

complacency. All this may be considered by some as fashionable ease of manner ; but, certainly, the *tout ensemble* is far from interesting or graceful.

Not only appearances, but the comfort of a young lady in public, depends upon her having an unexceptionable escort or *chaperon*, to whom she may have recourse upon any dilemma, and whose experience and greater knowledge of the world may be useful to her in assisting her out of her difficulties. Her mother is, of course, the best escort she can have ; but if circumstances prevent her from accompanying her daughter, a near relation or an intimate friend should supply her place.

**Visiting the Sick.**—This is a duty from which no lady should shrink under the excuse of the danger of contagion to which it exposes them, which is an alarm more imaginary than real. To visit the bed of sickness and poverty united affords an impressive lesson even to an unreflecting mind. Sufferings, unalleviated by the comforts which competency bestows, cannot fail to awaken the tenderest feelings of compassion within us ; and, at the same time, grateful sentiments will naturally arise, when we compare the superior mercies which we enjoy, with the deprivations of health and the necessitous state we behold in others. If we have, at any time, suffered ourselves to repine, or to indulge an impatience of temper when undergoing temporary affliction, no volume that we can peruse will so sensibly arouse us to the sense of our error, as the spectacle which indigence presents to us, when it is conjoined with bodily infirmity. In remembering our happier lot, we cannot refrain from asking ourselves, " Are we more worthy than these sufferers, since our condition is so much superior ?" The question is rarely answered with self-satisfaction. Conscience tells us, that discontent has often pervaded our hearts ; and that, when thwarted in some petty scheme or desire, we have indulged in useless repining. We have never yet visited the indigent sick, nor witnessed any of the trials of poverty, without self-condemnation for the unwilling submission with which we have met the few trials of our lives, nor without forming resolutions for the better ordering of the temper and disposition in future ; and we are persuaded that you, too, would never regret visiting these scenes of affliction, or any of those receptacles which benevolence has provided for the relief of the diseased, or for the support of the infirm, even though they tacitly admonish and reprehend you for impatience under your own sufferings.

While these scenes reprove the children of prosperity, they are a balm to those who are grieving under the trials to which "flesh is heir to." The benevolent satisfaction which springs from the desire to comfort and alleviate the affliction of others removes a portion of our own, and aids our exertions to resume the usual equanimity of our spirits.

If, in the midst of joy, surrounded by all the delights of prosperity, such melancholy scenes present themselves to your view, do not turn from them with disgust, but allow them, for a time, to temper the gaiety of your heart, and to cast a serious colouring over your thoughts ; they will check the feverishness of prosperity, as cooling showers temper summer heats. They will remind you of the precariousness of health, and of the shortness of life ; that neither the one nor the other should be trifled away, nor wasted on sublunary pleasures ; and they will admonish you to prepare for, and, meekly, to endure interruptions to the one, and teach you to adorn, gracefully, with sober virtues, the decline of the latter.

**Sickness of Servants.**—Servants, when ill, require the same kind of management as children. They are often very wayward, and unwilling to take the medicines prescribed for them. On this account, these should be given to them either by the mistress, or by a superior servant who can be depended upon, and who will not, from false kindness, permit them to practise any

deception in this respect. Their aid, also, is requisite to look after other servants when they are ill ; for, if left to themselves, they will seldom, on the approach of recovery, show either prudence or forbearance in the choice and quantity of their food. A sick servant should be seen at least once in the day by her mistress ; and, if possible, also, when the medical visit is paid. It is part of the domestic duty of a lady, to ascertain the exact state of any invalid amongst her household. When there is a want either of comforts or of cleanliness in the sick room, or any inattention towards the invalid from her fellow-servants, the censure belongs undoubtedly to the head of the family, whose general superintendence would have secured the sick person from neglect, and whose example would have shamed into kindness all the unfeeling or careless members of her family.

It is a provoking characteristic of servants, that they allow themselves to be completely overtaken by illness, before they will mention it, or give way to it in the least. By neglecting to take early notice of disease, and refusing alleviation from medicine and other means, it gains power ; and, thus, the patient's sufferings and the general inconvenience of the family are augmented, merely, we believe, from the dread of being doctored.

If the illness of a servant be of short duration, the work may probably be managed amongst the other servants ; but if it be protracted, it will be found advisable to fill up the place with a temporary assistant, lest the other servants become discontented or overworked.

Want of gratitude in servants, who have experienced the greatest kindness during illness, is the complaint of many, and there are instances to justify the assertion, although, no doubt, there are as many proofs of grateful attachment to weigh in the opposite balance. Yet, if we do meet with ingratitude, our cares, and desire to do good should not be diminished, since in no instance can the failings of others justify any omissions in kindness or duty on our part.

The expenses attendant on the illness of a domestic should undoubtedly be defrayed by her employer. We think there are very few cases in which the medical debt of a servant, falling ill while discharging her duty to her employers, should the expense be met of her removal into the country, provided change of air is deemed necessary for the re-establishment of health. On recovering from acute diseases, this change is generally very desirable ; but unless the friends of the servant, to whom it is natural she should wish to be removed, live in good air, and are able to provide her with suitable nourishment, her strength may, perhaps, return to her more rapidly, by remaining in her place, in possession of the comforts necessary for the entire restoration of her health.

**Hints to Lady Equestrians.**—The art of horsemanship does not consist in merely knowing how to mount, how to hold the reins, how to sit with security and grace, nor how to compel the horse to walk that canters or gallops at the will of the rider. All these are indispensable. But there is also the art of drawing forth the *willing* obedience of the animal. This is to be obtained only by a kind, temperate, and uniform treatment, and by a thorough knowledge of his habits and instincts. How different is a ride on a well-kept, well-used horse, who feels that he carries a *friend*, to one on a broken-spirited or timid creature, in whom ill-usage has produced many defects. In the former case, the exercise is as great a pleasure to the horse as to his rider. He sniffs the air, he pricks up his ears, he throws forward his feet with energy. Life has to him delights beyond his stall and his corn. The horse is naturally gentle, intelligent, and affectionate ; but these qualities are not sufficiently studied or appreciated. He is usually regarded merely as a means of health and pleasure to his owner, and not often is either gratitude, kindness, or sympathy extended to him in return.

Occasionally horses are found vicious and unmanageable ; but defects of temper may generally be traced to the ill-treatment of some reckless master, some cruel trainer, or some ignorant groom. Even in these cases, mild, but firm treatment, may render him gentle and tractable.

SADDLING.—In saddling, the groom very frequently flings the saddle on the horse's back, and at once proceeds to tighten the girths to the extent required. This causes the animal great inconvenience, which he resents by throwing back his ears, and trying to bite or kick his tormentor ; for which he is corrected in very strong language, if not by a blow, and his temper ruffled, to the discomfort of his rider. The horse, being accustomed to such rough treatment, endeavours, by puffing himself out, to lessen, in some degree, the distress experienced from this mode of saddling ; and, in consequence, when the rider has been on the road some half hour, she finds her seat become loose and unsteady. Should the horse start or shy, and the rider be inexperienced, she may lose her balance (in which case the saddle will turn round) and be precipitated to the ground.

The humane and experienced groom will place the saddle lightly on the back of the horse, patting him kindly as he does so. Then, drawing up the girths to within two holes of the required tightness, will so leave it for a quarter of an hour. By this time the saddle will be warm, when it may be tightened as much as necessary, without pain or discomfort to the animal, and, moreover, greatly lessening the chances of a wrung back or withers.

A lady's saddle should be placed more backward on the horse than a gentleman's, to keep the heavy weight of the iron as far from the withers as possible.

MOUNTING, AND USE OF THE REINS.—In mounting, place the left foot in the hand of the groom, resting the right hand on the pommel of the saddle. Spring lightly, but surely, into the seat, neither throwing too much weight on the hand of the assistant, nor pulling at the saddle ; both are ungraceful, and, after a little practice, unnecessary. Let the groom arrange the habit carefully between the foot and the stirrup. If well arranged at first, it ought to remain so during the ride. The habit should never be pinned under the foot ; it is sure to tear the skirt, and prevent it falling gracefully and easily. Seat yourself rather backward on the saddle, taking care that the figure be erect, and the shoulders perfectly square with your seat. Take the reins in the left hand. If you ride on the curb, raise that first, leaving the left rein outside the hand, or between the third and fourth fingers —the right side of the rein between the first and second fingers. Then raise the snaffle, leaving the left rein outside the hand, and the right with the curb, between the first and second fingers. Leave the snaffle looser than the curb, so as to hang gracefully in a festoon from the bit. Double all the four reins together over the forefinger, placing the thumb firmly on them.

Should you prefer riding on the snaffle, which, to an inexperienced rider, is perhaps safer, and certainly, in such a case, preferable for the horse, reverse the instructions above given, taking up the snaffle first, &c.—keep the elbows close to the body—not in young lady fashion, so as to form a triangle with the waist, by which rounding and stooping of the shoulders is produced, and all power over the horse lost. The hands should always be kept low, as near the saddle as possible. In guiding the horse by the rein, use the hand only, from the wrist downwards. Never use the arms. If you wish your horse to move to the right, bend the hand slightly inwards towards the body, so as to tighten the right rein, and loosen the left. If you wish him to move to the left, depress your hand slightly, which will tighten the left rein and loosen the right. In both cases, keep the wrist unmoved. It should be done by the hand alone, and imperceptibly—

a slight balancing motion of the body, so slight as to be *felt*, not *seen*, should accompany the action of the hand.

The management of the reins is the greatest difficulty in horsemanship, and, by some persons, it is a difficulty never altogether overcome. Do not pull at a horse's mouth. Work the reins continually very gently, and easily, but let there be no strain on him, or he will certainly learn to pull, and lose the graceful easy carriage of his head. A thoroughbred horse should have his mouth so light, that he may be ridden with a piece of packthread. But a bad rider may teach him to pull, in a very few lessons. By working the mouth is meant a light wavy motion of the hand, not tiring to the rider, and pleasing to the horse—to be acquired by practice and attention only.

The reins should never be required to assist the seat—we mean that perfect balance that enables the rider to do what she will, without interfering with the action of the horse. The perfect rider should be able to bend her body down to the stirrup on the left side, or down to the girth on the right, to throw her arms over-head, and yet her horse not swerve in the least. A lady who has a perfect seat may throw her stirrup aside, and her reins across her horse's neck, and yet be able to guide him by the mere balance of her body, whether in walking, cantering, trotting, or galloping.

We had almost forgotten to mention the whip. It should be carried in the right hand, and simply as an ornament. A good rider never requires it ; a kind rider will never use it. The man who strikes the willing creature who carries him through heat and cold, through wind and rain, in spite of fatigue or thirst, degrades himself by the act. A lady—a *lady*, uses the hand that holds the whip but to pat and encourage. "Poor fellow ! Good horse !" will do more with the noble animal than the blow.

CANTERING.—On first setting forth, the horse should be allowed to walk a short distance. Some riders gather up their reins hastily, and before they have secured them properly, allow the animal to trot or canter off. Such a proceeding is often productive of mischief, sometimes of accident. A lady's horse should canter with the right foot. The left, produces a rough unpleasant motion and ungraceful appearance. The whole body is jerked at every stride. Should the animal have been trained to canter with the left foot, a little perseverance will soon teach him better. Hold the rein so as to tighten it slightly on the left side of the mouth, touch (not hit) him gently on the right shoulder with the whip—sit well back in the saddle, so as not to throw weight on the shoulder. The horse will soon understand what is required of him. But if he does not, try again after an interval of a few minutes. Straighten the reins immediately he throws out the right foot. Pat and encourage him with kind words, but repeat the operation should he change his feet, which he may do before getting accustomed to his new step. The considerate rider will not compel him to canter too long at a time, for it is very fatiguing. That it is so, is easily proved by the fact that the steed of a lady, too fond of cantering, becomes weak in the forelegs, or what is commonly called " groggy."

TROTTING.—Trotting, if well performed, is very graceful, but is more difficult to acquire than cantering. The rider should sit slightly more forward than for cantering, on, but not more forward than, the centre of the seat, pressing the knee firmly against the saddle, and keeping the foot perfectly straight (rather turned in than out) in the stirrup. She must rise slightly with every step of the animal, taking care to keep the shoulders quite square with the horse. To lean over one side or the other, be the inclination ever so slight, or to bring forward one shoulder more than the other, has a very bad appearance. A good horsewoman will avoid the common error of leaning forward when trotting. It is not only very un-

graceful, but in the attitude nearly all power is lost. The arms are comparatively useless. Should the horse stumble, the rider risks being thrown over his head. Her position deprives her of the power of assisting her horse to rise, whilst the additional weight thrown on his shoulders prevents him from helping himself. At all times, the broad part of the foot only should rest on the iron of the stirrup.

SHYING.—Should a horse shy, he does it generally from timidity. The common practice of forcing a horse to approach very near the object of alarm is a foolish and useless abuse of power. He should be encouraged by words and patting on the neck, and above all by the fearlessness of his rider. A horse soon learns to depend greatly on his mistress. Should she start, or feel timid, he perceives it immediately, and will prick up his ears and look about him for the cause. On the other hand, we have known many real dangers encountered with safety, through the rider having sufficient presence of mind to break out into a snatch of song (all horses like singing), which has diverted his attention from the object of fear.

REARING.—Should a horse rear, lean the body forward, loosing the reins at the same moment ; press both hands, if necessary, on the mane. Should a horse however rear so as to endanger the safety of the rider, loosen well the rein, pass the whip from the right hand to the left, double up the right hand to a fist, and hit him between the ears. Show no fear, but trot on as though nothing had occurred. Turn his head towards home, and he will be certain to repeat his feat on a future occasion ! The above is rarely necessary, and should only be done in a case of urgency.

A lady rode a spirited thoroughbred horse. She had been ill for a short time, and the groom had been ordered to exercise him every day. Recovered from her indisposition, the lady again mounted her favourite. She had not proceeded far on her ride, before she encountered one of those high trucks often seen in country towns. At sight of this the horse reared fearfully. His rider pressed all her weight on him, and he descended, but only to rise still higher. As she cast up her eyes, she saw his fore-feet pawing the air above her head. He stood so erect, that she almost fell backwards. The bystanders screamed—the groom rode up: "Drop off, ma'am! oh, pray drop off!" he exclaimed, adding, in the excitement of the moment, a truth he might have concealed, "I always do." The lady fortunately preserved her presence of mind; she shifted her whip, and struck the horse with all her force between the ears. He descended instantly. Then (it was the first and last time she ever struck him) she beat him with her whip, and rode on as though nothing had happened. On enquiry, it was discovered that the groom had taken the horse out for exercise three times, had each time encountered a truck, and had each time dropped off behind when the horse reared, which he did at first through fear, but afterwards through "trickiness," for the purpose of getting home.

KICKING.—Should a horse kick, take care to keep him well in hand. He cannot kick, unless he throws his head down; and he cannot do that if the reins are held carelessly loose. A practised rider can always tell when a horse is about to kick, by a peculiar motion of his body. It is instantaneous, but unmistakable. The best-tempered horse may kick occasionally, from a rub of the saddle, or pressure on the withers. The animal should not be beaten, but the cause of his misconduct inquired into.

DISMOUNTING.—The ride being over, the horse should stand in the stable with the girths loosened, but the saddle untouched on his back, for at least twenty minutes, when it may be removed without inconvenience. Should the animal, if usually quiet, have misbehaved in any manner, the cause will generally appear as soon as the saddle is removed. Snatching the saddle from the horse's back while it is still heated, often produces swellings, particularly if the skin be at all irritated by friction. The saddle should be sponged and dried, either in the sun, or by the harness-room or kitchen-fire, before being put away. This precaution prevents the stuffing from hardening. A humane rider will always attend to the lining of the saddle, for a wrung back must be sad pain. A horse will shrink from the slightest touch of a finger on the injured part; what must, then, be the torture of the weight of a saddle and rider? We owe much pleasure to our saddle-horse; should we not do all we can to preserve him from pain?

With horses, anything can be achieved by gentleness and consideration—not the consideration of weakness, usually termed "spoiling," but the consideration prompted by admiration and love for God's creatures—pity for helplessness—and that true generosity which should always accompany power. The following instance will exemplify our meaning. A beautiful Irish mare, almost thoroughbred, had been ridden as a hunter, and afterwards by a lady. Being somewhat too high in her paces, it was intended to put her with another into harness. Immediately the coachman attached her to the carriage (an open one), she threw herself down on the stones of the stable-yard—she was whipped up, and again attached to the carriage, and again threw herself down. While the second course of whipping was being administered, a compassionate housemaid ran into the drawing room, and informed her mistress of what was going on. The lady immediately walked round through the garden, ordered the mare to be conveyed to the stable, and, on the following day, stood by the creature, feeding her with bread, and patting her silken neck while she was being attached to the carriage. Then, taking the reins in her own hand, slipping them through her fingers as she passed the animal, stroking and caressing her as she went, she drove out of the stable-yard to the great astonishment of the coachman. This creature in a few days became a perfectly trained carriage horse. She was, of course, awkward at first, but never obstinate.

**To Preserve a Bouquet.**—When you receive a bouquet, sprinkle it lightly with fresh water. Then put it into a vessel containing some soap-suds ; this will nutrify the roots, and keep the flowers bright as new. Take the bouquet out of the suds every morning and lay it sideways (the sock entering first) into clean water, keep it there a minute or two, then take it out, and sprinkle the flowers lightly by the hand with water. Replace it in the soap-suds, and it will bloom as fresh as when first gathered. The soap-suds need changing every three or four days. By observing these rules, a bouquet can be kept bright and beautiful for at least a month, and will last still longer in a very passable state ; but attention to the fair but frail creatures, as directed above, must be strictly observed, or all will perish.

**Peeling Potatoes.**—All the starch in potatoes is found very near the surface ; the heart contains but little nutriment. Ignorance of this fact may form a plausible excuse for those who cut off thick parings, but none to those who know better. Circulate the injunction, " pare thin the potato skin." Then, too, consider the economy of it.

**A Cheap and Efficient Filter.**—Procure a clean flower-pot (common kind), close the opening of the bottom by a piece of sponge, then place in the inside a layer of small stones, previously well cleaned by washing. This layer may be about two inches deep, the upper stones being very small. Next procure some freshly-burnt charcoal, which has not been kept in the dark or foul place, as it rapidly absorbs any strong smells, and so becomes tainted, and unfit for such purpose ; reduce this to powder, and mix it with about twice its bulk of clear, well-washed, sharp sand. With this mixture fill the pot to within a short distance of the top,

cover it with a layer of small stones. At intervals change the charcoal.

**Diptheria.**—This name was given to the disease on account of its tendency to form false membranes over the parts affected, which are the bronchial and respiratory passages. The progress of the disease is very rapid, and it commonly causes death by suffocation. A Mr. McDonald, who appears to have had considerable experience in diptheria, says, " The best line of action, I find, is as follows :—After a clearance of the bowels with calomel and rhubarb, I order strong beef tea, wine, and above all, Bass's pale ale ; the patients express themselves much relieved in the throat as it is swallowed, and feel greatly exhilarated after taking it. The medicine I find of most use is an ounce of the compound tincture of quinine, taken in wine and water, every four hours. As a local application (and it is by the personal inspection of the throat, and the personal use of the applications, that we may hope to benefit the sufferer), I find the best and most efficacious is equal parts of honey and concentrated muriatic acid, applied with a probang to the whole of the false membrane, about every sixth hour. As a gargle, borax and honey, mixed with a little brandy and water, is very useful ; and, after the stripping off of the false membranes, a gargle mixed with tannic acid and water affords great comfort."

**Married Women's Property Act.**—Whereas it is desirable to amend the law of property and contract with respect to married women :

Be it enacted by the Queen's most Excellent Majesty, by and with the advice and consent of the Lords Spiritual and Temporal, and Commons, in this present Parliament assembled, and by the authority of the same as follows :

Earnings of Married Women to be Deemed their Own Property.—1. The wages and earnings of any married woman in any employment, occupation, or trade in which she is engaged or which she carries on separately from her husband, and also any money or property so acquired by her through her husband, and also any money or property so acquired by her through the exercise of any literary, artistic, or scientific skill, and all investments of such wages, earnings, money, or property, shall be deemed and taken to be property held and settled to her separate use, independent of any husband.

DEPOSITS IN SAVINGS BANKS BY A MARRIED WOMAN TO BE DEEMED HER SEPARATE PROPERTY.—2. Deposits in savings banks in the name of a married woman, or in the name of a woman who may marry after such deposit or grant, shall be deemed to be the separate property of such woman, and the same shall be accounted for and paid to her as if she were an unmarried woman.

AS TO A MARRIED WOMAN'S PROPERTY IN THE FUNDS.—3. Any married woman, or any woman about to be married, may apply to the Governor and Company of the Bank of England by a form to be provided by the governor of each of the said company for that purpose, that any fund forming part of the public stocks and funds, and not being less than twenty pounds, to which the woman so applying is entitled, or which she is about to acquire, may be transferred to or made to stand in the books of the governor and company to whom such application is made in the name or intended name of the woman as a married woman entitled to her separate use, and on such sum being entered in the books of the said governor and company accordingly the same shall be transferred and the dividends paid as if she were an unmarried woman.

AS TO A MARRIED WOMAN'S PROPERTY IN A JOINT STOCK COMPANY OR A SOCIETY.—4. Any married woman, or any woman about to be married, may apply in writing to the managers of any incorporated or joint stock company that any fully paid up shares, or any debenture or debenture stock, or any stock of such company, to the holding of which no liability is attached, and to which the woman so applying is en-

titled, may be registered in the books of the said company in the name or intended name of the woman as a married woman entitled to her separate use, and the same upon being registered shall be deemed to be the separate property of such woman, and shall be transferred and the dividends and profits paid as if she were an unmarried woman.

DEPOSIT OF MONEYS IN FRAUD OF CREDITORS INVALID.—5. Nothing hereinbefore contained in reference to moneys deposited in or annuities granted by saving-banks or moneys invested in the funds or in shares or stock of any company shall as against creditors of the husband give validity to any deposit or investment of moneys of the husband made in fraud of such creditors, and any moneys so deposited or invested may be followed as if this Act had not passed.

PERSONAL PROPERTY NOT EXCEEDING £200 COMING TO A MARRIED WOMAN TO BE HER OWN.—6. When any woman married shall during her marriage become entitled to any personal property as next of kin or one of the next of kin of an intestate, or to any sum of money not exceeding two hundred pounds under any deed or will, such property shall belong to the woman for her separate use, and her receipts alone shall be a good discharge for the same.

FREEHOLD PROPERTY COMING TO A MARRIED WOMAN, RENTS AND PROFITS ONLY TO BE HER OWN.—7.—Where any freehold, copyhold, or customaryhold property shall descend upon any woman married as heiress or co-heiress of an intestate, the rents and profits of such property shall belong to such woman for her separate use.

HOW QUESTIONS AS TO OWNERSHIP OF PROPERTY ARE TO BE SETTLED.—8. In any question between husband and wife as to property declared by this Act to be the separate property of the wife, either party may apply to the judge of the County Court of the district in which either party resides, and thereupon the judge may make such order, direct such inquiry, and award such costs as he shall think fit.

MARRIED WOMEN MAY EFFECT POLICY OF INSURANCE.—9. A married woman may effect a policy of insurance upon her own life or the life of her husband for her separate use, and the same and all benefit thereof, if expressed on the face of it to be so effected, shall enure accordingly, and the contract in such policy shall be as valid as if made with an unmarried woman.

AS TO INSURANCE OF A HUSBAND FOR BENEFIT OF HIS WIFE.—10. A policy of insurance effected by any married man on his own life, and expressed upon the face of it to be for the benefit of his wife and children, or any of them, shall enure and be deemed a trust for the benefit of his wife for her separate use, and of his children, or any of them, according to the interest so expressed, and shall not, so long as any object of the trust remains, be subject to the control of her husband or of his creditors, or form part of his estate. When the sum secured by the policy becomes payable, or at any time previously, a trustee thereof may be appointed by the judge of the County Court of the district. If it shall be proved that the policy was effected and premiums paid by the husband with intent to defraud his creditors, they shall be entitled to receive out of the sum secured an amount equal to the premiums so paid.

MARRIED WOMEN MAY MAINTAIN AN ACTION.—11. A married woman may maintain an action in her own name for the recovery of any wages, earnings, money, and property by this Act declared to be her separate property, or of any property belonging to her before marriage, and which her husband shall, by writing under his hand, have agreed with her shall belong to her after marriage as her separate property, and she shall have in her own name the same remedies, civil and criminal, against all persons whomsoever for the protection and security of such wages, earnings, money, &c.

HUSBAND NOT TO BE LIABLE ON HIS WIFE'S CONTRACTS BEFORE HER MARRIAGE.—12. A husband shall not, by reason of any marriage which shall take place after this Act has come into operation, be liable for the debts of his wife contracted before marriage, but his wife shall be liable to be sued for, and any property belonging to her for her separate use shall be liable to satisfy such debts as if she had continued unmarried.

MARRIED WOMEN TO BE LIABLE TO THE PARISH FOR THE MAINTENANCE OF THEIR HUSBANDS.—13. Where in England the husband of any woman having separate property becomes chargeable to any union or parish, the justices having jurisdiction in such union or parish may, in petty sessions assembled, upon application of the guardians of the poor, issue a summons against the wife, and make and enforce such order against her for the maintenance of her husband.

MARRIED WOMEN TO BE LIABLE TO THE PARISH FOR THE MAINTENANCE OF THEIR CHILDREN.—14. A married woman having separate property shall be subject to all such liability for the maintenance of her children as a widow is now by law subject to for the maintenance of her children : provided always that nothing in this Act shall relieve her husband from any liability at present imposed upon him by law to maintain her children.

This Act does not extend to Scotland.

**Birthdays of the Queen and Royal Family**—Her Majesty, Alexandrina Victoria, Queen of Great Britain and Ireland ; born May 24, 1819 ; succeeded William IV. June 20, 1837 ; crowned June 28, 1838 ; married Feb. 10, 1840, to her cousin Prince Albert of Saxe-Coburg, whose lamented death occurred on the 14th of December, 1861. Issue of the marriage :—

H.R.H. Victoria Adelaide Mary Louisa, Princess Royal ; born November 21, 1840 ; married January 25, 1858, to H.R.H. Prince Frederick William of

Prussia, heir to the throne of the German empire.

H.R.H. Albert Edward, Prince of Wales, Duke of Saxony, Cornwall, and Rothesay, Earl of Dublin ; born November 9, 1841 ; married, March 10, 1863, to H.R.H. Princess Alexandra of Denmark.

H.R.H. Alice Maud Mary ; born April 25, 1843 ; married July 1, 1862, to Prince Louis of Hesse.

H.R.H. Alfred Ernest Albert, Duke of Edinburgh ; born August 6, 1844.

H.R.H. Helena Augusta Victoria ; born May 25, 1846 ; married July 5, 1866, to H.R.H. Prince Christian of Augustenburg.

H.R.H. Louisa Caroline Alberta ; born March 18, 1848 ; married Marquis of Lorne, 1871.

H.R.H. Arthur William Patrick Albert ; born May 1, 1850.

H.R.H. Leopold George Duncan Albert ; born April 7, 1853.

H.R.H. Beatrice Mary Victoria ; born April 14, 1857.

**County Courts.**—On Entering the Plaint, when the demand does not exceed £1—10d. ; and every additional £1, or less amount, 10d. (In Plaints for Recovery of Possession of Tenements, the poundage to be estimated on the weekly, monthly, or yearly rent of Tenement.)

Judgment by Consent—when the demand does not exceed £1—1s. ; and every additional £1, or less amount, 1s.

Every Hearing, with or without Jury, when the demand does not exceed £1 —2s. ; and every additional £1, or less amount, 2s.

Judgment by Default—when the demand does not exceed £1—1s. ; and every additional £1, or less amount, 1s.

Summons for Commitment—when the amount of the original demand remaining due shall not exceed £1—3d., and every additional £1, or less, 3d.

Hearing of Summons for Commitment—when the amount of the original demand remaining due shall not exceed £1—6d. ; and every additional £1, or less amount, 6d.

Warrant of Execution, or Commitment, or to Recover Possession—when the amount for which the Warrant issues shall not exceed £1—1s. 6d. ; and every additional £1, or less amount, 1s. 6d. (Warrants for Recovery of Possession of Tenements, to be charged on the weekly, monthly, quarterly, or yearly rent of Tenement.)

If the Plaintiff recovers less than the amount of his claim, so as to reduce the scale of costs, the Plaintiff to pay the difference, unless the reduction be caused by a set-off.

**The Weather.**—If the dew lie plentifully on the grass after a fair day, it is the sign of another ; if not, and there is no wind, rain must follow. A red evening sky portends fine weather ; but if it spreads too far upwards from the horizon in the evening, and especially in the morning, it foretells wind, or rain, or both. When the sky in windy weather is tinged with sea-green, the rain will increase ; if with deep blue it will be showery. When the clouds are formed like fleeces, but dense in the middle and bright towards the edges, with the sky bright, they are signs of frost, with hail, snow, or rain. Two currents of clouds always portend rain, and in summer thunder. If the moon looks pale and dim, expect rain ; if red, wind ; and if her natural colour, with a clear sky, fair weather.

**To Preserve the Colours of Dresses.**—The colours of merinos, mousseline-de-laines, ginghams, printed lawns, chintzes, &c., may be preserved by using water that is only milk-warm ; making a lather with white soap, *before* you put in the dress, instead of rubbing it on the material ; and stirring into it a first and second tub of water a large tablespoonful of ox-gall. The gall can be obtained from the butcher, and a bottle of it should always be kept in every house. No coloured articles should be allowed to remain long in the water. They must be washed fast, and then rinsed through two cold waters. Into each rinsing water, stir a teaspoonful of vinegar, which will help to brighten the colours ; and after rinsing hang them out immediately. When *ironing-dry,* (or still a little damp,) bring them in ; have irons ready heated, and iron them at once, as it injures the colours to allow them to remain damp too long, or to sprinkle and roll them up in a covering for ironing next day. If they cannot be conveniently ironed immediately, let them hang till they are *quite* dry ; and then damp and fold them on the following day, a quarter of an hour before ironing. The best way is not to do coloured dresses on the day of the general wash, but to give them a morning by themselves. They should only be undertaken in clear bright weather. If allowed to freeze, the colours will be irreparably injured. We need scarcely say that no coloured articles should ever be boiled or scalded. If you get from a shop a slip for testing the durability of colours, give it a fair trial by washing it as above ; afterwards, pinning it to the edge of a towel, and hanging it to dry. Some colours, (especially pinks and light greens,) though they may stand perfectly well in washing, will change as soon as a warm iron is applied to them ; the pink turning purplish, and the green bluish. No coloured article should be smoothed with a *hot* iron.

**Changes of Weather Indicated by the Clouds.**—1. The clouds, called Cirrus, appear early after serene weather ; they are, at first, indicated by a few threads pencilled as it were on the sky ; these increase in length, and new ones are, in the meantime, added laterally. Often the first formed threads serve as stems to support numerous branches, which in their turn give rise to others. Their duration is uncertain, varying, from a few minutes after their first appearance, to an extent of many hours. It is long when they appear alone, and at great heights ; and shorter when they are formed lower, and in the vicinity of other clouds. This modification, although in appearance almost motionless, is intimately connected with the motion of the atmosphere ; and

clouds of this kind have long been deemed a prognostic of the wind.

2. In fair weather, with light variable breezes, the sky is seldom quite clear from small groups of the oblique cirrus, which frequently come on from the leeward, and the direction of their increase is to the windward. Continued wet weather is attended with horizontal sheets of this cloud, which subside quickly, and pass to the cirro-stratus. The cirrus pointing upward, is a distant indication of rain ; and downward, a more immediate one of fair weather. Before storms they appear lower and denser, and usually in the quarter opposite to that from which the storm arises. Steady high winds are also preceded and attended by streaks running quite across the sky, in the direction they blow in. These, by an optical deception, appear to meet in the horizon.

3. The shooting or falling star, precedes a change of wind.

4. If clouds appear gradually to diminish, and dissolve into the air, so as to become invisible, it is an indication of fine weather.

5. If the sky, after being for a long time serene and blue, become fretted and spotted with undulated clouds, not unlike the waves of the sea, rain will speedily follow.

6. It not unfrequently happens that two different currents of clouds appear ; these are certain signs of rain, particularly if the lower current fly swiftly before the wind. Should two such currents appear during summer, or hot weather, they announce a speedy thunder storm.

7. When it rains with an east wind, it will probably continue for twenty-four hours.

8. While rain is falling, if any small space of the sky be observable, it is almost a certain sign that the rain will speedily cease.

9. When the solar rays break through the clouds, and are visible in the air, it shows that the atmosphere is filled with vapours, which will speedily be converted into rain.

COVER FOR A POLISHED BOX-IRON.

**Cover for a Polished Box-Iron.**—It is of great importance to keep a polished steel iron used for laces and fine muslins, protected from the air and damp ; it should, therefore, be provided with a cover. The one in our illustration is made of white frieze, in four pieces, put together according to that given above, and ornamented with scarlet star-braid, and a pattern worked in point rusze, with scarlet crewel. The cover, it may be seen, buttons on the top.

**Coloured Transparencies.**—Trace the subjoined design on a large square of moderately stout cardboard ; or, instead of a square, say a piece fourteen inches by eleven. The tracing should be as light as possible. With a sharp penknife cut round the entire outline, leaving the vase and flowers attached only at the base, A to A. It will be perceived that none of the pieces are entirely severed from one another, every one being joined at some place to the whole. Thus there is one continuous outline, but none of the other lines must touch it or each other. The centres of the leaves are cut through in the middle, but the cut does not extend to the sides. Colour the portion of the card indicated by the dotted lines F to G, on the opposite side of the card from which it is to be looked at, from B to C, and from D to E, with a smear of strong carmine, from C to D with sap green, from F to F cobalt blue, and all the rest of the edges within the dotted lines with a paler tint of green. The part round the vase is left uncoloured. Let the colours be both deep and full. They must be put on very strong in tint ; no skill is needed ; any one can do it well with a paint-brush. When completed, bend the group of flowers and vase the very least bit possible backwards through the aperture. In this state hold it up towards the light of a candle or single gas-burner, the coloured part turned towards the light. The effect is beautiful. Wall papers with floral designs will furnish ample models, or any vase or group of flowers, only in cutting them the operator must remember never to sever them entirely one from another. The best way to trace a pattern for this pur-

DESIGN FOR A TRANSPARENCY.

pose is to prick the design all over and dot through the pricked holes in pencil ; or use a tracing-paper made by scraping a quantity of black chalk or charcoal on a piece of writing-paper, and rubbing i well into the paper. Place this face downwards on the card. Having previously traced the design you wish to

W

produce on transparent tracing-paper, place it on the black, and with a sharp pencil mark the outline hard. Enough will remain on the card for the experimenter to lightly draw in the subject when the papers are removed. The less the outline which is drawn is visible, the better the effect. Busts and statues also form charming subjects, and may easily be traced from photographs.

**To Clean Feathers for Bedding.** —Mix well with a gallon of clear water one pound of quicklime ; and when the lime is precipitated in fine powder, pour off the clear lime-water for use at the time it is wanted. Put the feathers to be cleaned in a tub, and add to them a sufficient quantity of the clear lime-water, so as to cover them about three inches. The feathers, when thoroughly moistened, will sink down, and should remain in the lime-water for three or four days, after which, the foul liquor should be separated from them by laying them on a sieve. Afterwards, well wash them in clean water, and dry them on nets, about the same fineness as cabbage nets. Shake them from time to time on the nets ; as they dry, they will fall through the meshes, when collect them for use. The admission of air will be serviceable in the drying, and the whole process may be completed in about three weeks. The feathers thus prepared, want nothing further than beating, to be used either for beds, bolsters, pillows, &c.

**Vegetable Marrow.**—Cut a marrow into three or four slices, take out the seeds, and put them in boiling water with a small handful of salt, and let them boil for half an hour, longer, if the marrows are old. Serve them on toast and cover them with melted butter. If they are preferred mashed, they should be well drained when taken from the water, and beaten smooth with a wooden spoon, and seasoned with pepper and salt, and the dish garnished with toast sippets. Sometimes, when served in slices, they are covered with egg and bread-crumbs, and fried in boiling lard. Cooked **any** way, however, vegetable marrow is very nice eating, and unfortunately it is only in season for three months in the year, July, August, and September.

**Green Pea-Soup.**—Into half a gallon of water (stock, if at hand,) put a quart of *old* green peas, a slice or two of ham, two small onions, a little mint, and simmer the whole in a stewpan until the peas are done ; after that press them through a colander, or a fine-holed sieve, with the back of a wooden spoon. Separately, but simultaneously, boil a quart of *young* peas, with two lettuces, cut up small, and two ounces of butter ; when the young peas are done, add them to the older sort, and give them a boil up, and then serve. This soup is not often made in families, nor is it a very profitable one, nor simple in its preparation. If the soup, when done, is not considered thick enough, boil the crumb of a roll in a little of the soup, and rub it through a fine sieve, then add it to the soup, and boil. Serve very hot in a tureen with toasted bread.

**Pea Soup Without Meat.**—At p. 72 we gave an excellent receipt for this soup with meat, the following is for pea soup without meat :—Put one pound of split peas into a gallon of liquor in which a piece of salt beef or pork has been previously boiled ; add to this two onions and carrots, a little mint, and as much pepper and salt as the taste may approve. The vegetables, cut in small pieces, should be first fried in dripping for a quarter of an hour before putting them in with the liquor and the peas. When the ingredients are brought together in the saucepan, they will take a good three hours before the peas are nice and tender ; of course they should be well soaked, before boiling, for twelve hours, as mentioned in the previous receipt. When done, and taken up, crush the pulp of the peas through a sieve, return it to the soup, and let it boil for half an hour longer ; then again press the peas through a fine sieve, and serve them and the soup with toasted bread. This excellent soup can be made for the sum of five farthings a quart.

**Pease Pudding.**—The making of *Pease Pudding* may as well be noticed here. Dry before a fire a quart of split peas, and tie them up in a cloth, not too tight, just sufficient to give them a little play; then immerse them in a stewpan full of warm water, and let the peas boil until they are quite tender, when they should be removed from the cloth, and beaten up with salt and the yolks of two eggs, until the pudding is quite smooth, when it should be boiled in a cloth for another hour.

**Cucumbers, to Dress.**—After the cucumber is carefully peeled, cut it in thin slices, commencing at the thick end; if begun at the thin end a bitter taste is imparted to it throughout. Sprinkle pepper and salt over the slices, and put them into a shallow dish, and cover them with equal parts of salad-oil and vinegar, in which turn the slices about that they may become perfectly saturated. Be it observed, that the slices ought to be very evenly cut of a uniform thickness, and not some half as thick again as others. To avoid this imperfection to a dish of cucumber, as well as trouble to those who have to prepare it, an instrument has been made on purpose for slicing cucumbers; this will quickly cut them up into mere shavings of slices, with unerring exactitude in thickness. Cucumbers are in their prime of season from the middle of July to the end of September; forced ones are to be had from March to June. They are generally used with salads, salmon, and cheese.

**Dried Peas as an Article of Diet.** —Peas are a valuable article of diet, and their use might be extended with great advantage. For example, if your bread be made at home, sometimes add one pound of pea-meal to every stone of flour, and it will make the bread all the more nutritious. Peas are a very supporting food both for grown people and for children. Medical authority recommends that peas should be eaten once or twice a week throughout the year.

**To Prepare Good Stock.**—Broth, or, as it is termed, stock, is the base of all soups and gravies. The right and economical preparation of this material should be well understood by all housekeepers.

Old meat gives more flavour to broths than young meat, and brown than white.

The remains of roasted meat put into the stock-pot greatly improves the flavour of stock.

Meat should not be put into the stock while boiling, as this prevents the extraction of the juices.

Bones should always form a part of the stock-pot's contents; they are said to yield much more gelatine than is to be obtained from meat, two ounces of bones producing as much gelatine as one pound of meat; but as bones do not contain any flavouring matter, soup made entirely from them would, though nourishing, be tasteless.

The best kind of stock is made from beef, as it possesses more colour and flavour than other meats; veal lacks flavour, and mutton is apt to have a tallowy taste. Use fresh meat for stock, and mix various kinds; rabbit, old fowl, pigeons, or partridge, added to meat stock, greatly improve the flavour.

The liquor in which a joint of meat is boiled is good stock, to which bones well broken up should be added, along with gristle and cuttings of meat useless for other purposes.

As the scum rises be careful to skim it off; the stock must not be allowed to boil before this is thoroughly done, after which the salt and vegetables can be added. A tomato gives fine flavour. Any cutting of meat nicely broiled and put in is also an improvement.

Supposing stock has to be expressly made, the best way is to cut up the meat into small pieces, set it on in cold water, allowing one quart of water to one pound of meat. As the scum rises, skim carefully, then let it boil, add vegetables and seasoning, and simmer slowly for six hours.

Cow-heel jelly enriches soups, so also does butter. To preserve gravy meat it should be peppered and lightly fried.

Point Lace.—This lace, the most thoroughly English of any, is within the power of any lady to work, who possesses an ordinary amount of skill and patience with her needle. It has the advantages of durability and paramount beauty, and is therefore well worthy the little effort required for its manufacture. This exquisite lace is adapted to a variety of uses for dress adornment, or furniture decoration.

To make Mecklenburg lace, lay upon the pattern a piece of tracing cloth, and with fine pen and ink (liquid Indian ink is the best) trace over in outline the braids thereon ; then remove the tracing, and tack it upon leather, or any coloured substance, such as glazed cambric, and commence the work by tacking carefully the braids as you would for braiding a dress, beginning on the outer edge ; then whip carefully the curves to get them into the form indicated in your pattern. When these braids are firmly fastened down, commence the dotted bars ; with Taylor's Mecklenburg thread fasten with a button-hole stitch to make it firm ; at one edge of the braid lay two or three threads across ; and then (working from the left to right) half way close button-hole stitches ; then to form the dot, work one button-hole stitch on the top of each stitch, not drawing the thread tight, so as to form a loop, and in that loop work four tight button-hole stitches ; then one more button-hole stitch in the last of the row of stitches ; finish the bar with tight button-hole stitches.

DOTTED VENETIAN BARS.—When all the bars are complete, then with Evans'

point-lace cotton commence the stitch for largest opening

FAN LACE.—This is worked with six button-hole stitches ; then leave space for six ; then six stitches as before, and repeat till end of row ; in the next row five button-hole stitches on top of six in previous row, and leave space five on next, and so on ; next row is six stitches in the spaces left in previous rows : a space, six stitches, and repeat.

The stitch in other large opening is called—

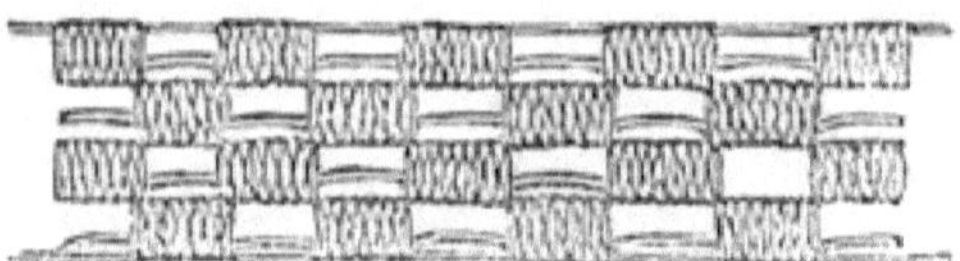

OPEN ENGLISH LACE—and is worked by placing threads across at equal distances, and then the reverse way, so as to form diamond spaces ; then twist the needle round the thread until you come to where they cross ; put your

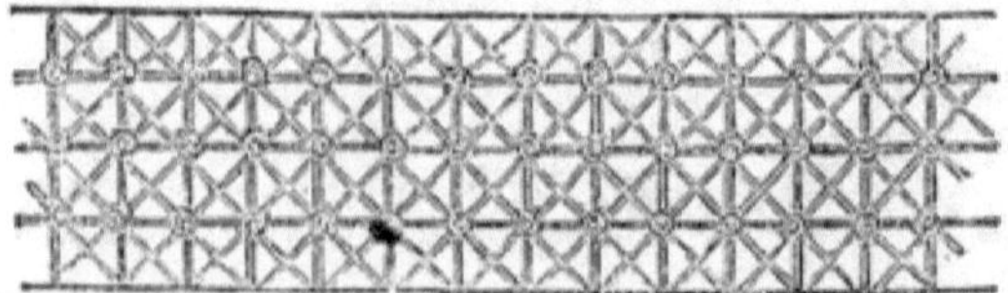

needle *under* the lower thread, over the next, and under the next; repeat this until the spot is as large as desired; then twist the needle round the thread until you come to the next crossing, when repeat.

The edge may be bought and sewn on, or worked; in this way one button-hole stitch, leaving it a little loose, and working four tight button-hole stitches into it, and repeat. This should be worked from left to right.

Those ladies who are in earnest to go into the fashionable accomplishment of point-lace making, should first visit Mr. William Barnard's Artistic Needlework Depository, 119, Edgware Road, London, where the most elegant designs and materials may be purchased, as well as the fullest instructions given.

**Lard.**—This is the fat of swine after being melted and separated from the flesh. In the pig, the fat differs from that of almost every other quadruped, as it covers the animal all over, and forms a thick layer between the flesh and the skin, not unlike the blubber in whales. Lard is used largely in medicine in the making of ointments. The prepared lard of the Pharmacopœia is made from the internal fat of the abdomen of the pig, perfectly fresh and removing as much of the membranes as possible. The fat is cut into small pieces and put into a vessel with cold water, having also a current of water running through it. It is then broken up with the hands so as to expose every part of it to the water, in order that everything soluble may be carried away. The water is then drained away by means of a sieve or cloth, and the fat liquefied at a heat not exceeding 212 degrees, and strained through flannel while hot; it is then put into a pan heated by steam, and kept at a temperature a little above 212 degrees, stirring it continually until it becomes clear and entirely free from water, and is then strained through flannel.

**Nasal Catarrh.**—Make a weak brine and snuff up the nostrils, and let it run down in the throat; also wet the head with the same. If persisted in a sufficient length of time, it will effectually cure nasal catarrh. It is said by a physician that the various mixtures sold as catarrh remedies, in many cases are only salt disguised so as not to be known.

**Chocolate Cream.**—Mix the yolks of six eggs strained with two ounces of pounded loaf sugar and three ounces of grated chocolate; add a pint of milk; set the mixture on the fire in a double saucepan, the outer one filled with hot water, and keep stirring till the cream thickens; dissolve a quarter of an ounce of isinglass, previously soaked, in a little milk; add this to the cream, strain it, pour it into a mould, and put it in a cold place or on ice to set.

**Hints for the Toilet.**—Too much attention cannot be paid to the arrangements of the toilet. Ladies' dresses should be chosen so as to produce an agreeable harmony. Never put on a dark-coloured bonnet with a light spring costume. Avoid uniting colours which will suggest an epigram; such as a straw-coloured dress with a green bonnet. The arrangement of the hair is most important. Whatever be your style of dress, avoid an excess of lace, and let flowers be few and choice. In a married woman a richer style of ornament is admissible. Costly elegance for her—for the young girl, a style of modest simplicity. The most elegant dress loses its character if it is not worn with grace. Young girls have often an air of constraint, and their dress seems to partake of their want of ease. In speaking of her toilet, a woman should not convey the idea that her whole skill consists in adjusting tastefully some trifling ornaments. A simple style of dress is an indication of modesty.

**Colours in Dress.**—Of all colours, perhaps the most trying to the complexion are the different shades of lilac and purple. The fashionable and really beautiful mauve and its varieties are, of course, included in this category. In accordance with the well-known law of optics that all colours, simple or compound, have a tendency to tint surrounding objects with a faint spectrum of their complementary colour, those above mentioned, which require for their harmony various tints of yellow and green, impart these supplementary colours to the complexion. It is scarcely necessary to observe that, of all complexions, those which turn upon the yellow are the most unpleasant in their effect—and probably for this reason, that in this climate it is always a sign of bad health.

But is there no means of harmonising colours so beautiful in themselves with the complexion, and so avoiding these ill effects? To a certain extent this may be done, and as follows :—

Should the complexion be dark, the purple tint may be dark also, because, by contrast, it makes the complexion appear fairer; if the skin be pale or fair, the tint should be lighter. In either case the colour should never be placed next the skin, but should be parted from it by the hair and by a ruche of tulle, which produce the neutralising effect of grey. Should the complexion still appear too yellow, green leaves or green ribbons may be worn as trimmings. These will often neutralise lilac and purple colours, and thus prevent their imparting an unfavourable hue to the skin.

Scarcely less difficult than mauve to harmonise with the complexion is the equally beautiful colour called " magenta." The complementary colour would be yellow-green ; magenta, therefore, requires very nice treatment to make it becoming. It must be subdued when near the skin, and this is best done by intermixture with black ; either by diminishing its brightness by nearly covering it with black lace, or by introducing the colour in very small quantity only. In connection with this colour, we have recently observed some curious effects. First, as to its appearance alone ; if in great quantity, the colour, though beautiful in itself, is glaring, and difficult to harmonise with its accompaniments. Secondly, as to its combination with black ; if the black

and the magenta-colour be in nearly equal quantities—such, for instance, as in checks of a square inch of each colour—the 'general effect is dull, and somewhat neutral. If, on the contrary, the checks consist of magenta and white, alternately, a bright effect will be produced. Again, if the ground be black, with very narrow stripes or cross-bars of magenta-colour, a bright, but yet subdued effect, will result. This last effect is produced on the principle that, as light is most brilliant when contrasted with a large portion of darkness—like the stars in a cloudless sky— so a small portion of bright colour is enhanced by contrast with a dark, and especially a black ground.

Yellow, also, is a difficult colour to harmonise with the complexion. A bright yellow, like that of the buttercup, contrasts well with black, and is becoming to brunettes, when not placed next the skin ; but pale yellow or greenish yellow suits no one, especially those with pale complexions. Its effect is to diffuse, by contrast, a purple hue over the complexion, and this is certainly no addition to beauty.

Besides the beautiful and permanent mauve and magenta colours, blue is favourable to most complexions ; light or sky-blue especially so to fair persons with golden hair ; fuller tints to those who are less fair, or in whom years have developed more of the colour of the sere and yellow leaf peculiar to autumn. It often happens, that as persons advance in years, colours which suited them in youth cease to be becoming ; pink, for instance, agrees well with a youthful complexion and fair skin, but it does not harmonise with the yellow tints of more advanced age ; in this case either sky-blue, or pure deep blue, will be substituted with advantage for pink.

These few instances will be sufficient to indicate some of the difficulties attending the right use of colour in dress.

Although broken colours next the skin—which of itself is a broken colour, as is also the hair—have a good effect, and help to clear up the complexion, pure colours are by no means to be excluded entirely from dress: what I mean to say is only that they should be employed with discretion, and always with a view to set off the wearer to the greatest advantage. They may thus be made to produce the best effect.

The coloured rosette, sometimes imitated by a thick cluster of artificial flowers of one colour, such as rose-buds, worn on the forehead or on the front of the rim of a hat, are very inartistic; artists always look upon a single patch of colour as a spot, or blot, which immediately attracts the eye, to the exclusion of everything else, thereby breaking up the repose of the subject or picture. To produce harmony, they consider that a colour should reappear, or be repeated, in different parts of the picture. This rule is founded on observation. Nature does not produce isolated specimens of the flowers which deck our fields and hedgerows, but scatters them over the soil more or less abundantly, and at greater or less intervals. Primroses and cowslips, buttercups and daisies, daffodils and harebells, come not in dense clusters like the nosegays we hold in our hands, nor singly, but each plant is separated from its kindred by the intervening green turf, and appears more beautiful in its emerald setting, while the frequent recurrence at uncertain intervals of the same colours and forms, gives pleasure to the eye; and the irregularity of the intervals between the plants produces variety. Applying these observations to the coloured rosette on the hat or forehead, a verdict of inharmonious must be returned against it. If the hat must have a coloured decoration, the colour should be repeated by binding the rim or crown of the hat with the same colour.

As the object of all decoration in dress is to improve, or to set off to the greatest advantage, the personal appearance of the wearer, it follows that the colours employed should be suitable to the complexion; and, as complexions are so various, it is quite impossible that the fashionable colour, though it may suit a few individuals, can be becoming to all. Instead, therefore, of blindly following fashion, as a sheep will follow the leader of the flock, even to destruction, we should like to see every lady select and wear the precise shade of colour which is not only best adapted to her peculiar complexion, but is in perfect harmony with the rest of her habiliments, and in accordance with her years and condition.

Table Poisons.—There are the buttercups to begin with, so caustic that the hands of children gathering them are sometimes inflamed, or even blistered. The deep colour of butter was ascribed to the eating of these flowers by the cows, wherefore they were called butter-flowers and butter-cups; but the cows know better than to eat them. The poisonous principle in buttercups is volatile, and disappears out of the herb in drying. Buttercups, therefore, are not only harmless when mixed with the grass in making hay, but even help to make the fodder nutritive by the large quantity of nutriment their stems contain.

It may be thought that we are safe among legumes, but we are not; we may eat beans and peas, but we had better avoid eating laburnum. The poisonous principle of the laburnum, cytisine, is contained in some other leguminous plants. In the laburnum it kills easily. There is much poison, too, in laburnum bark. The seeds of the yellow and of the rough-podded vetching may produce headache and sickness. The wild flower of the cucumber tribe, common in England, the bryony, is a powerful and highly irritant purgative. It is a quack herb medicine; its red berries produce very ill effects on children, who may chance to eat them.

In the parsley tribe there are some familiar wild flowers, very apt to be eaten, and very far from eatable. Carrots and parsnips, celery and fennel, belong to this family, and they are good to eat, of course; but there are other plants of this kind, which careless people may mistake for parsley, celery, or parsnips, and die of the blunder. Hemlock leaves have been eaten for parsley leaves, although very much darker and more glossy. Cows and goats will not eat hemlock, but sheep eat it unharmed. It kills man, when taken in a fatal dose, by its strong action on the nerves, producing insensibility, and palsy of the arms and legs. As a drug it is most dangerous, except in skilful hands. Then there is fool's parsley, which is decidedly poisonous, and much resembles common parsley.

But the most virulent of all the poisons of this sort, is the water dropwort, common on the banks of the Thames. When not in flower it resembles celery, and the roots may be mistaken easily for parsnip roots. The fine-leaved water-dropwort, and the common dropwort, are less poisonous, but not to be eaten without considerable danger. The similarity of the roots of the aconite, or monkshood of our gardens, to those of the horse-radish, has caused some fatal accidents, and the beautiful red berries of the belladonna, or deadly nightshade, have on several occasions lured children to destruction, so have those of the spotted arum, called " lords and ladies."

**A Hint to Musical Ladies.**—A lady who plays well on the piano-forte, and desires to make this accomplishment a source of pleasure and not annoyance to her friends, should be careful to adapt the style of her performance to the circumstance in which it is called for ; and should remember that a gay mixed company would be tired to death with one of those elaborate pieces which would delight the learned ears of a party of cognoscenti. It is from neglect of this consideration that many a really excellent performer makes her music a social grievance. Many a beautiful sonata or fantasia, to which at another time we should have listened with pleasure, has been thrown away upon a company, who either drowned it by their conversation, or sat during its continuance in constrained and wearied silence. We would never advise a performer to make a sacrifice to vulgarity or bad taste, but there is no want of pieces which combine brevity with excellence—contain in a small compass many beauties of melody, harmony, and modulation, and afford room for the display of brilliancy, taste, and expression on the part of the performer. A piece of this kind will not weary by its length those who do not care for music, while it will give pleasure to the most cultivated taste ; and with such things, therefore, every musical lady ought to be well provided.

**Wonders Revealed by the Telescope and Microscope.**—Dr. Chalmers, speaking of the advantages derived from the discovery of the telescope and microscope, says, " The one led me to see a system in every star. The other leads me to see a world in every atom. The one taught me that this mighty globe, with the whole burden of its people, and of its countries, is but a grain of sand on the high field of immensity. The other teaches me that every grain of sand may harbour within it the tribes and families of a busy population. The one told me of the insignificance of the world I tread upon. The other redeems it from all its insignificance ; for it tells me that in the leaves of every forest, and in the flowers of every garden, and in the waters of every rivulet, there are worlds teeming with life, and numberless as are the glories of the firmament. The one has suggested to me that beyond and above all that is visible to man, there may lie fields of creation which sweep immeasurably along, and carry the impress of the Almighty's hand to the remotest scenes of the universe. The other suggests to me, that within and beneath all that minuteness which the aided eye of man has been able to explore, there may lie a region of invisibles ; and that, could we draw aside the mysterious curtain which shrouds it from our senses, we might there see a theatre of as many wonders as astronomy has unfolded ; a universe within the compass of a point so small, as to elude all the powers of a microscope, but where the wonder-working God finds room for the exercise of all His attributes, where He can raise another mechanism of worlds, and fill and animate them all with the evidences of His glory."

The microscope is an optical instrument consisting of lenses or mirrors, by which minute objects are magnified, and thus rendered visible, so that their texture and structure can be examined. The microscope is of invaluable service in medical investigations, and in the detection of food adulteration, and of infinite interest in parlour pastime, revealing to us the myriad beauties of things invisible to the naked eye, while the telescope reveals the sublimity of the heavens, and brings to view the distant ships on the ocean.

Both these instruments are of great interest and importance to mankind.

But unfortunately they cannot always be depended upon, except they are purchased at the best makers, who have studied their theory, and brought the most perfect mechanical machinery to ensure the excellence of their manufacture. Those made by Messrs. F. Darton & Co., the well-known philosophical instrument manufacturers, 102, St. John Street Road, can always be relied on. The microscope could be made of great service in the education of the young, and we think it a great oversight that it is not introduced into schools and home education.

**To Roast and Prepare Coffee.—** The best mode of roasting, where it is done at home, is to dry the coffee first in an open vessel, until its colour is slightly changed. This allows the moisture to escape. Then cover it closely, and scorch it, keeping up a constant agitation, so that no portion of a kernel may be unequally heated. Too low and too slow a heat dries it up without producing the full aromatic flavour; while too great heat dissipates the oily matter, and leaves only bitter charred kernels. It should be heated so as to acquire a uniform deep cinnamon colour, and an oily appearance, but never a deep, dark brown colour. It should then be taken from the fire, and kept closely covered until cold, and further until used. While unroasted coffee improves by age, the roasted berries will very generally lose their aroma, if not covered very closely. The ground stuff kept on sale in barrels, boxes, or canisters, is not worthy the name of coffee.

Coffee should not be ground until just before using. If ground over night it should be covered; or, what is quite as well, put into the boiler, and covered with water. The water not only retains the valuable oil, and other aromatic elements, but also prepares it by soaking, for immediate boiling in the morning.

If the coffee pot be set on the range or stove, or near the fire, so as to be kept hot all night, preparatory to boiling in the morning, the beverage will be found, in the morning, rich, mellow, and of a most delicious flavour.

Coffee used at supper time should be placed on or near the fire immediately after dinner, and kept hot or simmering—not boiling—all the afternoon.

**Preparation of Whitewash.—** The following mode of preparing whitewash is strongly recommended :—Take a water-tight, clean barrel, or other suitable cask, and put into it half a bushel of lime. Slake it by pouring water over it, boiling hot, and in sufficient quantity to cover it five inches deep, and stir it briskly till thoroughly slaked. When the slaking has been effected, add two pounds of sulphate of zinc dissolved in water, and one of common salt. These will cause the wash to harden, and prevent its cracking, which gives an unseemly appearance to the work. If desirable, a beautiful cream colour may be communicated to the above wash by adding three pounds of yellow ochre; or a good pearl or lead colour, by the addition of lamp or ivory black. For fawn colour, add four pounds of umber, one pound Indian red, and one pound lampblack. This wash may be applied with a common whitewash-brush.

**Cream Sauce.**—Put two yelks of eggs in the bottom of a stew-pan, with the juice of a lemon, a quarter of a teaspoonful of salt, a little white pepper, and some fresh butter. Put it on a moderate fire and stir it till the butter is melted and thickened with the eggs. Take care that it does not become too hot ; if so, the egg will curdle. Then add half a pint of melted butter, stir together over the fire without permitting it to boil, pass it through a tammy into another stewpan, when wanted, stir it over the fire until hot. This sauce may be served with any boiled fish.

**Green Pea Soup Maigre.**—Take a pint and a half of young green peas, boil them in three quarts of water, with three or four sprigs of mint ; when done enough, strain them, then boil two quarts of old green peas in the same water, and rub them through a colander when done enough. Cut up a cucumber in slices, and some small young onions in slices about half an inch thick, the white part of a lettuce, and stew them till tender. Then add them to the young peas with about two ounces of butter rolled in flour. Then season to taste with a little cayenne pepper and salt. Beat some spinach and rub it through a sieve. Put it to the soup just before you take it off the fire, to make it green. Add a lump or two of white sugar. If peas are scarce, the shells of the green peas may be added, in place of the whole peas. If the flavour of meat is preferred, add either a bit of lean ham, or a hock of the ham, or root of a tongue, whichever is convenient.

**Drying Plants.**—There are so many ways of drying plants, that almost every botanist has a plan of his own. The only points to attend to, are to dry specimens quickly, thoroughly, and beneath a pressure that will not crush them. If they are succulent, or apt to cast their leaves, they should be dipped in boiling water previously to being placed under pressure. A good method is to place each specimen within a sheet of brown paper, and to interpose several empty sheets between each that is filled ; then to place them in a napkin press, and to press them gently for the first day or two, just enough to prevent the leaves and flowers from shrivelling. When the papers are quite damp, separate them, spread them on the floor of a room where they can become a little dry, and then gather them together, and place them in the press as before, rather increasing the pressure. This operation is repeated daily, till the plants are quite dry. A quicker and better, but more troublesome way, is to shift the plants daily out of their damp papers into hot and dry ones, immediately pressing them down ; but this is more inconvenient than the other.

**Domestic Economy.**—This should always be practised by persons with limited or fluctuating incomes. Extravagant parents must expect to have extravagant children, and, and when masters and mistresses do not economise, they can scarcely expect the servants to do so. Remember that there is a vast difference between economy and stinginess. Prudent persons generally set aside three twentieths of their yearly income for contingencies ; six-twentieths for household expenses ; three-twentieths for servants and amusement ; four-twentieths for the education of children, personal expenses, &c. ; and four-twentieths for rent, wear and tear of furniture, insurance, &c. For example —suppose that your income be £400 a year, you may expend £120 on food, and £60 on servants, &c. ; £80 on family and self, and the same sum for rent, &c. ; while you reserve £60 for an accumulating fund. If your income is fluctuating, set aside six-twentieths of it for a reserve fund.

**Watercress in Gardens.**—Nothing is easier than to have a good succession of this wholesome plant throughout the year. About the early part of March, says a contributor to a gardening journal, I procured a handful or two of healthy plants from a neighbouring brook, and having prepared two small beds of good loamy soil under an easterly wall, I cut the plants immediately into lengths of about three or four inches, preferring those pieces which had the appearance of a little white root attached, and planted them at once with a dibble, nearly up to the tops in rows, about eight inches apart, and six inches between the plants, watering them well, and shaded them with mats, supported on sticks just above the plants, for a few days. Every plant struck root, and soon began to grow. I kept the plants generally damp by applying the watering-pot nearly every day ; by the next month they were so much grown that I could nip off the tops, and supply a good plate-full for every day in the week. After the tops were first gathered, the plants threw out side shoots in abundance, and soon covered all the bed, and during the spring and summer produced a substantial crop, that there was some difficulty in keeping them down by constant gathering. The only time when they were not in so good flavour or condition was when inclined to seed. I let them all show for seed, and cut them off close to the ground, well weeding them, and surface-stirred the ground where I could. They soon made vigorous shoots, and have ever since supplied an abundance of as fine heads as any that come into the market, and that without any further attention than giving them water every day during dry weather.

**Low Fireplaces.**—The following observations by Dr. Arnott on the prevailing fashion of low grates, the reasons assigned being that a low fire burns better, or gives out more heat from the same quantity of fuel than a higher ; and, because lower and nearer the floor, that it must warm the carpet better, and so lessen the evil of cold feet, is worthy of attention :—" Both these suppositions are curious errors or delusions, having their origin in popular misconceptions respecting heat, and particularly respecting the radiation of heat. 1. The supposition that fuel burnt in a low fire gives out more heat has arisen from the experimenter not reflecting that his hand held over the low fire feels not only the heat radiated from the fire itself, but also that reflected from the hearth close beneath it, which second portion, if the grate were high, would have room to spread or radiate downwards and outwards to the more distant floor or carpet, and to warm them. 2. The notion that the fire, because near the floor, must warm the carpet more, springs from what may be called an error in the logic of the reasoner, who is assuming that the hearth, floor, and carpet, being parts of the same level, are in the same predicament—the truth being, however, that in such a case the hearth within the fender gets nearly all the downward rays, and the carpet almost none—as a candle held before a looking-glass at a moderate distance diffuses its heat pretty uniformly over the whole, but if moved close to one part of the glass it overheats, and probably cracks that part, leaving the rest unaffected. A low fire on a heated hearth is to the general floor or carpet of a room nearly what the sun, at the moment of rising or setting, is to the surface of a field. The rays are nearly all shooting upwards from the surface, and the few which approach it slant obliquely along, or nearly parallel to, the surface, without touching, and therefore without warming it. As would be anticipated by a person understanding the subject aright, low fires make cold feet very common, unless to those who sit near the fire with their feet on the fender ; but, deceived by their fallacious reasoning, the advocates are disposed to blame the state of their health or the weather as the cause, and they rejoice at having the low fire, which can quickly warm their feet, when placed near it. A company of such persons seen sitting close around their fire with thankfulness for its warmth near their feet might suggest the case of a party of good-natured people duped out of their property by a swindler, and afterwards gratefully accepting as charity from him a part of their own property." Other scientific men are of the same opinion.

**Throwing a Shoe after a Bridal Pair.**—The custom of " trashing," or pelting people with old shoes on their return from church on the wedding day is of very ancient date. There were certain offences which subjected the parties formerly to this disagreeable liability ; such as refusing to contribute to scholars' " potations," or other convivialities : but in process of time the reason of the thing became forgotten, and " trashing" was indiscriminately practised among the lower orders, turf-sods or mud being substituted for lack of old shoes, and generally thrown in jest and good humour rather than in anger or ill-will. Although it is true that an old shoe is to this day called " a trash," yet it did not, certainly, give the name to the nuisance. To " trash," originally signified to clog, encumber, or impede the progress of any one ; and agreeably to this explanation we find the rope tied by sportsmen round the necks of fleet pointers, to tire them well, and check their speed, is almost universally called the " trash-cord," or dog-trash. But why old shoes in particular were selected as the missiles for impeding the progress of newly-married persons it is now perhaps impossible to discover.

**Feather Baskets.**—Take the quill feathers of any bird whose plumage is variegated or beautiful ; for instance, that of the pheasant ; remove the bottom, or quill parts, and introduce the feathers into a piece of pasteboard, pierced for their reception, and cut to whatever form you may think fit ; bend a piece of wire into the same form, but rather larger than the bottom ; fix the ends together, and fasten the feathers into it at regular distances from each other. A handle of wire, or pasteboard, covered with a portion of skin with the feathers on it, may be added. The basket should be lined with coloured silk, or gold paper.

**Children's Playthings.**—Playthings that children make for themselves are a great deal better than those which are bought for them. They employ them a much longer time, they exercise ingenuity, and they really please them more. A little girl had better fashion her cups and saucers of acorns, than to have a set of earthen ones supplied. A boy takes ten times more pleasure in a little wooden cart he has pegged together, than he would in a painted and gilded carriage bought from the toy-shop ; and we do not believe that any expensive rocking-horse ever gave so much satisfaction, as we have seen a child in the country take with a cocoa-nut husk, which he had bridled and placed on four sticks. There is a peculiar satisfaction in inventing things for one's self. No matter though the construction be clumsy and awkward ; it employs time (which is a great object in childhood), and the pleasure the invention gives is the first impulse to ingenuity and skill. For this reason the making of little boats and mechanical toys should not be discouraged ; and when any difficulty occurs above the powers of a child, assistance should be cheerfully given. If the parents are able to explain the principles on which machines are constructed, the advantage will be tenfold.

**Filtered Water.**—The clearest and best water loses nothing of its goodness by filteration, but rather improves ; no house, therefore, should be without a filtering fountain. A very economical one may be made by taking out the head of a cask, setting it upright, and at a distance of about one-third from the bottom putting in a shelf or partition, pierced with small holes ; the shelf is then to be covered with a layer of clean, small pebbles, over which a quantity of fresh charcoal, made from wood or bones—the latter is preferable ; and fine sand should be laid to the depth of an inch, and then covered with another layer of pebbles ; over this should be placed another shelf, pierced with holes, to prevent the water which runs or is poured in, from disturbing the prepared bed of charcoal, and sand, and pebbles. At the bottom of the cask a tap is to be placed, to draw off the water as it is wanted. If it is intended to use rain-water, a pipe should communicate from the reservoir to the top of the cask, and in that case the top is to be fitted in, leaving only an opening for the pipe, and sufficient vent.

**Lamp Oil.**—The best lamp oil is that which is clear and nearly colourless, like water. None but the winter-strained oil should be used in cold weather. Thick, dark-coloured oil, burns badly (particularly if it is old), and there is no economy in trying to use it. Unless you require a great deal every night, it is well not to get more than two or three gallons at a time, as it spoils by keeping. Oil that has been kept for several months will frequently not burn at all. When that is found to be the case, it is best to empty it all out, clean thoroughly the can or jug that has contained it, and refill it with good fresh oil.

**Economical Use of Nutmegs.**— If a person begins to grate a nutmeg at the stalk end, it will prove hollow throughout ; whereas the same nutmeg, grated at the other end, would have proved sound and solid to the last. This circumstance may be accounted for thus :—The centre of a nutmeg consists of a number of fibres issuing from the stalk and its continuation through the centre of the fruit, the other ends of which fibres, though closely surrounded and pressed by the fruit, do not adhere to it. When the stalk is grated away, those fibres, having lost their hold, gradually drop out in succession, and the hollow continues right through the whole nut. By beginning at the contrary end, the fibres above-mentioned are grated off at their core end, with the surrounding fruit, and do not drop out and cause a hole.

Eating nutmegs, and similar things, is neither good for the health nor the complexion ; it interferes with the all-important process of digestion, destroying the refined sense of taste, which imparts a zest to the plainest morsel, often giving a disagreeable sallowness to the skin, and opening inroads to organic disease. Simple food is best—indulgence in stimulating food is bad.

**Cold from Damp Clothes.**—If the clothes which cover the body are damp, the moisture which they contain has a tendency to evaporate by the heat communicated to it by the body. The heat absorbed in the evaporation of the moisture contained in clothes, must be in part supplied by the body, and will have a tendency to reduce the temperature of the body in an undue degree, and thereby to produce cold. The effect of violent labour or exercise is to cause the body to generate heat much faster than it would do in a state of rest. Hence we see why, when the clothes have been rendered wet by rain or by perspiration, the taking of cold may be avoided by keeping the body in a state of exercise or labour till the clothes can be changed, or till they dry on the person ; for in this case, the heat carried off by the moisture in evaporating is simply supplied by the redundant heat generated by labour or exercise.

**To Destroy Blackbeetles.**—Several modes have been recommended to destroy them. A common trap, consisting of a glass pitfall, is sold in the shops. A very simple and inexpensive snare may be constructed at home in the following manner :—Cut four or five pieces of pasteboard, or strips of wood, and lay them slanting against the sides of an ordinary basin (taking care not to soil the sides, which must be perfectly clean and bright) a mixture of treacle and water, or beer and sugar. The beetles will be attracted by the syrup, and walking up the roadways made for them, fall headlong into the basin. Several of these traps being set night after night will ultimately put the whole of the insects in the housewife's power. Another plan, which may be pursued simultaneously with the above, is to place a few lumps of quicklime where the cockroaches frequent—about the hearth. Care must be taken, however, that children and ignorant persons do not burn their fingers with this substance. The beetle wafers sold in the shops to poison beetles are made by mixing equal weights of flour, sugar, and red lead ; but these wafers are liable to be picked up by children, and therefore objectionable.

**Custard for Pies.**—In a pint of good new milk, put two or three bitter almonds, a stick of cinnamon, a piece of lemon-peel, and seven or eight good-sized lumps of sugar ; let the whole simmer gently till the flavour is extracted, then strain and stir till cold. Beat the yolks of six eggs, and mix well with the milk, then stir the whole over a slow fire till it is about the thickness of rich cream. It may be flavoured with almond or rose water, of which one ounce will be sufficient.

**The Lips.**—Beautiful lips are regarded by all persons as indispensable requisites to prettiness in a lady. Nothing but excellent general health will impart to them that charming ruby tint which so delights the observer. It has been said, by the most reliable medical authorities, that a red under lip is one of the surest indications of good health ; and it may well be added, that it is one of the most irresistible fascinations of which a young lady can be possessed. The weather affects the lips of some persons to such an extent to disfigure their beauty, as well as to cause much pain from soreness. A strong wind, united with a cold atmosphere, will frequently cause so great an irritation of the delicate skin of the lips that weeks will sometimes elapse before the effects will be entirely effaced. Ladies should therefore be quite scrupulous in guarding their lips from cold and wind, especially in riding. In warm weather, cold water may be used in washing the face and lips without fear of their becoming chapped ; but in cold weather both cold or hot water, as also soap, should be avoided. Pure tepid rain water will be found to be the least irritating to a delicate complexion, and a preventive against chapped lips. Much may be done to restore the lips to their natural state, when they have become inflamed or chapped, by a timely application of some well-prepared emollient. An elegant lip-salve may be made in the following simple manner :—Put half-a-pound of fresh lard into a pan, with an ounce and a half of white wax ; set it on a slow fire till it is melted, then take a small tin dish, fill it with water, and add a few chips of alkanet root ; let the water boil till it becomes of a beautiful red colour, strain some of it, and mix it with the other ingredients according as may be desired ; scent it with some agreeable and favourite extract, and then pour it into small white jars or boxes.

**To Keep Silk and Velvet.**—Silk articles should not be kept in white paper, as the chloride of lime used in bleaching the paper will probably impair the colour of the silk. Brown or blue paper is better, and the yellowish, smooth India paper is best of all. Silks intended for dress should not be kept long in the house before they are made up, as lying in the folds will have a tendency to impair its durability, by causing it to cut or split, particularly if the silk has been thickened by gum. Thread lace veils are very easily cut. Dresses of velvet should not be laid by with any weight on them, for if the nap of thin velvet is laid down it is not possible to raise it up again. Hard silk should never be wrinkled, because the thread is easily broken in the crease, and it never can be rectified. The way to take wrinkles out of silk scarfs or handkerchiefs is to moisten the surface evenly with a spoon and some wheat glue, and then pin the silk with some toilet pins around the shelves or on a mattress or feather bed, taking pains to draw out the silk as soon as possible. When dry, the wrinkles will have disappeared. It is a nice job to dress light-coloured silk, and few should try it. Some silk articles should be moistened with weak glue or gum-water, and the wrinkles ironed out with a hot flat iron on the wrong side.

**Eyebrows and Eyelashes.**—The beauty of the eyebrows is held to consist in their being arched. In eyelashes, the height of their beauty consists in their being long and glossy. In the East the training of the eyelashes forms one of the peculiar cares of the toilette. In order to increase their length and brilliancy the Circassian ladies are said, frequently, that is ten or twelve times a year, to cut off the tips, the sharp points only, of their eyelashes. It is an operation requiring very considerable nicety, as if improperly performed it may be very injurious.

The eyebrows may be stained of a dark colour by various articles. The most simple are elderberriee or burnt cloves. A solution of green vitriol has also been recommended, which is applied by means of a brush ; the eyebrows having been previously washed by a decoction of galls.

**Hints on Letter-Writing.**—Few persons can write a letter themselves, or to satisfy others ; but the art is not difficult to acquire. It only needs practice and thought to become a ready writer, although it requires great talent to write letters of the highest order. Every one who is able to converse easily, ought to be able, and, with practice, would be able, to write a good letter, for letters should be written-conversation. Few persons are first-rate conversationists, but most persons of education can converse better than they can write. The reason is, that they are more natural in speaking than in writing. They utter their thoughts freely in speech, but strive to write elegantly ; and the consequence is, that they write artificially.

Begin your letter with the most important subject, and write all that you have to write upon it before you proceed to the next subject.

By paragraphing each subject, your letter will be better understood, and more easy to refer to. Each paragraph should be commenced at about an inch from the left edge of the paper as you face it.

Lord Chesterfield properly observes—" We must never offend against grammar, nor make use of words which are not really words. This is not all ; for not to speak ill is not sufficient ; we must speak well. Vulgarism in language is a distinguishing characteristic of bad company, and a bad education."

Avoid using unmeaning or vulgar phrases, as " You know," " You see," " So you see," &c. But do not strive to write " fine " language. Write good, strong, expressive English, such as you will find in Shakspere and the best writers. Many persons affect grandiloquent language, ponderous, but poor. With them everything is " splendid," " superb," " delicious," &c.

Lavater says—" Learn the value of a man's words and expressions, and you know him. Each man has a measure of his own for everything. This he offers you, inadvertently, in his words. He who has a superlative for everything, wants a measure for the great or small."

The pauses in speaking, and points in writing, are often at variance ; pauses belonging to the delivery of a sentence, and points to its grammatical construction. It is impossible to give precise rules for punctuation. The best authors differ materially in their practice. Good sense and consideration are more important than any mechanical rules. The best plan is to point in such a manner as to make the meaning clear, and to use too many points rather than too few.

Remember that putting words upon paper is a very different affair from uttering the same words, inasmuch as words spoken may be forgotten, or their precise meaning disputed or denied ; while a letter written remains indelible or unaltered. When you put your hand to an assertion or an opinion, it becomes your own, and you are held answerable for it. For these reasons you ought to use great caution in writing, even to your dearest friend, anything you should afterwards hesitate to acknowledge. To request your correspondent to burn a letter, is a plain confession that you have written something of which you are ashamed, or that you are afraid of its being known ; and, perhaps, the very circumstance of the request being made will induce the receiver to preserve the letter.

You should not forget that it is possible for your dearest friend to become your bitterest enemy, and especially so for your bitterest enemy to wish to be reconciled to you. Therefore write with warm but not foolish confidence to the friend, and with dignity instead of haughtiness to your enemy.

Use good paper. See that it is clean. Fold your letter neatly. These apparent trifles should be attended to, as many persons judge of a writer's character and habits by the appearance of her letter.

When you write to a person who is not bound to send an answer, and you wish for a reply, enclose a directed and stamped envelope.

Wives, in large family connections, where there are several of the same surname, are not distinguished by their own Christian names, but by those of their husbands, as " Mrs. George Johnson."

I am is used when addressing a person for the first time ; I remain, when subsequently addressing the same person. Or, " I have the honour to be," or to remain, &c., may always with propriety be used by an inferior addressing a superior.

The words *faithful, devoted, dutiful, obedient, humble, obliged,* &c., prefixed to the word *servant,* may be selected according as they are best suited to circumstances.

Whenever a doubt is entertained of the rank or title of the person addressed, it will be best to err on the safer side, and adopt the higher rank.

**Potichomanie.**—Rather a clumsy name given to an elegant art for ladies. It is really a mania for "potiches," the French designation for Chinese and Japanese vases ; but, more soberly, it is the art of imitating such vases. It is a pretty art when moderately indulged in, but is sometimes carried to an extent unsuitable alike to the purpose in view and to the materials employed. Although used to imitate every kind of porcelain and coloured earthenware, it is better fitted for large vases than for articles of smaller dimensions. There are two varieties of the art—potichomanie on wood and on glass ; the latter of which professes to look down with some contempt on the former. In the first-named variety, a vase or other article is fashioned in wood, and painted with wash-colour ; an Oriental pattern printed upon cloth is cut with scissors into proper form, and pasted upon the wash ; and the wash and the pattern or device are finally secured by varnish. The result, however, is seldom satisfactory ; the varnish cracks, the appearance is coarse and commonplace, and the delicate enamel-like surface of porcelain is not even faintly imitated. A better form of the art is that which involves the use of a vase or other article made of glass, more or less expensive than one of wood, according to circumstances. Barnard and Son, who supply the necessary materials, prepare a variety of designs or ornaments printed in colours, tubes of moist colours for grounding or foundation tints, bottles of varnish and gum, others of the essence of turpentine, brushes and pencils of various kinds, and fine sharp-pointed scissors. The designs depend for their excellence on the skill of the draughtsman and colourist, and on an appreciation of the direct object in view ; seeing that some are intended to imitate the fantastic ornamentation which we see on Chinese and Japanese vases, some the peculiar decorations of Dresden porcelain, some the landscapes and natural objects of Sevres porcelain ; while all the well-known ground-tints of rose de Pompadour, rose du Berri, &c., must be imitated in the colour-printing of the designs. As to the crystal vessels which are to be decorated, the lady artist has only to please her own taste in selection—chimney ornaments, table ornaments, toilet ornaments, or the like. Everything being at hand, one or more printed sheets are.

cut up, in such way as to isolate all the portions which are conjointly to make up the device. Taste in selection, and care in cutting, are necessary. Most of the coloured prints are prepared with a transparent adhesive composition on the surface, and the wetting this composition suffices to attach the composition to the glass; but where this is not the case, liquid glue is employed. The separate pieces are stuck to the inside of the glass, in order that the outside may retain its glossy surface. Every little piece must be made to adhere closely to the glass, and be pressed down carefully upon it by means of a cloth or a cloth or leather dabber. If the mouth of the vessel be too small to admit the hand, the ingenuity of the potichomanist will be somewhat taxed, but not hopelessly. When all the several sectional bits of paper ornament have been thus applied in their proper places, the whole interior of the vessel receives a coating of unalterable varnish or melted gum, to assist in fixing the paper to the glass, and to prevent the coloured composition subsequently applied from getting under the edges of the paper. This coloured composition is intended to imitate the ground tint or general colour of the species of porcelain selected. The colours require to be well prepared, and mixed with varnish or with essence of turpentine, according to the tint needed. The colour is applied either with a brush, as in ordinary painting, or else by pouring it into the vase, making it flow all over the interior, and pouring away the surplus. It generally requires a repetition of this process to render the tint clear and equable; and, indeed, this is the most critical feature in the art; for unless a near approach can be made to an imitation of the wonderful regularity of ground tint in good porcelain, the potichomanist had better modestly retire from the art altogether. Such, in a few words, are the leading features in a tasteful amusement, which a colour-maker once enthusiastically asserted, would, ere long, secure a place among

decorate arts; it would develop its resources in the embellishment of our apartments and furniture, and that we should see potichomanian artists honoured and praised. The prediction, however, has not yet been fulfilled; but the art is a pretty art nevertheless.

**Decalcomanie.**—This is another favourite art with ladies. It is a mode of decorating the panels of rooms, chair coverings, cloth, linen, silks, metals, and indeed almost all kinds of solid or opaque surfaces. It is effected by means of transferring. There must be, as in all these fancy arts, a storehouse of little aids for facilitating the work,—designs printed on paper, bottles of cement varnish, finishing varnish and detergent liquid, a roller, a few camel-hair pencils or brushes, a piece of cloth or leather, a sponge, an ivory knife, a pair of pincers, and a pair of scissors—all of which can be obtained in convenient boxes made for the purpose. The designs are printed on paper so prepared, that after the coloured surface has been cemented down upon wood, cloth, metal, &c., by means of varnish, the colours become transferred from the one surface to the other. The art is, in principle, diaphanie applied to an opaque instead of a transparent substance, with certain changes in plan and procedure depending on this difference. There are two kinds or classes of designs prepared for this purpose; one, intended to appear like ordinary pictures, is for applying to light-coloured surfaces, such as white wood, china, paper, &c.; the other, intended to present a kind of lustre or metallic hue, is for application to dark grounds, such as rosewood, japanned ware, brown or black woven fabrics, &c. The designs may be chosen in plenty from flowers, birds, figures, landscapes, imitations of Sevres porcelain, Chinese and other vase patterns, imitations of beautifully veined woods, arabesque or renaissance ornaments,—anything is available, provided that it is properly printed in colours, although in this, as in other things, good taste will produce wonders out of very slight materials. We may now watch the lady artist at her work. Let us say that a white earthenware or porcelain plate is to have a picture transferred to it. The selected design is cut with scissors nearly to the proper size and shape, and is well coated with varnish by means of a sable-hair pencil, every portion of the design receiving its due quota. The paper is not made use of immediately, but is allowed to remain a minute or two, until the varnish becomes slightly tacky to the fingers. The paper is then laid face downward upon the plate in its proper position ; a piece of cloth or leather, damp, but not actually wet, is laid upon it, and is pressed or rubbed down carefully, either with a roller or an ivory knife. The back of the paper is next moistened, and allowed to remain for a minute or two, by which time the paper itself is removed from the plate, leaving the colours of the device behind, as well as the varnish. This removal is effected either by the fingers only, or with the aid of pincers. The porcelain or earthenware plate, with the design thus transferred to its surface, is next washed carefully with water and a camel-hair brush, to remove spots and irregularities. When finally dried, a coat of varnish secures the whole work, and the fair artist has a pictorial dinner-plate at her disposal. If, instead of a hard surface of porcelain or earthenware, the transfer is made to a surface of silk or other soft material, the process is slightly modified. The silk is laid down on a piece of clean paper, the picture laid upon it face downwards, and the damping and pressing effected. Or else, as a more effective method in some cases, the face of the picture is coated with varnish, and the back is floated on the surface of warm water in a flat vessel ; in the course of a few minutes the picture is carefully lifted up, the superfluous moisture is absorbed by application of a sponge, the wet varnished surface is laid down on the silk, and in a very short time the paper may be pulled away, leaving the colour and the varnish behind it. A

learned professor of this art tells his lady pupils that " white biscuit china vases are very ornamental articles to work upon ; and glass potiche vases, being coloured in the inside white, green, blue, or any other colour, make very handsome ornaments when decorated. Also tea and coffee services of white earthenware or china ; white wood articles, such as screens, card-cases, and boxes ; straw dinner-mats, pieces of silk or cloth, slippers, hand-screens, sofa-cushions, scent-bags, ribbons, articles in ivory or wood ; indeed, it is difficult to say what ornamental article may not be thus decorated, from the panel of a room to the tiny articles upon the dressing-table. If you can paint in oil or water colours, sometimes the finished work may, by a few judicious touches with the appropriate colours, be improved ; but it is never absolutely necessary unless the work has been inexpertly performed." He is so enthusiastic in the matter, that he would have " every lady her own house decorator."

**The Truffle.**—The truffle is very much used in French cookery, though it is a very costly esculent. The root appears now to be indigenous to France, whence it is exported to all parts of Europe.

It is allowed that the very best truffles—those most acceptable to the epicure—are found at Perigord ; their perfume and fine flavour are said to be unparalleled. The blacker the root is in colour, the more highly it is prized ; while in Arabia preference is given to the white truffle, which is found in its deserts in great profusion. It is extensively used among the Bedouins, not as an article of luxury, but as a common necessary, like the potato among ourselves ; and when cooked in milk, it is said to be most palatable and nutritious. In India, where the same kind of esculent is found, it is turned to a different account ; it is distilled into a liquor which is highly prized by the natives.

The spot where a truffle-bed exists is generally known by the hollow sound which the ground emits on being tested, and on which frequently a swarm of large bottle-flies settles, being attracted by the scent of the root. It is a singular fact that all vegetation—all kinds of plants, flowers, and even the grass—is affect d by a sort of blight in the immediate vicinity of a truffle-bed. Pliny tells us that in his days the peasants who searched for truffles, to gratify the taste of the Roman aristocracy, were always accompanied by a swine, whose keen scent soon directed them to the hidden treasure. In the present day dogs of the spaniel breed, trained for the purpose, are used in searching for the underground vegetable. In those districts of France where the deposits are most extensive and prolific, numerous packs of dogs are kept by the peasantry, which are constantly employed in gathering the crop of truffles, if we may use this expression.

The truffle is considered by some to be a kind of mushroom or gall-nut, growing beneath the surface of the earth, on the root of the oak, just as real gall is formed on its branches.

**Dancing.**—It is a curious circumstance, that although dancing has been an institution among all nations from the earliest ages, the epochs of it are not very well known. Among the ancient peoples dancing was a necessary accompaniment of all religious and secular solemnities. The Egyptians not only danced at the festivals held in honour of their recovered Apis, but also, like the Greeks, regarded the art as a bodily exercise, and an indispensable part of every well-bred person's education. Dancing was performed in Egypt according to invariable laws and rules, from which no deviation was allowed.

It is probable that the Jews introduced the religious dances of the Egyptians into their ceremonies, and performed them on all joyful occasions. Thus a festival dance was ordained after the successful passage of the Red Sea, while the dance round the golden calf was merely an imitation of the Apis worship. From the description of the memorable dance which David performed before the ark "with all his might," we learn that the sacred dances of the Jews were not solemn stately measures, like those that take place in Catholic churches, but real dancing.

No nation, however, paid greater attention to choregraphy than the ancient Greeks, and with them it formed the most important branch of youthful education. They regarded it with such respect that the gods and goddesses were represented as dancers and inventors of ballets. The religious dances of the Greeks, however, must not be regarded as mere outbreaks of childish joy, but as complete pantomimic representations. Among the Greek dances, the Pyrrhic takes the first place ; it was a lively, impassioned dance, in which all the movements made in actual warfare were imitated, and it thus served as a species of drill. The chief comical dance was the Cordax, which we often find represented in old marbles. Sophocles the profound was a very celebrated dancer ; Epaminondas was renowned for his graceful movements ; while Socrates confirmed his fiery speech on behalf of choregraphy by learning his steps when well in years. Plato performed the Cyclian dances with a ballet of boys ; and Alcibiades delighted the populace by theatrical representations and dances, which excited the jealousy of his fellow-citizens.

In Rome, dancing was not so highly esteemed as in Greece ; many powerful voices were, indeed, at times raised against it ; but they could not put it down.

Among the numerous customs which the early Christians borrowed from the Pagan Church were masques and dances ; and in some of the oldest churches of Rome we find the choir to be an elevated stage, on which the priests performed the sacred dances every Sunday. The old bishops were indeed called " præsules," which, according to Scagliger, originally meant the leading dancer. It is probable that the successors of the

Apostles, and the first Bishops favoured dancing, because they knew that the Pagans were so attached to their religious rites, and could hardly give them up on joining the new Church. These Christian dances, however, did not for long remain proofs of religious zeal. As they most frequently took place at night, they eventually produced excesses, and the Church was obliged to interfere. Such hold had dancing obtained of the Christians, that in 692 it was found requisite to publish a Decree of the Council in prohibition. Special allusion was made in the decretal to the public or objectionable dances of women, and the festivities in honour of false gods. At the same time, the priesthood sedulously spread the opinion, that the Evil One was the patron of dancing ; and we find in a Breton ballad, that dancing was accursed since the day when the daughter of Herodias danced before the cruel king, who ordered, through her blandishments, the head of John the Baptist to be cut off.

It was not till the fifteenth century that the revival of dancing took place in Italy. On the celebration of the marriage between Galeazzo Sforza Duke of Milan, and Isabel of Arragon, in 1849, Virgouzo de Botta performed a grand ballet, which created considerable attention, and was imitated at other European Courts. The general impulse given to the arts of peace was favourable to choregraphy ; and this was especially the case at the Court of the Medici, where upwards of fifty young ladies of the highest families trod stately measures. The principal amusement was the so-called " Danses basses," in which the dancers did not rise above the ground, or either leap or hop. These were so solemn and stately, that at the Court of Charles IX. of France they were performed to Psalm tunes.

In Spain, dancing has been a national amusement from the earliest ages, and the descriptions which Roman authors have left us of the art of the Gaditanian dancers favour the assumption that the Spanish dances of those days, like the present Bolero and Fandango, were combined with animated movements and gesticulations, and accompanied by the sound of the castagnettes. During the sixteenth century, many new dances were invented which were considered improper, owing to their freer movements and suggestive poses, and which met with such favour from the multitude that they caused the older dances to be almost forgotten. Toward the middle of the seventeenth century, when through Philip the Fourth's love of splendour the external brilliancy of the dramatic performances was greatly heightened, the dances grew into lengthy ballets, which simply drove the simpler national dances from the stage. At the beginning of the last century the Seguidillas came into vogue in La Mancha. This dance soon spread over all the Spanish provinces ; and the Fandango is, in reality, only a modification of this dance. The character of the Fandango is at first gentle and tender, gradually attaining the extreme of Southern passion ; and in this lies its fascination, for the steps are extremely simple and inartistic. Formerly the nobility danced it in a dignified and ceremonious manner, and according to the rules prescribed by the stage, until it became popular, and was performed with more extravagant movements. The Bolero is a noble, modest, and more decent dance than the Fandango, and is also performed by two persons. Among other Spanish dances we may refer to the Cachuca. This dance is always performed by one gentleman or lady to the accompaniment of the castagnettes The name of the dance is applied to a beauty, and to anything that is graceful.

The first dances reached France from Italy in the reigns of Francis I. and Henry II., and Catherine de Medici did a great deal for them. She had heroic, gallant, grotesque, and allegorical ballets performed. She gradually added livelier dances, in which gentlemen, imitating professional dancers, were obliged to make leaps, and the ladies wore short dresses in order to show whether they kept time. Grand ballets and allegories took the place of tournaments, which had grown unfashionable since Henry II. lost his leg in one of them. In the year 1830 the Polka was discovered by a servant-girl in a Bohemian country town. She danced it for her own amusement, to a tune of her own composition; a schoolmaster wrote down the tune, and the new dance was soon after publicly performed.

What an important part dancing formerly played in England we may see from Shakspere's dramas, in which the poet allows no opportunity to escape for alluding to the dances of his day, or introducing them at proper places, as they so thoroughly suited the taste of Merry England in the olden time. Their number amazes us.

In Russia, nearly all the provinces have their own national dances, of which the Pigeon Dance and the Cossack are celebrated. The latter is performed by two persons, who move toward each other and retire, in turn, and accompany it with pantomimic gestures.

The dances of the Hungarians are of a most peculiar nature, and bear a distant resemblance to those of the Cossacks. The steps are performed with movements of the loins, turning in and out of the heels, beating together of the spurs, and striking of the hands on the boots. The most characteristic of these dances is the Czardas, which begins to a slow movement and gradually grows more excited. It is danced in every society.

The dances of the Poles resemble the Hungarian; and the audible beating of the heels together is a great point. The only exception to the rule is the Polonaise, which is still danced at some European balls, as is also the case with the Mazurka and Cracovienne. In Turkey, where any violent movement is considered improper, dancing is only performed by travelling bands. The public dancers are always present at Turkish festivals.

In modern Egypt, dances are only performed by the Ghawsi. The Ghaziehs (dancers) and Awalim (singers), who are among the prettiest women in Egypt, live deplorably in some district allotted to them. They are invited to the harems at festivities.

Such are the most remarkable epochs in the history of dancing, and we think they deserve preservation at the present day, when dancing seems to have disappeared from the scene. The headlong pace at which couples dash round the ball-room in the waltz, or the polka, renders it impossible to pay any attention to the steps; and even the quadrille, which might have afforded some opportunity for the display of grace, has yielded to the prevailing fastness of the age.

**Fish Gravy.**—Prepare three or four small eels, by skinning, cleaning, and cutting them into inch lengths; then place them in a stewpan, with sufficient water to cover them, adding to the water a little essence of anchovy, a few sweet herbs, mace, and lemon peel. Simmer the whole till the eels are drawn to the bottom of the pan; when the fish are nearly half done, add a thick crust of well toasted, but not burnt, bread. When the stewing is completed, strain it, and mix in a thickening composed of flour and butter, a little of each, and the gravy, which may advantageously accompany any kind of fresh fish, is quite ready.

**Mint Sauce.**—Wash, pick, and chop fine some fresh-gathered mint, and put it into a sauce tureen; be careful that the leaves are washed clean from grit and insects, and that they are picked from the stalks. To three tablespoonfuls of chopped mint put a gill of vinegar, and one ounce of white sugar; add these to the mint in the tureen, and stir altogether until the sugar is dissolved. Those who like this sauce sweet must increase the quantity of sugar, which should be pounded before adding to the mint, which, if not obtainable, mint vinegar makes a tolerable substitute. This sauce is improved by allowing the mint to soak a few hours in the vinegar for a few hours before wanted. This sauce is the invariable accompaniment to lamb, hot or cold, roast or boiled.

**English Omelet.**—Two eggs, a teaspoonful of finely-chopped parsley and thyme, the same quantity of chopped onion, salt, pepper, and two ounces of butter. Beat whites and yolks separately, the former to a stiff froth. Mix the herbs, pepper, and salt with the yolks. Put the onions and butter, into an omelet pan, and when the butter is melted, and very hot, mix whites and yolks together lightly; pour into the pan, and keep stirring the mixture with a spoon till it begins to set, then merely shake it till it is done. Omelets made by this recipe are equal to those made by French cooks. Do not turn the omelet in the pan, not even half over, but turn it out upside down; they are lighter so. A wood fire is best for cooking them over—light chips thrown on the fire, so as to make a good wood blaze. You can make " scrambled " or " buttered " eggs in the same way, by substituting a saucepan for the omelet-pan.

**Suet and Milk.**—This food is serviceable for children who dislike fat meat, but will take milk. In such cases the milk may fail to supply the system with a sufficient proportion of fat. The following preparation will be palatable, if given while it is warm :—Warm half a pint of new milk, and add to it a tablespoonful of suet very finely minced. When the suet is completely melted, skim the milk, and pour it into a warm cup. It may be sweetened with loaf-sugar.

**Management of Brooms.**—They should be put into boiling suds once a week, when they will become very tough, will not cut the carpet, last much longer, and always sweep like a new broom. A very dusty carpet may be cleaned by setting a pail of cold water out by the door, wet the broom in it, knock it to get off all the drops, sweep a yard or so, then wash the broom as before, and sweep again, being careful to shake all the drops off the broom, and not sweep far at a time. If done with care, it will clean a carpet very nicely, and you will be surprised at the quantity of dirt in the water. The water may need changing once or twice, if the carpet is very dusty. Snow sprinkled over a carpet and swept off before it has time to melt and dissolve, is also good for renovating a soiled carpet. Moistened Indian meal is used with good effect by some housekeepers.

**Buttermilk.**—This is advocated as food for very young children, in conjunction with rice or wheat-flour. Besides being easier of digestion, it is cheaper and less liable to adulteration than milk from the cow. Dr. Van Maanen, of Barneveld, says that buttermilk is invariably used by the children of that district, and with the best effects. They get through their infantile disorders with wonderful celerity. Scrofula is unknown, and the bills of mortality are reduced to a minimum, all owing, according to the doctor, to the use of buttermilk.

**Sponge Pudding.**—Butter a mould thickly, and fill it three parts full with small sponge cakes, soaked through with wine ; fill up the mould with a rich cold custard. Butter a paper and put on the mould ; then tie a floured cloth over it quite close, and boil it an hour. Turn out the pudding carefully, and pour some cold custard over it, or bake it, and serve with wine-sauce instead of custard.

**Raspberry Vinegar.**—Fill a large bowl with fresh-gathered raspberries, picked from their stalks, and cover the fruit with the best white vinegar ; let it steep for eight days, and then strain off the liquor carefully. Fill the bowl again with fresh fruit, and pour the liquor over it. Four days afterwards, change the fruit, and let the infusion stand for four days longer ; then strain the vinegar carefully through a jelly-bag until quite clear, and weigh the juice against its own weight in lump sugar. Boil it up for a few minutes with the sugar, removing the scum, and bottle it when cold. This syrup, mixed with water and lumps of ice, or soda-water, is very refreshing.

**To Keep Suet Sweet.**—Choose such as is freest from veins, &c. Set in a saucepan far from the fire to melt gradually. When melted, pour it into a pan of cold spring water : when hard, wipe it dry, fold it in white paper, put it into a linen bag and keep it in a cool place ; when to be used scrape it. By this process it will keep sweet for a year.

**Hints on Taking a House.**—GAS.—In some cases where gas is laid on in new houses, the fittings are left to be put in by the tenant ; in others they are supplied by the landlord, charged for as fixtures, the money being returned when the tenancy ends.

BLINDS.—The same plan is adopted in regard to Venetian blinds, and it is a saving one to tenants, as blinds and gas-fittings rarely suit any other house than the one for which they were originally intended. But when this is not the case, it will be found best and cheapest to have them supplied by a good house, where there is not only a choice of design, but where the work can be depended on. This advice is, however, to be taken with a grain of salt, and that is—get price lists and inspect for yourself before deciding.

BELLS.—In very small houses, it is not usual to hang any other than house-door or garden-gate bells ; still, if possible, there should be bells on each floor ringing to the lower passage. In regard to these, and the fixing of a LETTER-BOX, an incoming tenant might agree with a landlord to bear some part of the expense, because the comfort and saving of time are to the tenant's benefit.

SHELVES AND CLOSETS.—See that requisite closets and cupboards, as well as shelves, are in the house. If these should be deficient, the time to have them supplied is before you enter as tenant. If your requirements are reasonable, most landlords will attend to, and satisfy them, at least partially, *before* you take possession ; and, if you have reason to believe that your tenancy will be permanent, it is better to share some of the expenses with the landlord,

if all besides is suited to you, than to give up advantages for the sake of a pound or so.

GARDEN.—If the house should be in the suburbs, there will probably be a garden, or (if a new house), a piece of ground for one. In the first case, it is very probable that a piece of ground strewn and sown with building rubbish will be the plot that is to be converted into a garden. The landlord should remove the rubbish from the parts intended for beds, and lay down some foundation, as well as gravel for paths. Unless the house is a high-rented one, this is all that can be expected. If it be high-rented, landlords usually plan the garden and furnish it with grass and evergreens.

DUST-BIN.—Observe that this is put in a convenient place, where it will not annoy either the eye or the nose, and whence it can be emptied without the contents being carried through the house.

COAL-CELLAR.—This is another item of importance. See that it is so placed that the coals can be kept dry, and are within easy reach of the domestics.

REPAIRS.—Before taking a house, look well to all the locks, fastenings, &c., and see that everything is in good order before you enter ; make inquiries as far as you can, respecting the previous tenant, supposing that it has been occupied, and require to see the last receipts of rent and taxes, or at least have a reasonable assurance that there are no arrears.

LANDLORD.—It is also advisable to know something about the reputation of the landlord ; a little clever gossip, carried on with tact, will elicit quite as much as you want to know, the points interesting to you being, whether he is a man of respectable means and standing ; if he is careful and prompt in attending to needful repairs, &c. As a rule, avoid speculative builders for landlords ; they are always poor, generally in debt, and their houses are always changing hands. They usually employ either boys or unskilled labour, and, in consequence, their tenants' repairs are so badly executed that their houses are always either falling to decay from neglect, or kept in a constant confusion and discontent by the bungling and inefficient patching up of inexperienced workmen.

AGREEMENTS.—We give here only one word of advice. Never sign an agreement, or enter as a tenant in a house, before the landlord has entirely finished all you require him to do in it. At this moment we are suffering discomfort, the consequence of our own weak trust in the assurances of a promising landlord; and we repeat, if you wish for comfort in your home, see that all the landlord has to do to ensure it is done before you sign the agreement or enter the house as tenant.

**Laundry Blue.**—In the " getting up" of ladies' ornamental apparel and fine linen, too much attention cannot be paid to the qualities of the starch and the blue that are used, especially the latter article. The blues that are frequently in use positively dye and rot the clothes by some destructive mineral agent which they contain to produce intensity of colour. Thanks to an eminent French chemist, who has discovered the colour used by the old painters, and which in their day fetched fabulous prices, and to Messrs. Reckitt and Sons for utilising the discovery, and bringing this rare and beautiful colour within the reach of the very poorest, for it is sold in neat squares at one penny the ounce. But its cheapness, of course, was not the attractive feature that gained it admission into the laundry of H.R.H. the Princess of Wales, and other distinguished families ; it was for its durability, its purity of tint, and its freedom from any destructive ingredient. The " Paris Blue," introduced by Reckitt and Sons under that name, is used in the same manner as those old-fashioned blues it is fast superseding, only that its great strength requires less quantity than any other, and therefore it is more economical. It is unquestionably the best blue in domestic use. (*See* Starch.)

**Macaroni Soup.**—Boil a pound of the best macaroni in a quart of good stock till it is quite tender : then take out half, and put it into another stewpan. To the remainder add some more stock, and boil it till you can pulp all the macaroni through a fine sieve. Then put it to the two liquors, adding a pint or more of boiling hot cream, the macaroni that was first taken out, and half a pound of grated Parmesan cheese ; make it hot, but do not let it boil ; serve it with the crust of French roll, cut into small pieces.

**Vermicelli Soup.**—Break the vermicelli into three-inch lengths. It is not requisite to soak it ; rinse it, however, in water to get rid of the floury particles. Now put on the vermicelli, after thus prepared, in stock sufficient to cover it, and let it boil till quite tender, without dissolving. It will take a quarter of an hour to make tender, or a few minutes longer if it be very dry. Add this to some hot stock, and then serve. This soup, as well as macaroni, is sometimes dusted over with cheese.

**Fish Soup.**—Soak some crushed, dried peas, previously well washed, then put them to cook in warm spring or river water. After softening, pass them through a colander, so as to form a thin puree. Take afterwards some scraps of fresh fish, put them in a saucepan, with an onion stuck with one or two heads of cloves, slices of carrot and pot-herbs, salt and pepper ; moisten with half water and half broth ; add bread-crumbs and a lump of butter ; let the whole cook thoroughly, and then strain through a colander. In the South of France, this fish-soup, which everywhere can replace that of meat, is prepared with oil instead of butter.

**White and Brown Fish Stock.**—Take three pounds of silver eels, and cut them up into two-inch lengths, two pound of skate, and half a dozen flounders, cut into small pieces. Put them into a stewpan with water enough to cover them, season well with pepper and salt, and add a head of celery, two small onions, and a handful of sweet herbs, with two dozen cloves stuck round the onions ; cover the whole closely down, and gently stew for two hours. The only difference between white and brown stock is, that the latter is coloured by the fish that are used being first fried brown in flour and butter. Although our receipt specifies skate, flounders, and eels, we beg to observe that any fish, cooked or uncooked, will do for either white or brown fish stock. It is as well to know that neither sort will keep more than four days.

**Pepper-Pot.**—Stew gently a pound of pickled pork, and any roast meat bones that are to be had, in three or four quarts of water, with a few sliced onions, carrots, and turnips ; it should stew until the meat is tender ; then boil some spinach, and rub it through a fine-holed sieve ; withdraw the bones from the liquor, and put in the spinach, and season highly with cayenne. Cold mutton, lamb, or veal, minced, may be substituted for the pickled pork, stewed with any vegetables that may be in season ; the meat should be cut up into small pieces ; the meat from a cold fowl should be stewed with the pickled pork ; sometimes suet dumplings are boiled with the meat. A true pepper-pot should consist of a mixture of fish, flesh, and fowl, with vegetables, and the fish are invariably represented by minced lobster or crab, in similar proportions. Skim off the scum while the mixture is stewing. Rice is generally boiled with the other ingredients, but a nice savoury pepper-pot can be made without either lobster or crab. Strain off part of the gravy before serving, smooth the top, and with a salamander nicely brown it, and slightly pepper it with cayenne.

**Brown Soup.**—This soup is also the foundation of a variety of good brown soups. Cut up into very small pieces some lean beef from the shin, leg, ox-cheek, or any of the cheap, inferior parts ; also lean bacon, proportioned in quantity to the beef ; a quarter of a pound of bacon, to one pound of beef, is a good proportion. But half beef and half bacon may be used. Lay the pieces, with any other remnants of beef or bones, in a stewpan that has been rubbed round with an ounce or two of salt butter, and add half a tumbler of water to the meat. Let this stew gently, covered closely, until all the gravy is drawn out of the meat. Now pour in boiling water, as much as is required for the quantity of soup needed. To this add shred onions, sweet herbs, and a few cloves, then stew the whole together slowly for four or five hours. If the colour is not deep enough, add a little browning.

**To Roast a Haunch of Venison.** —When some country cousin presents us with a haunch, it is as well to know how to cook it. At p. 27 we have given the tests to choose venison by in the event of our aforesaid cousin forgetting us, and that we have to buy it. We have nothing to do here but to detail a process of cooking this aristocratic joint. Begin by trimming off the chine bone and the end of the knuckle, then wash it in cold milk and water, and wipe it thoroughly dry ; protect the joint with buttered paper before putting down to roast, to prevent the fat burning or scorching. Now arises a little difficulty for those who are not provided with a cradle-spit, for that is the only proper way to roast this joint, as it should be well balanced, and turn evenly ; if the spit is not to be had, why then the old familiar jack must be brought into requisition, and the best possible use made of it. Before putting the haunch down to roast, cover it with a paste of flour and water, then place it close to the fire to crust the paste, at the same time keeping the paper well basted, and therefore it should be stout, and securely tied over the paste ; after the haunch has been down an hour, move it further from the fire. It will take about three hours to roast ; just before taking it up, remove the paper covering, then baste the haunch with butter, draw it nearer the fire, and let it remain until a nice brown colour covers it, then dredge a little flour, and, when lightly browned all over, conclude that it is done. Send to table with a plain gravy, which should be made from the trimmings from the haunch, mixed with that in the dripping-pan. Currant jelly is usually served with it. Venison must be thoroughly roasted, and, to be assured of this, when the coating of paste and paper has been removed, it should be tested by inserting a skewer into the thickest part, and if it does not pass in easily, the joint must be put down again for further roasting.

**To Hash Venison.**—Cut the meat in sizeable pieces from the bones of the remains of any piece of venison, and place the latter and trimmings into a stewpan with some good stock ; then strain, and add a tablespoonful of mushroom ketchup, thicken with flour, then one boil up, and after the gravy has cooled, put the slices of venison into a pan, and when the whole is about to simmer, dish it, and serve hot with gravy.

**Mock-Turtle Soup.**—This is a very rich, nutritious soup, and rather an expensive one to make if prepared for the epicure. But our receipt will be found in practice a very good soup, and within the means of those for whom our volume is intended. Put in an earthen jar a small knuckle of veal, a large cow-heel, three onions, a bunch of herbs, a few cloves (which should be stuck round each onion), salt and pepper to taste, and about a gallon of cold water. Let this slowly boil for five hours and a half, then remove the jar from the hob, but it must not be uncovered till it is quite cold. After that, if the soup is wanted, remove the fat that may have caked at the top of the jar, strain the soup, and put it with the veal, and a dozen good-sized forcemeat balls, and the juice of a lemon, on the fire, and let the whole gently simmer for seven or eight minutes. Before the veal, however, is put on the fire again, it should be cut up into two-inch pieces, as near as possible square. A glass or two of sherry thrown into the soup while it is simmering, imparts a nice flavour to it, although it adds a trifle to the expense. But the

soup we have given the receipt for, including the wine, can be put on the table at the rate of about sixteenpence a quart.

**Mock-Turtle with Calf's Head.** —Proceed thus : Parboil the head without removing the skin, then take the meat from the bones, and cut it into small square pieces. Put them into the water the head has been parboiled in, adding a seasoning of mace, pepper, and cloves to your taste, and let it thoroughly boil. Prepare some flour, well-browned, adding as much butter as will make it rich ; add also some chopped onion which has been browned in slices, as well as some small portions of thyme and sweet marjoram ; then stir all together, put it into the pot containing the calf's head, and when it is enough cooked, add a little vinegar to the soup, and serve with white wine. A couple of hard-boiled eggs, chopped, and stirred into the soup, is a material improvement.

Mock-turtle will keep for several days —indeed it is improved by keeping, and will safely travel in jars. It is best wrapped up by setting the jar in boiling water. If only a portion of it is taken at a time, it should be thoroughly stirred up to get a proper share of the meat which has settled at the bottom.

**Brandy Sauce.**—One tablespoonful of pounded sugar, half a wine-glassfull each of brandy and sherry, and mix the same with half a pint of melted butter. When well mixed put it on the fire, and keep stirring it one way for fifteen minutes, or until it nearly comes to the point of boiling. This quantity is sufficient for a good-sized family plum-pudding, which may be either poured over it, or served in a tureen, at the discretion of those about to partake. As a rule, we think rich sauces are better served by themselves, for by some they are not liked, and with others they disagree.

**College Pudding.**—This is a very favourite currant pudding, which is thus made :—Take two pound of bread-crumbs, shred half a pound of suet, and mix with half a pound of currants, an ounce of each citron and orange peel, six ounces of sugar, two or three eggs, and a little nutmeg. Well mix these ingredients together, and make up the puddings to the size and shape of an egg. Having melted six ounces of butter in a frying-pan, when quite hot, stew the puddings in it over a stove, turning them in it three or four times till they are of a fine light brown. Mix a glass of brandy with the butter, and serve with sweet sauce for puddings (which see).

**Sweet Sauce for Puddings.**—Melt half a pound of fresh butter, to which add a tablespoonful of pounded sugar, and flavour the same with lemon peel and nutmeg. Simmer the whole for a few minutes, stirring the sauce one way. Another method of making this sauce, is, to boil a pint of new milk, mixing with it three eggs and a quarter of a pound of sugar ; stir the whole till it becomes of the consistence of cream, but it should not boil. Flavour with a tablespoonful of brandy and ground bitter almonds.

**Lemon Mince Pies.**—Weigh one pound of large lemons, cut them in half, squeeze out the juice, and pick the pulp from the skins ; boil them in water till tender, and pound them in a mortar ; add half a pound of white sugar, the same of currants, and of fresh beef suet minced, a little grated nutmeg, and citron cut small. Mix all these ingredients well, and fill the patty-pans with rather more of the mince than is usually put.

**To Prepare Buttered Toast.**— Hold the bread before a good clear fire, that it may be done as quickly as possible, and butter it the instant it is toasted. If this is not attended to, the toast, instead of eating light and crisp, will be tough and leathery. To prepare dry toast, if it is required to be crisp and thin, it should be put in the toast-rack, and placed before the fire some time before it is used. When thick toast, not too dry, is wanted, it should be served at once.

**Solid Custard.**—An ounce of isinglass, a quart of milk, half a dozen bitter almonds, pounded, the yolks of four eggs ; sugar to taste. Dissolve the isinglass in the milk and the pounded almonds ; put the mixture on the fire, and let it boil a few minutes ; pour it through a sieve, then add the yolks of the eggs well beaten ; put it on the fire until it thickens, stir it until nearly cold, and put it into a mould.

**Portable Soup.**—This soup is made in a few minutes, and it has other peculiar advantages to those ladies who prefer being their own cooks ; amongst others, it is always ready as good stock for gravies and sauces. Get about three pounds of shin of beef, and break the bones ; also a small knuckle of veal, and a large cow-heel ; immerse all the meat in a large saucepan, with water sufficient to cover it, adding four onions, and pepper and salt. Stew the meat to pieces, and then thoroughly strain it, and put it away in as cold a corner as the house commands, until the fat has caked on the top, which should be carefully removed, and then the soup returned to the stewpan, and rapidly boiled over a brisk fire ; the saucepan should be uncovered, and the soup boiled and stirred for six hours ; then pour it into a pan, and let it stand for a day, when it should be poured into a large-lipped basin ; boil enough water in the basin to reach as high outside the basin of soup which should invariably be placed in it, as the soup reaches inside ; keep the water boiling until the soup within the basin has reached a thick consistency ; it should then be spooned off into small pots, and put away in cool places ; tin canisters, if to be had, are better than pots. We have now distilled it to its essence, and a basin of good soup or gravy may be made in two or three minutes. It may be flavoured with any kind of herb the taste approves, by boiling the herbs, and straining them through water, make it boil, and then dissolve the soup in it.

**Rules for Frying.**—This mode of cooking is chiefly confined to fish, eggs, ham, onions, &c., but is not often resorted to for meat, except by the poor, whose appetites are generally superior to their sense of correct cookery. Frying meat is the least economical and nutritious of all known methods.

If, however, the frying-pan is occasionally pressed into the service for chops and steaks, it should be sufficiently large to allow the meat to lie flat at the bottom, while the fire should be free from blaze, although brisk.

In the case of lean meats, as veal cutlets, &c., the pan should be greased with butter or lard ; salt fat is apt to fly in the fire, and therefore dangerous to use.

Be careful not to fry in a stewpan, or, if so, with great care, and sufficient butter to save the tinning from melting.

A small shallow frying-pan is very useful to fry articles to be stewed ; this method differs from common frying, as it only requires butter enough to keep the article from sticking to the pan, and burning.

The fat used for frying must have left off bubbling and oe quite still before you put in the articles.

Bread crumbs for frying should be well dried before the fire or in a slack oven; any waste pieces of bread will do ; then pound them in a mortar and sift them, and preserve them till required for use. In frying, use a slice to lift the articies in and out.

When cutlets, and other fried things, are required to look particularly tempting, do them twice over with breadcrumbs and egg.

**Rules for Broiling.**—This is a very nutritious method of cooking meat. It requires a brisk and clear fire, moderated according to the article to be broiled. A mutton chop requires a clear but not a brisk fire, or the fat will be wasted before the lean is a quarter done ; while for a beef-steak the fire can neither be too hot nor too clear. Fish and underdone meat require but a steady fire.

When the bars of the gridiron are hot through, thoroughly wipe them, then smear them ever so little with suet, to prevent the meat from adhereing to the bars.

Meat while broiling should be frequently turned with a small pair of tongs ; a fork should never be used ; meat for the gridiron should range in thickness from three-quarters to an inch.

If the meat be thick, it must be placed at a greater distance, at first, from the fire, to warm it through ; if thin, the fire must be brisk, or the meat will be soddened, and inferior in colour.

Meat on the gridiron should never be cut to see whether it is done ; this can be ascertained by the smell, and by the small jets of steam puffing from the meat, which, if done, will feel firm if touched with the tongs. A hot plate should be ready to receive the meat directly it is taken from the gridiron.

A charcoal fire is best for broiling. To prevent the fat dripping into the fire set the gridiron aslant.

Butter rubbed on broiled meat will draw out the gravy ; ketchup, or other sauces, should be added hot.

**Rules for Stewing.**—This is the most economical mode of cooking meat, as many inferior parts, and old poultry, are thereby rendered tender and indigestible.

Earthenware vessels should have preference to metal ones, because they better retain their heat.

All articles for stewing should first be boiled gently, then skimmed and set aside in an even heat ; on this account charcoal makes the best fire for stewing.

Stewing should be slowly done, and then meat may even be stewed over and over again, without deterioration.

The process of stewing is best adapted for invalids, for it renders meat easy of digestion ; by it, moreover, the juice, or gravy, which is the more nutritive part, is retained, either in the meat itself, or in the liquor, which is taken with or without it.

Meat for stewing should be put into *cold* water, with only enough to cover it.

It should be thoroughly skimmed when it comes to the boil, and then simmered slowly until the meat is very tender, and the gelatinous portions thoroughly dissolved.

A stew should *never* boil. Nor does it require so great a heat as boiling All the nutritious elements are obtained by this process, too many of which evaporate in boiling and roasting.

**Rules for Boiling.**—The joint of meat should be put into boiling water, for hot water coagulates the albuminous constituents of meat, as the white of egg is set, and prevents the juices from escaping; but cold water softens the fibres, extracts the albumen and the nourishing juices, and renders the meat tasteless. During the time of cooking, however, the water should be kept under the boiling point until done, for to continue it at a boil hardens and spoils it.

**Rules for Roasting.**—This process of cooking especially requires care and great attention to the fire, which should be brisk, clear, and steady. Make up the fire a little longer than the joint, to ensure the ends being well done. In stirring the fire, be sure to remove the dripping-pan, to avoid ashes tumbling in with the gravy. Keep the fire well up in fuel to a strong equal heat.

Large joints should be kept at a moderate distance from the fire, and moved nearer by degrees; or the joint will only be half done through. When steam rises from the meat it is done.

Place paper over meat that is not very fat, to prevent burning; take off the same within the last hour, and dredge the joint with flour and salt.

Allow fifteen minutes to every pound of meat, and a quarter of an hour over. White meats, as lamb and veal, a little longer than the prescribed time for other meats.

Salt extracts the gravy, therefore do not sprinkle the meat with it.

Young meats do not require so much cooking as old.

The hook of the bottle-jack should be so placed as to take in a bone, and the thickest part of the joint hung downwards.

The joint should be first basted with fresh dripping, and then with its own gravy.

Roasting joints should be exposed to a quick fire, that the external surface may be made to contract at once, and the albumen to coagulate before it has had time to escape from within.

If meat is exposed to a slow fire, the pores remain open, the juice continues to flow from within as it is dried from the surface, and the flesh pines, and becomes hard, dry, and unsavoury.

**To Truss Larks, and all Small Birds.**—Pick them well, cut off their heads, and the pinions at the first joint. Flatten the breast-bone with the handle of a knife, turn the feet to the legs, and put one into the other. After the gizzard has been drawn, run a skewer through the middle of the body, and tie the same to the jack or spit during the roasting.

**To Truss and Roast Woodcocks and Snipes.**—These game-birds are never drawn, as the entrails are considered the best of the birds; after they have been plucked (in which great care must be taken, as they are very tender, especially after they have been hung), cut the pinions in the first joint, then flatten the breast-bone; turn the legs close to the thighs, and tie them together at the joints; place the thighs close to the pinions, into the latter put a skewer, and run it through the other pinion, the thighs, and the body. Skin the head, take out the eyes, and put the former on the point of the skewer. While roasting, place some toasted bread in the dripping-pan to catch the trail and gravy; well baste the birds during roasting; they will take about twenty minutes. Dish each bird on a separate piece of toast, and pour a little gravy over them. They are very troublesome to prepare for table, but they are delicious morsels, and worth the care, to those who have the time and who choose to devote a little of it to the cooking of snipes and woodcocks.

**Marmalades.**—These may be made with almost any kind of fruit, and they are usually prepared by boiling the fruit and sugar together to a pulp, stirring them while boiling ; it is kept in pots, which should not be covered until the marmalade is quite cold ; half a pound of sugar to every pound of fruit is the usual proportion.

**Orange Marmalade.**—Take equal weight of white sugar and sound Seville oranges, cut the rind thin, and place it in an iron pan, cover it with water, and boil till soft ; after straining it from the water, which should be preserved, cut up the peel into half-inch lengths, and return them to the water they were boiled in. Quarter the orange itself, after removing the outside white fluff or down, and scrape the orange from the fibry part of it ; put the latter with the seeds, and the orange pulp with the cut-up peel ; then with boiling water through a sieve wash the seeds, which will thicken to a jelly ; add it to the pulp and the strips of peel. Now put sugar and all in the preserving pan, boil forty minutes and in a few hours, to get cool and set, divide it off into pots.

**Seed Cake.**—Beat about one pound of fresh butter to a cream, and mix with it a pound of flour, three ounces of caraway seeds, one pound of sugar, and four eggs. When all is thoroughly beaten together, bake it in a tin, for two hours. These cakes are sometimes made with dough from the baker, but they are not so nice ; however, if it is used, cover it over, and set it in a warm place to rise, before mixing the ingredients.

**Sally-Lunn Tea-Cakes.**—Take a pint of milk, quite warm, a quarter of a pint of thick yeast ; put them into a pan with sufficient flour to make a thick batter, cover it over, set it in a warm place, and let it stand until it has risen as high as it will—about two hours it will take to accomplish this. Dissolve two ounces of lump sugar in a quarter of a pint of warm milk, and one egg well beaten ; add these to the batter. Then well rub a quarter of a pound of butter in sufficient flour to make a very light dough, knead for ten minutes, let it stand in a warm place for half an hour, then make up the cakes, put them on tins, let them stand a short time to rise, and bake them in a quick oven. Care should be taken not to put the yeast to the milk too hot nor too cold.

**Red and Black Currant Jam.**—Pluck the currants from the stalks, weigh them, and to each pound of fruit add twelve ounces of crushed sugar ; then put currants and sugar into a pan, and boil and stir them for forty minutes, removing any scum that may rise during the boiling. The jam is now fit for potting, but it should not be covered in until it is quite cold ; use oiled paper for the covers. Stretch the paper round the top of the pot, and, when dry, the covering will be quite hard and airtight.

**Raspberry Jam.**—Put the raspberries into the preserving-pan, mash them well up with a prong, and let them simmer for twenty minutes, stirring the while ; then add a pound of sugar to every pound of fruit, and a wineglassful of red currant juice, and when these are added to the raspberries, simmer again for half an hour. Pot it when cold, and tightly cover it with oiled paper.

**Preserved Rhubarb.**—Put an equal weight of rhubarb and sugar in a preserving-pan, after the rhubarb has been cut into inch pieces, and the sugar been clarified ; add a little water and ginger, and then put the rhubarb with the sugar, and simmer the whole for about three hours then pot it, and tie down when cold.

**Rules for Baking.**—This, like frying, is not a good process of cooking meat, with the exception, perhaps, of a leg of pork and a fillet of veal. But we do not advise the mode even for these joints, for meat loses one third in baking.

When, however, it is found necessary to resort to it, be particularly careful about the basting of it while in the oven, which will in a measure prevent burning or soddening, which baked meat is so liable to, and which tells so much against the process.

Some people give choice to a baked ham over a boiled one ; but we are not of them. If, however, baking a ham should be decided upon, it should be covered with a crust of flour and water, and baked in a slow oven.

For ordinary joints the oven should be brisk, but in the case of poultry it should be a little moderated.

**Treacle Pudding.**—Make a nice suet crust, and roll it out to a half inch thickness, then spread a quarter of a pound of treacle over it, close the edge securely, roll the paste up with the treacle, then tie it up in a cloth, put it into thoroughly boiling water, and keep it rapidly boiling for two hours and a half. This is called a roley-poley pudding, and, fortunately for the children, who have a great partiality for it, it is cheaply made ; at the cost of sixpence sufficient for half a dozen olive branches may be put on the table.

**Currant Dumpling.**—Take a pound of flour, and mix with the same a quarter of a pound of finely-chopped suet ; then add to them about a pound of currants, and make the whole into a dough with either milk or water ; then divide the whole into half a dozen dumplings, and put them into boiling water, and rapidly boil for half an hour. To prevent their sticking to the bottom of the pan, shake it occasionally. These dumplings may be boiled in floured cloths ; if this plan is chosen they will take twice the time to boil. Serve with cold butter, sugar, and slices of lemon.

**To Boil Salmon.**—After it has been well cleaned and scaled, so that no blood has been left inside, put it in a fish-kettle with sufficient cold water to cover it (boiling water makes the fish hard) ; add salt and a little vinegar, bring it quickly to a boil, take off the scum, and then simmer slowly. Allow from eight to ten minutes for each pound ; the test of being done is when the meat easily separates from the bones ; all meat should be thoroughly

done without being overdone ; the latter spoils the flavour, and makes it tasteless and insipid. When done, drain it, serve hot, with a garnish of parsley, and an accompaniment of plain melted butter.

**Cod's Head and Shoulders.**—The size and unequal thickness of cod generally prevents its being cooked whole. The head and shoulders is the piece that is commonly boiled, and in this manner :—begin by rubbing a little salt over the inside of the fish an hour before putting it in the fish-kettle ; tie it up with broad tape, lay it in sufficient water to cover it, adding six ounces of salt to each gallon of water ; do not pour the water on the cod for it might break it. When it comes gradually to a boil, draw it on one side to simmer for half an hour, which will be sufficient time to dress it ; while simmering, it is important to remove the scum as it rises. When taken up it should be well drained. Serve on a hot napkin, with a garnish of the liver, horseradish, and sliced lemon.

**Salt Cod.**—This is commonly an Ash Wednesday and Good Friday dish, and on these religious occasions it is both cheap and plentiful ; it is better known as " salt fish." It should be soaked in water for twelve hours preparatory to boiling : after it has soaked this time, put it into a fish-kettle with enough cold water to cover it, adding sufficient vinegar to give the fish a flavour ; it will be hard and tough if it boils fast ; simmer it gently for an hour, or until tender, occasionally removing the scum. Serve with plenty egg-sauce, parsnips, and fringe the dish with parsley sprigs.

**To Dress Cold Cod.**—Separate the cold fish to be dealt with into flakes, and fry them in butter with a sliced onion ; after the frying, the flakes should be simmered for ten minutes in a stewpan with a little butter rolled in flour, and half a pint of stock. Or, better still, begin thus :—Pick the flakes away from the bones, and skin them before they get cold. When wanted,

A YOUNG LADY'S APRON.

put them into a stewpan with what was left of the sauce with which they were originally served. Add a dozen oysters and the liquor. If those are not enough to moisten the fish, add a couple of spoonfuls of melted butter. Over a quiet fire carefully warm, and put it aside directly it is hot through. Surround a hot dish with some mashed potatoes, so as to leave a hollow in the middle, in which deposit the warmed fish and the sauce. Sprinkle over the fish some grated bread-crumbs, and set it for a few minutes in a quick oven, and, when nicely browned, it will be ready to serve.

**Model Pattern for a Young Lady's Apron.**—This elegant apron for a young lady fourteen to seventeen years of age, is composed of white percale, trimmed with embroidery, together with pockets.

**Model Pattern for a Lady's Cravat.**—The materials used for the cravat on p. 337, are composed of white percale, holland, or pique, and trimmed with scarlet, blue, or black braid; the escallops edged with the same. A bow of coloured ribbon on each shoulder.

**Cosmetics.**—There was a time when the chemical nature of things was not so well known as to day; when the

A LADY'S CRAVAT.

creamy whiteness of flake-white, or superior white-lead entered into the composition of pearl-powders. We need not pause to reprobate the great danger of employing this material for such a purpose, seeing that the employment is abandoned. Subsequently to the going out of white-lead as a face or pearl-powder, another metallic preparation—the trisnitrate of bismuth—came in. There is no metallic pigment so innocent that it can be laid on the skin continuously without incurring serious consequences. Pearl-powders, as now used, are variously made. Some are nothing else than powdered talc, or French chalk ; others a mixture of the same with common chalk ; a third order contains starch grains mingled with the preceding one, or both. By starch grains we would mean to signify the preparation called " violet powder," which really has no more to do with violets than with cabbages or cucumbers ; being really nothing else than starch grains odorised by orris-root, which smells not unlike violets.

The ladies of fashion of ancient Rome had as much inclination to make themselves " beautiful for ever" as the ladies of London or Paris of the present day. To preserve the complexion, recourse was had by the Roman ladies to a variety of cosmetics. Whilst sitting in their own apartments, and, above all, before retiring to rest at night, they would cover their faces with a paste made of wheat-flour, or of crumbs of bread well soaked. Others made an ointment of the suet extracted from the fleece of a fat ewe, twice washed and bleached in the sun, but still retaining a rank smell. Other cosmetics were more costly, and not unfrequently composed of singular ingredients, the specific virtues of which it is not easy to divine. The simplest was a lotion of asses' milk. Poppæa, Nero's wife, used to bathe in milk, five hundred asses being kept for the purpose. A certain fluid mixture much in vogue, was obtained by slowly boiling for forty days and nights the heel of a young white bull. Another was a kind of paste, in which white-lead predominated, that came from Rhodes, and imparted a dazzling whiteness to the skin, but had the effect of melting in the sun, or under the action of great heat. There was, likewise, a preparation of chalk steeped in acid, but which shunned all contact with water. Vermilion, too, was sometimes applied. The eyebrows and eyelids were commonly touched with a long pencil dipped in a paste, the colouring matter of which was soot or powdered charcoal, and occasionally saffron.

**To Dress Lobsters.**—Cut them in halves lengthways from the tail, break off the large claws, and crack them in three or four places without interfering with the meat, and then place the pieces on the dish as if they were again attached to the fish, so that it might have the appearance of not having been mutilated ; garnish the dish with parsley.

**To Dress Crabs.**—Scoop the fish out of the shell, and thoroughly amalgamate it with three tablespoonfuls each of vinegar and oil, and a little mustard ; after the fish has been mixed with the other ingredients, return it to the large shell, which should then rest upon the claws. Serve round the dish slices of lemon, and sprigs of parsley. If the crab has to be served hot, it should be heated before the fire, and served with some dry toast.

**To Boil Lobsters.**— Put them into boiling water with an ounce of salt ; while cooking they must be carefully watched to see that they are not over nor under-done ; they will take about half an hour. Lobsters that are bought in the shop, as a rule, are not boiled enough, and are in consequence hard and indigestible. After they have been sufficiently cooked, rub the shell with sweet oil to brighten its colour, taking care to wipe off the oil before bringing the lobster to table.

**Dripping Crust for Meat Pies and Puddings.**—All kinds of good meat fat may be made available for pie-crusts by clarifying, that is, melt it in boiling water, set it to cool, and then scrape away all the impurities that you will find settled on the under side of the solid cake of dripping formed on the top of the water. This process may have to be repeated if you wish to produce the finest dripping. The proportion to be used for ordinary pies and puddings, is a quarter of a pound of dripping to rather less than a pound of flour. Rub the fat well into the flour, mix the paste with water, and roll out to an inch thick ; break the other half of the fat in small bits, lay them on the paste, dust flour over them ; roll out the paste again, and shape as required ; or, if a richer crust is desired, cover the second rolled-out layer of paste with an ounce or two more of fat.

**Rump-Steak Pie.**—Of all meat-pies commend us to a well-made rump-steak pie, which is certainly the chief in substantial nourishing qualities. Cut the steak into narrow shapely pieces, and rub each piece over with mixed pepper and salt. Fill the dish three parts full of water, and insert a cup reversed. Cover with either a dripping or suet crust. A pie made with two pounds and a half of steak, requires two pounds of flour, mixed with fat in proportion, and half a pint of water to each pound of flour, as the crust should be rather thick, and the inside of the dish lined with the paste. To ensure the meat being done with the crust, we recommend that it should be first a little stewed, and the liquor thrown in the dish with the meat. The pie should be baked in a hot oven, when it will take about an hour and a half if the meat has been previously stewed, or a quarter of an hour beyond that time if the pie has been made with raw meat. Beef-steak pies may be flavoured with either oysters or mushrooms, but neither are essential, and only adds to the expense. A very nice pie may also be made with the remains of any underdone cold roast beef. Do not fail to make a hole in the centre of the crust, which may be ornamented or not, but we think meat pies bake better when the crust is left plain. We have said two pounds and a half of meat is sufficient for a small family, and so it is ; but we omitted to add that the size of the dish must be taken into consideration, for there must be meat enough put into it to fill it, in order that it shall support or raise the crust, and not allow it to sink in on the meat.

**Rump-Steak and Kidney Pudding.**—Cut up a pound and a half of meat into inch square pieces, with two sheep's kidneys, or the half of a bullock's, quartered. A pudding crust should be rather thicker than a pie-crust. Line the basin with a suet crust, then mix in the steak and kidney, seasoning each piece with some pepper and salt ; then put in half a pint of water, and cover with the crust, uniting the top crust with that which should be allowed to lap over with which the basin is lined. Now flour a clean cloth, after dipping it in hot water and wringing it out, and securely and tightly tie it round the basin, which should have a rim for that purpose, for it is all important that the water be kept out of the pudding, which should be put into boiling water, renewing the same as fast as it evaporates, or boils away, for the pudding should be kept covered with boiling water, and kept steadily on the boil for a good four hours. When done remove the cloth, and serve the pudding as quickly as possible in the basin. Of course the pudding, as well as the pie, may be enriched in flavour with the addition of a few oysters, but then oysters are scarce and expensive. Mushroom ketchup imparts a nice flavour to a beef-steak pie or pudding.

**Veal Pie.**—Veal cutlets are the best for a pie, a pound and a half or two pounds of which will be sufficient for four or five persons, especially if the veal be supplemented with a few slices of boiled ham. Proceed as follows :— put the ham and veal into a deep pie-dish in alternate layers, seasoning each piece of veal separately as it is laid in the dish ; mix in with the meat a couple of hard-boiled eggs, sliced, a table-spoonful of sweet herbs, and half a pint of water. Cover the whole with a puff-paste crust made thus :—carefully dry a pound of flour, and work the same into a smooth paste with less than half a pint of water ; roll out thin, and cover with a quarter of a pound of butter, broken into bits, and sifted over with flour ; fold it over, and roll out again, then cover the layer with a quarter of a pound of lard in bits, and well floured ; then fold over, and once more roll out, and spread over the paste two ounces of lard or butter, and finally roll it to the size of the pie-dish, either round or oval. The pie will take an hour and a half to bake in a brisk oven. The crust of a ham and veal pie is usually orna-mented in any way the cook's skill or fancy may suggest.

**Giblet Pie.**—Either duck or goose giblets will do for this pie, which should be made as follows :—After cleaning the giblets put them into a saucepan with some savoury herbs and an onion, adding a pint and a half of water, and simmer the whole gently for an hour, or a little longer. After that, throw up the giblets, and allow them to cool when they should be chopped into small pieces, and cut the gizzard, heart, and liver in slices, and put them in a pie-dish, with three or four pieces of a good rump-steak, which place at the bottom of the dish ; see that the steak and giblets are well salted and peppered ; then strain the gravy in which the gib-lets were stewed, and pour it over them in the dish ; cover with puff paste, and let it bake in a brisk oven for an hour and a half. A piece of buttered paper on the top of the crust will protect it from scorching or burning.

**To Broil Dried Haddock.**—They should be gradually warmed through before the fire or on the gridiron ; be particular that the fire is clear and not fierce ; baste with butter while cooking, and serve the fish as hot as possible. Another mode is, to skin the haddock before broiling, and roll it in bread-crumbs wetted with egg, and directly they are browned, serving them with egg-sauce. This second plan is more troublesome than remunerative.

**To Boil Turbot.**—Soak the fish for two or three hours in salt and water to remove the river slime ; then cut down the centre of the back nearly to the bone, but not to interfere with or re-move the fins ; then dissolve a quarter of a pound of salt in each gallon of cold water, adding a pinch of saltpetre ; lay turbot in a large saucepan (there are kettles made on purpose to boil this fish ; they are broad and shallow), and let it gradually come to a boil, skim-ming off any scum that may arise during the time ; if allowed to boil rapidly, the turbot would break, which would be a fatal mishap. In about half an hour after the water boils, the turbot will be done ; let it drain well before serving, and throw a hot cloth over the drainer ; place it on the table with lobster-sauce, melted butter, brown bread and cucum-ber ; arrange alternately round the dish slices of lemon and sprigs of parsley. Turbot is improved by keeping a day before boiling, longer if the weather be not too hot or muggy.

**To Boil Brill.**—In boiling brill nicely, one object should be to preserve its whiteness, which may be achieved by rubbing it with lemon-juice. Place the fish in a kettle with water enough to cover it, and a quarter of a pound of salt to each gallon of water, and slowly let it come to a boil, and then simmer for about twelve minutes, for a fish of medium size. Serve it accompanied with lobster-sauce and melted butter, and garnish the dish with parsley and horseradish. Many cooks boil brill in the same manner as turbot, and serve it with the same sauces, and the same garnish.

**To Boil Trout.**—Unlike most other kinds of fish, trout should be put into boiling water, with plenty of salt, and boil fast for a quarter of an hour. Sal-mon-trout can be boiled in the same way, after cleaning and scaling ; flavour the water with a little vinegar. When taking up be careful not to break the skin. Serve either with lobster or shrimp-sauce, or plain melted butter.

**To Fry Eels.**—Fried fish is very nice eating, but is not the most economical way of cooking it, for fish take so much fat to fry them properly : it is true, the same fat may be used again and again for fish, yet withal it is the most expensive method. To fry eels, first cut them into three-inch pieces, only scoring, not separating them ; dredge with flour, rub them over with egg and bread-crumbs, and fry in boiling lard to a nice brown, and serve with melted butter. There is no better way of frying them, and if they are carefully done, they will be found delicious to those who like eels.

**To Stew Eels.**—After well cleansing, cut the eels up into three-inch pieces, season them with pepper and salt, and put them in a stewpan ; pour over them a pint of stock, an onion and a piece of lemon-peel ; let them stew gently for half an hour, and then dish them with care, and after straining the gravy, pour it over the eels. A glass of port will improve the gravy if put into the stewpan with it.

**To Boil Salmon.**—After it has been well cleaned and scaled, so that no blood has been left inside, put it in a fish-kettle with sufficient cold water to cover it (boiling water makes the fish hard) ; add salt and a little vinegar, bring it quickly to a boil, take off the scum, and then gently simmer. Allow from eight to ten minutes for each pound ; the test of being done is when the meat easily separates from the bones ; all fish should be thoroughly done without being overdone ; the latter spoils the flavour, and makes it tasteless and insipid. When done, drain it, and serve hot, with a garnish of parsley and an accompaniment of plain melted butter.

**To Boil Mackerel.**—Soak first for a quarter of an hour in salt and water ; cleanse the fish inside and out, take out the roe and steep it in vinegar, and then replace it ; put it in lukewarm-water, and simmer very slowly for half an

hour ; to preserve it whole and unbroken, take it up directly it is done, which may be known with certainty when the tail splits. Serve on a hot cloth, with melted butter, and garnish the dish with parsley or fennel.

**To Fry Soles.**—Skin, wash, and wipe them dry, then smear them with the yolk of an egg, beaten up with bread-crumbs, and put them into a deep pan of boiling lard or dripping, and fry them a nice brown on both sides ; for this purpose they should be carefully turned so as not to break them ; dish them when taken from the pan, and put them before the fire to dry, or absorb the fat in which they have been fried ; a fine sole will take a quarter of an hour to fry and nicely brown.

**To Boil Soles.**—Wash and clean a large sole without disturbing the roe ; then lay it in a kettle of cold water sufficient to cover it, with a little salt and vinegar ; slowly let it come to a boil, carefully removing the scum as it rises ; after it has boiled, withdraw the kettle to the side of the fire to simmer, and in ten minutes it will be ready to take up ; it is usually served with lobster or shrimp-sauce.

**To Stew Soles.**—They should first be partially fried in lard or oil, and when about half fried, remove them from the pan, and put into it about a quart of water, three tablespoonfuls of anchovy, and a large onion, sliced ; after this has boiled for twenty minutes, put the sole or soles in again, and slowly stew them for half an hour, or less if they are small. When they have been removed, thicken the liquor with butter rolled in flour, then boil up, and having placed the soles in a dish, strain the liquor over them, and serve with shrimp or oyster-sauce.

**Rules for Making Soups.**—The delicate and proper blending of savours is the chief art of good soup-making. Be sure to skim the grease off the soup when it first boils, or it will not become clear. Throw in a little salt to bring up the scum. Remove ALL the fat. Be careful to simmer gently, and never allow soup to boil rapidly, it will spoil if this is not attended to.

Put the meat into cold water, and let it grow gradually warm. This dissolves the gelatine, allows the albumen to disengage, the scum to rise, and the heat to penetrate to the centre of the meat. But if the meat be put into hot water, or the soup over a hot fire to boil, the albumen coagulates, and the external surface of the meat is hardened ; the water is prevented from penetrating to the interior, and the nutritious part of the meat from disengaging itself. The broth will be without flavour, and the meat tough, if so managed  Allow two tablespoonfuls of salt to four quarts of soup, where there are many vegetables, and half a tablespoonful less where there are few.

One quart of water to one pound of meat is the proper and safe rule to observe.

Soup not made of meat previously cooked is as good, perhaps better, on the second day, if heated to the boiling point. If more water is needed, use boiling water, as cold or luke-warm spoils the soup. Some persons have thought potato water to be unhealthy ; do not, therefore, boil potatos in the soup, but, if required, boil them elsewhere, and add them when nearly cooked.

The water in which poultry or fresh meat is boiled should be saved for gravies or soups for the next day. If it is not needed in your own family give it to the poor. The bones, also, of roasts, with a little meat, make a soup ; and, if not required for this purpose, you may save them for the grease they contain.

**Chicken Pie.**—Cut up a couple of chicken, and put them in a deep pie-dish, alternating each layer with one or two slices of ham, to which add half a pint of water, and season with pepper, salt, and two blades of mace. If it is to be a raised pie-crust, the water should be omitted ; the pie we are describing is for a puff-paste crust. When the pie is ready, pour in at the hole made in the centre of the crust some hot beef gravy, well seasoned. The pie will not take more than an hour to bake in a moderately-heated oven. Cover the crust, which should be light, with buttered paper, to protect it from being scorched, for light pie-crusts, as a rule, bake sooner than the meat they cover. Chicken-pie is often reserved to be eaten cold ; when that is the case it should be served with the following salad :— hearts of lettuce, hard-boiled eggs, sliced, anchovies cut in strips, gherkins, and herbs, mixed with salad oil and vinegar. This delicate pie is more often bought for the races, parties, or picnics, than made at home, and it is cheaper to do so, but those who elect to be their own chicken pie-maker, we warn them that it is both troublesome and expensive.

**Lamb Pie.**—This is the most delicate amongst meat pies, and therefore requires more care in the making and baking. It may either be made of the breast, neck, or loin, but the breast is commonly preferred. After it has been cut up, each piece should be very lightly seasoned with pepper and salt ; put into the pie some hot gravy, and cover with a puff-crust, and bake in a quick oven for an hour and a quarter. To make it more savoury, a few oysters and their liquor may be put into the pie, as well as a little port wine, and a lamb's sweet-bread. It is quite as well to cover the crust with buttered paper, to protect from burning, a danger that attaches to all meat pies. For a LAMB PUDDING, the neck should be selected. When the basin has been filled with the meat, put in half a pint of water, and further proceed with the pudding according to the instructions given for a rump-steak and kidney pudding (p. 339), only that it will not take quite so long to boil ; like all other puddings, it must not be allowed to stop boiling for a minute until it is quite done.

**To Roast a Leg of Mutton.**—The leg should be hung in a cool place before roasting as long as it will keep free from taint, for newly-killed mutton is never tender. An eight-pound leg, before a clear brisk fire, will take about two hours to roast to meet the general taste, which is, that a little red gravy should flow from the joint when it is carved, and that it should never be over-done, except to meet some particular taste. It is a practice with some cooks, before roasting this joint, to immerse it in a saucepan of cold water, and parboil it by simmering, and when taken from the hot water immediately hung on the jack to roast; when this method is pursued, it will only take an hour and a quarter to roast before the fire. Basting should be persevered in during the whole time it is roasting. When the joint is done dredge a little salt over it, and then mix the dripping with a cupful of boiling water, salted, and pour it over the meat. Serve with its own gravy, red-currant jelly, and what vegetables may be in season.

**To Roast a Haunch of Mutton.** —This joint consists of the leg and part of the loin, cut so as to resemble a haunch of venison. It is the favourite and leading joint of mutton, and, when well cooked and served, is a very imposing family dish. It is of the first consideration to hang the haunch of venison as long as possible before roasting; if the weather be warm, pepper and ginger rubbed over it will protect it from flies, or, if the weather be heavy and moist, rubbing with sugar will prevent its turning sour. It should hang at least for forty-eight hours, and in the winter season a week's hanging will be none too long. When ready for roasting, paper the fat, and commence by placing the joint some distance from the fire: baste with its own dripping, and, about half an hour before it is done, remove the paper, draw the haunch closer to the fire for the purpose of finishing and browning. Before a favourable fire it will take about three hours. Finish off and serve the same as the leg.

**To Boil a Leg of Mutton.**—Cover the leg with boiling water; after it has once boiled up let it only simmer for about two hours, which will be sufficient for a leg of eight pounds; this joint is generally preferred somewhat under-done, so that when carved the red juices of the meat should mingle with the gravy in the dish; the two hours allowed must be reckoned from when the water boils up after the meat has been put into it; on no account let the meat boil rapidly, or it will harden; a little salt should be put into the water. Mashed turnips and caper sauce (see Sauces) are always served with boiled leg of mutton; the capers may be either thrown over the joint or sent to table in a tureen; the turnips and carrots (the latter are sometimes used) may be boiled with the meat. We deem this joint, whether roast or boiled, to be the most profitable that a family can sit down to, the bone weighing so little in comparison with the bulk of meat.

**Hashed Mutton.**—The remains of a cold leg or shoulder of mutton, especially if they are under-done, make a nice savoury dish if prepared in the following manner:—Cut the meat in neat uniform slices from the bones, trimming off all superfluous fat and gristle; chop the bones and fragments of the joint, put them into a stewpan with five or six whole peppers and allspice, half a head of celery, one onion, two ounces of butter, and a little flour to thicken; cover the whole with water, and simmer for one hour. Slice and fry the onion of a nice pale brown, and add it to the bones, &c. Stew for a quarter of an hour, strain the gravy, and let it cool; then skim off any particle of fat, and put it with the meat into a stewpan. Flavour with ketchup, tomato sauce, or any flavouring that may be preferred, and let the meat gradually warm through, but not boil, or it will harden. To hash meat properly, it should be laid in cold gravy, and only left on the fire long enough to warm through.

**To Roast Beef.**—With the exception of the round, the primest parts are roasted, the chief being the sirloin and ribs. Roasting joints should run about eight to ten pounds in weight. When a smaller joint is used it had better for the bones to be removed, and the meat rolled. It will be found the best economy to cut off the tops of ribs, salt them, and boil them, for if they are roasted with the joint they too frequently get shrivelled and burnt, and much good meat wasted.

Where fat prevails, it would be well to protect it with paper, removing the same when the meat is nearly done, and from this time dredge with flour until the roast is perfected. When done, empty the gravy from the dripping-pan into a basin, then remove the fat, and pour the gravy into a well-dish, garnishing the edge with finely-scraped horseradish.

Meat that is washed before roasting should always be well dried before putting down to the fire, which must be kept clear, and kept up to one height until the joint is done.

Allow a quarter of an hour to each pound of meat, which will be sufficient if the fire is properly attended to. The joint should remain near the fire till the outside is set, when it should be moved a little further back, and constantly basted with the dripping, as it falls, to the finish. These directions are applicable to other joints of beef as well as the sirloin and ribs.

**To Boil a Round of Beef.**—Salt for ten or twelve days, according to taste, about eight or nine pounds of the round ; then, after washing off the salt, skewer it in a round form. Put it in boiling water, and immediately it boils up, remove it on one side the fire, that it might only simmer until it is done. It will take about two hours and a quarter after it has commenced boiling. Clear the scum as it rises, or the joint will not look inviting when brought to table. Carrots, turnips, parsnips, and frequently suet dumplings, are served with this dish, and these may all be boiled with the meat if the size of the pot admits. This is a good family joint, being as much re-

lished cold as hot. When served, garnish the dish with carrots. The liquor the beef is boiled in should be preserved to a future day for pea-soup.

**To Boil Salt Beef.**—Wash the brine off, and put the joint into boiling water. Remove the scum as it rises. About twenty minutes to each pound of meat will be sufficient time for boiling, which should be gently and not rapidly done. If the joint be over salt, change the water when the meat is about a quarter done, or, better still, soak it for two or three hours in cold water before boiling.

Every kind of meat is best cooked by boiling gently, for rapid boiling spoils the meat ; salt meat should be very slowly boiled—indeed, it should only simmer.

Avoid hard water for boiling meat in. The water should always cover the meat, which should be wiped with a cloth when taken from the pot, and served as quickly as possible, with a little of the liquor, carrots, and suet dumplings.

**Stewed Rump Steak.**—The steak, say about two pounds, should be cut an inch thick, and rather lean ; before stewing, the steaks, cut into shapely pieces, should be fried in a bit of butter until they are evenly browned. After they have been taken from the pan, three carrots, turnips, and onions, all sliced, should be fried in the fat, and then the steaks and vegetables put into about half a pint of water, with a little salt and pepper, and a tablespoonful each of ketchup and flour, and let it slowly simmer for three hours ; the seasoning, and flour for thickening, should be added when the meat and vegetables are nearly done, and then rapidly boil the whole for three minutes. Skim off the fat, and serve.

**Caper Sauce for Boiled Mutton.**—Mix three tablespoonfuls of capers with half a pint of melted butter ; chop up the capers small, and add their liquor to them and the melted butter, stirring well the while, until the capers simmer for three minutes, when they may be served ; this sauce may be improved by the addition of a little chopped parsley, and a few bread-crumbs. Some persons prefer pickled nasturtium pods to be substituted for the capers. The quantity named in our receipt is sufficient to serve with a large leg of mutton.

**Caper Sauce for Fish.**—This sauce is not often served with fish, but when it is, it is thus prepared :—Take some melted butter, into which put a bit of glaze, and when the sauce is in a state of readiness, throw into it some capers, pepper and salt, and a tablespoonful of essence of anchovies.

**Imitation Caper Sauce.**—Boil a bunch of parsley down until it has lost its bright colour, then cut it up, put it into melted butter, with a pinch of salt, and a tablespoonful of vinegar, then boil up, and serve, when the sauce will hardly be known from that made with capers ; it may be used with either fish or meat.

**Bread Sauce.**—Boil some crumb of bread, with a finely-chopped onion, and a little white pepper ; when cooked, remove the onions and peppercorns, and put the bread, after it has been pulped through a sieve, into an earthenware pipkin with milk, a bit of salt butter, then stir it one way with a wooden spoon till it boils. The crumb of French rolls should be used for this sauce, and it should be cooked in boiling milk, and allowed to simmer on one side the fire until the bread evaporates the milk. Bread sauce is usually served with game or fowls, but it must be put on the table very hot. The bread, whether plain or fancy, used for this sauce, should be two or three days stale, and should remain in the milk for half an hour to soak before boiling, then beat it briskly with a fork until it is smooth, and without lumps. It will take an hour and a half to prepare. A richer bread sauce can be made by mixing a little cream with it before serving.

**Egg Sauce for Salt Fish.**—Boil three or four eggs quite hard, and then put them for ten or twelve minutes into cold water ; while the eggs are in the water, make half a pint of melted butter, then peel off the shells from the eggs, slice them, and when the butter is boiling, mix in the eggs with it, and stir them in it one way, and serve hot. If the sauce is required extra thick add an egg or two more than the number given to the same quantity of milk. Squeeze in some lemon juice, when liked, before serving. This is the proper sauce for salt fish, with which it is so necessary an accompaniment, that it should be made in abundance, so that it might not run short, and spoil the dinner. The eggs will take twenty-five minutes to harden.

**To Roast a Leg of Pork.**—Bear in mind that pork takes longer to cook than any other kind of meat : twenty-five minutes to the pound should be allowed, except for very young pork. The joints for roasting are the leg, the loin, the spare-rib, and the chine. In roasting the leg first equally score the rind, and stuff it with sage and onions, a few hours before hanging it on the jack ; an opening should be made about the knuckle for the reception of the stuffing. While the joint must be thoroughly done before serving, it should not be hung too near the fire, but steadily roasted at some distance before a good, but not a flaring fire, at the same time well basting it with its own fat and gravy. Serve with plenty apple sauce mixed with the gravy from the dripping-pan.

**To Roast Fore-Quarter of Lamb.**—Lamb requires very careful attention while cooking ; it should always be thoroughly done, and properly served. Mint-sauce is invariably served with hot or cold roast lamb. A fore-quarter, weighing eight or nine pounds, will require nearly two hours before a clear brisk fire, and constant basting ; it should not be put down too near the fire at first. When sufficiently done, the carver should separate the ribs from the shoulder ; but before it is quite done, lay in the dripping-pan two ounces of butter, squeeze a lemon, and season with pepper and salt ; this gravy should be placed in the dish with the lamb ; on no account send it to table with any red gravy in it.

**Boiled Leg of Lamb.**—First let it remain for half an hour in cold water sufficient to cover it, with a dessertspoonful of vinegar and two of salt ; after this soaking, dredge it with flour, then plunge it into boiling water, and boil gently for an hour and a half, if about six pounds, and it should not be heavier ; some cooks prefer boiling a leg of lamb sewn up in a thin cloth. Serve with melted butter, cauliflowers or spinach ; if white sauce is preferred to the melted butter throw it over the joint.

**To Stew a Breast of Lamb.**—Cut it into pieces, pepper and salt them, and stew in sufficient gravy to cover the meat until tender, or about an hour and a half ; then thicken the stock or gravy it has been boiled in with a little butter and flour, at the same time adding a glass of sherry, then boil it up for a minute and throw it over the meat. This dish is much improved by stewing mushrooms, spinach, or green peas with it, especially the latter.

**To Roast a Fillet of Veal.**—The prime joints of veal for roasting are the loin and the fillet. Prepare for roasting by first taking out the bone, and putting under the flap a stuffing of forcemeat ; then skewer the joint in a round form, sprinkle with flour, and then put it down to the fire, but at some distance at first, for it should be gradually cooked until it becomes a rich brown ; it must be constantly basted, and the caul covered with paper ; a fillet weighing nine pounds will require three hours. This joint depends much upon the stuffing, which should be abundant. A bit of bacon or pickled pork served with it is a welcome accompaniment, for veal in itself is tasteless and insipid eating ; with roast veal a lemon should never be forgotten.

**Days of the Week.**—SUNDAY.—This day was called by our Saxon ancestors, *Sunnan Dæg,* or sun's day, because it was dedicated to the worship of the sun. The idol of the sun was represented as " a halfe-naked man set upon a pillar ; his face, as it were, brightened with gleames of fire, and holding with both his armes stretched out, a burning wheele upon his breast ; the wheele being to signifie the course which he runneth about the world, and the fiery gleames and brightness, the light and heat wherewith he warmeth and comforteth the things that live and grow." The Romans called this day *Dies Solis.* Sunday, among Christians, has three denominations : the Sabbath, from its being the day of rest ; the Lord's Day, from its having been selected by the apostles as their peculiar time of meeting " to offer up their praises and thanksgivings for the inestimable benefits bestowed upon mankind, through Jesus Christ our Lord ;" and, lastly, and most commonly, it is called Sunday in compliance with the long-used and ordinary form of speech.

MONDAY.—Termed *Monan-Dæg* by the Saxons, was dedicated to the worship of the moon. " The form of this idoll seemeth very strange and ridiculous, for, being made for a woman, shee hath a short coat like a man ; but more strange it is to see her hood with such two long ears. The holding of a moone before her breast may seem to have been to express what she is ; but the reason of her chapron with long ears, as also of her short coat and pyked shoes, I doe not finde." By the Romans this day was called *Dies Lunæ,* being dedicated to the moon.

TUESDAY.—So named from *Tuysco,* the most ancient god of the Germans. He was " the father and conductor of the Germans, who, after his name, even unto this day, doe in their owne tongue call themselves *Tuytsh,* and their country of Germany *Tuytshland* : and the Netherlands using herein the D for the T, doe make it *Duytsh,* and *Duytshland,* both which appellations of the people and country I doe here write right, according as we in our English orthography would write them after our pronunciation." The Romans named this day *Dies Martis*, from its being dedicated to Mars.

WEDNESDAY.—A contraction of *Wodin's* or *Odin's* day. "Odin," says Dr. Henry, "is believed to be the name of the one true god among the first colonists who came from the east, and peopled Germany and Scandinavia, and among their posterity for several ages." But at length, a mighty conqueror, the leader of a new army of adventurers from the east, over-ran the north of Europe, erected a great empire, assumed the name of Odin, and claimed the honours which had been formerly paid to that deity From thenceforward that deified mortal, under the name of Odin or Wodin, became the chief object of the idolatrous worship of the Saxons and Danes in this island, as well as of many other nations. Having been a mighty and successful warrior, he was believed to be the god of war, who gave victory, and revived courage in the conflict. After civilising, in some measure, the countries which he conquered, and introducing arts formerly unknown, he was also worshipped as the god of arts and artists. In a word, to this Odin his deluded worshippers impiously ascribed all the attributes which belong only to the true God ; to him they built magnificent temples, offered many sacrifices, and consecrated the fourth day of the week, which is still called by his name in England, and in all other countries where he was formerly worshipped. Notwithstanding this, the founders of the whole of the Kingdoms of the Anglo-Saxon Heptarchy pretended to be descended from Woden, and some of them at the distance only of a few generations." The Romans dedicated this day to Mercury, from which cause it was named *Dies Mercurii.*

THURSDAY.—From *Thors-Day*, or the Thunderer's day. It was dedicated by the northern nations to the worship of Thor, the bravest of the sons of Odin. "The idol Thor was not only served and sacrificed unto of the ancient Pagan Saxons, but of all the Teutonic people of the Septentrionall regions, yea even of the people that dwelt beyond Thule or Island ; for in Gweeneland was he knowne and adored ; in memory whereof a promontory, or high poynt of land lying out into the sea at the said promontory, doth yet bear his name ; and the manner how he was made his picture doth declare. This great reputed god, being of more estimation than many of the rest of the like sort, though of as little worth as any of the meanest of that rabble, was majestically placed in a very large and spacious hall, and there set as if he had reposed himselfe upon a covered bed. On his head he wore a crown of gold, and round in a compass above, and about the same, were set or fixed twelve bright burnished golden starres. And in his right hand he held a kingly sceptre. He was of the seduced pagans believed to be of most marvellous power and might ; yea, and that there were no people throughout the whole world that were not subjected unto him, and did not owe him divine honour and service. That there was no puissance comparable to his. His dominion of all others farther extending itselfe, both in heaven and earth. That in the aire he governed the winds and the cloudes ; and being displeased did cause lightning, and tempest, with excessive raine, haile, and all ill weather ; but being well pleased, by the adoration, sacrifice, and service of his suppliants, he then bestowed upon them most faire and seasonable weather, and caused corne abundantly to growe, as all sortes of fruits, &c., and kept away the plague, and all other evill and infectious diseases. Of the weekly day that was dedicated unto his peculiar service we yet retain the name of Thursday, the which the Danes and Swedians doe yet call Thors-day. In the Netherlands it is yet called *Danders-dagh*, which being written according to our English orthography, is *Tyunders-day*, whereby it may appeare that they antiently therein intended the day of the God of *Thunder ;*

and in some of our old Saxon bookes I find it to have been written *Thunres-deagh*; so, as it seemeth, that the name of *Thor*, or *Thur*, was abbreviated of *Thunre*, which we now write *Thunder*." This day was named *Dies Jovis*, Jove's Day, by the Romans.

FRIDAY.—Was so named in honour of *Friga*, the wife of Odin. This goddess was the reputed giver of peace and plenty. The Romans dedicated Friday to Venus, whence its name of *Dies Veneris*; and that goddess having possessed many of the attributes for which Friga was most celebrated, several authors have supposed them originally to have meant the same divinity.

SATURDAY.—Or *Seater Dog*, so named from the idol Seater, worshipped by our Saxon ancestors. " He was leane of visage, having long haire and a long beard, and was bare-headed and bare-footed. In his left hand he held up a wheele, and in his right he carried a paile of water, wherein were flowers and fruites. His long coate was girded upon him with a towel of white linnen. His standing upon the sharpe finns of a fish (the pearch) was to signifie that the Saxons, for their serving him, should passe stedfastly and without harme in dangerous and difficult places. By the wheele was betokened the knit unity and conjoined concord of the Saxons, and their concurring together fn the running one course. By the girdle, which with the wind streamed from him, was signified the Saxon's freedom. By the paile with the flowers and fruites was declared that with kindly raine he would nourish the earth to bring forth such fruites and flowers. The seventh day was dedicated by the Romans to Saturn, and named in honour of him, *Dies Saturni.*

**Advent Sunday.**—This festival of the Church, always the nearest Sunday to the feast of St. Andrew (Nov. 30), whether before or after the Advent (literally the *coming*) is a term applied from an early period of ecclesiastical history to the four weeks preceding Christmas, which were observed with penance and devotion, in reference to the approaching birth of Christ. There are four Sundays in Advent, commencing with that, as we have remarked, nearest to the feast of St. Andrew.

**St. Agnes' Eve.**—The annals of canonisation in the Church of Rome present no image of greater purity and sweetness than St. Agnes. She is described as a very young and spotless maid, who suffered martyrdom in the tenth persecution under Diocletian, in the year 306. A few days after her death, her parents, going to her tomb, beheld a vision of angels (such is the legend), in the midst of which stood their daughter, with a snow-white lamb by her side. She is therefore usually represented with a lamb standing by her side. At Rome, on St. Agnes Day, Jan. 21, during mass, and while the *Agnus* is being sung, two lambs, as white as snow, and covered with finery, are brought in and laid upon the altar. Their fleeces are afterwards shorn, and converted into palls. In England, as much as elsewhere, it was customary for young women on St. Agnes' Eve to endeavour to divine who should be their husbands. The proper rite was to take a row of pins and pull them out one after another, saying a pater-noster, and sticking one pin in the sleeve; then going to rest without food, their dreams were expected to present to them the image of their future husband.

**All Fool's Day.**—We need hardly say that this day of trifling occurs on the 1st of April, which has been from the most ancient times set apart for the commission of various species of folly and practical joking. Its origin is unknown, but it is observed in many countries under different names. Whatever may have been its origin we can only say that it is more honoured in the breach than the observance. It is fast dying out.

**Quarter Days.—**

| | | |
|---|---|---|
| Lady Day | . . | 25th March. |
| Midsummer | . . | 24th June. |
| Michaelmas | . . | 29th Sep. |
| Christmas | . . | 25th Dec. |

**Calendar Months.—**

| | | |
|---|---|---|
| January | . . . | 31 days. |
| February | . . . | 28 „ |
| March | . . . | 31 „ |
| April | . . . . | 30 „ |
| May | . . . . | 31 „ |
| June | . . . | 30 „ |
| July | . . . . | 31 „ |
| August | . . . | 31 „ |
| September | . . . | 30 „ |
| October | . . . | 31 „ |
| November | . . . | 30 „ |
| December | . . . | 31 „ |

Thirty days have September,
April, June, and November,
All the rest have thirty-one ;
But Leap Year coming one in four,
Gives February one day more.

**Leap Year.**—This is found by dividing the date of the year by four. If there is no remainder it is Leap Year ; but if there be any remainder, it shows how many years it is after Leap Year.

**To Make Yeast.**—To any quantity of water desired add sufficient hops to make it very strong, and let it steep slowly for two or three hours. Then boil it a few minutes, strain out the hops, put the liquor back in the kettle, let it boil moderately, and add flour until a stiff batter is formed. When thoroughly scalded, put it in a jar to cool, and while a little warm, add yeast to ferment it. When well fermented, add to two quarts of the yeast half a teacupful of salt. Keep it in a cool place. A tablespoon twice filled will make sponge for a half-dozen loaves of bread. Yeast made in this way will not sour. Or boil one ounce of hops in a gallon of water until it is reduced to half a gallon, then strain it off through a hair sieve, and pour it boiling hot on a half quartern of flour, stirring well all the time ; mix in two tablespoonfuls of moist sugar ; when lukewarm, add a pint of old yeast to quicken, keeping it in a warm place while making. If no old yeast is at hand, half a pint of old ale will answer to quicken, or an ounce of German yeast. When made, reserve half a pint by bottling, and keep it in a cool place for your next making.

**The "Death-Watch."**—Superstitions have been associated with various insects, from the earliest times, and in all countries. The death's-head moth has been regarded as an unwelcome omen to the homes visited by it ; and the noise of the death-watch has been affirmed to "click the hour of death." Swift thus ridicules the superstition :

" A wood-worm that lies in old wood,
 like a hare in her form,
With teeth or with claws it will bite,
 it will scratch,
And chamber-maids christen this
 worm a death-watch ;
Because, like a watch, it will always
 cry, click,
And woe be to those in the house
 that are sick !
For sure as a gun they will give up
 the ghost,
If the maggot cries click, when it
 scratches the post.
But a kettle of scalding hot water injected,
Infallibly cures the timber affected :
The omen is broken, the danger is
 over,
The maggot will die, and the sick will
 recover !"

The noise of the wood-worm is produced by a species of small beetle of the timber-boring genus. In the spring these insects commence their ticking, as a call to each other. They beat with their heads, and though they are very " headstrong," they are less so than the people who cling to the stupid belief that their sound is a token of calamity.

**A Good Week's Work.—**
Sunday—Church doors enter in,
Rest from toil, repent of sin,
Strive a heavenly rest to win.
Monday—To your calling go ;
Serve the Lord, love friend and foe ;
To the tempter answer, " No."
Tuesday—Do what good you can :
Live in peace with God and man ;
Remember life is but a span.
Wednesday—Give away and earn ;
Teach some truth, some good thing
 learn ;
Joyfully good for ill return.

THURSDAY—Build your house upon
Christ the mighty Corner-stone ;
Whom God helps, his work is done.
FRIDAY—For the truth be strong ;
Own your fault if in the wrong,
Put a bridle on your tongue.
SATURDAY— Thank God and sing,
Tribute to His treasure bring ;
Be prepared for Terror's King !
Thus your hopes on Jesus cast,
Thus let all your weeks be passed,
And you shall be saved at last.

**To Destroy Weeds on Gravel Walks.**—Any manufacturing chemist will be glad to supply the residuum from the manufacture of ether at one halfpenny per pound. Mix six parts water with one part of this material in a glazed earthen vessel, then let two persons be employed, the one to pour the liquid from an earthen jug over the weedy walk, the other to well rub it in with a worn-out broom or scrubbing-brush ; no watering-pan to be used, or it would destroy it in an hour. Care, too, must be taken that it does not fall upon the clothes or hands, as the acid is extremely powerful. The weeds die almost immediately, nor will any for a long period spring again. It also utterly destroys the dwarf green moss, which is so apt to grow on walls in damp, shady places. Walks operated upon twice a-year in this way will effectually be kept clean and neat at a very slight cost. Care should be taken not to apply it within two inches of the edge of the lawn, lest it should destroy the grass.

**Whitsun Day.**—This festival of the Church is so called from this day being one of the stated times of baptism in the ancient Church, when those who were baptised put on white garments, as types of that spiritual purity they received in baptism. The day is designed to commemorate the descent of the Holy Spirit upon the Apostles on the day of Pentecost. Whit-Sunday, Monday, and Tuesday, these three days together are called Whitsuntide, and fall six weeks after Easter, which festival regulates all others in matter of time.

**Coffee.**—This is more stimulant, and more oppressive to the stomach, than tea. It is apt to constipate the bowels, and produce acidity and flatulence. It contains a greater quantity of extractive and resinous matter. Its use as a promoter of digestion is very questionable, if it be not positively clogging and injurious ; gratuitously absorbing the powers of the gastric juice, at the expense of the solid *ingesta*, besides introducing into the system a great amount of highly carbonised materials, only necessary in very low temperatures. Coffee should always be fresh roasted, and should be made by infusion. Boiling dissipates its aroma.

**Hints to Convalescents.**—Wasted energies are to be recruited, and the organs are to be prepared to encounter influences from which they have been withdrawn—influences of friends, society, visits, noise, light, cold, heat, meats, drinks, bodily labour, and mental toil. The fear of relapse necessitates that here, as in many things else, we advance step by step. Intellectual toil or exertion is to be avoided by convalescents, for its effects on the brain are too exciting. Perfect calm of the passions must also be observed.

**Michaelmas Day.**—This day, as most people know who have rent to pay, is one of the quarter days, and falls on the 29th of September. It is a great festival of the Romish and English churches. The popular custom of having a goose for dinner on this day thus originated :—Queen Elizabeth is said to have been eating her Michaelmas goose when she received intelligence of the defeat of the Spanish Armada. There have been other reasons assigned for this custom, but it seems to have arisen simply from the goose being at this time in finest condition for the table.

**Midsummer Day.**—This falls on the 24th of June, and is sometimes known as St. John's Day, being the nativity of St. John the Baptist. It is a time of high observance in Catholic countries. It was believed by the superstitious that on the eve of this day, by fasting and pulling certain herbs, it was possible to obtain an insight into futurity.

**Ash Wednesday.**—This is the first day in Lent, a holiday in the Church of England. The palms, or substitute branches, consecrated and used on Palm Sunday of one year, were kept till the present season of another, when they were burnt, and their ashes blessed by the priest, and sprinkled on the heads of the people ; hence the name given to the day. This sprinkling of ashes was performed with many ceremonies and great devotion. In England it is still a reason for the saying of the "Commination" in the Prayer Book, by which the doers of certain kinds of wickedness are cursed.

**Shrove Tuesday.**—This day is the herald of Lent, and has been from the earliest ages celebrated by feasting and merry-making. It is the concluding day of the time of Carnival, which in various Catholic countries is of greater or less extent, but celebrated with most distinction at Rome and Venice. The main distinction of Shrove Tuesday was the eating of pancakes, made with eggs and spice, and this custom still prevails.

**Palm Sunday.**—This day, the Sunday before Easter, is the commencement of Passion Week, and is therefore sometimes called Passion Sunday, in commemoration of the sufferings of our Saviour. In Catholic countries, on this day, the priests bless branches of palm, which are carried in procession in memory of those strewn before our Lord at the entrance into Jerusalem. After the procession is over the branches are burnt, and their ashes preserved for sprinkling on the heads of the people on Ash Wednesday.

**Candlemas Day.**—This holiday in the English church falls on the 2nd of February. The early fathers of the church held it in commemoration of Mary in the Temple, forty days after childbirth, as commanded by the law ; and it was their custom on this day to bless candles, and distribute the same among the people, by whom they were carried in solemn procession. The saying of Simeon, respecting the infant Christ, in the temple, that he would be a *light* to lighten the Gentiles, probably supplied an excuse for adopting the candle-bearing procession of the heathen, whose external religious practices the founders of the Romish Church made a practice of imitating.

**Test for Plate.**—The following process for testing the genuineness of silver plating on metals may be of value to many ladies. The metallic surface is carefully cleaned, and a drop of a cold, saturated solution of bichromate of potash, in nitric acid, is placed upon it, and immediately washed off with cold water. If silver, a blood-red spot of chromate of silver is formed ; on German silver or Britannia metal, the stain is brown or black.

**St. Swithin's Day.**—The legend of this day is (which falls on the 15th of July) that if it rains on it it will continue to rain for forty days afterwards. St. Swithin was Bishop of Winchester in the year 865, to which rank he was raised by King Ethelbert, the Dane, and was canonised by the pope. He was singular for his desire to be buried in the open churchyard, and not in the chancel of the minster, as was usual with other bishops, which request was complied with ; but the monks, on his being canonised, taking it into their heads that it was disgraceful for the saint to lie in the open churchyard, resolved to remove his body into the choir, which was to have been done with solemn procession on the 15th of July. It rained, however, so violently on that day, and for forty days succeeding, as had hardly ever been known, which made them set aside their design as heretical and blasphemous ; and instead they erected a chapel over his grave, at which many miracles are said to have been wrought. Churchill, Gay, Ben Jonson, and other poet satirists, have noticed St. Swithin with ridicule, which such superstitions deserve.

**St. Valentine's Day.**—The Fourteenth of February is a day of great expectation with lovers, and a day of misery for postmen, for a bag of letters of love is as heavy for them to carry, and takes as much walking to deliver, as a bag of letters devoted to commerce. Maidens' hearts leap with joy at the postman's imperative rat-tat at the knocker, and they are equally sad and disappointed if he passes the door without leaving a token of affection from somebody. Hearts are trumps, indeed, on St. Valentine's Day, and old and young amongst bachelors and spinsters are much disappointed if they have not a valentine of some sort—of course, always excepting those which maliciously point to personal defects.

The ice of many a courtship has been broken by a sweet valentine ! the heart of many a maiden won through the medium of those emblematic pictures and flattering rhymes sent on the day licensed to the revelations of love. Young men have been known never to have retired to rest at all on Valentine's Eve, but to have spent the night under their mistress' window for the purpose of gaining her first sweet glance in the morning. Juliet, of course, either by instinct or treachery, knew that her Romeo was "out in the cold," so at earliest dawn she would open her casement, claim him for her valentine, and give each other " sigh for sigh."

Girls, too, in order to avoid the sight of a disagreeable suitor, would shut themselves up for the entire morning. Others, by various clever stratagems— peeping through little friendly holes in the window-curtains—sitting with their eyes shut for hours, until they heard the wished-for step, or well-beloved voice, when they would issue forth to be embraced by their swain and called his Valentine !

We wish that all the old customs handed down to us and commonly observed by rich and poor, young and old, were as pure as the one dedicated to St. Valentine ! We are very sorry, however, to observe, that in cases too numerous, valentines, instead of breathing love and purity, are made the mediums of jealousy, spite and malice, and to wound a sensitive spirit by caricaturing personal deformities, committed by the hand of nature. This, if not positively wicked, is in the worst possible taste, and should always be discouraged.

A Valentine should be devoted to the purposes of a pure affection, couched in the sweetest language the writer has the capacity to pour out ; but above all things it should unmistakably breathe of sincerity.

May all our lady readers who are not already Hymen's prisoners, receive such Valentines, may they lead to marriage, and may they never regret St. Valentine's Day !

# INDEX.

## FRUIT JELLY.

Soak 1 oz. of Swinborne's Isinglass or 1 quart packet of Gelatine in 1 pint of cold water, add ½-pint of red currant jelly dissolved in ½-pint of hot water, with 4 ounces of loaf sugar and the juice and peel of 1 lemon, and stir over the fire till dissolved, strain through muslin and pour into a mould. Instead of currant jelly, a pint of any fruit syrup without sugar, or a pint of sweetened juice of any fresh fruit may be used; and whipped cream may be served with it the same as for claret jelly.

## LEMON CREAM.

Soak ¾-oz. of Swinborne's Isinglass or Gelatine in ½-pint of sherry or raisin wine, dissolve over the fire; add the juice of 2 lemons, with 6 ounces of loaf sugar rubbed over the rind of the lemons, and while hot pour the whole gently into 1 pint of cream, stir a short time and put into a mould.

## DUTCH FLUMMERY OR JAUNE-MANGE.

Soak 1 oz. of Swinborne's Isinglass or 1 quart packet of Gelatine in ½-pint of cold water. Beat up the yolks of 4 eggs with ½-pint of sherry or raisin wine, and add the juice and rinds of 2 lemons with 8 ounces of loaf sugar. Dissolve the soaked Isinglass in a saucepan and add all the other ingredients; mix well together and boil 1 minute, strain through muslin, stir occasionally till nearly cold, and then pour into a mould.

## BLANC-MANGE.

Soak 1 oz. of Swinborne's Isinglass or 1 quart packet of Gelatine in 1 quart of new milk for 20 minutes; then add 2 clean laurel leaves, boil for a few minutes, put in 6 ounces of loaf sugar and a little brandy; strain through muslin and stir occasionally till nearly cold, then pour into a mould.

N.B.—A richer blanc-mange is made by using half cream and half milk. Any flavouring may be substituted for the laurel leaves.

*For a 2 quart packet of Gelatine use double the quantities given.*

## SOUPS AND MEAT PIES

Are greatly improved by the addition of a little Gelatine previously soaked in cold water; about ½-ounce for an ordinary sized pie, and the same quantity for every quart of soup.

*NOTE.—Milk is rendered easier of digestion, and more nourishing for invalids and children, by dissolving a small quantity of Swinborne's Patent Refined Isinglass in it—or the Isinglass may be taken in broth or wine.*